D0948581

THE COMPLETE STORIES OF
Paul Laurence Dunbar

Paul Laurence Dunbar, Dayton, Ohio. Photograph by Josephine Watkins Lehman, ca. 1890–1900. *Courtesy of the Ohio Historical Society*

THE COMPLETE STORIES OF

Paul Laurence Dunbar

Edited by Gene Andrew Jarrett
and Thomas Lewis Morgan

Foreword by Shelley Fisher Fishkin

Ohio University Press   *Athens*

Ohio University Press, Athens, Ohio 45701
www.ohio.edu/oupress
Compilation © 2005 by Ohio University Press
Foreword © 2005 by Shelley Fisher Fishkin
Introduction © 2005 by Gene Andrew Jarrett and Thomas Lewis Morgan

Printed in the United States of America

Ohio University Press books are printed on acid-free paper ⊗ ™

12 11 10 09 08 07 06   5 4 3 2

"The Case of Cadwallader," "Jimmy Weedon's Contretemps," "A Prophesy
of Fate," "Sister Jackson's Superstitions," and "Ole Conju'in Joe" appear
courtesy of Ms. Mildred M. Norman, Ms. Gwendolyn Burton Raise, and
Sergeant F. C. William H. Smith, U.S. Army, retired.

The photographs of Paul Laurence Dunbar appear courtesy of the
Ohio Historical Society.

Library of Congress Cataloging-in-Publication Data
Dunbar, Paul Laurence, 1872–1906.
  [Short stories]
  The complete stories of Paul Laurence Dunbar / edited by Gene Andrew Jarrett
and Thomas Lewis Morgan ; foreword by Shelley Fisher Fishkin.
      p. cm.
  Includes bibliographical references and index.
  ISBN 0-8214-1644-8 (cloth : acid-free paper)
  1. African Americans—Fiction. I. Jarrett, Gene Andrew, 1975– II. Morgan,
Thomas Lewis, 1969– III. Title.
  PS1556.A4 2005
  813'.4—dc22

                                              2005025267

Contents

I: Collected Stories

Folks from Dixie (1898)

The Strength of Gideon and Other Stories (1900)

In Old Plantation Days (1903)

The Heart of Happy Hollow (1904)

II: Uncollected Stories

Dialect Stories (*New York Journal and Advertiser*, 1897)

"Ohio Pastorals" (*Lippincott's*, 1901)

Individual Stories (1890–1905)

Sources

Foreword

by Shelley Fisher Fishkin

One hundred years after his untimely death, we are still only beginning to understand what Paul Laurence Dunbar achieved during his life. Dunbar was the nation's first hugely successful African American author. His books were eagerly purchased by white and black readers alike, and he earned enough by his pen to buy his mother a handsome house on an oversized lot in his hometown of Dayton, Ohio. Much of the money that bought that house came from what magazine and book publishers paid him for the stories collected in this volume.

Dunbar was a commercial writer, an author who sought to sell his work in the marketplace. Yet he was also a self-aware writer who understood that his work was entering a highly charged and often offensive cultural conversation about African Americans that was going on around it. Was it possible to write commercial fiction that also redirected that conversation in productive ways? To what extent could a black writer at the turn of the century destabilize stereotypes—about black writers, and about black people generally—and still find a lucrative market for his fiction? The 103 short stories brought together for the first time in this book illuminate some of the ways that Dunbar responded to these challenges.

By bringing together Dunbar's extant apprentice-work and mature short fiction, this volume allows us to watch the author develop as a professional writer increasingly aware of the fact that the markets available to him demanded a range of subjects and styles. "The Tenderfoot," the first story he sold (to the A. N. Kellogg Newspaper Syndicate for six dollars in 1891) was a western tale set in a mining camp, narrated in the vernacular by a white miner, and featuring characters who were all white. A more mature "raceless" story like "The Lion Tamer," a graceful comedy of manners set in high society, shows that Dunbar remained comfortable, throughout his career, writing fiction in which race figured not at all. This volume also allows us to see the evolution of Dunbar's art in stories set in black communities and the increasing care he took in its presentation to the public. For example, a sequence of four of Dunbar's stories serialized in the *New York Journal and Advertiser* in 1897, which the newspaper subtitled variously as "A Human Nature Sketch of Real Darkey Life in New York," "A Character Sketch of Real Darky Life in New York" (for the second and third stories), and "A Darky Dialect Story," must have enhanced Dunbar's awareness of white America's curiosity about stories of black America, a vein he would mine with profit throughout his career; but it also probably served as a warning of media insensitivity to the nuances of prejudice, stereotype, and the writer's craft (Dunbar did not allow such a title to frame his work again).

Dunbar's stories reveal a writer aware that the nation's media often painted African Americans with broad brushes dipped in racist bigotry while whitewashing any moral lapse on the part of whites. For example, in "The Lynching of Jube

Benson," Dunbar writes dryly that the lynching of a blameless black man "was very quiet and orderly. There is no doubt that it was as the papers would have said, a gathering of the best citizens." Dunbar tackles media bias again in "The Tragedy at Three Forks," in which two unlucky innocent black men who happen to be passing through the area are summarily lynched by the "law-abiding citizens of Barlow County." Following the lynching, Dunbar writes, "Conservative editors wrote leaders about it in which they deplored the rashness of the hanging but warned the negroes that the only way to stop lynching was to quit the crimes of which they so often stood accused."

In addition to challenging "the papers" through sly irony, Dunbar's stories also displace, disrupt, or directly challenge stereotypes of African Americans that were commonly promulgated in newspapers and magazines. For example, in dozens of turn-of-the-century stories and sketches in magazines such as *Century*, *Scribner's*, and *Harper's*, African American religion was ridiculed and black preachers were presented as ignorant, pompous, self-important blowhards. Dunbar, by way of contrast, shows us black characters sincerely seeking faith ("Anner 'Lizer's Stumblin' Block"), black ministers sincerely devoted to communal uplift ("The Ordeal at Mt. Hope"), and black preachers preaching cogent, articulate, and effective sermons ("The Trial Sermons on Bull-Skin").

And at a time when degrading, minstrelsy-inflected stereotypes of black men as "sambos" or "zip coons" infested popular media and entertainment, Dunbar presented black men in a broad array of roles and relationships—such as a father surprised by the love he feels for his baby daughter ("Jimsella") and a con man who becomes the secret benefactor of an elderly woman who reminds him of his mother ("Aunt Mandy's Investment"). And at a time when "mammy" and "jezebel" stereotypes often defined the range of roles assigned to black women in popular culture, Dunbar often presented black women, as well, in some quite different roles—such as a psychologically abused wife who gains the courage to stand up to her husband and demand respect ("The Emancipation of Evalina Jones"). In the short fiction in this volume, Dunbar explores other themes involving black people that were absent from the columns of the national newspapers, the nostalgic Plantation Tradition tales that were so popular in the nation's magazines, or the ubiquitous latter-day versions of minstrel shows—themes like intergenerational conflict in black communities ("Old Abe's Conversion") or the discrimination black youth encountered in the job market ("One Man's Fortunes"), or the intricacies of black political life ("The Scapegoat"). He also explores the complexities of black-white relations among characters of a range of ages and occupations in multiple regions of the country and in varied venues—relations between children, between college students, or between employer and employee; relations in a private home, a law office, a political campaign, a court of law.

Dunbar's broader themes in these stories are not unlike those explored in fiction by his contemporaries, Mark Twain and Charles Chesnutt: themes like the temptations of power and pride, the seductions of hypocrisy, the persistence of human gullibility, and the ways in which racism derailed the promise of freedom and equality in American society. But while collections of stories by Twain and Chesnutt have long been in print, collections of Dunbar's stories have not; the obscurity of his short fiction has helped prevent Dunbar from being recognized as a writer tilling adjacent fields. *The Complete Stories* may encourage us to see resonances with Chesnutt and Twain that we may not have noted before. For example, "The Ingrate," Dunbar's 1899 story of the trickster-master tricked by the poker-faced trickster-slave, prefigures one of Charles Chesnutt's most acclaimed stories, "The Passing of Grandison," which was published in *The Wife of His Youth and Other Stories of the Color Line* the same year—but several months *after* Dunbar's story appeared in *New England Magazine*. Both stories satirize the self-serving rationalizations of "kind" slaveholders while portraying the resourcefulness and cunning of slaves who used whatever limited freedom and knowledge of the world they had to make their way North to freedom. There are shades of Mark Twain's famous story "The Man That Corrupted Hadleyburg" in Dunbar's story "The Mission of Mr. Scatters," which appeared several years later. Dunbar's story focuses on a black community's willingness to be duped by a charming black confidence man; like Twain's "Hadleyburg," it is a tale about a mysterious stranger who disrupts a complacent community's equilibrium with the seductive promise of great wealth. The ingratiating stranger's knowledge of the community and fake accent remind one a bit of the duke and the king in the Wilks episode of *Huckleberry Finn*, while the community's response to a man believed to be associated with great wealth is reminiscent of Twain's story "The Million-Pound Bank-Note." Readers who relish the ironies of Twain's *Pudd'nhead Wilson* will appreciate the satiric twist with which Dunbar ends this story: the black con man wins a "not guilty" verdict in a white courtroom by playing on the vanities of the white power structure with a virtuosity that stuns his black victims.

The Complete Stories allows us to see Dunbar writing in a variety of registers —sentimental, satiric, nostalgic, and sardonic. It allows us to see him experimenting with a broad range of vernaculars, and exploring subjects and themes that are both familiar and fresh. It might even suggest new perspectives on some of his most famous poems. For example, the clever dissimulation that animates a story like "The Ingrate" might add to our insight into Dunbar's poem "We Wear the Mask," while the several stories noted above involving black preachers might be fruitfully compared and contrasted with the preacher we encounter in "An Antebellum Sermon."

Dunbar turned out vast quantities of poetry and prose as if his life depended on it—and, indeed, it did. During most of his adult life, his writing, along with his public readings from his work, was (with the exception of a brief stint working at the Library of Congress) his principal source of support. Not all of these stories are memorable. Some are, to be sure, pedestrian and formulaic. But others are well-crafted gems. *The Complete Stories* allows us to see the range and versatility of this intriguing writer in unprecedented ways, enriching our understanding of Dunbar's achievements as a literary artist. This collection should be welcomed by anyone who cares about American literary history.

Acknowledgments

Certain individuals played a central role in the conception and production of this book. Shelley Fisher Fishkin moderated a roundtable on Paul Laurence Dunbar at the 2004 American Literature Association conference that inspired us to publish Dunbar's short stories. Since that time, Fishkin has provided encouragement, wonderful advice, and a foreword that succinctly captures the importance of Dunbar to American literary and cultural studies. Eugene Metcalf's meticulous bibliography, *Paul Laurence Dunbar* (Metuchen, NJ: Scarecrow Press, 1975), and his thoughtful responses to our queries were invaluable to our recovery of Dunbar's uncollected stories and to our ultimate organization of the book. Herbert Woodward Martin provided prompt and courteous responses to our frequent queries, and shared with us his extensive knowledge about Dunbar.

We are grateful for the assistance provided by the Ohio Historical Society, which maintains the Paul Laurence Dunbar Collection. Specifically, Elizabeth L. Plummer answered our numerous questions about Dunbar, and Duryea Kemp supplied the images that grace our book. The Interlibrary Loan Staff at the University of Tennessee, namely Elizabeth Berney and Kathleen Bailey, worked tirelessly to locate obscure and out-of-print sources.

At Ohio University Press, Gillian Berchowitz welcomed our ideas from the very beginning, and she helped sustain our excitement throughout the long, arduous process of researching, examining, transcribing, and copyediting the stories. Nancy Basmajian's excellent copyediting skills helped clarify, simplify, and focus the writing in our introduction; she and her editorial team also admirably waded through and corrected what must have seemed like endless pages of dense dialect.

Finally, we would like to thank our families, colleagues, and friends for their love and support.

o delited requarent – simply informed for press & a few literary friends J.B. Pond

Lyceum · Theatre

. . . . DANIEL FROHMAN, MANAGER

Tuesday Afternoon, Sept. 8th, from 3 to 4,

Paul Laurence Dunbar,

THE YOUNG NEGRO POET,

WILL GIVE AN HOUR'S

Readings and Recitations

FROM HIS OWN WRITINGS.

Address J. B. POND, Sole Manager,

Everett House, New York.

Flyer announcing an appearance by Paul Laurence Dunbar on September 8, 1896, at the Lyceum Theatre (most likely in New York City), with a handwritten note signed by his manager, J. B. Pond: "No tickets required—simply informal for press & a few literary friends." *The Paul Laurence Dunbar Papers*, roll 3, frame 207. *Courtesy of the Ohio Historical Society*

Introduction

Paul Laurence Dunbar (1872–1906) was one of the most prolific and versatile writers in American literary history. When he died five months before his thirty-fourth birthday, Dunbar had published four novels, four books of short stories, fourteen books of poetry, and numerous songs, dramatic works, short stories, poems, and essays in several American periodicals. At the time of his death, Dunbar was the greatest African American literary artist the nation had ever seen. The complexity of Dunbar's oeuvre and the range of his professional accomplishments should have led, in the century after his death, to commensurately rich and sophisticated critical approaches to his life and work.

In retrospect, that has not been the case. Scholars most often connect Dunbar's legacy to two books of poems he published in 1896, *Majors and Minors* and *Lyrics of Lowly Life,* because William Dean Howells, the so-called Dean of American Letters, wrote a laudatory review of the former in the June 27, 1896, issue of *Harper's Weekly* and adapted that review for the introduction he wrote for the latter. In the review, Howells praises *Majors and Minors* and, in effect, puts Dunbar on the mainstream literary map of America. Howells presents a special "negro poet" to readers in the United States and around the world, a Negro poet whose "negro pieces . . . are of like impulse and inspiration with the work of [Robert] Burns when he was most Burns, when he was most Scotch, when he was most peasant," and who, like Burns, "was least himself [when] he wrote literary English" (630). Howells's review specified Dunbar's niche in American letters as the "first man of his color to study his race objectively, to analyze it to himself, and then to represent it in art as he felt it and found it to be; to represent it humorously, yet tenderly, and above all so faithfully that we know the portrait to be undeniably like." For Howells, it was Dunbar's supposedly objective portrayal of African Americans speaking in dialect that made his representations both faithful and artistic.

Although Howells wrote with the best of intentions, Dunbar's supposed objective analysis of African American life became, for several contemporaneous literary critics and commercial marketplaces, the standard for determining the realistic nature and aesthetic value of "blackness" in literature. Eventually, this representational category limited Dunbar's own ability to deviate from the accepted protocols of African American literature, and subsequently reduced the complexity of his legacy to a rigid dichotomy. It has been argued that Dunbar was torn between, on the one hand, fulfilling certain cultural conventions of minstrelsy in order to make money and appease literary critics, and, on the other, heeding personal impulses to write poetry in the style of the Romantics. Dunbar was torn, in other words, between selling out to a racist market for blackface humor and dialect and practicing a sort of literary assimilationism that in itself was racist, because it privileged traditionally white-authored poetry as the best that Western literature had to offer. Scholars—and, indirectly, classroom teachers and students—have continued to frame their studies of Dunbar in terms of such poetic ambivalence, even when the literary text in question is not Dunbar's poetry. In short, the binary between informal and formal English into which Dunbar's poetry has often been put has incorrectly dictated the scholarly interpretations of his fiction. Consequently, we tend to come away with rather limited conceptual and generic approaches to Dunbar's literary life and legacy.[1]

The Complete Stories of Paul Laurence Dunbar addresses this tendency by focusing on Dunbar's gifts as a writer of short fiction. The collection reprints stories by Dunbar that have already appeared in previous editions as well as those that have remained out of print from their initial publication until now. The first section comprises the collected stories of Dunbar, reprinting the four collections of short stories he published during his lifetime: *Folks from Dixie* (1898), *The Strength of Gideon and Other Stories* (1900), *In Old Plantation Days* (1903), and *The Heart of Happy Hollow* (1904).[2] The second section comprises the uncollected stories—stories Dunbar did not include in his published collections.[3] Included in this second section are four dialect stories that Dunbar serialized in the *New York Journal and Advertiser* in 1897 and that are reprinted for the first time in our collection; and "Ohio Pastorals," five stories that Dunbar serialized in *Lippincott's Magazine* in 1901.

In the past, Dunbar's short fiction has come across as fragmented partially because it appeared in several competing anthologies of American literature and collections of Dunbar's writings.[4] Consequently, these anthologies and collections have made it rather difficult to make the necessary thematic connections between and among Dunbar's short stories. These books have also misrepresented Dunbar's short stories as only a minor part of his literary output, when in fact they constituted an important aspect of his experimentations with literary form. We can even go so far to assert that Dunbar's short stories reflect his most significant and sustained engagement with the literary conventions that ultimately frustrated his efforts at writing poetry, the novel, and plays. By reprinting 103 stories that Dunbar published between 1890 and 1905,[5] and by providing an editorial introduction that identifies the main themes and implications, *The Complete Stories of Paul Laurence Dunbar* makes Dunbar's entire oeuvre of short fiction available in one convenient and definitive volume for the first time.

I

Paul Laurence Dunbar was all too aware of the limitations William Dean Howells's review of *Majors and Minors* imposed on his abilities as a literary artist. In a letter to a friend on March 15, 1897, Dunbar observes:

> One critic says a thing and the rest hasten to say the same thing, in many instances using the identical words. I see now very clearly that Mr. Howells has done me ir-

revocable harm in the dictum he laid down regarding my dialect verse. I am afraid that it will even influence English criticism, although what notices I have here have shown a different trend. (73)

Howells's prescriptions concerning Dunbar's dialect poetry conditioned the ways in which other critics at the time and later would read his work. Critics' repetition of "identical words" and similar sentiments about Dunbar's writing not only indicated the value of his work in the public sphere but also restricted his ability to address social issues in his writing. As he noted earlier in the letter: "I am so glad also that you too can see and appreciate the utter hollowness of the most of American book criticism" (73). Unfortunately for Dunbar, this "hollowness" did matter to the general reading public. Dunbar realized the adverse effect of Howells's "dictums" only when it was too late to do anything about it.

In part, Dunbar's apprehension concerned the racial politics of American literary culture. Realism, ascendant as a literary practice and tradition in the 1890s, advocated the presentation of personal knowledge as the basis for fictional representation. In the case of African American authors, however, this personal knowledge also had to conform to the stereotypical norms that had already been institutionalized by the tenets of realism. As an anonymous literary review from the *Bookman* in September 1896 attested, "Mr. Dunbar, as his pleasing, manly, and not unrefined face shows, is a poet of the African race; and this novel and suggestive fact at once places his work upon a peculiar footing of interest, of study, and of appreciative welcome" (19). Dunbar's poetry was a "welcome" addition to American literature, but his race placed "his work upon a peculiar footing" in comparison to his Anglo-American contemporaries. The novelty of race lent significance to Dunbar's poetry for this reviewer. If Dunbar had been a white man, then "he would have received little or no consideration in a hurried weighing of the mass of contemporary verse" (19). Both Howells and the anonymous reviewer directly linked Dunbar's role in the literary realm to his racial or ethnic background. The aesthetic categories used to evaluate his writing were explicitly connected to his identity as an African American.

While critics positioned Dunbar's poetry in relation to his identity, his first three novels—*The Uncalled* (1898), *The Love of Landry* (1900), and *The Fanatics* (1901)—were criticized for their departure from the traditionally accepted subject matter of African American authors. Dunbar's decision to use what critics perceived to be white characters in his first three novels did not correspond with cultural expectations. Grace Isabel Colbron's *Bookman* review of *The Uncalled* asserts:

It is therefore no belittling of the true literary value of Paul Dunbar's earlier work, his exquisite poems, and the sketches in *Folks from Dixie*, to say that they touched us so deeply because they gave us what we asked for—the glow of a warm heart thrown on a little and hitherto almost unknown corner of our country's many-sided life. When this promising poet, from whom we expected work of increasing power along the same lines, forsakes his own people, and gives us pictures of the life of the white inhabitants of an Ohio town, he challenges us to judge him without the plea of his especial fitness for the work. [. . . A]s Mr. Dunbar finds for his hero at last the vocation for which he is truly "called," so he himself should return to those lines along which, as we have already indicated, lie his best chances of actual, not relative success. (339, 341)[6]

The review of *The Love of Landry* in the *New York Times* notes that "the story is more conventional than Mr. Dunbar's former work" before moving on to observe that "it is to be hoped Mr. Dunbar will not forsake his own province for one which he must share with so many other writers of romance" (902). Similarly, the anonymous reviewer of *The Love of Landry* for the *Bookman* states that "[i]t is quite natural that Mr. Dunbar should have certain limitations when he endeavours to portray the characters of those not of his own race" (512). Arguably, these critics were celebrating the distinctive perspective available to Dunbar as an African American author. It is more likely, however, that the remonstration to remain in "his own province" of representational subject matter, a province "he was so eminently fitted" to fulfill (Colbron, 338–39), was more a criticism than a compliment.

By contrast, Dunbar's short fiction did not elicit such lukewarm reviews—quite the opposite, as we shall discuss later. That few scholars have examined this body of work—as opposed to his poetry and his fourth novel, *The Sport of the Gods* (1902)—means that the critical connections between Dunbar's short stories and the rest of his oeuvre remain underdeveloped. These connections, when illuminated, deepen and broaden our understanding of Dunbar's literary strategies and goals, particularly in the context of the short story form. These connections also enable us to diversify the textual, historical, cultural, and sociological approaches that can be applied to Dunbar's work. A significant addition to American letters at the turn of the twentieth century, Dunbar's short stories offer keen insight into American race relations as well as the problems African Americans faced in the nineteenth and early twentieth centuries.

Literary fame distinguished Dunbar's own relationship to the short story, as opposed to how it functioned for other African American authors at the turn of the twentieth century, such as Charles Chesnutt, Pauline Hopkins, and Frances Ellen Watkins Harper. Although Dunbar was still bound by the period's representational norms for African Americans in fiction, his preeminence allowed him to more liberally experiment with different literary forms and themes. This latitude is most evident in his short fiction, where his most serious political interventions occur. Dunbar's collections of short stories contain an eclectic mix of literary strategies. They include stories that run from the traditional nostalgic plantation narrative extolling the virtues of humble and faithful slaves, to stories that more directly question the lack of cultural-national citizenship accorded to African Americans. In general, Dunbar complicates the simplistic caricatures of African Americans at the turn of the century, revealing the nuances of racial identity and reflecting the elaborate and provocative structure of America's racial landscape.

Dunbar's short stories enabled him to escape the socially compromised iconography, themes, and discourse of racial representation. Although the short story made use of the same kind of racial stereotypes found in American novels or poetry, its widely accepted designation as entertaining and apolitical provided a smokescreen for Dunbar's own experimentation with literary form and racial politics. We need to keep in mind that the short story was considered a genre "lower" than the novel in the period, and critical peer reviews in periodicals focused on providing authors the feedback required for improving their stories or their literary skills in general. Dunbar capitalized on the period's conception of the genre as literary training ground for authors in order to interrogate the pastoral boundaries, vis-à-vis the slave plantation, that circumscribed representations of blacks in American fiction.

Throughout his collections Dunbar interspersed so-called plantation stories that either conformed to or deviated from the pastoral standards by which African Americans were often viewed. First, there are the stories that conform to pastoral definitions of African American life. These are the stories that too readily lend themselves to the traditional critical interpretation of Dunbar as merely pandering to white expectations of blacks.[7] At the same time, there are also stories that undermine the pastoral logic used to depict African Americans.[8] These stories seemingly adhere to the public stereotypes of African Americans, but, upon closer examination, the black characters respond to racism and racial prejudice in active and progressive ways.

In addition to the plantation stories, there are stories by Dunbar that expand the representations of African Americans. For example, "Little Africa" stories set in Dalesford, Ohio, break from the traditional pastoral images of African Americans.[9] Several stories set in other urban areas such as the tenements of New York and Washington, D.C., present the positive abilities of African Americans while modifying the protocols of local color.[10] Occasionally, such stories perpetuate the racial stereotypes of the period; however, they also rethink the traditional literary location of African Americans within the rural South.[11] Presenting African American characters as an integral component of larger urban centers allowed Dunbar to critique in subtle ways the mores that configured African American identity and the politics of race in American society.

Dunbar's apparent inconsistency—his tendency toward stereotypical literary depictions, on the one hand, and his incorporation here and there of more serious racial-political discourse, on the other—points to his personal and professional obligations to the commercial marketplace for African American literature. Peter Revell has suggested that Dunbar's private arrangements in about 1898 with the editor of the *Saturday Evening Post* (George Horace Lorimer) to submit literary material compelled him to resort to the most publishable or marketable means of African American characterization in the 1890s: minstrelsy (Revell, 108). This agreement resulted in his third collection, *In Old Plantation Days,* which he dedicated to this editor and which, as we shall soon see, resumes the literary strategies of *The Strength of Gideon.* By this time, both critical acclaim and commercial success had already begun to reward the poet's command of what James Weldon Johnson called minstrel "humor and pathos" (41). Such qualities were also attributed to the so-called plantation tradition of postbellum Anglo-American literature, which tended to romanticize, sentimentalize, and thereby recuperate nostalgia for the inequitable race relations that thrived in the Old South.[12] To an extent, Dunbar fell onto his own sword in reintroducing some of the tradition's formulaic themes with his racially "authentic" pen—namely, the orthography of black dialect, racial stereotypes, and generally conciliatory interracial relationships. A victim of his own success, he boxed himself into a literary paradigm that overshadowed the diversity of his literary skills and racial-political thought while offering him the best means of earning money. While Dunbar accepted these terms for the sake of achieving financial security, he was more proactive and subtle about inserting his own political views than many critics, then and since, have given him credit for.

One skill overshadowed is his experimentation with white narrators and characters in his short fiction—an experimentation more liberal, in fact, than that found in his novels.[13] By probing the relationships between the races in more critical depth than perhaps any other author of his era, Dunbar uncovers the specific tensions that existed between whites and blacks and that resulted from inequities in social power. For example, Dr. Melville, Dunbar's white narrator in "The Lynching of Jube Benson," contained in *The Heart of Happy Hollow,* recognizes too late his complicity with the tenets of white supremacy. Further, Dunbar clearly posits that whites and blacks are influenced by the same set of cultural forces. Also in that collection, "The Promoter" depicts how Mr. Buford learns dubious business practices from his interactions with whites: "Truly he had profited by the examples of the white men for whom he had so long acted as messenger and factotum."

Finally, there are a good number of stories that test the political limitations African Americans faced while dealing with white society.[14] Dunbar's decision about where to place such stories within the collections demonstrates his conscious effort to soften those stories' inherently scathing critiques of the values within or imposed on African American life and of those underwriting black-white race relations. The frontloading of stereotypical stories in *The Strength of Gideon,* for example, belies the subtle racial-political critiques and depictions of African Americans that appear thereafter in the collection. Indeed, such nuanced stories defy the blanket praise of the stereotypes that characterize both the immediate reviews of *The Strength of Gideon* and the criticism of Dunbar's short fiction in subsequent literary history. Four of the sixteen reviews that appeared in U.S. periodicals commended Dunbar's realistic "command of humor and pathos."[15] But hardly any noticed how, much less considered why, certain stories by Dunbar document the social, economic, and political power that whites held over blacks in U.S. society. Within this context of pseudodocumentary realism, Dunbar complicates not only the conventions of racial representation in literature, but also the portrayal of his stories as merely selling out to the critics and the marketplace.

II

A closer look at the individual collections shows how Dunbar combined his literary strategies. Dunbar's first collection of stories, *Folks from Dixie,* was published in 1898, earlier in the same year that his first novel, *The Uncalled,* came out. Both appeared under the imprint of Dodd, Mead and Company. Dunbar dedicated *Folks from Dixie* to Henry A. Tobey, a longtime friend and supporter; it was Tobey who had helped finance the publication of first *Oak and Ivy* and later *Majors and Minors,* and it was also Tobey who suggested that Dunbar send a copy of *Majors and Minors* to James Herne, a well-known actor who was performing in Toledo. Herne "read the book, wrote enthusiastically to Dunbar, and passed the book on to William Dean Howells" (Revell, 45). The rest, as they say, was history.

Folks from Dixie contains twelve stories. One of them, "Anner 'Lizer's Stumblin' Block," had been published in the May 1895 *Independent,* and two others were published as the collection was in press: "The Deliberation of Mr. Dunkin" in the April 1898 *Cosmopolitan* and "A Family Feud" in the April 1898 *Outlook.* The collection was Dunbar's first extended experiment with the short story form; his earlier published stories were mostly attempts to develop his prose-writing abilities.[16] *Folks from Dixie* presents one of Dunbar's initial attempts to break out of the "objective" literary model that Howells's review had created for him.

The majority of the stories in *Folks from Dixie* deal with plantation settings and themes. Only three, "Anner 'Lizer's Stumblin' Block," "A Family Feud," and "The Intervention of Peter," are set in the pre–Civil War period. But of the first nine stories, all except "Jimsella" are set in the rural South. The first story, "Anner 'Lizer's Stumblin' Block," is a traditional plantation story narrating Anner 'Lizer's struggles to keep both her faith and her man. The second story, "The Ordeal at Mt. Hope," is also set in the rural South, but in the postbellum period. It chronicles Reverend Howard Dokesbury's attempts to bring change to the town of Mt. Hope. Dokesbury, recently sent to Mt. Hope from his Northern college, notes that the "environment" of the town is the largest force that he has to combat in helping to improve the lot of his fellow African Americans. Thinking of the proper course of action required to help Elias, the son of the couple he is staying with, Dokesbury observes:

> He could not talk to Elias. He could not lecture him. He would only be dashing his words against the accumulated evil of years of bondage as the ripples of a summer sea beat against a stone wall. It was not the wickedness of this boy he was fighting or even the wrongdoing of Mt. Hope. It was the aggregation of the evils of the fathers, the grandfathers, the masters and mistresses of these people. Against this what could talk avail?

Instead, Dokesbury realizes that he must use his own actions to inspire the changes that he desires. Dokesbury's success in awakening Mt. Hope points to the transformation African Americans can accomplish when they are given not only something to aspire to but the practical means to achieve it. Dunbar's story takes a productive slant on a traditionally negative topic—black Southern poverty—and invests it with a positive outcome. His story posits an affirmative vision for his white readers while also giving them a clear sense that the social environment and the tangible past have shaped and influenced Southern blacks in ways that need to be acknowledged. After "The Ordeal at Mt. Hope," Dunbar includes two more postbellum plantation stories in "The Colonel's Awakening" and "The Trial Sermons on Bull-Skin" before turning to the crowded urban space of New York City in "Jimsella."

"Jimsella" builds on the sentiments of "The Ordeal at Mt. Hope." Mandy Mason, the story's main protagonist, struggles with the different living conditions presented in the urban North: "here it was all very different: one room in a crowded tenement house, and the necessity of grinding day after day to keep the wolf—a very terrible and ravenous wolf—from the door." However, as the overriding narrative voice makes clear, it is not Mandy's "inherent" laziness or lack of trying that makes her present conditions difficult; she is, after all, "only a simple, honest countrywoman." Instead, it is the environment that has shaped Mandy in the rural South. Before she travels to the North with Jim, "the first twenty years of her life conditions had not taught her the necessity of thrift." Mandy and Jim struggle to survive, especially when Jim takes to "wandering." Hope is rekindled with the birth of their child, Jimsella. Not only does the arrival of the child stop Jim's wandering ways; both parents find the hope and courage that they lacked at the beginning of the story. Moreover, Dunbar frames the story around a strong black female character; it is Mandy's attempt to struggle on after Jim's initial absence that creates the possibility for a positive conclusion. The next four stories, however, use the "humor and pathos" noted by contemporary reviewers. "Mt. Pisgah's Christmas 'Possum," "A Family Feud," "Aunt Mandy's Investment," and "The Intervention of Peter" follow the more traditional use of minstrel-like black characters that are overly comical or overly faithful to whites.

Dunbar saves his most interesting stories for the end of the collection. After having appealed to the racist sensibilities of his white readers, Dunbar offers two stories, "Nelse Hatton's Vengeance" and "At Shaft 11," as his most pointed commentary on the social conditions that African Americans faced. "Nelse Hatton's Vengeance" concerns an industrious and successful ex-slave who becomes the "soundest and most highly respected" citizen of Dexter, Ohio. Nelse lives in an all-white neighborhood in one of the nicest houses, earning the respect of his white neighbors. The title comes into play when a vagrant who asks Nelse for a meal turns out to be Nelse's former childhood master. Instead of acting out his desired revenge on his former master, Nelse responds with sympathy and kindness. Nelse's actions could be read as another of Dunbar's capitulations to African American servility, but Nelse does express a larger racial anger over his earlier treatment, and his former master acknowledges the complaints. Nelse's ability to act humanely toward those who have previously wronged him suggests that reconciliation between whites and blacks is possible if both are willing to meet halfway.

The next story, "At Shaft 11," deals with labor agitation in a mining town in West Virginia. When black workers take over for striking whites, violence between the two groups ensues. Only the actions of white protagonist Jason Andrews prevent more bloodshed. While the story offers a seemingly negative portrayal of labor issues, Dunbar highlights the necessity of establishing equal rights for blacks before workers' rights can be resolved. Andrews's decision to stand up for the black workers and against the unionist activities of his former fellow workers is grounded in these sentiments. As he tells the white owners of the mine, "I am with you as long as you are in the right." Dunbar's story mediates the interactions between whites and blacks in a productive and judicious manner. At the conclusion of the story, whites and blacks continue to work together at the mine.

Dunbar's portrayal of the white labor agitator in "At Shaft 11" as "so perfectly plausible, so smooth, and so clear," takes on a larger meaning when juxtaposed with the description of Mr. Ruggles, a black confidence man in "Aunt Mandy's Investment." Ruggles's motto is "It is better to be plausible than right," and as the narrator informs us, "[h]e was seldom right, but he was always plausible." The tensions between plausibility and being "right" operate in both stories. Dunbar uses the abuses of plausibility between blacks to construct a humorous conclusion in "Aunt Mandy's Investment," but in "At Shaft 11" the plausibility of whites leads to violence against blacks. In sum, blacks and whites are equally guilty of using misleading rhetoric to accomplish individual goals. While not an explicit point of either story, such careful intertextual connections point out how Dunbar used his collections to intervene in the larger public discussions about the social relationships between blacks and whites. Curiously, Dunbar concludes the collection with "The Deliberation of Mr. Dunkin," a story set in Miltonville, Kentucky, that unthreateningly—that is, humorously—narrates Mr. Dunkin's courting of the town's new schoolteacher.

Several other intertextual threads and themes, often introduced as sly narrative asides, critique the perceived roles of blacks in American life. One of the more subtle examples refers to the negative representation of blacks in the popular press. In "The Ordeal at Mt. Hope," Rev. Howard Dokesbury observes "a group of idle Negroes exchanging rude badinage with their white counterparts across the street." The narrator then provides the following gloss of this exchange: "After a while this bantering interchange would grow more keen and personal, a free-for-all friendly fight would follow, and the newspaper correspondent in that section would write it up as a 'race war.'" The sensationalized representation of the "free-for-all friendly fight" as a "race war" by the "newspaper correspondent" points to the ways in which press representations exacerbated the tensions between whites and blacks in ways that disproportionately affected blacks.

In "Nelse Hatton's Vengeance," Dunbar also touches on the hackneyed use of literary convention. Describing Nelse Hatton's living room, the narrator observes: "If this story were chronicling the doings of some fanciful Negro, or some really rude plantation hand, it might be said that the 'front room was filled with a conglomeration of cheap but pretentious furniture, and the walls covered with gaudy prints'—this seems to be the usual phrase. But in it the chronicler too often forgets how many Negroes were house-servants, and from close contact with their master's families imbibed aristocratic notions and quiet but elegant tastes." Here, the narrator calls attention to the specific distinctions that are being expressed in the text between "the chronicler" who uses "the traditional phrase" and the narrator who knows better than to make such gross overgeneralizations. Further, in drawing social and economic distinctions between Nelse, on the one hand, and "some fanciful Negro, or some really rude plantation hand," on the other, the narrator also documents the actual differences from stereotypical norms that Nelse represents.

Reviews of *Folks from Dixie* were mostly favorable. Critics read Dunbar's short stories through the lens of Howells's review, some going so far as to quote Howells directly. As the anonymous reviewer for the *New York Times* notes, "[Dunbar] has treated the negro 'objectively,' as Mr. Howells says, with perfect truth and sympathy, but without a trace of sentimentality" (397). Dunbar's racial identity was also a topic of discussion. George Preston observes that "the work is notable as the first expression in national prose fiction of the inner life of the American negro" (348). The anonymous reviewer in the *Independent* states that "his insight into negro character is refreshingly clear, while his way of putting things avoids in most places the conventional stumbling-blocks of so-called 'dialect' writers" (726). Reviewers generally responded most positively to the humorous stories. The review in the *Independent* proclaims, "[T]here is pathos in some of them; but we like the humor better" (726), while the review in *Outlook* asserts that Dunbar "has humor in abundance, freshness of style, and sympathy of the best and truest" (86). The connections made in these reviews between race, "objectivity," and humor in Dunbar's stories reiterate the norms used to define African Americans in literature and in the larger public sphere.

However, critics singled out three stories: "The Ordeal at Mt. Hope," "Jimsella," and "Nelse Hatton's Vengeance." George Preston begins his comments on "The Ordeal at Mt. Hope" by reinforcing racist beliefs about blacks, bemoaning the "beautiful maternity of the grotesque black mother and the grim dignity of the repulsive black father" (348). But he recognizes Dunbar's portrayal of the influence of environment. Preston notes that Dokesbury's "ordeal is the struggle to raise his people" from "the aggregation of the evils done by the fathers, the grandfathers, the masters and mistresses of these people." Preston also favorably comments on "Jimsella," calling it an example of "the common destiny of humanity" (349). While he is overly sentimental in his observations, lamenting that the characters have drifted "from a plantation home of comparative comfort to the rigorous poverty of a New York tenement," he does acknowledge that the conclusion strikes a "universal" note. Finally, the review in the *Critic* observes that "light is thrown on the relations of the two races, black and white" (413) in "Nelse Hatton's Vengeance," while the reviewer from the *New York Times* calls the story "nobly conceived" (397). The critical response to these three stories points out that Dunbar's narrative strategies were having their intended effects. Humor and race were the main features that critics emphasized, but some also observed that more was going on in his collection. Taken as a whole, Dunbar's first collection was both a success and a failure. While his work was still marked by the terms that Howells had set out for his poetry, Dunbar did get some critics to look beyond the humorous facade of his initial stories. The stereotypical African American characters and idyllic settings found in Dunbar's collection appealed to "a huge audience for a literature of escape into a pre–Civil War, exotic South that, all but 'lost,' was now the object of nostalgia" in the postbellum decades (Blight, 211). Several of Dunbar's stories, however, defy this literary paradigm, which remained popular at the turn of the century, by illustrating the complexity of race relations in certain environments.

In the year following publication of these reviews of *Folks from Dixie,* Dunbar was editing the proofs of his second book of short stories, *The Strength of Gideon,* and writing *The Love of Landry,* a novel based on the medical trip he took to Colorado in late 1898 to recover from tuberculosis. The two books differed remarkably in both their literary nature and their public reception, analogous to the difference between *Folks from Dixie* and *The Uncalled.* Both *Folks from Dixie* and *The Strength of Gideon* are collections of short stories focusing on the trials and tribulations of African America. By contrast, both *The Uncalled* and *The Love of Landry* are novels that avoid any sustained discussion of this subject, focusing respectively on the local color of the Midwest (Ohio) and the West (Colorado). Although the New York–based publisher, Dodd, Mead and Company, released all four books with comparable marketing engines, *Folks from Dixie* outsold *The Uncalled,* and more critics praised *The Strength of Gideon* than *The Love of Landry.*[17]

There is a plausible explanation for the difference in the critical and public receptions of *Folks from Dixie* and *The Strength of Gideon,* on the one hand, and *The Uncalled* and *The Love of Landry,* on the other. The two books of short stories met the public expectation that African American literature should, at the very minimum, venture a realistic representation of African American life, and at its very best, appear to inscribe this representation within the cultural politics of minstrelsy. Comprising twenty stories that cover the antebellum period, *The Strength of Gideon,* like *Folks from Dixie,* concentrates mostly on African Americans in the South, but also includes stories about those who were trying to navigate the urban terrains and free societies of the Northeast. The title story captures the political-ideological tension between the African American accommodation of white privilege and the assertion among slaves of racial equality in spite of this privilege.

Gideon, a devoutly religious slave, has developed unwavering commitments to his master, his own wife, and his race. But when the master asks Gideon to promise to help take care of the "women folks" on the plantation, the slave experiences a crisis of loyalty. The prospect of emancipation inspires the slaves on the plantation, including Gideon's wife, to consider fleeing Northward and securing their own freedom. In the face of this smoldering resistance to the status quo, Gideon demonstrates the "strength" to remain faithful to his promise. Implicit in this loyalty is Gideon's belief that the conditions of slavery, however problematic, have not yet proven so unbearable as to warrant his own flight.

"Viney's Free Papers" echoes "The Strength of Gideon." Ben Raymond is a slave who secures the manumission paperwork for his wife, Viney, who then threatens to leave him when he resists the idea of achieving freedom in the North. Many manumitted slaves were traveling to the North, but if freedom could not be experienced in the South, where the slaves were born and reared, Ben argued, it should not be experienced at all. Again, an unshakable fidelity to the family heritage and social stability of slavery trumps the desire for freedom. This story is not new in African American literary history; Booker T. Washington has told it.[18] The appearance of this kind of story in *The Strength of Gideon*, as opposed to the more revolutionary and volatile narrative of slave insurrection (such as Nat Turner's) to secure freedom, certainly could have impressed on readers in Dunbar's era a highly conciliatory, if unbalanced, picture of slave life. Humorous punch lines in the stories of *The Strength of Gideon*, of course, encourage readers knowledgeable about African American history to cast a doubtful eye on this entertaining picture of racial conciliation. But Dunbar's overt catering to accommodationist or gradualist sensibilities—that is, the doctrines of accommodating white privilege and of advocating a gradual approach to racial equality—betrays the more skeptical stance he consistently held in his nonfictional essays about racial injustice and the importance of expeditious African American intellectual and cultural progress, or racial uplift.[19]

Despite probably boosting the critical and commercial success of *The Strength of Gideon*, reviews of the collection reduce its complexity. They are consistent with the longstanding critical reputation of the volume as a formulaic compendium of "plantation" stories and of its author as a novice at prose.[20] Almost all the reviews laud the book's realistic depictions of African Americans: the stories express "the character, feeling and sentiment of the southern darkey." The "plantation tales show the Negro in his truest light—fervid, credulous, full of rich, unconscious humor; lazy sometimes, but capable of dog-like faithfulness." And the stories "are correct reflections of the Negro dialect and habits and thoughts of the southern darkey" (qtd. in Metcalf, 136–38).[21] The interspersion throughout the book of E. W. Kemble's caricatures of the African Americans featured in the stories certainly contributed to such impressions.

A closer look at *The Strength of Gideon* reveals that most of these reviews miss crucial indications of Dunbar's resistance to pastoral and minstrel imagery. Only one review, however uneven, demonstrates an understanding of the complexity of Dunbar's literary project and his imagination of a multifaceted white audience. Appearing in the *New York Times* (May 19, 1900), the review states that the stories of *The Strength of Gideon*

> will be read with interest we can hardly doubt. That they will awaken antagonism in some quarters is equally certain. They bid strongly for sympathy for the col-

ored man in his struggle with the conditions which freedom has imposed upon him, and for that very reason they will evoke nothing but growls from that still considerable class of persons who cannot see anything good in a "nigger."

Indeed, it is at this class that the stories are written. Mr. Dunbar is most influential when he is engaged in telling something which goes to show that the negro cannot make the battle of life as a free man except in the face of social disabilities which affect him at every step. He cannot hope to get such employment as a white man of similar education and ability, simply because the white man conceives the permission of such employment as recognizing a social equality. (324)

By treating the more overt signs of racism, "The Tragedy at Three Forks," for example, indeed shows those "social disabilities" which affect African Americans. The story revolves around white mob violence and the consequent lynching of two Negroes prematurely accused of burning a respected white family out of its home. Several other stories in *The Strength of Gideon* portray African American resilience and perseverance in the face of social and cultural difficulties. In "The Ingrate," a story recalling the centrality of literacy to securing freedom in the antebellum slave narrative, a boy teaches himself to read while serving as an accountant for his master. Eventually he runs away, and his literacy qualifies him for the position of Union army sergeant during the Civil War. "The Finish of Patsy Barnes," furthermore, concerns a boy who learns to tend and ride race horses, despite the oppression of blacks in the racing industry, in order to pay for the care of his sick mother. Finally, "Silas Jackson" follows the journey of a Southern country boy to a faraway aristocratic hotel and resort where, through hard work and humility, he "refines" his interpersonal and verbal skills and ascends to a managerial position. He later volunteers as leading tenor of the hotel's quartet, traveling to Northern cities to perform, but eventually his singing talents decline and he returns to his home to persevere as a field worker. Dunbar's collection also features more educated African Americans struggling to understand U.S. social, political, and legal strategies of racial uplift, such as those in "One Man's Fortunes," "Mr. Cornelius Johnson, Office-Seeker," "A Mess of Pottage," and "A Council of State."

These and other stories in *The Strength of Gideon* focus on the lives of African American men, but a few other stories offer notable portrayals of comparably strong and fearless African American women, a theme Dunbar would accentuate in *In Old Plantation Days*. "The Case of 'Ca'line'" displays a "kitchen monologue" in which a servant openly criticizes her master and mistress's timid disenchantment with her work around the house. This was the humorous story that Dunbar frequently read to audiences when he toured the country (Cunningham, 201). The namesake of "Mammy Peggy's Pride," "a typical mammy of the old south," overcomes her residential pride to help consummate a rather complex courtship between her mistress, distraught over selling their homestead, and the young gentleman who bought it. This nuanced characterization, along with those of other African Americans in *The Strength of Gideon*, indicates Dunbar's constant negotiation of the literary politics of racial representation, even if only to serve as the backdrop to stories about folk-religious practices in the black church or about the moral and philosophical crises whites faced as they grappled with the question of slavery.[22]

The title of *In Old Plantation Days*, published three years after *The Strength of Gideon*, captures the generic limitations within which Dunbar wrote. According to some scholars, the collection represents one of his "chief" contributions to the plantation tradition of American literature (Brawley, 96; Revell, 108). Indeed, the collection of twenty-five stories revisits several of the same formulaic literary strategies and themes that entertained white readers of *Folks from Dixie* and *The Strength of Gideon*. But *In Old Plantation Days* differs from these collections in two main respects, one organizational and the other thematic. First, most of the stories are set on one specific plantation, that of Stuart Mordaunt, and the geographic restriction to the Mordaunt plantation lends organizational coherence to the collection. Mordaunt is a master often kindhearted and open-minded toward his family and slaves, and these traits help nurture a plantation atmosphere in which blacks and whites generally get along, respect one another, and form a tight social unit. *In Old Plantation Days* covers a variety of topics, including the jolly interactions between and among masters and slaves, the social role of conjure, and the power of music. The cameo appearances of protagonists and the recurrence throughout the stories of geographic, social, cultural, and religious markers facilitate transitions from one story to the next.[23]

The second unique feature of *In Old Plantation Days* is its attention to the gender politics of the slave community, especially the responsibilities and respectability of black women as they keep plantation life stable and functional for its residents. The opening story, "Aunt Tempe's Triumph," captures the degree of assertiveness, if not stereotypical sassiness, that the black women in the volume tend to express toward their black male counterparts or even toward their masters and mistresses. Similar in its argumentative nature to "The Case of 'Ca'line'" in *The Strength of Gideon*, "Aunt Tempe's Triumph" is framed by Aunt Tempe's willingness to debate Mordaunt on whether she, the mammy of his daughter, deserves more than he does the traditional right to "give her away" in her upcoming wedding—a role customarily fulfilled by the bride's father. Despite Aunt Tempe's reputed skill in intimidating other slaves or manipulating Mordaunt and his family until she gets her own way, he does not give in. Ultimately, she intervenes in the wedding ceremony, just before Mordaunt's cue, to give the daughter away. Aunt Tempe's attitude has analogues elsewhere in *In Old Plantation Days*: the sharp tongues of Martha in "The Memory of Martha," Aunt Fanny in "The Brief Cure of Aunt Fanny," Anna Maria in "The Way of a Woman," as well as Maria Ann Gibbs and Lucindy Woodyard in "The Defection of Maria Ann Gibbs" are notable examples.

To characterize Aunt Tempe as merely troublesome would be premature, however. Her character is more subtle than one might expect. "Aunt Tempe's Revenge" shows Aunt Tempe's more considerate and emotional side. Contrary to the expectations of Mordaunt and probably even the reader of this story, she tries to convince her master to buy Tom, the son of her estranged husband who has abandoned her for another woman living at a nearby plantation, so that a young woman on the

Mordaunt plantation can marry him. Aunt Tempe implores Mordaunt to ignore his own policy of forbidding his slaves to marry slaves residing on other plantations. (Mordaunt denounces the slave trade.) In the end his conscience convinces him to do precisely this. Mordaunt hands Aunt Tempe the money to forward to a slave trader for the acquisition of Tom.

The other black women of *In Old Plantation Days,* mentioned above, are comparably multidimensional. Martha inspires her husband, Ben, to play the banjo in order to sustain her before she dies. After her death she lives on in Ben's mind until he conjures up her memory by playing the banjo for old times' sake. Aunt Fanny, initially bitter and resentful at aging and relinquishing to an upstart her role as head cook on the plantation, becomes a pathetic figure slowly losing the fight against rheumatism and debilitating illnesses. Anna Maria ultimately agrees to marry her lover, Gabe, but only after her repeated rejections urge him to improve his interpersonal and verbal skills. Finally, Maria Ann Gibbs and Lucindy Woodyard have historically competed for the hearts and minds of a church congregation, but their public tussle in a fundraising challenge further undermines their relationship and concludes with Maria's defection from the church.

As serious as these stories might seem, Dunbar threads them with wonderful humor. One of the funnier stories is "A Lady Slipper." Dely saves her mistress, Emily, from the embarrassment and the sense of betrayal inherent in explaining to Robert, a man courting her, that she has encouraged another "oft-rejected lover," Nelson, to grovel in the dirt in order to win the right to own her sexy slipper. Dely persuades Robert's gullible and reckless younger brother to steal this slipper back for "luck cakes" (they provide long-lasting luck if eaten). In another story, "The Trouble about Sophiny," Sophiny strings along a coachman and a butler who desire to escort her to the great ball. Eventually and unfortunately, she tells them, after they have needlessly boxed each other into aches and pains, that she has already agreed to go with a field hand.

Aside from portraying the wit, savvy, and humor of black women, *In Old Plantation Days* also pays great attention to folk religion and the black church. Religious society in the slave quarters, we learn, tends to exhibit the kind of problems found in any society, including envy and sin. In "The Walls of Jericho," Reverend Parker is distressed to watch the members of his congregation trickle out to attend the church of a rival preacher, Reverend Johnson, who revels in and stokes Parker's jealousy. Only after what seems like the divine intervention of an earthquake—which is really Parker's young masters sneaking through nearby woodland and cutting down trees to cause a disturbance—does the congregation deem Johnson's leadership questionable and return to Parker's church.

Parker, like Mordaunt, makes cameo appearances in other stories. In many of the stories he is about eighty years of age, but in one story, "How Brother Parker Fell from Grace," he is as young as twenty-eight and as imperfect as any other person on the plantation. Parker is a talented preacher, yet also a young man full of such egotism and pride that he commits the sin of playing cards when challenged. The shame he experiences afterward almost paralyzes his will to return to the pulpit. However, the encouragement he receives from, of all people, his master, Mordaunt, illustrates two things. First, it emphasizes the theme of religious self-redemption pervading *In Old Plantation Days,* a divergence from the more critical stance on religion that Dunbar takes in, say, *The Strength of Gideon.* Second, it reiterates the supportive relationship possible between whites and religious slaves. (In "The Walls of Jericho," Reverend Johnson, a "free negro," receives the permission needed to hold meetings next to the Mordaunt estate.)

Dunbar's imagination of the bond between masters and slaves contrasts with the history of masters being resistant to slave religion. Christianity in particular bolstered African American social and spiritual networks, and as early as the late eighteenth century it had proven philosophically incompatible with the principles of enslavement.[24] Thus the collegiality between Mordaunt and Parker—and between other whites and blacks, masters and slaves, in *In Old Plantation Days*—subordinates this history of interracial tension to the possibilities of interracial conciliation. In this regard, Dunbar arguably plays into the hands of the plantation tradition. One could also maintain, however, that *In Old Plantation Days* differs from this tradition because such conciliation is not the end in itself. Upon heeding Mordaunt's encouraging words, Reverend Parker returns to the pulpit to preach to the black faithful. The white man, in other words, serves black moral, religious, and political interests that reinforce communal networks within a peculiar institution predicated on tearing them down. The recurrence of this plot line, albeit under various narrative guises, encodes polemical subtexts within stories that seem to pander to contemporaneous and mostly white sensibilities of racism or racial prejudice.

Unsurprisingly, as in the case of Dunbar's previous two collections of short stories, *In Old Plantation Days* sold well. Sales were especially brisk during the Christmas season of 1903 (Gentry, 102). Certain reviewers picked up on the optimistic theme of potential interracial peace. One critic characterized these as "good stories, such as tend to the encouragement of good feelings between races—black and white" (qtd. in Metcalf, 147). Others noticed the utter palatability of the stories. The collection, according to one critic, comprises "scenes from slavery in its least tragic aspect," and this deviance from the historical record results in tales wherein "the tone of the narration is admirable" and "the humor unforced" (148). However, not all reviewers enjoyed the book. For one, the "picture of plantation life on the whole seems rather weak and superficial," and *In Old Plantation Days* proves that Dunbar should stick to what he knows best: poetry.[25] Of course, despite his literary reputation as a poet, Dunbar continued to write, compile, and publish short stories—in fact, another sixteen for his final collection, *The Heart of Happy Hollow.*

The Heart of Happy Hollow was published in 1904 by Dodd, Mead and Company. As his correspondence from the period attests, Dunbar's deteriorating health left him unable to deal with the rigors of prose writing except at very short sittings. His last novel, *The Sport of the Gods,* had come in 1902; between 1902 and his death, *In Old Plantation Days* and *The Heart of Happy Hollow* would be the only prose he published in book form. However, *The Heart of Happy Hollow* was an important contribution to Dunbar's work in the short story. Leaving behind the pastoral setting that had dominated *In Old Plantation Days*, Dunbar focuses primarily on portraying African Americans in towns and cities. As he wrote in a draft of an undated letter to Edward H. Dodd of Dodd, Mead and Company, this collection would focus on the "modern Negro" and his "Tales of Little Africa."[26] Ostensibly his most complex collection for the ways in which it positions blacks as the inhabitants of traditionally white urban space, it is also more subdued in tone than either *Folks from Dixie* or *The Strength of Gideon*.

The collection contained mainly new material: of the sixteen stories, only one, "A Defender of the Faith," had been previously published. Compared to *The Strength of Gideon*, of which eight of the twenty stories had been previously published, and *In Old Plantation Days*, of which fifteen of the twenty-five stories had been previously published,[27] *The Heart of Happy Hollow* offered a new body of work and marked Dunbar's most explicit confrontation with the public conception of African Americans.

The collection's title may sound faintly reminiscent of Dunbar's previous plantation setting, but his foreword clearly suggests otherwise: "Happy Hollow; are you wondering where it is? Wherever Negroes colonise [*sic*] in the cities or villages, north or south." In "Happy Hollow," Dunbar imagines a postbellum world in which the folk past influences the development of black urban consciousness: "wherever the hod carrier, the porter, the waiter are the society men of the town; wherever the picnic and the excursion are the chief summer diversion, and the revival the winter time of repentance, wherever the cheese cloth veil obtains at a wedding, and the little white hearse goes by with blacks mourners in the one carriage behind, there—there—is Happy Hollow." For the most part, the book's characters are neither simply heroic, tragic, pathetic, nor humorous, but shaped by their circumstances in various ways. More restrained or subdued than Dunbar's previous collections of short stories, *The Heart of Happy Hollow* does not argue for black humanity but instead accepts it as a given and proceeds to an analysis of the nature and implications of black struggles with white racism. Humor is still used in the collection, but it is removed from the outright minstrel humor of black caricature. As well, Dunbar has inverted the focus of his previous collections. Rather than foregrounding mostly pastoral settings for his stories with a few selected deviations, the majority of the stories deal with larger town or urban settings that have their own distinctive and developed African American communities.[28]

"The Scapegoat," the first story of the collection, chronicles the life of Mr. Robinson Asbury,[29] a black man whose lowly beginnings do not impede his upward climb in the town of Cadgers, and focuses on both class politics within the African American community as well as the white exploitation of blacks in general. Asbury's growing influence is exploited by white politicians in the town: "It was [Asbury's] wisdom rather more than his morality that made the party managers after a while cast their glances toward him as *a man who might be useful to their interests*. It would be well to have a man—a shrewd, powerful man—down in that part of the town who could carry his people's vote in his vest pocket" (italics added). Asbury proves an apt choice; as his reputation continues to grow, the lower-class black community he lives in assumes that "he will move uptown," as after all, "that's the way with a coloured man when he gets a start." However, Asbury stays put, vowing to "never desert the people who have done so much to elevate me." When Asbury's political influence begins to threaten the "better class of Negroes—by that is meant those who were particularly envious of Asbury's success," he is labeled "an enemy to his race" by members of the "better class" for "catering" to the lower class. After the election, in which the white politicians Asbury works for are triumphant, the opposing side declares fraud, and Asbury is sacrificed by his own party to "give the people some tangible evidence of their own yearnings for purity." Asbury is found guilty and sentenced to a year in prison, but not before he reveals "the men behind the throne." When Asbury returns to Cadgers after his sentence, his previous allies, both black and white, assume that he is a crushed man. In the following election, however, Asbury turns the tables on those who had made him a scapegoat for their own ends, and "[n]ot one of the party that had damned Robinson Asbury was left in power."

"The Scapegoat" captures the complexity of the American political scene. Given the chance to succeed, Asbury negotiates his own compromise with the town's political networks by both taking their offerings and attempting to represent his constituents. Once stripped of the laurels of his position, however, Asbury still serves those he represents, galvanizing the black lower class to use its political power to address social wrongs. While critiquing the excesses of politically motivated self-interest, the story suggests that the class consciousness of both blacks and whites can conspire in the exploitation of lower-class blacks.

Another story from the collection, "The Mission of Mr. Scatters," plays with a similar theme, but offers a different outcome. In the Southern town of Miltonville,[30] a town that has a well-developed black society, a black confidence man, Mr. Scatters, pretends to be a Cuban national in charge of executing the last will of John Jackson, brother to Miltonville's Isaac Jackson. Scatters is caught in his attempt to bilk black citizens out of their money, but the white courts defer his punishment when he appeals to the vanity and cupidity of the Southern aristocracy. His defense, directed at the whites who make up the court, enacts the social and political power that whites have over blacks by blaming blacks for "their" own inequality: "Gentlemen, I maintain that instead of imprisoning you should thank me for what I have done. Have I not taught your community a lesson? Have I not put a check upon their credulity and made them wary of unheralded strangers?" Scatters successfully plays upon white Southern vanity, correctly gauging the machinations of white justice by appealing to, as he puts it, "men of mercy" to protect him from the "vindictiveness" of his black victims. Scatters's ploy has its intended effect: not only are the judge and jury suitably impressed, the narrative assessment of white sentiments posits that "Scatters had taught the darkies a lesson." Scatters, through his understanding of the operations of white power and privilege, exonerates himself at the expense of his black peers.

"Old Abe's Conversion" differs from Dunbar's previous approaches to religion in his short fiction. Here, the tensions between the old, rural-based folk versions of religion portrayed through emotional excess and a connection to the natural world, and the new, urban-based versions portrayed through education and public service, are presented through the relationship between a father, Abram Dixon, and his son, Robert Dixon. Robert's desire to attend college for religious training is viewed by his father and the town of Danvers as "an attempt to force Providence. If Robert were called to preach, they said, he would be endowed with the power from on high, and no intervention of the schools was necessary." However, the point is not to excoriate the past or glorify the present. As the narrator makes clear, Robert visits his parents "intending to avoid rather than combat [their] prejudices. There was no condescension in his thought of them and their ways. They were different; that was all. He had learned new ways. They had retained the old." Rather, Dunbar portrays both sets of religious practices as serving the needs of their respective constituents. The generational shift in values associated with religious practice comes to a head when Robert stands in for his father at the pulpit. Robert maintains his composure in the face of Danvers's collective scorn for his form of faith, and makes his father promise to visit him in the city. Abram's experiences in the city allow him to better understand Robert's different approach to religion, and he comes away feeling like a new convert. In the balance created between Robert and Abram, Dunbar portrays religion as more important than the struggle over the way faith is practiced. It is instead a union of the particular needs of the community with the guidance of faith required to develop true religious sentiments.

The Heart of Happy Hollow addresses serious political questions larger than those tackled in previous collections, but there are still stories designed to entertain readers. "A Matter of Doctrine" plays with the religious faith of the town's black preacher, Rev. Jasper Hayward, who uses his position to gain his own ends. "The Race Question" is a dialect piece set at the racetrack that chronicles a preacher watching his son sin in the exact same ways that he did as a younger man. The only previously published story from the collection, "A Defender of the Faith," is a Christmas story that has a white female newspaper reporter, Arabella Coe, sacrificing her scant savings to insure that a group of black youngsters keep their faith in Santa Claus. Dunbar presents Coe as a sympathetic character, but as with *Folks from Dixie,* he also casts barbs at her for being a reporter. Coe is, after all, in the black tenements looking for a suitable Christmas story to publish. When she overhears the children's conversation concerning their dubious faith in Santa Claus, the narrator asserts, "It was not a very polite thing for Miss Coe to do, but then Miss Coe was a reporter and reporters are not scrupulous about being polite when there is anything to hear." Coe compensates the children for the story she overhears—she literally pays for the local color she receives—with gifts that they otherwise could not have afforded. Finally, Dunbar obviously wrote "Cahoots" to entertain; indeed, it recalls the kind of stories characteristic of the plantation tradition of Anglo-American literature.

"Cahoots" does, however, allow Dunbar to segue into the two stories that deal with the rural South, "The Wisdom of Silence" and "The Lynching of Jube Benson." Both stories undercut the authority of the pastoral even as they seem to conform to its conventions. "The Wisdom of Silence" portrays the efforts of Jeremiah Anderson to better his lot in the rural South. He buys land, works his way out of debt, and prospers. But when fire destroys his farm, he turns to Samuel Brabant, his former master, for financial assistance to begin again. Initially sounding rather Washingtonian in his seeming decree to "cast down your buckets where you are," Dunbar depicts the series of miscommunications that led to the estranged relationship between Anderson and Brabant, as well as the inordinate amount of pride that Anderson takes in his own accomplishments. The ultimate reconciliation between the two indicates not only the danger of pride, but also the necessity of productive interactions between whites and blacks. As in "Nelse Hatton's Vengeance" from *The Folks from Dixie,* Dunbar makes the point that such interactions, while humbling to both sides, will ultimately lead to better relations between the two races.

"The Lynching of Jube Benson"[31] is Dunbar's most provocative story dealing with the influence of pastoral norms on the lives of African Americans. The story is told by a white narrator, Dr. Melville, who recounts his participation in the lynching of an innocent black man. In presenting Melville's complicity with the stereotypical beliefs that dictate black and white relationships, Dunbar exposes how and why these norms generate violence against blacks. The story's pastoral setting no longer authorizes the iconography and implications of black bodies; instead, it ascribes stereotypes to whites, as evidenced by Melville's recognition of his own animalistic behavior. The ringing of "Blood guilty!" in Melville's ears at the story's conclusion places the responsibility for refiguring racial reasoning in the hands of whites.

"The Lynching of Jube Benson" also participates in Dunbar's ongoing critique of the negative ways blacks are portrayed in the media. Dr. Melville observes that the lynching "was very quiet and orderly. There was no doubt that it was as the papers would have said, a gathering of the best citizens." Melville's original understanding of blacks, presented as a mix of "tradition" and a "false education" in the previous paragraph, highlights the learned social values that led him and his fellow citizens to act as they did. His wry connection between the events that occurred and the way that the press would have presented them foregrounds his own complicity in the events that lead up to Jube's death, inverting the meaning of his actual comments: the "best citizens" have become the very creatures they accused blacks of being. Melville's belated feelings of guilt and his recognition of his culpability are further complicated by the presence of Handon Gay, "the ambitious young reporter" who surreptitiously records the story for his own use without Melville's awareness. While one of the characters in the story understands the larger cost of racialized thinking, the other continues to exploit violence against blacks as a form of entertainment.

The critical assessments of *The Heart of Happy Hollow* were mixed. Positive reviews include the *Boston Journal*'s opinion that "Mr. Dunbar has written nothing better than this volume" and the *Detroit Free Press*'s belief that "[i]f these stories go for anything it is to show that the same heart beats in man's breast whether his skin is black or white." These two reviews commend Dunbar's collection as his best work, the second going so far as to gesture to the overriding humanity portrayed in the stories. Negative or less encouraging reviews include the *Cleveland Leader*'s remark that Dunbar "keeps to his own people whose nature he knows so well" (rpt. in Metcalf, 148–49).[32] Another is the assertion of the *New York Times:* "Just in proportion as the stories stick to the negro and the negro quarter they are good stories" (916). The first review echoes the sentiments of previous reviews of Dunbar's novels, in which Dunbar is gently reminded to remain in "his own province" (Colbron, 338). The second builds upon these reactions by drawing overly fine lines in Dunbar's collection. All of the stories deal with black characters, but the white narrative voices in stories like "The Lynching of Jube Benson" appear to these reviewers as inappropriate. As the reviewer asserts, "The author puts the story in the mouth of one of the participators in the imagined lynching, but it [. . .] bears no relationship to the real facts in a horrible business." Instead, the reviewer's main interest is in highlighting the stories that contain an image of the "real negro," stories like "The Race Question," which narrates the "monologue of an old darky" and presents how "all negroes over thirty-five are apt to be in the South," and "One Christmas at Shiloh," which portrays "negroes exactly as they are." Stories such as "The Scapegoat" and "The Mission of Mr. Scatters" are further criticized for their aesthetic deficiencies when they do not fulfill the traditional Southern roles expected of blacks. Taken together, these reviews communally narrate the tensions that Dunbar faced as an author who was looking for the acceptance and recognition of his artistic vision while being further reminded of the conventional role he was expected to fulfill.

III

The second section of the collection, devoted to Dunbar's uncollected stories, offers an uneven mix of literary skill. Containing both his earliest forays into fiction writing and some of his later and more interesting experimentations with the short story form, the uncollected stories highlight the distance that Dunbar traveled in his short but productive career. More important, they provide a better historical context for understanding the development of Dunbar's struggles with the publishing industry, specifically as it affected his ability to produce work that was rewarding both financially and artistically.

The section begins with a series of four stories published in the *New York Journal and Advertiser* from September 26 to October 17, 1897, which the newspaper billed as a "Notable Series of Negro Dialect Stories by the Greatest Writer the Colored Race Has Ever Produced." The representational limitations suggested by the description belie the complexity of the stories, which mark Dunbar's earliest attempts at presenting African Americans in an urban context. At times the stories uncritically pander to racial stereotypes, but at others they productively shift African American characters from the rural South to the urban North. Characters long to leave the South, but also desire to return after experiencing life in the urban North, as in the story "Buss Jinkins Up Nawth." The other stories feature different types of black trickster figures, some of whom, like John Jackson in "Yellowjack's Game of Craps," conform to racial caricatures of blacks, while others more closely resemble George Johnson in "How George Johnson 'Won Out,'" who merely uses his wiles to get the girl.

Further complicating the stories are the personal comments that passed between Dunbar and Alice Ruth Moore while the series was being published.[33] Dunbar revealed his own disdain for the stories, highlighting the financial interest that drove him to produce them. As he writes to Moore on September 26, 1897, "If you look in today's *Journal* you will see and [disap]prove of the first of my Tenderloin stories, but go on disapproving dear, I am getting money for it that means help toward a cozy nest for my singing bird" (195–96). Moore is less forgiving of the artistic prostitution his work reproduces. On October 21, 1897, she replies:

> *don't, don't* write any more such truck as you've been putting in the *Journal*. Now this is between us as between husband and wife. To everyone else I champion your taste, even to Sallie. I argue from all sorts of premises your right to do as you please —but to you darling, I must say—*don't*. I know it means money and a speedier union for us, but sometimes money isn't all. It is not fair to prostitute your art for "filthy lucre," is it? I shall be glad when the sixth story comes out.[34] It will be such a relief, for every Sunday I find myself asking "what next." (216)

Moore urges Dunbar to maintain his artistic integrity, even as Dunbar is aware that she will not approve of the stories that he has created. This tension highlights the complex array of forces that Dunbar faced as an artist. As Dunbar responded to Moore on October 24, 1897: "So you see we must marry soon even if I have to write trash for the *Journal* in order to do it" (221).

The *New York Journal and Advertiser* stories provide insight into the compromises required to succeed as an African American author at the turn of the twentieth century. When juxtaposed with his personal correspondence, they trace Dunbar's negotiations of the literary marketplace, his learning of the ropes in a world that had particular views about the role of blacks in the publishing world. Dunbar's personal and professional interests troubled his ability to produce fiction that effectively dealt with the American racial scene; the social and cultural values held by Gilded Age America further circumscribed and complicated this process. Dunbar was expected to conform to the accepted literary norms in ways that did not affect white authors, at least if he wanted to remain in the good graces of editors and his reading public. Understanding Dunbar's specific negotiation of the literary marketplace requires that we pay attention to the external factors that influenced his work—his failures as well as his successes—when assessing his position in American literary history.

The second group of stories marks Dunbar's turn to local color fiction without the protocols of racial realism. From August until December 1901, Dunbar published a series entitled "Ohio Pastorals" in *Lippincott's Monthly Magazine: A Popular Journal of General Literature, Science, and Politics*. From May 1898 until March 1905, *Lippincott's* was one of Dunbar's magazines of choice. During this period he published twelve poems, eleven short stories, and two novels in the magazine.[35] A reputable periodical established in 1868, based in Philadelphia, and published by J. B. Lippincott Company, *Lippincott's* featured authors ranging from Oscar Wilde and Arthur Conan Doyle to Anna Katherine Green and Stephen Crane (Mott, 400).[36] Alongside such fin-de-siècle British and American figures, Dunbar was the sole African American writer whom the magazine welcomed as a frequent literary contributor (Brawley, vii; Mott, 400). The reasons were simple: Not only was Dunbar prolific, he was achieving great milestones for African American writers. Dunbar was, quite simply, the most successful African American literary artist the nation had ever seen.[37] Reveling in this idea, *Lippincott's* tended to publish Dunbar's fiction with headlines of his previous two or three works, in some instances mentioning that a particular work had appeared in the magazine itself.

However, Dunbar's contributions to *Lippincott's* remain marginal in Dunbar criticism and African American literary criticism in general.[38] A few facts might begin to shed light on this situation. The twelve poems Dunbar printed in *Lippincott's* between November 1900 and November 1905 range from the lyric to narrative verse; touch on such themes as love and sorrow, nature and spirituality; and adopt classical rhyme schemes. But these poems were hardly ever in black dialect. Reminiscent of British Romantic and Victorian literature, these poems were published in spite and because of Dunbar's status as "Poet Laureate of the Negro Race" or "Robert Burns of Negro Poetry" (Revell, 164, 166). These names, which hail Dunbar as a writer of authentic "black" dialect literature, belie the fact that only 30 percent of the poems in Dunbar's first three books of poetry were verses in dialect—and not even all *black* dialect, for that matter—while the rest were poems in formal English.[39]

Most American critics panned this imbalance. Since black dialect and plantation imagery determined the commercialism of African American writing at the time, critics tended to praise this part of Dunbar's early poetic work and dismiss the rest. Dunbar, however, defied the expectation that he should produce only literature of black dialect. He wrote texts avoiding not only black dialect and plantation imagery but also conventional African American characters, settings, and vernacular in general. Along with his Romantic and Victorian poetry, for example, Dunbar's first three novels—*The Uncalled, The Love of Landry,* and *The Fanatics* —feature racially unmarked, neutral, or white protagonists, while assuming the traditional forms of local color, realism, and/or naturalism. The contemporary dismissal of these works as well as this kind of work persuaded Dunbar to publish books in the plantation tradition for financial security.[40] Yet for a certainly lesser sum, he mostly avoided the plantation tradition in *Lippincott's*. The Philadelphia magazine, according to one *Nation* reporter in 1873, fostered "comparative freedom from staleness and familiar routine" (qtd. in Mott, 399). For Dunbar, in the last few years before his death, the magazine likewise represented one of the few and last places where he could write on his own terms.

Written by Dunbar at the request of the editor of *Lippincott's* (Cunningham, 222), the "Ohio Pastorals" series includes five short stories that appeared in consecutive months from August to December in 1901: "The Mortification of the Flesh," "The Independence of Silas Bollender," "The White Counterpane," "The Minority Committee," and "The Visiting of Mother Danbury." Dunbar identifies neither the characters nor the settings of the stories in explicit racial terms. Rather, "Ohio Pastorals" are wonderful local color narratives about an Ohio village, featuring characters that Dunbar had included in other stories he had published in *Lippincott's*. The first two stories focus on two friends who reside in a small Ohio town and grapple with the politics of marriage, powerful women, male individualism, and provincialism. The third concerns a mother's attempts to cope with the potential loss of the son she struggled to raise and support to a woman ironically similar to her in strength and will. The fourth deals with the generational conflict between older and younger townsfolk over whether to purchase an organ to modernize hymnal accompaniment for church service. And the fifth story concentrates on two grandmothers disagreeing over how to care for their grandchild, who eventually dies of an illness. Several protagonists make cameo appearances in these five stories, creating a sense of narrative continuity despite the actual serial format. As a whole, the magazine stories potentially form the basis of a short story collection in the Ohioan local color tradition of his first novel, also first released in the magazine, *The Uncalled*.

As a native Ohioan writing about Ohio in his *Lippincott's* fiction, Dunbar could have earned critical acclaim for his regional authenticity. After all, the regional origin and experiences of authors had then determined the exactitude, the credibility, and the aesthetic worth of their local color literature.[41] Yet his *Lippincott's* writing attracted little attention in the early 1900s; scholarly silence still envelops this work today.

The rest of the uncollected stories offer a structure as uneven as that of these first two groups of stories. Of the remainder, the first four are from the *Dayton Tattler*, a newspaper Dunbar edited during high school (1890) that was designed to cater to the interests of the black community. The stories themselves are rather pedestrian, focusing on mainly humorous incidents. The next two play on the general fascination with the West and Manifest Destiny in the American imagination. These initial publications are among Dunbar's earliest attempts to learn the unwritten rules of the publishing world. In all of them, race is conspicuously absent. While at times clunky and formulaic, they do present a writer learning his craft. Like the "Ohio Pastoral" series, ten of the final fifteen stories, written after he had better developed his skills, also use racially unmarked characters. Several, in fact, use the same set of characters, further developing the setting initially created for *Lippincott's*.

In some of the other uncollected stories, Dunbar develops certain themes that recur in his later works, such as the implications of cultural and class differences, the politics of gender, and the significance of religion. "Jimmy Weedon's Contretemps" features a young New York socialite who has a "predilection for low life," but unlike his fiancée, Helen, Jimmy was "honest in his motives for slumming": "Never for an instant did he soothe his conscience or excuse his tastes, by thinking that he was searching for types or studying conditions." By comparison, Helen and her friends tour the "amusement places of the lower classes" in order to confirm the debased nature of its inhabitants. Just as one of Helen's friends, during the tour, observes that "[o]ne couldn't conceive of a person in our class enjoying this," Jimmy appears dancing, effectively ending his engagement with Helen as well as her group's smug sense of composure. The story thus concludes with a deprecation of upper-class pretensions.[42]

In another story, Dunbar probes the gender politics of the African American community. "The Emancipation of Evalina Jones" is a "Little Africa" tale that features a strong female character who turns the tables on her derisive husband. Jim, her husband, forces Evalina to stay home and work during Emancipation Day celebrations so that he can go out with another woman. Ultimately, Jim's actions push Evalina too far. Evalina's final declaration in the story, "This is the fust 'Mancipation Day I've had since I ma'ied you, but I want you to know I'se stood all I'se goin' to stan' f'om you, an' evah day's goin' to be 'Mancipation Day aftah this," links the postbellum problem of women's equality with the antebellum issue of slavery. After all, Evalina's marriage has not allowed her to enjoy the benefits of the annual Emancipation Day celebration. In making this connection, Dunbar points out that freedom must be experienced by both men and women to have any real meaning..

In "Lafe Halloway's Two Fights" Dunbar connects religious faith to personal triumph. Lafe's conversion to the church is threatened when Tom Randall, a moral backslider who tries to drag others down with him, taunts Lafe into a fight by insulting his girlfriend, Alice Staniland. Tom's actions mortify Lafe, especially after a church elder witnesses the conflict. Rather than shrink from his vows to the church, Lafe admits the error of his ways, apologizes to Randall, and asks his church for forgiveness. This second fight—an internal, spiritual, and moral fight—allows Lafe to overcome the circumstances that initially portended his downfall.

Understanding Dunbar's careful packaging of the different literary strategies in his short story collections gives us better insight into his negotiation of the social, cultural, and racial-political boundaries that African American authors of his period faced. Specifically, through literature he critiqued the "coon-era" culture of caricature that infringed on African American claims to racial uplift (Wonham, 55). In stories that took political risks, Dunbar articulated the social and racial limitations that existed for African Americans, while developing multidimensional and positive portrayals of African Americans in order to revise the literary norms of racial representation. The thematic diversity of Dunbar's short fiction goes beyond the scope and range of most other writers, black and white, at the turn of the twentieth century. While at certain times he may have pandered to mainstream literary interests, at others his short stories succinctly exposed and explored the complexities of American racial politics. Dunbar's short fiction enables us to rethink and appreciate the nature and legacy of his contributions to African American literature and American literature in general.

Notes

1. James Weldon Johnson argues in his preface to *The Book of American Negro Poetry* (1922) that Dunbar's dialect poems tended to assign the stereotypical temperaments of "humor" and "pathos" to African Americans (41). Thomas Millard Henry in "Old School of Negro 'Critics' Hard on Paul Laurence Dunbar" (1924), disagrees with Johnson by criticizing the African American writers of *The Crisis*—Johnson, William Stanley Braithwaite, and W. E. B. Du Bois— for failing to accord Dunbar the respect he deserves. For summaries of arguments for why Dunbar was progressive or retrograde in the African American poetic tradition, see Braxton, xxix; Jones, 185; Simon, 118; Story, 54; Nettels, 83–85; and Revell, 162–75.

2. The four collections have been reprinted previously; in particular, several reprints marked the renewed scholarly interest in Dunbar during the late 1960s and early 1970s, approximately a century after his birth. *Folks from Dixie* was reprinted in 1902 (London: H. R. Allenson), 1968 (Upper Saddle River, NJ: Gregg Press), and 1969 (New York: Negro Universities Press; Miami, FL: Mnemosyne Publishing Inc.; New York: New American Library; Freeport, NY: Books for Libraries Press). *The Strength of Gideon* was reprinted in 1969 (New York: Arno Press; Miami, FL: Mnemosyne Publishing Inc.) and 1970 (Freeport, NY: Books for Libraries Press). *In Old Plantation Days* was reprinted in 1969 (New York: Negro Universities Press). And *The Heart of Happy Hollow* was reprinted in 1969 (New York: Negro Universities Press) and 1970 (Freeport, NY: Books for Libraries Press). The papers published in Martin, ed., *A Singer in the Dawn* represent lectures delivered during the Centenary Conference celebrating the life and work of Dunbar (13).

3. Listed in order of first publication, these thirty-one stories appeared individually in editions of *Werner's Readings and Recitations* and in such periodicals as *Dayton (Ohio) Tattler, Independent, New York Journal and Advertiser, Cosmopolitan, Outlook, Lippincott's Monthly Magazine, Current Literature, Saturday Evening Post, New England Magazine, New York Evening Post, The People's Monthly, San Francisco Post, Boston Beacon, Smart Set, Pittsburgh Chronicle Telegraph, Metropolitan Magazine, San Francisco Chronicle, St. Louis Mirror,* and *Era.*

4. See Wiggins; Brawley, *The Best Stories*; J. Martin and Hudson; as well as H. Martin and Primeau.

5. Not included in this number are the references to several additional stories that are found in Dunbar's correspondence. For example, in a September 13, 1892, letter to the C. C. Hunt American Press Association, Dunbar asks for the return of a story titled "Race for Revenge" (*The Life and Works of Paul Laurence Dunbar,* roll 3, Paul Laurence Dunbar Section of the Schomburg Calendar of Manuscripts, Dunbar 2); a note on the back of a letter lists the following stories as returned: "A Monologue," "The Party," and "The Haunted Plantation," as well as two undecipherable titles (the same list also included "Ole Conjurin' [Conju'in] Joe," a story found in manuscript form in the University of Dayton Rare Books Collection and published for the first time in Herbert Woodward Martin and Ronald Primeau's *In His Own Voice*) (Dunbar, *The Paul Laurence Dunbar Papers,* roll 1, frame 183); and finally, a February 20, 1900, letter from *The Writer: A Monthly Magazine for Literary Workers* that discusses a story that deals with "the central idea [. . .] of having the devil in the form of a fascinating young woman tempt an impecunious young man" (roll 1, frame 402). In addition, there are several fragments of stories in both manuscript and handwritten form on roll 4 of *The Paul Laurence Dunbar Papers,* including such titles as "A Detective Story," "Dialogue Between Four Friends," "A Man Named Ben Adams," "Murder Story," and "Reginald Vere." The recent publication of "Ole Conju'in Joe"

(2002) by Martin and Primeau points to the possibility that more of Dunbar's short stories remain to be rediscovered.

6. Colbron connects Dunbar's race and his aesthetic abilities elsewhere in the review as well. Earlier she states that *The Uncalled* "is an earnest work worthy of being taken seriously, and yet in the reading of it there are moments when we do well to remember the difficulties of race and environment with which the author had to struggle. We recognise [*sic*] then, that what for another would be but mediocrity may be credited as an achievement to Mr. Dunbar" (338). She further expounds on the "race characteristics" needed to succeed when she states "[t]he Anglo-Saxon race is more inclined to the narration of impersonal outward fact and action, than to the analyzing of mental torment" (339). Just in case readers miss the point that Colbron is making in the review, one of Dunbar's dialect poems, "Christmas is A-Comin'," appears right below the review, reinforcing Dunbar's supposedly correct role in "representing" race.

7. See "The Colonel's Awakening," "Mt. Pisgah's Christmas 'Possum," "Aunt Tempe's Revenge," "How Brother Parker Fell from Grace," and "Cahoots."

8. See "The Intervention of Peter," "The Last Fiddling of Mordaunt's Jim," "The Stanton Coachman," and "Who Stand for the Gods."

9. See "The Finish of Patsy Barnes," "A Mess of Pottage," "A Judgment of Paris," "Silent Sam'el," and "The Promoter."

10. Stories set in New York include "Jimsella," "An Old-Time Christmas," "The Faith Cure Man," and "The Trustfulness of Polly"; stories set in Washington, D.C., include "Mr. Cornelius Johnson, Office-Seeker," "The Boy and the Bayonet," and "The Finding of Martha." One of Dunbar's earliest attempts at presenting African Americans as part of the local color space of the city is seen in a series of four stories he published in the *New York Journal and Advertiser* from September 26 to October 17, 1897. While these stories do pander to racial stereotypes, at the same time they shift the African American characters in them from the rural South to the urban North. Other urban stories include "The Ordeal at Mt. Hope," "Nelse Hatton's Vengeance," "A Council of State," and "The Scapegoat."

11. For additional commentary on the ways that Dunbar's short stories offer an in-depth analysis of American social space, see the "Introduction to the Short Stories" in *The Paul Laurence Dunbar Reader,* edited by Jay Martin and Gossie H. Hudson, 63–66.

12. The plantation tradition referred mostly to the popular literature produced by Anglo-American Southerners, including the poetry of Thomas Dunn English, the brothers Sidney and Clifford Lanier, and Irwin Russell; the novels of George Tucker, James Ewell Heath, Harriet Beecher Stowe, Francis Hopkinson Smith, and Mark Twain; and the shorter fiction of John Esten Cooke, John Pendleton Kennedy, William Gilmore Simms, and most notably Joel Chandler Harris and Thomas Nelson Page. While these works are not entirely homogeneous, Blight suggests that their plot constructions, characterizations, settings, symbolism, and themes consistently romanticize the plantation societies and cultures of the Old South to communicate and alleviate national anxieties over sectional reunion between the South and the North. For general discussions of the imagery of the plantation tradition, see F. Gaines, S. Brown, Mixon, Wagner, Tracy, and Blight.

13. See "A Family Feud," "The Lynching of Jube Benson," "At Shaft 11," and "The Tragedy at Three Forks."

14. See "A Mess of Pottage," "Mr. Cornelius Johnson, Office-Seeker," "One Man's Fortune," "A Council of State," and "The Scapegoat."

15. This is another example of the critical repetition of "identical words" that Dunbar continued to negotiate in the literary realm.

16. Dunbar's initial forays into the short story form will be discussed in section III of the introduction.

17. For the comparison of sales between *Folks from Dixie* and *The Uncalled,* see Cunningham, 191. For the contrast in the reviews between *The Strength of Gideon* and *The Love of Landry,* see Metcalf, 136–40.

18. One has only to turn to Booker T. Washington's *Up from Slavery* (1901) for the story of slaves who preferred to stay on the plantation rather than enjoy emancipation.

19. Dunbar viewed the world through racial uplift ideology. As early as 1890, at the age of eighteen and as the only African American student at Dayton's Central High School, he published an editorial in the *Dayton Tattler* (December 13, 1890) pleading with local African American readers to subscribe to that newspaper, which would keep them abreast of the progress of African American communities in Dayton, in the state of Ohio, and in other regions of the United States. Essays Dunbar wrote later in life in this same vein include "Of Negro Journals" (1894), "England as Seen by a Black Man" (1897), "Recession Never" (1898), and "The Negroes of the Tenderloin: Paul Laurence Dunbar Sees Peril for His Race in Life in the City" (1898) (rpt. in J. Martin and Hudson).

20. For examples of such deprecations, see Brawley, 96, 104; Revell, 108, 113; and the remarkable silence around Dunbar's short stories in J. Martin, *A Singer in the Dawn.*

21. The four reviews employing the language of "humor and pathos" include those in the *New York Times* (March 10, 1900), the *Washington (D.C.) Post* (May 14, 1900), the *Louisville Christian Observer* (June 13, 1900), and the *Cedar Rapids (Iowa) Republican* (June 23, 1900). The three excerpted reviews belong to the *Philadelphia Times* (May 19, 1900), the *New York Commercial Advertiser* (June 1, 1900), and the *Cedar Rapids (Iowa) Republican* (June 23, 1900).

22. For the critique of the role of religion in the black community, see "The Fruitful Sleeping of the Rev. Elisha Edwards," "Jim's Probation," "The Strength of Gideon," "Uncle Simon's Sundays Out," and "A Mess of Pottage." For an exemplary analysis of the crisis whites faced on the issue of slavery, see "The Ingrate."

23. For the best stories about interactions between and among masters and slaves, see "A Supper by Proxy," "The Trouble about Sophiny," and "Mr. Groby's Slippery Gift." For conjure, see "The Conjuring Contest," "Dandy Jim's Conjure Scare," and "The Brief Cure of Aunt Fanny." For the power of music, see "The Last Fiddling of Mordaunt's Jim" and "The Memory of Martha."

24. For more information about the incompatibility of Christianity and slavery, see Raboteau, 290–318.

25. Respectively, the three reviews come from the *New York Times* (October 31, 1903), the *Nation,* February 18, 1904, 134, and the *Critic* 44 (May 1904): 476.

26. Quoted from the notebooks kept by Dunbar's secretary, in *The Paul Laurence Dunbar Papers,* roll 1, frame 805.

27. See Metcalf, 77–80.

28. Of the sixteen stories, only three, "Cahoots," "The Wisdom of Silence," and "The Lynching of Jube Benson," deal with what can be considered "pastoral" settings, and of these three, only "Cahoots" leaves the pastoral framing intact at the end of the story.

29. Of particular interest is Dunbar's emphasis of "Mr." in Asbury's title; he is not the traditional lowly servant figure, but one who has claim to his designation.

30. Miltonville is the home of Mr. Dunkin from "The Deliberation of Mr. Dunkin" in *Folks from Dixie.*

31. For an excellent reading of Dunbar's manipulation of narrative masking in "The Lynching of Jube Benson," see Gavin Jones's chapter on Dunbar, "Paul Laurence Dunbar and the Authentic Black Voice," in *Strange Talk.*

32. The reviews making these observations are from the *Detroit Free Press* (December 11, 1904), the *Boston Journal* (December 13, 1904), and the *Cleveland Leader* (December 4, 1904).

33. At this point, Paul and Alice were not yet married; in fact, part of Dunbar's motivation for writing these stories was to obtain enough money so that he could marry Alice. See Metcalf's "The Letters of Paul and Alice: A Private History."

34. To the best of our knowledge, only four of these stories were published.

35. The twelve poems are "The Tryst" (November 1900): 772; "To a Captious Critic" (October 1901): 493; "A Roadway" (January 1902): 114; "Differences" (March 1902): 325; "Lyrics of Love and Sorrow" (December 1902): 732; "Summer in the South" (September 1903): 378; "Forever" (June 1904): 670; "The Farm Child's Lullaby" (August 1904): 201; "Twilight" (October 1904): 497; "Compensation" (December 1904): 786; "Rain-Songs" (February 1905): 214; and "Day" (November 1905): 629. The eleven short stories are "The End of the Chapter" (April 1899): 532–34; "The Strength of Gideon" (October 1899); the five stories of "Ohio Pastorals"

(August–December 1901); "The Finding of Martha" (March 1902): 375–84; "The Vindication of Jared Hargot" (March 1904): 374–81; "The Way of Love" (January 1905): 68–73; and "The Churching of Grandma Pleasant" (March 1905): 337–42. The two novels are *The Uncalled* (May 1898): 579–669 and *The Sport of the Gods* (May 1901): 515–94.

36. For more information about the establishment of *Lippincott's* in the late nineteenth century, see Mott, 396–401.

37. According to biographer Virginia Cunningham, Dunbar's third book of poems, *Lyrics of Lowly Life* (1896), made him the first African American to earn cash advances (four hundred dollars) and royalties (almost 18 percent) from a major publisher (Dodd, Mead, and Company) (153).

38. According to Kallenbach, 32–33, and our own research, three of Dunbar's twelve *Lippincott's* poems have been reprinted in anthologies of African American literature since 1924. Of the *Lippincott's* short stories, "The Strength of Gideon" was reprinted in Dunbar's *The Strength of Gideon and Other Stories* (1900), while "The Finding of Martha" reappeared in *In Old Plantation Days* (1903). The first "Ohio Pastorals" story, "The Mortification of the Flesh," has been reprinted in Turner (1969, 1970). The two *Lippincott's* novels, *The Uncalled* and *The Sport of the Gods,* have been reprinted as books in 1898 and 1902, respectively, and a few times thereafter with his other novels. Aside from Brawley's allusion to "Ohio Pastorals" in his introduction to *The Best Short Stories of Paul Laurence Dunbar* (1938), in which he dismisses the stories as without "racial interest" (vi–vii), no scholarly work has yet examined Dunbar's *Lippincott's* oeuvre as a single body of work.

39. In the wake of Howells's review of Dunbar's *Majors and Minors,* Dunbar ascended to the throne of "Poet Laureate of the Negro Race," or "the Robert Burns of Negro Poetry," the latter name referring to the great late-eighteenth-century Scottish dialect poet with whom Howells compared Dunbar in the review. Various critics and artists, black and white, employed these terms either appreciatively or disparagingly.

40. Books written for financial gain include his books of short stories, as well as such poetry collections as *Poems of Cabin and Field* (1899), *Candle-Lightin' Time* (1901), *Chris'mus Is A-Comin' and Other Poems* (1905), *Howdy, Honey, Howdy* (1905), *A Plantation Portrait* (1905), and *Joggin' Erlong* (1906).

41. In their classic anthology of the genre, *American Local Color Stories,* editors Harry R. Warfel and G. Harrison Orians introduce the aesthetic contingency of local colorism on regional authenticity: "Merit depends upon an author's knowledge, insight, and artistry" (x). Warfel and Orians reiterate the long-standing definitions of local colorism established in early nineteenth-century France ("*la couleur locale*") and refashioned toward the end of the century by such American authors as James Lane Allen and Hamlin Garland.

42. See also H. Martin and Primeau's comments on this story in *In His Own Voice,* 218–19.

Editors' Note

We have altered the texts minimally, only to correct typographical errors and mis-spellings, as well as to standardize contemporary contractions. We have also placed in brackets words that are illegible in the original text. The original versions of the stories have been reprinted, but if necessary, discrepancies between these and sub-sequently published versions of the text have been noted. The stories appearing in *Folks from Dixie, The Strength of Gideon, In Old Plantation Days, The Heart of Happy Hollow,* the *New York Journal and Advertiser* series, and "Ohio Pastorals" are reprinted in the order in which they were arranged in the books or series. The individual stories are reprinted in the order in which they were first published in periodicals. We have chosen to exclude from the four collections of stories the il-lustrations by E. W. Kemble (*Folks from Dixie, The Strength of Gideon,* and *The Heart of Happy Hollow*) and by B. Martin Justice (*In Old Plantation Days*). Kem-ble and Justice's caricatures of African American protagonists in Dunbar's stories mirrored the racist images circulating in American popular culture at the turn of the century. The illustrations reflect the kind of misreading that Dunbar tried to address and refute during much of his professional career and that subsequent lit-erary scholars have tried to critique and revise. For this reason, our expurgation of the illustrations from *The Complete Stories of Paul Laurence Dunbar* is intended to allow readers to interpret and assess Dunbar's stories on their own terms and merits.

I

Collected Stories

Folks from Dixie

Anner 'Lizer's Stumblin' Block

IT WAS WINTER. The gray old mansion of Mr. Robert Selfridge, of Fayette County, Ky., was wrapped in its usual mantle of winter sombreness, and the ample plantation stretching in every direction thereabout was one level plain of unflecked whiteness. At a distance from the house the cabins of the negroes stretched away in a long, broken black line that stood out in bold relief against the extreme whiteness of their surroundings.

About the centre of the line, as dark and uninviting as the rest, with its wide chimney of scrap limestone turning clouds of dense smoke into the air, stood a cabin.

There was nothing in its appearance to distinguish it from the other huts clustered about. The logs that formed its sides were just as seamy, the timbers of the roof had just the same abashed, brow-beaten look; and the keenest eye could not have detected the slightest shade of difference between its front and the bare, unwhitewashed fronts of its scores of fellows. Indeed, it would not have been mentioned at all, but for the fact that within its confines lived and thrived the heroine of this story.

Of all the girls of the Selfridge estate, black, brown, or yellow, Anner 'Lizer was, without dispute, conceded to be the belle. Her black eyes were like glowing coals in their sparkling brightness; her teeth were like twin rows of shining ivories; her brown skin was as smooth and soft as silk; and the full lips that enclosed her gay and flexile tongue were tempting enough to make the heart of any dusky swain throb and his mouth water.

Was it any wonder, then, that Sam Merritt—strapping, big Sam, than whom there was not a more popular man on the place—should pay devoted court to her?

Do not gather from this that it was Sam alone who paid his *devoirs* to this brown beauty. Oh, no! Anner 'Lizer was the "bright, particular star" of that plantation, and the most desired of all blessings by the young men thereabout. But Sam, with his smooth but fearless ways, Sam, with his lightsome foot, so airy in the dance, Sam, handsome Sam, was the all-preferred. If there was a dance to go to, a corn-husking to attend, a social at the rude little log church, Sam was always the lucky man who was alert and *able* to possess himself of Anner 'Lizer's "comp'ny." And so, naturally, people began to connect their names, and the rumour went forth, as rumours will, that the two were engaged; and, as far as engagements went among the slaves in those days, I suppose it was true. Sam had never exactly prostrated himself at his sweetheart's feet and openly declared his passion; nor had she modestly snickered behind her fan, and murmured yes in the approved fashion of the present. But he had looked his feelings, and she had looked hers; while numerous little attentions bestowed on each other, too subtle to be detailed, and the attraction which kept them constantly together, were earnests of their intentions more weighty than words could give. And so, let me say, without further explanation, that Sam and Anner 'Lizer were engaged. But when did the course of true love ever run smooth?

There was never a time but there were some rocks in its channel around which the little stream had to glide or over which it had to bound and bubble; and thus it was with the loves of our young friends. But in this case the crystal stream seemed destined neither to bound over nor glide by the obstacle in its path, but rather to let its merry course be checked thereby.

It may, at first, seem a strange thing to say, but it was nevertheless true, that the whole sweep and torrent of the trouble had rise in the great religious revival that was being enthusiastically carried on at the little Baptist meeting-house. Interest, or, perhaps more correctly speaking, excitement ran high, and regularly as night came round all the hands on the neighbouring plantations flocked to the scene of their devotions.

There was no more regular attendant at these meetings, nor more deeply interested listener to the pastor's inflammatory exhortations, than Anner 'Lizer. The weirdness of the scene and the touch of mysticism in the services—though, of course, she did not analyse it thus—reached her emotional nature and stirred her being to its depths. Night after night found her in her pew, the third bench from the rude pulpit, her large eyes, dilated to their fullest capacity, following the minister through every motion, seeming at times in their steadfastness to look through him and beyond to the regions he was describing,—the harp-ringing heaven of bliss or the fire-filled home of the damned.

Now Sam, on the other hand, could not be induced to attend these meetings; and when his fellow-servants were at the little church praying, singing, and shouting, he was to be found sitting in one corner of his cabin, picking his banjo, or scouring the woods, carrying axe and taper, and, with a dog trotting at his heels, hunting for that venison of the negro palate,—'coon.

Of course this utter irreverence on the part of her lover shocked Anner 'Lizer; but she had not entered far enough into the regions of the ecstasy to be a proselyte; so she let Sam go his way, albeit with reluctance, while she went to church unattended. But she thought of Sam; and many a time when she secretly prayed to get religion she added a prayer that she might retain Sam.

He, the rogue, was an unconscious but pronounced sceptic; and day by day, as Anner 'Lizer became more and more possessed by religious fervour, the breach between them widened; still widening gradually until the one span that connected the two hearts was suddenly snapped asunder on the night when Anner 'Lizer went to the mourner's bench.

She had not gone to church with that intention; indeed not, although she had long been deeply moved by a consciousness of her lost estate. But that night, when the preacher had pictured the boundless joys of heaven, and then, leaning over the pulpit and stretching out his arms before him, had said in his softest tone, "Now come, won't you, sinnahs? De Lawd is jes' on de othah side; jes' one step away, waitin' to receibe you. Won't you come to him? Won't you tek de chance o' becomin' j'int 'ars o' dat beautiful city whar de streets is gol' an' de gates is pearl? Won't you come to him, sinnah? Don't you see de pityin' look he's a-givin' you, a-sayin' Come, come?" she lost herself. Some irresistible power seemed dominating her, and she arose and went forward, dropping at the altar amid a great shouting and clapping of hands and cries of "Bless de Lawd, one mo' recruit fu' de Gospel ahmy."

Some one started the hymn, "We'll bow around the altar," and the refrain was taken up by the congregation with a fervour that made the rafters of the little edifice ring again.

The conquest of Anner 'Lizer, the belle of that section of Kentucky, was an event of great moment; and in spite of the concentration of the worshippers' minds on their devotions, the unexpected occurrence called forth a deal of discussion among the brothers and sisters. Aunt Hannah remarked to Aunt Maria, over the back of the seat, that she "nevah knowed de gal was unner c'nviction." And Aunt Maria answered solemnly, "You know, sistah, de Lawd wuks in a myste'ious way his wondahs to pu'fo'm."

Meanwhile the hymn went on, and above it rose the voice of the minister: "We want all de Christuns in de house to draw up aroun' de altah, whar de fiah is bu'nin': you know in de wintah time when hit's col' you crowds up clost to de fiah-place; so now ef you wants to git spi'tually wa'm, you mus' be up whar de fiah is." There was a great scrambling and shuffling of feet as the members rose with one accord to crowd, singing, around the altar.

Two of the rude benches had been placed end to end before the pulpit, so that they extended nearly the full width of the little church; and at these knelt a dozen or more mourners, swaying and writhing under the burden of their sins.

The song being ended, the preacher said: "Brer' Adams, please tek up de cross." During the momentary lull that intervened between the end of the song and the prayer, the wails and supplications of the mourners sounded out with weird effect. Then Brer' Adams, a white-haired patriarch, knelt and " took up the cross."

Earnestly he besought the divine mercy in behalf of "de po' sinnahs, a-rollin' an' a-tossin' in de tempes' of dere sins. Lawd," he prayed, "come down dis evenin' in Sperit's powah to seek an' to save-ah; let us heah de rumblin' of yo' cha'iot wheels-ah lak de thundah f'om Mount Sinai-ah; oh, Lawd-ah, convert mou'nahs an' convict sinnahs-ah ; show 'em dat dey mus' die an' cain't lib an' atter death to judg-a-ment; tu'n 'em aroun' befo' it is evahlastin' an' eternally too late." Then warming more and more, and swaying his form back and forth, as he pounded the seat in emphasis, he began to wail out in a sort of indescribable monotone: "O Lawd, save de mou'nah!"

"Save de mou'nah!" came the response from all over the church.

"He'p 'em out of de miah an' quicksan's of dere sins!"

"He'p, Lawd!"

"And place deir feet upon de evahlastin' an' eternal rock-ah!"

"Do, Lawd!"

"O Lawd-ah, shake a dyin' sinnah ovah hell an' fo'bid his mighty fall-ah!"

"O Lawd, shake 'em!" came from the congregation.

By this time every one was worked up to a high state of excitement, and the prayer came to an end amid great commotion. Then a rich, mellow voice led out with:

> "Sabe de mou'nah jes' now,
> Sabe de mou'nah jes' now,
> Sabe de mou'nah jes' now,
> Only trust Him jes' now,
> Only trust Him jes' now,
> He'p de sinnah jes' now;"

and so to indefinite length the mournful minor melody ran along like a sad brook flowing through autumn woods, trying to laugh and ripple through tears.

Every now and then some mourner would spring half up, with a shriek, and then sink down again trembling and jerking spasmodically. "He's a-doubtin', he's a-doubtin'!" the cry would fly around; "but I tell you he purt' nigh had it that time."

Finally, the slender form of Anner 'Lizer began to sway backward and forward, like a sapling in the wind, and she began to mourn and weep aloud.

"Praise de Lawd!" shouted Aunt Hannah, "de po' soul's gittin' de evidence: keep on, honey, de Lawd ain't fa' off." The sudden change attracted considerable attention, and in a moment a dozen or more zealous altarworkers gathered around Anner 'Lizer, and began to clap and sing with all their might, keeping time to the melodious cadence of their music with heavy foot-pats on the resounding floor.

> "Git on boa'd-ah, little childering,
> Git on boa'd-ah, little childering,
> Git on boa'd-ah, little childering,
>   Dere's room fo' many mo'.

> "De gospel ship is sailin',
> It's loaded down wid souls.
> If you want to mek heab'n yo' happy home,
> You mus' ketch it 'fo' it goes.
>   Git on boa'd, etc.

> "King Jesus at de hellum,
> Fu' to guide de ship erright.
> We gwine fu' to put into heab'n's po't

Wid ouah sails all shinin' white.
    Git on boa'd," etc.

With a long dwell on the last word of the chorus, the mellow cadence of the song died away.

"Let us bow down fu' a season of silent praar," said the minister.

"Lawd, he'p us to pray," responded Uncle Eben Adams.

The silence that ensued was continually broken by the wavering wail of the mourners. Suddenly one of them, a stalwart young man, near the opening of the aisle, began to writhe and twist himself into every possible contortion, crying: "O Lawd, de devil's a-ridin' me; tek him off—tek him off!"

"Tek him off, Lawd!" shouted the congregation.

Then suddenly, without warning, the mourner rose straight up into the air, shouting, "Hallelujah, hallelujah, hallelujah!"

"He's got it—he's got it!" cried a dozen eager worshippers, leaping to their feet and crowding around the happy convert; "bless de Lawd, he's got it." A voice was raised, and soon the church was ringing with

"Loose him and let him go,
    Let him shout to glory."

On went the man, shouting "Hallelujah," shaking hands, and bounding over seats in the ecstasy of his bliss.

His conversion kindled the flame of the meeting and set the fire going. You have seen corn in the popper when the first kernel springs up and flares open, how quickly the rest follow, keeping up the steady pop, pop, pop; well, just so it was after this first conversion. The mourners popped up quickly and steadily as the strength of the spiritual fire seemed to reach their swelling souls. One by one they left the bench on which, figuratively speaking, they may be said to have laid down their sins and proclaimed themselves possessors of religion; until, finally, there was but one left, and that one—Anner 'Lizer. She had ceased from her violent activity, and seemed perfectly passive now.

The efforts of all were soon concentrated on her, and such stamping and clapping and singing was never heard before. Such cries of "Jes' look up, sistah, don't you see Him at yo' side? Jes' reach out yo' han' an' tech de hem of His ga'ment. Jes' listen, sistah, don't you heah de angels singin'? don't you heah de rumblin' of de cha'iot wheels? He's a-comin', He's a-comin', He's a-comin'!"

But Anner 'Lizer was immovable; with her face lying against the hard bench, she moaned and prayed softly to herself. The congregation redoubled its exertions, but all to no effect, Anner 'Lizer wouldn't "come thoo."

It was a strange case.

Aunt Maria whispered to her bosom friend: "You min' me, Sistah Hannah, dere's sump'n' on dat gal's min'." And Aunt Hannah answered: "I believe you."

Josephine, or more commonly Phiny, a former belle whom Anner 'Lizer's superior charms had deposed, could not lose this opportunity to have a fling at her successful rival. Of course such cases of vindictiveness in women are rare, and Phiny was exceptional when she whispered to her fellow-servant, Lucy: "I reckon she'd git 'ligion if Sam Me'itt was heah to see her." Lucy snickered, as in duty bound, and whispered back: "I wisht you'd heish."

Well, after all their singing, in spite of all their efforts, the time came for closing the meeting and Anner 'Lizer had not yet made a profession.

She was lifted tenderly up from the mourner's bench by a couple of solicitous sisters, and after listening to the preacher's exhortation to "pray constantly, thoo de day an' thoo de night, in de highways an' de byways an' in yo' secret closet," she went home praying in her soul, leaving the rest of the congregation to loiter along the way and gossip over the night's events.

ALL THE NEXT day Anner 'Lizer, erstwhile so cheerful, went about her work sad and silent; every now and then stopping in the midst of her labours and burying her face in her neat white apron to sob violently. It was true, as Aunt Hannah expressed, that "de Sperit had sholy tuk holt of dat gal wid a powahful han'."

All of her fellow-servants knew that she was a mourner, and with that characteristic reverence for religion which is common to all their race, and not lacking even in the most hardened sinner among them, they respected her feelings. Phiny alone, when she met her, tossed her head and giggled openly. But Phiny's actions never troubled Anner 'Lizer, for she felt herself so far above her. Once, though, in the course of the day, she had been somewhat disturbed, when she had suddenly come upon her rival, standing in the spring-house talking and laughing with Sam. She noticed, too, with a pang, that Phiny had tied a bow of red ribbon on her hair. She shut her lips and only prayed the harder. But an hour later, somehow, a ribbon as red as Phiny's had miraculously attached itself to her thick black plaits. Was the temporal creeping in with the spiritual in Anner 'Lizer's mind? Who can tell? Perhaps she thought that, while cultivating the one, she need not utterly neglect the other; and who says but that she was right?

Uncle Eben, however, did not take this view of the matter when he came hobbling up in the afternoon to exhort her a little. He found Anner 'Lizer in the kitchen washing dishes. Engrossed in the contemplation of her spiritual state, or praying for deliverance from the same, through the whole day she had gone about without speaking to any one. But with Uncle Eben it was, of course, different; for he was a man held in high respect by all the negroes and, next to the minister, the greatest oracle in those parts; so Anner 'Lizer spoke to him.

"Howdy, Uncl' Eben," she said, in a lugubrious tone, as the old man hobbled in and settled down in a convenient corner.

"Howdy, honey, howdy," he replied, crossing one leg over the other, as he unwound his long bandana, placed it in his hat, and then deposited his heavy cane on the white floor. "I jes' thought I'd drap in to ax you how do you do to-day?"

"Po' enough, Uncl' Eben, fu' sho."

"Ain't foun' no res' fu' yo' soul yit?"

"No res' yit," answered Anner 'Lizer, again applying the apron to her already swollen eyes.

"Um-m," sighed the old man, meditatively tapping his foot; and then the gay flash of Anner 'Lizer's ribbon caught his eye and he gasped: "Bless de Lawd, Sis 'Lizer; you don't mean to tell me dat you's gwin 'bout heah seekin' wid yo' har tied up in ribbon? Whut! tek it off, honey, tek it off; ef yo' wants yo' soul saved, tek it off!"

Anner 'Lizer hesitated, and raised her eyes in momentary protest; but they met the horrified gaze of the old man, and she lowered them again as her hand went reluctantly up to her head to remove the offending bit of finery.

"You see, honey," Uncle Eben went on, "when you sta'ts out on de Christian jou'ney, you's got to lay aside evry weight dat doeth so easy beset you an' keeps you f'om pergressin'; y' ain't got to think nothin' 'bout pussunal 'dornment ; you's jes' got to shet yo' eyes an' open yo' hea't an' say, Lawd, come; you mustn't wait fu' to go to chu'ch to pray, nuther, you mus' pray anywhar an' ev'rywhar. Why, when I was seekin', I ust to go 'way off up in de big woods to pray, an' dere's whar de Lawd answered me, an' I'm a-rejoicin' to-day in de powah of de same salvation. Honey, you's got to pray, I tell you. You's got to brek de backbone of yo' pride an' pray in earnes'; an' ef you does dat, you'll git he'p, fu' de Lawd is a praar-heahin' Lawd an' plenteous in mussy."

Anner 'Lizer listened attentively to the exhortation, and evidently profited by it; for soon after Uncle Eben's departure she changed her natty little dress for one less pretentious, and her dainty, frilled white muslin apron gave way to a broad dark calico one. If grace was to be found by self-abnegation in the matter of dress, Anner 'Lizer was bound to have it at any price.

As afternoon waned and night came on, she grew more and more serious, and more frequent recourse was had to the corner of her apron. She even failed to see Phiny when that enterprising young person passed her, decked out in the whitest of white cuffs and collars setting off in pleasant contrast her neat dark dress. Phiny giggled again and put up her hand, ostensibly to brush some imaginary dust from her bosom, but really to show her pretty white cuffs with their big bone buttons. But it was all lost on Anner 'Lizer; her gaze was downcast and her thoughts far away. If any one was ever "seekin'" in earnest, this girl was.

Night came, and with it the usual services. Anner 'Lizer was one of the earliest of the congregation to arrive, and she went immediately to the mourner's bench. In the language of the congregation, "Eldah Johnsing sholy did preach a powahful sermon" that night. More sinners were convicted and brought to their knees, and, as before, these recruits were converted and Anner 'Lizer left. What was the matter?

That was the question which every one asked, but there were none found who could answer it. The circumstance was all the more astounding from the fact that this unsuccessful mourner had not been a very wicked girl. Indeed, it was to have been expected that she might shake her sins from her shoulders as she would discard a mantle, and step over on the Lord's side. But it was not so.

But when a third night came and passed with the same result, it became the talk of three plantations. To be sure, cases were not lacking where people had "mourned" a week, two weeks, or even a month; but they were woful sinners and those were times of less spiritual interest; but under circumstances so favourable as were now presented, that one could long refrain from "gittin' religion" was the wonder of all. So, after the third night, everybody wondered and talked, and not a few began to lean to Phiny's explanation, that "de ole snek in de grass had be'n a-goin' on doin' all her dev'ment on de sly, so's *people* wouldn't know it; but de *Lawd* he did, an' he payin' her up fu' it now."

Sam Merritt alone did not talk, and seemed perfectly indifferent to all that was said; when he was in Phiny's company and she rallied him about the actions of his "gal," he remained silent.

On the fourth night of Anner 'Lizer's mourning, the congregation gathered as usual at the church. For the first half-hour all went on as usual, and the fact that Anner 'Lizer was absent caused no remark, for every one thought she would come in later. But time passed and she did not come. "Eldah Johnsing's" flock became agitated. Of course there were other mourners, but the one particular one was absent; hence the dissatisfaction. Every head in the house was turned toward the door, whenever it was opened by some late comer; and around flew the whisper, "I wunner ef she's quit mou'nin'; you ain't heerd of her gittin' 'ligion, have you?" No one had.

Meanwhile the object of their solicitude was praying just the same, but in a far different place. Grasping, as she was, at everything that seemed to give her promise of relief, somehow Uncle Eben's words had had a deep effect upon her. So, when night fell and her work was over, she had gone up into the woods to pray. She had prayed long without success, and now she was crying aloud from the very fulness of her heart, "O Lawd, sen' de light—sen' de light!" Suddenly, as if in answer to her prayer, a light appeared before her some distance away.

The sudden attainment of one's desires often shocks one; so with our mourner. For a moment her heart stood still and the thought came to her to flee; but her mind flashed back over the words of one of the hymns she had heard down at church, "Let us walk in de light;" and she knew that before she walked in the light she must walk toward it. So she rose and started in the direction of the light. How it flickered and flared, disappeared and reappeared, rose and fell, even as her spirits, as she stumbled and groped her way over fallen logs and through briers. Her limbs were bruised and her dress torn by the thorns. But she heeded it not, she had fixed her eye—physical and spiritual—on the light before her. It drew her with an irresistible fascination. Suddenly she stopped. An idea had occurred to her! Maybe this light was a Jack-o'-lantern! For a moment she hesitated, then promptly turned her pocket wrong side out, murmuring, "De Lawd'll tek keer o' me." On she started; but, lo! the light had disappeared! What! had the turning of the pocket indeed worked so potent a charm?

But no! it reappeared as she got beyond the intervention of a brush pile which had obscured it. The light grew brighter as she grew fainter; but she clasped her hands and raised her eyes in unwavering faith, for she found that the beacon did not recede, but glowed with a steady and stationary flame.

As she drew near, the sound of sharp strokes came to her ears, and she wondered. Then, as she slipped into the narrow circle of light, she saw that it was made by a taper which was set on a log. The strokes came from a man who was chopping down a tree in which a 'coon seemed to have taken refuge. It needed no second glance at the stalwart shoulders to tell her that the man was—Sam. Her step attracted his attention, and he turned.

"Sam!"

"Anner 'Lizer!"

And then they both stood still, too amazed to speak. Finally she walked across to where he was standing, and said: "Sam, I didn't come out heah to fin' you, but de Lawd has 'p'inted it so, 'ca'se he knowed I orter speak to you." Sam leaned hopelessly on his axe; he thought she was going to exhort him.

Anner 'Lizer went on: "Sam, you's my stumblin' block in de highroad to salvation; I's be'n tryin' to git 'ligion fu' fou' nights, an' I cain't do it jes' on yo' 'count; I prays an' I prays, an' jes' as I's a'mos' got it, jes' as I begin to heah de cha'iot wheels a-rollin', yo' face comes right in 'tween an' drives it all away. Tell me, now, Sam, so's to put me out ov my 'spense, does you want to ma'y me, er is you goin' to ma'y Phiny? I jes' wants you to tell me, not dat I keers pussonally, but so's my min' kin be at res' spi'tu'lly, an' I kin git 'ligion. Jes' say yes er no; I wants to be settled one way er 't other."

"Anner 'Lizer," said Sam, reproachfully, "you know I wants to ma'y you jes' ez soon ez Mas' Rob'll let me."

"Dere now," said Anner 'Lizer, "bless de Lawd!" And, somehow, Sam had dropped the axe and was holding her in his arms.

It boots not whether the 'coon was caught that night or not; but it is a fact that Anner 'Lizer set the whole place afire by getting religion at home early the next morning. And the same night the minister announced "dat de Lawd had foun' out de sistah's stumblin' block an' removed it f'om de path."

The Ordeal at Mt. Hope

"AND THIS IS Mt. Hope," said the Rev. Howard Dokesbury to himself as he descended, bag in hand, from the smoky, dingy coach, or part of a coach, which was assigned to his people, and stepped upon the rotten planks of the station platform. The car he had just left was not a palace, nor had his reception by his fellow-passengers or his intercourse with them been of such cordial nature as to endear them to him. But he watched the choky little engine with its three black cars wind out of sight with a look as regretful as if he were witnessing the departure of his dearest friend. Then he turned his attention again to his surroundings, and a sigh welled up from his heart. "And this is Mt. Hope," he repeated. A note in his voice indicated that he fully appreciated the spirit of keen irony in which the place had been named.

The colour scheme of the picture that met his eyes was in dingy blacks and grays. The building that held the ticket, telegraph, and train despatchers' offices was a miserably old ramshackle affair, standing well in the foreground of this scene of gloom and desolation. Its windows were so coated with smoke and grime that they seemed to have been painted over in order to secure secrecy within. Here and there a lazy cur lay drowsily snapping at the flies, and at the end of the station, perched on boxes or leaning against the wall, making a living picture of equal laziness, stood a group of idle Negroes exchanging rude badinage with their white counterparts across the street.

After a while this bantering interchange would grow more keen and personal, a free-for-all friendly fight would follow, and the newspaper correspondent in that section would write it up as a "race war." But this had not happened yet that day.

"This is Mt. Hope," repeated the new-comer; "this is the field of my labours."

Rev. Howard Dokesbury, as may already have been inferred, was a Negro,— there could be no mistake about that. The deep dark brown of his skin, the rich over-fulness of his lips, and the close curl of his short black hair were evidences that admitted of no argument. He was a finely proportioned, stalwart-looking man, with a general air of self-possession and self-sufficiency in his manner. There was firmness in the set of his lips. A reader of character would have said of him, "Here is a man of solid judgment, careful in deliberation, prompt in execution, and decisive."

It was the perception in him of these very qualities which had prompted the authorities of the little college where he had taken his degree and received his theological training, to urge him to go among his people at the South, and there to exert his powers for good where the field was broad and the labourers few.

Born of Southern parents from whom he had learned many of the superstitions and traditions of the South, Howard Dokesbury himself had never before been below Mason and Dixon's line. But with a confidence born of youth and a consciousness of personal power, he had started South with the idea that he knew the people with whom he had to deal, and was equipped with the proper weapons to cope with their shortcomings.

But as he looked around upon the scene which now met his eye, a doubt arose in his mind. He picked up his bag with a sigh, and approached a man who had been standing apart from the rest of the loungers and regarding him with indolent intentness.

"Could you direct me to the house of Stephen Gray?" asked the minister.

The interrogated took time to change his position from left foot to right and to shift his quid, before he drawled forth, "I reckon you's de new Mefdis preachah, huh?"

"Yes," replied Howard, in the most conciliatory tone he could command, "and I hope I find in you one of my flock."

"No, suh, I's a Babtist myse'f. I wa'n't raised up no place erroun' Mt. Hope; I'm nachelly f'om way up in Adams County. Dey jes' sont me down hyeah to fin' you an' to tek you up to Steve's. Steve, he's workin' to-day an' couldn't come down."

He laid particular stress upon the "to-day," as if Steve's spell of activity were not an everyday occurrence.

"Is it far from here?" asked Dokesbury.

"'T ain't mo' 'n a mile an' a ha'f by de shawt cut."

"Well, then, let's take the short cut, by all means," said the preacher.

They trudged along for a while in silence, and then the young man asked, "What do you men about here do mostly for a living?"

"Oh, well, we does odd jobs, we saws an' splits wood an' totes bundles, an' some of 'em raises gyahden, but mos' of us, we fishes. De fish bites an' we ketches 'em. Sometimes we eats 'em an' sometimes we sells 'em; a string o' fish'll bring a peck o' co'n any time."

"And is that all you do?"

"'Bout."

"Why, I don't see how you live that way."

"Oh, we lives all right," answered the man; "we has plenty to eat an' drink, an' clothes to wear, an' some place to stay. I reckon folks ain't got much use fu' nuffin' mo'."

Dokesbury sighed. Here indeed was virgin soil for his ministerial labours. His spirits were not materially raised when, some time later, he came in sight of the house which was to be his abode. To be sure, it was better than most of the houses which he had seen in the Negro part of Mt. Hope; but even at that it was far from being good or comfortable-looking. It was small and mean in appearance. The weather boarding was broken, and in some places entirely fallen away, showing the great unhewn logs beneath; while off the boards that remained the whitewash had peeled in scrofulous spots.

The minister's guide went up to the closed door, and rapped loudly with a heavy stick.

"G' 'way f'om dah, an' quit you' foolin'," came in a large voice from within.

The guide grinned, and rapped again. There was a sound of shuffling feet and the pushing back of a chair, and then the same voice saying: "I bet I'll mek you git away f'om dat do'."

"Dat's A'nt Ca'line," the guide said, and laughed.

The door was flung back as quickly as its worn hinges and sagging bottom would allow, and a large body surmounted by a face like a big round full moon presented itself in the opening. A broomstick showed itself aggressively in one fat shiny hand.

"It's you, Tom Scott, is it—you trif'nin'—" and then, catching sight of the stranger, her whole manner changed, and she dropped the broomstick with an embarrassed "'Scuse me, suh."

Tom chuckled all over as he said, "A'nt Ca'line, dis is yo' new preachah."

The big black face lighted up with a broad smile as the old woman extended her hand and enveloped that of the young minister's.

"Come in," she said, "I's mighty glad to see you—that no-'count Tom come put' nigh mekin' me 'spose myse'f." Then turning to Tom, she exclaimed with good-natured severity, "An' you go 'long, you scoun'll you!"

The preacher entered the cabin—it was hardly more—and seated himself in the rush-bottomed chair which A'nt Ca'line had been industriously polishing with her apron.

"An' now, Brothah—"

"Dokesbury," supplemented the young man.

"Brothah Dokesbury, I jes' want you to mek yo'se'f at home right erway. I know you ain't use to ouah ways down hyeah; but you jes' got to set in an' git ust to 'em. You mus'n't feel bad ef things don't go yo' way f'om de ve'y fust. Have you got a mammy?"

The question was very abrupt, and a lump suddenly jumped up in Dokesbury's throat and pushed the water into his eyes. He did have a mother away back there at home. She was all alone, and he was her heart and the hope of her life.

"Yes," he said, "I've got a little mother up there in Ohio."

"Well, I's gwine to be yo' mothah down hyeah; dat is, ef I ain't too rough an' common fu' you."

"Hush!" exclaimed the preacher, and he got up and took the old lady's hand in both of his own. "You shall be my mother down here; you shall help me, as you have done to-day. I feel better already."

"I knowed you would"; and the old face beamed on the young one. "An' now jes' go out de do' dah an' wash yo' face. Dey's a pan an' soap an' watah right dah, an' hyeah's a towel; den you kin go right into yo' room, fu' I knows you want to be erlone fu' a while. I'll fix yo' suppah while you rests."

He did as he was bidden. On a rough bench outside the door, he found a basin and a bucket of water with a tin dipper in it. To one side, in a broken saucer, lay a piece of coarse soap. The facilities for copious ablutions were not abundant, but one thing the minister noted with pleasure: the towel, which was rough and hurt his skin, was, nevertheless, scrupulously clean. He went to his room feeling fresher and better, and although he found the place little and dark and warm, it too was clean, and a sense of its homeness began to take possession of him.

The room was off the main living-room into which he had been first ushered. It had one small window that opened out on a fairly neat yard. A table with a chair before it stood beside the window, and across the room—if the three feet of space which intervened could be called "across"—stood the little bed with its dark calico quilt and white pillows. There was no carpet on the floor, and the absence of a washstand indicated very plainly that the occupant was expected to wash outside. The young minister knelt for a few minutes beside the bed, and then rising cast himself into the chair to rest.

It was possibly half an hour later when his partial nap was broken in upon by the sound of a gruff voice from without saying, "He's hyeah, is he—oomph. Well, what's he ac' lak? Want us to git down on ouah knees an' crawl to him? If he do, I reckon he'll fin' dat Mt. Hope ain't de place fo' him."

The minister did not hear the answer, which was in a low voice and came, he conjectured, from Aunt 'Ca'line'; but the gruff voice subsided, and there was the sound of footsteps going out of the room. A tap came on the preacher's door, and he opened it to the old woman. She smiled reassuringly.

"Dat 'uz my ol' man," she said. "I sont him out to git some wood, so's I'd have time to post you. Don't you mind him; he's lots mo' ba'k dan bite. He's one o' dese little yaller men, an' you know dey kin be powahful contra'y when dey sets dey hai'd to it. But jes' you treat him nice an' don't let on, an' I'll be boun' you'll bring him erroun' in little er no time."

The Rev. Mr. Dokesbury received this advice with some misgiving. Albeit he had assumed his pleasantest manner when, after his return to the living-room, the little "yaller" man came through the door with his bundle of wood.

He responded cordially to Aunt Caroline's, "Dis is my husband, Brothah Dokesbury," and heartily shook his host's reluctant hand.

"I hope I find you well, Brother Gray," he said.

"Moder't, jes' moder't," was the answer.

"Come to suppah now, bofe o' you," said the old lady, and they all sat down to the evening meal, of crisp bacon, well-fried potatoes, egg-pone, and coffee.

The young man did his best to be agreeable, but it was rather discouraging to receive only gruff monosyllabic rejoinders to his most interesting observations. But the cheery old wife came bravely to the rescue, and the minister was continually floated into safety on the flow of her conversation. Now and then, as he talked, he could catch a stealthy upflashing of Stephen Gray's eye, as suddenly lowered again, that told him that the old man was listening. But, as an indication that they would get on together, the supper, taken as a whole, was not a success. The evening that followed proved hardly more fortunate. About the only remarks that could be elicited from the "little yaller man" were a reluctant "oomph" or "oomph-uh."

It was just before going to bed that, after a period of reflection, Aunt Caroline began slowly: "We got a son"—her husband immediately bristled up and his eyes flashed, but the old woman went on; "he named 'Lias, an' we thinks a heap o' 'Lias, we does; but—" the old man had subsided, but he bristled up again at the word— "he ain't jes' whut we want him to be." Her husband opened his mouth as if to speak in defence of his son, but was silent in satisfaction at his wife's explanation: "'Lias ain't bad; he jes' ca'less. Sometimes he stays at home, but right sma't o' de time he stays down at"—she looked at her husband and hesitated—"at de colo'ed s'loon. We don't lak dat. It ain't no fitten place fu' him. But 'Lias ain't bad, he jes' ca'less, an' me an' de ol' man we 'membahs him in ouah pra'ahs, an' I jes' t'ought I'd ax you to 'membah him too, Brothah Dokesbury."

The minister felt the old woman's pleading look and the husband's intense gaze upon his face, and suddenly there came to him an intimate sympathy in their trouble and with it an unexpected strength.

"There is no better time than now," he said, "to take his case to the Almighty Power; let us pray."

Perhaps it was the same prayer he had prayed many times before; perhaps the words of supplication and the plea for light and guidance were the same; but somehow to the young man kneeling there amid those humble surroundings, with the sorrow of these poor ignorant people weighing upon his heart, it seemed very different. It came more fervently from his lips, and the words had a deeper meaning. When he arose, there was a warmth at his heart just the like of which he had never before experienced.

Aunt Caroline blundered up from her knees, saying, as she wiped her eyes, "Blessed is dey dat mou'n, fu' dey shall be comfo'ted." The old man, as he turned to go to bed, shook the young man's hand warmly and in silence; but there was a moisture in the old eyes that told the minister that his plummet of prayer had sounded the depths.

Alone in his own room Howard Dokesbury sat down to study the situation in which he had been placed. Had his thorough college training anticipated specifically any such circumstance as this? After all, did he know his own people? Was it possible that they could be so different from what he had seen and known? He had always been such a loyal Negro, so proud of his honest brown; but had he been mistaken? Was he, after all, different from the majority of the people with whom he was supposed to have all thoughts, feelings, and emotions in common?

These and other questions he asked himself without being able to arrive at any satisfactory conclusion. He did not go to sleep soon after retiring, and the night brought many thoughts. The next day would be Saturday. The ordeal had already begun,—now there were twenty-four hours between him and the supreme trial. What would be its outcome? There were moments when he felt, as every man, howsoever brave, must feel at times, that he would like to shift all his responsibilities and go away from the place that seemed destined to tax his powers beyond their capability of endurance. What could he do for the inhabitants of Mt. Hope? What was required of him to do? Ever through his mind ran that world-old question: "Am I my brother's keeper?" He had never asked, "Are these people my brothers?"

He was up early the next morning, and as soon as breakfast was done, he sat down to add a few touches to the sermon he had prepared as his introduction. It was not the first time that he had retouched it and polished it up here and there. Indeed, he had taken some pride in it. But as he read it over that day, it did not sound to him as it had sounded before. It appeared flat and without substance. After a while he laid it aside, telling himself that he was nervous and it was on this account that he could not see matters as he did in his calmer moments. He told himself, too, that he must not again take up the offending discourse until time to use it, lest the discovery of more imaginary flaws should so weaken his confidence that he would not be able to deliver it with effect.

In order better to keep his resolve, he put on his hat and went out for a walk through the streets of Mt. Hope. He did not find an encouraging prospect as he went along. The Negroes whom he met viewed him with ill-favour, and the whites who passed looked on him with unconcealed distrust and contempt. He began to feel lost, alone, and helpless. The squalor and shiftlessness which were plainly in evidence about the houses which he saw filled him with disgust and a dreary hopelessness.

He passed vacant lots which lay open and inviting children to healthful play; but instead of marbles or leap-frog or ball, he found little boys in ragged knicker-bockers huddled together on the ground, "shooting craps" with precocious avidity and quarrelling over the pennies that made the pitiful wagers. He heard glib profanity rolling from the lips of children who should have been stumbling through baby catechisms; and his heart ached for them.

He would have turned and gone back to his room, but the sound of shouts, laughter, and the tum-tum of a musical instrument drew him on down the street. At the turn of a corner, the place from which the noise emanated met his eyes. It was a rude frame building, low and unpainted. The panes in its windows whose places had not been supplied by sheets of tin were daubed a dingy red. Numerous kegs and bottles on the outside attested the nature of the place. The front door was open, but the interior was concealed by a gaudy curtain stretched across the entrance within. Over the door was the inscription, in straggling characters, "Sander's Place"; and when he saw half-a-dozen Negroes enter, the minister knew instantly that he now beheld the colored saloon which was the frequenting-place of his hostess's son 'Lias; and he wondered, if, as the mother said, her boy was not bad, how anything good could be preserved in such a place of evil.

The cries and boisterous laughter mingled with the strumming of the banjo and the shuffling of feet told him that they were engaged in one of their rude hoe-down dances. He had not passed a dozen paces beyond the door when the music was suddenly stopped, the sound of a quick blow followed, then ensued a scuffle, and a young fellow half ran, half fell through the open door. He was closely followed by a heavily built ruffian who was striking him as he ran. The young fellow was very much the weaker and slighter of the two, and was suffering great punishment. In an instant all the preacher's sense of justice was stung into sudden life. Just as the brute was about to give his victim a blow that would have sent him into the gutter, he felt his arm grasped in a detaining hold and heard a commanding voice,—"Stop!"

He turned with increased fury upon this meddler, but his other wrist was caught and held in a vice-like grip. For a moment the two men looked into each other's eyes. Hot words rose to the young man's lips, but he choked them back. Until this moment he had deplored the possession of a spirit so easily fired that it had been a test of his manhood to keep from "slugging" on the football field; now he was glad of it. He did not attempt to strike the man, but stood holding his arms and meeting the brute glare with manly flashing eyes. Either the natural cowardice of the bully or something in his new opponent's face had quelled the big fellow's spirit, and he said doggedly: "Lemme go. I wasn't a-go'n' to kill him nohow, but ef I ketch him dancin' with my gal anymo', I'll—" He cast a glance full of malice at his victim, who stood on the pavement a few feet away, as much amazed as the dumfounded crowd which thronged the door of "Sander's Place." Loosing his hold, the preacher turned, and, putting his hand on the young fellow's shoulder, led him away.

For a time they walked on in silence. Dokesbury had to calm the tempest in his breast before he could trust his voice. After a while he said: "That fellow was making it pretty hot for you, my young friend. What had you done to him?"

"Nothin'," replied the other. "I was jes' dancin' 'long an' not thinkin' 'bout him, when all of a sudden he hollered dat I had his gal an' commenced hittin' me."

"He's a bully and a coward, or he would not have made use of his superior strength in that way. What's your name, friend?"

"'Lias Gray," was the answer, which startled the minister into exclaiming,—

"What! are you Aunt Caroline's son?"

"Yes, suh, I sho is; does you know my mothah?"

"Why, I'm stopping with her, and we were talking about you last night. My name is Dokesbury, and I am to take charge of the church here."

"I thought mebbe you was a preachah, but I couldn't scarcely believe it after I seen de way you held Sam an' looked at him."

Dokesbury laughed, and his merriment seemed to make his companion feel better, for the sullen, abashed look left his face, and he laughed a little himself as he said: "I wasn't a-pesterin' Sam, but I tell you he pestered me mighty."

Dokesbury looked into the boy's face,—he was hardly more than a boy,—lit up as it was by a smile, and concluded that Aunt Caroline was right. 'Lias might be 'ca'less', but he wasn't a bad boy. The face was too open and the eyes too honest for that. 'Lias wasn't bad; but environment does so much, and he would be if something were not done for him. Here, then, was work for a pastor's hands.

"You'll walk on home with me, 'Lias, won't you?"

"I reckon I mout ez well," replied the boy. "I don't stay erroun' home ez much ez I oughter."

"You'll be around more, of course, now that I am there. It will be so much less lonesome for two young people than for one. Then, you can be a great help to me, too."

The preacher did not look down to see how wide his listener's eyes grew as he answered: "Oh, I ain't fittin' to be no he'p to you, suh. Fust thing, I ain't nevah got religion, an' then I ain't well larned enough."

"Oh, there are a thousand other ways in which you can help, and I feel sure that you will."

"Of co'se, I'll do de ve'y bes' I kin."

"There is one thing I want you to do soon, as a favour to me."

"I can't go to de mou'nah's bench," cried the boy, in consternation.

"And I don't want you to," was the calm reply.

Another look of wide-eyed astonishment took in the preacher's face. These were strange words from one of his guild. But without noticing the surprise he had created, Dokesbury went on: "What I want is that you will take me fishing as soon as you can. I never get tired of fishing and I am anxious to go here. Tom Scott says you fish a great deal about here."

"Why, we kin go dis ve'y afternoon," exclaimed 'Lias, in relief and delight; "I's mighty fond o' fishin', myse'f."

"All right; I'm in your hands from now on."

'Lias drew his shoulders up, with an unconscious motion. The preacher saw it, and mentally rejoiced. He felt that the first thing the boy beside him needed was a consciousness of responsibility, and the lifted shoulders meant progress in that direction, a sort of physical straightening up to correspond with the moral one.

On seeing her son walk in with the minister, Aunt 'Ca'line's' delight was boundless. "La! Brothah Dokesbury," she exclaimed, "wha'd you fin' dat scamp?"

"Oh, down the street here," the young man replied lightly. "I got hold of his name and made myself acquainted, so he came home to go fishing with me."

"'Lias is pow'ful fon' o' fishin', hisse'f. I 'low he kin show you some mighty good places. Cain't you, 'Lias?"

"I reckon."

'Lias was thinking. He was distinctly grateful that the circumstances of his meeting with the minister had been so deftly passed over. But with a half idea of the superior moral responsibility under which a man in Dokesbury's position laboured, he wondered vaguely—to put it in his own thought-words—"ef de preachah hadn't put' nigh lied." However, he was willing to forgive this little lapse of veracity, if such it was, out of consideration for the anxiety it spared his mother.

When Stephen Gray came in to dinner, he was no less pleased than his wife to note the terms of friendship on which the minister received his son. On his face was the first smile that Dokesbury had seen there, and he awakened from his taciturnity and proffered much information as to the fishing-places thereabout. The young minister accounted this a distinct gain. Anything more than a frowning silence from the "little yaller man" was gain.

The fishing that afternoon was particularly good. Catfish, chubs, and suckers were landed in numbers sufficient to please the heart of any amateur angler.

'Lias was happy, and the minister was in the best of spirits, for his charge seemed promising. He looked on at the boy's jovial face, and laughed within himself; for, mused he, "it is so much harder for the devil to get into a cheerful heart than into a sullen, gloomy one." By the time they were ready to go home Howard* Dokesbury had received a promise from 'Lias to attend service the next morning and hear the sermon.

There was a great jollification over the fish supper that night, and 'Lias and the minister were the heroes of the occasion. The old man again broke his silence, and recounted, with infinite dryness, ancient tales of his prowess with rod and line; while Aunt 'Ca'line' told of famous fish suppers that in the bygone days she had cooked for "de white folks." In the midst of it all, however, 'Lias disappeared. No one had noticed when he slipped out, but all seemed to become conscious of his absence about the same time. The talk shifted, and finally simmered into silence.

When the Rev. Mr. Dokesbury went to bed that night, his charge had not yet returned.

*Original reads "Harold Dokesbury." We have standardized the character's name to "Howard Dokesbury" throughout the story.

The young minister woke early on the Sabbath morning, and he may be forgiven that the prospect of the ordeal through which he had to pass drove his care for 'Lias out of mind for the first few hours. But as he walked to church, flanked on one side by Aunt Caroline in the stiffest of ginghams and on the other by her husband stately in the magnificence of an antiquated "Jim-swinger," his mind went back to the boy with sorrow. Where was he? What was he doing? Had the fear of a dull church service frightened him hack to his old habits and haunts? There was a new sadness at the preacher's heart as he threaded his way down the crowded church and ascended the rude pulpit.

The church was stiflingly hot, and the morning sun still beat relentlessly in through the plain windows. The seats were rude wooden benches, in some instances without backs. To the right, filling the inner corner, sat the pillars of the church, stern, grim, and critical. Opposite them, and, like them, in seats at right angles to the main body, sat the older sisters, some of them dressed with good old-fashioned simplicity, while others yielding to newer tendencies were gotten up in gaudy attempts at finery. In the rear seats a dozen or so much beribboned mulatto girls tittered and giggled, and cast bold glances at the minister.

The young man sighed as he placed the manuscript of his sermon between the leaves of the tattered Bible. "And this is Mt. Hope," he was again saying to himself.

It was after the prayer and in the midst of the second hymn that a more pronounced titter from the back seats drew his attention. He raised his head to cast a reproving glance at the irreverent, but the sight that met his eyes turned that look into one of horror. 'Lias had just entered the church, and with every mark of beastly intoxication was staggering up the aisle to a seat, into which he tumbled in a drunken heap. The preacher's soul turned sick within him, and his eyes sought the face of the mother and father. The old woman was wiping her eyes, and the old man sat with his gaze bent upon the floor, lines of sorrow drawn about his wrinkled mouth.

All of a sudden a great revulsion of feeling came over Dokesbury. Trembling he rose and opened the Bible. There lay his sermon, polished and perfected. The opening lines seemed to him like glints from a bright cold crystal. What had he to say to these people, when the full realisation of human sorrow and care and of human degradation had just come to him? What had they to do with firstlies and secondlies, with premises and conclusions? What they wanted was a strong hand to help them over the hard places of life and a loud voice to cheer them through the dark. He closed the book again upon his precious sermon. A something new had been born in his heart. He let his glance rest for another instant on the mother's pained face and the father's bowed form, and then turning to the congregation began, "Come unto me, all ye that labour and are heavy laden, and I will give you rest. Take my yoke upon you, and learn of me: for I am meek and lowly in heart: and ye shall find rest unto your souls." Out of the fulness of his heart he spoke unto them. Their great need informed his utterance. He forgot his carefully turned sentences and perfectly rounded periods. He forgot all save that here was the well-being of a community put into his hands whose real condition he had not even suspected until now. The situation wrought him up. His words went forth like winged fire, and the emotional people were moved beyond control. They shouted, and clapped their hands, and praised the Lord loudly.

When the service was over, there was much gathering about the young preacher, and handshaking. Through all 'Lias had slept. His mother started toward him; but the minister managed to whisper to her, "Leave him to me." When the congregation had passed out, Dokesbury shook 'Lias. The boy woke, partially sobered, and his face fell before the preacher's eyes.

"Come, my boy, let's go home." Arm in arm they went out into the street, where a number of scoffers had gathered to have a laugh at the abashed boy; but Howard Dokesbury's strong arm steadied his steps, and something in his face checked the crowd's hilarity. Silently they cleared the way, and the two passed among them and went home.

The minister saw clearly the things which he had to combat in his community, and through this one victim he determined to fight the general evil. The people with whom he had to deal were children who must be led by the hand. The boy lying in drunken sleep upon his bed was no worse than the rest of them. He was an epitome of the evil, as his parents were of the sorrows, of the place.

He could not talk to Elias. He could not lecture him. He would only be dashing his words against the accumulated evil of years of bondage as the ripples of a summer sea beat against a stone wall. It was not the wickedness of this boy he was fighting or even the wrongdoing of Mt. Hope. It was the aggregation of the evils of the fathers, the grandfathers, the masters and mistresses of these people. Against this what could talk avail?

The boy slept on, and the afternoon passed heavily away. Aunt Caroline was finding solace in her pipe, and Stephen Gray sulked in moody silence beside the hearth. Neither of them joined their guest at evening service.

He went, however. It was hard to face those people again after the events of the morning. He could feel them covertly nudging each other and grinning as he went up to the pulpit. He chided himself for the momentary annoyance it caused him. Were they not like so many naughty, irresponsible children?

The service passed without unpleasantness, save that he went home with an annoyingly vivid impression of a yellow girl with red ribbons on her hat, who pretended to be impressed by his sermon and made eyes at him from behind her handkerchief.

On the way to his room that night, as he passed Stephen Gray, the old man whispered huskily, "It's de fus' time 'Lias evah done dat."

It was the only word he had spoken since morning.

A sound sleep refreshed Dokesbury, and restored the tone to his overtaxed nerves. When he came out in the morning, Elias was already in the kitchen. He too had slept off his indisposition, but it had been succeeded by a painful embarrassment that proved an effectual barrier to all intercourse with him. The minister talked lightly and amusingly, but the boy never raised his eyes from his plate, and only spoke when he was compelled to answer some direct questions.

Howard Dokesbury knew that unless he could overcome this reserve, his power over the youth was gone. He bent every effort to do it.

"What do you say to a turn down the street with me?" he asked as he rose from breakfast.

'Lias shook his head.

"What! You haven't deserted me already?"

The older people had gone out, but young Gray looked furtively about before he replied: "You know I ain't fittin' to go out with you—aftah—aftah—yestiddy."

A dozen appropriate texts rose in the preacher's mind, but he knew that it was not a preaching time, so he contented himself with saying,—

"Oh, get out! Come along!"

"No, I cain't. I cain't. I wisht I could! You needn't think I's ashamed, 'cause I ain't. Plenty of 'em git drunk, an' I don't keer nothin' 'bout dat"—this in a defiant tone.

"Well, why not come along, then?"

"I tell you I cain't. Don't ax me no mo'. It ain't on my account I won't go. It's you."

"Me! Why, I want you to go."

"I know you does, but I mustn't. Cain't you see that dey'd be glad to say dat—dat you was in cahoots wif me an' you tuk yo' dram on de sly?"

"I don't care what they say so long as it isn't true. Are you coming?"

"No, I ain't."

He was perfectly determined, and Dokesbury saw that there was no use arguing with him. So with a resigned "All right!" he strode out the gate and up the street, thinking of the problem he had to solve.

There was good in Elias Gray, he knew. It was a shame that it should be lost. It would be lost unless he were drawn strongly away from the paths he was treading. But how could it be done? Was there no point in his mind that could be reached by what was other than evil? That was the thing to be found out. Then he paused to ask himself if, after all, he were not trying to do too much,—trying, in fact, to play Providence to Elias. He found himself in voluntarily wanting to shift the responsibility of planning for the youth. He wished that something entirely independent of his intentions would happen.

Just then something did happen. A piece of soft mud hurled from some unknown source caught the minister square in the chest, and spattered over his clothes. He raised his eyes and glanced about quickly, but no one was in sight. Whoever the foe was, he was securely ambushed.

"Thrown by the hand of a man," mused Dokesbury, "prompted by the malice of a child."

He went on his way, finished his business, and returned to the house.

"La, Brothah Dokesbury!" exclaimed Aunt Caroline, "what's de mattah 'f yo' shu't bosom?"

"Oh, that's where one of our good citizens left his card."

"You don' mean to say none o' dem low-life scoun'els—"

"I don't know who did it. He took particular pains to keep out of sight."

"'Lias!" the old woman cried, turning on her son, "wha' 'd you let Brothah Dokesbury go off by hisse'f fu'? Whyn't you go 'long an' tek keer o' him?"

The old lady stopped even in the midst of her tirade, as her eyes took in the expression on her son's face.

"I'll kill some o' dem damn—"

"'Lias!"

"'Scuse me, Mistah Dokesbury, but I feel lak I'll bus' ef I don' 'spress myse'f. It makes me so mad. Don't you go out o' hyeah no mo' 'dout me. I'll go 'long an' I'll brek somebody's haid wif a stone."

"'Lias! how you talkin' fo' de ministah?"

"Well, dat's whut I'll do, 'cause I kin out-th'ow any of 'em an' I know dey hidin'-places."

"I'll be glad to accept your protection," said Dokesbury.

He saw his advantage, and was thankful for the mud,—the one thing that without an effort restored the easy relations between himself and his protégé.

Ostensibly these relations were reversed, and Elias went out with the preacher as a guardian and protector. But the minister was laying his nets. It was on one of these rambles that he broached to 'Lias a subject which he had been considering for some time.

"Look here, 'Lias," he said, "what are you going to do with that big back yard of yours?"

"Oh, nothin'. 'T ain't no 'count to raise nothin' in."

"It may not be fit for vegetables, but it will raise something."

"What?"

"Chickens. That's what."

Elias laughed sympathetically.

"I'd lak to eat de chickens I raise. I wouldn't want to be feedin' de neighbourhood."

"Plenty of boards, slats, wire, and a good lock and key would fix that all right."

"Yes, but whah 'm I gwine to git all dem things?"

"Why, I'll go in with you and furnish the money, and help you build the coops. Then you can sell chickens and eggs, and we'll go halves on the profits."

"Hush, man!" cried 'Lias, in delight.

So the matter was settled, and, as Aunt Caroline expressed it, "Fu' a week er sich a mattah, you nevah did see sich ta'in' down an' buildin' up in all yo' bo'n days."

'Lias went at the work with zest, and Dokesbury noticed his skill with tools. He let fall the remark: "Say, 'Lias, there's a school near here where they teach carpentering; why don't you go and learn?"

"What I gwine to do with bein' a cyahpenter?"

"Repair some of these houses around Mt. Hope, if nothing more," Dokesbury responded, laughing; and there the matter rested.

The work prospered, and as the weeks went on, 'Lias' enterprise became the town's talk. One of Aunt Caroline's patrons who had come with some orders about work regarded the changed condition of affairs, and said, "Why, Aunt Caroline, this doesn't look like the same place. I'll have to buy some eggs from you; you keep your yard and hen-house so nice, it's an advertisement for the eggs."

"Don't talk to me nothin' 'bout dat ya'd, Miss Lucy," Aunt Caroline had retorted. "Dat 'long to 'Lias an' de preachah. Hit dey doin's. Dey done mos' nigh drove me out wif dey cleanness. I ain't nevah seed no sich ca'in' on in my life befo'. Why, my 'Lias done got right brigity an' talk about bein' somep'n'."

Dokesbury had retired from his partnership with the boy save in so far as he acted as a general supervisor. His share had been sold to a friend of 'Lias, Jim Hughes. The two seemed to have no other thought save of raising, tending, and selling chickens.

Mt. Hope looked on and ceased to scoff. Money is a great dignifier, and Jim and 'Lias were making money. There had been some sniffs when the latter had hinged the front gate and whitewashed his mother's cabin, but even that had been accepted now as a matter of course.

Dokesbury had done his work. He, too, looked on, and in some satisfaction.

"Let the leaven work," he said, " and all Mt. Hope must rise."

It was one day, nearly a year later, that "old lady Hughes" dropped in on Aunt Caroline for a chat.

"Well, I do say, Sis' Ca'line, dem two boys o' ourn done sot dis town on fiah."

"What now, Sis' Lizy?"

"Why, evah sence 'Lias tuk it into his haid to be a cyahpenter an' Jim 'cided to go 'long an' lu'n to be a blacksmif, some o' dese hyeah othah young people's been tryin' to do somep'n'."

"All dey wanted was a staht."

"Well, now will you b'lieve me, dat no-'count Tom Johnson done opened a fish sto', an' he has de boys an' men bring him dey fish all de time. He give 'em a little somep'n' fu' dey ketch, den he go sell 'em to de white folks."

"Lawd, how long!"

"An' what you think he say?"

"I do' know, sis'."

"He say ez soon 'z he git money enough, he gwine to dat school whah 'Lias an' Jim gone an' lu'n to fahm scientific."

"Bless de Lawd! Well, 'um, I don' put nothin' pas' de young folks now."

Mt. Hope had at last awakened. Something had come to her to which she might aspire,—something that she could understand and reach. She was not soaring, but she was rising above the degradation in which Howard Dokesbury had found her. And for her and him the ordeal had passed.

The Colonel's Awakening

IT WAS THE morning before Christmas. The cold winter sunlight fell brightly through the window into a small room where an old man was sitting. The room, now bare and cheerless, still retained evidences of having once been the abode of refinement and luxury. It was the one open chamber of many in a great rambling old Virginia house, which in its time had been one of the proudest in the county. But it had been in the path of the hurricane of war, and had been shorn of its glory as a tree is stripped of its foliage. Now, like the bare tree, dismantled, it remained, and this one old man, with the aristocratic face, clung to it like the last leaf.

He did not turn his head when an ancient serving-man came in and began laying the things for breakfast. After a while the servant spoke: "I got a monst'ous fine breakfus' fu' you dis mo'nin', Mas' Estridge. I got fresh aigs, an' beat biscuits, an Lize done fried you a young chicken dat'll sholy mek yo' mouf worter."

"Thank you, Ike, thank you," was the dignified response. "Lize is a likely girl, and she's improving in her cooking greatly."

"Yes, Mas' Estridge, she sho is a mighty fine ooman."

"And you're not a bad servant yourself, Ike," the old man went on, with an air of youthful playfulness that ill accorded with his aged face. "I expect some day you'll be coming around asking me to let you marry Lize, eh! What have you got to say to that?"

"I reckon dat's right, mastah, I reckon dat's mighty nigh right."

"Well, we shall see about it when the time comes; we shall see about it."

"Lawd, how long!" mumbled the old servant to himself as he went on about his work. "Ain't Mas' Bob nevah gwine to git his almanec straight? He been gwine on dis way fu' ovah twenty yeahs now. He cain't git it thoo' his haid dat time been a-passin'. Hyeah I done been ma'ied to Lize fu' lo dese many yeahs, an' we've got ma'ied chillum, but he still think I's a-cou'tin' huh."

To Colonel Robert Estridge time had not passed and conditions had not changed for a generation. He was still the gallant aristocrat he had been when the war broke out,—a little past the age to enlist himself, but able and glad to give two sons to the cause of the South. They had gone out, light-hearted and gay, and brave in their military trappings and suits of gray. The father had watched them away with moist eyes and a swelling bosom. After that the tide of war had surged on and on, had even rolled to his very gates, and the widowed man watched and waited for it to bring his boys back to him. One of them came. They brought him back from the valley of the Shenandoah, and laid him in the old orchard out there behind the house. Then all the love of the father was concentrated upon the one remaining son, and his calendar could know but one day and that the one on which his Bob, his namesake and his youngest, should return to him. But one day there came to him the news that his boy had fallen in the front of a terrific fight, and in the haste of retreat he had been buried with the unknown dead. Into that trench, among the unknown, Colonel Robert Estridge had laid his heart, and there it had stayed. Time stopped, and his faculties wandered. He lived always in the dear past. The present and future were not. He did not even know when the fortunes of war brought an opposing host to his very doors. He was unconscious of it all when they devoured his substance like a plague of locusts. It was all a blank to him when the old manor house was fired and he was like to lose his possessions and his life. When his servants left him he did not know, but sat and gave orders to the one faithful retainer as though he were ordering the old host of blacks. And so for more than a generation he had lived.

"Hope you gwine to enjoy yo' Christmas Eve breakfus', Mas' Estridge," said the old servant.

"Christmas Eve, Christmas Eve? Yes, yes, so it is. To-morrow is Christmas Day, and I'm afraid I have been rather sluggish in getting things ready for the celebration. I reckon the darkies have already begun to jubilate and to shirk in consequence, and I won't be able to get a thing done decently for a week."

"Don't you bother 'bout none o' de res', Mas' Estridge; you kin 'pend on me —I ain't gwine to shu'k even ef 't is Christmus."

"That's right, Ike. I can depend upon you. You're always faithful. Just you get things done up right for me, and I'll give you that broadcloth suit of mine. It's most as good as new."

"Thanky, Mas' Bob, thanky." The old Negro said it as fervently as if he had not worn out that old broadcloth a dozen years ago.

"It's late and we've got to hurry if we want things prepared in time. Tell Lize that I want her to let herself out on that dinner. Your Mas' Bob and your Mas' Stanton are going to be home to-morrow and I want to show them that their father's house hasn't lost any of the qualities that have made it famous in Virginia for a hundred years. Ike, there ain't anything in this world for making men out of boys like making them feel the debt they owe to their name and family."

"Yes, suh, Mas' Bob an' Mas' Stant sholy is mighty fine men."

"There ain't two finer in the whole country, sir,—no, sir, not in all Virginia, and that of necessity means the whole country. Now, Ike, I want you to get out some of that wine up in the second cellar, and when I say some I mean plenty. It ain't seen the light for years, but it shall gurgle into the glasses to-morrow in honour of my sons' home-coming. Good wine makes good blood, and who should drink good wine if not an Estridge of Virginia, sir, eh, Ike?"

The wine had gone to make good cheer when a Federal regiment had lighted its campfires on the Estridge lawn, but old Ike had heard it too often before and knew his business too well to give any sign.

"I want you to take some things up to Miss Clarinda Randolph to-morrow, too, and I've got a silver snuffbox for Thomas Daniels. I can't make many presents this year. I've got to devote my money to the interest of your young masters."

There was a catch in the Negro's voice as he replied, "Yes, Mas' Estridge, dey needs it mos', dey needs it mos'."

The old colonel's spell of talking seldom lasted long, and now he fell to eating in silence; but his face was the face of one in a dream. Ike waited on him until he had done, and then, clearing the things away, slipped out, leaving him to sit and muse in his chair by the window.

"Look hyeah, Lize," said the old servant, as he entered his wife's cabin a little later. "Pleggoned ef I didn't come purt' nigh brekin' down dis mo'nin'."

"Wha' 's de mattah wif you, Ike?"

"Jes' a-listenin' to ol' Mas' a-sittin' dah a-talkin' lak it was de ol' times,— a-sendin' messages to ol' Miss Randolph, dat's been daid too long to talk about, an' to Mas' Tom Daniels, dat went acrost de wateh ruther 'n tek de oaf o' 'legiance."

"Oomph," said the old lady, wiping her eyes on her cotton apron.

"Den he expectin' Mas' Bob an Mas' Stant home to-morrer. 'Clah to goodness, when he say dat I lak to hollahed right out."

"Den you would 'a' fixed it, wouldn't you? Set down an' eat yo' breakfus', Ike, an' don't you nevah let on when Mas' Estridge talkin', you jes' go 'long 'bout yo' wuk an' keep yo' mouf shet, 'ca'se ef evah he wake up now he gwine to die right straight off."

"Lawd he'p him not to wake up den, 'ca'se he ol', but we needs him. I do' know whut I'd do ef I didn't have Mas' Bob to wuk fu'. You got ol' Miss Randolph's present ready fu' him?"

"Co'se I has. I done made him somep'n' diffunt dis yeah."

"Made him somep'n' diffunt—whut you say, Lize?" exclaimed the old man, laying his knife and fork on his plate and looking up at his wife with wide-open eyes. "You ain't gwine change afteh all dese yeahs?"

"Yes. I jes' pintly had to. It's been de same thing now fu' mo' 'n twenty yeahs."

"Whut you done made fu' him?"

"I's made him a comfo't to go roun' his naik."

"But, Lize, ol' Miss Cla'indy allus sont him gloves knit wif huh own han'. Ain't you feared Mas' Estridge gwine to 'spect?"

"No, he ain't gwine to 'spect. He don't tek no notice o' nuffin', an' he jes' pintly had to have dat comfo't fu' his naik, 'ca'se he boun' to go out in de col' sometime er ruther an' he got plenty gloves."

"I's feared," said the old man, sententiously, "I's mighty feared. I wouldn't have Mastah know we been doin' fu' him an' a-sendin' him dese presents all dis time fu' nuffin' in de worl'. It 'u'd hu't him mighty bad."

"He ain't foun' out all dese yeahs, an' he ain't gwine fin' out now." The old man shook his head dubiously, and ate the rest of his meal in silence.

It was a beautiful Christmas morning as he wended his way across the lawn to his old master's room, bearing the tray of breakfast things and "ol' Miss Randolph's present,"—a heavy home-made scarf. The air was full of frosty brightness. Ike was happy, for the frost had turned the persimmons. The 'possums had gorged themselves, and he had one of the fattest of them for his Christmas dinner. Colonel Estridge was sitting in his old place by the window. He crumbled an old yellow envelope in his hand as Ike came in and set the things down. It looked like the letter which had brought the news of young Robert Estridge's loss, but it could not be, for the old man sitting there had forgotten that and was expecting the son home on that day.

Ike took the comforter to his master, and began in the old way: "Miss Cla'iny Randolph mek huh comperments to you, Mas' Bob, an' say—" But his master had turned and was looking him square in the face, and something in the look checked his flow of words. Colonel Estridge did not extend his hand to take the gift. "Clarinda Randolph," he said, "always sends me gloves." His tone was not angry, but it was cold and sorrowful. "Lay it down," he went on more kindly and pointing to the comforter, "and you may go now. I will get whatever I want from the table." Ike did not dare to demur. He slipped away, embarrassed and distressed.

"Wha' 'd I tell you?" he asked Lize, as soon as he reached the cabin. "I believe he done woke up." But the old woman could only mourn and wring her hands.

"Well, nevah min'," said Ike, after his first moment of sad triumph was over. "I guess it wasn't the comfo't nohow, 'ca'se I seed him wif a letteh when I went in, but I didn't 'spicion nuffin' tell he look at me an' talk jes' ez sensible ez me er you."

It was not until dinner-time that Ike found courage to go back to his master's room, and then he did not find him sitting in his accustomed place, nor was he on the porch or in the hall.

Growing alarmed, the old servant searched high and low for him, until he came to the door of a long-disused room. A bundle of keys hung from the keyhole.

"Hyeah's whah he got dat letteh," said Ike. "I reckon he come to put it back." But even as he spoke, his eyes bulged with apprehension. He opened the door farther, and went in. And there at last his search was ended. Colonel Estridge was on his knees before an old oak chest. On the floor about him were scattered pair on pair of home-knit gloves. He was very still. His head had fallen forward on the edge of the chest. Ike went up to him and touched his shoulder. There was no motion in response. The black man lifted his master's head. The face was pale and cold and lifeless. In the stiffening hand was clenched a pair of gloves,—the last Miss Randolph had ever really knit for him. The servant lifted up the lifeless form, and laid it upon the bed. When Lize came she would have wept and made loud lamentations, but Ike checked her. "Keep still," he said. "Pray if you want to, but don't hollah. We ought to be proud, Lize." His shoulders were thrown back and his head was up. "Mas' Bob's in glory. Dis is Virginia's Christmas gif' to Gawd!"

The Trial Sermons on Bull-Skin

THE CONGREGATION ON Bull-Skin Creek was without a pastor. You will probably say that this was a deficiency easily remedied among a people who possess so much theological material. But you will instantly perceive how different a matter it was, when you learn that the last shepherd who had guided the flock at Bull-Skin had left that community under a cloud. There were, of course, those who held with the departed minister, as well as those who were against him; and so two parties arose in the church, each contending for supremacy. Each party refused to endorse any measure or support any candidate suggested by the other; and as neither was strong enough to run the church alone, they were in a state of inactive equipoise very gratifying to that individual who is supposed to take delight in the discomfort of the righteous.

It was in this complicated state of affairs that Brother Hezekiah Sneedon, who was the representative of one of the candidates for the vacant pastorate, conceived and proposed a way out of the difficulty. Brother Sneedon's proposition was favourably acted upon by the whole congregation, because it held out the promise of victory to each party. It was, in effect, as follows:

Each faction—it had come to be openly recognised that there were two factions —should name its candidate, and then they should be invited to preach, on successive Sundays, trial sermons before the whole congregation, the preacher making the better impression to be called as pastor.

"And," added Brother Sneedon, pacifically, "in ordah dat dis little diffunce between de membahs may be settled in ha'mony, I do hope an' pray dat de pahty dat fin's itse'f outpreached will give up to de othah in Christun submission, an' th'ow in all deir might to hol' up de han's of whatever pastor de Lawd may please to sen'."

Sister Hannah Williams, the leader of the opposing faction, expressed herself as well pleased with the plan, and counselled a like submission to the will of the majority. And thus the difficulty at Bull-Skin seemed in a fair way to settlement. But could any one have read that lady's thoughts as she wended her homeward way after the meeting, he would have had some misgivings concerning the success of the proposition which she so willingly endorsed. For she was saying to herself,—

"Uh huh! ol' Kiah Sneedon thinks he's mighty sma't, puttin' up dat plan. Reckon he thinks ol' Abe Ma'tin kin outpreach anything near an' fur, but ef Brothah 'Lias Smith don't fool him, I ain't talkin'."

And Brother Sneedon himself was not entirely guiltless of some selfish thought as he hobbled away from the church door.

"Ann," said he to his wife, "I wunner ef Hannah Williams ca'culates dat 'Lias Smith kin beat Brother Abe Ma'tin preachin', ki yi! but won't she be riley when she fin's out how mistaken she is? Why, dey ain't nobody 'twixt hyeah an' Louisville kin beat Brothah Abe Ma'tin preachin'. I's hyeahed dat man preach 'twell de winders rattled an' it seemed lak de skies mus' come down anyhow, an' sinnahs was a-fallin' befo' de Wo'd lak leaves in a Novembah blas'; an' she 'lows to beat him, oomph!" The "oomph" meant disgust, incredulity, and, above all, resistance.

The first of the momentous Sundays had been postponed two weeks, in order, it was said, to allow the members to get the spiritual and temporal elements of the church into order that would be pleasing to the eyes of a new pastor. In reality, Brother Sneedon and Sister Williams used the interval of time to lay their plans and to marshal their forces. And during the two weeks previous to the Sunday on which, by common consent, it had been agreed to invite the Reverend Elias Smith to preach, there was an ominous quiet on the banks of Bull-Skin,—the calm that precedes a great upheaval, when clouds hang heavy with portents and forebodings, but silent withal.

But there were events taking place in which the student of diplomacy might have found food for research and reflection. Such an event was the taffy-pulling which Sister Williams' daughters, Dora and Caroline, gave to the younger members of the congregation on Thursday evening. Such were the frequent incursions of Sister Williams herself upon the domains of the neighbours, with generous offerings of "a taste o' my ketchup" or "a sample o' my jelly." She did not stop with rewarding her own allies, but went farther, gift-bearing, even into the camp of the enemy himself.

It was on Friday morning that she called on Sister Sneedon. She found the door ajar and pushed it open, saying, "You see, Sis' Sneedon, I's jes' walkin' right in."

"Oh, it's you, Sis' Williams; dat's right, come in. I was jes' settin' hyeah sawtin' my cyahpet rags, de mof do seem to pestah 'em so. Tek dis cheer"—industriously dusting one with her apron. "How you be'n sence I seen you las'?"

"Oh, jes' sawt o' so."

"How's Do' an' Ca'line?"

"Oh, Ca'line's peart enough, but Do's feelin' kind o' peekid."

"Don't you reckon she grow too fas'?"

"'Spec' dat's about hit; dat gal do sutny seem to run up lak a weed."

"It don't nevah do 'em no good to grow so fas', hit seem to tek away all deir strengf."

"Yes, 'm, it sholy do; gals ain't whut dey used to be in yo' an' my day, nohow."

"Lawd, no; dey's ez puny ez white folks now."

"Well, dem sholy is lovely cyahpet rags—put' nigh all wool, ain't dey?"

"Yes, ma'am, dey is wool, evah speck an' stitch; dey ain't a bit o' cotton among 'em. I ain't lak some folks; I don't b'lieve in mixin' my rags evah-which-way. Den when you gits 'em wove have de cyahpet wah in holes, 'cause some'll stan' a good deal o' strain an' some won't; yes, 'm, dese is evah one wool."

"An' you sholy have be'n mighty indust'ous in gittin' 'em togethah."

"I's wo'ked ha'd an' done my level bes', dat's sho."

"Dat's de mos' any of us kin do. But I mustn't be settin' hyeah talkin' all day an' keepin' you f'om yo' wo'k. Why, la! I'd mos' nigh fu'got what I come fu'—I jes' brung you ovah a tas'e o' my late greens. I knows how you laks greens, so I thought mebbe you'd enjoy dese."

"Why, sho enough; now ain't dat good o' you, Sis' Williams? Dey's right wa'm, too, an' tu'nip tops—bless me! Why, dese mus' be de ve'y las' greens o' de season."

"Well, I reely don't think you'll fin' none much latah. De fros' had done teched dese, but I kin' o' kivered 'em up wif leaves ontwell dey growed up wuf cuttin'."

"Well, I knows I sholy shell relish dem." Mrs. Sneedon beamed as she emptied the dish and insisted upon washing it for her visitor to take home with her. "Fu'," she said, by way of humour, "I's a mighty po' han' to retu'n nice dishes when I gits 'em in my cu'boa'd once."

Sister Williams rose to go. "Well, you'll be out to chu'ch Sunday to hyeah Broth' 'Lias Smith; he's a powahful man, sho."

"Dey do tell me so. I'll be thah. You kin 'pend on me to be out whenevah thah's to be any good preachin'."

"Well, we kin have dat kin' o' preachin' all de time ef we gits Broth' 'Lias Smith."

"Yes, 'm."

"Dey ain't no 'sputin' he'll be a movin' powah at Bull-Skin."

"Yes, 'm."

"We sistahs'll have to ban' togethah an' try to do whut is bes' fu' de chu'ch."

"Yes, 'm."

"Co'se, Sistah Sneedon, ef you's pleased wif his sermon, I suppose you'll be in favoh o' callin' Broth' 'Lias Smith."

"Well, Sis' Williams, I do' know; you see Hezekier's got his hea't sot on Broth' Abe Ma'tin fum Dokesville; he's mighty sot on him, an' when he's sot he's sot, an' you know how it is wif us women when de men folks says dis er dat."

Sister Williams saw that she had overshot her mark. "Oh, hit's all right, Sis' Sneedon, hit's all right. I jes' spoke of it a-wunnerin'. What we women folks wants to do is to ban' togethah to hol' up de han' of de pastah dat comes, whoms'ever he may be."

"Dat's hit, dat's hit," assented her companion; "an' you kin 'pend on me thah, fu' I's a powahful han' to uphol' de ministah whoms'ever he is."

"An' you right too, fu' dey's de shepuds of de flock. Well, I mus' be goin'—come ovah."

"I's a-comin'—come ag'in yo'se'f, goodbye."

As soon as her visitor was gone, Sister Sneedon warmed over the greens and sat down to the enjoyment of them. She had just finished the last mouthful when her better half entered. He saw the empty plate and the green liquor. Evidently he was not pleased, for be it said that Brother Sneedon had himself a great tenderness for turnip greens.

"Wha'd you git dem greens?" he asked.

"Sistah Hannah Williams brung 'em ovah to me."

"Sistah Hannah—who?" ejaculated he.

"Sis' Williams, Sis' Williams, you know Hannah Williams."

"What! dat wolf in sheep's clothin' dat's a-gwine erroun' a-seekin' who she may devowah, an' you hyeah a-projickin' wif huh, eatin' de greens she gives you! How you know whut's in dem greens?"

"Oh, g'long, 'Kiah, you so funny! Sis' Williams ain't gwine conju' nobidy."

"You hyeah me, you hyeah me now. Keep on foolin' wif dat ooman, she'll have you crawlin' on yo' knees an' ba'kin, lak a dog. She kin do it, she kin do it, fu' she's long-haided, I tell you."

"Well, ef she wants to hu't me it's done, fu' I's eat de greens now."

"Yes," exclaimed Brother Sneedon, "you eat 'em up lak a hongry hog an' never saved me a smudgeon."

"Oomph! I thought you's so afeard o' gittin' conju'ed."

"Heish up! you's allus tryin' to raise some kin' er contentions in de fambly. I nevah seed a ooman lak you." And old Hezekiah strode out of the cabin in high dudgeon.

And so, smooth on the surface, but turbulent beneath, the stream of days flowed on until the Sunday on which Reverend Elias Smith was to preach his trial sermon. His fame as a preacher, together with the circumstances surrounding this particular sermon, had brought together such a crowd as the little church on Bull-Skin had never seen before even in the heat of the most successful revivals. Outsiders had come from as far away as Christiansburg, which was twelve, and Fox Run, which was fifteen miles distant, and the church was crowded to the doors.

Sister Williams with her daughters Dora and Caroline were early in their seats. Their ribbons were fluttering to the breeze like the banners of an aggressive host. There were smiles of anticipated triumph upon their faces. Brother and Sister Sneedon arrived a little later. They took their seat far up in the "amen corner," directly behind the Williams family. Sister Sneedon sat very erect and looked about her, but her spouse leaned his chin upon his cane and gazed at the floor, nor did he raise his head, when, preceded by a buzz of expectancy, the Reverend Elias Smith, accompanied by Brother Abner Williams, who was a local preacher, entered and ascended to the pulpit, where he knelt in silent prayer.

At the entrance of their candidate, the female portion of the Williams family became instantly alert.

They were all attention when the husband and father arose and gave out the hymn: "Am I a Soldier of the Cross?" They joined lustily in the singing, and at the lines, "Sure I must fight if I would reign," their voices rose in a victorious swell far above the voices of the rest of the congregation. Prayer followed, and then Brother Williams rose and said,—

"Brothahs an' sistahs, I teks gret pleasuah in interducin' to you Eldah Smith, of Dokeville, who will preach fu' us at dis howah. I want to speak fu' him yo' pra'ful attention." Sister Williams nodded her head in approval, even this much was good; but Brother Sneedon sighed aloud.

The Reverend Elias Smith arose and glanced over the congregation. He was young, well-appearing, and looked as though he might have been unmarried. He announced his text in a clear, resonant voice: "By deir fruits shell you know dem."

The great change that gave to the blacks fairly trained ministers from the schools had not at this time succeeded their recently accomplished emancipation. And the sermon of Elder Smith was full of all the fervour, common-sense, and rude eloquence of the old plantation exhorter. He spoke to his hearers in the language that they understood, because he himself knew no other. He drew his symbols and illustrations from the things which he saw most commonly about him,—things which he and his congregation understood equally well. He spent no time in dallying about the edge of his subject, but plunged immediately into the middle of things, and soon had about him a shouting, hallooing throng of frantic people. Of course it was the Williams faction who shouted. The spiritual impulse did not seem to reach those who favoured Brother Sneedon's candidate. They sat silent and undemonstrative. That earnest disciple himself still sat with his head bent upon his cane, and still at intervals sighed audibly. He had only raised his head once, and that was when some especially powerful period in the sermon had drawn from the partner of his joys and sorrows an appreciative "Oomph!" Then the look that he shot forth from his eyes, so full of injury, reproach, and menace, repressed her noble rage and settled her back into a quietude more consonant with her husband's ideas.

Meanwhile, Sister Hannah Williams and her sylph-like daughters "Do" and "Ca'line" were in an excess of religious frenzy. Whenever any of the other women in the congregation seemed to be working their way too far forward, those enthusiastic sisters shouted their way directly across the approach to the pulpit, and held place there with such impressive and menacing demonstrativeness that all comers were warned back. There had been times when, actuated by great religious fervour, women had ascended the rostrum and embraced the minister. Rest assured, nothing of that kind happened in this case, though the preacher waxed more and more eloquent as he proceeded,—an eloquence more of tone, look, and gesture than of words. He played upon the emotions of his willing hearers, except those who had steeled themselves against his power, as a skilful musician upon the strings of his harp. At one time they were boisterously exultant, at another they were weeping and moaning, as if in the realisation of many sins. The minister himself lowered his voice to a soft rhythmical moan, almost a chant, as he said,—

"You go 'long by de road an you see an ol' shabby tree a-standin' in de o'chud. It ain't ha'dly got a apple on it. Its leaves are put' nigh all gone. You look at de branches, dey's all rough an' crookid. De tree's all full of sticks an' stones an' wiah an' ole tin cans. Hit's all bruised up an' hit's a ha'd thing to look at altogether. You look at de tree an' whut do you say in yo' hea't? You say de tree ain't no 'count, fu' 'by deir fruits shell you know dem.' But you wrong, my frien's, you wrong. Dat tree did ba' good fruit, an' by hits fruit was hit knowed. John tol' Gawge an' Gawge tol' Sam, an' evah one dat passed erlong de road had to have a shy at dat fruit. Dey be'n th'owin' at dat tree evah sence hit begun to ba' fruit, an' dey's 'bused hit so dat hit couldn't grow straight to save hits life. Is dat whut's de mattah wif you, brothah, all bent ovah yo' staff an' a-groanin' wif yo' burdens? Is dat whut's de mattah wif you, brothah, dat yo' steps are a-weary an' you's longin' fu' yo' home? Have dey be'n th'owin' stones an' cans at you? Have dey be'n beatin' you wif sticks? Have dey tangled you up in ol' wiah twell you couldn't move han' ner foot? Have de way be'n all trouble? Have de sky be'n all cloud? Have de sun refused to shine an' de day be'n all da'kness? Don't git werry, be consoled. Whut de mattah! Why, I tell you you ba'in' good fruit, an' de debbil cain't stan' it—'By deir fruits shell you know dem.'

"You go 'long de road a little furder an' you see a tree standin' right by de fence. Standin' right straight up in de air, evah limb straight out in hits place, all de leaves green an' shinin' an' lovely. Not a stick ner a stone ner a can in sight. You look 'way up in de branches, an' dey hangin' full o' fruit, big an' roun' an' solid. You look at dis tree an' whut now do you say in yo' hea't? You say dis is a good tree, fu' 'by deir fruits shell you know dem.' But you wrong, you wrong ag'in, my frien's. De apples on dat tree are so sowah dat dey'd puckah up yo mouf wuss'n a green pu'simmon, an' evahbidy knows hit, by hits fruit is hit knowed. Dey don't want none o' dat fruit, an' dey pass hit by an' don't bothah dey haids about it.

"Look out, brothah, you gwine erlong thoo dis worl' sailin' on flowery beds of ease. Look out, my sistah, you's a-walkin' in de sof' pafs an' a-dressin' fine. Ain't nobidy a-troublin' you, nobidy ain't a-backbitin' you, nobidy ain't a-castin' yo' name out as evil. You all right an' movin' smoov. But I want you to stop an' 'zamine yo'se'ves. I want you to settle whut kin' o' fruit you ba'in', whut kin' o' light you showin' fo'f to de worl'. An' I want you to stop an' tu'n erroun' when you fin' out dat you ba'in' bad fruit, an' de debbil ain't bothahed erbout you 'ca'se he knows you his'n anyhow. 'By deir fruits shell you know dem.'"

The minister ended his sermon, and the spell broke. Collection was called for and taken, and the meeting dismissed.

"Wha' 'd you think o' dat sermon?" asked Sister Williams of one of her good friends; and the good friend answered,—

"Tsch, pshaw! dat man jes' tuk his tex' at de fust an' nevah lef' it."

Brother Sneedon remarked to a friend: "Well, he did try to use a good deal o' high langgidge, but whut we want is grace an' speritual feelin'."

The Williams faction went home with colours flying. They took the preacher to dinner. They were exultant. The friends of Brother Sneedon were silent but thoughtful.

It was true, beyond the shadow of a doubt, that the Reverend Elias Smith had made a wonderful impression upon his hearers,—an impression that might not entirely fade away before the night on which the new pastor was to be voted for. Comments on the sermon did not end with the closing of that Sabbath day. The discussion of its excellences was prolonged into the next week, and continued with a persistency dangerous to the aspirations of any rival candidate. No one was more fully conscious of this menacing condition of affairs than Hezekiah Sneedon himself. He knew that for the minds of the people to rest long upon the exploits of Elder Smith would be fatal to the chances of his own candidate; so he set about inventing some way to turn the current of public thought into another channel. And nothing but a powerful agency could turn it. But in fertility of resources Hezekiah Sneedon was Napoleonic. Though his diplomacy was greatly taxed in this case, he came out victorious and with colours flying when he hit upon the happy idea of a "'possum supper." That would give the people something else to talk about beside the Reverend Elias Smith and his wonderful sermon. But think not, O reader, that the intellect that conceived this new idea was so lacking in the essential qualities of diplomacy as to rush in his substitute, have done with it, and leave the public's attention to revert to its former object. Brother Sneedon was too wary for this. Indeed, he did send his invitations out early to the congregation; but this only aroused discussion and created anticipation which was allowed to grow and gather strength until the very Saturday evening on which the event occurred.

Sister Hannah Williams saw through the plot immediately, but she could not play counter, so she contented herself with saying: "Dat Hezikiah Sneedon is sholy de bigges' scamp dat evah trod shoe-leathah." But nevertheless, she did not refuse an invitation to be present at the supper. She would go, she said, for the purpose of seeing "how things went on." But she added, as a sort of implied apology to her conscience, "and den I's powahful fond o' 'possum, anyhow."

In inviting Sister Williams, Brother Sneedon had taken advantage of the excellent example which that good woman had set him, and was carrying the war right into the enemy's country; but he had gone farther in one direction, and by the time the eventful evening arrived had prepared for his guests a *coup d'état* which was unanticipated even by his own wife.

He had been engaged in a secret correspondence, the result of which was seen when, just after the assembling of the guests in the long, low room which was parlour, sitting, and dining room in the Sneedon household, the wily host ushered in and introduced to the astonished people the Reverend Abram Martin. They were not allowed to recover from their surprise before they were seated at the table, grace said by the reverend brother, and the supper commenced. And such a supper as it was,—one that could not but soften the feelings and touch the heart of any Negro. It was a supper that disarmed opposition. Sister Hannah was seated at the left of Reverend Abram Martin, who was a fluent and impressive talker; and what with his affability and the delight of the repast, she grew mollified and found herself laughing and chatting. The other members of her faction looked on, and, seeing her pleased with the minister, grew pleased themselves. The Reverend Abram Martin's magnetic influence ran round the board like an electric current.

He could tell a story with a dignified humour that was irresistible,—and your real Negro is a lover of stories and a teller of them. Soon, next to the 'possum, he was the centre of attraction around the table, and he held forth while the diners listened respectfully to his profound observations or laughed uproariously at his genial jokes. All the while Brother Sneedon sat delightedly by, watchful, but silent, save for the occasional injunction to his guests to help themselves. And they did so with a gusto that argued well for their enjoyment of the food set before them. As the name by which the supper was designated would imply, 'possum was the principal feature, but, even after including the sweet potatoes and brown gravy, that was not all. There was hog jole and cold cabbage, ham and Kentucky oysters, more widely known as chittlings. What more there was it boots not to tell. Suffice it to say that there was little enough of anything left to do credit to the people's dual powers of listening and eating, for in all this time the Reverend Abram Martin had not abated his conversational efforts nor they their unflagging attention.

Just before the supper was finished, the preacher was called upon, at the instigation of Hezekiah Sneedon, of course, to make a few remarks, which he proceeded to do in a very happy and taking vein. Then the affair broke up, and the people went home with myriad comments on their tongues. But one idea possessed the minds of all, and that was that the Reverend Abram Martin was a very able man, and charming withal.

It was at this hour, when opportunity for sober reflection returned, that Sister Williams first awakened to the fact that her own conduct had compromised her cause. She did not sleep that night—she lay awake and planned, and the result of her planning was a great fumbling the next morning in the little bag where she kept her earnings, and the despatching of her husband on an early and mysterious errand.

The day of meeting came, and the church presented a scene precisely similar to that of the previous Sunday. If there was any difference, it was only apparent in the entirely alert and cheerful attitude of Brother Sneedon and the reversed expressions of the two factions. But even the latter phase was not so marked, for the shrewd Sister Williams saw with alarm that her forces were demoralised. Some of them were sitting near the pulpit with expressions of pleasant anticipation on their faces, and as she looked at them she groaned in spirit. But her lips were compressed in a way that to a close observer would have seemed ominous, and ever and anon she cast anxious and expectant glances toward the door. Her husband sat upon her left, an abashed, shamefaced expression dominating his features. He continually followed her glances toward the door with a furtive, half-frightened look; and when Sneedon looked his way, he avoided his eye.

That arch schemer was serene and unruffled. He had perpetrated a stroke of excellent policy by denying himself the pleasure of introducing the new minister, and had placed that matter in the hands of Isaac Jordan, a member of the opposing faction and one of Sister Williams' stanchest supporters. Brother Jordan was pleased and flattered by the distinction, and converted.

The service began. The hymn was sung, the prayer said, and the minister, having been introduced, was already leading out from his text, when, with a rattle and bang that instantly drew every eye rearward, the door opened and a man entered. Apparently oblivious to the fact that he was the centre of universal attention, he came slowly down the aisle and took a seat far to the front of the church. A gleam of satisfaction shot from the eye of Sister Williams, and with a sigh she settled herself in her seat and turned her attention to the sermon. Brother Sneedon glanced at the new-comer and grew visibly disturbed. One sister leaned over and whispered to another,—

"I wunner whut Bud Lewis is a-doin' hyeah?"

"I do' know," answered the other, "but I do hope an' pray dat he won't git into none o' his shoutin' tantrums to-day."

"Well, ef he do, I's a-leavin' hyeah, you hyeah me," rejoined the first speaker.

The sermon had progressed about one-third its length, and the congregation had begun to show frequent signs of awakening life, when on an instant, with startling suddenness, Bud Lewis sprang from his seat and started on a promenade down the aisle, swinging his arms in sweeping semi-circles, and uttering a sound like the incipient bellow of a steamboat. "Whough! Whough!" he puffed, swinging from side to side down the narrow passageway.

At the first demonstration from the new-comer, people began falling to right and left out of his way. The fame of Bud Lewis' "shoutin' tantrums" was widespread, and they who knew feared them. This unregenerate mulatto was without doubt the fighting man of Bull-Skin.

While, as a general thing, he shunned the church, there were times when a perverse spirit took hold of him, and he would seek the meeting-house, and promptly, noisily, and violently "get religion." At these times he made it a point to knock people helter-skelter, trample on tender toes, and do other mischief, until in many cases the meeting broke up in confusion. The saying finally grew to be proverbial among the people in the Bull-Skin district that they would rather see a thunderstorm than Bud Lewis get religion.

On this occasion he made straight for the space in front of the pulpit, where his vociferous hallelujahs entirely drowned the minister's voice; while the thud, thud, thud of his feet upon the floor, as he jumped up and down, effectually filled up any gap of stillness which his hallelujahs might have left.

Hezekiah Sneedon knew that the Reverend Mr. Martin's sermon would be ruined, and he saw all his cherished hopes destroyed in a moment. He was a man of action, and one glance at Sister Williams' complacent countenance decided him. He rose, touched Isaac Jordan, and said, "Come on, let's hold him." Jordan hesitated a minute; but his leader was going on, and there was nothing to do but to follow him. They approached Lewis, and each seized an arm. The man began to struggle. Several other men joined them and laid hold on him.

"Quiet, brother, quiet," said Hezekiah Sneedon; "dis is de house o' de Lawd."

"You lemme go," shrieked Bud Lewis. "Lemme go, I say."

"But you mus' be quiet, so de res' o' de congregation kin hyeah."

"I don't keer whethah dey hyeahs er not. I reckon I kin shout ef I want to." The minister had paused in his sermon, and the congregation was alert.

"Brother, you mus' not distu'b de meetin'. Praise de Lawd all you want to, but give somebidy else a chance too."

"I won't, I won't; lemme go. I's paid fu' shoutin', an' I's gwine to shout." Hezekiah Sneedon caught the words, and he followed up his advantage.

"You's paid fu' shoutin'! Who paid you?"

"Hannah Williams, dat's who! Now you lemme go; I's gwine to shout."

The effect of this declaration was magical. The brothers, by their combined efforts, lifted the struggling mulatto from his feet and carried him out of the chapel, while Sister Williams' face grew ashen in hue.

The congregation settled down, and the sermon was resumed. Disturbance and opposition only seemed to have heightened the minister's power, and he preached a sermon that is remembered to this day on Bull-Skin. Before it was over, Bud Lewis' guards filed back into church and listened with enjoyment to the remainder of the discourse.

The service closed, and under cover of the crowd that thronged about the altar to shake the minister's hand Hannah Williams escaped.

As the first item of business at the church meeting on the following Wednesday evening, she was formally "churched" and expelled from fellowship with the flock at Bull-Skin for planning to interrupt divine service. The next business was the unanimous choice of Reverend Abram Martin for the pastorate of the church.

Jimsella

No one could ever have accused Mandy Mason of being thrifty. For the first twenty years of her life conditions had not taught her the necessity for thrift. But that was before she had come North with Jim. Down there at home one either rented or owned a plot of ground with a shanty set in the middle of it, and lived off the products of one's own garden and coop. But here it was all very different: one room in a crowded tenement house, and the necessity of grinding day after day to keep the wolf—a very terrible and ravenous wolf—from the door. No wonder that Mandy was discouraged and finally gave up to more than her old shiftless ways.

Jim was no less disheartened. He had been so hopeful when he first came, and had really worked hard. But he could not go higher than his one stuffy room, and the food was not so good as it had been at home. In this state of mind, Mandy's shiftlessness irritated him. He grew to look on her as the source of all his disappointments. Then, as he walked Sixth or Seventh Avenue, he saw other coloured women who dressed gayer than Mandy, looked smarter, and did not wear such great shoes. These he contrasted with his wife, to her great disadvantage.

"Mandy," he said to her one day, "why don't you fix yo'se'f up an' look like people? You go 'roun' hyeah lookin' like I dunno what."

"Whyn't you git me somep'n' to fix myse'f up in?" came back the disconcerting answer.

"Ef you had any git up erbout you, you'd git somep'n' fu' yo'se'f an' not wait on me to do evahthing."

"Well, ef I waits on you, you keeps me waitin', fu' I ain' had nothin' fit to eat ner waih since I been up hyeah."

"Nev' min'! You's mighty free wid yo' talk now, but some o' dese days you won't be so free. You's gwine to wake up some mo'nin' an' fin' dat I's lit out; dat's what you will."

"Well, I 'low nobody ain't got no string to you."

Mandy took Jim's threat as an idle one, so she could afford to be independent. But the next day had found him gone. The deserted wife wept for a time, for she had been fond of Jim, and then she set to work to struggle on by herself. It was a dismal effort, and the people about her were not kind to her. She was hardly of their class. She was only a simple, honest countrywoman, who did not go out with them to walk the avenue.

When a month or two afterward the sheepish Jim returned, ragged and dirty, she had forgiven him and taken him back. But immunity from punishment spoiled him, and hence of late his lapses had grown more frequent and of longer duration.

He walked in one morning, after one of his absences, with a more than usually forbidding face, for he had heard the news in the neighbourhood before he got in. During his absence a baby had come to share the poverty of his home. He thought with shame at himself, which turned into anger, that the child must be three months old and he had never seen it.

"Back ag'in, Jim?" was all Mandy said as he entered and seated himself sullenly.

"Yes, I's back, but I ain't back fu' long. I jes' come to git my clothes. I's a-gwine away fu' good."

"Gwine away ag'in! Why, you been gone fu' nigh on to fou' months a'ready. Ain't you nevah gwine to stay home no mo'?"

"I tol' you I was gwine away fu' good, didn't I? Well, dat's what I mean."

"Ef you didn't want me, Jim, I wish to Gawd dat you'd 'a' lef' me back home among my folks, whaih people knowed me an' would 'a' give me a helpin' han'. Dis hyeah No'f ain't no fittin' place fu' a lone colo'ed ooman less'n she got money."

"It ain't no place fu' nobody dat's jes' lazy an' no 'count."

"I ain't no 'count. I ain't wuffless. I does de bes' I kin. I been wo'kin' like a dog to try an' keep up while you trapsein' 'roun', de Lawd knows whaih. When I was single I could git out an' mek my own livin'. I didn't ax nobody no odds; but you wa'n't satisfied ontwell I ma'ied you, an' now, when I's tied down wid a baby, dat's de way you treats me."

The woman sat down and began to cry, and the sight of her tears angered her husband the more.

"Oh, cry!" he exclaimed. "Cry all you want to. I reckon you'll cry yo' fill befo' you gits me back. What do I keer about de baby! Dat's jes' de trouble. It wa' n't enough fu' me to have to feed an' clothe you a-layin' 'roun' doin' nothin', a baby had to go an' come too."

"It's yo'n, an' you got a right to tek keer of it, dat's what you have. I ain't a-gwine to waih my soul-case out a-tryin' to pinch along an' sta've to def at las'. I'll kill myse'f an' de chile, too, fus'."

The man looked up quickly. "Kill yo'se'f," he said. Then he laughed. "Who evah hyeahed tell of a niggah killin' hisse'f?"

"Nev' min', nev' min', you jes' go on yo' way rejoicin'. I 'spect you runnin' 'roun' aftah somebody else—dat's de reason you cain't nevah stay at home no mo'."

"Who tol' you dat?" exclaimed the man, fiercely. "I ain't runnin' aftah nobody else—'t ain't none o' yo' business ef I is."

The denial and implied confession all came out in one breath.

"Ef hit ain't my bus'ness, I'd like to know whose it gwine to be. I's yo' lawful wife an' hit's me dat's a-sta'vin' to tek keer of yo' chile."

"Doggone de chile; I's tiahed o' hyeahin' 'bout huh."

"You done got tiahed mighty quick when you ain't nevah even seed huh yit. You done got tiahed quick, sho."

"No, an' I do' want to see huh, neithah."

"You do' know nothin' 'bout de chile, you do' know whethah you wants to see huh er not."

"Look hyeah, ooman, don't you fool wid me. I ain't right, nohow!"

Just then, as if conscious of the hubbub she had raised, and anxious to add to it, the baby awoke and began to wail. With quick mother instinct, the black woman went to the shabby bed, and, taking the child in her arms, began to croon softly to it: "Go s'eepy, baby; don' you be 'f'aid; mammy ain' gwine let nuffin' hu't you, even ef pappy don' wan' look at huh li'l face. Bye, bye, go s'eepy, mammy's li'l gal." Unconsciously she talked to the baby in a dialect that was even softer than usual. For a moment the child subsided, and the woman turned angrily on her husband: "I don' keer whethah you evah sees dis chile er not. She's a blessed li'l angel, dat's what she is, an' I'll wo'k my fingahs off to raise huh, an' when she grows up, ef any nasty niggah comes erroun' mekin' eyes at huh, I'll tell huh 'bout huh pappy an' she'll stay wid me an' be my comfo't."

"Keep yo' comfo't. Gawd knows I do' want huh."

"De time'll come, though, an' I kin wait fu' it. Hush-a-bye, Jimsella."

The man turned his head slightly.

"What you call huh?"

"I calls huh Jimsella, dat's what I calls huh, 'ca'se she de ve'y spittin' image of you. I gwine to jes' lun to huh dat she had a pappy, so she know she's a hones' chile an' kin hol' up huh haid."

"Oomph!"

They were both silent for a while, and then Jim said, "Huh name ought to be Jamsella—don't you know Jim's sho't fu' James?"

"I don't keer what it's sho't fu'." The woman was holding the baby close to her breast and sobbing now. "It wasn't no James dat come a-cou'tin' me down home. It was jes' plain Jim. Dat's what de mattah, I reckon you done got to be James." Jim didn't answer, and there was another space of silence, only interrupted by two or three contented gurgles from the baby.

"I bet two bits she don't look like me," he said finally, in a dogged tone that was a little tinged with curiosity.

"I know she do. Look at huh yo'se'f."

"I ain' gwine look at huh."

"Yes, you's 'fraid—dat's de reason."

"I ain' 'fraid nuttin' de kin'. What I got to be 'fraid fu'? I reckon a man kin look at his own darter. I will look jes' to spite you."

He couldn't see much but a bundle of rags, from which sparkled a pair of beady black eyes. But he put his finger down among the rags. The baby seized it and gurgled. The sweat broke out on Jim's brow.

"Cain't you let me hold de baby a minute?" he said angrily. "You must be 'fraid I'll run off wid huh." He took the child awkwardly in his arms.

The boiling over of Mandy's clothes took her to the other part of the room, where she was busy for a few minutes. When she turned to look for Jim, he had slipped out, and Jimsella was lying on the bed trying to kick free of the coils which swaddled her.

At supper-time that evening Jim came in with a piece of "shoulder-meat" and a head of cabbage.

"You'll have to git my dinnah ready fu' me to ca'y to-morrer. I's wo'kin' on de street, an' I cain't come home twell night."

"Wha', what!" exclaimed Mandy, "den you ain' gwine leave, aftah all."

"Don't bothah me, ooman," said Jim. "Is Jimsella 'sleep?"

Mt. Pisgah's Christmas 'Possum

NO MORE HAPPY expedient for raising the revenues of the church could have been found than that which was evolved by the fecund brain of the Reverend Isaiah Johnson. Mr. Johnson was wise in his day and generation. He knew his people, their thoughts and their appetites, their loves and their prejudices. Also he knew the way to their hearts and their pocketbooks.

As far ahead as the Sunday two weeks before Christmas, he had made the announcement that had put the congregation of Mt. Pisgah church into a flurry of anticipatory excitement.

"Brothahs an' sistahs," he had said, "you all reckernizes, ez well ez I does, dat de revenues of dis hyeah chu'ch ain't whut dey ought to be. De chu'ch, I is so'y to say, is in debt. We has a mo'gage on ouah buildin', an' besides de int'rus' on dat, we has fuel to buy an' lightin' to do. Fu'thahmo', we ain't paid de sexton but twenty-five cents on his salary in de las' six months. In conserquence of de same, de dus' is so thick on de benches dat ef you'd jes' lay a clof ovah dem, dey'd be same ez upholstahed fu'niture. Now, in o'dah to mitigate dis condition of affairs, yo' pastoh has fo'med a plan which he wishes to p'nounce dis mo'nin' in yo' hyeahin' an' to ax yo' 'proval. You all knows dat Chris'mus is 'proachin', an' I reckon dat you is all plannin' out yo' Chris'mus dinnahs. But I been a-plannin' fu' you when you was asleep, an' my idee is dis,—all of you give up yo' Chris'mus dinnahs, tek fifteen cents er a qua'tah apiece an' come hyeah to chu'ch an' have a 'possum dinnah."

"Amen!" shouted one delighted old man over in the corner, and the whole congregation was all smiles and acquiescent nods.

"I puceive on de pa't of de cong'egation a disposition to approve of de pastoh's plan."

"Yes, yes, indeed," was echoed on all sides.

"Well, den I will jes' tek occasion to say fu'thah dat I already has de 'possums, fo' of de fattes' animals I reckon you evah seen in all yo' bo'n days, an' I's gwine to tu'n 'em ovah to Brothah Jabez Holly to tek keer of dem an' fatten 'em wuss ag'in de happy day."

The eyes of Jabez Holly shone with pride at the importance of the commission assigned to him. He showed his teeth in a broad smile as he whispered to his neighbour, 'Lishy Davis, "I 'low when I gits thoo wif dem 'possums dey won't be able to waddle"; and 'Lishy slapped his knee and bent double with appreciation. It was a happy and excited congregation that filed out of Mt. Pisgah church that Sunday morning, and how they chattered! Little knots and clusters of them, with their heads together in deep converse, were gathered all about, and all the talk was of the coming dinner. This, as has already been said, was the Sunday two weeks before Christmas. On the Sunday following, the shrewd, not to say wily, Mr. Johnson delivered a stirring sermon from the text, "He prepareth a table before me in the presence of mine enemies," and not one of his hearers but pictured the Psalmist and his brethren sitting at a 'possum feast with the congregation of a rival church looking enviously on. After the service that day, even the minister sank into insignificance beside his steward, Jabez Holly, the custodian of the 'possums. He was the most sought man on the ground.

"How dem 'possums comin' on?" asked one.

"Comin' on!" replied Jabez. "'Comin' on' ain't no name fu' it. Why, I tell you, dem animals is jes' a-waddlin' a'ready."

"O-o-mm!" groaned a hearer, "Chris'mus do seem slow a-comin' dis yeah."

"Why, man," Jabez went on, "it 'u'd mek you downright hongry to see one o' dem critters. Evah time I looks at 'em I kin jes' see de grease a-drippin' in de pan, an' dat skin all brown an' crispy, an' de smell a-risin' up—"

"Heish up, man!" exclaimed the other; "ef you don't, I'll drap daid befo' de time comes."

"Huh-uh! no, you won't; you know dat day's wuf livin' fu'. Brothah Jackson, how'd yo' crap o' sweet pertaters tu'n out dis yeah?"

"Fine, fine! I's got dem mos' plenteous in my cellah."

"Well, don't eat em too fas' in de nex' week, 'ca'se we 'spects to call on you fu' some o' yo' bes'. You know dem big sweet pertaters cut right in two and laid all erroun' de pan teks up lots of de riches' grease when ol' Mistah 'Possum git too wa'm in de oven an' git to sweatin' it out."

"Have mercy!" exclaimed the impressionable one. "I know ef I don't git erway f'om dis chu'ch do' right now, I'll be foun' hyeah on Chris'mus day wif my mouf wide open."

But he did not stay there until Christmas morning, though he arrived on that momentous day bright and early like most of the rest. Half the women of the church had volunteered to help cook the feast, and the other half were there to see it done right; so by the time for operations to commence, nearly all of Mt. Pisgah's congregation was assembled within its chapel walls. And what laughing and joking there was!

"O-omph!" exclaimed Sister Green, "I see Brothah Bill Jones' mouf is jes' sot fu' 'possum now."

"Yes, indeed, Sis' Green; hit jes' de same's a trap an' gwine to spring ez soon ez dey any 'possum in sight."

"Hyah, hyah, you ain't de on'iest one in dat fix, Brothah Jones; I see some mo' people roun' hyeah lookin' mighty 'spectious."

"Yes, an' I's one of 'em," said some one else. "I do wish Jabez Holly 'ud come on, my mouf's jest p'intly worterin'."

"Let's sen' a c'mittee aftah him, dat'll be a joke." This idea was taken up, and with much merriment the committee was despatched to find and bring in the delinquent Jabez.

Every one who has ever cooked a 'possum—and who has not?—knows that the animal must be killed the day before and hung out of doors over night to freeze "de wil' tas'e outen him." This duty had been intrusted to Jabez, and shouts of joy went up from the assembled people when he appeared, followed by the committee and bearing a bag on his shoulder. He set the bag on the floor, and as the crowd closed round him, he put his arm far down into it, and drew forth by the tail a beautiful white fat cleaned 'possum.

"O-om, jes' look at dat! Ain't dat a possum fu' you? Go on, Brothah Jabez, let's see anothah." Jabez hesitated.

"Dat's one 'possum dah, ain't it?" he said.

"Yes, yes, go on, let's see de res'." Those on the inside of the circle were looking hard at Jabez.

"Now, dat's one 'possum," he repeated.

"Yes, yes, co'se it is." There was breathless expectancy.

"Well, dat's all dey is."

The statement fell like a thunder-clap. No one found voice till the Reverend Isaiah Johnson broke in with, "Wha', what dat you say, Jabez Holly?"

"I say dat's all de 'possum dey is, dat's what I say."

"Whah's dem othah 'possums, huh! whah's de res'?"

"I put 'em out to freeze las' night, an' de dogs got 'em."

A groan went up from the disappointed souls of Mt. Pisgah. But the minister went on: "Whah 'd you hang dem?"

"Up ag'in de side o' de house."

"How 'd de dogs git 'em dah?"

"Mebbe it mout 'a' been cats."

"Why didn't dey git dat un?"

"Why, why—'ca'se—'ca'se—Oh, don't questun me, man. I want you to know dat I's a honer'ble man."

"Jabez Holly," said the minister, impressively, "don't lie hyeah in de sanctua'y. I see 'possum grease on yo' mouf."

Jabez unconsciously gave his lips a wipe with his sleeve. "On my mouf, on my mouf!" he exclaimed. "Don't you say you see no 'possum grease on my mouf! I mek you prove it. I's a honer'ble man, I is. Don't you 'cuse me of nuffin'!"

Murmurs had begun to arise from the crowd, and they had begun to press in upon the accused.

"Don't crowd me!" he cried, his eyes bulging, for he saw in the faces about him the energy of attack which should have been directed against the 'possum all turned upon him. "I didn't eat yo' ol' 'possum, I do' lak 'possum nohow."

"Hang him," said some one, and the murmur rose louder as the culprit began to be hustled. But the preacher's voice rose above the storm.

"Ca'm yo'se'ves, my brethren," he said; "let us thank de Lawd dat one 'possum remains unto us. Brothah Holly has been put undah a gret temptation, an' we believe dat he has fell; but it is a jedgment. I ought to knowed bettah dan to 'a' trusted any colo'ed man wif fo' 'possums. Let us not be ha'd upon de sinnah. We mus' not be violent, but I tu'ns dis assembly into a chu'ch meetin' of de brothahs to set on Brothah Holly's case. In de mean time de sistahs will prepah de remainin' 'possum."

The church-meeting promptly found Brother Holly guilty of having betrayed his trust, and expelled him in disgrace from fellowship with Mt. Pisgah church.

The excellence of the one 'possum which the women prepared only fed their angry feelings, as it suggested what the whole four would have been; but the hungry men, women, and children who had foregone their Christmas dinners at home ate as cheerfully as possible, and when Mt. Pisgah's congregation went home that day, salt pork was in great demand to fill out the void left by the meagre fare of Christmas 'possum.

A Family Feud

I WISH I could tell you the story as I heard it from the lips of the old black woman as she sat bobbing her turbaned head to and fro with the motion of her creaky little rocking-chair, and droning the tale forth in the mellow voice of her race. So much of the charm of the story was in that voice, which even the cares of age had not hardened.

It was a sunny afternoon in late November, one of those days that come like a backward glance from a reluctantly departing summer. I had taken advantage of the warmth and brightness to go up and sit with old Aunt Doshy on the little porch that fronted her cottage. The old woman had been a trusted house-servant in one of the wealthiest of the old Kentucky families, and a visit to her never failed to elicit some reminiscence of the interesting past. Aunt Doshy was inordinately proud of her family, as she designated the Venables, and was never weary of detailing accounts of their grandeur and generosity. What if some of the harshness of reality was softened by the distance through which she looked back upon them; what if the glamour of memory did put a halo round the heads of some people who were never meant to be canonised? It was all plain fact to Aunt Doshy, and it was good to hear her talk. That day she began:—

"I reckon I hain't never tol' you 'bout ole Mas' an' young Mas' fallin' out, has I? Hit's all over now, an' things is done change so dat I reckon eben ef ole Mas' was libin', he wouldn't keer ef I tol', an' I knows young Mas' Tho'nton wouldn't. Dey ain't nuffin' to hide 'bout it nohow, 'ca'se all quality families has de same kin' o' 'spectable fusses.

"Hit all happened 'long o' dem Jamiesons whut libed jinin' places to our people, an' whut ole Mas' ain't spoke to fu' nigh onto thutty years. Long while ago, when Mas' Tom Jamieson an' Mas' Jack Venable was bofe young mans, dey had a qua'l 'bout de young lady dey bofe was a-cou'tin', an' by-an'-by dey had a du'l an' Mas' Jamieson shot Mas' Jack in de shouldah, but Mas' Jack ma'ied de lady, so dey was eben. Mas' Jamieson ma'ied too, an' after so many years dey was bofe wid'ers, but dey ain't fu'give one another yit. When Mas' Tho'nton was big enough to run erroun', ole Mas' used to try to 'press on him dat a Venable mus' n' never put his foot on de Jamieson lan'; an' many a tongue-lashin' an' sometimes wuss de han's on our place got fu' mixin' wif de Jamieson servants. But, la! young Mas' Tho'nton was wuss 'n de niggers. Evah time he got a chance he was out an' gone, over lots an' fiel's an' into de Jamieson ya'd a-playin' wif little Miss Nellie, whut was Mas' Tom's little gal. I never did see two chillun so 'tached to one another. Dey used to wander erroun', han' in han', lak brother an' sister, an' dey'd cry lak dey little hea'ts 'u'd brek ef either one of dey pappys seed 'em an' pa'ted 'em.

"I 'member once when de young Mastah was erbout eight year ole, he was a-settin' at de table one mo'nin' eatin' wif his pappy, when all of er sudden he pause an' say, jes' ez solerm-lak, 'When I gits big, I gwine to ma'y Nellie.' His pappy jump lak he was shot, an' tu'n right pale, den he say kin' o' slow an' gaspy-lak, 'Don't evah let me hyeah you say sich a thing ergin, Tho'nton Venable. Why, boy, I'd raver let evah drap o' blood outen you, dan to see a Venable cross his blood wif a Jamieson.'

"I was jes' a-bringin' in de cakes whut Mastah was pow'ful fon' of, an' I could see bofe dey faces. But, la! honey, dat chile didn't look a bit skeered. He jes' sot dah lookin' in his pappy's face,—he was de spittin' image of him, all 'cept his eyes, dey was his mother's,—den he say, 'Why, Nellie's nice,' an' went on eatin' a aig. His pappy laid his napkin down an' got up an' went erway f'om de table. Mas' Tho'nton say, 'Why, father didn't eat his cakes.' 'I reckon yo' pa ain't well,' says I, fu' I knowed de chile was innercent.

"Well, after dat day, ole Mas' tuk extry pains to keep de chillun apa't—but 't wa' n't no use. 'T ain't never no use in a case lak dat. Dey jes' would be together, an' ez de boy got older, it seemed to grieve his pappy mighty. I reckon he didn't lak to jes' fu'bid him seein' Miss Nellie, fu' he know how haidstrong Mas' Tho'nton was, anyhow. So things kep' on dis way, an' de boy got handsomer evah day. My, but his pappy did set a lot o' sto' by him. Dey wasn't nuffin' dat boy eben wished fu' dat his pappy didn't gin him. Seemed lak he fa'ly wushipped him. He'd jes' watch him ez he went erroun' de house lak he was a baby yit. So hit mus' 'a' been putty ha'd wif Mas' Jack when hit come time to sen Mas' Tho'nton off to college. But he never showed it. He seed him off wif a cheerful face, an' nobidy would 'a' ever guessed dat it hu't him; but dat afternoon he shet hisse'f up an' hit was th'ee days befo' anybody 'cept me seed him, an' nobidy 'cept me knowed how his vittels come back not teched. But after de fus' letter come, he got better. I hyeahd him a-laffin' to hisse'f ez he read it, an' dat day he et his dinner.

"Well, honey, dey ain't no tellin' whut Mas' Jack's plans was, an' hit ain't fu' me to try an' guess 'em; but ef he had sont Mas' Tho'nton erway to brek him off f'om Miss Nellie, he mout ez well 'a' let him stayed at home; fu' Jamieson's Sal whut nussed Miss Nellie tol' me dat huh mistis got a letter f'om Mas' Tho'nton evah day er so. An' when he was home fu' holidays, you never seed nuffin' lak it. Hit was jes' walkin' er ridin' er dribin' wif dat young lady evah day of his life. An' dey did look so sweet together dat it seemed a shame to pa't 'em—him wif his big brown eyes an sof' curly hair an' huh all white an' gentle lak a little dove. But de ole Mas' couldn't see hit dat erway, an' I knowed dat hit was a-troublin' him mighty bad. Ez well ez he loved his son, hit allus seemed lak he was glad when de holidays was over an' de boy was back at college.

"Endurin' de las' year dat de young Mastah was to be erway, his pappy seemed lak he was jes' too happy an' res'less fu' anything. He was dat proud of his son, he didn't know whut to do. He was allus tellin' visitors dat come to de house erbout him, how he was a 'markable boy an' was a-gwine to be a honour to his name. An' when 'long to'ds de ve'y end of de term, a letter come sayin' dat Mas' Tho'nton had done tuk some big honour at de college, I jes' thought sho Mas' Jack 'u'd plum bus' hisse'f, he was so proud an' tickled. I hyeahd him talkin' to his ole frien'

Cunnel Mandrey an' mekin' great plans 'bout whut he gwine to do when his son come home. He gwine tek him trav'lin' fus' in Eur'p, so's to 'finish him lak a Venable ought to be finished by seein' somep'n' of de worl''—' dem's his ve'y words. Den he was a-gwine to come home an' 'model de house an' fit it up, 'fu'—I never shell fu'git how he said it,—'fu' I 'spec' my son to tek a high place in de society of ole Kintucky an' to mo' dan surstain de reputation of de Venables.' Den when de las' day come an' young Mastah was home fu' sho, so fine an' clever lookin' wif his new mustache—sich times ez dey was erbout dat house nobidy never seed befo'. All de frien's an' neighbours, 'scusin', o' co'se, de Jamiesons, was invited to a big dinner dat lasted fu' hours. Dey was speeches by de gent'men, an' evahbidy drinked de graderate's health an' wished him good luck. But all de time I could see dat Mas' Tho'nton wasn't happy, dough he was smilin' an' mekin' merry wif evahbidy. It 'pressed me so dat I spoke erbout hit to Aunt Emmerline. Aunt Emmerline was Mas' Tho'nton's mammy, an' sence he'd growed up, she didn't do much but he'p erroun' de house a little.

"'You don' mean to tell me dat you noticed dat too?' says she when I tol' huh erbout it.

"'Yes, I did,' says I, 'an' I noticed hit strong.'

"'Dey's somep'n' ain't gwine right wif my po' chile,' she say, 'an' dey ain't no tellin' whut it is.'

"'Hain't you got no idee, Aunt Emmerline?' I say.

"'La! chile,' she say in a way dat mek me think she keepin' somep'n' back, 'la! chile, don' you know young mans don' come to dey mammys wif dey secuts lak dey do when dey's babies? How I gwine to know whut's pesterin' Mas' Tho'nton?'

"Den I knowed she was hidin' somep'n', an' jes' to let huh know dat I'd been had my eyes open too, I say slow an' 'pressive lak, 'Aunt Emmerline, don' you reckon hit Miss Nellie Jamieson?' She jumped lak she was skeered, an' looked at me right ha'd; den she say, 'I ain' reck'nin' nuffin' 'bout de white folks' bus'ness.' An' she pinched huh mouf up right tight, an' I couldn't git another word outen huh; but I knowed dat I'd hit huh jes' erbout right.

"One mo'nin' erbout a week after de big dinner, jes' ez dey was eatin', Mas' Tho'nton say, 'Father, I'd lak to see you in de liberry ez soon ez you has de time. I want to speak to you 'bout somep'n' ve'y impo'tant.' De ole man look up right quick an' sha'p, but he say ve'y quiet lak, 'Ve'y well, my son, ve'y well; I's at yo' service at once.'

"Dey went into de liberry, an' Mas' Tho'nton shet de do' behin' him. I could hyeah dem talkin' kin' o' low while I was cl'arin' erway de dishes. After while dey 'menced to talk louder. I had to go out an' dus' de hall den near de liberry do', an' once I hyeahd ole Mas' say right sho't an' sha'p, 'Never!' Den young Mas' he say, 'But evah man has de right to choose fu' his own se'f.'

"'Man, man!' I hyeahd his pappy say in a way I had never hyeahd him use to his son befo', 'evah male bein' dat wahs men's clothes an' has a mustache ain't a man.'

"'Man er whut not,' po' young Mastah's voice was a-tremblin', 'I am at leas' my father's son an' I deserve better dan dis at his han's.' I hyeahd somebody a-walkin' de flo', an' I was feared dey'd come out an' think dat I was a-listenin', so I dus'es on furder down de hall, an' didn't hyeah no mo' ontwell Mas' Tho'nton come hurryin' out an' say, 'Ike, saddle my hoss.' He was ez pale ez he could be, an' when he spoke sho't an rough lak dat, he was so much lak his father dat hit skeered me. Ez soon ez his hoss was ready, he jumped into de saddle an' went flyin' outen de ya'd lak mad, never eben lookin' back at de house. I didn't see Mas' Jack fu' de res' of de day, an' he didn't come in to suppah. But I seed Aunt Emmerline an' I knowed dat she had been somewhah an' knowed ez much ez I did erbout whut was gwine on, but I never broached a word erbout hit to huh. I seed she was oneasy, but I kep' still 'twell she say, 'Whut you reckon keepin' Mas' Tho'nton out so late?' Den I jes say, 'I ain't reck'nin' 'bout de white folks' bus'ness.' She looked a little bit cut at fus', den she jes' go on lak nuffin' hadn't happened: 'I's mighty 'sturbed 'bout young Mas'; he never stays erway f'om suppah 'dout sayin' somep'n'.'

"'Oh, I reckon he kin fin' suppah somewhah else.' I says dis don't keer lak jes' fu' to lead huh on.

"'I ain't so much pestered 'bout his suppah,' she say; 'I's feared he gwine do somep'n' he hadn't ought to do after dat qua'l 'twixt him an' his pappy.'

"'Did dey have a qua'l?' says I.

"'G' long!' Aunt Emmerline say, 'you wasn't dus'in' one place in de hall so long fu' nuffin'. You knows an' I knows eben ef we don't talk a heap. I's troubled myse'f. Hit jes in dat Venable blood to go right straight an' git Miss Nellie an' ma'y huh right erway, an' ef he do it, I p'intly know his pa'll never fu'give him.' Den Aunt Emmerline 'mence to cry, an' I feel right sorry fu' huh, 'ca'se Mas' Tho'nton huh boy, an' she think a mighty heap o' him.

"Well, we hadn't had time to say much mo' when we hyeahd a hoss gallopin' into de ya'd. Aunt Emmerline jes' say, 'Dat's Giner'al's lope!' an' she bus' outen de do'. I waits, 'spectin' huh to come back an' say dat Mas' Tho'nton done come at las'. But after while she come in wif a mighty long face an' say, 'Hit's one o' Jamieson's darkies; he brung de hoss back an' a note Mas' gin him fu' his pappy. Mas' Tho'nton done gone to Lexin'ton wif Miss Nellie an' got ma'ied.' Den she jes' brek down an' 'mence a-cryin' ergin an' a-rockin' huhse'f back an fofe an' sayin', 'Oh, my po' chile, my po' boy, whut's to 'come o' you!'

"I went upstairs an' lef' huh—we bofe stayed at de big house—but I didn't sleep much, 'ca'se all thoo de night I could hyeah ole Mas' a-walkin' back an' fofe ercross his flo', an' when Aunt Emmerline come up to baid, she mou'ned all night, eben in huh sleep. I tell you, honey, dem was mou'nin' times.

"Nex' mo'nin' when ole Mas' come down to brekfus', he looked lak he done had a long spell o' sickness. But he wasn't no man to 'spose his feelin's. He never let on, never eben spoke erbout Mas' Tho'nton bein' erway f'om de table. He didn't eat much, an' fin'ly I see him look right long an' stiddy at de place whah Mas' Tho'nton used to set an' den git up an' go 'way f'om de table. I knowed dat he was done filled up. I went to de liberry do' an' I could hyeah him sobbin' lak a chile. I tol' Aunt Emmerline 'bout it, but she jes' shuck huh haid an' didn't say nuffin' a'-tall.

"Well, hit went dis erway fu' 'bout a week. Mas' Jack was gittin' paler an' paler evah day, an' hit jes' 'menced to come to my min' how ole he was. One day Aunt Emmerline say she gwine erway, an' she mek Jim hitch up de spring wagon an' she dribe on erway by huhse'f. Co'se, now, Aunt Emmerline she do putty much ez she please, so I don't think nuffin' 'bout hit. When she come back, 'long to'ds ebenin', I say, 'Aunt Emmerline, whah you been all day?'

"'Nemmine, honey, you see,' she say, an' laff. Well, I ain't seed nobidy laff fu' so long dat hit jes' mek me feel right wa'm erroun' my hea't, an' I laff an' keep on laffin' jes' at nuffin'.

"Nex' mo'nin' Aunt Emmerline mighty oneasy, an' I don' know whut de matter ontwell I hyeah some un say, 'Tek dat hoss, Ike, an' feed him, but keep de saddle on.' Aunt Emmerline jes' fa'ly fall out de do' an' I lak to drap, 'ca'se hit's Mas' Tho'nton's voice. In a minute he come to me an' say, 'Doshy, go tell my father I'd lak to speak to him.'

"I don' skeercely know how I foun' my way to de liberry, but I did. Ole Mas' was a-settin' dah wif a open book in his han', but his eyes was jes' a-starin' at de wall, an' I knowed he wasn't a-readin'. I say, 'Mas' Jack,' an' he sta't jes' lak he rousin' up, 'Mas' Jack, Mas' Tho'nton want to speak to you.' He jump up quick, an' de book fall on de flo', but he grab a cheer an' stiddy hisse'f. I done tol' you Mas' Jack wasn't no man to 'spose his feelin's. He jes' say, slow lak he hol'in' hisse'f, 'Sen' him in hyeah.' I goes back an' 'livers de message, den I flies roun' to de po'ch whah de liberry winder opens out, 'ca'se, I ain't gwine lie erbout it, I was mighty tuk up wif all dis gwine on an' I wanted to see an' hyeah,—an' who you reckon 'roun' dah but Aunt Emmerline! She jes' say, 'S-sh!' ez I come 'roun', an' clas' huh han's. In a minute er so, de liberry do' open an' Mas' Tho'nton come in. He shet hit behin' him, an' den stood lookin' at his pa, dat ain't never tu'ned erroun' yit. Den he say sof', 'Father.' Mas' Jack tu'ned erroun' raal slow an' look at his son fu' a while. Den he say, 'Do you still honour me wif dat name?' Mas' Tho'nton got red in de face, but he answer, 'I don' know no other name to call you.'

"'Will you set down?' Mas' speak jes' lak he was a-talkin' to a stranger.

"'Ef you desiah me to.' I see Mas' Tho'nton was a-bridlin' up too. Mas' jes' th'owed back his haid an' say, 'Fa' be it f'om any Venable to fu'git cou'tesy to his gues'.' Young Mas' moved erway f'om de cheer whah he was a-gwine to set, an' his haid went up. He spoke up slow an' delibut, jes' lak his pa, "I do not come, suh, in dat cha'acter, I is hyeah ez yo' son.'

"Well, ole Mas' eyes fa'ly snapped fiah. He was white ez a sheet, but he still spoke slow an' quiet, hit made me creep, 'You air late in 'memberin' yo' relationship, suh.'

"'I hab never fu'got it.'

"'Den, suh, you have thought mo' of yo' rights dan of yo' duties.' Mas' Jack was mad an' so was Mas' Tho'nton; he say, 'I didn't come hyeah to 'scuss dat.' An' he tu'ned to'ds de do'. I hyeah Aunt Emmerline groan jes' ez Mas' say, 'Well, whut did you come fu'?'

"'To be insulted in my father's house by my father, an' I's got all dat I come fu'!' Mas' Tho'nton was ez white ez his pa now, an' his han' was on de do'-knob. Den all of a sudden I hyeah de winder go up, an' I lak to fall over gittin' outen de way to keep f'om bein' seed. Aunt Emmerline done opened de winder an' gone in. Dey bole tu'ned an' looked at huh s'prised lak, an' Mas' Jack sta'ted to say somep'n', but she th'owed up huh han' an' say 'Wait!' lak she owned de house. 'Mas' Jack,' she say, 'you an' Mas' Tho'nton ain't gwine pa't dis way. You mus' n't. You's father an' son. You loves one another. I knows I ain't got no bus'ness meddlin' in yo' 'fairs, but I cain't see you all qua'l dis way. Mastah, you's bofe stiffnecked. You's bofe wrong. I know Mas' Tho'nton didn't min' you, but he didn't mean no ha'm—he couldn't he'p it—it was in de Venable blood, an' you mus' n't 'spise him fu' it.'

"'Emmerline'—ole Mas' tried to git in a word, but she wouldn't let him.

"'Yes, Mastah, yes, but I nussed dat boy an' tuk keer o' him when he was a lit-tle bit of a he'pless thing; an' when his po' mammy went to glory, I 'member how she look up at me wif dem blessed eyes o' hern an' lay him in my arms an' say, "Emmerline, tek keer o'my baby." I's done it, Mastah, I's done it de bes' I could. I's nussed him thoo sickness when hit seemed lak his little soul mus' foller his mother anyhow, but I's seen de look in yo' eyes, an' prayed to God to gin de chile back to you. He done it, he done it, an' you sha'n't th'ow erway de gif' of God!' Aunt Emmerline was a-cryin' an' so was Mas' Tho'nton. Ole Mas' mighty red, but he clared his th'oat an' said wif his voice tremblin', 'Emmerline, leave de room.' De ole ooman come out a-cryin' lak huh hea't 'u'd brek, an' jes' ez de do' shet behin' huh, ole Mas' brek down an' hol' out his arms, cryin', 'My son, my son.' An' in a minute he an' Mas' Tho'nton was a-hol'in' one another lak dey'd never let go, an' his pa was a-pattin' de boy's haid lak he was a baby. All of a sudden ole Mas' hel' him off an' looked at him an' say, 'Dat ole fool talkin' to me erbout yo' mother's eyes, an' you stannin' hyeah a-lookin' at me wif 'em.' An' den he was a-cryin' ergin, an' dey was bofe huggin'.

"Well, after while dey got all settled down, an' Mas' Tho'nton tol' his pa how Aunt Emmerline drib to Lexin'ton an' foun' him an' made him come home. 'I was wrong, father,' he say, 'but I reckon ef it hadn't 'a' been fu' Aunt Emmerline, I would 'a' stuck it out.'

"'It was in de Venable blood,' his pa say, an' dey bofe laff. Den ole Mas' say, kin' o' lak it hu't him, 'An' whah's yo' wife?' Young Mas' got mighty red ergin ez he answer, 'She ain't fu' erway.'

"'Go bring huh,' Mas' Jack say.

"Well, I reckon Mas' Tho'nton lak to flew, an' he had Miss Nellie dah in lit-tle er no time. When dey come, Mas' he say, 'Come hyeah,' den he pause awhile—'my daughter.' Den Miss Nellie run to him, an' dey was another cryin' time, an' I went on to my work an' lef' 'em talkin' an' laffin' an' cryin'.

"Well, Aunt Emmerline was skeered to def. She jes' p'intly knowed dat she was gwine to git a tongue-lashin'. I don' know whether she was mos' skeered er mos' happy. Mas' sont fu' huh after while, an' I listened when she went in. He was tryin' to talk an' look pow'ful stern, but I seed a twinkle in his eye. He say, 'I want you to know, Emmerline, dat hit ain't yo' place to dictate to yo' mastah whut he shell do—Shet up, shet up! I don' want a word outen you. You been on dis place so long, an' been bossin' de other darkies an' yo' Mas' Tho'nton erroun' so long, dat I 'low you think you own de place. Shet up, not a word outen you! Ef you an' yo' young Mas' 's a-gwine to run dis place, I reckon I'd better step out. Humph! You was so sma't to go to Lexin'ton de other day, you kin go back dah ergin. You seem to think you's white, an' hyeah's de money to buy a new dress fu' de ole fool darky dat nussed yo' son an' made you fu'give his foo'ishness when you wanted to be a fool yo'se'f.' His voice was sof' ergin, an' he put de money in Aunt Emmerline's han' an' pushed huh out de do', huh a-cryin' an' him put' nigh it.

"After dis, Mas Jack was jes bent an' boun' dat de young people mus' go on a weddin' trip. So dey got ready, an' Miss Nellie went an' tol' huh pa goo'bye. Min' you, dey hadn't been nuffin' said 'bout him an' Mas' not bein' frien's. He done fu'give Miss Nellie right erway fu' runnin' off. But de mo'nin' dey went erway, we all was out in de ya'd, an' Aunt Emmerline settin' on de seat wif Jim, lookin' ez proud ez you please. Mastah was ez happy ez a boy. 'Emmerline,' he hollahs ez dey drib off, 'tek good keer o' dat Venable blood.' De ca'iage stopped ez it went out de gate, an' Mas' Tom Jamieson kissed his daughter. He had rid up de road to see de las' of huh. Mastah seed him, an' all of a sudden somep'n' seemed to tek holt o' him an' he hollahed, 'Come in, Tom.'

"'Don' keer ef I do,' Mas' Jamieson say, a-tu'nin' his hoss in de gate. 'You Venables has got de res' o' my fambly.' We all was mos' s'prised to def.

"Mas' Jamieson jumped offen his hoss, an' Mas' Venable come down de steps to meet him. Dey shuk han's, an' Mas' Jack say, 'Dey ain't no fool lak a ole fool.'

"'An' fu' unekaled foo'ishness,' Mas' Tom say, 'reckermen' me to two ole fools.' Dey went into de house a-laffin', an' I knowed hit was all right 'twixt 'em, fu' putty soon I seed Ike out in de ya'd a-getherin' mint."

Aunt Mandy's Investment

THE COLOURED AMERICAN Investment Company was organised for the encouragement and benefit of the struggling among Americans of African descent; at least, so its constitution said. Though truth was, Mr. Solomon Ruggles, the efficient president and treasurer of the institution, usually represented the struggling when there were any benefits to receive.

Indeed, Mr. Ruggles was the Coloured American Investment Company. The people whom he persuaded to put their money into his concern were only accessories. Though a man of slight education, he was possessed of a liberal amount of that shrewd wit which allows its possessor to feed upon the credulity of others.

Mr. Ruggles's motto was "It is better to be plausible than right," and he lived up to his principles with a fidelity that would have been commendable in a better cause. He was seldom right, but he was always plausible. No one knew better than he how to bring out the good point of a bad article. He would have sold you a blind horse and convinced you that he was doing you a favour in giving you an animal that would not be frightened by anything he saw. No one but he could have been in a city so short a time and yet gained to such an extent the confidence and cash of the people about him.

When a coloured man wishes to start a stock company, he issues a call and holds a mass meeting. This is what Solomon Ruggles did. A good many came. Some spoke for and some against the movement, but the promoter's plausible argument carried the day.

"Gent'men," he said, "my fellow colo'ed brotheren, I jest want to say this to you, that we Af'-Americans been ca'yin' a leaky bucket to the well too long. We git the stream from the ground, an' back to the ground it goes befoah we kin git any chance to make use o' what we've drawed. But, not to speak in meterphers, this is what I mean. I mean that we work for the white folks for their money. All they keer about us is ouah work, an' all we keer about them is their money; but what do we do with it when we git it? I'll tell you what we do with it; we take an' give it right back to the white folks fu' somef'n' or other we want, an' so they git ouah labour, an' ouah money too. Ain't that the truth?"

There were cries of "Yes, indeed, that's so; you're right, sho!"

"Well, now, do you want this hyeah thing to go on?"

"No!" from a good many voices.

"Then how are we going to stop it?" Mr. Ruggles paused. No one answered. "Why," he resumed, "by buyin' from ourselves, that's how. We all put in so much ev'ry week till we git enough to buy things of ouah own; then we'll jest pat'onise ouahselves. Don't you see it can't fail?"

The audience did.

Brother Jeremiah Buford rose and "hea'tily concuhed in what the brothah had said"; and dapper little Spriggins, who was said to be studying law, and to be altogether as smart as a whip, expressed his pleasure that a man of such enterprise had come among them to wake the coloured people up to a sense of their condition and to show them a way out of it. So the idea which had been formulated in the fecund brain of Solomon Ruggles became a living, active reality. His project once on foot, it was easy enough to get himself elected president and treasurer. This was quite little enough to do for a man whose bright idea might make them all rich, so thought the stockholders or prospective stockholders who attended the meeting, and some who came to scoff remained to pay. It was thus that the famous Coloured Improvement Company sprang into life.

It was a Saturday afternoon of the third week after the formation of the company that Mr. Ruggles sat in the "firm's" office alone. There was a cloud upon his face. It was the day when most of the stockholders brought in their money, but there had been a picnic the day before, and in consequence a distinct falling off in the receipts of the concern. This state of affairs especially annoyed the president and treasurer, because that dual official had just involved himself in some new obligations on the strength of what that day would bring him. It was annoying. Was it any wonder, then, that his brow cleared and a smile lightened up his rather pleasant features when the door opened and an old woman entered?

"Ah, madam, good afternoon," said the Coloured American Investment Company, rubbing its hands; "and what kin I do fer you?"

The old lady timidly approached the table which the official used as a desk. "Is you Mistah Ruggles?" she asked.

"I have the honah to bear that name," was the bland response.

"Well, I got a little money dat I wants to 'vest in yo' comp'ny. I's hyeahd tell dat ef you put yo' money in dere hit jes' lays and grows."

"That's the princerple we go on, to take small investments and give back big profits."

"Well, I's sho' dat my 'vestment's small 'nough, but I been savin' it a mighty long while." The old woman drew a weather-beaten purse from her pocket, and Solomon Ruggles's eyes glistened with expectation as he saw it. His face fell, though, when he saw that it held but little. However, every little helps, and he brightened again as the old lady counted, slowly and tremblingly, the small store of only five dollars in all.

Ruggles took the money in his eager palms. "Of course, Mrs.—"

"Mandy Smif's my name."

"Of course, we can't promise you no fortune in return fu' an investment of fi' dollahs, but we'll do the bes' we kin fu' you."

"I do' want no fortune ner nothin' lak dat. What I wants is a little mo' money—'cause—'cause I got a boy; he allus been a good boy to me an' tuk keer o' me, but he thought he would do bettah out West, so he went out dere, an' fu' a while he got along all right an' sent me money reg'lar. Den he took down sick an' got out o' work. It was ha'd fu' me to git along 'dout his he'p, 'cause I's old. But dat ain't what hu'ts me. I don' keer nuffin' 'bout myse'f. I's willin' to sta've ef I could jes' sen' fu' dat boy an' bring him home so's I could nuss him. Dat's de reason I's a-'vestin' dis money."

Solomon Ruggles fingered the bills nervously.

"You know when a boy's sick dey ain't nobidy kin nuss lak his own mothah kin, fu' she nussed him when he was a baby; he's pa't o' huh, an' she knows his natur'. Yo' mothah livin', Mistah Ruggles?"

"Yes, 'way down South—she's ve'y ol'."

"I reckon some o' us ol' folks does live too long past dey times."

"No, you don't; you couldn't. I wish to God the world was full of jest sich ol' people as you an' my mothah is."

"Bless you, honey, I laks to hyeah you talk dat way 'bout yo' mammy. I ain' 'fred to trus' my money wif no man dat knows how to 'spect his mothah." The old woman rose to go. Ruggles followed her to the door. He was trembling with some emotion. He shook the investor warmly by the hand as he bade her good-bye. "I shall do the ve'y bes' I kin fu' you," he said.

"How soon kin I hyeah 'bout it?"

"I've took yo' address, an' you kin expect to hyeah from me in a week's time— that's sooner than we do anything fu' most of ouah customers."

"Thanky, sir, fu' the favour; thanky, an' good-bye, Mistah Ruggles."

The head of the company went in and sat for a long time dreaming over his table.

A week later an angry crowd of coloured investors stood outside the office of the Coloured Improvement Company. The office was closed to all business, and diligent search failed to reveal the whereabouts of Mr. Solomon Ruggles. The investors knew themselves to be the victims of a wily swindler, and they were furious. Dire imprecations were hurled at the head of the defaulting promoter. But, as the throng was spending its breath in vain anger, an old woman with smiling face worked her way through them toward the door.

"Let me th'oo," she said; " I want to fin' Mistah Ruggles."

"Yes, all of us do. Has he cheated you, too, Auntie?"

"Cheated me? What's de matter wif you, man? I put fi' dollahs in hyeah las' week, an' look at dat!"

The old woman waved some bills in the air and a letter with them. Some one took it from her hand and read:—

DEAR MRS. SMITH,—I am glad to say that yore int'rust 'cumulated faster than usu'l, so I kan inklose you heerwith $15. I am sorry I shall not see you again, az I am kalled away on bizness.

Very respectably yores,
S. RUGGLES.

The men looked at each other in surprise, and then they began to disperse. Some one said: "I reckon he mus' be all right, aftah all. Aunt Mandy got huh div'den'."

"I reckon he's comin' back all right," said another.

But Mr. Ruggles did not come back.

The Intervention of Peter

No one knows just what statement it was of Harrison Randolph's that Bob Lee doubted. The annals of these two Virginia families have not told us that. But these are the facts:—

It was at the home of the Fairfaxes that a few of the sons of the Old Dominion were giving a dinner,—not to celebrate anything in particular, but the joyousness of their own souls,—and a brave dinner it was. The courses had come and gone, and over their cigars they had waxed more than merry. In those days men drank deep, and these men were young, full of the warm blood of the South and the joy of living. What wonder then that the liquor that had been mellowing in the Fairfax cellars since the boyhood of their revolutionary ancestor should have its effect upon them?

It is true that it was only a slight thing which Bob Lee affected to disbelieve, and that his tone was jocosely bantering rather than impertinent. But sometimes Virginia heads are not less hot than Virginia hearts. The two young men belonged to families that had intermarried. They rode together. They hunted together, and were friends as far as two men could be who had read the message of love in the dark eyes of the same woman. So perhaps there was some thought of the long-contested hand of Miss Sallie Ford in Harrison Randolph's mind when he chose to believe that his honour had been assailed.

His dignity was admirable. There was no scene to speak of. It was all very genteel.

"Mr. Lee," he said, "had chosen to doubt his word, which to a gentleman was the final insult. But he felt sure that Mr. Lee would not refuse to accord him a gentleman's satisfaction." And the other's face had waxed warm and red and his voice cold as he replied: "I shall be most happy to give you the satisfaction you demand."

Here friends interposed and attempted to pacify the two. But without avail. The wine of the Fairfaxes has a valiant quality in it, and these two who had drunken of it could not be peaceably reconciled.

Each of the young gentlemen nodded to a friend and rose to depart. The joyous dinner-party bade fair to end with much more serious business.

"You shall hear from me very shortly," said Randolph, as he strode to the door.

"I shall await your pleasure with impatience, sir, and give you such a reply as even you cannot disdain."

It was all rather high-flown, but youth is dramatic and plays to the gallery of its own eyes and ears. But to one pair of ears there was no ring of anything but tragedy in the grandiloquent sentences. Peter, the personal attendant of Harrison Randolph, stood at the door as his master passed out, and went on before him to hold his stirrup. The young master and his friend and cousin, Dale, started off briskly and in silence, while Pete, with wide eyes and disturbed face, followed on behind. Just as they were turning into the avenue of elms that led to their own house, Randolph wheeled his horse and came riding back to his servant.

"Pete," said he, sternly, "what do you know?"

"Nuffin', Mas' Ha'ison, nuffin' 't all. I do' know nuffin'."

"I don't believe you." The young master's eyes were shining through the dusk. "You're always slipping around spying on me."

"Now dah you goes, Mas' Randolph. I ain't done a t'ing, and you got to 'mence pickin' on me—"

"I just want you to remember that my business is mine."

"Well, I knows dat."

"And if you do know anything, it will be well for you to begin forgetting right now." They were at the door now and in the act of dismounting. "Take Bess around and see her attended to. Leave Dale's horse here, and—I won't want you any more to-night."

"Now how does you an' Mas' Dale 'spect dat you gwine to wait on yo'se'ves to-night?"

"I shall not want you again to-night, I tell you."

Pete turned away with an injured expression on his dark face. "Bess," he said to the spirited black mare as he led her toward the stables, "you jes' bettah t'ank yo' Makah dat you ain't no human-bein', 'ca'se human-bein's is cur'ous articles. Now you's a hoss, ain't you? An' dey say you ain't got no soul, but you got sense, Bess, you got sense. You got blood an' fiah an' breedin' in you too, ain't you? Co'se you has. But you knows how to answah de rein. You's a high steppah, too: but you don' go to work an' try to brek yo' naik de fus' chanst you git. Bess, I 'spect you 'ca'se you got jedgment, an' you don' have to have a black man runnin' 'roun aftah you all de time plannin' his haid off jes' to keep you out o' trouble. Some folks dat's human-bein's does. Yet an' still, Bess, you ain't nuffin' but a dumb beas', so dey says. Now, what I gwine to do? Co'se dey wants to fight. But whah an' when an' how I gwine to stop hit? Do' want me to wait on him to-night, huh! No, dey want to mek dey plans an' do' want me 'roun' to hyeah, dat's what's de mattah. Well, I lay I'll hyeah somep'n' anyhow."

Peter hurried through his work and took himself up to the big house and straight to his master's room. He heard voices within, but though he took many liberties with his owner, eavesdropping was not one of them. It proved too dangerous. So, though "he kinder lingered on the mat, some doubtful of the sekle," it was not for long, and he unceremoniously pushed the door open and walked in. With a great show of haste, he made for his master's wardrobe and began busily searching among the articles therein. Harrison Randolph and his cousin were in the room, and their conversation, which had been animated, suddenly ceased when Peter entered.

"I thought I told you I didn't want you any more to-night."

"I's a-lookin' fu' dem striped pants o' yo'n. I want to tek 'em out an' bresh 'em: dey's p'intly a livin' sight."

"You get out o' here."

"But, Mas' Ha'ison, now—now—look—a—hyeah—"

"Get out, I tell you—"

Pete shuffled from the room, mumbling as he went: "Dah now, dah now! driv' out lak a dog! How's I gwine to fin' out anyt'ing dis away? It do 'pear lak Mas' Ha'ison do try to gi'e me all de trouble he know how. Now he plannin' an' projickin' wif dat cousin Dale, an' one jes' ez scattah-brained ez de othah. Well, I 'low I got to beat dey time somehow er ruther."

He was still lingering hopeless and worried about the house when he saw young Dale Randolph come out, mount his horse and ride away. After a while his young master also came out and walked up and down in the soft evening air. The rest of the family were seated about on the broad piazza.

"I wonder what is the matter with Harrison to-night," said the young man's father, "he seems so preoccupied."

"Thinking of Sallie Ford, I reckon," some one replied; and the remark passed with a laugh. Pete was near enough to catch this, but he did not stop to set them right in their conjectures. He slipped into the house as noiselessly as possible.

It was less than two hours after this when Dale Randolph returned and went immediately to his cousin's room, where Harrison followed him.

"Well?" said the latter, as soon as the door closed behind them.

"It's all arranged, and he's anxious to hurry it through for fear some one may interfere. Pistols, and to-morrow morning at daybreak."

"And the place?"

"The little stretch of woods that borders Ford's Creek. I say, Harrison, it isn't too late to stop this thing yet. It's a shame for you two fellows to fight. You're both too decent to be killed for a while yet."

"He insulted me."

"Without intention, every one believes."

"Then let him apologise."

"As well ask the devil to take Communion."

"We'll fight then."

"All right. If you must fight, you must. But you'd better get to bed; for you'll need a strong arm and a steady hand to-morrow."

If a momentary paleness struck into the young fellow's face, it was for a moment only, and he set his teeth hard before he spoke.

"I am going to write a couple of letters," he said, "then I shall lie down for an hour or so. Shall we go down and drink a steadier?"

"One won't hurt, of course."

"And, by the way, Dale, if I—if it happens to be me to-morrow, you take Pete— he's a good fellow."

The cousins clasped hands in silence and passed out. As the door closed behind them, a dusty form rolled out from under the bed, and the disreputable, eavesdropping, backsliding Pete stood up and rubbed a sleeve across his eyes.

"It ain't me dat's gwine to be give to nobody else. I hates to do it, but dey ain't no othah way. Mas' Ha'ison cain't be spaihed." He glided out mysteriously, some plan of salvation working in his black head.

JUST BEFORE DAYBREAK next morning, three stealthy figures crept out and made their way toward Ford's Creek. One skulked behind the other two, dogging their steps and taking advantage of the darkness to keep very near to them. At the grim trysting-place they halted and were soon joined by other stealthy figures, and together they sat down to wait for the daylight. The seconds conferred for a few minutes. The ground was paced off, and a few low-pitched orders prepared the young men for business.

"I will count three, gentlemen," said Lieutenant Custis. "At three, you are to fire."

At last daylight came, gray and timid at first, and then red and bold as the sun came clearly up. The pistols were examined and the men placed face to face.

"Are you ready, gentlemen?"

But evidently Harrison Randolph was not. He was paying no attention to the seconds. His eyes were fixed on an object behind his opponent's back. His attitude relaxed and his mouth began twitching. Then he burst into peals of laughter.

"Pete," he roared, "drop that and come out from there!" and away he went into another convulsion of mirth. The others turned just in time to see Pete cease his frantic grimaces of secrecy at his master, and sheepishly lower an ancient fowling-piece which he had had levelled at Bob Lee.

"What were you going to do with that gun levelled at me?" asked Lee, his own face twitching.

"I was gwine to fiah jes' befo' dey said free. I wa'n't gwine to kill you, Mas' Bob. I was on'y gwine to lame you."

Another peal of laughter from the whole crowd followed this condescending statement.

"You unconscionable scoundrel, you! If I was your master, I'd give you a hundred lashes."

"Pete," said his master, "don't you know that it is dishonourable to shoot a man from behind? You see you haven't in you the making of a gentleman."

"I do' know nuffin' 'bout mekin' a gent'man, but I does know how to save one dat's already made."

The prime object of the meeting had been entirely forgotten. They gathered around Pete and examined the weapon.

"Gentlemen," said Randolph, "we have been saved by a miracle. This old gun, as well as I can remember and count, has been loaded for the past twenty-five years, and if Pete had tried to fire it, it would have torn up all of this part of the county." Then the eyes of the two combatants met. There was something irresistibly funny in the whole situation, and they found themselves roaring again. Then, with one impulse, they shook hands without a word.

And Pete led the way home, the willing butt of a volume of good-natured abuse.

Nelse Hatton's Vengeance

It was at the close of a summer day, and the sun was sinking dimly red over the hills of the little Ohio town which, for convenience, let us call Dexter.

The people had eaten their suppers, and the male portion of the families had come out in front of their houses to smoke and rest or read the evening paper. Those who had porches drew their rockers out on them, and sat with their feet on the railing. Others took their more humble positions on the front steps, while still others, whose houses were flush with the street, went even so far as to bring their chairs out upon the sidewalk, and over all there was an air of calmness and repose save when a glance through the open doors revealed the housewives busy at their evening dishes, or the blithe voices of the children playing in the street told that little Sally Waters was a-sitting in a saucer or asserted with doubtful veracity that London Bridge was falling down. Here and there a belated fisherman came straggling up the street that led from the river, every now and then holding up his string of slimy, wiggling catfish in answer to the query "Wha' 'd you ketch?"

To one who knew the generous and unprejudiced spirit of the Dexterites, it was no matter of wonder that one of their soundest and most highly respected citizens was a coloured man, and that his home should nestle unrebuked among the homes of his white neighbours.

Nelse Hatton had won the love and respect of his fellow-citizens by the straightforward honesty of his conduct and the warmth of his heart. Everybody knew him. He had been doing chores about Dexter,—cutting grass in summer, cleaning and laying carpets in the spring and fall, and tending furnaces in the winter,—since the time when, a newly emancipated man, he had passed over from Kentucky into Ohio. Since then through thrift he had attained quite a competence, and, as he himself expressed it, "owned some little propity." He was one among the number who had arisen to the dignity of a porch; and on this evening he was sitting thereon, laboriously spelling out the sentences in the *Evening News*—his reading was a *post-bellum* accomplishment—when the oldest of his three children, Theodore, a boy of twelve, interrupted him with the intelligence that there was an "old straggler at the back door."

After admonishing the hope of his years as to the impropriety of applying such a term to an unfortunate, the father rose and sought the place where the "straggler" awaited him.

Nelse's sympathetic heart throbbed with pity at the sight that met his eye. The "straggler," a "thing of shreds and patches," was a man about his own age, nearing fifty; but what a contrast he was to the well-preserved, well-clothed black man! His gray hair straggled carelessly about his sunken temples, and the face beneath it was thin and emaciated. The hands that pulled at the fringe of the ragged coat were small and bony. But both the face and the hands were clean, and there was an open look in the bold, dark eye.

In strong contrast, too, with his appearance was the firm, well-modulated voice, somewhat roughened by exposure, in which he said, "I am very hungry; will you give me something to eat?" It was a voice that might have spoken with authority. There was none of the beggar's whine in it. It was clear and straightforward; and the man spoke the simple sentence almost as if it had been a protest against his sad condition.

"Jes' set down on the step an' git cool," answered Nelse, "an' I'll have something put on the table."

The stranger silently did as he was bidden, and his host turned into the house.

Eliza Hatton had been quietly watching proceedings, and as her husband entered the kitchen she said, "Look a-here, Nelse, you shorely ain't a-goin' to have that tramp in the kitchen a-settin' up to the table?"

"Why, course," said Nelse; "he's human, ain't he?"

"That don't make no difference. I bet none of these white folks round here would do it."

"That ain't none of my business," answered her husband. "I believe in every person doin' their own duty. Put somethin' down on the table; the man's hungry. An' don't never git stuck up, 'Lizy; you don't know what our children have got to come to."

Nelse Hatton was a man of few words; but there was a positive manner about him at times that admitted neither argument nor resistance.

His wife did as she was bidden, and then swept out in the majesty of wounded dignity, as the tramp was ushered in and seated before the table whose immaculate white cloth she had been prudent enough to change for a red one.

The man ate as if he were hungry, but always as if he were a hungry gentleman. There was something in his manner that impressed Nelse that he was not feeding a common tramp as he sat and looked at his visitor in polite curiosity. After a somewhat continued silence he addressed the man: "Why don't you go to your own people when you're hungry instead of coming to us coloured folks?"

There was no reproof in his tone, only inquiry.

The stranger's eyes flashed suddenly.

"Go to them up there?" he said; "never. They would give me my supper with their hypocritical patronage and put it down to charity. You give me something to eat as a favour. Your gift proceeds from disinterested kindness; they would throw me a bone because they thought it would weigh something in the balance against their sins. To you I am an unfortunate man; to them I am a tramp."

The stranger had spoken with much heat and no hesitation; but his ardour did not take the form of offence at Nelse's question. He seemed perfectly to comprehend the motive which actuated it.

Nelse had listened to him with close attention, and at the end of his harangue he said, "You hadn't ought to be so hard on your own people; they mean well enough."

"My own people!" the stranger flashed back. "My people are the people of the South,—the people who have in their veins the warm, generous blood of Dixie!"

"I don't see what you stay in the North fur ef you don't like the people."

"I am not staying; I'm getting away from it as fast as I can. I only came because I thought, like a lot of other poor fools, that the North had destroyed my fortunes and it might restore them; but five years of fruitless struggle in different places out of Dixie have shown me that it isn't the place for a man with blood in his veins. I thought that I was reconstructed; but I'm not. My State didn't need it, but I did."

"Where're you from?"

"Kentucky; and there's where I'm bound for now. I want to get back where people have hearts and sympathies."

The coloured man was silent. After a while he said, and his voice was tremulous as he thought of the past, "I'm from Kintucky, myself."

"I knew that you were from some place in the South. There's no mistaking our people, black or white, wherever you meet them. Kentucky's a great State, sir. She didn't secede; but there were lots of her sons on the other side. I was; and I did my duty as clear as I could see it."

"That's all any man kin do," said Nelse; "an' I ain't a-blamin' you. I lived with as good people as ever was. I know they wouldn't 'a' done nothin' wrong ef they'd 'a' knowed it; an' they was on the other side."

"You've been a slave, then?"

"Oh, yes, I was born a slave; but the War freed me."

"I reckon you wouldn't think that my folks ever owned slaves; but they did. Everybody was good to them except me, and I was young and liked to show my authority. I had a little black boy that I used to cuff around a good deal, altho' he was near to me as a brother. But sometimes he would turn on me and give me the trouncing that I deserved. He would have been skinned for it if my father had found it out; but I was always too much ashamed of being thrashed to tell."

The speaker laughed, and Nelse joined him. "Bless my soul!" he said, "ef that ain't jes' the way it was with me an' my Mas' Tom—"

"Mas' Tom!" cried the stranger; "man, what's your name?"

"Nelse Hatton," replied the Negro.

"Heavens, Nelse! I'm your young Mas' Tom. I'm Tom Hatton; don't you know me, boy?"

"You can't be—you can't be!" exclaimed the Negro.

"I am, I tell you. Don't you remember the scar I got on my head from falling off old Baldy's back? Here it is. Can't you see?" cried the stranger, lifting the long hair away from one side of his brow. "Doesn't this convince you?"

"It's you—it's you; 't ain't nobody else but Mas' Tom!" and the ex-slave and his former master rushed joyously into each other's arms.

There was no distinction of colour or condition there. There was no thought of superiority on the one hand, or feeling of inferiority on the other. They were simply two loving friends who had been long parted and had met again.

After a while the Negro said, "I'm sure the Lord must 'a' sent you right here to this house, so's you wouldn't be eatin' off o' none o' these poor white people 'round here."

"I reckon you're religious now, Nelse; but I see it ain't changed your feeling toward poor white people."

"I don't know about that. I used to be purty bad about 'em."

"Indeed you did. Do you remember the time we stoned the house of old Nat, the white wood-sawyer?"

"Well, I reckon I do! Wasn't we awful, them days?" said Nelse, with forced contrition, but with something almost like a chuckle in his voice.

And yet there was a great struggle going on in the mind of this black man. Thirty years of freedom and the advantages of a Northern State made his whole soul revolt at the word "master." But that fine feeling, that tender sympathy, which is natural to the real Negro, made him hesitate to make the poor wreck of former glory conscious of his changed estate by using a different appellation. His warm sympathies conquered.

"I want you to see my wife and boys, Mas' Tom," he said, as he passed out of the room.

Eliza Hatton sat in her neatly appointed little front room, swelling with impotent rage.

If this story were chronicling the doings of some fanciful Negro, or some really rude plantation hand, it might be said that the "front room was filled with a conglomeration of cheap but pretentious furniture, and the walls covered with gaudy prints"—this seems to be the usual phrase. But in it the chronicler too often forgets how many Negroes were house-servants, and from close contact with their master's families imbibed aristocratic notions and quiet but elegant tastes.

This front room was very quiet in its appointments. Everything in it was subdued except—Mrs. Hatton. She was rocking back and forth in a light little rocker that screeched the indignation she could not express. She did not deign to look at Nelse as he came into the room; but an acceleration of speed on the part of the rocker showed that his presence was known.

Her husband's enthusiasm suddenly died out as he looked at her; but he put on a brave face as he said,—

"'Lizy, I bet a cent you can't guess who that pore man in there is."

The rocker suddenly stopped its violent motion with an equally violent jerk, as the angry woman turned upon her husband.

"No, I can't guess," she cried; "an' I don't want to. It's enough to be settin' an on'ry ol' tramp down to my clean table, without havin' me spend my time guessin' who he is."

"But look a-here, 'Lizy, this is all different; an' you don't understand."

"Don't care how different it is, I do' want to understand."

"You'll be mighty su'prised, I tell you."

"I 'low I will; I'm su'prised already at you puttin' yourself on a level with tramps." This with fine scorn.

"Be careful, 'Lizy, be careful; you don't know who a tramp may turn out to be."

"That ol' humbug in there has been tellin' you some big tale, an' you ain't got no more sense 'an to believe it; I 'spect he's crammin' his pockets full of my things now. Ef you don't care, I do."

The woman rose and started toward the door, but her husband stopped her, "You mustn't go out there that way," he said. "I want you to go out, you an' the childern; but I want you to go right—that man is the son of my ol' master, my young Mas' Tom, as I used to call him."

She fell back suddenly and stared at him with wide-open eyes.

"Your master!"

"Yes, it's young Mas' Tom Hatton."

"An' you want me an' the childern to see him, do you?"

"Why, yes, I thought—"

"Humph! that's the slave in you yet," she interrupted. "I thought thirty years had made you free! Ain't that the man you told me used to knock you 'round so?"

"Yes, 'Lizy; but—"

"Ain't he the one that made you haul him in the wheelbar', an' whipped you because you couldn't go fast enough?"

"Yes, yes; but that—"

"Ain't he the one that lef' that scar there?" she cried, with a sudden motion of her hand toward his neck.

"Yes," said Nelse, very quietly; but he put his hand up and felt the long, cruel scar that the lash of a whip had left, and a hard light came into his eyes.

His wife went on: "An' you want to take me an' the childern in to see that man? No!" The word came with almost a snarl. "Me an' my childern are free born, an', ef I kin help it, they sha'n't never look at the man that laid the lash to their father's back! Shame on you, Nelse, shame on you, to want your childern, that you're tryin' to raise independent,—to want 'em to see the man that you had to call 'master'!"

The man's lips quivered, and his hand opened and shut with a convulsive motion; but he said nothing.

"What did you tell me?" she asked. "Didn't you say that if you ever met him again in this world you'd—"

"Kill him!" burst forth the man; and all the old, gentle look had gone out of his face, and there was nothing but fierceness and bitterness there, as his mind went back to his many wrongs.

"Go on away from the house, 'Lizy," he said hoarsely; "if anything happens, I do' want you an' the childern around."

"I do' want you to kill him, Nelse, so you'll git into trouble; but jes' give him one good whippin' for those he used to give you."

"Go on away from the house;" and the man's lips were tightly closed. She threw a thin shawl over her head and went out.

As soon as she had gone Nelse's intense feeling got the better of him, and, falling down with his face in a chair, he cried, in the language which the Sunday sermons had taught him, "Lord, Lord, thou hast delivered mine enemy into my hands!"

But it was not a prayer; it was rather a cry of anger and anguish from an over-burdened heart. He rose, with the same hard gleam in his eyes, and went back toward the kitchen. One hand was tightly clinched till the muscles and veins stood out like cords, and with the other he unconsciously fingered the lash's scar.

"Couldn't find your folks, eh, Nelse?" said the white Hatton.

"No," growled Nelse; and continued hurriedly, "Do you remember that scar?"

"Well enough—well enough," answered the other, sadly; "and it must have hurt you, Nelse."

"Hurt me! yes," cried the Negro.

"Ay," said Tom Hatton, as he rose and put his hand softly on the black scar; "and it has hurt me many a day since, though time and time again I have suffered pains that were as cruel as this must have been to you. Think of it, Nelse; there have been times when I, a Hatton, have asked bread of the very people whom a few years ago I scorned. Since the War everything has gone against me. You do not know how I have suffered. For thirty years life has been a curse to me; but I am going back to Kentucky now, and when I get there I'll lay it down without a regret."

All the anger had melted from the Negro's face, and there were tears in his eyes as he cried, "You sha'n't do it, Mas' Tom,—you sha'n't do it."

His destructive instinct had turned to one of preservation.

"But, Nelse, I have no further hopes," said the dejected man.

"You have, and you shall have. You're goin' back to Kentucky, an' you're goin' back a gentleman. I kin he'p you, an' I will; you're welcome to the last I have."

"God bless you, Nelse—"

"Mas' Tom, you used to be jes' about my size, but you're slimmer now; but— but I hope you won't be mad ef I ask you to put on a suit o' mine. It's put' nigh brand-new, an'—"

"Nelse, I can't do it! Is this the way you pay me for the blows—"

"Heish your mouth; ef you don't I'll slap you down!" Nelse said it with mock solemnity, but there was an ominous quiver about his lips.

"Come in this room, suh;" and the master obeyed. He came out arrayed in Nelse's best and newest suit. The coloured man went to a drawer, over which he bent laboriously. Then he turned and said: "This'll pay your passage to Kentucky, an' leave somethin' in your pocket besides. Go home, Mas' Tom,—go home!"

"Nelse, I can't do it; this is too much!"

"Doggone my cats, ef you don't go on—"

The white man stood bowed for a moment; then, straightening up, he threw his head back. "I'll take it, Nelse; but you shall have every cent back, even if I have to sell my body to a medical college and use a gun to deliver the goods! Good-bye, Nelse, God bless you! good-bye."

"Good-bye, Mas' Tom, but don't talk that way; go home. The South is changed, an' you'll find somethin' to suit you. Go home—go home; an' ef there's any of the folks a-livin', give 'em my love, Mas' Tom—give 'em my love—good-bye —good-bye!"

The Negro leaned over the proffered hand, and his tears dropped upon it. His master passed out, and he sat with his head bowed in his hands.

After a long while Eliza came creeping in.

"Wha' 'd you do to him, Nelse—wha' 'd you do to him?" There was no answer. "Lawd, I hope you ain't killed him," she said, looking fearfully around. "I don't see no blood."

"I ain't killed him," said Nelse. "I sent him home—back to the ol' place."

"You sent him home! how'd you send him, huh?"

"I give him my Sunday suit and that money—don't git mad, 'Lizy, don't git mad—that money I was savin' for your cloak. I couldn't help it, to save my life. He's goin' back home among my people, an' I sent 'em my love. Don't git mad an' I'll git you a cloak anyhow."

"Pleggone the cloak!" said Mrs. Hatton, suddenly, all the woman in her rising in her eyes. "I was so 'fraid you'd take my advice an' do somethin' wrong. Ef you're happy, Nelse, I am too. I don't grudge your master nothin'—the ol' devil! But you're jes' a good-natured, big-hearted, weak-headed ol' fool!" And she took his head in her arms.

Great tears rolled down the man's cheeks, and he said: "Bless God, 'Lizy, I feel as good as a young convert."

At Shaft 11

NIGHT FALLS EARLY over the miners' huts that cluster at the foot of the West Virginia mountains. The great hills that give the vales their shelter also force upon them their shadow. Twilight lingers a short time, and then gives way to that black darkness which is possible only to regions in the vicinity of high and heavily wooded hills.

Through the fast-gathering gloom of a mid-spring evening, Jason Andrews, standing in his door, peered out into the open. It was a sight of rugged beauty that met his eyes as they swept the broken horizon. All about the mountains raised their huge forms,—here bare, sharp, and rocky; there undulating, and covered with wood and verdure, whose various shades melted into one dull, blurred, dark green, hardly distinguishable in the thick twilight. At the foot of the hills all was in shadow, but their summits were bathed in the golden and crimson glory of departing day.

Jason Andrews, erstwhile foreman of Shaft 11, gazed about him with an eye not wholly unappreciative of the beauty of the scene. Then, shading his eyes with one brawny hand, an act made wholly unnecessary by the absence of the sun, he projected his vision far down into the valley.

His hut, set a little way up the mountain-side, commanded an extended view of the road, which, leaving the slope, ran tortuously through the lower land. Evidently something that he saw down the road failed to please the miner, for he gave a low whistle and re-entered the house with a frown on his face.

"I'll be goin' down the road a minute, Kate," he said to his wife, throwing on his coat and pausing at the door. "There's a crowd gathered down toward the settlement. Somethin' 's goin' on, an' I want to see what's up." He slammed the door and strode away.

"Jason, Jason," his wife called after him, "don't you have nothin' to do with their goin's-on, neither one way nor the other. Do you hear?"

"Oh, I'll take care o' myself." The answer came back out of the darkness.

"I do wish things would settle down some way or other," mused Mrs. Andrews. "I don't see why it is men can't behave themselves an' go 'long about their business, lettin' well enough alone. It's all on account o' that pesky walkin' delegate too. I wisht he'd 'a' kept walkin'. If all the rest o' the men had had the commonsense that Jason has, he wouldn't never 'a' took no effect on them. But most of 'em must set with their mouths open like a lot o' ninnies takin' in everything that come their way, and now here's all this trouble on our hands."

There were indeed troublous times at the little mining settlement. The men who made up the community were all employees, in one capacity or another, of the great Crofton West Virginia Mining Co. They had been working on, contented and happy, at fair wages and on good terms with their employers, until the advent among them of one who called himself, alternately, a benefactor of humanity and a labour agitator. He proceeded to show the men how they were oppressed, how they were withheld from due compensation for their labours, while the employers rolled in the wealth which the workers' hands had produced. With great adroitness of argument and elaboration of phrase, he contrived to show them that they were altogether the most ill-treated men in America. There was only one remedy for the misery of their condition, and that was to pay him two dollars and immediately organise a local branch of the Miners' Labour Union. The men listened. He was so perfectly plausible, so smooth, and so clear. He found converts among them. Some few combated the man's ideas, and none among these more forcibly than did Jason Andrews, the foreman of Shaft 11. But the heresy grew, and the opposition was soon overwhelmed. There are always fifty fools for every fallacy. Of course, the thing to do was to organise against oppression, and accordingly, amid great enthusiasm, the union was formed. With the exception of Jason Andrews, most of the men, cowed by the majority opposed to them, yielded their ground and joined. But not so he. It was sturdy, stubborn old Scotch blood that coursed through his veins. He stayed out of the society even at the expense of the friendship of some of the men who had been his friends. Taunt upon taunt was thrown into his face.

"He's on the side of the rich. He's for capital against labour. He's in favour of supporting a grinding monopoly." All this they said in the ready, pat parlance of their class; but the foreman went his way unmoved, and kept his own counsel.

Then, like the falling of a thunderbolt, had come the visit of the "walking-delegate" for the district, and his command to the men to "go out." For a little time the men demurred; but the word of the delegate was law. Some other company had failed to pay its employees a proper price, and the whole district was to be made an example of. Even while the men were asking what it was all about, the strike was declared on.

The usual committee, awkward, shambling, hat in hand, and uncomfortable in their best Sunday clothes, called upon their employers to attempt to explain the grievances which had brought about the present state of affairs. The "walking-delegate" had carefully prepared it all for them, with the new schedule of wages based upon the company's earnings.

The three men who had the local affairs of the company in charge heard them through quietly. Then young Harold Crofton, acting as spokesman, said, "Will you tell us how long since you discovered that your wages were unfair?"

The committee severally fumbled its hat and looked confused. Finally Grierson, who had been speaking for them, said: "Well, we've been thinkin' about it fur a good while. Especially ever sence, ahem—"

"Yes," went on Crofton, "to be plain and more definite, ever since the appearance among you of Mr. Tom Daly, the agitator, the destroyer of confidence between employer and employed, the weasel who sucks your blood and tells you that he is doing you a service. You have discovered the unfairness of your compensation since making his acquaintance."

"Well, I guess he told us the truth," growled Grierson.

"That is a matter of opinion."

"But look what you all are earnin'."

"That's what we're in the business for. We haven't left comfortable homes in the cities to come down to this hole in the mountains for our health. We have a right to earn. We brought capital, enterprise, and energy here. We give you work and pay you decent wages. It is none of your business what we earn." The young man's voice rose a little, and a light came into his calm gray eyes. "Have you not been comfortable? Have you not lived well and been able to save something? Have you not been treated like men? What more do you want? What real grievance have you? None. A scoundrel and a sneak has come here, and for his own purposes aroused your covetousness. But it is unavailing, and," turning to his colleagues, "these gentlemen will bear me out in what I say,—we will not raise your wages one-tenth of one penny above what they are. We will not be made to suffer for the laxity of other owners, and if within three hours the men are not back at work, they may consider themselves discharged." His voice was cold, clear, and ringing.

Surprised, disappointed, and abashed, the committee heard the ultimatum, and then shuffled out of the office in embarrassed silence. It was all so different from what they had expected. They thought that they had only to demand and their employers would accede rather than have the work stop. Labour had but to make a show of resistance and capital would yield. So they had been told. But here they were, the chosen representatives of labour, skulking away from the presence of capital like felons detected. Truly this was a change. Embarrassment gave way to anger, and the miners who waited the report of their committee received a highly coloured account of the stand-offish way in which they had been met. If there had been anything lacking to inflame the rising feelings of the labourers, this new evidence of the arrogance of plutocrats supplied it, and with one voice the strike was confirmed.

Soon after the three hours' grace had passed, Jason Andrews received a summons to the company's office.

"Andrews," said young Crofton, "we have noticed your conduct with gratitude since this trouble has been brewing. The other foremen have joined the strikers and gone out. We know where you stand and thank you for your kindness. But we don't want it to end with thanks. It is well to give the men a lesson and bring them to their senses, but the just must not suffer with the unjust. In less than two days the mine will be manned by Negroes with their own foreman. We wish to offer you a place in the office here at the same wages you got in the mine."

The foreman raised his hand in a gesture of protest. "No, no, Mr. Crofton. That would look like I was profiting by the folly of the men. I can't do it. I am not in their union, but I will take my chances as they take theirs."

"That's foolish, Andrews. You don't know how long this thing may last."

"Well, I've got a snug bit laid by, and if things don't brighten in time, why, I'll go somewhere else."

"We'd be sorry to lose you, but I want you to do as you think best. This change may cause trouble, and if it does, we shall hope for your aid."

"I am with you as long as you are in the right."

The miner gave the young man's hand a hearty grip and passed out.

"Steel," said Crofton the younger.

"Gold," replied his partner.

"Well, as true as one and as good as the other, and we are both right."

As the young manager had said, so matters turned out. Within two days several car-loads of Negroes came in and began to build their huts. With the true racial instinct of colonisation, they all flocked to one part of the settlement. With a wisdom that was not entirely instinctive, though it may have had its origin in the Negro's social inclination, they built one large eating-room a little way from their cabin and up the mountain-side. The back of the place was the bare wall of a sheer cliff. Here their breakfasts and suppers were to be taken, the midday meal being eaten in the mine.

The Negro who held Jason Andrews' place as foreman of Shaft 11, the best yielding of all the mines, and the man who seemed to be the acknowledged leader of all the blacks, was known as big Sam Bowles. He was a great black fellow, with a hand like a sledge-hammer, but with an open, kindly face and a voice as musical as a lute.

On the first morning that they went in a body to work in the mines, they were assailed by the jeers and curses of the strikers, while now and then a rock from the hand of some ambushed foe fell among them. But they did not heed these things, for they were expected.

For several days nothing more serious than this happened, but ominous mutterings foretold the coming storm. So matters stood on the night that Jason Andrews left his cabin to find out what was "up."

He went on down the road until he reached the outskirts of the crowd, which he saw to be gathered about a man who was haranguing them. The speaker proved to be "Red" Cleary, one of Daly's first and most ardent converts. He had worked the men up to a high pitch of excitement, and there were cries of, "Go it, Red, you're on the right track!" "What's the matter with Cleary? He's all right!" and, "Run the niggers out. That's it!" On the edge of the throng, half in the shadow, Jason Andrews listened in silence, and his just anger grew.

The speaker was saying, "What are we white men goin' to do? Set still an' let niggers steal the bread out of our mouths? Ain't it our duty to rise up like free Americans an' drive 'em from the place? Who dares say no to that?" Cleary made the usual pause for dramatic effect and to let the incontrovertibility of his argument sink into the minds of his hearers. The pause was fatal. A voice broke the stillness that followed his question, "I do!" and Andrews pushed his way through the crowd to the front. "There ain't anybody stealin' the bread out of our mouths, niggers ner nobody else. If men throw away their bread, why, a dog has the right to pick it up."

There were dissenting murmurs, and Cleary turned to his opponent with a sneer. "Humph, I'd be bound for you, Jason Andrews, first on the side of the bosses and then takin' up for the niggers. Boys, I'll bet he's a Republican!" A laugh greeted this sally. The red mounted into the foreman's face and made his tan seem darker.

"I'm as good a Democrat as any of you," he said, looking around, "and you say that again, Red Cleary, and I'll push the words down your throat with my fist."

Cleary knew his man and turned the matter off. "We don't care nothin' about what party you vote with. We intend to stand up for our rights. Mebbe you've got something to say ag'in that."

"I've got something to say, but not against any man's rights. There's men here that have known me and are honest, and they will say whether I've acted on the square or not since I've been among you. But there is right as well as rights. As for the niggers, I ain't any friendlier to 'em than the rest of you. But I ain't the man to throw up a job and then howl when somebody else gets it. If we don't want our hoe-cake, there's others that do."

The plain sense of Andrews' remarks calmed the men, and Cleary, seeing that his power was gone, moved away from the centre of the crowd, "I'll settle with you later," he muttered, as he passed Jason.

"There ain't any better time than now," replied the latter, seizing his arm and drawing him back.

"Here, here, don't fight," cried some one. "Go on, Cleary, there may be something better than a fellow-workman to try your muscle on before long." The crowd came closer and pushed between the two men. With many signs of reluctance, but willingly withal, Cleary allowed himself to be hustled away. The crowd dispersed, but Jason Andrews knew that he had only temporarily quieted the turmoil in the breasts of the men. It would break out very soon again, he told himself. Musing thus, he took his homeward way. As he reached the open road on the rise that led to his cabin, he heard the report of a pistol, and a shot clipped a rock three or four paces in front of him.

"With the compliments of Red Cleary," said Jason, with a hard laugh. "The coward!"

All next day, an ominous calm brooded over the little mining settlement. The black workmen went to their labours unmolested, and the hope that their hardships were over sprang up in the hearts of some. But there were two men who, without being informed, knew better. These were Jason Andrews and big Sam, and chance threw the two together. It was as the black was returning alone from the mine after the day's work was over.

"The strikers didn't bother you any to-day, I noticed," said Andrews.

Sam Bowles looked at him with suspicion, and then, being reassured by the honest face and friendly manner, he replied: "No, not to-day, but there ain't no tellin' what they'll do to-night. I don't like no sich sudden change."

"You think something is brewing, eh?"

"It looks mighty like it, I tell you."

"Well, I believe that you're right, and you'll do well to keep a sharp lookout all night."

"I, for one, won't sleep," said the Negro.

"Can you shoot?" asked Jason.

The Negro chuckled, and, taking a revolver from the bosom of his blouse, aimed at the top of a pine-tree which had been grazed by lightning, and showed white through the fading light nearly a hundred yards away. There was a crack, and the small white space no larger than a man's hand was splintered by the bullet.

"Well, there ain't no doubt that you can shoot, and you may have to bring that gun of yours into action before you expect. In a case like this it's your enemy's life against yours."

Andrews kept on his way, and the Negro turned up to the large supper-room. Most of them were already there and at the meal.

"Well boys," began big Sam, "you'd just as well get it out of your heads that our trouble is over here. It's jest like I told you. I've been talkin' to the fellow that used to have my place,—he ain't in with the rest of the strikers,—an' he thinks that they're goin' to try an' run us out to-night. I'd advise you, as soon as it gets dark-like, to take what things you want out o' yore cabins an' bring 'em up here. It won't do no harm to be careful until we find out what kind of a move they're goin' to make."

The men had stopped eating, and they stared at the speaker with open mouths. There were some incredulous eyes among the gazers, too.

"I don't believe they'd dare come right out an' do anything," said one.

"Stay in yore cabin, then," retorted the leader angrily.

There was no more demur, and as soon as night had fallen, the Negroes did as they were bidden, though the rude, ill-furnished huts contained little or nothing of value. Another precaution taken by the blacks was to leave short candles burning in their dwellings so as to give the impression of occupancy. If nothing occurred during the night, the lights would go out of themselves and the enemy would be none the wiser as to their vigilance.

In the large assembly room the men waited in silence, some drowsing and some smoking. Only one candle threw its dim circle of light in the centre of the room, throwing the remainder into denser shadow. The flame flickered and guttered. Its wavering faintness brought out the dark strained faces in fantastic relief, and gave a weirdness to the rolling white eyeballs and expanded eyes. Two hours passed. Suddenly, from the window where big Sam and a colleague were stationed, came a warning "S-sh!" Sam had heard stealthy steps in the direction of the nearest cabin. The night was so black that he could see nothing, but he felt that developments were about to begin. He could hear more steps. Then the men heard a cry of triumph as the strikers threw themselves against the cabin doors, which yielded easily. This was succeeded from all parts by exclamations of rage and disappointment. In the assembly room the Negroes were chuckling to themselves. Mr. "Red" Cleary had planned well, but so had Sam Bowles.

After the second cry there was a pause, as if the men had drawn together for consultation. Then some one approached the citadel a little way and said: "If you niggers'll promise to leave here to-morrow morning at daylight, we'll let you off this time. If you don't, there won't be any of you to leave to-morrow."

Some of the blacks were for promising, but their leader turned on them like a tiger. "You would promise, would you, and then give them a chance to whip you out of the section! Go, all of you that want to; but as for me, I'll stay here an' fight it out with the blackguards."

The man who had spoken from without had evidently waited for an answer. None coming, his footsteps were heard retreating, and then, without warning, there was a rattling fusillade. Some of the shots crashed through the thin pine boarding, and several men were grazed. One struck the man who stood at big Sam's side at the window. The blood splashed into the black leader's face, and his companion sunk to the floor with a groan. Sam Bowles moved from the window a moment and wiped the blood drops from his cheek. He looked down upon the dead man as if the deed had dazed him. Then, with a few sharp commands, he turned again to the window.

Some over-zealous fool among the strikers had fired one of the huts, and the growing flames discovered their foes to the little garrison.

"Put out that light," ordered big Sam. "All of you that can, get to the two front windows—you, Toliver, an' you, Moten, here with me. All the rest of you lay flat on the floor. Now, as soon as that light gets bright, pick out yore man,—don't waste a shot, now—fire!" Six pistols spat fire out into the night. There were cries of pain and the noise of scurrying feet as the strikers fled pell-mell out of range.

"Now, down on the floor!" commanded Sam.

The order came not a moment too soon, for an answering volley of shots penetrated the walls and passed harmlessly over the heads of those within. Meanwhile, some one seeing the mistake of the burning cabin had ordered it extinguished; but this could not be done without the workmen being exposed to the fire from the blacks' citadel. So there was nothing to do save to wait until the shanty had burned down. The dry pine was flaming brightly now, and lit up the scene with a crimson glare. The great rocks and the rugged mountain-side, with patches of light here and there contrasting with the deeper shadows, loomed up threatening and terrible, and the fact that behind those boulders lay armed men thirsty for blood made the scene no less horrible.

In his cabin, farther up the mountain side, Jason Andrews had heard the shouts and firing, seen the glare of the burning cabin through his window, and interpreted it aright. He rose and threw on his coat.

"Jason," said his wife, "don't go down there. It's none of your business."

"I'm not going down there, Kate," he said; "but I know my duty and have got to do it."

The nearest telegraph office was a mile away from his cabin. Thither Jason hurried. He entered, and, seizing a blank, began to write rapidly, when he was interrupted by the voice of the operator, "It's no use, Andrews, the wires are cut." The foreman stopped as if he had been struck; then, wheeling around, he started for the door just as Crofton came rushing in.

"Ah, Andrews, it's you, is it?—and before me. Have you telegraphed for troops?"

"It's no use, Mr. Crofton, the wires are cut."

"My God!" exclaimed the young man, "what is to be done? I did not think they would go to this length."

"We must reach the next station and wire from there."

"But it's fifteen miles away on a road where a man is liable to break his neck at any minute."

"I'll risk it, but I must have a horse."

"Take mine. He's at the door,—God speed you." With the word, Jason was in the saddle and away like the wind.

"He can't keep that pace on the bad ground," said young Crofton, as he turned homeward.

At the centre of strife all was still quiet. The fire had burned low, and what remained of it cast only a dull light around. The assailants began to prepare again for action.

"Here, some one take my place at the window," said Sam. He left his post, crept to the door and opened it stealthily, and, dropping on his hands and knees, crawled out into the darkness. In less than five minutes he was back and had resumed his station. His face was expressionless. No one knew what he had done until a new flame shot athwart the darkness, and at sight of it the strikers burst into a roar of rage. Another cabin was burning, and the space about for a hundred yards was as bright as day. In the added light, two or three bodies were distinguishable upon the ground, showing that the shots of the blacks had told. With deep chagrin the strikers saw that they could do nothing while the light lasted. It was now nearly midnight, and the men were tired and cramped in their places. They dared not move about much, for every appearance of an arm or a leg brought a shot from the besieged. Oh for the darkness, that they might advance and storm the stronghold! Then they could either overpower the blacks by force of numbers, or set fire to the place that held them and shoot them down as they tried to escape. Oh for darkness!

As if the Powers above were conspiring against the unfortunates, the clouds, which had been gathering dark and heavy, now loosed a downpour of rain which grew fiercer and fiercer as the thunder crashed down from the mountains echoing and re-echoing back and forth in the valley. The lightning tore vivid, zigzag gashes in the inky sky. The fury of the storm burst suddenly, and before the blacks could realise what was happening, the torrent had beaten the fire down, and the way between them and their enemies lay in darkness. The strikers gave a cheer that rose even over the thunder.

As THE YOUNG manager had said, the road over which Jason had to travel was a terrible one. It was rough, uneven, and treacherous to the step even in the light of day. But the brave man urged his horse on at the best possible speed. When he was half-way to his destination, a sudden drop in the road threw the horse and he went over the animal's head. He felt a sharp pain in his arm, and he turned sick and dizzy, but, scrambling to his feet, he mounted, seized the reins in one hand, and was away again. It was half-past twelve when he staggered into the telegraph office. "Wire—quick!" he gasped. The operator who had been awakened from a nap by the clatter of the horse's hoofs, rubbed his eyes and seized a pencil and blank.

"Troops at once—for God's sake—troops at once—Crofton's mine riot— murder being done!" and then, his mission being over, nature refused longer to resist the strain and Jason Andrews swooned.

His telegram had been received at Wheeling, and another ordering the instant despatch of the nearest militia, who had been commanded to sleep in their armories in anticipation of some such trouble, before a physician had been secured for Andrews. His arm was set and he was put to bed. But, loaded on flat-cars and whatever else came handy, the troops were on their way to the scene of action.

While this was going on, the Negroes had grown disheartened. The light which had disclosed to them their enemy had been extinguished, and under cover of the darkness and storm they knew their assailants would again advance. Every flash of lightning showed them the men standing boldly out from their shelter.

Big Sam turned to his comrades. "Never say die, boys," he said. "We've got jest one more chance to scatter 'em. If we can't do it, it's hand to hand with twice our number. Some of you lay down on the floor here with your faces jest as clost to the door as you can. Now some more of you kneel jest above. Now above them some of you bend, while the rest stand up. Pack that door full of gun muzzles while I watch things outside." The men did as he directed, and he was silent for a while. Then he spoke again softly: "Now they're comin'. When I say 'Ready!' open the door, and as soon as a flash of lightning shows you where they are, let them have it."

They waited breathlessly.

"Now, ready!"

The door was opened, and a moment thereafter the glare of the lightning was followed by another flash from the doorway. Groans, shrieks, and curses rang out as the assailants scampered helter-skelter back to their friendly rocks, leaving more of their dead upon the ground behind them.

"That was it," said Sam. "That will keep them in check for a while. If we can hold 'em off until daybreak, we are safe."

The strikers were now angry and sore and wet through. Some of them were wounded. "Red" Cleary himself had a bullet through his shoulder. But his spirits were not daunted, although six of his men lay dead upon the ground. A long consultation followed the last unsuccessful assault. At last Cleary said: "Well, it won't do any good to stand here talkin'. It's gettin' late, an' if we don't drive 'em out to-night, it's all up with us an' we'd jest as well be lookin' out fur other diggin's. We've got to crawl up as near as we can an' then rush 'em. It's the only way, an' what we ought to done at first. Get down on your knees. Never mind the mud—better have it under you than over you." The men sank down, and went creeping forward like a swarm of great ponderous vermin. They had not gone ten paces when some one said, "Tsch! what is that?" They stopped where they were. A sound came to their ears. It was the laboured puffing of a locomotive as it tugged up the incline that led to the settlement. Then it stopped. Within the room they had heard it, too, and there was as great suspense as without.

With his ear close to the ground, "Red" Cleary heard the tramp of marching men, and he shook with fear. His fright was communicated to the others, and with one accord they began creeping back to their hiding-places. Then, with a note that was like the voice of God to the besieged, through the thunder and rain, a fife took up the strains of "Yankee Doodle" accompanied by the tum-tum of a sodden drum. This time a cheer went up from within the room,—a cheer that directed the steps of the oncoming militia.

"It's all up!" cried Cleary, and, emptying his pistol at the wood fort, he turned and fled. His comrades followed suit. A bullet pierced Sam Bowles's wrist. But he did not mind it. He was delirious with joy. The militia advanced and the siege was lifted. Out into the storm rushed the happy blacks to welcome and help quarter their saviours. Some of the Negroes were wounded, and one dead, killed at the first fire. Tired as the men were, they could not sleep, and morning found them still about their fires talking over the night's events. It found also many of the strikers missing besides those who lay stark on the hillside.

For the next few days the militia took charge of affairs. Some of the strikers availed themselves of the Croftons' clemency, and went back to work along with the blacks; others moved away.

When Jason Andrews was well enough to be moved, he came back. The Croftons had already told of his heroism, and he was the admiration of white and black alike. He has general charge now of all the Crofton mines, and his assistant and stanch friend is big Sam.

The Deliberation of Mr. Dunkin

MILTONVILLE HAD JUST risen to the dignity of being a school town. Now, to the uninitiated and unconcerned reader this may appear to be the most unimportant statement in the world; but one who knows Miltonville, and realises all the facts in the case, will see that the simple remark is really fraught with mighty import.

When for two years a growing village has had to crush its municipal pride and send its knowledge-seeking youth to a rival town two miles away, when that rival has boasted and vaunted its superiority, when a listless school-board has been un-successfully prodded, month after month, then the final decision in favour of the institution and the renting of a room in which to establish it is no small matter. And now Fox Run, with its most plebeian name but arrogantly aristocratic community, could no longer look down upon Miltonville.

The coloured population of this town was sufficiently large and influential to merit their having a member on the school-board. But Mr. Dunkin, the incumbent, had found no employment for his energies until within the last two months, when he had suddenly entered the school fight with unwonted zest. Now it was an assured thing, and on Monday Miss Callena Johnson was to start the fountain of knowledge a-going. This in itself was enough to set the community in a commotion.

Much had been heard of Miss Callena before she had been selected as the guiding genius of the new venture. She had even visited Fox Run, which prided itself greatly on the event. Flattering rumours were afloat in regard to her beauty and brilliancy. She was from Lexington. What further recommendation as to her personal charms did she need? She was to come in on Saturday evening, and as the railroad had not deigned to come nearer to Miltonville than Fox Run station,—another thorn in the side of the Miltonvillians,—Mr. Dunkin, as the important official in the affair, was delegated to go and bring the fair one into her kingdom.

Now, Mr. Dunkin was a man of deliberation. He prided himself upon that. He did nothing in a hurry. Nothing came from him without due forethought. So, in this case, before going for Miss Callena, he visited Mr. Alonzo Taft. Who was Mr. Taft? Of course you have never been to Miltonville or you would never have asked that question. Mr. Alonzo Taft was valet to Major Richardson, who lived in the great house on the hill overlooking the town. He not only held this distinguished position in that aristocratic household, but he was the black beau ideal and social mentor for all the town.

Him, then, did Mr. Dunkin seek, and delivered himself as follows: "Mistah Taf', you reco'nise de dooty dat is laid upon me by bein' a membah of de school-boa'd. I has got to go to de depot aftah Miss Callena Johnson to-morrow aftah-noon. Now, Mistah Taf', I is a delibut man myse'f. I is mighty keerful what I does an' how I does it. As you know, I ain't no man fu' society, an' conserkently I is not convusant wid some of de manipulations of comp'ny. So I t'ought I'd come an' ax yo' advice about sev'al t'ings,—what to waih, an' which side o' de wagon to have Miss Callena on, an' how to he'p huh in, an' so fofe."

"Why, of co'se, Mr Dunkin," said the elegant Alonzo, "I shell be happy to administah any instructions to you dat lies within my powah."

Mr. Taft was a perfect second edition of Major Richardson bound in black hide.

"But," he went on in a tone of dignified banter, "we shell have to keep a eye on you prosp'ous bachelors. You may be castin' sheep-eyes at Miss Callena."

"Dat 'u'd be mo' nachul an' fittener in a young man lak you," said Mr. Dunkin, deliberately.

"Oh, I has been located in my affections too long to lif' anchor now."

"You don' say," said the "prosp'ous bachelor," casting a quick glance at the speaker.

"Yes, indeed, suh."

So they chatted on, and in the course of time the deliberate Dunkin got such information as he wished, and departed in the happy consciousness that on the morrow he should do the proper and only the proper thing.

After he was gone, Alonzo Taft rubbed his chin and mused: "I wonder what ol' man Dunkin's got in his head. Dey say he's too slow an' thinks too long evah to git married. But you watch dem thinkin' people when dey do make up deir minds."

On the morrow, when Mr. Dunkin went forth, he outshone Solomon in all his glory. When he came back, the eyes of all the town saw Miss Callena Johnson, beribboned and smiling, sitting on his right and chatting away vivaciously. As to her looks, the half had not been told. As to her manners, those smiles and head-tossings gave promise of unheard-of graces, and the hearts of all Miltonville throbbed as one.

Alonzo Taft was lounging carelessly on the corner as the teacher and her escort passed along. He raised his hat to them with that sweeping, graceful gesture which was known to but two men in that vicinity, himself and Major Richardson.

After some hesitation as to which hand should retain the reins, Mr. Dunkin returned the salute.

The next day being Sunday, and universal calling-day in Miltonville, Eli Thompson's house, where Miss Callena had taken up her abode, was filled with guests. All the beaux in town were there, resplendent in their Sunday best. Many a damsel sat alone that afternoon whose front room no Sunday before had seen untenanted. Mr. Taft was there, and also one who came early and stayed late,— Mr. Dunkin. The younger men thought that he was rather overplaying his rôle of school trustee. He was entirely too conscientious as to his duty to Miss Callena. What the young beaux wanted to know was whether it was entirely in his official position that he sat so long with Miss Callena that first Sabbath.

On Monday morning the school opened with great *éclat*. There were exercises. The trustee was called upon to make a speech, and, as speechmaking is the birthright of his race, acquitted himself with credit. The teacher was seen to smile at him as he sat down.

Now, under ordinary circumstances a smile is a small thing. It is given, taken, and forgotten all in a moment. At other times it is the keynote to the tragedy or comedy of a life. Miss Callena's smile was like an electric spark setting fire to a whole train of combustibles. Those who saw it marvelled and told their neighbours, and their neighbours asked them what it meant. Before night, that smile and all the import it might carry was the town's talk.

Alonzo Taft had seen it. Unlike the others, he said nothing to his neighbours. He questioned himself only. To him that smile meant familiarity, good-fellowship, and a thorough mutual understanding. He looked into the dark, dancing eyes of Miss Callena, and in spite of his statement of a few days ago that he had been located too long to "lif' anchor," he felt a pang at his heart that was like the first stab of jealousy. So he was deeply interested that evening when Maria, his fellow-servant, told him that Mr. Dunkin was waiting to see him. He hurried through with his work, even leaving a speck of lint on the major's coat,—an unprecedented thing, —and hastened down to his guest.

A look of great seriousness and determination was fixed upon the features of the "prosp'ous bachelor" as his host made his appearance and invited him up to his room.

Mr. Dunkin was well seated and had his pipe going before he began: "Mistah Taf', I allus has 'lowed dat you was a sensible young man an' a pu'son of mo' dan o'dina'y intel'gence."

"You flattah me, Mistah Dunkin, you flattah me, suh."

"Now I's a man, Mistah Taf', dat don't do nuffin' in a hu'y. I don' mek up my min' quick 'bout myse'f ner 'bout othah people. But when my min' is made up, it's made up. Now I come up hyeah to cornfide in you 'bout somep'n'. I was mighty glad to hyeah you say de othah day dat yo' 'fections was done sot an' located, because hit meks me free to talk to you 'bout a mattah, seein' dat hit's a mattah of my own 'fections."

"This is ve'y int'rustin', Mistah Dunkin; go on."

"I's a-cornfidin' in you because you is a young man of presentment an' knows jes' how to pu'sue a co'se of cou'tin'. I unnerstan' dat you is ingaged to Miss Marfy Madison."

Mr. Taft smiled with a sudden accession of modesty, either real or assumed.

"Now, I ain't nevah had no experunce in cou'tin' ladies, because I nevah 'spected to ma'y. But hit's nachul dat a man should change his min', Mistah Taf', 'specially 'bout sich a mattah as matermony."

"Nothin' mo' nachul in de world."

"So, when I seed dat it was pos'ble to bring sich a young lady as I hyeahed Miss Callena Johnson was, to Miltonville, by jes' havin' a school, I wo'ks to have de school."

"Oh, dat's de reason you commence to tek sich a int'rus', huh!" The expression slipped from Alonzo's lips.

"Don' narrow me down, Mistah Taf', don' narrow me down! Dat was one o' de reasons. Howsomevah, we has de school an' Miss Callena is hyeah. So fa' my wo'k is good. But I 'low dat no man dat ain't experunced in cou'tin' ort to tek de 'sponsibility alone."

"Of co'se not!" said Alonzo.

"So I t'ought I'd ax you to he'p me by drappin' roun' to Miss Callena's 'casionally an' puttin' in a word fu' me. I unnerstan' dat women-folks laks to hyeah 'bout de man dat's cou'tin' dem, f'om de outside. Now, you kin be of gret suhvice to me, an' you won't lose nothin' by it. Jes' manage to let Miss Callena know 'bout my propity, an' 'bout my hogs an' my hosses an' my chickens, an' dat I's buyin' mo' lan'. Drap it kind o' delikit lak. Don' mention my name too often. Will you he'p me out dat-away?"

"W'y, co'se I will, Mr. Dunkin. It'll gi' me gret pleasuah to he'p you in dis way, an' I'll be jes' as delikit as anybody kin."

"Dat's right; dat's right."

"I won't mention yo' name too much."

"Dat's right."

"I'll jes' hint an' hint an' hint."

"Dat's right. You jes' got it right ezactly, an' you sha'n't lose nothin' by it, I tell you."

The "prosp'ous bachelor" rose in great elation, and shook Mr. Taft's hand vigorously as he departed.

"Miss Marfy, Miss Callena: Miss Callena, Miss Marfy," repeated Mr. Taft, as he stood musing after his visitor had gone.

It may have been zeal in the cause of his good friend, or it may have been some very natural desire for appreciation of his own merits, that prompted Alonzo Taft to dress with such extreme care for his visit to Miss Callena Johnson on the next night. He did explain his haste to make the call by telling himself that if he was going to do anything for Mr. Dunkin he had better be about it. But this anxiety on his protégé's account did not explain why he put on his fawn-coloured waistcoat, which he had never once worn when visiting Miss Martha, nor why he needed to be so extraordinarily long in tying his bow tie. His beaver was rubbed and caressed until it shone again. Major Richardson himself had not looked better in that blue Prince Albert coat, when it was a year newer. Thus arrayed, stepping manfully and twirling a tiny cane, did the redoubtable Mr. Taft set out for the conquest of Miss Callena Johnson. It is just possible that it was Alonzo's absorption in his own magnificence that made him forgetfully walk down the very street on which Miss Martha Madison's cottage was situated. Miss Martha was at the gate. He looked up and saw her, but too late to retreat.

"La! Mistah Taf'," said Miss Martha, smiling as she opened the gate for him. "I wasn't expectin' you dis evenin'. Walk right in."

"I—I—I—thank you, Miss Marfy, thank you," replied the dark beau, a bit confused but stepping through the gateway. "It's a mighty fine evenin' we're havin'."

"I don't wunner you taken yo'se'f out fu' a walk. I was thinkin' 'bout goin' out myse'f ontwell I seen you comin' along. You mus' 'a' been mighty tuk up wif de weathah, 'cause you hahdly knowed when you got to de gate. I thought you was a-goin' to pass on by."

"Oh, I couldn't pass dis gate. I'm so used to comin' hyeah dat I reckon my feet 'u'd jes' tu'n up de walk of dey own accord."

"Dey didn't tu'n up dat walk much Sunday. Whaih was you all day aftah mo'nin' chu'ch? I 'spected you up in de aft'noon."

"I—I—would 'a' been"—Mr. Taft was beginning to writhe upon his chair— "but I had to go out to mek some calls."

"Oh, yes" retorted Miss Martha, good-naturedly, "I reckon you was one o' dem gent'mans dat was settin' up at de schoolteachah's house."

" I fu' one was callin' on Miss Callena. Hit's only propah when a strange lady come to town fu' de gent'men to call an' pay deir 'spects."

"I reckon hit ain't propah fu' de gent'mans to tek none o' de ladies to call."

"I ain't 'scussin' dat," said Mr Taft, with some acerbity.

"Of co'se you ain't. Well, hit ain't none o' my bus'ness, to be sho. I ain't thinkin' nothin' 'bout myse'f or none o' de things you been sayin' to me. But all I got to say is, you bettah leave Miss Callena, as you call huh, alone, 'cause evah-body say ol' man Dunkin got his eyes sot on huh, an' he gwine to win. Dey do say, too, dat he outsot you all, Sunday."

Nothing could have hurt Alonzo Taft's pride more than this, or more thoroughly aroused his dignity.

"Ef I wanted Miss Callena Johnson," he said, "I wouldn't stan' back fu' nobody like ol' man Dunkin."

"I reckon you wouldn't, but you might set in an' git jes' nachully sot back;" and Martha laughed maliciously.

"I ain't boastin' 'bout what I could do ef I had a min' to, but I 'low ef I wan'ed to set my cap fu' any young lady, I wouldn't be feared o' no ol' man dat don't know nothin' but hogs an' chickens."

"Nevah min'! Dem hogs an' chickens fetches money, an' dat's what yo' fine city ladies wants, an' don't you fu'git it."

"Money ain't a-gwine to mek no ol' man young."

"De ol' man wa'n't too ol' to outset you all young men anyhow."

"Dey's somep'n' mo' to cou'tin' 'sides settin'."

"Yes, but a long set an' a long pocket is mighty big evidence."

"I don't keer ef it is. Wha—what's de use of argyin'? I do' want Miss Callena nohow—I do' want huh."

"You stahted de argyment; I didn't staht it. You ain't goin', is you?"

"I got to go," said Alonzo, with his hand on the door-knob; "I done ovah-stayed my time now."

"Whaih you gwine to?"

"I—I—oh, I'm goin' down de street. Don' ax whaih I'm a-goin' to, Miss Marfy; it ain't good raisin'."

"I unnerstan' you, 'Lonzo Taf'. I unnerstood you when you fus' come in, all rigged out in yo' fines' clothes. You did 'n' 'low to stop hyeah nohow. You gwine down to see dat teachah, dat's whaih you gwine."

"Well, s'posin' I am, s'posin' I am?"

"Well, s'posin' you is," repeated Miss Martha. "Why, go on. But I hope you won't run acrost ol' man Dunkin ag'in an' git outsot."

"I ain't afeard o' runnin' acrost ol' man Dunkin," said Alonzo, as he went out; and he smiled an inscrutable smile.

Martha watched him as he went down the street and faded into the darkness. Then she went in and locked her door.

"I don't keer," she said to herself, " I don't keer a bit. Ef he wants huh, he kin go 'long an' git huh. I 'low she'll be glad enough to have him. I ain't gwine to try an' hol' him a bit." Then, to fortify her resolution, she buried her face in her apron and sobbed out the fulness of her heart.

Mr. Taft's good-humour and gallantry came back to him as he knocked at Eli Thompson's door and asked for the teacher. Yes, she was in, and came smiling into the front room to see him. He carefully picked his phrases of greeting, shook her hand gently, and hoped that she was enjoying good health.

Alonzo rather prided himself on the elegance of his conversation. His mind rebelled against the idea of having to talk hogs to this divine creature, and for some one else besides.

"Reely, Miss Callena, I do' know as de gent'men ought to bothah you by callin' 'roun' in de evenin'. Haid wo'k is so hahd dat aftah yo' dooties endurin' de day you mus' be mos' nigh wo' out when night comes."

"Oh, I assure you you are wrong, Mr Taft. I am not very tired, and if I were there is nothing that rests the mind like agreeable company." And oh, the ravishing smile as she said this! Alonzo felt his head going.

"I don't reckon even agreeable company 'u'd res' me aftah lahourin' wif some o' de childern you've got in yo' school; I knows 'em."

"Well, it's true they're not all of them saints."

"No, indeed, they're not saints. I don't see how a slendah, delikit lady like yo'se'f kin manage 'em, 'less 'n you jes' 'spire 'em wif respect."

"I can see already," she answered, "that it is going to take something more than inspiration to manage the rising generation of Miltonville."

Here was Alonzo's opportunity. He cast his eyes romantically toward the ceiling.

"I c'nfess," he said, "dat I am one o' dem dat believes dat yo' sex ought to be mo' fu' o'nament. You ought to have de strong ahms of a man to pertect you an' manage fu' you."

If that was a twinkle which for an instant lightened the dark eyes of Miss Callena, Mr. Taft did not see it, for his own orbs were still feelingly contemplating the ceiling.

"Ah, yes," sighed the teacher, "the strong arms of man would save poor woman a great deal; but it is always the same difficulty, to find them both strong and willing."

"Oh, I know ef you was de lady in question, dey'd be plenty dat was willin' right hyeah in dis town." Alonzo went on impetuously, "Men dat owns houses an' lan' an' hosses an' hogs, even dey'd be willin' ef it was you."

Miss Callena's eyes were discreetly cast down.

"Oh, you flatter me, Mr. Taft."

"Flattah you! No, ma'am. You don't know lak I do. You have sholy brought new life into dis hyeah town, an' all Miltonville'll tek off its hat to you. Dat's de way we feel to'ds you."

"I am sure I appreciate these kind words of yours, and I hope that I shall he able to keep the good opinion of Miltonville."

"Jes' as Miltonville hopes dat it may be pu'mitted to keep you," said Alonzo, gallantly. And so the conversation went along merrily.

It was after ten o'clock before the enamoured caller could tear himself away from the soft glance and musical voice of the teacher. Then he told her: "Miss Callena, I sholy have injoyed dis evenin'. It has been one of de most unctious in all my life. I shell nevah fu'git it so long as I am pu'mitted to remain on dis earth."

In return, she said that the pleasure had been mutual, and it had been so kind of him to come in and take her mind off the cares of the day, and she did so hope that he would call again.

Would he call again! Could he stay away?

He went away walking on air. The beaver was tilted far back on his head, and the cane was more furiously twirled. The blue Prince Albert was thrown wide, showing the fawn-coloured waistcoat in all its glory.

"Miss Callena, Miss Marfy, Mr. Dunkin an' me!" said Mr. Taft; and he chuckled softly to himself. Then he added: "Well, I did speak 'bout de hosses an' de hogs an' de lan', didn't I; well, what mo' could I do? Of co'se, I didn't say whose dey was; but he didn't want me to mention no names—jes' to hint, an' I did hint. Nobody couldn't ask no mo' dan dat."

Thus does that duplicity which is resident in the hearts of men seek to deceive even itself, making shining virtues of its shadiest acts.

In the days that ensued, Alonzo availed himself of Miss Callena's invitation to call, and went often. If he was trying or had succeeded in deceiving himself as to his feelings, in the minds of two sagacious women there was yet no doubt about his intentions. The clear eyes of the teacher could do something besides sparkle; they could see. And she wondered and smiled at the beau's veiled wooing. From the first gorgeous moment of the fawn-coloured waistcoat and the blue Prince Albert, the other woman, Martha, had seen through her recreant lover as by inspiration. She constantly brooded over his infidelity. He had entirely deserted her now, not even making any pretence of caring what she thought of him. For a while the girl went stolidly about her own business, and tried to keep her mind from dwelling on him. But his elegance and grace would come back to her with the memory of their pleasant days of courtship, and fill her heart with sorrow. Did she care for him still? Of course she did. The admission hurt her pride, but fostered in her a strong determination. If she did love him and had dared to confess so much to herself, she had already reached the lowest depths of humiliations. It could be no worse to make an effort to retain her lover. This resolution gave her warrant to accost Mr. Dunkin the next time she saw him pass the house.

"Howdy, Mistah Dunkin?—how you come on?"

"Jes' tol'able, Miss Marfy. How's yo'se'f?"

"Mode't', thanky, jes' mode't'. How de school-house come on?"

"Oh, hit's p'ogressin' mos' salub'ious, thanky, ma'am."

"I would ax you how de teachah, but hit do seem dat Mistah Taf' done beat yo' time so claih dat you wouldn't know nothin' 'bout it."

"Haw, haw, Miss Marfy, you shuly is de beatenes' one to have yo' joke."

"I 'claih to goodness, Mistah Dunkin, I's s'prised at a man o' yo' position lettin' Mistah Taf' git de bes' of him dat way."

"Nemmine, Miss Marfy, I 'low dat young man o' yo'n done let out my secut, but you cain't rig me 'bout hit."

"I don't unnerstan' you. What young man, an' what secut?"

"Oh, I reckon you an' Mistah Taf' 'll soon be man an' wife, an' hit ain't no hahm fu' de wife to know what de husban' know."

"I do' know huccome you say dat; Mistah Taf' don' have nothin' to say to me; he cou'tin' Miss Callena Johnson."

"Don' have nothin' to say to you! Cou'tin Miss Callena!"

"Dat's de reason I wants to know huccome you back out."

"Back out! Who back out? Me back out? I ain't nevah backed out: Mistah Taf' foolin' you."

"'T ain' me he's a-foolin'. He may be foolin' some folks, but hit ain't Marfy Jane Madison. La, Mistah Dunkin, I knows colo'ed folks, I kin shet my eyes an' put my han's on 'em in de da'k. Co'se hit ain't none o' my business, but I know he ain't puttin' on his bes' clothes, an' gwine to see dat teachah th'ee times a week, 'less 'n he got notions in his haid. 'T ain't in human natur, leastways not colo'ed human natur as I knows it. 'T ain' me he's a-foolin'."

"Do he put on his best clothes an' go th'ee times a week?"

"Dat he do, an' ca'ies huh flowahs f'om ol' Major Richardson's pusservatory besides, an' you ain't makin' a move."

"Ain't Mistah Taf' nevah tol' you nothin'?"

"Tol' me nothin'! No, suhree. What he got to tell me?"

"Uh huh!" said Mr. Dunkin, thoughtfully. "Well, good-night, Miss Marfy. I's glad I seed you; but I mus' be gittin' along. I got to delibe'ate ovah dis question."

"Oh, yes; you go on an delibe'ate, dat's right, an' while you delibe'atin', Mistah Taf' he walk off wid de lady. But 't ain't none o' my business, 't ain't none o' my business."

Mr. Dunkin deliberated as he walked down the street. Could there be any truth in Martha Madison's surmises? He had talked with Alonzo only the day before, and been assured that everything was going right. Could it be that his lieutenant was playing him false? Some suspicious circumstances now occurred to his mind. When he had spoken of going himself to see Miss Callena, he remembered now how Alonzo had insisted that he had matters in such a state that the interference of Mr. Dunkin just at that point would spoil everything. It looked dark. His steps were taking him toward Major Richardson's. He heard a footstep, and who should be coming toward him, arrayed even as Martha Madison had said, but the subject of his cogitations? Mr. Dunkin thought he saw Alonzo start as their eyes met. He had a bouquet in his hand.

"Hey ho, 'Lonzo. Gwine down to Miss Callena's?"

"Why—why—ye'—yes. I jes' thought I would walk down that way in yo' int'rus'."

"My! but you sholy has got yo'se'f up fit to kill."

"When de genul sen's his messengers out to negoterate, dey mus' go in full unifo'm, so's to impress de people dat dey genul is somebody."

"Jesso," assented the elder man, "but I don't want you to be waihin' out yo' clothes in my suhvice, 'Lonzo."

"Oh, dat's all right, Mistah Dunkin; hit's a pleasuah, I assuah you."

"How's things comin' on, anyhow, down to Miss Callena's?"

"Couldn't be bettah, suh; dey's most puspicious. Hit'll soon be time fu' you to come in an' tek mattahs in yo' own han's."

"Do you tell Miss Callena 'bout de houses an' lan'?"

"Oh, yes; I tells huh all about dat."

"What she say?"

"Oh, she jes' smiles."

"I reckon you tol' huh 'bout de hogs an' de chickens an' de hosses?"

"Yes, indeed, I sholy done dat."

"What she do den?"

"She jes' smiled."

"Did you th'ow out a hint 'bout me buyin' mo' lan'?"

"Why, co'se I wa' n't go'n' to leave dat paht out."

"Well, den, what did she say?"

"She smiled ag'in."

"Huh! she mus' be a gone smiler. 'Pears to me, 'Lonzo, 'bout time she *sayin'* somep'n'."

"Oh, she smile 'cause she kin do dat so purty, dat's de reason she smile."

"Uh huh! Well, go 'long, I mus' be gittin' home."

Alonzo Taft smiled complacently as he passed on. "Yes," he said to himself, "it'll soon be time fu' Mistah Dunkin to come in an' tek mattahs in his own han's. It'll soon be time."

He had lost all scruples at his course, and ceased self-questioning.

Mr. Dunkin gave no sign of perturbation of mind as he walked down the street to his cottage. He walked neither faster nor slower than he had gone before seeing Martha Madison. But when he sank down into the depths of his arm-chair in the privacy of his own apartment, he said: "Miss Marfy say dat while I delibe'atin' Mistah Taf' walk off wif de lady. Huh uh! Well, I jes' delibe'ate a little mo' while I's a-changin' my clothes."

Who shall tell of the charms which Miss Callena displayed that night,—how her teeth gleamed and her eyes sparkled and her voice was alternately merry or melting? It is small wonder that the heart of Alonzo Taft throbbed, and that words of love rushed to his lips and burst into speech. But even then some lingering sense of loyalty made his expressions vague and ambiguous. There was the sea before him, but he hated, nay, feared to plunge in. Miss Callena watched him as he dallied upon the shore of an open declaration, and admired a timidity so rare in a man of Taft's attainments.

"I know you boun' to look down on me, Miss Callena," he said, with subdued ardour, "'cause I'm a ign'ant man. I ain't had no ejication nor no schoolin'. I'm jes' a se'f-made man. All I know I've lunned f'om de white folks I've wo'ked fu'."

"It isn't always education that makes the man, Mr. Taft," said the school-teacher, encouragingly. "I've seen a great many men in my life who had all the education and schooling that heart could wish, but when that was said, all was said. They hadn't anything here." She pressed her hand feelingly and impressively upon her heart. "It's the noble heart, after all, that makes the real man."

Mr. Taft also pressed his hand against his heart and sighed. They were both so absorbed that neither of them saw the shadow that fell on the floor from a form that stood in the doorway.

"As for being self-made," Miss Callena went on, "why, Mr. Taft, what can be nobler or better for a man to know than that all he has he has got by his own efforts?"

The shadow disappeared, and the form receded from the doorway as the suitor was saying: "I tek no credit to myse'f fu' what I've got, neither in sense or money. But I am glad to say dat I wo'ked fu' everything myse'f."

"You have reason to be proud of such a fact."

They were visibly warming up. Alonzo moved his chair a little nearer, and possessed himself of Miss Callena's hand. She did not draw it away nor repulse him. She even hung her head. Yes, the proud, educated, queenly Callena Johnson hung her head. Meanwhile, in the darkness of the doorway the form stood and glowered upon them.

"Miss Callena, at a time like dis, I hates to talk to you about de o'dina'y things of life, but when anything se'ious arises, it is allus well fu' de pahties to know each othah's circumstances."

"You are a very sensible man, Mr. Taft."

"Call me 'Lonzo," he murmured, patting her hand. "But, as I was going to say, it's necessary dat you should know de circumstances of anybody who wanted to ax fu' dis han' dat I'm a-holdin'."

Miss Callena turned her head away and was silent. In fact, she held her breath.

"Miss Johnson—Callena—what 'u'd you think of a nice cottage wif no encumbrances on it, a couple o' nice hosses, a cow an' ha'f a dozen of de fines' hogs in Miltonville—"

"An' all o' dem mine!" thundered the voice of the form, striding into the middle of the room.

Miss Callena shrieked. Alonzo had been about falling on his knees, but he assumed an erect position with an alacrity that would have done credit to a gymnast.

"Co'se, of co'se, Mistah Dunkin! I was jes' a-comin' to dat!"

"I jes' come down fu' feah you'd fu'git to tell Miss Callena who all dem things 'longed to, an' who's a-layin' dem at huh feet," said Mr. Dunkin.

"I 'low Miss Callena unnerstan' dat," said Mr. Taft, bobbing his head sheepishly.

"I don't remember that Mr. Taft explained this before," said Miss Johnson, turning coldly from him. "Do have a seat, dear Mr. Dunkin."

Alonzo saw with grief that the idol of his heart had transferred her affectionate smiles to the rightful owner of the other property that had been in question. He made his stay short, leaving Mr. Dunkin in undisputed possession of the field.

That gentleman took no further time for deliberation. He promptly proposed and was accepted. Perhaps even the romantic Miss Callena had an eye to the main chance.

The day after the announcement of the engagement, he met his erstwhile lieutenant on the street.

"Well, well, Mistah Dunkin, we winned huh, didn't we?" said Alonzo.

"'Lonzo Taf'," said Mr. Dunkin, deliberately, "I fu'give you, but you ain't de man I teken you to be."

The Strength of Gideon
and Other Stories

The Strength of Gideon

OLD MAM' HENRY, and her word may be taken, said that it was "De powerfulles' sehmont she ever had hyeahd in all huh bo'n days." That was saying a good deal, for the old woman had lived many years on the Stone place and had heard many sermons from preachers, white and black. She was a judge, too.

It really must have been a powerful sermon that Brother Lucius preached, for Aunt Doshy Scott had fallen in a trance in the middle of the aisle, while "Merlatter Mag," who was famed all over the place for having white folk's religion and never "waking up," had broken through her reserve and shouted all over the camp ground.

Several times Cassie had shown signs of giving way, but because she was frail some of the solicitous sisters held her with self-congratulatory care, relieving each other now and then, that each might have a turn in the rejoicings. But as the preacher waded out deeper and deeper into the spiritual stream, Cassie's efforts to make her feelings known became more and more decided. He told them how the spears of the Midianites had "clashed upon de shiels of de Gideonites, an' aftah while, wid de powah of de Lawd behin' him, de man Gideon triumphed mightily," and swaying then and wailing in the dark woods, with grim branches waving in the breath of their own excitement, they could hear above the tumult the clamor of the fight, the clashing of the spears, and the ringing of the shields. They could see the conqueror coming home in triumph. Then when he cried, "A-who, I say, a-who is in Gideon's ahmy to-day?" and the wailing chorus took up the note, "A-who!" it was too much even for frail Cassie, and, deserted by the so-licitous sisters, in the words of Mam' Henry, "she broke a-loose, and faihly tuk de place."

Gideon had certainly triumphed, and when a little boy baby came to Cassie two or three days later, she named him Gideon in honor of the great Hebrew war-rior whose story had so wrought upon her. All the plantation knew the spiritual significance of the name, and from the day of his birth the child was as one set apart to a holy mission on earth.

86

Say what you will of the influences which the circumstances surrounding birth have upon a child, upon this one at least the effect was un-mistakable. Even as a baby he seemed to realize the weight of responsibility which had been laid upon his little black shoulders, and there was a complacent dignity in the very way in which he drew upon the sweets of his dirty sugar-teat when the maternal breast was far off bending over the sheaves of the field.

He was a child early destined to sacrifice and self-effacement, and as he grew older and other youngsters came to fill Cassie's cabin, he took up his lot with the meekness of an infantile Moses. Like a Moses he was, too, leading his little flock to the promised land, when he grew to the age at which, barefooted and one-shifted, he led or carried his little brothers and sisters about the quarters. But the "promised land" never took him into the direction of the stables, where the other picaninnies worried the horses, or into the region of the hen-coops, where egg-sucking was a common crime.

No boy ever rolled or tumbled in the dirt with a heartier glee than did Gideon, but no warrior, not even his illustrious prototype himself, ever kept sterner discipline in his ranks when his followers seemed prone to overstep the bounds of right. At a very early age his shrill voice could be heard calling in admonitory tones, caught from his mother's very lips, "You 'Nelius, don' you let me ketch you th'owin' at ol' mis' guinea-hens no mo'; you hyeah me?" or "Hi'am, you come offen de top er dat shed 'fo' you fall an' brek yo' naik all to pieces."

It was a common sight in the evening to see him sitting upon the low rail fence which ran before the quarters, his shift blowing in the wind, and his black legs lean and bony against the whitewashed rails, as he swayed to and fro, rocking and singing one of his numerous brothers to sleep, and always his song was of war and victory, albeit crooned in a low, soothing voice. Sometimes it was "Turn Back Pharaoh's Army," at others "Jinin' Gideon's Band." The latter was a favorite, for he seemed to have a proprietary interest in it, although, despite the martial inspiration of his name, "Gideon's band" to him meant an aggregation of people with horns and fiddles.

Steve, who was Cassie's man, declared that he had never seen such a child, and, being quite as religious as Cassie herself, early began to talk Scripture and religion to the boy. He was aided in this when his master, Dudley Stone, a man of the faith, began a little Sunday class for the religiously inclined of the quarters, where the old familiar stories were told in simple language to the slaves and explained. At these meetings Gideon became a shining light. No one listened more eagerly to the teacher's words, or more readily answered his questions at review. No one was wider-mouthed or whiter-eyed. His admonitions to his family now took on a different complexion, and he could be heard calling across a lot to a mischievous sister, "Bettah tek keer daih, Lucy Jane, Gawd's a-watchin' you; bettah tek keer."

The appointed man is always marked, and so Gideon was by always receiving his full name. No one ever shortened his scriptural appellation into Gid. He was always Gideon from the time he bore the name out of the heat of camp-meeting fervor until his master discovered his worthiness and filled Cassie's breast with pride by taking him into the house to learn "mannahs and 'po'tment."

As a house servant he was beyond reproach, and next to his religion his Mas' Dudley and Miss Ellen claimed his devotion and fidelity. The young mistress and young master learned to depend fearlessly upon his faithfulness.

It was good to hear old Dudley Stone going through the house in a mock fury, crying, "Well, I never saw such a house; it seems as if there isn't a soul in it that can do without Gideon. Here I've got him up here to wait on me, and it's Gideon here and Gideon there, and every time I turn around some of you have sneaked him off. Gideon, come here!" And the black boy smiled and came.

But all his days were not days devoted to men's service, for there came a time when love claimed him for her own, when the clouds took on a new color, when the sough of the wind was music in his ears, and he saw heaven in Martha's eyes. It all came about in this way.

Gideon was young when he got religion and joined the church, and he grew up strong in the faith. Almost by the time he had become a valuable house servant he had grown to be an invaluable servant of the Lord. He had a good, clear voice that could lead a hymn out of all the labyrinthian wanderings of an ignorant congregation, even when he had to improvise both words and music; and he was a mighty man of prayer. It was thus he met Martha. Martha was brown and buxom and comely, and her rich contralto voice was loud and high on the sisters' side in meeting time. It was the voices that did it at first. There was no hymn or "spiritual" that Gideon could start to which Martha could not sing an easy blending second, and never did she open a tune that Gideon did not swing into it with a wonderfully sweet, flowing, natural bass. Often he did not know the piece, but that did not matter, he sang anyway. Perhaps when they were out he would go to her and ask, "Sis' Martha, what was that hymn you stahrted to-day?" and she would probably answer, "Oh, dat was jes' one o' my mammy's ol' songs."

"Well, it sholy was mighty pretty. Indeed it was."

"Oh, thanky, Brothah Gidjon, thanky."

Then a little later they began to walk back to the master's house together, for Martha, too, was one of the favored ones, and served, not in the field, but in the big house.

The old women looked on and conversed in whispers about the pair, for they were wise, and what their old eyes saw, they saw.

"Oomph," said Mam' Henry, for she commented on everything, "dem too is jes' natchelly singin' demse'ves togeddah."

"Dey's lak de mo'nin' stahs," interjected Aunt Sophy.

"How 'bout dat?" sniffed the older woman, for she objected to any one's alluding to subjects she did not understand.

"Why, Mam' Henry, ain' you nevah hyeahd tell o' de mo'nin' stahs whut sung deyse'ves togeddah?"

"No, I ain't, an' I been livin' a mighty sight longah'n you, too. I knows all 'bout when de stahs fell, but dey ain' nevah done no singin' dat I knows 'bout."

"Do heish, Mam' Henry, you sho' su'prises me. W'y, dat ain' happenin's, dat's Scripter."

"Look hyeah, gal, don't you tell me dat's Scripter, an' me been a-settin' undah de Scripter fu' nigh onto sixty yeah."

"Well, Mam' Henry, I may 'a' been mistook, but sho' I took hit fu' Scripter. Mebbe de preachah I hyeahd was jes' inlinin'."

"Well, wheddah hit's Scripter er not, dey's one t'ing su'tain, I tell you,—dem two is singin' deyse'ves togeddah."

"Hit's a fac', an' I believe it."

"An' it's a mighty good thing, too. Brothah Gidjon is de nicest house dahky dat I ever hyeahd tell on. Dey jes' de same diffunce 'twixt him an' de othah house-boys as dey is 'tween real quality an' strainers—he got mannahs, but he ain't got aihs."

"Heish, ain't you right!"

"An' while de res' of dem ain' thinkin' 'bout nothin' but dancin' an' ca'in' on, he makin' his peace, callin', an' 'lection sho'."

"I tell you, Mam' Henry, dey ain' nothin' like a spichul named chile."

"Humph! g'long, gal; 'tain't in de name; de biggest devil I evah knowed was named Moses Aaron. 'Tain't in de name, hit's all in de man hisse'f."

But notwithstanding what the gossips said of him, Gideon went on his way, and knew not that the one great power of earth had taken hold of him until they gave the great party down in the quarters, and he saw Martha in all her glory. Then love spoke to him with no uncertain sound.

It was a dancing-party, and because neither he nor Martha dared countenance dancing, they had strolled away together under the pines that lined the white road, whiter now in the soft moonlight. He had never known the pinecones smell so sweet before in all his life. She had never known just how the moonlight flecked the road before. This was lovers' lane to them. He didn't understand why his heart kept throbbing so furiously, for they were walking slowly, and when a shadow thrown across the road from a by-standing bush frightened her into pressing close up to him, he could not have told why his arm stole round her waist and drew her slim form up to him, or why his lips found hers, as eye looked into eye. For their simple hearts love's mystery was too deep, as it is for wiser ones.

Some few stammering words came to his lips, and she answered the best she could. Then why did the moonlight flood them so, and why were the heavens so full of stars? Out yonder in the black hedge a mocking-bird was singing, and he was translating—oh, so poorly—the song of their hearts. They forgot the dance, they forgot all but their love.

"An' you won't ma'y nobody else but me, Martha?"

"You know I won't, Gidjon."

"But I mus' wait de yeah out?"

"Yes, an' den don't you think Mas' Stone'll let us have a little cabin of ouah own jest outside de quahtahs?"

"Won't it be blessid? Won't it be blessid?" he cried, and then the kindly moon went under a cloud for a moment and came out smiling, for he had peeped through and had seen what passed. Then they walked back hand in hand to the dance along the transfigured road, and they found that the first part of the festivities were over, and all the people had sat down to supper. Every one laughed when they went in. Martha held back and perspired with embarrassment. But even though he saw some of the older heads whispering in a corner, Gideon was not ashamed. A new light was in his eyes, and a new boldness had come to him. He led Martha up to the grinning group, and said in his best singing voice, "Whut you laughin' at? Yes, I's popped de question, an' she says 'Yes,' an' long 'bout a yeah f'om now you kin all 'spec' a' invitation." This was a formal announcement. A shout arose from the happy-go-lucky people, who sorrowed alike in each other's sorrows, and joyed in each other's joys. They sat down at a table, and their health was drunk in cups of cider and persimmon beer.

Over in the corner Mam' Henry mumbled over her pipe, "Wha'd I tell you? wha'd I tell you?" and Aunt Sophy replied, "Hit's de pa'able of de mo'nin' stahs."

"Don't talk to me 'bout no mo'nin' stahs," the mammy snorted; "Gawd jes' fitted dey voices togeddah, an' den j'ined dey hea'ts. De mo'nin' stahs ain't got nothin' to do wid it."

"Mam' Henry," said Aunt Sophy, impressively, "you's a' oldah ooman den I is, an' I ain' sputin' hit; but I say dey done 'filled Scripter 'bout de mo'nin' stahs; dey's done sung deyse'ves togeddah."

The old woman sniffed.

The next Sunday at meeting some one got the start of Gideon, and began a new hymn. It ran:

"At de ma'ige of de Lamb, oh Lawd,
      God done gin His 'sent.
 Dey dressed de Lamb all up in white,
      God done gin His 'sent.
 Oh, wasn't dat a happy day,
 Oh, wasn't dat a happy day, Good Lawd,
 Oh, wasn't dat a happy day,
      De ma'ige of de Lamb!"

The wailing minor of the beginning broke into a joyous chorus at the end, and Gideon wept and laughed in turn, for it was his wedding-song.

The young man had a confidential chat with his master the next morning, and the happy secret was revealed.

"What, you scamp!" said Dudley Stone. "Why, you've got even more sense than I gave you credit for; you've picked out the finest girl on the plantation, and the one best suited to you. You couldn't have done better if the match had been made for you. I reckon this must be one of the marriages that are made in heaven. Marry her, yes, and with a preacher. I don't see why you want to wait a year."

Gideon told him his hopes of a near cabin.

"Better still," his master went on; "with you two joined and up near the big house, I'll feel as safe for the folks as if an army was camped around, and, Gideon, my boy,"—he put his arms on the black man's shoulders,—"if I should slip away some day—"

The slave looked up, startled.

"I mean if I should die—I'm not going to run off, don't be alarmed—I want you to help your young Mas' Dud look after his mother and Miss Ellen; you hear? Now that's the one promise I ask of you,—come what may, look after the women folks." And the man promised and went away smiling.

His year of engagement, the happiest time of a young man's life, began on golden wings. There came rumors of war, and the wings of the glad-hued year drooped sadly. Sadly they drooped, and seemed to fold, when one day, between the rumors and predictions of strife, Dudley Stone, the old master, slipped quietly away out into the unknown.

There were wife, daughter, son, and faithful slaves about his bed, and they wept for him sincere tears, for he had been a good husband and father and a kind master. But he smiled, and, conscious to the last, whispered to them a cheery good-bye. Then, turning to Gideon, who stood there bowed with grief, he raised one weak finger, and his lips made the word, "Remember!"

They laid him where they had laid one genertion after another of the Stones and it seemed as if a pall of sorrow had fallen upon the whole place. Then, still grieving, they turned their long-distracted attention to the things that had been going on around, and lo! the ominous mutterings were loud, and the cloud of war was black above them.

It was on an April morning when the storm broke, and the plantation, master and man, stood dumb with consternation, for they had hoped, they had believed, it would pass. And now there was the buzz of men who talked in secret corners. There were hurried saddlings and feverish rides to town. Somewhere in the quarters was whispered the forbidden word "freedom," and it was taken up and dropped breathlessly from the ends of a hundred tongues. Some of the older ones scouted it, but from some who held young children to their breasts there were deep-souled prayers in the dead of night. Over the meetings in the woods or in the log church a strange reserve brooded, and even the prayers took on a guarded tone. Even from the fulness of their hearts, which longed for liberty, no open word that could offend the mistress or the young master went up to the Almighty. He might know their hearts, but no tongue in meeting gave vent to what was in them, and even Gideon sang no more of the gospel army. He was sad because of this new trouble coming hard upon the heels of the old, and Martha was grieved because he was.

Finally the trips into town budded into something, and on a memorable evening when the sun looked peacefully through the pines, young Dudley Stone rode into the yard dressed in a suit of gray, and on his shoulders were the straps of office. The servants gathered around him with a sort of awe and followed him until he alighted at the porch. Only Mam' Henry, who had been nurse to both him and his sister, dared follow him in. It was a sad scene within, but such a one as any Southern home where there were sons might have shown that awful year. The mother tried to be brave, but her old hands shook, and her tears fell upon her son's brown head, tears of grief at parting, but through which shone the fire of a noble pride. The young Ellen hung about his neck with sobs and caresses.

"Would you have me stay?" he asked her.

"No! no! I know where your place is, but oh, my brother!"

"Ellen," said the mother in a trembling voice, "you are the sister of a soldier now."

The girl dried her tears and drew herself up.

"We won't burden your heart, Dudley, with our tears, but we will weight you down with our love and prayers."

It was not so easy with Mam' Henry. Without protest, she took him to her bosom and rocked to and fro, wailing "My baby! my baby!" and the tears that fell from the young man's eyes upon her grey old head cost his manhood nothing.

Gideon was behind the door when his master called him. His sleeve was traveling down from his eyes as he emerged.

"Gideon," said his master, pointing to his uniform, "you know what this means?"

"Yes, suh."

"I wish I could take you along with me. But—"

"Mas' Dud," Gideon threw out his arms in supplication.

"You remember father's charge to you, take care of the women-folks." He took the servant's hand, and, black man and white, they looked into each other's eyes, and the compact was made. Then Gideon gulped and said "Yes, suh" again.

Another boy held the master's horse and rode away behind him when he vaulted into the saddle, and the man of battle-song and warrior name went back to mind the women-folks.

Then began the disintegration of the plantation's population. First Yellow Bob slipped away, and no one pursued him. A few blamed him, but they soon followed as the year rolled away. More were missing every time a Union camp lay near, and great tales were told of the chances for young negroes who would go as body-servants to the Yankee officers. Gideon heard all and was silent.

Then as the time of his marriage drew near he felt a greater strength, for there was one who would be with him to help him keep his promise and his faith.

The spirit of freedom had grown strong in Martha as the days passed, and when her lover went to see her she had strange things to say. Was he going to stay? Was he going to be a slave when freedom and a livelihood lay right within his grasp? Would he keep her a slave? Yes, he would do it all—all.

She asked him to wait.

Another year began, and one day they brought Dudley Stone home to lay beside his father. Then most of the remaining negroes went. There was no master now. The two bereaved women wept, and Gideon forgot that he wore the garb of manhood and wept with them.

Martha came to him.

"Gidjon," she said, "I's waited a long while now. Mos' eve'ybody else is gone. Ain't you goin'?"

"No."

"But, Gidjon, I wants to be free. I know how good dey've been to us; but, oh, I wants to own myse'f. They're talkin' 'bout settin' us free every hour."

"I can wait."

"They's a camp right near here."

"I promised."

"The of'cers wants body-servants, Gidjon—"

"Go, Martha, if you want to, but I stay."

She went away from him, but she or some one else got word to young Captain Jack Griswold of the near camp that there was an excellent servant on the plantation who only needed a little persuading, and he came up to see him.

"Look here," he said, "I want a body-servant. I'll give you ten dollars a month."

"I've got to stay here."

"But, you fool, what have you to gain by staying here?"

"I'm goin' to stay."

"Why, you'll be free in a little while, anyway."

"All right."

"Of all fools," said the Captain. "I'll give you fifteen dollars."

"I do' want it."

"Well, your girl's going, anyway. I don't blame her for leaving such a fool as you are."

Gideon turned and looked at him.

"The camp is going to be moved up on this plantation, and there will be a requisition for this house for officers' quarters, so I'll see you again," and Captain Griswold went his way.

Martha going! Martha going! Gideon could not believe it. He would not. He saw her, and she confirmed it. She was going as an aid to the nurses. He gasped, and went back to mind the women-folks.

They did move the camp up nearer, and Captain Griswold came to see Gideon again, but he could get no word from him, save "I'm goin' to stay," and he went away in disgust, entirely unable to understand such obstinacy, as he called it.

But the slave had his moments alone, when the agony tore at his breast and rended him. Should he stay? The others were going. He would soon be free. Every one had said so, even his mistress one day. Then Martha was going. "Martha! Martha!" his heart called.

The day came when the soldiers were to leave, and he went out sadly to watch them go. All the plantation, that had been white with tents, was dark again, and everywhere were moving, blue-coated figures.

Once more his tempter came to him. "I'll make it twenty dollars," he said, but Gideon shook his head. Then they started. The drums tapped. Away they went, the flag kissing the breeze. Martha stole up to say good-bye to him. Her eyes were overflowing, and she clung to him.

"Come, Gidjon," she plead, "fu' my sake. Oh, my God, won't you come with us—it's freedom." He kissed her, but shook his head.

"Hunt me up when you do come," she said, crying bitterly, "fu' I do love you, Gidjon, but I must go. Out yonder is freedom," and she was gone with them.

He drew out a pace after the troops, and then, turning, looked back at the house. He went a step farther, and then a woman's gentle voice called him, "Gideon!" He stopped. He crushed his cap in his hands, and the tears came into his eyes. Then he answered, "Yes, Mis' Ellen, I's a-comin'."

He stood and watched the dusty column until the last blue leg swung out of sight and over the grey hills the last drum-tap died away, and then turned and re-traced his steps toward the house.

Gideon had triumphed mightily.

Mammy Peggy's Pride

IN THE FAILING light of the midsummer evening, two women sat upon the broad veranda that ran round three sides of the old Virginia mansion. One was young and slender with the slightness of delicate girlhood. The other was old, black and ample,—a typical mammy of the old south. The girl was talking in low, subdued tones touched with a note of sadness that was strange in one of her apparent youth, but which seemed as if somehow in consonance with her sombre garments.

"No, no, Peggy," she was saying, "we have done the best we could, as well as even papa could have expected of us if he had been here. It was of no use to keep struggling and straining along, trying to keep the old place from going, out of a sen-timent, which, however honest it might have been, was neither common sense nor practical. Poor people, and we are poor, in spite of the little we got for the place, cannot afford to have feelings. Of course I hate to see strangers take possession of the homestead, and—and—papa's and mamma's and brother Phil's graves are out there on the hillside. It is hard,—hard, but what was I to do? I couldn't plant and hoe and plow, and you couldn't, so I am beaten, beaten." The girl threw out her hands with a despairing gesture and burst into tears.

Mammy Peggy took the brown head in her lap and let her big hands wander softly over the girl's pale face. "Sh,—sh," she said as if she were soothing a baby, "don't go on lak dat. W'y whut's de mattah wid you, Miss Mime? 'Pears lak you done los' all yo' spe'it. Whut you reckon yo' pappy 'u'd t'ink ef he could see you ca'in'on dis away? Didn' he put his han' on yo' haid an' call you his own brave little gal, jes befo', jes' befo'—he went?"

The girl raised her head for a moment and looked at the old woman.

"Oh, mammy, mammy," she cried, "I have tried so hard to be brave—to be really my father's daughter, but I can't, I can't. Everything I turn my hand to fails. I've tried sewing, but here every one sews for herself now. I've even tried writing," and here a crimson glow burned in her cheeks, "but oh, the awful regularity with which everything came back to me. Why, I even put you in a story, Mammy Peggy, you dear old, good, unselfish thing, and the hard-hearted editor had the temerity to decline you with thanks."

"I wouldn't 'a' nevah lef' you nohow, honey."

Mima laughed through her tears. The strength of her first grief had passed, and she was viewing her situation with a whimsical enjoyment of its humorous points.

"I don't know," she went on, "it seems to me that it's only in stories themselves that destitute young Southern girls get on and make fame and fortune with their pens. I'm sure I couldn't."

"Of course you couldn't. Whut else do you 'spect? Whut you know 'bout mekin' a fortune? Ain't you a Ha'ison? De Ha'isons nevah was no buyin' an' sellin', mekin' an' tradin' fambly. Dey was gent'men an' ladies f'om de ve'y fus' beginnin'."

"Oh what a pity one cannot sell one's quality for daily bread, or trade off one's blue blood for black coffee."

"Miss Mime, is you out o' yo' haid?" asked Mammy Peggy in disgust and horror.

"No, I'm not, Mammy Peggy, but I do wish that I could traffic in some of my too numerous and too genteel ancestors instead of being compelled to dispose of my ancestral home and be turned out into the street like a pauper."

"Heish, honey, heish, I can' stan' to hyeah you talk dat-away. I's so'y to see dee ol' place go, but you got to go out of it wid yo' haid up, jes' ez ef you was gwine away fo' a visit an' could come back w'en evah you wanted to."

"I shall slink out of it like a cur. I can't meet the eyes of the new owner; I shall hate him."

"W'y, Miss Mime, whaih's yo' pride? Whaih's yo' Ha'ison pride?"

"Gone, gone with the deed of this house and its furniture. Gone with the money I paid for the new cottage and its cheap chairs."

"Gone, hit ain' gone, fu' ef you won't let on to have it, I will. I'll show dat new man how yo' pa would 'a' did ef he'd 'a' been hyeah."

"What, you, Mammy Peggy?"

"Yes, me, I ain' a-gwine to let him t'ink dat de Ha'isons didn' have no quality."

"Good, mammy, you make me remember who I am, and what my duty is. I shall see Mr. Northcope when he comes, and I'll try to make my Harrison pride sustain me when I give up to him everything I have held dear. Oh, mammy, mammy!"

"Heish, chile, sh, sh, er go on, dat's right, yo' eyes is open now an' you kin cry a little weenty bit. It'll do you good. But when dat new man comes I want mammy's lamb to look at him an' hol' huh haid lak' huh ma used to hol' hern, an' I reckon Mistah No'thcope gwine to withah away."

And so it happened that when Bartley Northcope came the next day to take possession of the old Virginia mansion he was welcomed at the door, and ushered into the broad parlor by Mammy Peggy, stiff and unbending in the faded finery of her family's better days.

"Miss Mime'll be down in a minute," she told him, and as he sat in the great old room, and looked about him at the evidences of ancient affluence, his spirit was subdued by the silent tragedy which his possession of it evinced. But he could not but feel a thrill at the bit of comedy which is on the edge of every tragedy, as he thought of Mammy Peggy and her formal reception. "She let me into my own house," he thought to himself, "with the air of granting me a favor." And then there was a step on the stair; the door opened, and Miss Mima stood before him, proud, cold, white, and beautiful.

He found his feet, and went forward to meet her. "Mr. Northcope," she said, and offered her hand daintily, hesitatingly. He took it, and thought, even in that flash of a second, what a soft, tiny hand it was.

"Yes," he said, "and I have been sitting here, overcome by the vastness of your fine old house."

The "your" was delicate, she thought, but she only said, "Let me help you to recovery with some tea. Mammy will bring some," and then she blushed very red. "My old nurse is the only servant I have with me, and she is always mammy to me." She remembered, and throwing up her proud little head rang for the old woman.

Directly, Mammy Peggy came marching in like a grenadier. She bore a tray with the tea things on it, and after she had set it down hovered in the room as if to chaperon her mistress. Bartley felt decidedly uncomfortable. Mima's manners were all that politeness could require, but he felt as if she resented his coming even to his own, and he knew that mammy looked upon him as an interloper.

Mima kept up well, only the paleness of her face showed what she felt at leaving her home. Her voice was calm and impassive, only once it trembled, when she wished that he would be as happy in the house as she had been.

"I feel very much like an interloper," he said, "but I hope you won't feel yourself entirely shut out from your beautiful home. My father, who comes on in a few days is an invalid, and gets about very little, and I am frequently from home, so pray make use of the grounds when you please, and as much of the house as you find convenient."

A cold "thank you" fell from Mima's lips, but then she went on, hesitatingly, "I should like to come sometimes to the hill, out there behind the orchard." Her voice choked, but she went bravely on, "Some of my dear ones are buried there."

"Go there, and elsewhere, as much as you please. That spot shall be sacred from invasion."

"You are very kind," she said and rose to go. Mammy carried away the tea things, and then came and waited silently by the door.

"I hope you will believe me, Miss Harrison," said Bartley, as Mima was starting, "when I say that I do not come to your home as a vandal to destroy all that makes its recollection dear to you; for there are some associations about it that are almost as much to me as to you, since my eyes have been opened."

"I do not understand you," she replied.

"I can explain. For some years past my father's condition has kept me very closely bound to him, and both before and after the beginning of the war, we lived abroad. A few years ago, I came to know and love a man, who I am convinced now was your brother. Am I mistaken in thinking that you are a sister of Philip Harrison?"

"No, no, he was my brother, my only brother."

"I met him in Venice just before the war and we came to be dear friends. But in the events that followed so tumultuously, and from participation in which, I was cut off by my father's illness, I lost sight of him."

"But I don't believe I remember hearing my brother speak of you, and he was not usually reticent."

"You would not remember me as Bartley Northcope, unless you were familiar with the very undignified sobriquet with which your brother nicknamed me," said the young man smiling.

"Nickname—what, you are not, you can't be 'Budge'?"

"I am 'Budge' or 'old Budge' as Phil called me."

Mima had her hand on the door-knob, but she turned with an impulsive motion and went back to him. "I am so glad to see you," she said, giving him her hand again, and "Mammy," she called, "Mr. Northcope is an old friend of brother Phil's!"

The effect of this news on mammy was like that of the April sun on an icicle. She suddenly melted, and came overflowing back into the room, her smiles and grins and nods trickling everywhere under the genial warmth of this new friendliness. Before one who had been a friend of "Mas' Phil's," Mammy Peggy needed no pride.

"La, chile," she exclaimed, settling and patting the cushions of the chair in which he had been sitting, "w'y didn' you say so befo'?"

"I wasn't sure that I was standing in the house of my old friend. I only knew that he lived somewhere in Virginia."

"He is among those out on the hill behind the orchard," said Mima, sadly. Mammy Peggy wiped her eyes, and went about trying to add some touches of comfort to the already perfect room.

"You have no reason to sorrow, Miss Harrison," said Northcope gently, "for a brother who died bravely in battle for his principles. Had fate allowed me to be here I should have been upon the other side, but believe me, I both understand and appreciate your brother's heroism."

The young girl's eyes glistened with tears, through which glowed her sisterly pride.

"Won't you come out and look at his grave?"

"It is the desire that was in my mind."

Together they walked out, with mammy following, to the old burying plot. All her talk was of her brother's virtues, and he proved an appreciative listener. She pointed out favorite spots of her brother's childhood as they passed along, and indicated others which his boyish pranks had made memorable, though the eyes of the man were oftener on her face than on the landscape. But it was with real sympathy and reverence that he stood with bared head beside the grave of his friend, and the tears that she let fall unchecked in his presence were not all tears of grief.

They did not go away from him that afternoon until Mammy Peggy, seconded by Mima, had won his consent to let the old servant come over and "do for him" until he found suitable servants.

"To think of his having known Philip," said Mima with shining eyes as they entered the new cottage, and somehow it looked pleasanter, brighter and less mean to her than it had ever before.

"Now s'posin' you'd 'a' run off widout seein' him, whaih would you been den? You wouldn' nevah knowed whut you knows."

"You're right, Mammy Peggy, and I'm glad I stayed and faced him, for it doesn't seem now as if a stranger had the house, and it has given me a great pleasure. It seemed like having Phil back again to have him talked about so by one who lived so near to him."

"I tell you, chile," mammy supplemented in an oracular tone, "de right kin' o' pride allus pays." Mima laughed heartily. The old woman looked at her bright face. Then she put her big hand on the girl's small one. It was trembling. She shook her head. Mima blushed.

Bartley went out and sat on the veranda a long time after they were gone. He took in the great expanse of lawn about the house, and the dark background of the pines in the woods beyond. He thought of the conditions through which the place had become his, and the thought saddened him, even in the first glow of the joy of possession. Then his mind went on to the old friend who was sleeping his last sleep back there on the sun-bathed hill. His recollection went fondly over the days of their comradeship in Venice, and colored them anew with glory.

"These Southerners," he mused aloud, "cannot understand that we sympathize with their misfortunes. But we do. They forget how our sympathies have been trained. We were first taught to sympathize with the slave, and now that he is free, and needs less, perhaps, of our sympathy, this, by a transition, as easy as it is natural, is transferred to his master. Poor, poor Phil!"

There was a strange emotion, half-sad, half-pleasant tugging at his heart. A mist came before his eyes and hid the landscape for a moment.

And he, he referred it all to the memories of the brother. Yes, he thought he was thinking of the brother, and he did not notice or did not pretend to notice that a pair of appealing eyes looking out beneath waves of brown hair, that a soft, fair hand, pressed in his own, floated nebulously at the back of his consciousness.

It was not until he had set out to furnish his house with a complement of servants against the coming of his father that Bartley came to realize the full worth of Mammy Peggy's offer to "do for him." The old woman not only got his meals and kept him comfortable, trudging over and back every day from the little cottage, but she proved invaluable in the choice of domestic help. She knew her people there-abouts, just who was spry, and who was trifling, and with the latter she would have nothing whatever to do. She acted rather as if he were a guest in his own house, and what was more would take no pay for it. Of course there had to be some re-turn for so much kindness, and it took the form of various gifts of flowers and fruit from the old place to the new cottage. And sometimes when Bartley had for-gotten to speak of it before mammy had left, he would arrange his baskets and carry his offering over himself. Mima thought it was very thoughtful and kind of him, and she wondered on these occasions if they ought not to keep Mr. North-cope to tea, and if mammy would not like to make some of those nice muffins of hers that he had liked so, and mammy always smiled on her charge, and said, "Yes, honey, yes, but hit do 'pear lak' dat Mistah No'thcope do fu'git mo' an' mo' to sen' de t'ings ovah by me w'en I's daih."

But mammy found her special charge when the elder Northcope came. It seemed that she could never do enough for the pale, stooped old man, and he de-clared that he had never felt better in his life than he grew to feel under her touch. An injury to his spine had resulted in partially disabling him, but his mind was a rich store of knowledge, and his disposition was tender and cheerful. So it pleased his son sometimes to bring Mima over to see him.

The warm, impulsive heart of the Southern girl went out to him, and they be-came friends at once. He found in her that soft, caressing, humoring quality that even his son's devotion could not supply, and his superior age, knowledge and wis-dom made up to her the lost father's care for which Peggy's love illy substituted. The tenderness grew between them. Through the long afternoons she would read to him from his favorite books, or would listen to him as he talked of the lands where he had been, and the things he had seen. Sometimes Mammy Peggy grum-bled at the reading, and said it "wuz jes' lak' doin' hiahed wo'k," but Mima only laughed and went on.

Bartley saw the sympathy between them and did not obtrude his presence, but often in the twilight when she started away, he would slip out of some corner and walk home with her.

These little walks together were very pleasant, and on one occasion he had asked her the question that made her pale and red by turns, and sent her heart beating with convulsive throbs that made her gasp.

"Maybe I'm over soon in asking you, Mima dear," he faltered, "but—but, I couldn't wait any longer. You've become a part of my life. I have no hope, no joy, no thought that you are not of. Won't you be my wife?"

They were pausing at her gate, and she was trembling from what emotion he only dared guess. But she did not answer. She only returned the pressure of his hand, and drawing it away, rushed into the house. She durst not trust her voice. Bartley went home walking on air.

Mima did not go directly to Mammy Peggy with her news. She must compose herself first. This was hard to do, so she went to her room and sat down to think it over.

"He loves me, he loves me," she kept saying to herself and with each repetition of the words, the red came anew into her cheeks. They were still a suspicious hue when she went into the kitchen to find mammy who was slumbering over the waiting dinner. "What meks you so long honey," asked the old woman, coming wide awake out of her cat-nap.

"Oh,—I—I—I don't know," answered the young girl, blushing furiously, "I—I stopped to talk."

"Why dey ain' no one in de house to talk to. I hyeahed you w'en you come home. You have been a powahful time sence you come in. Whut meks you so red?" Then a look of intelligence came into mammy's fat face. "Oomph," she said.

"Oh mammy, don't look that way, I couldn't help it. Bartley—Mr. Northcope has asked me to be his wife."

"Asked you to be his wife! Oomph! Whut did you tell him?"

"I didn't tell him anything. I was so ashamed I couldn't talk. I just ran away like a silly."

"Oomph," said mammy again, "an' whut you gwine to tell him?"

"Oh, I don't know. Don't you think he's a very nice young man, Mr. Northcope, mammy? And then his father's so nice."

Mammy's face clouded. "I doan' see whaih yo' Ha'ison pride is," she said; "co'se, he may be nice enough, but does you want to tell him yes de fust t'ing, so's he'll t'ink dat you jumped at de chanst to git him an' git back in de homestid?"

"Oh, mammy," cried Mima; she had gone all white and cold.

"You do' know nothin' 'bout his quality. You a Ha'ison yo'se'f. Who is he to be jumped at an' tuk at de fust axin'? Ef he wants you ve'y bad he'll ax mo' dan once."

"You needn't have reminded me, mammy, of who I am," said Mima. "I had no intention of telling Mr Northcope yes. You needn't have been afraid for me." She fibbed a little, it is to be feared.

"Now don't talk dat 'way, chile. I know you laks him, an' I do' want to stop you f'om tekin' him. Don't you say no, ez ef you wasn' nevah gwine to say nothin' else. You jes' say a hol'in' off no."

"I like Mr. Northcope as a friend, and my no to him will be final."

The dinner did not go down very well with Mima that evening. It stopped in her throat, and when she swallowed, it brought the tears to her eyes. When it was done, she hurried away to her room.

She was so disappointed, but she would not confess it to herself, and she would not weep. "He proposed to me because he pitied me, oh, the shame of it! He turned me out of doors, and then thought I would be glad to come back at any price."

When he read her cold formal note, Bartley knew that he had offended her, and the thought burned him like fire. He cursed himself for a blundering fool. "She was only trying to be kind to father and me," he said, "and I have taken advantage of her goodness." He would never have confessed to himself before that he was a coward. But that morning when he got her note, he felt that he could not face her just yet, and commending his father to the tender mercies of Mammy Peggy and the servants, he took the first train to the north.

It would be hard to say which of the two was the most disappointed when the truth was known. It might better be said which of the three, for Mima went no more to the house, and the elder Northcope fretted and was restless without her. He availed himself of an invalid's privilege to be disagreeable, and nothing Mammy Peggy could do now would satisfy him. Indeed, between the two, the old woman had a hard time of it, for Mima was tearful and morose, and would not speak to her except to blame her. As the days went on she wished to all the powers that she had left the Harrison pride in the keeping of the direct members of the family. It had proven a dangerous thing in her hands.

Mammy soliloquized when she was about her work in the kitchen. "Men ain' whut dey used to be," she said, "who'd 'a' t'ought o' de young man a runnin' off dat away jes' 'cause a ooman tol' him no. He orter had sense enough to know dat a ooman has sev'al kin's o' noes. Now ef dat 'ud 'a' been in my day he'd 'a' jes' stayed away to let huh t'ink hit ovah an' den come back an' axed huh ag'in. Den she could 'a' said yes all right an' proper widout a belittlin' huhse'f. But 'stead o' dat he mus' go a ta'in' off jes' ez soon ez de fus' wo'ds come outen huh mouf. Put' nigh brekin' huh hea't. I clah to goodness, I nevah did see sich ca'in's on."

Several weeks passed before Bartley returned to his home. Autumn was painting the trees about the place before the necessity of being at his father's side called him from his voluntary exile. And then he did not go to see Mima. He was still bowed with shame at what he thought his unmanly presumption, and he did not blame her that she avoided him.

His attention was arrested one day about a week after his return by the peculiar actions of Mammy Peggy. She hung around him, and watched him, following him from place to place like a spaniel.

Finally he broke into a laugh and said, "Why, what's the matter, Aunt Peggy, are you afraid I'm going to run away?"

"No, I ain' afeared o' dat," said mammy, meekly, "but I been had somepn' to say to you dis long w'ile."

"Well, go ahead, I'm listening."

Mammy gulped and went on. "Ask huh ag'in," she said, "it were my fault she tol' you no. I 'minded huh o' huh fambly pride an' tol' huh to hol' you off less'n you'd t'ink she wan'ed to jump at you."

Bartley was on his feet in a minute.

"What does this mean," he cried, "Is it true, didn't I offend her?"

"No, you didn' 'fend huh. She's been pinin' fu' you, 'twell she's growed right peekid."

"Sh, auntie, do you mean to tell me that Mim—Miss Harrison cares for me?"

"You go an' ax huh ag'in."

Bartley needed no second invitation. He flew to the cottage. Mima's heart gave a great throb when she saw him coming up the walk, and she tried to harden herself against him. But her lips would twitch, and her voice would tremble as she said, "How do you do, Mr. Northcope?"

He looked keenly into her eyes.

"Have I been mistaken, Mima," he said, "in believing that I greatly offended you by asking you to be my wife? Do you—can you care for me, darling?"

The words stuck in her throat, and he went on, "I thought you were angry with me because I had taken advantage of your kindness to my father, or presumed upon any kindness that you may have felt for me out of respect to your brother's memory. Believe me, I was innocent of any such intention."

"Oh, it wasn't—it wasn't that!" she gasped.

"Then won't you give me a different answer," he said, taking her hand.

"I can't, I can't," she cried.

"Why, Mima?" he asked.

"Because—"

"Because of the Harrison pride?"

"Bartley!"

"Your Mammy Peggy has confessed all to me."

"Mammy Peggy!"

"Yes."

She tried hard to stiffen herself. "Then it is all out of the question," she began.

"Don't let any little folly or pride stand between us," he broke in, drawing her to him.

She gave up the struggle, and her head dropped upon his shoulder for a moment. Then she lifted her eyes, shining with tears to his face, and said, "Bartley, it wasn't my pride, it was Mammy Peggy's."

He cut off further remarks.

When he was gone, and mammy came in after a while, Mima ran to her crying.

"Oh, mammy, mammy, you bad, stupid, dear old goose!" and she buried her head in the old woman's lap.

"Oomph," grunted mammy, "I said de right kin' o' pride allus pays. But de wrong kin'—oomph, well, you'd bettah look out!"

Viney's Free Papers

Part I

THERE WAS JOY in the bosom of Ben Raymond. He sang as he hoed in the field. He cheerfully worked overtime and his labors did not make him tired. When the quitting horn blew he executed a double shuffle as he shouldered his hoe and started for his cabin. While the other men dragged wearily over the ground he sprang along as if all day long he had not been bending over the hoe in the hot sun, with the sweat streaming from his face in rivulets.

And this had been going on for two months now—two happy months—ever since Viney had laid her hand in his, had answered with a coquettish "Yes," and the master had given his consent, his blessing and a five-dollar bill.

It had been a long and trying courtship—that is, it had been trying for Ben, because Viney loved pleasure and hungered for attention and the field was full of rivals. She was a merry girl and a pretty one. No one could dance better; no girl on the place was better able to dress her dark charms to advantage or to show them off more temptingly. The toss of her head was an invitation and a challenge in one, and the way she smiled back at them over her shoulder, set the young men's heads dancing and their hearts throbbing. So her suitors were many. But through it all Ben was patient, unflinching and faithful, and finally, after leading him a life full of doubt and suspense, the coquette surrendered and gave herself into his keeping.

She was maid to her mistress, but she had time, nevertheless, to take care of the newly whitewashed cabin in the quarters to which Ben took her. And it was very pleasant to lean over and watch him at work making things for the little house— a chair from a barrel and a wonderful box of shelves to stand in the corner. And she knew how to say merry things, and later outside his door Ben would pick his banjo and sing low and sweetly in the musical voice of his race. Altogether such another honeymoon there had never been.

For once the old women hushed up their prophecies of evil, although in the beginning they had shaken their wise old turbaned heads and predicted that marriage with such a flighty creature as Viney could come to no good. They had said among themselves that Ben would better marry some good, solid-minded, strong-armed girl who would think more about work than about pleasures and coquetting.

"I 'low, honey," an old woman had said, "she'll mek his heart ache many a time. She'll comb his haid wid a three-legged stool an' bresh it wid de broom. Uh, huh—putty, is she? You ma'y huh 'cause she putty. Ki-yi! She fix you! Putty women fu' putty tricks."

And the old hag smacked her lips over the spice of malevolence in her words. Some women—and they are not all black and ugly—never forgive the world for letting them grow old.

But, in spite of all prophecies to the contrary, two months of unalloyed joy had passed for Ben and Viney, and to-night the climax seemed to have been reached. Ben hurried along, talking to himself as his hoe swung over his shoulder.

"Kin I do it?" he was saying. "Kin I do it?" Then he would stop his walk and his cogitations would bloom into a mirthful chuckle. Something very pleasant was passing through his mind.

As he approached, Viney was standing in the door of the little cabin, whose white sides with green Madeira clambering over them made a pretty frame for the dark girl in her print dress. The husband bent double at sight of her, stopped, took off his hat, slapped his knee, and relieved his feelings by a sounding "Who-ee!"

"What's de mattah wid you, Ben? You ac' lak you mighty happy. Bettah come on in hyeah an' git yo' suppah fo' hit gits col'."

For answer, the big fellow dropped the hoe and, seizing the slight form in his arms, swung her around until she gasped for breath.

"Oh, Ben," she shrieked, "you done tuk all my win'!"

"Dah, now," he said, letting her down; "dat's what you gits fu' talkin' sassy to me!"

"Nev' min'; I'm goin' to fix you fu' dat fus' time I gits de chanst—see ef I don't."

"Whut you gwine do? Gwine to pizen me?"

"Worse'n dat!"

"Wuss'n dat? Whut you gwine fin' any wuss'n pizenin' me, less'n you conjuh me?"

"Huh uh—still worse'n dat. I'm goin' to leave you."

"Huh uh—no you ain', 'cause any place you'd go you wouldn' no more'n git dah twell you'd tu'n erroun' all of er sudden an' say, 'Why, dah's Ben!' an' dah I'd be."

They chattered on like children while she was putting the supper on the table and he was laying his hot face in the basin beside the door.

"I got great news fu' you," he said, as they sat down.

"I bet you ain' got nothin' of de kin'."

"All right. Den dey ain' no use in me a tryin' to 'vince you. I jes' be wastin' my bref."

"Go on—tell me, Ben."

"Huh uh—you bet I ain', an' ef I tell you you lose de bet."

"I don' keer. Ef you don' tell me, den I know you ain' got no news worth tellin'."

"Ain' got no news wuff tellin'! Who-ee!"

He came near choking on a gulp of coffee, and again his knee suffered from the pounding of his great hands.

"Huccume you so full of laugh to-night?" she asked, laughing with him.

"How you 'spec' I gwine tell you dat less'n I tell you my sec'ut?"

"Well, den, go on—tell me yo' sec'ut."

"Huh uh. You done bet it ain' wuff tellin'."

"I don't keer what I bet. I wan' to hyeah it now. Please, Ben, please!"

"Listen how she baig! Well, I gwine tell you now. I ain' gwine tease you no mo'."

She bent her head forward expectantly.

"I had a talk wid Mas' Raymond to-day," resumed Ben.

"Yes?"

"An' he say he pay me all my back money fu' ovahtime."

"Oh!"

"An' all I gits right along he gwine he'p me save, an' when I git fo' hund'ed dollahs he gwine gin me de free papahs fu' you, my little gal."

"Oh, Ben, Ben! Hit ain' so, is it?"

"Yes, hit is. Den you'll be you own ooman—leas'ways less'n you wants to be mine."

She went and put her arms around his neck. Her eyes were sparkling and her lips quivering.

"You don' mean, Ben, dat I'll be free?"

"Yes, you'll be free, Viney. Den I's gwine to set to wo'k an' buy my free papahs."

"Oh, kin you do it—kin you do it—kin you do it?"

"Kin I do it?" he repeated. He stretched out his arm, with the sleeve rolled to the shoulder, and curved it upward till the muscles stood out like great knots of oak. Then he opened and shut his fingers, squeezing them together until the joints cracked. "Kin I do it?" He looked down on her calmly and smiled simply, happily.

She threw her arms around his waist and sank on her knees at his feet sobbing.

"Ben, Ben! My Ben! I nevah even thought of it. Hit seemed so far away, but now we're goin' to be free—free, free!"

He lifted her up gently.

"It's gwine to tek a pow'ful long time," he said.

"I don' keer," she cried gaily. "We know it's comin' an' we kin wait."

The woman's serious mood had passed as quickly as it had come, and she spun around the cabin, executing a series of steps that set her husband a-grin with admiration and joy.

And so Ben began to work with renewed vigor. He had found a purpose in life and there was something for him to look for beyond dinner, a dance and the end of the day. He had always been a good hand, but now he became a model—no shirking, no shiftlessness—and because he was so earnest his master did what he could to help him. Numerous little plans were formulated whereby the slave could make or save a precious dollar.

Viney, too, seemed inspired by a new hope, and if this little house had been pleasant to Ben, nothing now was wanting to make it a palace in his eyes. Only one sorrow he had, and that one wrung hard at his great heart—no baby came to them—but instead he made a great baby of his wife, and went on his way hiding his disappointment the best he could. The banjo was often silent now, for when he came home his fingers were too stiff to play; but sometimes, when his heart ached for the laughter of a child, he would take down his old friend and play low, soothing melodies until he found rest and comfort.

Viney had once tried to console him by saying that had she had a child it would have taken her away from her work, but he had only answered, "We could a' stood that."

But Ben's patient work and frugality had their reward, and it was only a little over three years after he had set out to do it that he put in his master's hand the price of Viney's freedom, and there was sound of rejoicing in the land. A fat shoat, honestly come by—for it was the master's gift—was killed and baked, great jugs of biting persimmon beer were brought forth, and the quarters held high carnival to celebrate Viney's new-found liberty.

After the merrymakers had gone, and when the cabin was clear again, Ben held out the paper that had been on exhibition all evening to Viney.

"Hyeah, hyeah's de docyment dat meks you yo' own ooman. Tek it."

During all the time that it had been out for show that night the people had looked upon it with a sort of awe, as if it was possessed of some sort of miraculous power. Even now Viney did not take hold of it, but shrunk away with a sort of gasp.

"No, Ben, you keep it. I can't tek keer o' no sich precious thing ez dat. Put hit in yo' chist."

"Tek hit and feel of hit, anyhow, so's you'll know dat you're free."

She took it gingerly between her thumb and forefinger. Ben suddenly let go.

"Dah, now," he said; "you keep dat docyment. It's yo's. Keep hit undah yo' own 'sponsibility."

"No, no, Ben!" she cried. "I jes' can't!"

"You mus'. Dat's de way to git used to bein' free. Whenevah you looks at yo'se'f an' feels lak you ain' no diff'ent f'om whut you been you tek dat papah out an' look at hit, an' say to yo'se'f, 'Dat means freedom.'"

Carefully, reverently, silently Viney put the paper into her bosom.

"Now, de nex' t'ing fu' me to do is to set out to git one dem papahs fu' myse'f. Hit'll be a long try, 'cause I can't buy mine so cheap as I got yo's, dough de Lawd knows why a great big ol' hunk lak me should cos' mo'n a precious mossell lak you."

"Hit's because dey's so much of you, Ben, an' evah bit of you's wo'th its weight in gol'."

"Heish, chile! Don' put my valy so high, er I'll be twell jedgment day a-payin' hit off."

Part II

So Ben went forth to battle for his own freedom, undaunted by the task before him, while Viney took care of the cabin, doing what she could outside. Armed with her new dignity, she insisted upon her friends' recognizing the change in her condition.

Thus, when Mandy so far forgot herself as to address her as Viney Raymond, the new free woman's head went up and she said with withering emphasis:

"Mis' Viney Allen, if you please!"

"Viney Allen!" exclaimed her visitor. "Huccum you's Viney Allen now?"

"'Cause I don' belong to de Raymonds no mo', an' I kin tek my own name now."

"Ben 'longs to de Raymonds, an' his name Ben Raymond an' you his wife. How you git aroun' dat, Mis' Viney Allen?"

"Ben's name goin' to be Mistah Allen soon's he gits his free papahs."

"Oomph! You done gone now! Yo' naik so stiff you can't ha'dly ben' it. I don' see how dat papah mek sich a change in anybody's actions. Yo' face ain' got no whitah."

"No, but I's free, an' I kin do as I please."

Mandy went forth and spread the news that Viney had changed her name from Raymond to Allen. "She's Mis' Viney Allen, if you please!" was her comment. Great was the indignation among the older heads whose fathers and mothers and grandfathers before them had been Raymonds. The younger element was greatly amused and took no end of pleasure in repeating the new name or addressing each other by fantastic cognomens. Viney's popularity did not increase.

Some rumors of this state of things drifted to Ben's ears and he questioned his wife about them. She admitted what she had done,

"But, Viney," said Ben, "Raymond's good enough name fu' me."

"Don' you see, Ben," she answered, "dat I don' belong to de Raymonds no mo', so I ain' Viney Raymond. Ain' you goin' change w'en you git free?"

"I don' know. I talk about dat when I's free, and freedom's a mighty long, weary way off yet."

"Evahbody dat's free has dey own name, an' I ain' nevah goin' feel free's long ez I's a-totin' aroun' de Raymonds' name."

"Well, change den," said Ben; "but wait ontwell I kin change wid you."

Viney tossed her head, and that night she took out her free papers and studied them long and carefully.

She was incensed at her friends that they would not pay her the homage that she felt was due her. She was incensed at Ben because he would not enter into her feelings about the matter. She brooded upon her fancied injuries, and when a chance for revenge came she seized upon it eagerly.

There were two or three free negro families in the vicinity of the Raymond place, but there had been no intercourse between them and the neighboring slaves. It was to these people that Viney now turned in anger against her own friends. It first amounted to a few visits back and forth, and then, either because the association became more intimate or because she was instigated to it by her new companions, she refused to have anything more to do with the Raymond servants. Boldly and without concealment she shut the door in Mandy's face, and, hearing this, few of the others gave her a similar chance.

Ben remonstrated with her, and she answered him:

"No, suh! I ain' goin' 'sociate wid slaves! I's free!"

"But you cuttin' out yo' own husban'."

"Dat's diff'ent. I's jined to my husban'." And then petulantly: "I do wish you'd hu'y up an' git yo' free papahs, Ben."

"Dey'll be a long time a-comin'," he said; "yeahs f'om now. Mebbe I'd abettah got mine fust."

She looked up at him with a quick, suspicious glance. When she was alone again she took her papers and carefully hid them.

"I's free," she whispered to herself, "an' I don' expec' to nevah be a slave no mo'."

She was further excited by the moving North of one of the free families with which she had been associated. The emigrants had painted glowing pictures of the Eldorado to which they were going, and now Viney's only talk in the evening was of the glories of the North. Ben would listen to her unmoved, until one night she said:

"You ought to go North when you gits yo' papahs."

Then he had answered her, with kindling eyes:

"No, I won't go Nawth! I was bo'n an' raised in de Souf, an' in de Souf I stay ontwell I die. Ef I have to go Nawth to injoy my freedom I won't have it. I'll quit wo'kin fu' it."

Ben was positive, but he felt uneasy, and the next day he told his master of the whole matter, and Mr. Raymond went down to talk to Viney.

She met him with a determination that surprised and angered him. To everything he said to her she made but one answer: "I's got my free papahs an' I's a-goin' Nawth."

Finally her former master left her with the remark:

"Well, I don't care where you go, but I'm sorry for Ben. He was a fool for working for you. You don't half deserve such a man."

"I won' have him long," she flung after him, with a laugh.

The opposition with which she had met seemed to have made her more obstinate, and in spite of all Ben could do, she began to make preparations to leave him. The money for the chickens and eggs had been growing and was to have gone toward her husband's ransom, but she finally sold all her laying hens to increase the amount. Then she calmly announced to her husband:

"I's got money enough an' I's a-goin' Nawth next week. You kin stay down hyeah an' be a slave ef you want to, but I's a-goin' Nawth."

"Even ef I wanted to go Nawth you know I ain' half paid out yit."

"Well, I can't he'p it. I can't spen' all de bes' pa't o' my life down hyeah where dey ain' no 'vantages."

"I reckon dey's 'vantages everywhah fu' anybody dat wants to wu'k."

"Yes, but what kin' o' wages does yo' git? Why, de Johnsons say dey had a lettah f'om Miss Smiff an' dey's gettin' 'long fine in de Nawth."

"De Johnsons ain' gwine?"

"Si Johnson is—"

Then the woman stopped suddenly.

"Oh, hit's Si Johnson? Huh!"

"He ain' goin' wid me. He's jes' goin' to see dat I git sta'ted right aftah I git thaih."

"Hit's Si Johnson?" he repeated.

"'Tain't," said the woman. "Hit's freedom."

Ben got up and went out of the cabin.

"Men's so 'spicious," she said. "I ain' goin' Nawth 'cause Si's a-goin'—I ain't."

When Mr. Raymond found out how matters were really going he went to Ben where he was at work in the field.

"Now, look here, Ben," he said. "You're one of the best hands on my place and I'd be sorry to lose you. I never did believe in this buying business from the first, but you were so bent on it that I gave in. But before I'll see her cheat you out of your money I'll give you your free papers now. You can go North with her and you can pay me back when you find work."

"No," replied Ben doggedly. "Ef she cain't wait fu' me she don' want me, an' I won't foller her erroun' an' be in de way."

"You're a fool!" said his master.

"I loves huh," said the slave. And so this plan came to naught.

Then came the night on which Viney was getting together her belongings. Ben sat in a corner of the cabin silent, his head bowed in his hands. Every once in a while the woman cast a half-frightened glance at him. He had never once tried to oppose her with force, though she saw that grief had worn lines into his face.

The door opened and Si Johnson came in. He had just dropped in to see if everything was all right. He was not to go for a week.

"Let me look at yo' free papahs," he said, for Si could read and liked to show off his accomplishment at every opportunity. He stumbled through the formal document to the end, reading at the last: "This is a present from Ben to his beloved wife, Viney."

She held out her hand for the paper. When Si was gone she sat gazing at it, trying in her ignorance to pick from the, to her, senseless scrawl those last words. Ben had not raised his head.

Still she sat there, thinking, and without looking her mind began to take in the details of the cabin. That box of shelves there in the corner Ben had made in the first days they were together. Yes, and this chair on which she was sitting—she remembered how they had laughed over its funny shape before he had padded it with cotton and covered it with the piece of linsey "old Mis'" had given him. The very chest in which her things were packed he had made, and when the last nail was driven he had called it her trunk, and said she should put her finery in it when she went traveling like the white folks. She was going traveling now, and Ben— Ben? There he sat across from her in his chair, bowed and broken, his great shoulders heaving with suppressed grief.

Then, before she knew it, Viney was sobbing, and had crept close to him and put her arms around his neck. He threw out his arms with a convulsive gesture and gathered her up to his breast, and the tears gushed from his eyes.

When the first storm of weeping had passed Viney rose and went to the fireplace. She raked forward the coals.

"Ben," she said, "hit's been dese pleggoned free papahs. I want you to see 'em bu'n."

"No, no!" he said. But the papers were already curling, and in a moment they were in a blaze.

"Thaih," she said, "thaih, now, Viney Raymond!"

Ben gave a great gasp, then sprang forward and took her in his arms and kicked the packed chest into the corner.

And that night singing was heard from Ben's cabin and the sound of the banjo.

The Fruitful Sleeping of
the Rev. Elisha Edwards

THERE WAS GREAT commotion in Zion Church, a body of Christian worshippers, usually noted for their harmony. But for the last six months, trouble had been brewing between the congregation and the pastor. The Rev. Elisha Edwards had come to them two years before, and he had given good satisfaction as to preaching and pastoral work. Only one thing had displeased his congregation in him, and that was his tendency to moments of meditative abstraction in the pulpit. However much fire he might have displayed before a brother minister arose to speak, and however much he might display in the exhortation after the brother was done with the labors of hurling phillipics against the devil, he sat between in the same way, with head bowed and eyes closed.

There were some who held that it was a sign in him of deep thoughtfulness, and that he was using these moments for silent prayer and meditation. But others, less generous, said that he was either jealous of or indifferent to other speakers. So the discussion rolled on about the Rev. Elisha, but it did not reach him and he went on in the same way until one hapless day, one tragic, one never-to-be-forgotten day. While Uncle Isham Dyer was exhorting the people to repent of their sins, the disclosure came. The old man had arisen on the wings of his eloquence and was painting hell for the sinners in the most terrible colors, when to the utter surprise of the whole congregation, a loud and penetrating snore broke from the throat of the pastor of the church. It rumbled down the silence and startled the congregation into sudden and indignant life like the surprising cannon of an invading host. Horror-stricken eyes looked into each other, hands were thrown into the air, and heavy lips made round O's of surprise and anger. This was his meditation. The Rev. Elisha Edwards was asleep!

Uncle Isham Dyer turned around and looked down on his pastor in disgust, and then turned again to his exhortations, but he was disconcerted, and soon ended lamely.

As for the Rev. Elisha himself, his snore rumbled on through the church, his head drooped lower, until with a jerk, he awakened himself. He sighed religiously, patted his foot upon the floor, rubbed his hands together, and looked complacently over the aggrieved congregation. Old ladies moaned and old men shivered, but the pastor did not know what they had discovered, and shouted Amen, because he thought something Uncle Isham had said was affecting them. Then, when he arose to put the cap sheaf on his local brother's exhortations, he was strong, fiery, eloquent, but it was of no use. Not a cry, not a moan, not an Amen could he gain from his congregation. Only the local preacher himself, thinking over the scene which had just been enacted, raised his voice, placed his hands before his eyes, and murmured, "Lord he'p we po' sinnahs!"

Brother Edwards could not understand this unresponsiveness on the part of his people. They had been wont to weave and moan and shout and sigh when he spoke to them, and when, in the midst of his sermon, he paused to break into spirited song, they would join with him until the church rang again. But this day, he sang alone, and ominous glances were flashed from pew to pew and from aisle to pulpit. The collection that morning was especially small. No one asked the minister home to dinner, an unusual thing, and so he went his way, puzzled and wondering.

Before church that night, the congregation met together for conference. The exhorter of the morning himself opened proceedings by saying, "Brothahs an' sistahs, de Lawd has opened ouah eyes to wickedness in high places."

"Oom—oom—oom, he have opened ouah eyes," moaned an old sister.

"We have been puhmitted to see de man who was intrusted wid de guidance of dis flock a-sleepin' in de houah of duty, an' we feels grieved ter-night."

"He sholy were asleep," sister Hannah Johnson broke in, "dey ain't no way to 'spute dat, dat man sholy were asleep."

"I kin testify to it," said another sister, "I p'intly did hyeah him sno', an' I hyeahed him sno't w'en he waked up."

"An' we been givin' him praise fu' meditation," pursued Brother Isham Dyer, who was only a local preacher, in fact, but who had designs on ordination, and the pastoring of Zion Church himself.

"It ain't de sleepin' itse'f," he went on, "ef you 'member in de Gyarden of Gethsemane, endurin' de agony of ouah Lawd, dem what he tuk wid him fu' to watch while he prayed, went to sleep on his han's. But he fu'give 'em, fu' he said,

'De sperit is willin' but de flesh is weak.' We know dat dey is times w'en de eyes grow sandy, an' de haid grow heavy, an' we ain't accusin' ouah brothah, nor a-blamin' him fu' noddin'. But what we do blame him fu' is fu' 'ceivin' us, an' mekin' us believe he was prayin' an' meditatin', w'en he wasn' doin' a blessed thing but snoozin'."

"Dat's it, dat's it," broke in a chorus of voices. "He 'ceived us, dat's what he did."

The meeting went stormily on, the accusation and the anger of the people against the minister growing more and more. One or two were for dismissing him then and there, but calmer counsel prevailed and it was decided to give him another trial. He was a good preacher they had to admit. He had visited them when they were sick, and brought sympathy to their afflictions, and a genial presence when they were well. They would not throw him over, without one more chance, at least, of vindicating himself.

This was well for the Rev. Elisha, for with the knowledge that he was to be given another chance, one trembling little woman, who had listened in silence and fear to the tirades against him, crept out of the church, and hastened over in the direction of the parsonage. She met the preacher coming toward the church, hymn-book in hand, and his Bible under his arm. With a gasp, she caught him by the arm, and turned him back.

"Come hyeah," she said, "come hyeah, dey been talkin' 'bout you, an' I want to tell you."

"Why, Sis' Dicey," said the minister complacently, "what is the mattah? Is you troubled in sperit?"

"I's troubled in sperit now," she answered, "but you'll be troubled in a minute. Dey done had a church meetin' befo' services. Dey foun' out you was sleepin' dis mornin' in de pulpit. You ain't only sno'ed, but you sno'ted, an' dey 'lowin' to give you one mo' trial, an' ef you falls f'om grace agin, dey gwine ax you fu' to 'sign f'om de pastorship."

The minister staggered under the blow, and his brow wrinkled. To leave Zion Church. It would be very hard. And to leave there in disgrace; where would he go? His career would be ruined. The story would go to every church of the connection in the country, and he would be an outcast from his cloth and his kind. He felt that it was all a mistake after all. He loved his work, and he loved his people. He wanted to do the right thing, but oh, sometimes, the chapel was hot and the hours were long. Then his head would grow heavy, and his eyes would close, but it had been only for a minute or two. Then, this morning, he remembered how he had tried to shake himself awake, how gradually, the feeling had overcome him. Then—then —he had snored. He had not tried wantonly to deceive them, but the Book said, "Let not thy right hand know what thy left hand doeth." He did not think it necessary to tell them that he dropped into an occasional nap in church. Now, however, they knew all.

He turned and looked down at the little woman, who waited to hear what he had to say.

"Thankye, ma'am, Sis' Dicey," he said. "Thankye, ma'am. I believe I'll go back an' pray ovah this subject." And he turned and went back into the parsonage.

Whether he had prayed over it or whether he had merely thought over it, and made his plans accordingly, when the Rev. Elisha came into church that night, he walked with a new spirit. There was a smile on his lips, and the light of triumph in his eyes. Throughout the Deacon's long prayer, his loud and insistent Amens precluded the possibility of any sleep on his part. His sermon was a masterpiece of fiery eloquence, and as Sister Green stepped out of the church door that night, she said, "Well, ef Brothah Eddards slep' dis mornin', he sholy prached a wakenin' up sermon ter-night." The congregation hardly remembered that their pastor had ever been asleep. But the pastor knew when the first flush of enthusiasm was over that their minds would revert to the crime of the morning, and he made plans accordingly for the next Sunday which should again vindicate him in the eyes of his congregation.

The Sunday came round, and as he ascended to the pulpit, their eyes were fastened upon him with suspicious glances. Uncle Isham Dyer had a smile of triumph on his face, because the day was a particularly hot and drowsy one. It was on this account, the old man thought, that the Rev. Elisha asked him to say a few words at the opening of the meeting. "Shirkin' again," said the old man to himself, "I reckon he wants to go to sleep again, but ef he don't sleep dis day to his own confusion, I ain't hyeah." So he arose, and burst into a wonderful exhortation on the merits of a Christian life.

He had scarcely been talking for five minutes, when the ever watchful congregation saw the pastor's head droop, and his eyes close. For the next fifteen minutes, little or no attention was paid to Brother Dyer's exhortation. The angry people were nudging each other, whispering, and casting indignant glances at the sleeping pastor. He awoke and sat up, just as the exhorter was finishing in a fiery period. If those who watched him, were expecting to see any embarrassed look on his face, or show of timidity in his eyes, they were mistaken. Instead, his appearance was one of sudden alertness, and his gaze that of a man in extreme exaltation. One would have said that it had been given to him as to the inspired prophets of old to see and to hear things far and beyond the ken of ordinary mortals. As Brother Dyer sat down, he arose quickly and went forward to the front of the pulpit with a firm step. Still, with the look of exaltation on his face, he announced his text, "Ef he sleep he shell do well."

The congregation, which a moment before had been all indignation, suddenly sprang into the most alert attention. There was a visible pricking up of ears as the preacher entered into his subject. He spoke first of the benefits of sleep, what it did for the worn human body and the weary human soul, then turning off into a half-humorous, half-quizzical strain, which was often in his sermons, he spoke of how many times he had to forgive some of those who sat before him to-day for nodding in their pews; then raising his voice, like a good preacher, he came back to his text, exclaiming, "But ef he sleep, he shell do well."

He went on then, and told of Jacob's sleep, and how at night, in the midst of his slumbers the visions of angels had come to him, and he had left a testimony behind him that was still a solace to their hearts. Then he lowered his voice and said:

"You all condemns a man when you sees him asleep, not knowin' what visions is a-goin' thoo his mind, nor what feelin's is a-goin thoo his heart. You ain't conside'in' that mebbe he's a-doin' mo' in the soul wo'k when he's asleep then when he's awake. Mebbe he sleep, w'en you think he ought to be up a-wo'kin'. Mebbe he slumber w'en you think he ought to be up an' erbout. Mebbe he sno' an' mebbe he sno't, but I'm a-hyeah to tell you, in de wo'ds of the Book, that they ain't no 'sputin' 'Ef he sleep, he shell do well!'"

"Yes, Lawd!" "Amen!" "Sleep on Ed'ards!" some one shouted. The church was in smiles of joy. They were rocking to and fro with the ecstasy of the sermon, but the Rev. Elisha had not yet put on the cap sheaf.

"Hol' on," he said, "befo' you shouts er befo' you sanctions. Fu' you may yet have to tu'n yo' backs erpon me, an' say, 'Lawd he'p the man!' I's a-hyeah to tell you that many's the time in this very pulpit, right under yo' very eyes, I has gone f'om meditation into slumber. But what was the reason? Was I a-shirkin' er was I lazy?"

Shouts of "No! No!" from the congregation.

"No, no," pursued the preacher, "I wasn't a-shirkin' ner I wasn't a-lazy, but the soul within me was a wo'kin' wid the min', an' as we all gwine ter do some day befo' long, early in de mornin', I done fu'git this ol' body. My haid fall on my breas', my eyes close, an' I see visions of anothah day to come. I see visions of a new Heaven an' a new earth, when we shell all be clothed in white raimen', an' we shell play ha'ps of gol', an' walk de golden streets of the New Jerusalem! That's what been a runnin' thoo my min', w'en I set up in the pulpit an' sleep under the Wo'd; but I want to ax you, was I wrong? I want to ax you, was I sinnin'? I want to p'int you right hyeah to the Wo'd, as it are read out in yo' hyeahin' ter-day, 'Ef he sleep, he shell do well.'"

The Rev. Elisha ended his sermon amid the smiles and nods and tears of his congregation. No one had a harsh word for him now, and even Brother Dyer wiped his eyes and whispered to his next neighbor, "Dat man sholy did sleep to some pu'pose," although he knew that the dictum was a deathblow to his own pastoral hopes. The people thronged around the pastor as he descended from the pulpit, and held his hand as they had done of yore. One old woman went out, still mumbling under her breath, "Sleep on, Ed'ards, sleep on."

There were no more church meetings after that, and no tendency to dismiss the pastor. On the contrary, they gave him a donation party next week, at which Sister Dicey helped him to receive his guests.

The Ingrate

I

Mr. Leckler was a man of high principle. Indeed, he himself had admitted it at times to Mrs. Leckler. She was often called into counsel with him. He was one of those large souled creatures with a hunger for unlimited advice, upon which he never acted. Mrs. Leckler knew this, but like the good, patient little wife that she was, she went on paying her poor tribute of advice and admiration. To-day her husband's mind was particularly troubled,—as usual, too, over a matter of principle. Mrs. Leckler came at his call.

"Mrs. Leckler," he said, "I am troubled in my mind. I—in fact, I am puzzled over a matter that involves either the maintaining or relinquishing of a principle."

"Well, Mr. Leckler?" said his wife, interrogatively.

"If I had been a scheming, calculating Yankee, I should have been rich now; but all my life I have been too generous and confiding. I have always let principle stand between me and my interests." Mr. Leckler took himself all too seriously to be conscious of his pun, and went on: "Now this is a matter in which my duty and my principles seem to conflict. It stands thus: Josh has been doing a piece of plastering for Mr. Eckley over in Lexington, and from what he says, I think that city rascal has misrepresented the amount of work to me and so cut down the pay for it. Now, of course, I should not care, the matter of a dollar or two being nothing to me; but it is a very different matter when we consider poor Josh." There was deep pathos in Mr. Leckler's tone. "You know Josh is anxious to buy his freedom, and I allow him a part of whatever he makes; so you see it's he that's affected. Every dollar that he is cheated out of cuts off just so much from his earnings, and puts further away his hope of emancipation."

If the thought occurred to Mrs. Leckler that, since Josh received only about one-tenth of what he earned, the advantage of just wages would be quite as much her husband's as the slave's, she did not betray it, but met the naïve reasoning with the question, "But where does the conflict come in, Mr. Leckler?"

"Just here. If Josh knew how to read and write and cipher—"

"Mr. Leckler, are you crazy!"

"Listen to me, my dear, and give me the benefit of your judgment. This is a very momentous question. As I was about to say, if Josh knew these things, he could protect himself from cheating when his work is at too great a distance for me to look after it for him."

"But teaching a slave—"

"Yes, that's just what is against my principles. I know how public opinion and the law look at it. But my conscience rises up in rebellion every time I think of that poor black man being cheated out of his earnings. Really, Mrs. Leckler, I think I may trust to Josh's discretion, and secretly give him such instructions as will permit him to protect himself."

"Well, of course, it's just as you think best," said his wife.

"I knew you would agree with me," he returned. "It's such a comfort to take counsel with you, my dear!" And the generous man walked out on to the veranda, very well satisfied with himself and his wife, and prospectively pleased with Josh. Once he murmured to himself, "I'll lay for Eckley next time."

Josh, the subject of Mr. Leckler's charitable solicitations, was the plantation plasterer. His master had given him his trade, in order that he might do whatever such work was needed about the place; but he became so proficient in his duties, having also no competition among the poor whites, that he had grown to be in great demand in the country thereabout. So Mr. Leckler found it profitable, instead of letting him do chores and field work in his idle time, to hire him out to neighboring farms and planters. Josh was a man of more than ordinary intelligence; and when he asked to be allowed to pay for himself by working overtime, his master readily agreed,—for it promised more work to be done, for which he could allow the slave just what he pleased. Of course, he knew now that when the black man began to cipher this state of affairs would be changed; but it would mean such an increase of profit from the outside, that he could afford to give up his own little peculations. Anyway, it would be many years before the slave could pay the two thousand dollars, which price he had set upon him. Should he approach that figure, Mr. Leckler felt it just possible that the market in slaves would take a sudden rise.

When Josh was told of his master's intention, his eyes gleamed with pleasure, and he went to his work with the zest of long hunger. He proved a remarkably apt pupil. He was indefatigable in doing the tasks assigned him. Even Mr. Leckler, who had great faith in his plasterer's ability, marveled at the speed which he had acquired the three R's. He did not know that on one of his many trips a free negro had given Josh the rudimentary tools of learning, and that since the slave had been adding to his store of learning by poring over signs and every bit of print that he could spell out. Neither was Josh so indiscreet as to intimate to his benefactor that he had been anticipated in his good intentions.

It was in this way, working and learning, that a year passed away, and Mr. Leckler thought that his object had been accomplished. He could safely trust Josh to protect his own interests, and so he thought that it was quite time that his servant's education should cease.

"You know, Josh," he said, "I have already gone against my principles and against the law for your sake, and of course a man can't stretch his conscience too far, even to help another who's being cheated; but I reckon you can take care of yourself now."

"Oh, yes, suh, I reckon I kin," said Josh.

"And it wouldn't do for you to be seen with any books about you now."

"Oh, no, suh, su't'n'y not." He didn't intend to be seen with any books about him.

It was just now that Mr. Leckler saw the good results of all he had done, and his heart was full of a great joy, for Eckley had been building some additions to his house, and sent for Josh to do the plastering for him. The owner admonished his slave, took him over a few examples to freshen his memory, and sent him forth with glee. When the job was done, there was a discrepancy of two dollars in what Mr. Eckley offered for it and the price which accrued from Josh's measurements. To the employer's surprise, the black man went over the figures with him and convinced him of the incorrectness of the payment,—and the additional two dollars were turned over.

"Some o' Leckler's work," said Eckley, "teaching a nigger to cipher! Close-fisted old reprobate,—I've a mind to have the law on him."

Mr. Leckler heard the story with great glee. "I laid for him that time—the old fox." But to Mrs. Leckler he said: "You see, my dear wife, my rashness in teaching Josh to figure for himself is vindicated. See what he has saved for himself."

"What did he save?" asked the little woman indiscreetly.

Her husband blushed and stammered for a moment, and then replied, "Well, of course, it was only twenty cents saved to him, but to a man buying his freedom every cent counts; and after all, it is not the amount, Mrs. Leckler, it's the principle of the thing."

"Yes," said the lady meekly.

II

Unto the body it is easy for the master to say, "Thus far shalt thou go, and no far-ther." Gyves, chains and fetters will enforce that command. But what master shall say unto the mind, "Here do I set the limit of your acquisition. Pass it not"? Who shall put gyves upon the intellect, or fetter the movement of thought? Joshua Leck-ler, as custom denominated him, had tasted of the forbidden fruit, and his appetite had grown by what it fed on. Night after night he crouched in his lonely cabin, by the blaze of a fat pine brand, poring over the few books that he had been able to secure and smuggle in. His fellow-servants alternately laughed at him and wondered why he did not take a wife. But Joshua went on his way. He had no time for marry-ing or for love; other thoughts had taken possession of him. He was being swayed by ambitions other than the mere fathering of slaves for his master. To him his slav-ery was deep night. What wonder, then, that he should dream, and that through the ivory gate should come to him the forbidden vision of freedom? To own himself, to be master of his hands, feet, of his whole body—something would clutch at his heart as he thought of it; and the breath would come hard between his lips. But he met his master with an impassive face, always silent, always docile; and Mr. Leck-ler congratulated himself that so valuable and intelligent a slave should be at the same time so tractable. Usually intelligence in a slave meant discontent; but not so with Josh. Who more content than he? He remarked to his wife:

"You see, my dear, this is what comes of treating even a nigger right."

Meanwhile the white hills of the North were beckoning to the chattel, and the north winds were whispering to him to be a chattel no longer. Often the eyes that looked away to where freedom lay were filled with a wistful longing that was tragic in its intensity, for they saw the hardships and the difficulties between the slave and his goal and, worst of all, an iniquitous law,—liberty's compromise with bondage, that rose like a stone wall between him and hope,—a law that degraded every free-thinking man to the level of a slave-catcher. There it loomed up before him, for-midable, impregnable, insurmountable. He measured it in all its terribleness, and paused. But on the other side there was liberty; and one day when he was away at work, a voice came out of the woods and whispered to him "Courage!"—and on that night the shadows beckoned him as the white hills had done, and the forest called to him, "Follow."

"It seems to me that Josh might have been able to get home to-night," said Mr. Leckler, walking up and down his veranda; "but I reckon it's just possible that he got through too late to catch a train." In the morning he said: "Well, he's not here yet; he must have had to do some extra work. If he doesn't get here by evening, I'll run up there."

In the evening, he did take the train for Joshua's place of employment, where he learned that his slave had left the night before. But where could he have gone? That no one knew, and for the first time it dawned upon his master that Josh had run away. He raged; he fumed; but nothing could be done until morning, and all the time Leckler knew that the most valuable slave on his plantation was working his way toward the North and freedom. He did not go back home, but paced the floor all night long. In the early dawn he hurried out, and the hounds were put on the fugitive's track. After some nosing around they set off toward a stretch of woods. In a few minutes they came yelping back, pawing their noses and rubbing their heads against the ground. They had found the trail, but Josh had played the old slave trick of filling his tracks with cayenne pepper. The dogs were soothed, and taken deeper into the wood to find the trail. They soon took it up again, and dashed away with low bays. The scent led them directly to a little wayside station about six miles distant. Here it stopped. Burning with the chase, Mr. Leckler has-tened to the station agent. Had he seen such a negro? Yes, he had taken the north-bound train two nights before.

"But why did you let him go without a pass?" almost screamed the owner.

"I didn't," replied the agent. "He had a written pass, signed James Leckler, and I let him go on it."

"Forged, forged!" yelled the master. "He wrote it himself."

"Humph!" said the agent, "how was I to know that? Our niggers round here don't know how to write."

Mr. Leckler suddenly bethought him to hold his peace. Josh was probably now in the arms of some northern abolitionist, and there was nothing to be done now but advertise; and the disgusted master spread his notices broadcast before starting for home. As soon as he arrived at his house, he sought his wife and poured out his griefs to her.

"You see, Mrs. Leckler, this is what comes of my goodness of heart. I taught that nigger to read and write, so that he could protect himself,—and look how he uses his knowledge. Oh, the ingrate, the ingrate! The very weapon which I give him to defend himself against others he turns upon me. Oh, it's awful,—awful! I've always been too confiding. Here's the most valuable nigger on my plantation gone,—gone, I tell you,—and through my own kindness. It isn't his value, though, I'm thinking so much about. I could stand his loss, if it wasn't for the principle of the thing, the base ingratitude he has shown me. Oh, if I ever lay hands on him again!" Mr. Leckler closed his lips and clenched his fist with an eloquence that laughed at words.

Just at this time, in one of the underground railway stations, six miles north of the Ohio, an old Quaker was saying to Josh: "Lie still,—thee'll be perfectly safe there. Here comes John Trader, our local slave catcher, but I will parley with him and send him away. Thee need not fear. None of thy brethren who have come to us have ever been taken back to bondage.—Good-evening, Friend Trader!" and Josh heard the old Quaker's smooth voice roll on, while he lay back half smothering in a bag, among other bags of corn and potatoes.

It was after ten o'clock that night when he was thrown carelessly into a wagon and driven away to the next station, twenty-five miles to the northward. And by such stages, hiding by day and traveling by night, helped by a few of his own people who were blessed with freedom, and always by the good Quakers wherever found, he made his way into Canada. And on one never-to-be-forgotten morning he stood up, straightened himself, breathed God's blessed air, and knew himself free!

III

To Joshua Leckler this life in Canada was all new and strange. It was a new thing for him to feel himself a man and to have his manhood recognized by the whites with whom he came into free contact. It was new, too, this receiving the full measure of his worth in work. He went to his labor with a zest that he had never known before, and he took a pleasure in the very weariness it brought him. Ever and anon there came to his ears the cries of his brethren in the South. Frequently he met fugitives who, like himself, had escaped from bondage; and the harrowing tales that they told him made him burn to do something for those whom he had left behind him. But these fugitives and the papers he read told him other things. They said that the spirit of freedom was working in the United States, and already men were speaking out boldly in behalf of the manumission of the slaves; already there was a growing army behind that noble vanguard, Sumner, Phillips, Douglass, Garrison. He heard the names of Lucretia Mott and Harriet Beecher Stowe, and his heart swelled, for on the dim horizon he saw the first faint streaks of dawn.

So the years passed. Then from the surcharged clouds a flash of lightning broke, and there was the thunder of cannon and the rain of lead over the land. From his home in the North he watched the storm as it raged and wavered, now threatening the North with its awful power, now hanging dire and dreadful over the South. Then suddenly from out the fray came a voice like the trumpet tone of God to him: "Thou and thy brothers are free!" Free, free, with the freedom not cherished by the few alone, but for all that had been bound. Free, with the freedom not torn from the secret night, but open to the light of heaven.

When the first call for colored soldiers came, Joshua Leckler hastened down to Boston, and enrolled himself among those who were willing to fight to maintain their freedom. On account of his ability to read and write and his general intelligence, he was soon made an orderly sergeant. His regiment had already taken part in an engagement before the public roster of this band of Uncle Sam's niggers, as they were called, fell into Mr. Leckler's hands. He ran his eye down the column of names. It stopped at that of Joshua Leckler, Sergeant, Company F. He handed the paper to Mrs. Leckler with his finger on the place:

"Mrs. Leckler," he said, "this is nothing less than a judgment on me for teaching a nigger to read and write. I disobeyed the law of my state and, as a result, not only lost my nigger, but furnished the Yankees with a smart officer to help them fight the South. Mrs. Leckler, I have sinned—and been punished. But I am content, Mrs. Leckler; it all came through my kindness of heart,—and your mistaken advice. But, oh, that ingrate, that ingrate!"

The Case of "Ca'line"

A Kitchen Monologue

THE MAN OF the house is about to go into the dining-room when he hears voices that tell him that his wife has gone down to give the "hired help" a threatened going over. He quietly withdraws, closes the door noiselessly behind him and listens from a safe point of vantage.

One voice is timid and hesitating; that is his wife. The other is fearlessly raised; that is her majesty, the queen who rules the kitchen, and from it the rest of the house.

This is what he overhears:

"Well, Mis' Ma'tin, hit do seem lak you jes' bent an' boun' to be a-fin'in' fault wid me w'en de Lawd knows I's doin' de ve'y bes' I kin. What 'bout de brekfus'? De steak too done an' de 'taters ain't done enough! Now, Miss Ma'tin, I jes' want to show you I cooked dat steak an' dem 'taters de same lengt' o' time. Seems to me dey ought to be done de same. Dat uz a thick steak, an' I jes' got hit browned thoo nice. What mo'd you want?

"You didn't want it fried at all? Now, Mis' Ma'tin, 'clah to goodness! Who evah hyeah de beat o' dat? Don't you know dat fried meat is de bes' kin' in de worl'? W'y, de las' fambly dat I lived wid—dat uz ol' Jedge Johnson—he said dat I beat anybody fryin' he evah seen; said I fried evahthing in sight, an' he said my fried food stayed by him longer than anything he evah e't. Even w'en he paid me off he said it was 'case he thought somebody else ought to have de benefit of my wunnerful powahs. Huh, ma'am, I's used to de bes'. De Jedge paid me de highes' kin' o' comperments. De las' thing he say to me was, 'Ca'line, Ca'line,' he say, 'yo' cookin' is a pa'dox. It is crim'nal, dey ain't no 'sputin' dat, but it ain't action'ble.' Co'se, I didn't unnerstan' his langidge, but I knowed hit was comperments, 'case his wife, Mis' Jedge Johnson, got right jealous an' told him to shet his mouf.

"Dah you goes. Now, who'd 'a' thought dat a lady of yo' raisin' an unner-stannin' would 'a' brung dat up. De mo'nin' you come an' ketch me settin' down an' de brekfus not ready, I was a-steadyin'. I's a mighty han' to steady, Mis' Ma'tin. 'Deed I steadies mos' all de time. But dat mo'nin' I got to steadyin' an' aftah while I sot down an' all my troubles come to my min'. I sho' has a heap o' trouble. I jes' sot thaih a-steadyin' 'bout 'em an' a-steadyin' tell bime-by, hyeah you comes.

"No, ma'am, I wasn't 'sleep. I's mighty apt to nod w'en I's a-thinkin'. It's a kin' o' keepin' time to my idees. But bless yo' soul I wasn't 'sleep. I shets my eyes so's to see to think bettah. An' aftah all, Mistah Ma'tin wasn't mo' 'n half an houah late dat mo'nin' nohow, 'case w'en I did git up I sholy flew. Ef you jes' 'membahs 'bout my steadyin' we ain't nevah gwine have no trouble long's I stays hyeah.

"You say dat one night I stayed out tell one o'clock. W'y—oh, yes. Dat uz Thu'sday night. W'y la! Mis' Ma'tin, dat's de night my s'ciety meets, de Af'Ame'i-can Sons an' Daughtahs of Judah. We had to 'nitianate a new can'date dat night, an' la! I wish you'd 'a' been thaih, you'd 'a' killed yo'self a-laffin'.

"You nevah did see sich ca'in's on in all yo' bo'n days. It was pow'ful funny. Broth' Eph'am Davis, he's ouah Mos' Wusshipful Rabbi, he says hit uz de mos' s'cessful 'nitination we evah had. Dat can'date pawed de groun' lak a hoss an' tried to git outen de winder. But I got to be mighty keerful how I talk: I do' know whethah you 'long to any secut s'cieties er not. I wouldn't been so late even fu' dat, but Mistah Hi'am Smif, he gallanted me home an' you know a lady boun' to stan' at de gate an' talk to huh comp'ny a little while. You know how it is, Mis' Ma'tin.

"I been en'tainin' my comp'ny in de pa'lor? Co'se I has; you wasn't usin' it. What you s'pose my frien's 'u'd think ef I'd ax 'em in de kitchen w'en dey wasn't no one in de front room? Co'se I ax 'em in de pa'lor. I do' want my frien's to think

I's wo'kin' fu' no low-down people. W'y, Miss 'Liza Harris set down an' played mos' splendid on yo' pianna, an' she compermented you mos' high. S'pose I'd a tuck huh in de kitchen, whaih de comperments come in?

"Yass'm, yass'm, I does tek home little things now an' den, dat I does, an' I ain't gwine to 'ny it. I jes' says to myse'f, I ain't wo'kin' fu' no strainers lak de people nex' do', what goes into tantrums ef de lady what cooks fu' 'em teks home a bit o' sugar. I 'lows to myse'f I ain't wo'kin' fu' no sich folks; so sometimes I teks home jes' a weenchy bit o' somep'n' dat nobody couldn't want nohow, an' I knows you ain't gwine 'ject to dat. You do 'ject, you do 'ject! Huh!

"I's got to come an' ax you, has I? Look a-hyeah, Mis' Ma'tin, I know has to wo'k in yo' kitchen. I know I has to cook fu' you, but I want you to know dat even ef I does I's a lady. I's a lady, but I see you do' know how to 'preciate a lady w'en you meets one. You kin jes' light in an' git yo' own dinner. I wouldn't wo'k fu' you ef you uz made o' gol'. I nevah did lak to wo'k fu' strainers, nohow.

"No, ma'am, I cain't even stay an' git de dinner. I know w'en I been insulted. Seems lak ef I stay in hyeah another minute I'll bile all over dis kitchen.

"Who excited? Me excited? No, I ain't excited. I's mad. I do' lak nobody pesterin' 'roun' my kitchen, nohow, huh, uh, honey. Too many places in dis town waitin' fu' Ca'line Mason.

"No, indeed, you needn't 'pologize to me! needn't 'pologize to me! I b'lieve in people sayin' jes' what dey mean, I does.

"Would I stay, ef you 'crease my wages? Well—I reckon I could, but I—but I do' want no foolishness."

(Sola.) "Huh! Did she think she was gwine to come down hyeah an' skeer me, huh, uh? Whaih's dat fryin' pan?"

The man of the house hears the rustle of his wife's skirts as she beats a retreat and he goes upstairs and into the library whistling, "See, the Conquering Hero Comes."

The Finish of Patsy Barnes

HIS NAME WAS Patsy Barnes, and he was a denizen of Little Africa. In fact, he lived on Douglass Street. By all the laws governing the relations between people and their names, he should have been Irish—but he was not. He was colored, and very much so. That was the reason he lived on Douglass Street. The negro has very strong within him the instinct of colonization and it was in accordance with this that

Patsy's mother had found her way to Little Africa when she had come North from Kentucky.

Patsy was incorrigible. Even into the confines of Little Africa had penetrated the truant officer and the terrible penalty of the compulsory education law. Time and time again had poor Eliza Barnes been brought up on account of the short-comings of that son of hers. She was a hard-working, honest woman, and day by day bent over her tub, scrubbing away to keep Patsy in shoes and jackets, that would wear out so much faster than they could be bought. But she never murmured, for she loved the boy with a deep affection, though his misdeeds were a sore thorn in her side.

She wanted him to go to school. She wanted him to learn. She had the notion that he might become something better, something higher than she had been. But for him school had no charms; his school was the cool stalls in the big livery stable near at hand; the arena of his pursuits its sawdust floor; the height of his ambi-tion, to be a horseman. Either here or in the racing stables at the Fair-grounds he spent his truant hours. It was a school that taught much, and Patsy was as apt a pupil as he was a constant attendant. He learned strange things about horses, and fine, sonorous oaths that sounded eerie on his young lips, for he had only turned into his fourteenth year.

A man goes where he is appreciated; then could this slim black boy be blamed for doing the same thing? He was a great favorite with the horsemen, and picked up many a dime or nickel for dancing or singing, or even a quarter for warming up a horse for its owner. He was not to be blamed for this, for, first of all, he was born in Kentucky, and had spent the very days of his infancy about the paddocks near Lexington, where his father had sacrificed his life on account of his love for horses. The little fellow had shed no tears when he looked at his father's bleeding body, bruised and broken by the fiery young two-year-old he was trying to subdue. Patsy did not sob or whimper, though his heart ached, for over all the feeling of his grief was a mad, burning desire to ride that horse.

His tears were shed, however, when, actuated by the idea that times would be easier up North, they moved to Dalesford. Then, when he learned that he must leave his old friends, the horses and their masters, whom he had known, he wept. The comparatively meagre appointments of the Fair-grounds at Dalesford proved a poor compensation for all these. For the first few weeks Patsy had dreams of running away—back to Kentucky and the horses and stables. Then after a while he settled himself with heroic resolution to make the best of what he had, and with a mighty effort took up the burden of life away from his beloved home.

Eliza Barnes, older and more experienced though she was, took up her burden with a less cheerful philosophy than her son. She worked hard, and made a scanty livelihood, it is true, but she did not make the best of what she had. Her complain-ings were loud in the land, and her wailings for her old home smote the ears of any who would listen to her.

They had been living in Dalesford for a year nearly, when hard work and ex-posure brought the woman down to bed with pneumonia. They were very poor—

too poor even to call in a doctor, so there was nothing to do but to call in the city physician. Now this medical man had too frequent calls into Little Africa, and he did not like to go there. So he was very gruff when any of its denizens called him, and it was even said that he was careless of his patients.

Patsy's heart bled as he heard the doctor talking to his mother:

"Now, there can't be any foolishness about this," he said. "You've got to stay in bed and not get yourself damp."

"How long you think I got to lay hyeah, doctah?" she asked.

"I'm a doctor, not a fortune-teller," was the reply. "You'll lie there as long as the disease holds you."

"But I can't lay hyeah long, doctah, case I ain't got nuffin' to go on."

"Well, take your choice: the bed or the boneyard."

Eliza began to cry.

"You needn't sniffle," said the doctor; " I don't see what you people want to come up here for anyhow. Why don't you stay down South where you belong? You come up here and you're just a burden and a trouble to the city. The South deals with all of you better, both in poverty and crime." He knew that these people did not understand him, but he wanted an outlet for the heat within him.

There was another angry being in the room, and that was Patsy. His eyes were full of tears that scorched him and would not fall. The memory of many beautiful and appropriate oaths came to him; but he dared not let his mother hear him swear. Oh! to have a stone—to be across the street from that man!

When the physician walked out, Patsy went to the bed, took his mother's hand, and bent over shamefacedly to kiss her. He did not know that with that act the Recording Angel blotted out many a curious damn of his.

The little mark of affection comforted Eliza unspeakably. The mother-feeling overwhelmed her in one burst of tears. Then she dried her eyes and smiled at him.

"Honey," she said; "mammy ain' gwine lay hyeah long. She be all right putty soon."

"Nevah you min'," said Patsy with a choke in his voice. "I can do somep'n', an' we'll have anothah doctah."

"La, listen at de chile; what kin you do?"

"I'm goin' down to McCarthy's stable and see if I kin git some horses to exercise."

A sad look came into Eliza's eyes as she said:

"You'd bettah not go, Patsy; dem hosses'll kill you yit, des lak dey did yo' pappy."

But the boy, used to doing pretty much as he pleased, was obdurate, and even while she was talking, put on his ragged jacket and left the room.

Patsy was not wise enough to be diplomatic. He went right to the point with McCarthy, the liveryman.

The big red-faced fellow slapped him until he spun round and round. Then he said, "Ye little devil, ye, I've a mind to knock the whole head off o' ye. Ye want harses to exercise, do ye? Well git on that 'un, an' see what ye kin do with him."

The boy's honest desire to be helpful had tickled the big, generous Irishman's peculiar sense of humor, and from now on, instead of giving Patsy a horse to ride now and then as he had formerly done, he put into his charge all the animals that needed exercise.

It was with a king's pride that Patsy marched home with his first considerable earnings.

They were small yet, and would go for food rather than a doctor, but Eliza was inordinately proud, and it was this pride that gave her strength and the desire of life to carry her through the days approaching the crisis of her disease.

As Patsy saw his mother growing worse, saw her gasping for breath, heard the rattling as she drew in the little air that kept going her clogged lungs, felt the heat of her burning hands, and saw the pitiful appeal in her poor eyes, he became convinced that the city doctor was not helping her. She must have another. But the money?

That afternoon, after his work with McCarthy, found him at the Fair-grounds. The spring races were on, and he thought he might get a job warming up the horse of some independent jockey. He hung around the stables, listening to the talk of men he knew and some he had never seen before. Among the latter was a tall, lanky man, holding forth to a group of men.

"No, suh," he was saying to them generally, "I'm goin' to withdraw my hoss, because thaih ain't nobody to ride him as he ought to be rode. I haven't brought a jockey along with me, so I've got to depend on pick-ups. Now, the talent's set agin my hoss, Black Boy, because he's been losin' regular, but that hoss has lost for the want of ridin', that's all."

The crowd looked in at the slim-legged, raw boned horse, and walked away laughing.

"The fools!" muttered the stranger. "If I could ride myself I'd show 'em!"

Patsy was gazing into the stall at the horse.

"What are you doing thaih," called the owner to him.

"Look hyeah, mistah," said Patsy, "ain't that a bluegrass hoss?"

"Of co'se it is, an' one o' the fastest that evah grazed."

"I'll ride that hoss, mistah."

"What do you know 'bout ridin'?"

"I used to gin'ally be' roun' Mistah Boone's paddock in Lexington, an'—"

"Aroun' Boone's paddock—what! Look here, little nigger, if you can ride that hoss to a winnin' I'll give you more money than you ever seen before."

"I'll ride him."

Patsy's heart was beating very wildly beneath his jacket. That horse. He knew that glossy coat. He knew that raw-boned frame and those flashing nostrils. That black horse there owed something to the orphan he had made.

The horse was to ride in the race before the last. Somehow out of odds and ends, his owner scraped together a suit and colors for Patsy. The colors were maroon and green, a curious combination. But then it was a curious horse, a curious rider, and a more curious combination that brought the two together.

Long before the time for the race Patsy went into the stall to become better acquainted with his horse. The animal turned its wild eyes upon him and neighed. He patted the long, slender head, and grinned as the horse stepped aside as gently as a lady.

"He sholy is full o' ginger," he said to the owner, whose name he had found to be Brackett.

"He'll show 'em a thing or two," laughed Brackett.

"His dam was a fast one," said Patsy, unconsciously.

Brackett whirled on him in a flash. "What do you know about his dam?" he asked.

The boy would have retracted, but it was too late. Stammeringly he told the story of his father's death and the horse's connection therewith.

"Well," said Brackett, "if you don't turn out a hoodoo, you're a winner, sure. But I'll be blessed if this don't sound like a story! But I've heard that story before. The man I got Black Boy from, no matter how I got him, you're too young to understand the ins and outs of poker, told it to me."

When the bell sounded and Patsy went out to warm up, he felt as if he were riding on air. Some of the jockeys laughed at his get-up, but there was something in him—or under him, maybe—that made him scorn their derision. He saw a sea of faces about him, then saw no more. Only a shining white track loomed ahead of him, and a restless steed was cantering with him around the curve. Then the bell called him back to the stand.

They did not get away at first, and back they trooped. A second trial was a failure. But at the third they were off in a line as straight as a chalk-mark. There were Essex and Firefly, Queen Bess and Mosquito, galloping away side by side, and Black Boy a neck ahead. Patsy knew the family reputation of his horse for endurance as well as fire, and began riding the race from the first. Black Boy came of blood that would not be passed, and to this his rider trusted. At the eighth the line was hardly broken, but as the quarter was reached Black Boy had forged a length ahead, and Mosquito was at his flank. Then, like a flash, Essex shot out ahead under whip and spur, his jockey standing straight in the stirrups.

The crowd in the stand screamed; but Patsy smiled as he lay low over his horse's neck. He saw that Essex had made his best spurt. His only fear was for Mosquito, who hugged and hugged his flank. They were nearing the three-quarter post, and he was tightening his grip on the black. Essex fell back; his spurt was over. The whip fell unheeded on his sides. The spurs dug him in vain.

Black Boy's breath touches the leader's ear. They are neck and neck—nose to nose. The black stallion passes him.

Another cheer from the stand, and again Patsy smiles as they turn into the stretch. Mosquito has gained a head. The colored boy flashes one glance at the horse and rider who are so surely gaining upon him, and his lips close in a grim line. They are half-way down the stretch, and Mosquito's head is at the stallion's neck.

For a single moment Patsy thinks of the sick woman at home and what that race will mean to her, and then his knees close against the horse's sides with a firmer dig. The spurs shoot deeper into the steaming flanks. Black Boy shall win; he must win. The horse that has taken away his father shall give him back his mother. The stallion leaps away like a flash, and goes under the wire—a length ahead.

Then the band thundered, and Patsy was off his horse, very warm and very happy, following his mount to the stable. There, a little later, Brackett found him. He rushed to him, and flung his arms around him.

"You little devil," he cried, "you rode like you were kin to that hoss! We've won! We've won!" And he began sticking banknotes at the boy. At first Patsy's eyes bulged, and then he seized the money and got into his clothes.

"Goin' out to spend it?" asked Brackett.

"I'm goin' for a doctah fu' my mother," said Patsy, "she's sick."

"Don't let me lose sight of you."

"Oh, I'll see you again. So long," said the boy.

An hour later he walked into his mother's room with a very big doctor, the greatest the druggist could direct him to. The doctor left his medicines and his orders, but, when Patsy told his story, it was Eliza's pride that started her on the road to recovery. Patsy did not tell his horse's name.

One Man's Fortunes

Part I

WHEN BERTRAM HALLIDAY left the institution which, in the particular part of the middle west where he was born, was called the state university, he did not believe, as young graduates are reputed to, that he had conquered the world and had only to come into his kingdom. He knew that the battle of life was, in reality, just beginning and, with a common sense unusual to his twenty-three years but born out of the exigencies of a none-too-easy life, he recognized that for him the battle would be harder than for his white comrades.

Looking at his own position, he saw himself the member of a race dragged from complacent savagery into the very heat and turmoil of a civilization for which it was in nowise prepared; bowed beneath a yoke to which its shoulders were not fitted, and then, without warning, thrust forth into a freedom as absurd as it was startling and overwhelming. And yet, he felt, as most young men must feel, an individual strength that would exempt him from the workings of the general law.

His outlook on life was calm and unfrightened. Because he knew the dangers that beset his way, he feared them less. He felt assured because with so clear an eye he saw the weak places in his armor which the world he was going to meet would attack, and these he was prepared to strengthen. Was it not the fault of youth and self-confessed weakness, he thought, to go into the world always thinking of it as a foe? Was not this great Cosmopolis, this dragon of a thousand talons kind as well as cruel? Had it not friends as well as enemies? Yes. That was it: the outlook of young men, of colored young men in particular, was all wrong,—they had gone at the world in the wrong spirit. They had looked upon it as a terrible foeman and forced it to be one. He would do it, oh, so differently. He would take the world as a friend. He would even take the old, old world under his wing.

They sat in the room talking that night, he and Webb Davis and Charlie McLean. It was the last night they were to be together in so close a relation. The commencement was over. They had their sheepskins. They were pitched there on the bed very carelessly to be the important things they were,—the reward of four years digging in Greek and Mathematics.

They had stayed after the exercises of the day just where they had first stopped. This was at McLean's rooms, dismantled and topsy-turvy with the business of packing. The pipes were going and the talk kept pace. Old men smoke slowly and in great whiffs with long intervals of silence between their observations. Young men draw fast and say many and bright things, for young men are wise,—while they are young.

"Now, it's just like this," Davis was saying to McLean, "Here we are, all three of us turned out into the world like a lot of little sparrows pitched out of the nest, and what are we going to do? Of course it's easy enough for you, McLean, but what are my grave friend with the nasty black briar, and I, your humble servant, to do? In what wilderness are we to pitch our tents and where is our manna coming from?"

"Oh, well, the world owes us all a living," said McLean.

"Hackneyed, but true. Of course it does; but every time a colored man goes around to collect, the world throws up its hands and yells 'insolvent'—eh, Halliday?"

Halliday took his pipe from his mouth as if he were going to say something. Then he put it back without speaking and looked meditatively through the blue smoke.

"I'm right," Davis went on, "to begin with, we colored people haven't any show here. Now, if we could go to Central or South America, or some place like that,— but hang it all, who wants to go thousands of miles away from home to earn a little bread and butter?"

"There's India and the young Englishmen, if I remember rightly," said McLean.

"Oh, yes, that's all right, with the Cabots and Drake and Sir John Franklin behind them. Their traditions, their blood, all that they know makes them willing to go 'where there ain't no ten commandments and a man can raise a thirst,' but for me, home, if I can call it home."

"Well, then, stick it out."

"That's easy enough to say, McLean; but ten to one you've got some snap picked out for you already, now 'fess up, ain't you?"

"Well, of course I'm going in with my father, I can't help that, but I've got—"

"To be sure," broke in Davis, "you go in with your father. Well, if all I had to do was to step right out of college into my father's business with an assured salary, however small, I shouldn't be falling on my own neck and weeping to-night. But that's just the trouble with us; we haven't got fathers before us or behind us, if you'd rather."

"More luck to you, you'll be a father before or behind some one else; you'll be an ancestor."

"It's more profitable being a descendant, I find."

A glow came into McLean's face and his eyes sparkled as he replied: "Why, man, if I could, I'd change places with you. You don't deserve your fate. What is before you? Hardships, perhaps, and, long waiting. But then, you have the zest of the fight, the joy of the action and the chance of conquering. Now what is before me,—me, whom you are envying? I go out of here into a dull counting-room. The way is prepared for me. Perhaps I shall have no hardships, but neither have I the joy that comes from pains endured. Perhaps I shall have no battle, but even so, I lose the pleasure of the fight and the glory of winning. Your fate is infinitely to be preferred to mine."

"Ah, now you talk with the voluminous voice of the centuries," bantered Davis. "You are but echoing the breath of your Nelsons, your Cabots, your Drakes and your Franklins. Why, can't you see, you sentimental idiot, that it's all different and has to be different with us? The Anglo-Saxon race has been producing that fine frenzy in you for seven centuries and more. You come, with the blood of merchants, pioneers and heroes in your veins, to a normal battle. But for me, my forebears were savages two hundred years ago. My people learn to know civilization by the lowest and most degrading contact with it, and thus equipped or unequipped I tempt, an abnormal contest. Can't you see the disproportion?"

"If I do, I can also see the advantage of it."

"For the sake of common sense, Halliday," said Davis, turning to his companion, "don't sit there like a clam; open up and say something to convince this Don Quixote who, because he himself, sees only windmills, cannot be persuaded that we have real dragons to fight."

"Do you fellows know Henley?" asked Halliday, with apparent irrelevance.

"I know him as a critic," said McLean.

"I know him as a name," echoed the worldly Davis, "but—"

"I mean his poems," resumed Halliday, "he is the most virile of the present-day poets. Kipling is virile, but he gives you the man in hot blood with the brute in him to the fore; but the strong masculinity of Henley is essentially intellectual. It is the mind that is conquering always."

"Well, now that you have settled the relative place in English letters of Kipling and Henley, might I be allowed humbly to ask what in the name of all that is good has that to do with the question before the house?"

"I don't know your man's poetry," said McLean, "but I do believe that I can see what you are driving at."

"Wonderful perspicacity, oh, youth!"

"If Webb will agree not to run, I'll spring on you the poem that seems to me to strike the keynote of the matter in hand."

"Oh, well, curiosity will keep me. I want to get your position, and I want to see McLean annihilated."

In a low, even tone, but without attempt at dramatic effect, Halliday began to recite:

"Out of the night that covers me,
    Black as the pit from pole to pole,
I thank whatever gods there be
    For my unconquerable soul!

"In the fell clutch of circumstance,
    I have not winced nor cried aloud.
Under the bludgeonings of chance,
    My head is bloody, but unbowed.

"Beyond this place of wrath and tears
    Looms but the horror of the shade,
And yet the menace of the years
    Finds, and shall find me unafraid.

"It matters not how strait the gate,
    How charged with punishments the scroll,
I am the master of my fate,
    I am the captain of my soul."

"That's it," exclaimed McLean, leaping to his feet, "that's what I mean. That's the sort of a stand for a man to take."

Davis rose and knocked the ashes from his pipe against the window-sill. "Well, for two poetry-spouting, poetry-consuming, sentimental idiots, commend me to you fellows. 'Master of my fate, captain of my soul,' be dashed! Old Jujube, with his bone-pointed hunting spear, began determining a couple of hundred years ago what I should be in this year of our Lord one thousand eight hundred and ninety-four. J. Webb Davis, senior, added another brick to this structure, when he was picking cotton on his master's plantation forty years ago."

"And now," said Halliday, also rising, "don't you think it fair that you should start out with the idea of adding a few bricks of your own, and all of a better make than those of your remote ancestor, Jujube, or that nearer one, your father?"

"Spoken like a man," said McLean.

"Oh, you two are so hopelessly young," laughed Davis.

Part II

After the two weeks' rest which he thought he needed, and consequently promised himself, Halliday began to look about him for some means of making a start for that success in life which he felt so sure of winning.

With this end in view he returned to the town where he was born. He had settled upon the law as a profession, and had studied it for a year or two while at college. He would go back to Broughton now to pursue his studies, but of course, he needed money. No difficulty, however, presented itself in the getting of this for he knew several fellows who had been able to go into offices, and by collecting and similar duties make something while they studied. Webb Davis would have said, "but they were white," but Halliday knew what his own reply would have been: "What a white man can do, I can do."

Even if he could not go to studying at once, he could go to work and save enough money to go on with his course in a year or two. He had lots of time before him, and he only needed a little start. What better place then, to go to than Broughton, where he had first seen the light? Broughton, that had known him, boy and man. Broughton that had watched him through the common school and the high school, and had seen him go off to college with some pride and a good deal of curiosity. For even in middle west towns of such a size, that is, between seventy and eighty thousand souls, a "smart negro" was still a freak.

So Halliday went back home because the people knew him there and would respect his struggles and encourage his ambitions.

He had been home two days, and the old town had begun to take on its remembered aspect as he wandered through the streets and along the river banks. On this second day he was going up Main street deep in a brown study when he heard his name called by a young man who was approaching him, and saw an outstretched hand.

"Why, how de do, Bert, how are you? Glad to see you back. I hear you have been astonishing them up at college."

Halliday's reverie had been so suddenly broken into that for a moment, the young fellow's identity wavered elusively before his mind and then it materialized, and his consciousness took hold of it. He remembered him, not as an intimate, but as an acquaintance whom he had often met upon the football and baseball fields.

"How do you do? It's Bob Dickson," he said, shaking the proffered hand, which at the mention of the name, had grown unaccountably cold in his grasp.

"Yes, I'm Mr. Dickson," said the young man, patronizingly. "You seem to have developed wonderfully, you hardly seem like the same Bert Halliday I used to know."

"Yes, but I'm the same Mr. Halliday."

"Oh—ah—yes," said the young man, "well, I'm glad to have seen you. Ah—good-bye, Bert."

"Good-bye, Bob."

"Presumptuous darky!" murmured Mr. Dickson.

"Insolent puppy!" said Mr. Halliday to himself.

But the incident made no impression on his mind as bearing upon his status in the public eye. He only thought the fellow a cad, and went hopefully on. He was rather amused than otherwise. In this frame of mind, he turned into one of the large office-buildings that lined the street and made his way to a business suite over whose door was the inscription, "H. G. Featherton, Counsellor and Attorney-at-Law." Mr. Featherton had shown considerable interest in Bert in his school days, and he hoped much from him.

As he entered the public office, a man sitting at the large desk in the centre of the room turned and faced him. He was a fair man of an indeterminate age, for you could not tell whether those were streaks of grey shining in his light hair, or only the glint which it took on in the sun. His face was dry, lean and intellectual. He smiled now and then, and his smile was like a flash of winter lightning, so cold and quick it was. It went as suddenly as it came, leaving the face as marbly cold and impassive as ever. He rose and extended his hand, "Why—why—ah—Bert, how de do, how are you?"

"Very well, I thank you, Mr. Featherton."

"Hum, I'm glad to see you back, sit down. Going to stay with us, you think?"

"I'm not sure, Mr. Featherton; it all depends upon my getting something to do."

"You want to go to work, do you? Hum, well, that's right. It's work makes the man. What do you propose to do, now since you've graduated?"

Bert warmed at the evident interest of his old friend. "Well, in the first place, Mr. Featherton," he replied, "I must get to work and make some money. I have heard of fellows studying and supporting themselves at the same time, but I musn't expect too much. I'm going to study law."

The attorney had schooled his face into hiding any emotion he might feel, and it did not betray him now. He only flashed one of his quick cold smiles and asked,

"Don't you think you've taken rather a hard profession to get on in?"

"No doubt. But anything I should take would be hard. It's just like this, Mr. Featherton," he went on, "I am willing to work and to work hard, and I am not looking for any snap."

Mr. Featherton was so unresponsive to this outburst that Bert was ashamed of it the minute it left his lips. He wished this man would not be so cold and polite and he wished he would stop putting the ends of his white fingers together as carefully as if something depended upon it.

"I say the law is a hard profession to get on in, and as a friend I say that it will be harder for you. Your people have not the money to spend in litigation of any kind."

"I should not cater for the patronage of my own people alone."

"Yes, but the time has not come when a white person will employ a colored attorney."

"Do you mean to say that the prejudice here at home is such that if I were as competent as a white lawyer a white person would not employ me?"

"I say nothing about prejudice at all. It's nature. They have their own lawyers; why should they go outside of their own to employ a colored man?"

"But I am of their own. I am an American citizen, there should be no thought of color about it."

"Oh, my boy, that theory is very nice, but State University democracy doesn't obtain in real life."

"More's the pity, then, for real life."

"Perhaps, but we must take things as we find them, not as we think they ought to be. You people are having and will have for the next ten or a dozen years the hardest fight of your lives. The sentiment of remorse and the desire for atoning which actuated so many white men to help negroes right after the war has passed off without being replaced by that sense of plain justice which gives a black man his due, not because of, nor in spite of, but without consideration of his color."

"I wonder if it can be true, as my friend Davis says, that a colored man must do twice as much and twice as well as a white man before he can hope for even equal chances with him? That white mediocrity demands black genius to cope with it?"

"I am afraid your friend has philosophized the situation about right."

"Well, we have dealt in generalities," said Bert, smiling, "let us take up the particular and personal part of this matter. Is there any way you could help me to a situation?"

"Well,—I should be glad to see you get on, Bert, but as you see, I have nothing in my office that you could do. Now, if you don't mind beginning at the bottom—"

"That's just what I expected to do."

"—Why I could speak to the head-waiter of the hotel where I stay. He's a very nice colored man and I have some influence with him. No doubt Charlie could give you a place."

"But that's a work I abhor."

"Yes, but you must begin at the bottom, you know. All young men must."

"To be sure, but would you have recommended the same thing to your nephew on his leaving college?"

"Ah—ah—that's different."

"Yes," said Halliday, rising, "it is different. There's a different bottom at which black and white young men should begin, and by a logical sequence, a different top to which they should aspire. However, Mr. Featherton, I'll ask you to hold your offer in abeyance. If I can find nothing else, I'll ask you to speak to the head-waiter. Good-morning."

"I'll do so with pleasure," said Mr. Featherton, "and good-morning."

As the young man went up the street, an announcement card in the window of a publishing house caught his eye. It was the announcement of the next Sunday's number in a series of addresses which the local business men were giving before the Y. M. C. A. It read, "'How a Christian young man can get on in the law' —an address by a Christian lawyer—H. G. Featherton."

Bert laughed. "I should like to hear that address," he said. "I wonder if he'll recommend them to his head-waiter. No, 'that's different.' All the addresses and all the books written on how to get on, are written for white men. We blacks must solve the question for ourselves."

He had lost some of the ardor with which he had started out but he was still full of hope. He refused to accept Mr. Featherton's point of view as general or final. So he hailed a passing car that in the course of a half hour set him down at the door of the great factory which, with its improvements, its army of clerks and employees, had built up one whole section of the town. He felt especially hopeful in attacking this citadel, because they were constantly advertising for clerks and their placards plainly stated that preference would be given to graduates of the local high school. The owners were philanthropists in their way. Well, what better chance could there be before him? He had graduated there and stood well in his classes, and besides, he knew that a number of his classmates were holding good positions in the factory. So his voice was cheerful as he asked to see Mr. Stockard, who had charge of the clerical department.

Mr. Stockard was a fat, wheezy young man, with a reputation for humor based entirely upon his size and his rubicund face, for he had really never said anything humorous in his life. He came panting into the room now with a "Well, what can I do for you?"

"I wanted to see you about a situation"—began Halliday.

"Oh, no, no, you don't want to see me," broke in Stockard, "you want to see the head janitor."

"But I don't want to see the head janitor. I want to see the head of the clerical department."

"You want to see the head of the clerical department!"

"Yes, sir, I see you are advertising for clerks with preference given to the high school boys. Well, I am an old high school boy, but have been away for a few years at college."

Mr. Stockard opened his eyes to their widest extent, and his jaw dropped. Evidently he had never come across such presumption before.

"We have nothing for you," he wheezed after awhile.

"Very well, I should be glad to drop in again and see you," said Halliday, moving to the door. "I hope you will remember me if anything opens."

Mr. Stockard did not reply to this or to Bert's good-bye. He stood in the middle of the floor and stared at the door through which the colored man had gone, then he dropped into a chair with a gasp.

"Well, I'm dumbed!" he said.

A doubt had begun to arise in Bertram Halliday's mind that turned him cold and then hot with a burning indignation. He could try nothing more that morning. It had brought him nothing but rebuffs. He hastened home and threw himself down on the sofa to try and think out his situation.

"Do they still require of us bricks without straw? I thought all that was over. Well, I suspect that I will have to ask Mr. Featherton to speak to his head-waiter in my behalf. I wonder if the head-waiter will demand my diploma. Webb Davis, you were nearer right than I thought."

He spent the day in the house thinking and planning.

Part III

Halliday was not a man to be discouraged easily, and for the next few weeks he kept up an unflagging search for work. He found that there were more Feathertons and Stockards than he had ever looked to find. Everywhere that he turned his face, anything but the most menial work was denied him. He thought once of going away from Broughton, but would he find it any better anywhere else, he asked himself? He determined to stay and fight it out there for two reasons. First, because he held that it would be cowardice to run away, and secondly, because he felt that he was not fighting a local disease, but was bringing the force of his life to bear upon a national evil. Broughton was as good a place to begin curative measures as elsewhere.

There was one refuge which was open to him, and which he fought against with all his might. For years now, from as far back as he could remember, the colored graduates had "gone South to teach." This course was now recommended to him. Indeed, his own family quite approved of it, and when he still stood out against the scheme, people began to say that Bertram Halliday did not want work; he wanted to be a gentleman.

But Halliday knew that the South had plenty of material, and year by year was raising and training her own teachers. He knew that the time would come, if it were not present when it would be impossible to go South to teach, and he felt it to be essential that the North should be trained in a manner looking to the employment of her own negroes. So he stayed. But he was only human, and when the tide of talk anent his indolence began to ebb and flow about him, he availed himself of the only expedient that could arrest it.

When he went back to the great factory where he had seen and talked with Mr. Stockard, he went around to another door and this time asked for the head janitor. This individual, a genial Irishman, took stock of Halliday at a glance.

"But what do ye want to be doin' sich wurruk for, whin ye've been through school?" he asked.

"I am doing the only thing I can get to do," was the answer.

"Well," said the Irishman, "ye've got sinse, anyhow."

Bert found himself employed as an under janitor at the factory at a wage of nine dollars a week. At this, he could pay his share to keep the house going, and save a little for the period of study he still looked forward to. The people who had accused him of laziness now made a martyr of him, and said what a pity it was for a man with such an education and with so much talent to be so employed menially.

He did not neglect his studies, but read at night, whenever the day's work had not made both brain and body too weary for the task.

In this way his life went along for over a year when one morning a note from Mr. Featherton summoned him to that gentleman's office. It is true that Halliday read the note with some trepidation. His bitter experience had not yet taught him how not to dream. He was not yet old enough for that. "Maybe," he thought, "Mr. Featherton has relented, and is going to give me a chance anyway. Or perhaps he wanted me to prove my metal before he consented to take me up. Well, I've tried to do it, and if that's what he wanted, I hope he's satisfied." The note which seemed written all over with joyful tidings shook in his hand.

The genial manner with which Mr. Featherton met him reaffirmed in his mind the belief that at last the lawyer had determined to give him a chance. He was almost deferential as he asked Bert into his private office, and shoved a chair forward for him.

"Well, you've been getting on, I see," he began.

"Oh, yes," replied Bert, "I have been getting on by hook and crook."

"Hum, done any studying lately?"

"Yes, but not as much as I wish to. Coke and Wharton aren't any clearer to a head grown dizzy with bending over mops, brooms and heavy trucks all day."

"No, I should think not. Ah—oh—well, Bert, how should you like to come into my office and help around, do such errands as I need and help copy my papers?"

"I should be delighted."

"It would only pay you five dollars a week, less than what you are getting now, I suppose, but it will be more genteel."

"Oh, now, that I have had to do it, I don't care so much about the lack of gentility of my present work, but I prefer what you offer because I shall have a greater chance to study."

"Well, then, you may as well come in on Monday. The office will be often in your charge, as I am going to be away a great deal in the next few months. You know I am going to make the fight for nomination to the seat on the bench which is vacant this fall."

"Indeed. I have not so far taken much interest in politics, but I will do all in my power to help you with both nomination and election."

"Thank you," said Mr. Featherton, "I am sure you can be of great service to me as the vote of your people is pretty heavy in Broughton. I have always been a friend to them, and I believe I can depend upon their support. I shall be glad of any good you can do me with them."

Bert laughed when he was out on the street again. "For value received," he said. He thought less of Mr Featherton's generosity since he saw it was actuated by self-interest alone, but that in no wise destroyed the real worth of the opportunity that was now given into his hands. Featherton, he believed, would make an excellent judge, and he was glad that in working for his nomination his convictions so aptly fell in with his inclinations.

His work at the factory had put him in touch with a larger number of his people than he could have possibly met had he gone into the office at once. Over them, his naturally bright mind exerted some influence. As a simple laborer he had fellowshipped with them but they acknowledged and availed themselves of his leadership, because they felt instinctively in him a power which they did not have. Among them now he worked sedulously. He held that the greater part of the battle would be in the primaries, and on the night when they convened, he had his friends out in force in every ward which went to make up the third judicial district. Men who had never seen the inside of a primary meeting before were there actively engaged in this.

The *Diurnal* said next morning that the active interest of the hard-working, church-going colored voters, who wanted to see a Christian judge on the bench had had much to do with the nomination of Mr. Featherton.

The success at the primaries did not tempt Halliday to relinquish his efforts on his employer's behalf. He was indefatigable in his cause. On the west side where the colored population had largely colonized, he made speeches and held meetings clear up to election day. The fight had been between two factions of the party and after the nomination it was feared that the defection of the part defeated in the primaries might prevent the ratification of the nominee at the polls. But before the contest was half over all fears for him were laid. What he had lost in the districts where the skulking faction was strong, he made up in the wards where the colored vote was large. He was overwhelmingly elected.

Halliday smiled as he sat in the office and heard the congratulations poured in upon Judge Featherton.

"Well, it's wonderful," said one of his visitors, "how the colored boys stood by you."

"Yes, I have been a friend to the colored people, and they know it," said Featherton.

It would be some months before His Honor would take his seat on the bench, and during that time, Halliday hoped to finish his office course.

He was surprised when Featherton came to him a couple of weeks after the election and said, "Well, Bert, I guess I can get along now. I'll be shutting up this office pretty soon. Here are your wages and here is a little gift I wish to add out of respect to you for your kindness during my run for office."

Bert took the wages, but the added ten dollar note he waved aside. "No, I thank you, Mr. Featherton," he said, "what I did, I did from a belief in your fitness for the place, and out of loyalty to my employer. I don't want any money for it."

"Then let us say that I have raised your wages to this amount."

"No, that would only be evasion. I want no more than you promised to give me."

"Very well, then accept my thanks, anyway."

What things he had at the office Halliday took away that night. A couple of days later he remembered a book which he had failed to get and returned for it. The office was as usual. Mr. Featherton was a little embarrassed and nervous. At Halliday's desk sat a young white man about his own age. He was copying a deed for Mr. Featherton.

Part IV

Bertram Halliday went home, burning with indignation at the treatment he had received at the hands of the Christian judge.

"He has used me as a housemaid would use a lemon," he said, "squeezed all out of me he could get, and then flung me into the street. Well, Webb was nearer right than I thought."

He was now out of everything. His place at the factory had been filled, and no new door opened to him. He knew what reward a search for work brought a man of his color in Broughton, so he did not bestir himself to go over the old track again. He thanked his stars that he, at least, had money enough to carry him away from the place and he determined to go. His spirit was quelled, but not broken.

Just before leaving, he wrote to Davis.

"My dear Webb!" the letter ran, "you, after all, were right. We have little or no show in the fight for life among these people. I have struggled for two years here at Broughton, and now find myself back where I was when I first stepped out of school with a foolish faith in being equipped for something. One thing, my eyes have been opened anyway, and I no longer judge so harshly the shiftless and unambitious among my people. I hardly see how a people, who have so much to contend with and so little to hope for, can go on striving and aspiring. But the very fact that they do, breeds in me a respect for them. I now see why so many promising young men, class orators, valedictorians and the like fall by the wayside and are never heard from after commencement day. I now see why the sleeping and dining-car companies are supplied by men with better educations than half the passengers whom they serve. They get tired of swimming always against the tide, as who would not? and are content to drift.

"I know that a good many of my friends would say that I am whining. Well, suppose I am, that's the business of a whipped cur. The dog on top can bark, but the under dog must howl.

"Nothing so breaks a man's spirit as defeat, constant, unaltering, hopeless defeat. That's what I've experienced. I am still studying law in a half-hearted way for I don't know what I am going to do with it when I have been admitted. Diplomas don't draw clients. We have been taught that merit wins. But I have learned that the adages, as well as the books and the formulas were made by and for others than us of the black race.

"They say, too, that our brother Americans sympathize with us, and will help us when we help ourselves. Bah! The only sympathy that I have ever seen on the part of the white man was not for the negro himself, but for some portion of white blood that the colored man had got tangled up in his veins.

"But there, perhaps my disappointment has made me sour, so think no more of what I have said. I am going now to do what I abhor. Going South to try to find a school. It's awful. But I don't want any one to pity me. There are several thousands of us in the same position.

"I am glad you are prospering. You were better equipped than I was with a deal of materialism and a dearth of ideals. Give us a line when you are in good heart.

"Yours, HALLIDAY.

"P. S.—Just as I finished writing I had a note from Judge Featherton offering me the court messengership at five dollars a week. I am twenty-five. The place was held before by a white boy of fifteen. I declined. 'Southward Ho!'"

Davis was not without sympathy as he read his friend's letter in a city some distance away. He had worked in a hotel, saved money enough to start a barber-shop and was prospering. His white customers joked with him and patted him on the back, and he was already known to have political influence. Yes, he sympathized with Bert, but he laughed over the letter and jingled the coins in his pockets.

"Thank heaven," he said, "that I have no ideals to be knocked into a cocked hat. A colored man has no business with ideals—not in *this* nineteenth century!"

Jim's Probation

FOR SO LONG a time had Jim been known as the hardest sinner on the plantation that no one had tried to reach the heart under his outward shell even in camp-meeting and revival times. Even good old Brother Parker, who was ever looking after the lost and straying sheep, gave him up as beyond recall.

"Dat Jim," he said, "Oomph, de debbil done got his stamp on dat boy, an' dey ain' no use in tryin' to scratch hit off."

"But Parker," said his master, "that's the very sort of man you want to save. Don't you know it's your business as a man of the gospel to call sinners to repentance?"

"Lawd, Mas' Mordaunt," exclaimed the old man, "my v'ice done got hoa'se callin' Jim, too long ergo to talk erbout. You jes' got to let him go 'long, maybe some o' dese days he gwine slip up on de gospel an' fall plum' inter salvation."

Even Mandy, Jim's wife, had attempted to urge the old man to some more active efforts in her husband's behalf. She was a pillar of the church herself, and was woefully disturbed about the condition of Jim's soul. Indeed, it was said that half of the time it was Mandy's prayers and exhortations that drove Jim into the woods with his dog and his axe, or an old gun that he had come into possession of from one of the younger Mordaunts.

Jim was unregenerate. He was a fighter, a hard drinker, fiddled on Sunday, and had been known to go out hunting on that sacred day. So it startled the whole place when Mandy announced one day to a few of her intimate friends that she believed "Jim was under conviction." He had stolen out hunting one Sunday night and in passing through the swamp had gotten himself thoroughly wet and chilled, and this had brought on an attack of acute rheumatism, which Mandy had pointed out to him as a direct judgment of heaven. Jim scoffed at first, but Mandy grew more and more earnest, and finally, with the racking of the pain, he waxed serious and determined to look to the state of his soul as a means to the good of his body.

"Hit do seem," Mandy said, "dat Jim feel de weight o' his sins mos' powahful."

"I reckon hit's de rheumatics," said Dinah.

"Don' mek no diffunce what de inst'ument is," Mandy replied, "hit's de 'sult, hit's de 'sult."

When the news reached Stuart Mordaunt's ears he became intensely interested. Anything that would convert Jim, and make a model Christian of him would be providential on that plantation. It would save the overseers many an hour's worry; his horses, many a secret ride; and the other servants, many a broken head. So he again went down to labor with Parker in the interest of the sinner.

"Is he mou'nin' yit?" said Parker.

"No, not yet, but I think now is a good time to sow the seeds in his mind."

"Oomph," said the old man, "reckon you bettah let Jim alone twell dem sins o' his'n git him to tossin' an' cryin' an' a mou'nin'. Den'll be time enough to strive wid him. I's allus willin' to do my pa't, Mas' Stuart, but w'en hit comes to ol' time sinnahs lak Jim, I believe in layin' off, an' lettin' de sperit do de strivin'.'"

"But Parker," said his master, "you yourself know that the Bible says that the spirit will not always strive."

"Well, la den, mas', you don' spec' I gwine outdo de sperit."

But Stuart Mordaunt was particularly anxious that Jim's steps might be turned in the right direction. He knew just what a strong hold over their minds the Negroes' own emotional religion had, and he felt that could he once get Jim inside the pale of the church, and put him on guard of his salvation, it would mean the loss of fewer of his shoats and pullets. So he approached the old preacher, and said in a confidential tone,

"Now look here, Parker, I've got a fine lot of that good old tobacco you like so up to the big house, and I'll tell you what I'll do. If you'll just try to work on Jim, and get his feet in the right path, you can come up and take all you want."

"Oom-oomph," said the old man, "dat sho' is monst'ous fine terbaccer, Mas' Stua't."

"Yes, it is, and you shall have all you want of it."

"Well, I'll have a little wisit wid Jim, an' des' see how much he 'fected, an' if dey any stroke to be put in fu' de gospel ahmy, you des' count on me ez a mighty strong wa'ior. Dat boy been layin' heavy on my mind fu' lo, dese many days."

As a result of this agreement, the old man went down to Jim's cabin on a night when that interesting sinner was suffering particularly from his rheumatic pains.

"Well, Jim," the preacher said, "how you come on?"

"Po'ly, po'ly," said Jim, "I des' plum' racked an' 'stracted f'om haid to foot."

"Uh, huh, hit do seem lak to me de Bible don' tell nuffin' else but de trufe."

"What de Bible been sayin' now?" asked Jim suspiciously.

"Des' what it been sayin' all de res' o' de time. 'Yo' sins will fin' you out.'"

Jim groaned and turned uneasily in his chair. The old man saw that he had made a point and pursued it.

"Don' you reckon now, Jim, ef you was a bettah man dat you wouldn' suf-fah so?"

"I do' know, I do' know nuffin' 'bout hit."

"Now des' look at me. I ben a-trompin' erlong in dis low groun' o' sorrer fu' mo' den seventy yeahs, an' I hain't got a ache ner a pain. Nevah had no rheumat-ics in my life, an' yere you is, a young man, in a mannah o' speakin', all twinged up wid rheumatics. Now what dat p'int to? Hit mean de Lawd tek keer o' dem dat's his'n. Now Jim, you bettah come ovah on de Lawd's side, an' git erway f'om yo' ebil doin's."

Jim groaned again, and lifted his swollen leg with an effort just as Brother Parker said, "Let us pray."

The prayer itself was less effective than the request was just at that time for Jim was so stiff that it made him fairly howl with pain to get down on his knees. The old man's supplication was loud, deep, and diplomatic, and when they arose from their knees there were tears in Jim's eyes, but whether from cramp or contri-tion it is not safe to say. But a day or two after, the visit bore fruit in the appear-ance of Jim at meeting where he sat on one of the very last benches, his shoulders hunched, and his head bowed, unmistakable signs of the convicted sinner.

The usual term of mourning passed, and Jim was converted, much to Mandy's joy, and Brother Parker's delight. The old man called early on his master after the meeting, and announced the success of his labors. Stuart Mordaunt himself was no less pleased than the preacher. He shook Parker warmly by the hand, patted him on the shoulder, and called him a "sly old fox." And then he took him to the cup-board, and gave him of his store of good tobacco, enough to last him for months. Something else, too, he must have given him, for the old man came away from the cupboard grinning broadly, and ostentatiously wiping his mouth with the back of his hand.

"Great work you've done, Parker, a great work."

"Yes, yes, Mas'," grinned the old man, "now ef Jim can des' stan' out his p'o-bation, hit'll be montrous fine."

"His probation!" exclaimed the master.

"Oh yes suh, yes suh, we has all de young convu'ts stan' a p'obation o' six months, fo' we teks 'em reg'lar inter de chu'ch. Now ef Jim will des' stan' strong in de faif—"

"Parker," said Mordaunt, "you're an old wretch, and I've got a mind to take every bit of that tobacco away from you. No. I'll tell you what I'll do."

He went back to the cupboard and got as much again as he had given Parker, and handed it to him saying,

"I think it will be better for all concerned if Jim's probation only lasts two months. Get him into the fold, Parker, get him into the fold!" And he shoved the ancient exhorter out of the door.

It grieved Jim that he could not go 'possum hunting on Sundays any more, but shortly after he got religion, his rheumatism seemed to take a turn for the bet-ter and he felt that the result was worth the sacrifice. But as the pain decreased in his legs and arms, the longing for his old wicked pleasures became stronger and stronger upon him though Mandy thought that he was living out the period of his probation in the most exemplary manner, and inwardly rejoiced.

It was two weeks before he was to be regularly admitted to church fellowship. His industrious spouse had decked him out in a bleached cotton shirt in which to attend divine service. In the morning Jim was there. The sermon which Brother Parker preached was powerful, but somehow it failed to reach this new convert. His gaze roved out of the window toward the dark line of the woods beyond, where the frost still glistened on the trees and where he knew the persimmons were hanging ripe. Jim was present at the afternoon service also, for it was a great day; and again, he was preoccupied. He started and clasped his hands together until the bones cracked, when a dog barked somewhere out on the hill. The sun was going down over the tops of the woodland trees, throwing the forest into gloom, as they came out of the log meeting-house. Jim paused and looked lovingly at the scene, and sighed as he turned his steps back toward the cabin.

That night Mandy went to church alone. Jim had disappeared. Nowhere around was his axe, and Spot, his dog, was gone. Mandy looked over toward the woods whose tops were feathered against the frosty sky, and away off, she heard a dog bark.

Brother Parker was feeling his way home from meeting late that night, when all of a sudden, he came upon a man creeping toward the quarters. The man had an axe and a dog, and over his shoulders hung a bag in which the outlines of a 'possum could be seen.

"Hi, oh, Brothah Jim, at it agin?"

Jim did not reply. "Well, des' heish up an' go 'long. We got to mek some 'low-ances fu' you young convu'ts. W'en you gwine cook dat 'possum, Brothah Jim?"

"I do' know, Brothah Pahkah. He so po', I 'low I haveter keep him and fatten him fu' awhile."

"Uh, huh! well, so long, Jim."

"So long, Brothah Pahkah." Jim chuckled as he went away. "I 'low I fool dat ol' fox. Wanter come down an' eat up my one little 'possum, do he? huh, uh!"

So that very night Jim scraped his possum, and hung it out-of-doors, and the next day, brown as the forest whence it came, it lay on a great platter on Jim's table. It was a fat possum too. Jim had just whetted his knife, and Mandy had just finished the blessing when the latch was lifted and Brother Parker stepped in.

"Hi, oh, Brothah Jim, I's des' in time."

Jim sat with his mouth open. "Draw up a cheer, Brothah Pahkah," said Mandy. Her husband rose, and put his hand over the possum.

"Wha—wha'd you come hyeah fu'?" he asked.

"I thought I'd des' come in an' tek a bite wid you."

"Ain' gwine tek no bite wid me," said Jim.

"Heish," said Mandy, "wha' kin' o' way is dat to talk to de preachah?"

"Preachah er no preachah, you hyeah what I say," and he took the possum, and put it on the highest shelf.

"Wha's de mattah wid you, Jim; dat's one o' de' 'quiahments o' de chu'ch."

The angry man turned to the preacher.

"Is it one o' de 'quiahments o' de chu'ch dat you eat hyeah ter-night?"

"Hit sholy am usual fu' de shepherd to sup wherevah he stop," said Parker suavely.

"Ve'y well, ve'y well," said Jim, "I wants you to know dat I 'specs to stay out o' yo' chu'ch. I's got two weeks mo' p'obation. You tek hit back, an' gin hit to de nex' niggah you ketches wid a 'possum."

Mandy was horrified. The preacher looked longingly at the possum, and took up his hat to go.

There were two disappointed men on the plantation when he told his master the next day the outcome of Jim's probation.

Uncle Simon's Sundays Out

MR. MARSTON SAT upon his wide veranda in the cool of the summer Sabbath morning. His hat was off, the soft breeze was playing with his brown hair, and a fragrant cigar was rolled lazily between his lips. He was taking his ease after the fashion of a true gentleman. But his eyes roamed widely, and his glance rested now on the blue-green sweep of the great lawn, again on the bright blades of the growing corn, and anon on the waving fields of tobacco, and he sighed a sigh of ineffable content. The breath had hardly died on his lips when the figure of an old man appeared before him, and, hat in hand, shuffled up the wide steps of the porch.

It was a funny old figure, stooped and so one-sided that the tail of the long and shabby coat he wore dragged on the ground. The face was black and shrewd, and little patches of snow-white hair fringed the shiny pate.

"Good-morning, Uncle Simon," said Mr. Marston, heartily.

"Mornin' Mas' Gawge. How you come on?"

"I'm first-rate. How are you? How are your rheumatics coming on?"

"Oh, my, dey's mos' nigh well. Dey don' trouble me no mo'!"

"Most nigh well, don't trouble you any more?"

"Dat is none to speak of."

"Why, Uncle Simon, who ever heard tell of a man being cured of his aches and pains at your age?"

"I ain' so powahful ol', Mas', I ain' so powahful ol'."

"You're not so powerful old! Why, Uncle Simon, what's taken hold of you? You're eighty if a day."

"Sh—sh, talk dat kin' o' low, Mastah, don' 'spress yo'se'f so loud!" and the old man looked fearfully around as if he feared some one might hear the words.

The master fell back in his seat in utter surprise.

"And, why, I should like to know, may I not speak of your age aloud?"

Uncle Simon showed his two or three remaining teeth in a broad grin as he answered:

"Well, Mastah, I's 'fraid ol' man Time mought hyeah you an' t'ink he done let me run too long." He chuckled, and his master joined him with a merry peal of laughter.

"All right, then, Simon," he said, "I'll try not to give away any of your secrets to old man Time. But isn't your age written down somewhere?"

"I reckon it's in dat ol' Bible yo' pa gin me."

"Oh, let it alone then, even Time won't find it there."

The old man shifted the weight of his body from one leg to the other and stood embarrassedly twirling his ancient hat in his hands. There was evidently something more that he wanted to say. He had not come to exchange commonplaces with his master about age or its ailments.

"Well, what is it now, Uncle Simon?" the master asked, heeding the servant's embarrassment, "I know you've come up to ask or tell me something. Have any of your converts been backsliding, or has Buck been misbehaving again?"

"No, suh, de converts all seem to be stan'in' strong in de faif, and Buck, he actin' right good now."

"Doesn't Lize bring your meals regular, and cook them good?"

"Oh, yes, suh, Lize ain' done nuffin'. Dey ain' nuffin' de mattah at de quahtahs, nuffin' 't'al."

"Well, what on earth then—"

"Hol' on, Mas', hol' on! I done tol' you dey ain' nuffin' de mattah 'mong de people, an' I ain' come to 'plain 'bout nuffin'; but—but—I wants to speak to you 'bout somefin' mighty partic'ler."

"Well, go on, because it will soon be time for you to be getting down to the meeting-house to exhort the hands."

"Dat's jes' what I want to speak 'bout, dat 'zortin'."

"Well, you've been doing it for a good many years now."

"Dat's de very idee, dat's in my haid now. Mas' Gawge, huccume you read me so nigh right?"

"Oh, that's not reading anything, that's just truth. But what do you mean, Uncle Simon, you don't mean to say that you want to resign. Why what would your old wife think if she was living?"

"No, no, Mas' Gawge, I don't ezzactly want to 'sign, but I'd jes' lak to have a few Sundays off."

"A few Sundays off! Well, now, I do believe that you are crazy. What on earth put that into your head?"

"Nuffin', Mas' Gawge, I wants to be away f'om my Sabbaf labohs fu' a little while, dat's all."

"Why, what are the hands going to do for some one to exhort them on Sunday. You know they've got to shout or burst, and it used to be your delight to get them stirred up until all the back field was ringing."

"I do' say dat I ain' gwine try an' do dat some mo', Mastah, min' I do' say dat. But in de mean time I's got somebody else to tek my place, one dat I trained up in de wo'k right undah my own han'. Mebbe he ain' endowed wif de sperrit as I is, all men cain't be gifted de same way, but dey ain't no sputin' he is powahful. Why, he can handle de Scriptures wif bof han's, an' you kin hyeah him prayin' fu' two miles."

"And you want to put this wonder in your place?"

"Yes, suh, fu' a while, anyhow."

"Uncle Simon, aren't you losing your religion?"

"Losin' my u'ligion? Who, me losin' my u'ligion! No, suh."

"Well, aren't you afraid you'll lose it on the Sundays that you spend out of your meeting-house?"

"Now, Mas' Gawge, you a white man, an' you my mastah, an' you got larnin'. But what kin' o' argyment is dat? Is dat good jedgment?"

"Well, now if it isn't, you show me why, you're a logician." There was a twinkle in the eye of George Marston as he spoke.

"No, I ain' no 'gician, Mastah," the old man contended. "But what kin' o' u'ligion you spec' I got anyhow? Hyeah me been sto'in' it up fu' lo, dese many yeahs an' ain' got enough to las' ovah a few Sundays. What kin' o u'ligion is dat?"

The master laughed, "I believe you've got me there, Uncle Simon; well go along, but see that your flock is well tended."

"Thanky, Mas' Gawge, thanky. I'll put a shepherd in my place dat'll put de food down so low dat de littles' lambs kin enjoy it, but'll mek it strong enough fu' de oldes' ewes." And with a profound bow the old man went down the steps and hobbled away.

As soon as Uncle Simon was out of sight, George Marston threw back his head and gave a long shout of laughter.

"I wonder," he mused, "what crotchet that old darkey has got into his head now. He comes with all the air of a white divine to ask for a vacation. Well, I reckon he deserves it. He had me on the religious argument, too. He's got his grace stored." And another peal of her husband's laughter brought Mrs. Marston from the house.

"George, George, what is the matter. What amuses you so that you forget that this is the Sabbath day?"

"Oh, don't talk to me about Sunday any more, when it comes to the pass that the Reverend Simon Marston wants a vacation. It seems that the cares of his parish have been too pressing upon him and he wishes to be away for some time. He does not say whether he will visit Europe or the Holy Land, however, we shall expect him to come back with much new and interesting material for the edification of his numerous congregation."

"I wish you would tell me what you mean by all this."

Thus adjured, George Marston curbed his amusement long enough to recount to his wife the particulars of his interview with Uncle Simon.

"Well, well, and you carry on so, only because one of the servants wishes his Sundays to himself for awhile? Shame on you!"

"Mrs. Marston," said her husband, solemnly, "you are hopeless—positively, undeniably, hopeless. I do not object to your failing to see the humor in the situation, for you are a woman; but that you should not be curious as to the motives which actuate Uncle Simon, that you should be unmoved by a burning desire to know why this staunch old servant who has for so many years pictured hell each Sunday to his fellow-servants should wish a vacation—that I can neither understand nor forgive."

"Oh, I can see why easily enough, and so could you, if you were not so intent on laughing at everything. The poor old man is tired and wants rest, that's all." And Mrs. Marston turned into the house with a stately step, for she was a proud and dignified lady

"And that reason satisfies you? Ah, Mrs. Marston, Mrs. Marston, you discredit your sex!" her husband sighed, mockingly after her.

There was perhaps some ground for George Marston's perplexity as to Uncle Simon's intentions. His request for "Sundays off" was so entirely out of the usual order of things. The old man, with the other servants on the plantation had been bequeathed to Marston by his father. Even then, Uncle Simon was an old man, and for many years in the elder Marston's time had been the plantation exhorter. In this position he continued, and as his age increased, did little of anything else. He had a little log house built in a stretch of woods convenient to the quarters, where Sunday after Sunday he held forth to as many of the hands as could be encouraged to attend.

With time, the importance of his situation grew upon him. He would have thought as soon of giving up his life as his pulpit to any one else. He was never absent a single meeting day in all that time. Sunday after Sunday he was in his place expounding his doctrine. He had grown officious, too, and if any of his congregation were away from service, Monday morning found him early at their cabins to find out the reason why.

After a life, then, of such punctilious rigidity, it is no wonder that his master could not accept Mrs. Marston's simple excuse for Uncle Simon's dereliction, "that the old man needed rest." For the time being, the good lady might have her way, as all good ladies should, but as for him, he chose to watch and wait and speculate.

Mrs. Marston, however, as well as her husband, was destined to hear more that day of Uncle Simon's strange move, for there was one other person on the place who was not satisfied with Uncle Simon's explanation of his conduct, and yet could not as easily as the mistress formulate an opinion of her own. This was Lize, who did about the quarters and cooked the meals of the older servants who were no longer in active service.

It was just at the dinner hour that she came hurrying up to the "big house," and with the freedom of an old and privileged retainer went directly to the dining-room.

"Look hyeah, Mis' M'ree," she exclaimed, without the formality of prefacing her remarks, "I wants to know whut's de mattah wif Brothah Simon—what mek him ac' de way he do?"

"Why, I do not know, Eliza, what has Uncle Simon been doing?"

"Why, some o' you all mus' know, lessn' he couldn' 'a' done hit. Ain' he ax you nuffin', Marse Gawge?"

"Yes, he did have some talk with me."

"Some talk! I reckon he did have some talk wif somebody!"

"Tell us, Lize," Mr. Marston said, "what has Uncle Simon done?"

"He done brung somebody else, dat young Merrit darky, to oc'py his pu'pit. He in'juce him, an' 'en he say dat he gwine be absent a few Sundays, an' 'en he tek hissef off, outen de chu'ch, widout even waitin' fu' de sehmont."

"Well, didn't you have a good sermon?"

"It mought 'a' been a good sehmont, but dat ain' whut I ax you. I want to know whut de mattah wif Brothah Simon."

"Why, he told me that the man he put over you was one of the most powerful kind, warranted to make you shout until the last bench was turned over."

"Oh, some o' dem, dey shouted enough, dey shouted dey fill. But dat ain' whut I's drivin' at yit. Whut I wan' 'o know, whut mek Brothah Simon do dat?"

"Well, I'll tell you, Lize," Marston began, but his wife cut him off.

"Now, George," she said, "you shall not trifle with Eliza in that manner." Then turning to the old servant, she said: "Eliza, it means nothing. Do not trouble your-self about it. You know Uncle Simon is old; he has been exhorting for you now for many years, and he needs a little rest these Sundays. It is getting toward mid-summer, and it is warm and wearing work to preach as Uncle Simon does."

Lize stood still, with an incredulous and unsatisfied look on her face. After a while she said, dubiously shaking her head:

"Huh uh! Miss M'ree, dat may 'splain t'ings to you, but hit ain' mek 'em light to me yit."

"Now, Mrs. Marston"—began her husband, chuckling.

"Hush, I tell you, George. It's really just as I tell you, Eliza, the old man is tired and needs rest!"

Again the old woman shook her head, "Huh uh," she said, "ef you'd' a' seen him gwine lickety split outen de meetin'-house you wouldn' a thought he was so tiahed."

Marston laughed loud and long at this. "Well, Mrs. Marston," he bantered, "even Lize is showing a keener perception of the fitness of things than you."

"There are some things I can afford to be excelled in by my husband and my servants. For my part, I have no suspicion of Uncle Simon, and no concern about him either one way or the other."

"'Scuse me, Miss M'ree," said Lize, " I didn' mean no ha'm to you, but I ain' a trustin' ol' Brothah Simon, I tell you."

"I'm not blaming you, Eliza; you are sensible as far as you know."

"Ahem," said Mr. Marston.

Eliza went out mumbling to herself, and Mr. Marston confined his attentions to his dinner; he chuckled just once, but Mrs. Marston met his levity with something like a sniff.

On the first two Sundays that Uncle Simon was away from his congregation nothing was known about his whereabouts. On the third Sunday he was reported to have been seen making his way toward the west plantation. Now what did this old man want there? The west plantation, so called, was a part of the Marston domain, but the land there was worked by a number of slaves which Mrs. Marston had brought with her from Louisiana, where she had given up her father's gorgeous home on the Bayou Lafourche, together with her proud name of Marie St. Pierre for George Marston's love. There had been so many bickerings between the Marston servants and the contingent from Louisiana that the two sets had been separated, the old remaining on the east side and the new ones going to the west. So, to those who had been born on the soil the name of the west plantation became a reproach. It was a synonym for all that was worldly, wicked and unregenerate. The east plantation did not visit with the west. The east gave a dance, the west did not attend. The Marstons and St. Pierres in black did not intermarry. If a Marston died, a St. Pierre did not sit up with him. And so the division had kept up for years.

It was hardly to be believed then that Uncle Simon Marston, the very patriarch of the Marston flock, was visiting over the border. But on another Sunday he was seen to go straight to the west plantation.

At her first opportunity Lize accosted him:—

"Look a-hyeah, Brothah Simon, whut's dis I been hyeahin 'bout you, huh?"

"Well, sis' Lize, I reckon you'll have to tell me dat yo'se'f, 'case I do' know. Whut you been hyeahin'?"

"Brothah Simon, you's a ol' man, you's ol'."

"Well, sis' Lize, dah was Methusalem."

"I ain' jokin', Brothah Simon, I ain' jokin', I's a talkin' right straightfo'wa'd. Yo' conduc' don' look right. Hit ain' becomin' to you as de shepherd of a flock."

"But whut I been doin', sistah, whut I been doin'?"

"You know."

"I reckon I do, but I wan' see whethah you does er not."

"You been gwine ovah to de wes' plantation, dat's whut you been doin'. You can' 'ny dat, you's been seed!"

"I do' wan' 'ny it. Is dat all?"

"Is dat all!" Lize stood aghast. Then she said slowly and wonderingly, "Brothah Simon, is you losin' yo' senses er yo' grace?"

"I ain' losin' one ner 'tothah, but I do' see no ha'm in gwine ovah to de wes' plantation."

"You do' see no ha'm in gwine ovah to de wes' plantation! You stan' hyeah in sight o' Gawd an' say dat?"

"Don't git so 'cited, sis' Lize, you mus' membah dat dey's souls on de wes' plantation, jes' same as dey is on de eas'."

"Yes, an' dey's souls in hell, too," the old woman fired back.

"Cose dey is, but dey's already damned; but dey's souls on de wes' plantation to be saved."

"Oomph, uh, uh, uh!" grunted Lize.

"You done called me de shepherd, ain't you, sistah? Well, sayin' I is, when dey's little lambs out in de col' an' dey ain' got sense 'nough to come in, er dey do' know de way, whut do de shepherd do? Why, he go out, an' he hunt up de po' shiverin', bleatin' lambs and brings 'em into de fol'. Don't you bothah 'bout de wes' plantation, sis' Lize." And Uncle Simon hobbled off down the road with surprising alacrity, leaving his interlocutor standing with mouth and eyes wide open.

"Well, I nevah!" she exclaimed when she could get her lips together, "I do believe de day of jedgmen' is at han'."

Of course this conversation was duly reported to the master and mistress, and called forth some strictures from Mrs. Marston on Lize's attempted interference with the old man's good work.

"You ought to be ashamed of yourself, Eliza, that you ought. After the estrangement of all this time if Uncle Simon can effect a reconciliation between the west and the east plantations, you ought not to lay a straw in his way. I am sure there is more of a real Christian spirit in that than in shouting and singing for hours, and then coming out with your heart full of malice. You need not laugh, Mr. Marston, you need not laugh at all. I am very much in earnest, and I do hope that Uncle Simon will continue his ministrations on the other side. If he wants to, he can have a room built in which to lead their worship."

"But you do' want him to leave us altogethah?"

"If you do not care to share your meeting-house with them, they can have one of their own."

"But, look hyeah, Missy, dem Lousiany people, dey bad—an' dey hoodoo folks, an' dey Cath'lics—"

"Eliza!"

"'Scuse me, Missy, chile, bless yo' hea't, you know I do' mean no ha'm to you. But somehow I do' feel right in my hea't 'bout Brothah Simon."

"Never mind, Eliza, it is only evil that needs to be watched, the good will take care of itself."

It was not one, nor two, nor three Sundays that Brother Simon was away from his congregation, but six passed before he was there again. He was seen to be very busy tinkering around during the week, and then one Sunday he appeared suddenly in his pulpit. The church nodded and smiled a welcome to him. There was no change in him. If anything he was more fiery than ever. But, there was a change. Lize, who was news-gatherer and carrier extraordinary, bore the tidings to her owners. She burst into the big house with the cry of "Whut I tell you! Whut I tell you!"

"Well, what now," exclaimed both Mr. and Mrs. Marston.

"Didn' I tell you ol' Simon was up to some'p'n?"

"Out with it," exclaimed her master, "out with it, I knew he was up to something, too."

"George, try to remember who you are."

"Brothah Simon come in chu'ch dis mo'nin' an' he 'scended up de pulpit—"

"Well, what of that, are you not glad he is back?"

"Hol' on, lemme tell you—he 'scended up de pu'pit, an' 'menced his disco'se. Well, he hadn' no sooner got sta'ted when in walked one o' dem brazen Lousiany wenches—"

"Eliza!"

"Hol' on, Miss M'ree, she walked in lak she owned de place, an' flopped huhse'f down on de front seat."

"Well, what if she did," burst in Mrs. Marston, "she had a right. I want you to understand, you and the rest of your kind, that that meeting-house is for any of the hands that care to attend it. The woman did right. I hope she'll come again."

"I hadn' got done yit, Missy. Jes' ez soon ez de sehmont was ovah, whut mus' Brothah Simon, de 'zortah, min' you, whut mus' he do but come hoppin' down f'om de pu'pit, an' beau dat wench home! 'Scorted huh clah 'crost de plantation befo' evahbody's face. Now whut you call dat?"

"I call it politeness, that is what I call it. What are you laughing at, Mr. Marston? I have no doubt that the old man was merely trying to set an example of courtesy to some of the younger men, or to protect the woman from the insults that the other members of the congregation would heap upon her. Mr. Marston, I do wish you would keep your face serious. There is nothing to laugh at in this matter. A worthy old man tries to do a worthy work, his fellow-servants cavil at him, and his master, who should encourage him, laughs at him for his pains."

"I assure you, my dear, I'm not laughing at Uncle Simon."

"Then at me, perhaps; that is infinitely better."

"And not at you, either; I'm amused at the situation."

"Well, Manette ca'ied him off dis mo'nin'," resumed Eliza.

"Manette!" exclaimed Mrs. Marston.

"It was Manette he was a beauin'. Evahbody say he likin' huh moughty well, an' dat he look at huh all th'oo preachin'."

"Oh my! Manette's one of the nicest girls I brought from St. Pierre. I hope—oh, but then she is a young woman, she would not think of being foolish over an old man."

"I do' know, Miss M'ree. De ol' men is de wuss kin'. De young oomans knows how to tek de young mans, 'case dey de same age, an' dey been lu'nin' dey tricks right along wif dem'; but de ol' men, dey got sich a long sta't ahaid, dey been lu'nin so long. Ef I had a darter, I wouldn' be afeard to let huh tek keer o' huhse'f wif a young man, but ef a ol' man come a cou'tin' huh, I'd keep my own two eyes open."

"Eliza, you're a philosopher," said Mr. Marston. "You're one of the few reasoners of your sex."

"It is all nonsense," said his wife. "Why Uncle Simon is old enough to be Manette's grandfather."

"Love laughs at years."

"And you laugh at everything."

"That's the difference between love and me, my dear Mrs. Marston."

"Do not pay any attention to your master, Eliza, and do not be so suspicious of every one. It is all right. Uncle Simon had Manette over, because he thought the service would do her good."

"Yes'm, I 'low she's one o' de young lambs dat he gone out in de col' to fotch in. Well, he tek'n' moughty good keer o' dat lamb."

Mrs. Marston was compelled to laugh in spite of herself. But when Eliza was gone, she turned to her husband, and said:

"George, dear, do you really think there is anything in it?"

"I thoroughly agree with you, Mrs. Marston, in the opinion that Uncle Simon needed rest, and I may add on my own behalf, recreation."

"Pshaw! I do not believe it."

All doubts, however, were soon dispelled. The afternoon sun drove Mr. Marston to the back veranda where he was sitting when Uncle Simon again approached and greeted him.

"Well, Uncle Simon, I hear that you're back in your pulpit again?"

"Yes, suh, I's done 'sumed my labohs in de Mastah's vineya'd."

"Have you had a good rest of it?"

"Well, I ain' ezzackly been restin'," said the aged man, scratching his head. "I's been pu'su'in' othah 'ployments."

"Oh, yes, but change of work is rest. And how's the rheumatism, now, any better?"

"Bettah? Why, Mawse Gawge, I ain' got a smidgeon of hit. I's jes' limpin' a leetle bit on 'count o' habit."

"Well, it's good if one can get well, even if his days are nearly spent."

"Heish, Mas' Gawge. I ain' t'inkin' 'bout dyin'."

"Aren't you ready yet, in all these years?"

"I hope I's ready, but I hope to be spaihed a good many yeahs yit."

"To do good, I suppose?"

"Yes, suh; yes, suh. Fac' is, Mawse Gawge, I jes' hop up to ax you some'p'n."

"Well, here I am."

"I want to ax you—I want to ax you—er—er—I want—"

"Oh, speak out. I haven't time to be bothering here all day."

"Well, you know, Mawse Gawge, some o' us ain' nigh ez ol' ez dey looks."

"That's true. A person, now, would take you for ninety, and to my positive knowledge, you're not more than eighty-five."

"Oh, Lawd, Mastah, do heish."

"I'm not flattering you, that's the truth."

"Well, now, Mawse Gawge, couldn' you mek me look lak eighty-fo', an' be a little youngah?"

"Why, what do you want to be younger for?"

"You see, hit's jes' lak dis, Mawse Gawge. I come up hyeah to ax you—I want —dat is—me an' Manette, we wants to git ma'ied."

"Get married!" thundered Marston. "What you, you old scarecrow, with one foot in the grave!"

"Heish, Mastah, 'buse me kin' o' low. Don't th'ow yo' words 'roun' so keer-less."

"This is what you wanted your Sundays off for, to go sparking around—you an exhorter, too."

"But I's been missin' my po' ol' wife so much hyeah lately."

"You've been missing her, oh, yes, and so you want to get a woman young enough to be your granddaughter to fill her place."

"Well, Mas' Gawge, you know, ef I is ol' an' feeble, ez you say, I need a strong young han' to he'p me down de hill, an' ef Manette don' min' spa'in a few mont's er yeahs—"

"That'll do, I'll see what your mistress says. Come back in an hour."

A little touched, and a good deal amused, Marston went to see his wife. He kept his face straight as he addressed her. "Mrs. Marston, Manette's hand has been proposed for."

"George!"

"The Rev. Simon Marston has this moment come and solemnly laid his heart at my feet as proxy for Manette."

"He shall not have her, he shall not have her!" exclaimed the lady, rising angrily.

"But remember, Mrs. Marston, it will keep her coming to meeting."

"I do not care; he is an old hypocrite, that is what he is."

"Think, too, of what a noble work he is doing. It brings about a reconciliation between the east and west plantations, for which we have been hoping for years. You really oughtn't to lay a straw in his way."

"He's a sneaking, insidious, old scoundrel."

"Such poor encouragement from his mistress for a worthy old man, who only needs rest!"

"George!" cried Mrs. Marston, and she sank down in tears, which turned to convulsive laughter as her husband put his arm about her and whispered, "He is showing the true Christian spirit. Don't you think we'd better call Manette and see if she consents? She is one of his lambs, you know."

"Oh, George, George, do as you please. If the horrid girl consents, I wash my hands of the whole affair."

"You know these old men have been learning such a long while."

By this time Mrs. Marston was as much amused as her husband. Manette was accordingly called and questioned. The information was elicited from her that she loved "Brothah Simon" and wished to marry him.

"'Love laughs at age,'" quoted Mr. Marston again when the girl had been dismissed. Mrs. Marston was laughingly angry, but speechless for a moment. Finally she said: "Well, Manette seems willing, so there is nothing for us to do but to consent, although, mind you, I do not approve of this foolish marriage, do you hear?"

After a while the old man returned for his verdict. He took it calmly. He had expected it. The disparity in the years of him and his betrothed did not seem to strike his consciousness at all. He only grinned.

"Now look here, Uncle Simon," said his master, "I want you to tell me how you, an old, bad-looking, half-dead darky won that likely young girl."

The old man closed one eye and smiled. "Mastah, I don' b'lieve you looks er-roun' you," he said. "Now, 'mongst white folks, you knows a preachah 'mongst de ladies is mos' nigh i'sistible, but 'mongst col'ed dey ain't no pos'ble way to git er-roun' de gospel man w'en he go ahuntin' fu' anything."

Mr. Cornelius Johnson, Office-Seeker

IT WAS A beautiful day in balmy May and the sun shone pleasantly on Mr. Cornelius Johnson's very spruce Prince Albert suit of grey as he alighted from the train in Washington. He cast his eyes about him, and then gave a sigh of relief and satisfaction as he took his bag from the porter and started for the gate. As he went along, he looked with splendid complacency upon the less fortunate mortals who were streaming out of the day coaches. It was a Pullman sleeper on which he had come in. Out on the pavement he hailed a cab, and giving the driver the address of a hotel, stepped in and was rolled away. Be it said that he had cautiously inquired about the hotel first and found that he could be accommodated there.

As he leaned back in the vehicle and allowed his eyes to roam over the streets, there was an air of distinct prosperity about him. It was in evidence from the tips of his ample patent-leather shoes to the crown of the soft felt hat that sat rakishly upon his head. His entrance into Washington had been long premeditated, and he had got himself up accordingly.

It was not such an imposing structure as he had fondly imagined, before which the cab stopped and set Mr. Johnson down. But then he reflected that it was about the only house where he could find accommodation at all, and he was content. In Alabama one learns to be philosophical. It is good to be philosophical in a place where the proprietor of a café fumbles vaguely around in the region of his hip pocket and insinuates that he doesn't want one's custom. But the visitor's ardor was not cooled for all that. He signed the register with a flourish, and bestowed a liberal fee upon the shabby boy who carried his bag to his room.

"Look here, boy," he said, "I am expecting some callers soon. If they come, just send them right up to my room. You take good care of me and look sharp when I ring and you'll not lose anything."

Mr. Cornelius Johnson always spoke in a large and important tone. He said the simplest thing with an air so impressive as to give it the character of a pronouncement. Indeed, his voice naturally was round, mellifluous and persuasive. He carried himself always as if he were passing under his own triumphal arch. Perhaps, more than anything else, it was these qualities of speech and bearing that had made him invaluable on the stump in the recent campaign in Alabama. Whatever it was that held the secret of his power, the man and principles for which he had labored triumphed, and he had come to Washington to reap his reward. He had been assured that his services would not be forgotten, and it was no intention of his that they should be.

After a while he left his room and went out, returning later with several gentlemen from the South and a Washington man. There is some freemasonry among these office-seekers in Washington that throws them inevitably together. The men with whom he returned were such characters as the press would designate as "old wheel-horses" or "pillars of the party." They all adjourned to the bar, where they had something at their host's expense. Then they repaired to his room, whence for the ensuing two hours the bell and the bell-boy were kept briskly going.

The gentleman from Alabama was in his glory. His gestures as he held forth were those of a gracious and condescending prince. It was his first visit to the city, and he said to the Washington man: "I tell you, sir, you've got a mighty fine town here. Of course, there's no opportunity for anything like local pride, because it's the outsiders, or the whole country, rather, that makes it what it is, but that's nothing. It's a fine town, and I'm right sorry that I can't stay longer."

"How long do you expect to be with us, Professor?" inquired Col. Mason, the horse who had bent his force to the party wheel in the Georgia ruts.

"Oh, about ten days, I reckon, at the furthest. I want to spend some time sightseeing. I'll drop in on the Congressman from my district to-morrow, and call a little later on the President."

"Uh, huh!" said Col. Mason. He had been in the city for some time.

"Yes, sir, I want to get through with my little matter and get back home. I'm not asking for much, and I don't anticipate any trouble in securing what I desire. You see, it's just like this, there's no way for them to refuse us. And if any one deserves the good things at the hands of the administration, who more than we old campaigners, who have been helping the party through its fights from the time that we had our first votes?"

"Who, indeed?" said the Washington man.

"I tell you, gentlemen, the administration is no fool. It knows that we hold the colored vote down there in our vest pockets and it ain't going to turn us down."

"No, of course not, but sometimes there are delays—"

"Delays, to be sure, where a man doesn't know how to go about the matter. The thing to do, is to go right to the centre of authority at once. Don't you see?"

"Certainly, certainly," chorused the other gentlemen.

Before going, the Washington man suggested that the newcomer join them that evening and see something of society at the capital. "You know," he said, "that outside of New Orleans, Washington is the only town in the country that has any colored society to speak of, and I feel that you distinguished men from different sections of the country owe it to our people that they should be allowed to see you. It would be an inspiration to them."

So the matter was settled, and promptly at 8:30 o'clock Mr. Cornelius Johnson joined his friends at the door of his hotel. The grey Prince Albert was scrupulously buttoned about his form, and a shiny top hat replaced the felt of the afternoon. Thus clad, he went forth into society, where he need be followed only long enough to note the magnificence of his manners and the enthusiasm of his reception when he was introduced as Prof. Cornelius Johnson, of Alabama, in a tone which insinuated that he was the only really great man his state had produced.

It might also be stated as an effect of this excursion into Vanity Fair, that when he woke the next morning he was in some doubt as to whether he should visit his Congressman or send for that individual to call upon him. He had felt the subtle flattery of attention from that section of colored society which imitates—only imitates, it is true, but better than any other, copies—the kindnesses and cruelties, the niceties and deceits, of its white prototype. And for the time, like a man in a fog, he had lost his sense of proportion and perspective. But habit finally triumphed, and he called upon the Congressman, only to be met by an under-secretary who told him that his superior was too busy to see him that morning.

"But—"

"Too busy," repeated the secretary.

Mr. Johnson drew himself up and said: "Tell Congressman Barker that Mr. Johnson, Mr. Cornelius Johnson, of Alabama, desires to see him. I think he will see me."

"Well, I can take your message," said the clerk, doggedly, "but I tell you now it won't do you any good. He won't see any one."

But, in a few moments an inner door opened, and the young man came out followed by the desired one. Mr. Johnson couldn't resist the temptation to let his eyes rest on the underling in a momentary glance of triumph as Congressman Barker hurried up to him, saying: "Why, why, Cornelius, how'do? how'do? Ah, you came about that little matter, didn't you? Well, well, I haven't forgotten you; I haven't forgotten you."

The colored man opened his mouth to speak, but the other checked him and went on: "I'm sorry, but I'm in a great hurry now. I'm compelled to leave town to-day, much against my will, but I shall be back in a week; come around and see me then. Always glad to see you, you know. Sorry I'm so busy now; good-morning, good-morning."

Mr. Johnson allowed himself to be guided politely, but decidedly, to the door. The triumph died out of his face as the reluctant good-morning fell from his lips. As he walked away, he tried to look upon the matter philosophically. He tried to reason with himself—to prove to his own consciousness that the Congressman was very busy and could not give the time that morning. He wanted to make himself believe that he had not been slighted or treated with scant ceremony. But, try as he would, he continued to feel an obstinate, nasty sting that would not let him rest, nor forget his reception. His pride was hurt. The thought came to him to go at once to the President, but he had experience enough to know that such a visit would be vain until he had seen the dispenser of patronage for his district. Thus, there was nothing for him to do but to wait the necessary week. A whole week! His brow knitted as he thought of it.

In the course of these cogitations, his walk brought him to his hotel, where he found his friends of the night before awaiting him. He tried to put on a cheerful face. But his disappointment and humiliation showed through his smile, as the hollows and bones through the skin of a cadaver.

"Well, what luck?" asked Col. Mason, cheerfully.

"Are we to congratulate you?" put in Mr. Perry.

"Not yet, not yet, gentlemen. I have not seen the President yet. The fact is—ahem—my Congressman is out of town."

He was not used to evasions of this kind, and he stammered slightly and his yellow face turned brick-red with shame.

"It is most annoying," he went on, "most annoying. Mr. Barker won't be back for a week, and I don't want to call on the President until I have had a talk with him."

"Certainly not," said Col. Mason, blandly. "There will be delays." This was not his first pilgrimage to Mecca.

Mr. Johnson looked at him gratefully. "Oh, yes; of course, delays," he assented; "most natural. Have something."

At the end of the appointed time, the office-seeker went again to see the Congressman. This time he was admitted without question, and got the chance to state his wants. But somehow, there seemed to be innumerable obstacles in the way. There were certain other men whose wishes had to be consulted; the leader of one of the party factions, who, for the sake of harmony, had to be appeased. Of course, Mr. Johnson's worth was fully recognized, and he would be rewarded according to his deserts. His interests would be looked after. He should drop in again in a day or two. It took time, of course, it took time.

Mr. Johnson left the office unnerved by his disappointment. He had thought it would be easy to come up to Washington, claim and get what he wanted, and, after a glance at the town, hurry back to his home and his honors. It had all seemed so easy—before election; but now—

A vague doubt began to creep into his mind that turned him sick at heart. He knew how they had treated Davis, of Louisiana. He had heard how they had once kept Brotherton, of Texas—a man who had spent all his life in the service of his party—waiting clear through a whole administration, at the end of which the opposite party had come into power. All the stories of disappointment and disaster that he had ever heard came back to him, and he began to wonder if some one of these things was going to happen to him.

Every other day for the next two weeks, he called upon Barker, but always with the same result. Nothing was clear yet, until one day the bland legislator told him that considerations of expediency had compelled them to give the place he was asking for to another man.

"But what am I to do?" asked the helpless man.

"Oh, you just bide your time. I'll look out for you. Never fear."

Until now, Johnson had ignored the gentle hints of his friend, Col. Mason, about a boarding-house being more convenient than a hotel. Now, he asked him if there was a room vacant where he was staying, and finding that there was, he had his things moved thither at once. He felt the change keenly, and although no one really paid any attention to it, he believed that all Washington must have seen it, and hailed it as the first step in his degradation.

For a while the two together made occasional excursions to a glittering palace down the street, but when the money had grown lower and lower Col. Mason had the knack of bringing "a little something" to their rooms without a loss of dignity. In fact, it was in these hours with the old man, over a pipe and a bit of something, that Johnson was most nearly cheerful. Hitch after hitch had occurred in his plans, and day after day he had come home unsuccessful and discouraged. The crowning disappointment, though, came when, after a long session that lasted even up into the hot days of summer, Congress adjourned and his one hope went away. Johnson saw him just before his departure, and listened ruefully as he said: "I tell you, Cornelius, now, you'd better go on home, get back to your business and come again next year. The clouds of battle will be somewhat dispelled by then and we can see clearer what to do. It was too early this year. We were too near the fight still, and there were party wounds to be bound up and little factional sores that had to be healed. But next year, Cornelius, next year we'll see what we can do for you."

His constituent did not tell him that even if his pride would let him go back home a disappointed applicant, he had not the means wherewith to go. He did not tell him that he was trying to keep up appearances and hide the truth from his wife, who, with their two children, waited and hoped for him at home.

When he went home that night, Col. Mason saw instantly that things had gone wrong with him. But here the tact and delicacy of the old politician came uppermost and, without trying to draw his story from him—for he already divined the situation too well—he sat for a long time telling the younger man stories of the ups and downs of men whom he had known in his long and active life.

They were stories of hardship, deprivation and discouragement. But the old man told them ever with the touch of cheeriness and the note of humor that took away the ghastly hopelessness of some of the pictures. He told them with such feeling and sympathy that Johnson was moved to frankness and told him his own pitiful tale.

Now that he had some one to whom he could open his heart, Johnson himself was no less willing to look the matter in the face, and even during the long summer days, when he had begun to live upon his wardrobe, piece by piece, he still kept up; although some of his pomposity went, along with the Prince Albert coat and the shiny hat. He now wore a shiny coat, and less showy head-gear. For a couple of weeks, too, he disappeared, and as he returned with some money, it was fair to presume that he had been at work somewhere, but he could not stay away from the city long.

It was nearing the middle of autumn when Col. Mason came home to their rooms one day to find his colleague more disheartened and depressed than he had ever seen him before. He was lying with his head upon his folded arm, and when he looked up there were traces of tears upon his face.

"Why, why, what's the matter now?" asked the old man. "No bad news, I hope."

"Nothing worse than I should have expected," was the choking answer. "It's a letter from my wife. She's sick and one of the babies is down, but"—his voice broke—"she tells me to stay and fight it out. My God, Mason, I could stand it if she whined or accused me or begged me to come home, but her patient, long-suffering bravery breaks me all up."

Col. Mason stood up and folded his arms across his big chest. "She's a brave little woman," he said, gravely. "I wish her husband was as brave a man." Johnson raised his head and arms from the table where they were sprawled, as the old man went on: "The hard conditions of life in our race have taught our women a patience and fortitude which the women of no other race have ever displayed. They have taught the men less, and I am sorry, very sorry. The thing, that as much as anything else, made the blacks such excellent soldiers in the civil war was their patient endurance of hardship. The softer education of more prosperous days seems to have weakened this quality. The man who quails or weakens in this fight of ours against adverse circumstances would have quailed before—no, he would have run from an enemy on the field."

"Why, Mason, your mood inspires me. I feel as if I could go forth to battle cheerfully." For the moment, Johnson's old pomposity had returned to him, but in the next, a wave of despondency bore it down. "But that's just it; a body feels as if he could fight if he only had something to fight. But here you strike out and hit—nothing. It's only a contest with time. It's waiting—waiting—waiting!"

"In this case, waiting is fighting."

"Well, even that granted, it matters not how grand his cause, the soldier needs his rations."

"Forage," shot forth the answer like a command.

"Ah, Mason, that's well enough in good country; but the army of office-seekers has devastated Washington. It has left a track as bare as lay behind Sherman's troopers." Johnson rose more cheerfully. "I'm going to the telegraph office," he said as he went out.

A few days after this, he was again in the best of spirits, for there was money in his pocket.

"What have you been doing?" asked Mr. Toliver.

His friend laughed like a boy. "Something very imprudent, I'm sure you will say. I've mortgaged my little place down home. It did not bring much, but I had to have money for the wife and the children, and to keep me until Congress assembles; then I believe that everything will be all right."

Col. Mason's brow clouded and he sighed.

On the reassembling of the two Houses, Congressman Barker was one of the first men in his seat. Mr. Cornelius Johnson went to see him soon.

"What, you here already, Cornelius?" asked the legislator.

"I haven't been away," was the answer.

"Well, you've got the hang-on, and that's what an officer-seeker needs. Well, I'll attend to your matter among the very first. I'll visit the President in a day or two."

The listener's heart throbbed hard. After all his waiting, triumph was his at last.

He went home walking on air, and Col. Mason rejoiced with him. In a few days came word from Barker: "Your appointment was sent in to-day. I'll rush it through on the other side. Come up to-morrow afternoon."

Cornelius and Mr. Toliver hugged each other.

"It came just in time," said the younger man; "the last of my money was about gone, and I should have had to begin paying off that mortgage with no prospect of ever doing it."

The two had suffered together, and it was fitting that they should be together to receive the news of the long-desired happiness; so arm in arm they sauntered down to the Congressman's office about five o'clock the next afternoon. In honor of the occasion, Mr. Johnson had spent his last dollar in redeeming the grey Prince Albert and the shiny hat. A smile flashed across Barker's face as he noted the change.

"Well, Cornelius," he said, "I'm glad to see you still prosperous-looking, for there were some alleged irregularities in your methods down in Alabama, and the Senate has refused to confirm you. I did all I could for you, but—"

The rest of the sentence was lost, as Col. Mason's arms received his friend's fainting form.

"Poor devil!" said the Congressman. "I should have broken it more gently."

Somehow Col. Mason got him home and to bed, where for nine weeks he lay wasting under a complete nervous give-down. The little wife and the children came up to nurse him, and the woman's ready industry helped him to such creature comforts as his sickness demanded. Never once did she murmur; never once did her faith in him waver. And when he was well enough to be moved back, it was money that she had earned, increased by what Col. Mason, in his generosity of spirit, took from his own narrow means, that paid their second-class fare back to the South.

During the fever-fits of his illness, the wasted politician first begged piteously that they would not send him home unplaced, and then he would break out in the most extravagant and pompous boasts about his position, his Congressman and his influence. When he came to himself, he was silent, morose, and bitter. Only once did he melt. It was when he held Col. Mason's hand and bade him good-bye. Then the tears came into his eyes, and what he would have said was lost among his broken words.

As he stood upon the platform of the car as it moved out, and gazed at the white dome and feathery spires of the city, growing into grey indefiniteness, he ground his teeth, and raising his spent hand, shook it at the receding view. "Damn you! damn you!" he cried. "Damn your deceit, your fair cruelties; damn you, you hard, white liar!"

An Old-Time Christmas

WHEN THE HOLIDAYS came round the thoughts of 'Liza Ann Lewis always turned to the good times that she used to have at home when, following the precedent of anti-bellum days, Christmas lasted all the week and good cheer held sway. She remembered with regret the gifts that were given, the songs that were sung to the tinkling of the banjo and the dances with which they beguiled the night hours. And the eating! Could she forget it? The great turkey, with the fat literally bursting from him; the yellow yam melting into deliciousness in the mouth; or in some more fortunate season, even the juicy 'possum grinning in brown and greasy death from the great platter.

In the ten years she had lived in New York, she had known no such feast-day. Food was strangely dear in the Metropolis, and then there was always the weekly rental of the poor room to be paid. But she had kept the memory of the old times green in her heart, and ever turned to it with the fondness of one for something irretrievably lost.

That is how Jimmy came to know about it. Jimmy was thirteen and small for his age, and he could not remember any such times as his mother told him about. Although he said with great pride to his partner and rival, Blinky Scott, "Chee, Blink, you ought to hear my ol' lady talk about de times dey have down w'ere we come from at Christmas; N'Yoick ain't in it wid dem, you kin jist bet." And Blinky, who was a New Yorker clear through with a New Yorker's contempt for anything outside of the city, had promptly replied with a downward spreading of his right hand, "Aw fu'git it!"

Jimmy felt a little crest-fallen for a minute, but he lifted himself in his own estimation by threatening to "do" Blinky and the cloud rolled by.

'Liza Ann knew that Jimmy couldn't ever understand what she meant by an old-time Christmas unless she could show him by some faint approach to its merry-making, and it had been the dream of her life to do this. But every year she had failed, until now she was a little ahead.

Her plan was too good to keep, and when Jimmy went out that Christmas eve morning to sell his papers, she had disclosed it to him and bade him hurry home as soon as he was done, for they were to have a real old-time Christmas.

Jimmy exhibited as much pleasure as he deemed consistent with his dignity and promised to be back early to add his earnings to the fund for celebration.

When he was gone, 'Liza Ann counted over her savings lovingly and dreamed of what she would buy her boy, and what she would have for dinner on the next day. Then a voice, a colored man's voice, she knew, floated up to her. Some one in the alley below her window was singing "The Old Folks at Home."

"All up an' down the whole creation,
Sadly I roam,

Still longing for the old plantation,
An' for the old folks at home."

She leaned out of the window and listened and when the song had ceased and she drew her head in again, there were tears in her eyes—the tears of memory and longing. But she crushed them away, and laughed tremulously to herself as she said, "What a reg'lar ol' fool I'm a-gittin' to be." Then she went out into the cold, snow-covered streets, for she had work to do that day that would add a mite to her little Christmas store.

Down in the street, Jimmy was calling out the morning papers and racing with Blinky Scott for prospective customers; these were only transients, of course, for each had his regular buyers whose preferences were scrupulously respected by both in agreement with a strange silent compact.

The electric cars went clanging to and fro, the streets were full of shoppers with bundles and bunches of holly, and all the sights and sounds were pregnant with the message of the joyous time. People were full of the holiday spirit. The papers were going fast, and the little colored boy's pockets were filling with the desired coins. It would have been all right with Jimmy if the policeman hadn't come up on him just as he was about to toss the "bones," and when Blinky Scott had him "faded" to the amount of five hard-earned pennies.

Well, they were trying to suppress youthful gambling in New York, and the officer had to do his duty. The others scuttled away, but Jimmy was so absorbed in the game that he didn't see the "cop" until he was right on him, so he was "pinched." He blubbered a little and wiped his grimy face with his grimier sleeve until it was one long, brown smear. You know this was Jimmy's first time.

The big blue-coat looked a little bit ashamed as he marched him down the street, followed at a distance by a few hooting boys. Some of the holiday shoppers turned to look at them as they passed and murmured, "Poor little chap; I wonder what he's been up to now." Others said sarcastically, "It seems strange that 'copper' didn't call for help." A few of his brother officers grinned at him as he passed, and he blushed, but the dignity of the law must be upheld and the crime of gambling among the news-boys was a growing evil.

Yes, the dignity of the law must be upheld, and though Jimmy was only a small boy, it would be well to make an example of him. So his name and age were put down on the blotter, and over against them the offence with which he was charged. Then he was locked up to await trial the next morning.

"It's shameful," the bearded sergeant said, "how the kids are carryin' on these days. People are feelin' pretty generous, an' they'll toss 'em a nickel er a dime fur their paper an' tell 'em to keep the change fur Christmas, an' foist thing you know the little beggars are shootin' craps er pitchin' pennies. We've got to make an example of some of 'em."

'Liza Ann Lewis was tearing through her work that day to get home and do her Christmas shopping, and she was singing as she worked some such old song as she used to sing in the good old days back home. She reached her room late and tired, but happy. Visions of a "wakening up" time for her and Jimmy were in her mind. But Jimmy wasn't there.

"I wunner whah that little scamp is," she said, smiling; "I tol' him to hu'y home, but I reckon he's stayin' out latah wid de evenin' papahs so's to bring home mo' money."

Hour after hour passed and he did not come; then she grew alarmed. At two o'clock in the morning she could stand it no longer and she went over and awakened Blinky Scott, much to that young gentleman's disgust, who couldn't see why any woman need make such a fuss about a kid. He told her laconically that "Chimmie was pinched fur t'rowin' de bones."

She heard with a sinking heart and went home to her own room to walk the floor all night and sob.

In the morning, with all her Christmas savings tied up in a handkerchief, she hurried down to Jefferson Market court room. There was a full blotter that morning, and the Judge was rushing through with it. He wanted to get home to his Christmas dinner. But he paused long enough when he got to Jimmy's case to deliver a brief but stern lecture upon the evil of child-gambling in New York. He said that as it was Christmas Day he would like to release the prisoner with a reprimand, but he thought that this had been done too often and that it was high time to make an example of one of the offenders.

Well, it was fine or imprisonment. 'Liza Ann struggled up through the crowd of spectators and her Christmas treasure added to what Jimmy had, paid his fine and they went out of the court room together.

When they were in their room again she put the boy to bed, for there was no fire and no coal to make one. Then she wrapped herself in a shabby shawl and sat huddled up over the empty stove.

Down in the alley she heard the voice of the day before singing:

> "Oh, darkies, how my heart grows weary,
> Far from the old folks at home."

And she burst into tears.

A Mess of Pottage

IT WAS BECAUSE the Democratic candidate for Governor was such an energetic man that he had been able to stir Little Africa, which was a Republican stronghold, from centre to circumference. He was a man who believed in carrying the war into the enemy's country. Instead of giving them a chance to attack him, he went directly into their camp, leaving discontent and disaffection among their allies. He believed in his principles. He had faith in his policy for the government of the State, and, more than all, he had a convincing way of making others see as he saw.

No other Democrat had ever thought it necessary to assail the stronghold of Little Africa. He had merely put it into his forecast as "solidly against," sent a little money to be distributed desultorily in the district, and then left it to go its way, never doubting what that way would be. The opposing candidates never felt that the place was worthy of consideration, for as the Chairman of the Central Committee said, holding up his hand with the fingers close together: "What's the use of wasting any speakers down there? We've got 'em just like that."

It was all very different with Mr. Lane.

"Gentlemen," he said to the campaign managers, "that black district must not be ignored. Those people go one way because they are never invited to go another."

"Oh, I tell you now, Lane," said his closest friend, "it'll be a waste of material to send anybody down there. They simply go like a flock of sheep, and nothing is going to turn them."

"What's the matter with the bellwether?" said Lane sententiously.

"That's just exactly what *is* the matter. Their bellwether is an old deacon named Isham Swift, and you couldn't turn him with a forty-horse-power crank."

"There's nothing like trying."

"There are many things very similar to failing, but none so bad."

"I'm willing to take the risk."

"Well, all right; but whom will you send? We can't waste a good man."

"I'll go myself."

"What, you?"

"Yes, I."

"Why, you'd be the laughing-stock of the State."

"All right; put me down for that office if I never reach the gubernatorial chair."

"Say, Lane, what was the name of that Spanish fellow who went out to fight windmills, and all that sort of thing?"

"Never mind, Widner; you may be a good political hustler, but you're dead bad on your classics," said Lane laughingly.

So they put him down for a speech in Little Africa, because he himself desired it.

Widner had not lied to him about Deacon Swift, as he found when he tried to get the old man to preside at the meeting. The Deacon refused with indignation at the very idea. But others were more acquiescent, and Mount Moriah church was hired at a rental that made the Rev. Ebenezer Clay and all his Trustees rub their hands with glee and think well of the candidate. Also they looked at their shiny coats and thought of new suits.

There was much indignation expressed that Mount Moriah should have lent herself to such a cause, and there were murmurs even among the congregation where the Rev. Ebenezer Clay was usually an unquestioned autocrat. But, because Eve was the mother of all of us and the thing was so new, there was a great crowd on the night of the meeting. The Rev. Ebenezer Clay presided. Lane had said, "If I can't get the bellwether to jump the way I want, I'll transfer the bell." This he had tried to do. The effort was very like him.

The Rev. Mr. Clay, looking down into more frowning faces than he cared to see, spoke more boldly than he felt. He told his people that though they had their own opinions and ideas, it was well to hear both sides. He said, "The brothah," meaning the candidate, "had a few thoughts to pussent," and he hoped they'd listen to him quietly. Then he added subtly: "Of co'se Brothah Lane knows we colo'ed folks're goin' to think our own way, anyhow."

The people laughed and applauded, and Lane went to his work. They were quiet and attentive. Every now and then some old brother grunted and shook his head. But in the main they merely listened.

Lane was pleasing, plausible and convincing, and the brass band which he had brought with him was especially effective. The audience left the church shaking their heads with a different meaning, and all the way home there were remarks such as, "He sholy tol' de truth," "Dat man was right," "They ain't no way to 'ny a word he said."

Just at that particular moment it looked very dark for the other candidate, especially as the brass band lingered around an hour or so and discoursed sweet music in the streets where the negroes most did congregate.

Twenty years ago such a thing could not have happened, but the ties which had bound the older generation irrevocably to one party were being loosed upon the younger men. The old men said "We know;" the young ones said "We have heard," and so there was hardly anything of the blind allegiance which had made even free thought seem treason to their fathers.

Now all of this was the reason of the great indignation that was rife in the breasts of other Little Africans and which culminated in a mass meeting called by Deacon Isham Swift and held at Bethel Chapel a few nights later. For two or three days before this congregation of the opposing elements there were ominous mutterings. On the streets little knots of negroes stood and told of the terrible thing that had taken place at Mount Moriah. Shoulders were grasped, heads were wagged and awful things prophesied as the result of this compromise with the general enemy. No one was louder in his denunciation of the treacherous course of the Rev. Ebenezer Clay than the Republican bellwether, Deacon Swift. He saw in it signs of the break-up of racial integrity and he bemoaned the tendency loud and long. His son Tom did not tell him that he had gone to the meeting himself and had been one of those to come out shaking his head in acquiescent doubt at the truths he had heard. But he went, as in duty bound, to his father's meeting.

The church was one thronging mass of colored citizens. On the platform, from which the pulpit had been removed, sat Deacon Swift and his followers. On each side of him were banners bearing glowing inscriptions. One of the banners which the schoolmistress had prepared read:

"His temples are our forts and towers which frown upon a tyrant foe."

The schoolmistress taught in a mixed school. They had mixed it by giving her a room in a white school where she had only colored pupils. Therefore she was loyal to her party, and was known as a woman of public spirit.

THE MEETING WAS an enthusiastic one, but no such demonstration was shown through it all as when old Deacon Swift himself arose to address the assembly. He put Moses Jackson in the chair, and then as he walked forward to the front of the platform a great, white-haired, rugged, black figure, he was heroic in his very crudeness. He wore a long, old Prince Albert coat, which swept carelessly about his thin legs. His turn-down collar was disputing territory with his tie and his waistcoat. His head was down, and he glanced out of the tower part of his eyes over the congregation, while his hands fumbled at the sides of his trousers in an embarrassment which may have been pretended or otherwise.

"Mistah Cheerman," he said, "fu' myse'f, I ain't no speakah. I ain't nevah been riz up dat way. I has plowed an' I has sowed, an' latah on I has laid cyahpets, an' I has whitewashed. But, ladies an' gent'men, I is a man, an' as a man I want to speak to you ter-night. We is lak a flock o' sheep, an' in de las' week de wolf has come among ouah midst. On evah side we has hyeahd de shephe'd dogs a-ba'kin' a-wa'nin' unto us. But, my f'en's, de cotton o' p'ospe'ity has been stuck in ouah eahs. Fu' thirty yeahs er mo', ef I do not disremember, we has walked de streets an' de by-ways o' dis country an' called ouahse'ves f'eemen. Away back yander, in de days of old, lak de chillen of Is'ul in Egypt, a deliv'ah came unto us, an Ab'aham Lincoln a-lifted de yoke f'om ouah shouldahs." The audience waked up and began swaying, and there was moaning heard from both Amen corners.

"But, my f'en's, I want to ax you, who was behind Ab'aham Lincoln? Who was it helt up dat man's han's when dey sent bayonets an' buttons to enfo'ce his word—umph? I want to—to know who was behin' him? Wasn' it de 'Publican pa'ty?" There were cries of "Yes, yes! dat's so!" One old sister rose and waved her sunbonnet.

"An' now I want to know in dis hyeah day o' comin' up ef we a-gwineter 'sert de ol' flag which waved ovah Lincoln, waved ovah Gin'r'l Butler, an' led us up straight to f'eedom? Ladies an' gent'men, an' my f'en's, I know dar have been suttain meetin's held lately in dis pa't o' de town. I know dar have been suttain cannerdates which have come down hyeah an' brung us de mixed wine o' Babylon. I know dar have been dem o' ouah own people who have drunk an' become drunk —ah! But I want to know, an' I want to ax you ter-night as my f'en's an' my broth-ahs, is we all a-gwineter do it—huh? Is we all a-gwineter drink o' dat wine? Is we all a-gwineter reel down de perlitical street, a-staggerin' to an' fro?—hum!"

Cries of "No! No! No!" shook the whole church.

"Gent'men an' ladies," said the old man, lowering his voice, "de pa'able has been 'peated, an' some o' us—I ain't mentionin' no names, an' I ain't a-blamin' no chu'ch—but I say dar is some o' us dat has sol' dere buthrights fu' a pot o' cabbage."

What more Deacon Swift said is hardly worth the telling, for the whole church was in confusion and little more was heard. But he carried everything with him, and Lane's work seemed all undone. On a back seat of the church Tom Swift, the son of the presiding officer, sat and smiled at his father unmoved, because he had gone as far as the sixth grade in school, and thought he knew more.

As the reporters say, the meeting came to a close amid great enthusiasm.

The day of election came and Little Africa gathered as usual about the polls in the precinct. The Republicans followed their plan of not bothering about the district. They had heard of the Deacon's meeting, and chuckled to themselves in their committee-room. Little Africa was all solid, as usual, but Lane was not done yet. His emissaries were about, as thick as insurance agents, and they, as well as the Republican workers, had money to spare and to spend. Some votes, which counted only for numbers, were fifty cents apiece, but when Tom Swift came down they knew who he was and what his influence could do. They gave him five dollars, and Lane had one more vote and a deal of prestige. The young man thought he was voting for his convictions.

He had just cast his ballot, and the crowd was murmuring around him still at the wonder of it—for the Australian ballot has tongues as well as ears—when his father came up, with two or three of his old friends, each with the old ticket in his hands. He heard the rumor and laughed. Then he came up to Tom.

"Huh," he said, "dey been sayin' 'roun' hyeah you voted de Democratic ticket. Go mek 'em out a lie."

"I did vote the Democratic ticket," said Tom steadily.

The old man fell back a step and gasped, as if he had been struck.

"You did?" he cried. "You did?"

"Yes," said Tom, visibly shaken; "every man has a right—"

"Evah man has a right to what?" cried the old man.

"To vote as he thinks he ought to," was his son's reply.

Deacon Swift's eyes were bulging and reddening.

"You—you tell me dat?" His slender form towered above his son's, and his knotted, toil-hardened hands opened and closed.

"You tell me dat? You with yo' bringin' up vote de way you think you're right? You lie! Tell me what dey paid you, or, befo' de Lawd, I'll taih you to pieces right hyeah!"

Tom wavered. He was weaker than his father. He had not gone through the same things, and was not made of the same stuff.

"They—they give me five dollahs," he said; "but it wa'n't fu' votin'."

"Fi' dollahs! fi' dollahs! My son sell hisse'f fu' fi' dollahs! an' forty yeahs ago I brung fifteen hun'erd, an' dat was only my body, but you sell body an' soul fu' fi' dollahs!"

Horror and scorn and grief and anger were in the old man's tone. Tears trickled down his wrinkled face, but there was no weakness in the grip with which he took hold of his son's arms.

"Tek it back to 'em!" he said. "Tek it back to 'em."

"But, pap—"

"Tek it back to 'em, I say, or yo' blood be on yo' own haid!"

And then, shamefaced before the crowd, driven by his father's anger, he went back to the man who had paid him and yielded up the precious bank-note. Then they turned, the one head-hung, the other proud in his very indignation, and made their way homeward.

There was prayer-meeting the next Wednesday night at Bethel Chapel. It was nearly over and the minister was about to announce the Doxology, when old Deacon Swift arose.

"Des' a minute, brothahs," he said. "I want to mek a 'fession. I was too ha'd an' too brash in my talk de othah night, an' de Lawd visited my sins upon my haid. He struck me in de bosom o' my own fambly. My own son went wrong. Pray fu' me!"

The Trustfulness of Polly

POLLY JACKSON WAS a model woman. She was practical and hard-working. She knew the value of a dollar, could make one and keep one, sometimes—fate permitting. Fate was usually Sam and Sam was Polly's husband. Any morning at six o'clock she might be seen, basket on arm, wending her way to the homes of her wealthy patrons for the purpose of bringing in their washing, for by this means did she gain her livelihood. She had been a person of hard common sense, which suffered its greatest lapse when she allied herself with the man whose name she bore. After that the lapses were more frequent.

How she could ever have done so no one on earth could tell. Sam was her exact opposite. He was an easy-going happy-go-lucky individual, who worked only when occasion demanded and inclination and the weather permitted. The weather was usually more acquiescent than inclination. He was sanguine of temperament, highly imaginative and a dreamer of dreams. Indeed, he just missed being a poet. A man who dreams takes either to poetry or policy. Not being able quite to reach the former, Sam had declined upon the latter, and, instead of meter, feet and rhyme, his mind was taken up with "hosses," "gigs" and "straddles."

He was always "jes' behin' dem policy sha'ks, an' I'll be boun', Polly, but I gwine to ketch 'em dis time."

Polly heard this and saw the same result so often that even her stalwart faith began to turn into doubt. But Sam continued to reassure her and promise that some day luck would change. "An' when hit do change," he would add, impressively, "it's gwine change fu' sho', an' we'll have one wakenin' up time. Den I bet you'll git dat silk dress you been wantin' so long."

Polly did have ambitions in the direction of some such finery, and this plea always melted her. Trust was restored again, and Hope resumed her accustomed place.

It was, however, not through the successful culmination of any of Sam's policy manipulations that the opportunity at last came to Polly to realize her ambitions. A lady for whom she worked had a second-hand silk dress, which she was willing to sell cheap. Another woman had spoken for it, but if Polly could get the money in three weeks she would let her have it for seven dollars.

To say that the companion of Sam Jackson jumped at the offer hardly indicates the attitude of eagerness with which she received the proposition.

"Yas'm, I kin sholy git dat much money together in th'ee weeks de way I's a-wo'kin'."

"Well, now, Polly, be sure; for if you are not prompt I shall have to dispose of it where it was first promised," was the admonition.

"Oh, you kin 'pend on me, Mis' Mo'ton; fu' when I sets out to save money I kin save, I tell you." Polly was not usually so sanguine, but what changes will not the notion of the possession of a brown silk dress trimmed with passementrie make in the disposition of a woman?

Polly let Sam into the secret, and, be it said to his credit, he entered into the plan with an enthusiasm no less intense than her own. He had always wanted to see her in a silk dress, he told her, and then in a quizzically injured tone of voice, "but you ought to waited tell I ketched dem policy sha'ks an' I'd 'a' got you a new one." He even went so far as to go to work for a week and bring Polly his earnings, of course, after certain "little debts" which he mentioned but did not specify, had been deducted.

But in spite of all this, when washing isn't bringing an especially good price; when one must eat and food is high; when a grasping landlord comes around once every week and exacts tribute for the privilege of breathing foul air from an alley in a room up four flights; when, I say, all this is true, and it generally is true in the New York tenderloin, seven whole dollars are not easily saved. There was much raking and scraping and pinching during each day that at night Polly might add a few nickels or pennies to the store that jingled in a blue jug in one corner of her closet. She called it her bank, and Sam had laughed at the conceit, telling her that that was one bank anyhow that couldn't "bust."

As the days went on how she counted her savings and exulted in their growth! She already saw herself decked out in her new gown, the envy and admiration of every woman in neighborhood. She even began to wish that she had a full-length glass in order that she might get the complete effect of her own magnificence. So saving, hoping, dreaming, the time went on until a few days before the limit, and there was only about a dollar to be added to make the required amount. This she could do easily in the remaining time. So Polly was jubilant.

Now everything would have been all right and matters would have ended happily if Sam had only kept on at work. But, no. He must needs stop, and give his mind the chance to be employed with other things. And that is just what happened. For about this time, having nothing else to do, like that old king of Bible renown, he dreamed a dream. But unlike the royal dreamer, he asked no seer or prophet to interpret his dream to him. He merely drove his hand down into his inside pocket, and fished up an ancient dream-book, greasy and tattered with use. Over this he pored until his eyes bulged and his hands shook with excitement.

"Got 'em at last!" he exclaimed. "Dey ain't no way fu' dem to git away f'om me. I's behind 'em. I's behind 'em I tell you," and then his face fell and he sat for a long time with his chin in his hand thinking, thinking.

"Polly," said he when his wife came in, "d'you know what I dremp 'bout las' night?"

"La! Sam Jackson, you ain't gone to dreamin' agin. I thought you done quit all dat foolishness."

"Now jes' listen at you runnin' on. You ain't never axed me what I dremp 'bout yit."

"Hit don' make much diffunce to me, less'n you kin dream 'bout a dollah mo' into my pocket."

"Dey has been sich things did," said Sam sententiously. He got up and went out. If there is one thing above another that your professional dreamer does demand, it is appreciation. Sam had failed to get it from Polly, but he found a balm for all his hurts when he met Bob Davis.

"What!" exclaimed Bob. "Dreamed of a nakid black man. Fu' de Lawd sake, Sam, don' let de chance pass. You got 'em dis time sho'. I'll put somep'n' on it myse'f. Wha'd you think ef we'd win de 'capital'?"

That was enough. The two parted and Sam hurried home. He crept into the house. Polly was busy hanging clothes on the roof. Where now are the guardian spirits that look after the welfare of trusting women? Where now are the enchanted belongings that even in the hands of the thief cry out to their unsuspecting owners? Gone. All gone with the ages of faith that gave them birth. Without an outcry, without even so much as a warning jingle, the contents of the blue jug and the embodied hope of a woman's heart were transferred to the gaping pocket of Sam Jackson. Polly went on hanging up clothes on the roof.

Sam chuckled to himself: "She won't never have a chanst to scol' me. I'll git de drawin's early dis evenin', an' go ma'chin' home wif a new silk fu' huh, an' money besides. I do' want my wife waihin' no white folks' secon'-han' clothes nohow. My, but won't she be su'prised an' tickled. I kin jes' see huh now. Oh, mistah policy-sha'k, I got you now. I been layin' fu' you fu' a long time, but you's my meat at las'."

He marched into the policy shop like a conqueror. To the amazement of the clerk, he turned out a pocketful of small coin on the table and played it all in "gigs," "straddles and combinations."

"I'll call on you about ha' pas' fou', Mr. McFadden," he announced exultantly as he went out.

"Faith, sor," said McFadden to his colleague, "if that nagur does ketch it he'll break us, sure."

Sam could hardly wait for half-past four. A minute before the time he burst in upon McFadden and demanded the drawings. They were handed to him. He held his breath as his eye went down the column of figures. Then he gasped and staggered weakly out of the room. The policy sharks had triumphed again.

Sam walked the streets until nine o'clock that night. He was afraid to go home to Polly. He knew that she had been to the jug and found—. He groaned, but at last his very helplessness drove him in. Polly, with swollen eyes, was sitting by the table, the empty jug lying on its side before her.

"Sam," she exclaimed, "whaih's my money? Whaih's my money I been wo'kin' fu' all dis time?"

"Why—Why, Polly—"

"Don' go beatin' 'roun' de bush. I want 'o know whaih my money is; you tuck it."

"Polly, I dremp—"

"I do' keer what you dremp, I want my money fu' my dress."

His face was miserable.

"I thought sho' dem numbers 'u'd come out, an'—"

The woman flung herself upon the floor and burst into a storm of tears. Sam bent over her. "Nemmine, Polly," he said. "Nemmine. I thought I'd su'prise you. Dey beat me dis time." His teeth clenched. "But when I ketch dem policy sha'ks—"

The Tragedy at Three Forks

It was a drizzly, disagreeable April night. The wind was howling in a particularly dismal and malignant way along the valleys and hollows of that part of Central Kentucky in which the rural settlement of Three Forks is situated. It had been "trying to rain" all day in a half-hearted sort of manner, and now the drops were flying about in a cold spray. The night was one of dense, inky blackness, occasionally relieved by flashes of lightning. It was hardly a night on which a girl should be out. And yet one was out, scudding before the storm, with clenched teeth and wild eyes, wrapped head and shoulders in a great blanket shawl, and looking, as she sped along like a restless, dark ghost. For her, the night and the storm had no terrors; passion had driven out fear. There was determination in her every movement, and purpose was apparent in the concentration of energy with which she set her foot down. She drew the shawl closer about her head with a convulsive grip, and muttered with a half sob, "'Tain't the first time, 'tain't the first time she's tried to take me down in comp'ny, but—" and the sob gave way to the dry, sharp note in her voice, "I'll fix her, if it kills me. She thinks I ain't her ekals, does she? 'Cause her pap's got money, an' has good crops on his lan', an' my pap ain't never had no luck, but I'll show 'er, I'll show 'er that good luck can't allus last. Pleg-take 'er, she's jealous, 'cause I'm better lookin' than she is, an' pearter in every way, so she tries to make me little in the eyes of people. Well, you'll find out what it is to be pore—to have nothin', Seliny Williams, if you live."

The black night hid a gleam in the girl's eyes, and her shawl hid a bundle of something light, which she clutched very tightly, and which smelled of kerosene.

The dark outline of a house and its outbuildings loomed into view through the dense gloom; and the increased caution with which the girl proceeded, together with the sudden breathless intentness of her conduct, indicated that it was with this house and its occupants she was concerned.

The house was cellarless, but it was raised at the four corners on heavy blocks, leaving a space between the ground and the floor, the sides of which were partly closed by banks of ashes and earth which were thrown up against the weatherboarding. It was but a few minutes' work to scrape away a portion of this earth, and push under the pack of shavings into which the mysterious bundle resolved itself. A match was lighted, sheltered, until it blazed, and then dropped among them. It took only a short walk and a shorter time to drop a handful of burning shavings into the hay at the barn. Then the girl turned and sped away, muttering: "I reckon I've fixed you, Seliny Williams, mebbe, next time you meet me out at a dance, you won't snub me; mebbe next time, you'll be ez pore ez I am, an'll be willin' to dance crost from even ole 'Lias Hunster's gal."

The constantly falling drizzle might have dampened the shavings and put out the fire, had not the wind fanned the sparks into too rapid a flame, which caught eagerly at shingle, board and joist until house and barn were wrapped in flames. The whinnying of the horses first woke Isaac Williams, and he sprang from bed at sight of the furious light which surrounded his house. He got his family up and out of the house, each seizing what he could of wearing apparel as he fled before the flames. Nothing else could be saved, for the fire had gained terrible headway, and its fierceness precluded all possibility of fighting it. The neighbors attracted by the lurid glare came from far and near, but the fire had done its work, and their efforts availed nothing. House, barn, stock, all, were a mass of ashes and charred cinders. Isaac Williams, who had a day before, been accounted one of the solidest farmers in the region, went out that night with his family—homeless.

Kindly neighbors took them in, and by morning the news had spread throughout all the country-side. Incendiarism was the only cause that could be assigned, and many were the speculations as to who the guilty party could be. Of course, Isaac Williams had enemies. But who among them was mean, ay, daring enough to perpetrate such a deed as this?

Conjecture was rife, but futile, until old 'Lias Hunster, who though he hated Williams, was shocked at the deed, voiced the popular sentiment by saying, "Look a here, folks, I tell you that's the work o' niggers, I kin see their hand in it."

"Niggers, o' course," exclaimed every one else. "Why didn't we think of it before? It's jest like 'em."

Public opinion ran high and fermented until Saturday afternoon when the county paper brought the whole matter to a climax by coming out in a sulphurous account of the affair, under the scarehead:

A TERRIBLE OUTRAGE!

MOST DASTARDLY DEED EVER COMMITTED IN THE HISTORY OF BARLOW COUNTY. A HIGHLY RESPECTED, UNOFFENDING AND WELL-BELOVED FAMILY BURNED OUT OF HOUSE AND HOME. NEGROES! UNDOUBTEDLY THE PERPETRATORS OF THE DEED!

The article went on to give the facts of the case, and many more supposed facts, which had originated entirely in the mind of the correspondent. Among these facts was the intelligence that some strange negroes had been seen lurking in the vicinity the day before the catastrophe and that a party of citizens and farmers were scouring the surrounding country in search of them. "They would, if caught," concluded the correspondent, "be summarily dealt with."

Notwithstanding the utter falsity of these statements, it did not take long for the latter part of the article to become a prophecy fulfilled, and soon, excited, inflamed and misguided parties of men and boys were scouring the woods and roads in search of strange "niggers." Nor was it long, before one of the parties raised the cry that they had found the culprits. They had come upon two strange negroes going through the woods, who seeing a band of mounted and armed men, had instantly taken to their heels. This one act had accused, tried and convicted them.

The different divisions of the searching patty came together, and led the negroes with ropes around their necks into the centre of the village. Excited crowds on the one or two streets which the hamlet boasted, cried "Lynch 'em, lynch 'em! Hang the niggers up to the first tree!"

Jane Hunster was in one of the groups, as the shivering negroes passed, and she turned very pale even under the sunburn that browned her face.

The law-abiding citizens of Barlow County, who composed the capturing party, were deaf to the admonitions of the crowd. They filed solemnly up the street, and delivered their prisoners to the keeper of the jail, sheriff, by courtesy, and scamp by the seal of Satan; and then quietly dispersed. There was something ominous in their very orderliness.

Late that afternoon, the man who did duty as prosecuting attorney for that county, visited the prisoners at the jail, and drew from them the story that they were farm-laborers from an adjoining county. They had come over only the day before, and were passing through on the quest for work; the bad weather and the lateness of the season having thrown them out at home.

"Uh, huh," said the prosecuting attorney at the conclusion of the tale, "your story's all right, but the only trouble is that it won't do here. They won't believe you. Now, I'm a friend to niggers as much as any white man can be, if they'll only be friends to themselves, an' I want to help you two all I can. There's only one way out of this trouble. You must confess that you did this."

"But Mistah," said the bolder of the two negroes, "how kin we 'fess, when we wasn' nowhahs nigh de place?"

"Now there you go with regular nigger stubbornness; didn't I tell you that that was the only way out of this? If you persist in saying you didn't do it, they'll hang you; whereas, if you own, you'll only get a couple of years in the 'pen.' Which 'ud you rather have, a couple o' years to work out, or your necks stretched?"

"Oh, we'll 'fess, Mistah, we'll 'fess we done it; please, please don't let 'em hang us!" cried the thoroughly frightened blacks.

"Well, that's something like it," said the prosecuting attorney as he rose to go. "I'll see what can be done for you."

With marvelous and mysterious rapidity, considering the reticence which a prosecuting attorney who was friendly to the negroes should display, the report got abroad that the negroes had confessed their crime, and soon after dark, ominous looking crowds began to gather in the streets. They passed and repassed the place, where stationed on the little wooden shelf that did duty as a doorstep, Jane Hunster sat with her head buried in her hands. She did not raise up to look at any of them, until a hand was laid on her shoulder, and a voice called her, "Jane!"

"Oh, hit's you, is it, Bud," she said, raising her head slowly, "howdy?"

"Howdy yoreself," said the young man, looking down at her tenderly.

"Bresh off yore pants an' set down," said the girl making room for him on the step. The young man did so, at the same time taking hold of her hand with awkward tenderness.

"Jane," he said, "I jest can't wait fur my answer no longer! you got to tell me to-night, either one way or the other. Dock Heaters has been a-blowin' hit aroun' that he has beat my time with you. I don't believe it Jane, fur after keepin' me waitin' all these years, I don't believe you'd go back on me. You know I've allus loved you, ever sence we was little children together."

The girl was silent until he leaned over and said in pleading tones, "What do you say, Jane?"

"I hain't fitten fur you, Bud."

"Don't talk that-a-way, Jane, you know ef you jest say 'yes,' I'll be the happiest man in the state."

"Well, yes, then, Bud, for you're my choice, even ef I have fooled with you fur a long time; an' I'm glad now that I kin make somebody happy." The girl was shivering, and her hands were cold, but she made no movement to rise or enter the house.

Bud put his arms around her and kissed her shyly. And just then a shout arose from the crowd down the street.

"What's that?" she asked.

"It's the boys gittin' worked up, I reckon. They're going to lynch them niggers to-night that burned ole man Williams out."

The girl leaped to her feet, "They mustn't do it," she cried. "They ain't never been tried!"

"Set down, Janey," said her lover, "they've owned up to it."

"I don't believe it," she exclaimed, "somebody's jest a lyin' on 'em to git 'em hung because they're niggers."

"Sh—Jane, you're excited, you ain't well; I noticed that when I first come to-night. Somebody's got to suffer fur that house-burnin', an' it might ez well be them ez anybody else. You mustn't talk so. Ef people knowed you wuz a standin' up fur niggers so, it 'ud ruin you."

He had hardly finished speaking, when the gate opened, and another man joined them.

"Hello, there, Dock Heaters, that you?" said Bud Mason.

"Yes, it's me. How are you, Jane?" said the newcomer.

"Oh, jest middlin', Dock, I ain't right well."

"Well, you might be in better business than settin' out here talkin' to Bud Mason."

"Don't know how as to that," said his rival, "seein' as we're engaged."

"You're a liar!" flashed Dock Heaters.

Bud Mason half rose, then sat down again; his triumph was sufficient without a fight. To him "liar" was a hard name to swallow without resort to blows, but he only said, his flashing eyes belying his calm tone, "Mebbe I am a liar, jest ast Jane."

"Is that the truth, Jane?" asked Heaters, angrily.

"Yes, hit is, Dock Heaters, an' I don't see what you've got to say about it; I hain't never promised you nothin' shore."

Heaters turned toward the gate without a word. Bud sent after him a mocking laugh, and the bantering words, "You'd better go down, an' he'p hang them niggers, that's all you're good fur." And the rival really did bend his steps in that direction.

Another shout arose from the throng down the street, and rising hastily, Bud Mason exclaimed, "I must be goin', that yell means business."

"Don't go down there, Bud!" cried Jane. "Don't go, fur my sake, don't go." She stretched out her arms, and clasped them about his neck.

"You don't want me to miss nothin' like that," he said as he unclasped her arms; "don't you be worried, I'll be back past here." And in a moment he was gone, leaving her cry of "Bud, Bud, come back," to smite the empty silence.

When Bud Mason reached the scene of action, the mob had already broken into the jail and taken out the trembling prisoners. The ropes were round their necks and they had been led to a tree.

"See ef they'll do any more house-burnin'!" cried one as the ends of the ropes were thrown over the limbs of the tree.

"Reckon they'll like dancin' hemp a heap better," mocked a second.

"Justice an' pertection!" yelled a third.

"The mills of the gods grind swift enough in Barlow County," said the school-master.

The scene, the crowd, the flaring lights and harsh voices intoxicated Mason, and he was soon the most enthusiastic man in the mob. At the word, his was one of the willing hands that seized the rope, and jerked the negroes off their feet into eternity. He joined the others with savage glee as they emptied their revolvers into the bodies. Then came the struggle for pieces of the rope as "keepsakes." The scramble was awful. Bud Mason had just laid hold of a piece and cut it off, when some one laid hold of the other end. It was not at the rope's end, and the other man also used his knife in getting a hold. Mason looked up to see who his antagonist was, and his face grew white with anger. It was Dock Heaters.

"Let go this rope," he cried.

"Let go yoreseif, I cut it first, an' I'm a goin' to have it."

They tugged and wrestled and panted, but they were evenly matched and neither gained the advantage.

"Let go, I say," screamed Heaters, wild with rage.

"I'll die first, you dirty dog!"

The words were hardly out of his mouth before a knife flashed in the light of the lanterns, and with a sharp cry, Bud Mason fell to the ground. Heaters turned to fly, but strong hands seized and disarmed him.

"He's killed him! Murder, murder!" arose the cry, as the crowd with terror-stricken faces gathered about the murderer and his victim.

"Lynch him!" suggested some one whose thirst for blood was not yet appeased.

"No," cried an imperious voice, "who knows what may have put him up to it? Give a white man a chance for his life."

The crowd parted to let in the town marshal and the sheriff who took charge of the prisoner, and led him to the little rickety jail, whence he escaped later that night; while others improvised a litter, and bore the dead man to his home.

The news had preceded them up the street, and reached Jane's ears. As they passed her home, she gazed at them with a stony, vacant stare, muttering all the while as she rocked herself to and fro, "I knowed it, I knowed it!"

The press was full of the double lynching and the murder. Conservative editors wrote leaders about it in which they deplored the rashness of the hanging but warned the negroes that the only way to stop lynching was to quit the crimes of which they so often stood accused. But only in one little obscure sheet did an editor think to say, "There was Salem and its witchcraft; there is the south and its lynching. When the blind frenzy of a people condemn a man as soon as he is accused, his enemies need not look far for a pretext!"

The Finding of Zach

THE ROOMS OF the "Banner" Club—an organization of social intent, but with political streaks—were a blaze of light that Christmas Eve night. On the lower floor some one was strumming on the piano, and upstairs, where the "ladies" sat, and where the Sunday smokers were held, a man was singing one of the latest coon songs. The "Banner" always got them first, mainly because the composers went there, and often the air of the piece itself had been picked out or patched together, with the help of the "Banner's" piano, before the song was taken out for somebody to set the "'companiment" to it.

The proprietor himself had just gone into the parlor to see that the Christmas decorations were all that he intended them to be when a door opened and an old man entered the room. In one hand he carried an ancient carpetbag, which he deposited on the floor, while he stared around at the grandeur of the place. He was a typical old uncle of the South, from the soles of his heavy brogans to the shiny top of his bald pate, with its fringe of white wool. It was plain to be seen that he was not a denizen of the town, or of that particular quarter. They do not grow old in the Tenderloin. He paused long enough to take in the appointments of the place, then, suddenly remembering his manners, he doffed his hat and bowed with old-fashioned courtesy to the splendid proprietor.

"Why, how'do, uncle!" said the genial Mr. Turner, extending his hand. "Where did you stray from?"

"Howdy, son, howdy," returned the old man gravely. "I hails f'om Miss'ippi myse'f, a mighty long ways f'om hyeah."

His voice and old-time intonation were good to listen to, and Mr. Turner's thoughts went back to an earlier day in his own life. He was from Maryland himself. He drew up a chair for the old man and took one himself. A few other men passed into the room and stopped to look with respectful amusement at the visitor. He was such a perfect bit of old plantation life and so obviously out of place in a Tenderloin club room.

"Well, uncle, are you looking for a place to stay?" pursued Turner.

"Not 'zackly, honey ; not 'zackly. I come up hyeah a-lookin' fu' a son o' mine dat been away f'om home nigh on to five years. He live hyeah in Noo Yo'k, an' dey tell me whaih I 'quiahed dat I li'ble to fin' somebody hyeah dat know him. So I jes' drapped in."

"I know a good many young men from the South. What's your son's name?"

"Well, he named aftah my ol' mastah, Zachariah Priestley Shackelford."

"Zach Shackelford!" exclaimed some of the men, and there was a general movement among them, but a glance from Turner quieted the commotion.

"Why, yes, I know your son," he said.

"He's in here almost every night, and he's pretty sure to drop in a little later on. He has been singing with one of the colored companies here until a couple of weeks ago."

"Heish up; you don't say so. Well! well! well! but den Zachariah allus did have a mighty sweet voice. He tu'k hit aftah his mammy. Well, I sholy is hopin' to see dat boy. He was allus my favorite, aldough I reckon a body ain' got no livin' right to have favorites among dey chilluns. But Zach was allus sich a good boy."

The men turned away. They could not remember a time since they had known Zach Shackelford when by any stretch of imagination he could possibly have been considered good. He was known as one of the wildest young bucks that frequented the club, with a deft hand at cards and dice and a smooth throat for whisky. But Turner gave them such a defiant glance that they were almost ready to subscribe to anything the old man might say.

"Dis is a mighty fine place you got hyeah. Hit mus' be a kind of a hotel or boa'din' house, ain't hit?"

"Yes, something like."

"We don' have nuffin' lak dis down ouah way. Co'se, we's jes' common folks. We wo'ks out in de fiel', and dat's about all we knows—fiel', chu'ch an' cabin. But I's mighty glad my Zach's gittin' up in de worl'. He nevah were no great han' fu' wo'k. Hit kin' o' seemed to go agin his natur'. You know dey is folks lak dat."

"Lots of 'em, lots of 'em," said Mr. Turner.

The crowd of men had been augmented by a party from out of the card room, and they were listening intently to the old fellow's chatter. They felt now that they ought to laugh, but somehow they could not, and the twitching of their careless faces was not from suppressed merriment.

The visitor looked around at them, and then remarked: "My, what a lot of boa'dahs you got."

"They don't all stay here," answered Turner seriously; "some of them have just dropped in to see their friends."

"Den I 'low Zach'll be drappin' in presently. You mus' 'scuse me fu' talkin' 'bout him, but I's mighty anxious to clap my eyes on him. I's been gittin' on right sma't dese las' two yeahs, an' my ol' ooman she daid an' gone, an' I kin' o' lonesome, so I jes' p'omised mysef' dis Crismus de gif' of a sight o' Zach. Hit do look foolish fu' a man ez ol' ez me to be a runnin' 'roun' de worl' a spen'in' money dis away, but hit do seem so ha'd to git Zach home."

"How long are you going to be with us?"

"Well, I 'specs to stay all o' Crismus week."

"Maybe—" began one of the men. But Turner interrupted him. "This gentleman is my guest. Uncle," turning to the old man, "do you ever—would you—er. I've got some pretty good liquor here, ah—"

Zach's father smiled a sly smile. "I do' know, suh," he said, crossing his leg high. "I's Baptis' mys'f, but 'long o' dese Crismus holidays I's right fond of a little toddy."

A half dozen eager men made a break for the bar, but Turner's uplifted hand held them. He was an autocrat in his way.

"Excuse me, gentlemen," he said, "but I think I remarked some time ago that Mr. Shackelford was my guest." And he called the waiter.

All the men had something and tapped rims with the visitor.

"'Pears to me you people is mighty clevah up hyeah; 'tain' no wondah Zachariah don' wan' to come home."

Just then they heard a loud whoop outside the door, and a voice broke in upon them singing thickly, "Oh, this spo'tin' life is surely killin' me." The men exchanged startled glances. Turner looked at them, and there was a command in his eye. Several of them hurried out, and he himself arose, saying: "I've got to go out for a little while, but you just make yourself at home, uncle. You can lie down right there on that sofa and push that button there—see, this way—if you want some more toddy. It shan't cost you anything."

"Oh, I'll res' myself, but I ain' gwine sponge on you dat away. I got some money," and the old man dug down into his long pocket. But his host laid a hand on his arm.

"Your money's no good up here."

"Wh—wh—why, I thought dis money passed any whah in de Nunited States!" exclaimed the bewildered old man.

"That's all right, but you can't spend it until we run out."

"Oh! Why, bless yo' soul, suh, you skeered me. You sho' is clevah."

Turner went out and came upon his emissaries, where they had halted the singing Zach in the hallway, and were trying to get into his muddled brain that his father was there.

"Wha'sh de ol' man doin' at de 'Banner,' gittin' gay in his ol' days? Hic."

That was enough for Turner to hear. "Look a-here," he said, "don't you get flip when you meet your father. He's come a long ways to see you, and I'm damned if he shan't see you right. Remember you're stoppin' at my house as long as the old man stays, and if you make a break while he's here I'll spoil your mug for you. Bring him along, boys."

Zach had started in for a Christmas celebration, but they took him into an empty room. They sent to the drug store and bought many things. When the young man came out an hour later he was straight, but sad.

"Why, Pap," he said when he saw the old man, "I'll be—"

"Hem!" said Turner.

"I'll be blessed!" Zach finished.

The old man looked him over. "Tsch! tsch! tsch! Dis is a Crismus gif' fu sho'!" His voice was shaking. "I's so glad to see you, honey; but chile, you smell lak a 'pothac'ay shop."

"I ain't been right well lately," said Zach sheepishly.

To cover his confusion Turner called for eggnog.

When it came the old man said: "Well, I's Baptis' myse'f, but seen' it's Crismus—"

Johnsonham, Junior

Now ANY ONE will agree with me that it is entirely absurd for two men to fall out about their names; but then, circumstances alter cases. It had its beginning in 1863, and it has just ended.

In the first place, Ike and Jim had been good friends on the plantation, but when the time came for them to leave and seek homes for themselves each wanted a name. The master's name was Johnson, and they both felt themselves entitled to it. When Ike went forth to men as Isaac Johnson, and Jim, not to be outdone, became James Johnsonham, the rivalry began. Each married and became the father of a boy who took his father's name.

When both families moved North and settled in Little Africa their children had been taught that there must be eternal enmity between them on account of their names, and just as lasting a friendship on every other score. But with boys it was natural that the rivalry should extend to other things. When they went to school it was a contest for leadership both in the classroom and in sports, and when Isaac Johnson left school to go to work in the brickyard, James Johnsonham, not to be outdone in industry, also entered the same field of labor.

Later, it was questioned all up and down Douglass Street, which, by the way, is the social centre of Little Africa—as to which of the two was the better dancer or the more gallant beau. It was a piece of good fortune that they did not fall in love with the same girl and bring their rivalry into their affairs of the heart, for they were only men, and nothing could have kept them friends. But they came quite as near it as they could, for Matilda Benson was as bright a girl as Martha Mason, and when Ike married her she was an even-running contestant with her friend, Martha, for the highest social honors of their own particular set.

It was a foregone conclusion that when they were married and settled they should live near each other. So the houses were distant from each other only two or three doors. It was because every one knew every one else's business in that locality that Sandy Worthington took it upon himself to taunt the two men about their bone of contention.

"Mr. Johnson," he would say, when, coming from the down-town store where he worked, he would meet the two coming from their own labors in the brickyard, "how are you an' Mistah Johnsonham mekin' it ovah yo' names?"

"Well, I don' know that Johnsonham is so much of a name," Ike would say; and Jim would reply: "I 'low it's mo' name than Johnson, anyhow."

"So is stealin' ham mo' than stealin'," was the other's rejoinder, and then his friends would double up with mirth.

Sometimes the victorious repartee was Jim's, and then the laugh was on the other side. But the two went at it all good-naturedly, until one day, one foolish day, when they had both stopped too often on the way home, Jim grew angry at some little fling of his friend's, and burst into hot abuse of him. At first Ike was only astonished, and then his eyes, red with the dust of the brick-field, grew redder, the veins of his swarthy face swelled, and with a "Take that, Mistah Johnsonham," he gave Jim a resounding thwack across the face.

It took only a little time for a crowd to gather, and, with their usual tormentor to urge them on, the men forgot themselves and went into the fight in dead earnest. It was a hard-fought battle. Both rolled in the dust, caught at each other's short hair, pummeled, bit and swore. They were still rolling and tumbling when their wives, apprised of the goings on, appeared upon the scene and marched them home.

After that, because they were men, they kept a sullen silence between them, but Matilda and Martha, because they were women, had much to say to each other, and many unpleasant epithets to hurl and hurl again across the two yards that intervened between them. Finally, neither little family spoke to the other. And then, one day, there was a great bustle about Jim's house. A wise old woman went waddling in, and later the doctor came. That night the proud husband and father was treating his friends, and telling them it was a boy, and his name was to be James Johnsonham, Junior.

For a week Jim was irregular and unsteady in his habits, when one night, full of gin and pride, he staggered up to a crowd which was surrounding his rival, and said in a loud voice, "James Johnsonham, Junior—how does that strike you?"

"Any bettah than Isaac Johnson, Junior?" asked some one, slapping the happy Ike on the shoulder as the crowd burst into a loud guffaw. Jim's head was sadly bemuddled, and for a time he gazed upon the faces about him in bewilderment. Then a light broke in upon his mind, and with a "Whoo-ee!" he said, "No!" Ike grinned a defiant grin at him, and led the way to the nearest place where he and his friends might celebrate.

Jim went home to his wife full of a sullen, heavy anger. "Ike Johnson got a boy at his house, too," he said, "an' he done put Junior to his name." Martha raised her head from the pillow and hugged her own baby to her breast closer.

"It do beat all," she made answer airily; "we can't do a blessed thing but them thaih Johnsons has to follow right in ouah steps. Anyhow, I don't believe their baby is no sich healthy lookin' chile as this one is, bress his little hea't! 'Cause I knows Matilda Benson nevah was any too strong."

She was right; Matilda Benson was not so strong. The doctor went oftener to Ike's house than he had gone to Jim's, and three or four days after an undertaker went in.

They tried to keep the news from Martha's ears, but somehow it leaked into them, and when Jim came home on that evening she looked into her husband's face with a strange, new expression.

"Oh, Jim," she cried weakly, "'Tildy done gone, an' me jes' speakin' ha'd 'bout huh a little while ago, an' that po' baby lef' thaih to die! Ain't it awful?"

"Nev' min'," said Jim, huskily; "nev' min', honey." He had seen Ike's face when the messenger had come for him at the brickyard, and the memory of it was like a knife at his heart.

"Jes' think, I said, only a day or so ago," Martha went on, "that 'Tildy wasn't strong; an' I was glad of it, Jim, I was glad of it! I was jealous of huh havin' a baby, too. Now she's daid, an' I feel jes' lak I'd killed huh. S'p'osin' God 'ud sen' a jedgment on me—s'p'osin' He'd take our little Jim?"

"Sh, sh, honey," said Jim, with a man's inadequacy in such a moment. "'Tain't yo' fault; you nevah wished huh any ha'm."

"No; but I said it, I said it!"

"Po' Ike," said Jim absently; "po' fellah!"

"Won't you go thaih," she asked, "an' see what you kin do fu' him?"

"He don't speak to me."

"You mus' speak to him; you got to do it, Jim; you got to."

"What kin I say? 'Tildy's daid."

She reached up and put her arms around her husband's brawny neck. "Go bring that po' little lamb hyeah," she said. "I kin save it, an' 'ten' to two. It'll be a sort of consolation fu' him to keep his chile."

"Kin you do that, Marthy?" he said. "Kin you do that?"

"I know I kin." A great load seemed to lift itself from Jim's heart as he burst out of the house. He opened Ike's door without knocking. The man sat by the empty fireplace with his head bowed over the ashes.

"Ike," he said, and then stopped.

Ike raised his head and glanced at him with a look of dull despair. "She's gone," he replied; "'Tildy's gone." There was no touch of anger in his tone. It was as if he took the visit for granted. All petty emotions had passed away before this great feeling which touched both earth and the beyond.

"I come fu' the baby," said Jim. "Marthy, she'll take keer of it."

He reached down and found the other's hand, and the two hard palms closed together in a strong grip. "Ike," he went on, "I'm goin' to drop the 'Junior' an' the 'ham,' an' the two little ones'll jes' grow up togethah, one o' them lak the othah."

The bereaved husband made no response. He only gripped the hand tighter. A little while later Jim came hastily from the house with something small wrapped closely in a shawl.

The Faith Cure Man

HOPE IS TENACIOUS. It goes on living and working when science has dealt it what should be its deathblow.

In the close room at the top of the old tenement house little Lucy lay wasting away with a relentless disease. The doctor had said at the beginning of the winter that she could not live. Now he said that he could do no more for her except to ease the few days that remained for the child.

But Martha Benson would not believe him. She was confident that doctors were not infallible. Anyhow, this one wasn't, for she saw life and health ahead for her little one.

Did not the preacher at the Mission Home say: "Ask, and ye shall receive?" and had she not asked and asked again the life of her child, her last and only one, at the hands of Him whom she worshipped?

No, Lucy was not going to die. What she needed was country air and a place to run about in. She had been housed up too much; these long Northern winters were too severe for her, and that was what made her so pinched and thin and weak. She must have air, and she should have it.

"Po' little lammie," she said to the child, "Mammy's little gal boun' to git well. Mammy gwine sen' huh out in de country when the spring comes, whaih she kin roll in de grass an' pick flowers an' git good an' strong. Don' baby want to go to de country? Don' baby want to see de sun shine?" And the child had looked up at her with wide, bright eyes, tossed her thin arms and moaned for reply.

"Nemmine, we gwine fool dat doctah. Some day we'll th'ow all his nassy medicine 'way, an' he come in an' say: 'Whaih's all my medicine?' Den we answeh up sma't like: 'We done th'owed it out. We don' need no nassy medicine.' Den he look 'roun' an' say: 'Who dat I see runnin' roun' de flo' hyeah, a-lookin' so fat?' an' you up an' say: 'Hit's me, dat's who 'tis, mistah doctor man!' Den he go out an' slam de do' behin' him. Ain' dat fine?"

But the child had closed her eyes, too weak even to listen. So her mother kissed her little thin forehead and tiptoed out, sending in a child from across the hall to take care of Lucy while she was at work, for sick as the little one was she could not stay at home and nurse her.

Hope grasps at a straw, and it was quite in keeping with the condition of Martha's mind that she should open her ears and her heart when they told her of the wonderful works of the faith-cure man. People had gone to him on crutches, and he had touched or rubbed them and they had come away whole. He had gone to the homes of the bed-ridden, and they had risen up to bless him. It was so easy for her to believe it all. The only religion she had ever known, the wild, emotional religion of most of her race, put her credulity to stronger tests than that. Her only question was, would such a man come to her humble room. But she put away even this thought. He must come. She would make him. Already she saw Lucy strong, and running about like a mouse, the joy of her heart and the light of her eyes.

As soon as she could get time she went humbly to see the faith doctor, and laid her case before him, hoping, fearing, trembling.

Yes, he would come. Her heart leaped for joy.

"There is no place," said the faith curist, "too humble for the messenger of heaven to enter. I am following One who went among the humblest and the lowliest, and was not ashamed to be found among publicans and sinners. I will come to your child, madam, and put her again under the law. The law of life is health, and no one who will accept the law need be sick. I am not a physician. I do not claim to be. I only claim to teach people how not to be sick. My fee is five dollars, merely to defray my expenses, that's all. You know the servant is worthy of his hire. And in this little bottle here I have an elixir which has never been known to fail in any of the things claimed for it. Since the world has got used to taking medicine we must make some concessions to its prejudices. But this in reality is not a medicine at all. It is only a symbol. It is really liquefied prayer and faith."

Martha did not understand anything of what he was saying. She did not try to; she did not want to. She only felt a blind trust in him that filled her heart with unspeakable gladness.

Tremulous with excitement, she doled out her poor dollars to him, seized the precious elixir and hurried away home to Lucy, to whom she was carrying life and strength. The little one made a weak attempt to smile at her mother, but the light flickered away and died into greyness on her face.

"Now mammy's little gal gwine to git well fu' sho'. Mammy done bring huh somep'n' good." Awed and reverent, she tasted the wonderful elixir before giving it to the child. It tasted very much like sweetened water to her, but she knew that it was not, and had no doubt of its virtues.

Lucy swallowed it as she swallowed everything her mother brought to her. Poor little one! She had nothing to buoy her up or to fight science with.

In the course of an hour her mother gave her the medicine again, and persuaded herself that there was a perceptible brightening in her daughter's face.

Mrs. Mason, Caroline's mother, called across the hall: "How Lucy dis evenin', Mis' Benson?"

"Oh, I think Lucy air right peart," Martha replied. "Come over an' look at huh."

Mrs. Mason came, and the mother told her about the new faith doctor and his wonderful powers.

"Why, Mis' Mason," she said, "'pears like I could see de change in de child de minute she swallowed dat medicine."

Her neighbor listened in silence, but when she went back to her own room it was to shake her head and murmur: "Po' Marfy, she jes' ez blind ez a bat. She jes' go 'long, holdin' on to dat chile wid all huh might, an' I see death in Lucy's face now. Dey ain't no faif nur prayer, nur Jack-leg doctors nuther gwine to save huh."

But Martha needed no pity then. She was happy in her self-delusion.

On the morrow the faith doctor came to see Lucy. She had not seemed so well that morning, even to her mother, who remained at home until the doctor arrived. He carried a conquering air, and a baggy umbrella, the latter of which he laid across the foot of the bed as he bent over the moaning child.

"Give me some brown paper," he commanded.

Martha hastened to obey, and the priestly practitioner dampened it in water and laid it on Lucy's head, all the time murmuring prayers—or were they incantations?—to himself. Then he placed pieces of the paper on the soles of the child's feet and on the palms of her hands, and bound them there.

When all this was done he knelt down and prayed aloud, ending with a peculiar version of the Lord's prayer, supposed to have mystic effect. Martha was greatly impressed, but through it all Lucy lay and moaned.

The faith curist rose to go. "Well, we can look to have her out in a few days. Remember, my good woman, much depends upon you. You must try to keep your mind in a state of belief. Are you saved?"

"Oh, yes, suh. I'm a puffessor," said Martha, and having completed his mission, the man of prayers went out, and Caroline again took Martha's place at Lucy's side.

In the next two days Martha saw, or thought she saw, a steady improvement in Lucy. According to instructions, the brown paper was moved every day, moistened, and put back.

Martha had so far spurred her faith that when she went out on Saturday morning she promised to bring Lucy something good for her Christmas dinner, and a pair of shoes against the time of her going out, and also a little doll. She brought them home that night. Caroline had grown tired and, lighting the lamp, had gone home.

"I done brung my little lady bird huh somep'n nice," said Martha, "here's a lil' doll and de lil' shoes, honey. How's de baby feel?" Lucy did not answer.

"You sleep?" Martha went over to the bed. The little face was pinched and ashen. The hands were cold.

"Lucy! Lucy!" called the mother. "Lucy! Oh, Gawd! It ain't true! She ain't daid! My little one, my las' one!"

She rushed for the elixir and brought it to the bed. The thin dead face stared back at her, unresponsive.

She sank down beside the bed, moaning. "Daid, daid, oh, my Gawd, gi' me back my chile! Oh, don't I believe you enough? Oh, Lucy, Lucy, my little lamb! I got you yo' gif'. Oh, Lucy!"

The next day was set apart for the funeral. The Mission preacher read: "The Lord giveth and the Lord taketh away, blessed be the name of the Lord," and some one said "Amen!" But Martha could not echo it in her heart. Lucy was her last, her one treasured lamb.

A Council of State

Part I

LUTHER HAMILTON WAS a great political power. He was neither representative in Congress, senator nor cabinet minister. When asked why he aspired to none of these places of honor and emolument he invariably shrugged his shoulders and smiled inscrutably. In fact, he found it both more pleasant and more profitable simply to boss his party. It gave him power, position and patronage, and yet put him under obligations to no narrow constituency.

As he sat in his private office this particular morning there was a smile upon his face, and his little eyes looked out beneath the heavy grey eyebrows and the massive cheeks with gleams of pleasure. His whole appearance betokened the fact that he was feeling especially good. Even his mail lay neglected before him, and his eyes gazed straight at the wall. What wonder that he should smile and dream. Had he not just the day before utterly crushed a troublesome opponent? Had he not ruined the career of a young man who dared to oppose him, driven him out of public life and forced his business to the wall? If this were not food for self-congratulation pray what is?

Mr. Hamilton's reverie was broken in upon by a tap at the door, and his secretary entered.

"Well, Frank, what is it now? I haven't gone through my mail yet."

"Miss Kirkman is in the outer office, sir, and would like to see you this morning."

"Oh, Miss Kirkman, heh; well, show her in at once."

The secretary disappeared and returned ushering in a young woman, whom the "boss" greeted cordially.

"Ah, Miss Kirkman, good-morning! Good-morning! Always prompt and busy, I see. Have a chair."

Miss Kirkman returned his greeting and dropped into a chair. She began at once fumbling in a bag she carried.

"We'll get right to business," she said. "I know you're busy, and so am I, and I want to get through. I've got to go and hunt a servant for Mrs. Senator Dutton when I leave here."

She spoke in a loud voice, and her words rushed one upon the other as if she were in the habit of saying much in a short space of time. This is a trick of speech frequently acquired by those who visit public men. Miss Kirkman's whole manner indicated bustle and hurry. Even her attire showed it. She was a plump woman, aged, one would say about thirty. Her hair was brown and her eyes a steely grey— not a bad face, but one too shrewd and aggressive perhaps for a woman. One might have looked at her for a long time and never suspected the truth, that she was allied to the colored race. Neither features, hair nor complexion showed it, but then "colored" is such an elastic word, and Miss Kirkman in reality was colored "for revenue only." She found it more profitable to ally herself to the less important race because she could assume a position among them as a representative woman, which she could never have hoped to gain among the whites. So she was colored, and, without having any sympathy with the people whom she represented, spoke for them and uttered what was supposed by the powers to be the thoughts that were in their breasts.

"Well, from the way you're tossing the papers in that bag I know you've got some news for me."

"Yes, I have, but I don't know how important you'll think it is. Here we are!" She drew forth a paper and glanced at it.

"It's just a memorandum, a list of names of a few men who need watching. The Afro-American convention is to meet on the 22d; that's Thursday of next week. Bishop Carter is to preside. The thing has resolved itself into a fight between those who are office-holders and those who want to be."

"Yes, well what's the convention going to do?"

"They're going to denounce the administration."

"Hem, well in your judgment, what will that amount to, Miss Kirkman?"

"They are the representative talking men from all sections of the country, and they have their following, and so there's no use disputing that they can do some harm."

"Hum, what are they going to denounce the administration for?"

"Oh, there's a spirit of general discontent, and they've got to denounce something, so it had as well be the administration as anything else."

There was a new gleam in Mr. Hamilton's eye that was not one of pleasure as he asked, "Who are the leaders in this movement?"

"That's just what I brought this list for. There's Courtney, editor of the *New York Beacon,* who is rabid; there's Jones of Georgia, Gray of Ohio—"

"Whew," whistled the boss, "Gray of Ohio, why he's on the inside."

"Yes, and I can't see what's the matter with him, he's got his position, and he ought to keep his mouth shut."

"Oh, there are ways of applying the screw. Go on."

"Then, too, there's Shackelford of Mississippi, Duncan of South Carolina, Stowell of Kentucky, and a lot of smaller fry who are not worth mentioning."

"Are they organized?"

"Yes, Courtney has seen to that, the forces are compact."

"We must split them. How is the bishop?"

"Neutral."

"Any influence?"

"Lots of it."

"How's your young man, the one for whom you've been soliciting a place—what's his name?"

Miss Kirkman did her womanhood the credit of blushing, "Joseph Aldrich, you mean. You can trust to me to see that he's on the right side."

"Happy is the man who has the right woman to boss him, and who has sense enough to be bossed by her; his path shall be a path of roses, and his bed a flowery bed of ease. Now to business. They must not denounce the administration. What are the conditions of membership in this convention?"

"Any one may be present, but it costs a fee of five dollars for the privilege of the floor."

Mr. Hamilton turned to the desk and made out a check. He handed it to Miss Kirkman, saying, "Cash this, and pack that convention for the administration. I look to you and the people you may have behind you to check any rash resolutions they may attempt to pass. I want you to be there every day and take notes of the speeches made, and their character and tenor. I shall have Mr. Richardson there also to help you. The record of each man's speech will be sent to his central committee, and we shall know how to treat him in the future. You know, Miss Kirkman, it is our method to help our friends and to crush our enemies. I shall depend upon you to let me know which is which. Good-morning."

"Good-morning, Mr. Hamilton."

"And, oh, Miss Kirkman, just a moment. Frank," the secretary came in, "bring me that jewel case out of the safe. Here, Miss Kirkman, Mrs. Hamilton told me if you came in to ask if you would mind running past the safety deposit vaults and putting these in for her?"

"Certainly not," said Miss Kirkman.

This was one of the ways in which Miss Kirkman was made to remember her race. And the relation to that race, which nothing in her face showed, came out strongly in her willingness thus to serve. The confidence itself flattered her, and she was never tired of telling her acquaintances how she had put such and such a senator's wife's jewels away, or got a servant for a cabinet minister.

When her other duties were done she went directly to a small dingy office building and entered a room, over which was the sign, "Joseph Aldrich, Counselor and Attorney at Law."

"How do, Joe."

"Why, Miss Kirkman, I'm glad to see you," said Mr. Aldrich, coming forward to meet her and setting a chair. He was a slender young man, of a complexion which among the varying shades bestowed among colored people is termed a light brown skin. A mustache and a short Vandyke beard partially covered a mouth inclined to weakness. Looking at them, an observer would have said that Miss Kirkman was the stronger man of the two.

"What brings you out this way to-day?" questioned Aldrich.

"I'll tell you. You've asked me to marry you, haven't you?"

"Yes."

"Well, I'm going to do it."

"Annie, you make me too happy."

"That's enough," said Miss Kirkman, waving him away. "We haven't any time for romance now. I mean business. You're going to the convention next week."

"Yes."

"And you're going to speak?"

"Of course."

"That's right. Let me see your speech."

He drew a typewritten manuscript from the drawer and handed it to her. She ran her eyes over the pages, murmuring to herself. "Uh, huh, 'wavering, weak, vacillating administration, have not given us the protection our rights as citizens demanded—while our brothers were murdered in the South. Nero fiddled while Rome burned, while this modern'—uh, huh, oh, yes, just as I thought," and with a sudden twist Miss Kirkman tore the papers across and pitched them into the grate.

"Miss Kirkman—Annie, what do you mean?"

"I mean that if you're going to marry me, I'm not going to let you go to the convention and kill yourself."

"But my convictions—"

"Look here, don't talk to me about convictions. The colored man is the under dog, and the under dog has no right to have convictions. Listen, you're going to the convention next week and you're going to make a speech, but it won't be that speech. I have just come from Mr. Hamilton's. That convention is to be watched closely. He is to have his people there and they are to take down the words of every man who talks, and these words will be sent to his central committee. The man who goes there with an imprudent tongue goes down. You'd better get to work and see if you can't think of something good the administration has done and dwell on that."

"Whew!"

"Well, I'm off."

"But Annie, about the wedding?"

"Good-morning, we'll talk about the wedding after the convention."

The door closed on her last words, and Joseph Aldrich sat there wondering and dazed at her manner. Then he began to think about the administration. There must be some good things to say for it, and he would find them. Yes, Annie was right—and wasn't she a hustler though?

Part II

It was on the morning of the 22d and near nine o'clock, the hour at which the convention was to be called to order. But Mr. Gray of Ohio had not yet gone in. He stood at the door of the convention hall in deep converse with another man. His companion was a young looking sort of person. His forehead was high and his eyes were keen and alert. The face was mobile and the mouth nervous. It was the face of an enthusiast, a man with deep and intense beliefs, and the boldness or, perhaps, rashness to uphold them.

"I tell you, Gray," he was saying, "it's an outrage, nothing less. Life, liberty, and the pursuit of happiness. Bah! It's all twaddle. Why, we can't even be secure in the first two, how can we hope for the last?"

"You're right, Elkins," said Gray, soberly, "and though I hold a position under the administration, when it comes to a consideration of the wrongs of my race, I cannot remain silent."

"I cannot and will not. I hold nothing from them, and I owe them nothing. I am only a bookkeeper in a commercial house, where their spite cannot reach me, so you may rest assured that I shall not bite my tongue."

"Nor shall I. We shall all be colored men here together, and talk, I hope, freely one to the other. Shall you introduce your resolution today?"

"I won't have a chance unless things move more rapidly than I expect them to. It will have to come up under new business, I should think."

"Hardly. Get yourself appointed on the committee on resolutions."

"Good, but how can I?"

"I'll see to that; I know the bishop pretty well. Ah, good-morning, Miss Kirkman. How do you do, Aldrich?" Gray pursued, turning to the newcomers, who returned his greeting, and passed into the hall.

"That's Miss Kirkman. You've heard of her. She fetches and carries for Luther Hamilton and his colleagues, and has been suspected of doing some spying, also."

"Who was that with her?"

"Oh, that's her man Friday; otherwise Joseph Aldrich by name, a fellow she's trying to make something of before she marries him. She's got the pull to do it, too."

"Why don't you turn them down?"

"Ah, my boy, you're young, you're young; you show it. Don't you know that a wind strong enough to uproot an oak only ripples the leaves of a creeper against the wall? Outside of the race that woman is really considered one of the leaders, and she trades upon the fact."

"But why do you allow this base deception to go?"

"Because, Elkins, my child," Gray put his hand on the other's shoulder with mock tenderness, "because these seemingly sagacious whites among whom we live are really a very credulous people, and the first one who goes to them with a good front and says 'Look here, I am the leader of the colored people; I am their oracle and prophet,' they immediately exalt and say 'That's so.' Now do you see why Miss Kirkman has a pull?"

"I see, but come on, let's go in; there goes the gavel."

The convention hall was already crowded, and the air was full of the bustle of settling down. When the time came for the payment of their fees, by those who wanted the privilege of the floor, there was a perfect rush for the secretary's desk. Bank notes fluttered everywhere. Miss Kirkman had on a suspiciously new dress and bonnet, but she had done her work well, nevertheless. She looked up into the gallery in a corner that overlooked the stage and caught the eye of a young man who sat there notebook in hand. He smiled, and she smiled. Then she looked over at Mr. Aldrich, who was not sitting with her, and they both smiled complacently. There's nothing like being on the inside.

After the appointment of committees, the genial bishop began his opening address, and a very careful, pretty address it was, too—well worded, well balanced, dealing in broad generalities and studiously saying nothing that would indicate that he had any intention of directing the policy of the meetings. Of course it brought forth all the applause that a bishop's address deserves, and the ladies in the back seats fluttered their fans, and said: "The dear man, how eloquent he is."

Gray had succeeded in getting Elkins placed on the committee on resolutions, but when they came to report, the fiery resolution denouncing the administration for its policy toward the negro was laid on the table. The young man had succeeded in engineering it through the committee, but the chairman decided that its proper place was under the head of new business, where it might be taken up in the discussion of the administration's attitude toward the negro.

"We are here, gentlemen," pursued the bland presiding officer, "to make public sentiment, but we must not try to make it too fast; so if our young friend from Ohio will only hold his resolution a little longer, it will be acted upon at the proper time. We must be moderate and conservative."

Gray sprang to his feet and got the chairman's eye. His face was flushed and he almost shouted: "Conservatism be hanged! We have rolled that word under our tongues when we were being trampled upon; we have preached it in our churches when we were being shot down; we have taught it in our schools when the right to use our learning was denied us, until the very word has come to be a reproach upon a black man's tongue!"

There were cries of "Order! Order!" and "Sit down!" and the gavel was rattling on the chairman's desk. Then some one rose to a point of order, so dear to the heart of the negro debater. The point was sustained and the Ohioan yielded the floor, but not until he had gazed straight into the eyes of Miss Kirkman as they rose from her notebook. She turned red. He curled his lip and sat down, but the blood burned in his face, and it was not the heat of shame, but of anger and contempt that flushed his cheeks.

This outbreak was but the precursor of other storms to follow. Every one had come with an idea to exploit or some proposition to advance. Each one had his panacea for all the aches and pains of his race. Each man who had paid his five dollars wanted his full five dollars' worth of talk. The chairman allowed them five minutes apiece, and they thought time dear at a dollar a minute. But there were speeches to be made for buncombe, and they made the best of the seconds. They howled, they raged, they stormed. They waxed eloquent or pathetic. Jones of Georgia was swearing softly and feelingly into Shackelford's ear. Shackelford was sympathetic and nervous as he fingered a large bundle of manuscript in his back pocket. He got up several times and called "Mr. Chairman," but his voice had been drowned in the tumult. Amid it all, calm and impassive, sat the man, who of all others was expected to be in the heat of the fray.

It had been rumored that Courtney of the *New York Beacon* had come to Washington with blood in his eyes. But there he sat, silent and unmoved, his swarthy, eagle-like face, with its frame of iron-grey hair as unchanging as if he had never had a passionate thought.

"I don't like Jim Courtney's silence," whispered Stowell to a colleague. "There's never so much devil in him as when he keeps still. You look out for him when he does open up."

But all the details of the convention do not belong to this narrative. It is hardly relevant, even, to tell how Stowell's prediction came true, and at the second day's meeting Courtney's calm gave way, and he delivered one of the bitterest speeches of his life. It was in the morning, and he was down for a set speech on "The Negro in the Higher Walks of Life." He started calmly, but as he progressed, the memory of all the wrongs, personal and racial that he had suffered; the knowledge of the disabilities that he and his brethren had to suffer, and the vision of toil unrequited, love rejected, and loyalty ignored, swept him off his feet. He forgot his subject, forgot everything but that he was a crushed man in a crushed race.

The auditors held their breath, and the reporters wrote much.

Turning to them he said, "And to the press of Washington, to whom I have before paid my respects, let me say that I am not afraid to have them take any word that I may say. I came here to meet them on their own ground. I will meet them with pen. I will meet them with pistol," and then raising his tall, spare form, he shouted, "Yes, even though there is but one hundred and thirty-five pounds of me, I will meet them with my fists!"

This was all very rash of Courtney. His paper did not circulate largely, so his real speech, which he printed, was not widely read, while through the columns of the local press, a garbled and distorted version of it went to every corner of the country. Purposely distorted? Who shall say? He had insulted the press; and then Mr. Hamilton was a very wealthy man.

When the time for the consideration of Elkins' resolution came, Courtney, Jones and Shackelford threw themselves body and soul into the fight with Gray and its author. There was a formidable array against them. All the men in office, and all of those who had received even a crumb of promise were for buttering over their wrongs, and making their address to the public a prophecy of better things.

Jones suggested that they send an apology to lynchers for having negroes where they could be lynched. This called for reproof from the other side, and the discussion grew hot and acrimonious. Gray again got the floor, and surprised his colleagues by the plainness of his utterances. Elkins followed him with a biting speech that brought Aldrich to his feet.

Mr. Aldrich had chosen well his time, and had carefully prepared his speech. He recited all the good things that the administration had done, hoped to do, tried to do, or wanted to do, and showed what a very respectable array it was. He counseled moderation and conservatism, and his peroration was a flowery panegyric of the "noble man whose hand is on the helm, guiding the grand old ship of state into safe harbor."

The office-holders went wild with enthusiasm. No self-interest there. The opposition could not argue that this speech was made to keep a job, because the speaker had none. Then Jim Courtney got up and spoiled it all by saying that it may be that the speaker had no job but wanted one.

Aldrich was not moved. He saw a fat salary and Annie Kirkman for him in the near future.

The young lady had done her work well, and when the resolution came to a vote it was lost by a good majority. Aldrich was again on his feet and offering another. The forces of the opposition were discouraged and disorganized, and they made no effort to stop it when the rules were suspended, and it went through on the first reading. Then the convention shouted, that is, part of it did, and Miss Kirkman closed her notebook and glanced up at the gallery again. The young man had closed his book also. Their work was done. The administration had not been denounced, and they had their black-list for Mr. Hamilton's knife.

There were some more speeches made, just so that the talkers should get their money's worth; but for the masses, the convention had lost its interest, and after a few feeble attempts to stir it into life again, a motion to adjourn was entertained. But, before a second appeared, Elkins arose and asked leave to make a statement. It was granted.

"Gentlemen," he said, "we have all heard the resolution which goes to the public as the opinion of the negroes of the country. There are some of us who do not believe that this expresses the feelings of our race, and to us who believe this, Mr. Courtney has given the use of his press in New York, and we shall print our resolution and scatter it broadcast as the minority report of this convention, but the majority report of the race."

Miss Kirkman opened her book again for a few minutes, and then the convention adjourned.

"I wish you'd find out, Miss Kirkman," said Hamilton a couple of days later, "just what firm that young Elkins works for."

"I have already done that. I thought you'd want to know," and she handed him a card.

"Ah, yes," he said. "I have some business relations with that firm. I know them very well. Miss Anderson," he called to his stenographer, "will you kindly take a letter for me. By the way, Miss Kirkman, I have placed Mr. Aldrich. He will have his appointment in a few days."

"Oh, thank you, Mr. Hamilton; is there anything more I can do for you?"

"Nothing. Good-morning."

"Good-morning."

A week later in his Ohio home William Elkins was surprised to be notified by his employers that they were cutting down forces, and would need his services no longer. He wrote at once to his friend Gray to know if there was any chance for him in Washington, and received the answer that Gray could hardly hold his own, as great pressure was being put upon him to force him to resign.

"I think," wrote Gray, "that the same hand is at the bottom of all our misfortunes. This is Hamilton's method."

Miss Kirkman and Mr. Aldrich were married two weeks from the day the convention adjourned. Mr. Gray was removed from his position on account of inefficiency. He is still trying to get back, but the very men to whom his case must go are in the hands of Mr. Hamilton.

Silas Jackson

SILAS JACKSON WAS a young man to whom many opportunities had come. Had he been a less fortunate boy, as his little world looked at it, he might have spent all his days on the little farm where he was born, much as many of his fellows did. But no, Fortune had marked him for her own, and it was destined that he should be known to fame. He was to know a broader field than the few acres which he and his father worked together, and where he and several brothers and sisters had spent their youth.

Mr. Harold Marston was the instrument of Fate in giving Silas his first introduction to the world. Marston, who prided himself on being, besides a man of leisure, something of a sportsman, was shooting over the fields in the vicinity of the Jackson farm. During the week he spent in the region, needing the services of a likely boy, he came to know and like Silas. Upon leaving, he said, "It's a pity for a boy as bright as you are to be tied down in this God-forsaken place. How'd you like to go up to the Springs, Si, and work in a hotel?"

The very thought of going to such a place, and to such work, fired the boy's imagination, although the idea of it daunted him.

"I'd like it powahful well, Mistah Ma'ston," he replied.

"Well, I'm going up there, and the proprietor of one of the best hotels, the Fountain House, is a very good friend of mine, and I'll get him to speak to his head waiter in your behalf. You want to get out of here, and see something of the world, and not stay cooped up with nothing livelier than rabbits, squirrels, and quail."

And so the work was done. The black boy's ambitions that had only needed an encouraging word had awakened into buoyant life. He looked his destiny squarely in the face, and saw that the great world outside beckoned to him. From that time his dreams were eagle-winged. The farm looked narrower to him, the cabin meaner, and the clods were harder to his feet. He learned to hate the plough that he had followed before in dumb content, and there was no longer joy in the woods he knew and loved. Once, out of pure joy of living, he had gone singing about his work; but now, when he sang, it was because his heart was longing for the city of his dreams, and hope inspired the song.

However, after Mr. Marston had been gone for over two weeks, and nothing had been heard from the Springs, the hope died in Silas's heart, and he came to believe that his benefactor had forgotten him. And yet he could not return to the old contentment with his mode of life. Mr. Marston was right, and he was "cooped up there with nothing better than rabbits, squirrels, and quail." The idea had never occurred to him before, but now it struck him with disconcerting force that there was something in him above his surroundings and the labor at which he toiled day by day. He began to see that the cabin was not over clean, and for the first time recognized that his brothers and sisters were positively dirty. He had always looked on it with unconscious eyes before, but now he suddenly developed the capacity for disgust.

When young 'Lishy, noticing his brother's moroseness, attributed it to his strong feeling for a certain damsel, Silas turned on him in a fury. Ambition had even driven out all other feelings, and Dely Manly seemed poor and commonplace to the dark swain, who a month before would have gone any length to gain a smile from her. He compared everything and everybody to the glory of what he dreamed the Springs and its inhabitants to be, and all seemed cheap beside.

Then on a day when his spirits were at their lowest ebb, a passing neighbor handed him a letter which he had found at the little village post office. It was addressed to Mr. Si Jackson, and bore the Springs postmark. Silas was immediately converted from a raw backwoods boy to a man of the world. Save the little notes that had been passed back and forth from boy to girl at the little log schoolhouse where he had gone four fitful sessions, this was his first letter, and it was the first time he had ever been addressed as "Mr." He swelled with a pride that he could not conceal, as with trembling hands he tore the missive open.

He read it through with glowing eyes and a growing sense of his own importance. It was from the head waiter whom Mr. Marston had mentioned, and was couched in the most elegant and high-sounding language. It said that Mr. Marston had spoken for Silas, and that if he came to the Springs, and was quick to learn, "to acquire knowledge," was the head waiter's phrase, a situation would be provided for him. The family gathered around the fortunate son, and gazed on him with awe when he imparted the good news. He became, on the instant, a new being to them. It was as if he had only been loaned to them, and was now being lifted bodily out of their world.

The elder Jackson was a bit doubtful about the matter.

"Of co'se ef you wants to go, Silas, I ain't a-gwine to gainsay you, an' I hope it's all right, but sence freedom dis hyeah piece o' groun's been good enough fu' me, an' I reckon you mought a' got erlong on it."

"But pap, you see it's diff'ent now. It's diff'ent, all I wanted was a chanst."

"Well, I reckon you got it, Si, I reckon you got it."

The younger children whispered long after they had gone to bed that night, wondering and guessing what the great place to which brother Si was going could be like, and they could only picture it as like the great white-domed city whose picture they had seen in the gaudy Bible foisted upon them by a passing agent.

As for Silas, he read and reread the letter by the light of a tallow dip until he was too sleepy to see, and every word was graven on his memory; then he went to bed with the precious paper under his pillow. In spite of his drowsiness, he lay awake for some time, gazing with heavy eyes into the darkness, where he saw the great city and his future; then he went to sleep to dream of it.

From then on, great were the preparations for the boy's departure. So little happened in that vicinity that the matter became a neighborhood event, and the black folk for three miles up and down the road manifested their interest in Silas's good fortune.

"I hyeah you gwine up to de Springs," said old Hiram Jones, when he met the boy on the road a day or two before his departure.

"Yes, suh, I's gwine up thaih to wo'k in a hotel. Mistah Ma'ston, he got me the job."

The old man reined in his horse slowly, and deposited the liquid increase of a quid of tobacco before he said; "I hyeah tell it's powahful wicked up in dem big cities."

"Oh, I reckon I ain't a-goin' to do nuffin wrong. I's goin' thaih to wo'k."

"Well, you has been riz right," commented the old man doubtfully, "but den, boys will be boys."

He drove on, and the prospect of a near view of wickedness did not make the Springs less desirable in the boy's eyes. Raised as he had been, almost away from civilization, he hardly knew the meaning of what the world called wickedness. Not that he was strong or good. There had been no occasion for either quality to develop; but that he was simple and primitive, and had been close to what was natural and elemental. His faults and sins were those of the gentle barbarian. He had not yet learned the subtler vices of a higher civilization.

Silas, however, was not without the pride of his kind, and although his father protested that it was a useless extravagance, he insisted upon going to the nearest village and investing part of his small savings in a new suit of clothes. It was quaint and peculiar apparel, but it was the boy's first "store suit," and it filled him with unspeakable joy. His brothers and sisters regarded his new magnificence with envying admiration. It would be a long while before they got away from bagging, homespun, and copperas-colored cotton, whacked out into some semblance of garments by their "mammy." And so, armed with a light bundle, in which were his few other belongings, and fearfully and wonderfully arrayed, Silas Jackson set out for the Springs. His father's parting injunctions were ringing in his ears, and the memory of his mammy's wet eyes and sad face lingered in his memory. She had wanted him to take the gaudy Bible away, but it was too heavy to carry, especially as he was to walk the whole thirty miles to the land of promise. At the last, his feeling of exaltation gave way to one of sorrow, and as he went down the road, he turned often to look at the cabin, until it faded from sight around the bend. Then a lump rose in his throat, and he felt like turning and running back to it. He had never thought the old place could seem so dear. But he kept his face steadily forward and trudged on toward his destiny.

The Springs was the fashionable resort of Virginia, where the aristocrats who thought they were ill went to recover their health and to dance. Compared with large cities of the North, it was but a small town, even including the transient population, but in the eyes of the rural blacks and the poor whites of the region, it was a place of large importance.

Hither, on the morning after his departure from the home gate, came Silas

Jackson, a little footsore and weary, but hopeful withal. In spite of the pains that he had put upon his dressing, he was a quaint figure on the city streets. Many an amused smile greeted him as he went his way, but he saw them not. Inquiring the direction, he kept on, until the many windows and broad veranda of the great hotel broke on his view, and he gasped in amazement and awe at the sight of it, and a sudden faintness seized him. He was reluctant to go on, but the broad grins with which some colored men who were working about the place regarded him, drove him forward, in spite of his embarrassment.

He found his way to the kitchen, and asked in trembling tones for the head waiter. Breakfast being over, that individual had leisure to come to the kitchen. There, with the grinning waiters about him, he stopped and calmly surveyed Silas. He was a very pompous head waiter.

Silas had never been self-conscious before, but now he became distressfully aware of himself—of his awkwardness, of his clumsy feet and dangling hands, of the difference between his clothes and the clothes of the men about him.

After a survey, which seemed to the boy of endless duration, the head waiter spoke, and his tone was the undisputed child of his looks.

"I pussoom," said Mr. Buckner, "that you are the pusson Mistah Ma'ston spoke to the p'op'ietor about?"

"Yes, suh, I reckon I is. He p'omised to git me a job up hyeah, an' I got yo' lettah—" here Silas, who had set his bundle on the floor in coming into the Presence, began to fumble in his pockets for the letter. He searched long in vain, because his hands trembled, and he was nervous under the eyes of this great personage who stood unmoved and looked calmly at him.

Finally the missive was found and produced, though not before the perspiration was standing thick on Silas's brow. The head waiter took the sheet.

"Ve'y well, suh, ve'y well. You are evidently the p'oper pusson, as I reco'nize this as my own chirography."

The up-country boy stood in awed silence. He thought he had never heard such fine language before.

"I ca'culate that you have nevah had no experience in hotel work," pursued Mr. Buckner somewhat more graciously.

"I's nevah done nuffin' but wo'k on a farm; but evahbody 'lows I's right handy." The fear that he would be sent back home without employment gave him boldness.

"I see, I see," said the head waiter. "Well, we'll endeavor to try an' see how soon you can learn. Mistah Smith, will you take this young man in charge, an' show him how to get about things until we are ready to try him in the dinin'-room?"

A rather pleasant-faced yellow boy came over to Silas and showed him where to put his things and what to do.

"I guess it'll be a little strange at first, if you've never been a hotel man, but you'll ketch on. Just you keep your eye on me."

All that day as Silas blundered about slowly and awkwardly, he looked with wonder and admiration at the ease and facility with which his teacher and the other men did their work. They were so calm, so precise, and so self-sufficient. He wondered if he would ever be like them, and felt very hopeless as the question presented itself to him.

They were a little prone to laugh at him, but he was so humble and so sensible that he thought he must be laughable; so he laughed a little shamefacedly at himself, and only tried the harder to imitate his companions. Once when he dropped a dish upon the floor, he held his breath in consternation, but when he found that no one paid any attention to it, he picked it up and went his way.

He was tired that night, more tired than ploughing had ever made him, and was thankful when Smith proposed to show him at once to the rooms apportioned to the servants. Here he sank down and fell into a doze as soon as his companion left him with the remark that he had some studying to do. He found afterward that Smith was only a temporary employee at the Springs, coming there during the vacations of the school which he attended, in order to eke out the amount which it cost him for his education. Silas thought this a very wonderful thing at first, but when he grew wiser, as he did finally, he took the point of view of most of his fellows and thought that Smith was wasting both time and opportunities.

It took a very short time for Silas's unfamiliarity with his surroundings to wear off, and for him to become acquainted with the duties of his position. He grew at ease with his work, and became a favorite both in dining-room and kitchen. Then began his acquaintance with other things, and there were many other things at the Springs which an unsophisticated young man might learn.

Silas's social attainments were lamentably sparse, but being an apt youngster, he began to acquire them, quite as he acquired his new duties, and different forms of speech. He learned to dance—almost a natural gift of the negro—and he was introduced into the subtleties of flirtation. At first he was a bit timid with the nurse-girls and maids whom the wealthy travelers brought with them, but after a few lessons from very able teachers, he learned the manly art of ogling to his own satisfaction, and soon became as proficient as any of the other black coxcombs.

If he ever thought of Dely Manly any more, it was with a smile that he had been able at one time to consider her seriously. The people at home, be it said to his credit, he did not forget. A part of his wages went back every month to help better the condition of the cabin. But Silas himself had no desire to return, and at the end of a year he shuddered at the thought of it. He was quite willing to help his father, whom he had now learned to call the "old man," but he was not willing to go back to him.

II

Early in his second year at the Springs Marston came for a stay at the hotel. When he saw his protégé, he exclaimed: "Why, that isn't Si, is it?"

"Yes, suh," smiled Silas.

"Well, well, well, what a change. Why, boy, you've developed into a regular fashion-plate. I hope you're not advertising for any of the Richmond tailors. They're terrible Jews, you know."

"You see, a man has to be neat aroun' the hotel, Mistah Ma'ston."

"Whew, and you've developed dignity, too. By the Lord Harry, if I'd have made that remark to you about a year and a half ago, there at the cabin, you'd have just grinned. Ah, Silas, I'm afraid for you. You've grown too fast. You've gained a certain poise and ease at the expense of—of—I don't know what, but something that I liked better. Down there at home you were just a plain darky. Up here you are trying to be like me, and you are colored."

"Of co'se, Mistah Ma'ston," said Silas politely but deprecatingly, "the worl' don't stan' still."

"Platitudes—the last straw!" exclaimed Mr. Marston tragically. "There's an old darky preacher up at Richmond who says it does, and I'm sure I think more of his old fog blasts than I do of your parrot tones. Ah! Si, this is the last time that I shall ever fool with good raw material. However, don't let this bother you. As I remember, you used to sing well. I'm going to have some of my friends up at my rooms to-night; get some of the boys together, and come and sing for us. And remember, nothing hifalutin; just the same old darky songs you used to sing."

"All right, suh, we'll be up."

Silas was very glad to be rid of his old friend, and he thought when Marston had gone that he was, after all, not such a great man as he had believed. But the decline in his estimation of Mr. Marston's importance did not deter him from going that night with three of his fellow-waiters to sing for that gentleman. Two of the quartet insisted upon singing fine music, in order to show their capabilities, but Silas had received his cue, and held out for the old songs. Silas Jackson's tenor voice rang out in the old plantation melodies with the force and feeling that old memories give. The concert was a great success, and when Marston pressed a generous bank note into his hand that night, he whispered, "Well, I'm glad there's one thing you haven't lost, and that's your voice."

That was the beginning of Silas's supremacy as manager and first tenor of the Fountain Hotel Quartet, and he flourished in that capacity for two years longer; then came Mr. J. Robinson Frye, looking for talent, and Silas, by reason of his prominence, fell in this way.

Mr. J. Robinson Frye was an educated and enthusiastic young mulatto gentleman, who, having studied music abroad, had made art his mistress. As well as he was able, he wore the shock of hair which was the sign manual of his profession. He was a plausible young man of large ideas, and had composed some things of which the critics had spoken well. But the chief trouble with his work was that his one aim was money. He did not love the people among whom American custom had placed him, but he had respect for their musical ability.

"Why," he used to exclaim in the sudden bursts of enthusiasm to which he was subject, "why, these people are the greatest singers on earth. They've got more emotion and more passion than any other people, and they learn easier. I could take a chorus of forty of them, and with two months' training make them sing the roof off the Metropolitan Opera house."

When Mr. Frye was in New York, he might be seen almost any day at the piano of one or the other of the negro clubs, either working at some new inspiration, or playing one of his own compositions, and all black clubdom looked on him as a genius.

His latest scheme was the training of a colored company which should do a year's general singing throughout the country, and then having acquired poise and a reputation, produce his own opera.

It was for this he wanted Silas, and in spite of the warning and protests of friends, Silas went with him to New York, for he saw his future loom large before him.

The great city frightened him at first, but he found there some, like himself, drawn from the smaller towns of the South. Others in the company were the relics of the old days of negro minstrelsy, and still others recruited from the church choirs in the large cities. Silas was an adaptable fellow, but it seemed a little hard to fall in with the ways of his new associates. Most of them seemed as far away from him in their knowledge of worldly things as had the waiters at the Springs a few years before. He was half afraid of the chorus girls, because they seemed such different beings from the nurse girls down home. However, there was little time for moping or regrets. Mr. Frye was, it must be said, an indefatigable worker. They were rehearsing every day. Silas felt himself learning to sing. Meanwhile, he knew that he was learning other things—a few more elegancies and vices. He looked upon the "rounders" with admiration and determined to be one. So, after rehearsals were over other occupations held him. He came to be known at the clubs and was quite proud of it, and he grew bolder with the chorus girls, because he was to be a star.

After three weeks of training, the company opened, and Silas, who had never sung anything heavier than "Bright Sparkles in the Churchyard," was dressed in a Fauntleroy suit, and put on to sing in a scene from "Rigoletto."

Every night he was applauded to the echo by "the unskilful," until he came to believe himself a great singer. This belief was strengthened when the girl who performed the Spanish dance bestowed her affections upon him. He was very happy and very vain, and for the first time he forgot the people down in a little old Virginia cabin. In fact, he had other uses for his money.

For the rest of the season, either on the road or in and about New York, he sang steadily. Most of the things for which he had longed and had striven had come to him. He was known as a rounder, his highest ambition. His waistcoats were the loudest to be had. He was possessed of a factitious ease and self-possession that was almost aggression. The hot breath of the city had touched and scorched him, and had dried up within him whatever was good and fresh. The pity of it was that he was proud of himself, and utterly unconscious of his own degradation. He looked upon himself as a man of the world, a fine product of the large opportunities of a great city.

Once in those days he heard of Smith, his old time companion at the Springs. He was teaching at some small place in the South. Silas laughed contemptuously when he heard how his old friend was employed. "Poor fellow," he said, "what a pity he didn't come up here, and make something out of himself, instead of starving down there on little or nothing," and he mused on how much better his fate had been.

The season ended. After a brief period of rest, the rehearsals for Frye's opera were begun. Silas confessed to himself that he was tired; he had a cough, too, but Mr. Frye was still enthusiastic, and this was to be the great triumph, both for the composer and the tenor.

"Why, I tell you, man," said Frye, "it's going to be the greatest success of the year. I am the only man who has ever put grand-opera effects into comic opera with success. Just listen to the chords of this opening chorus." And so he inspired the singer with some of his own spirit. They went to work with a will. Silas might have been reluctant as he felt the strain upon him grow, but that he had spent all his money, and Frye, as he expressed it, was "putting up for him," until the opening of the season.

Then one day he was taken sick, and although Frye fumed, the rehearsals had to go on without him. For awhile his companions came to see him, and then they gradually ceased to come. So he lay for two months. Even Sadie, his dancing sweetheart, seemed to have forgotten him. One day he sent for her, but the messenger returned to say she could not come, she was busy. She had married the man with whom she did a turn at the roof-garden. The news came, too, that the opera had been abandoned, and that Mr. Frye had taken out a company with a new tenor, whom he pronounced far superior to the former one.

Silas gazed blankly at the wall. The hollowness of his life all came suddenly before him. All his false ideals crumbled, and he lay there with nothing to hope for. Then came back the yearnings for home, for the cabin and the fields, and there was no disgust in his memory of them.

When his strength partly returned, he sold some of the few things that remained to him from his prosperous days, and with the money purchased ticket for home; then spent, broken, hopeless, all contentment and simplicity gone, he turned his face toward his native fields.

In Old Plantation Days

Aunt Tempe's Triumph

IT WAS IN the glow of an April evening when Aunt Tempe came out on the veranda to hold a conference with her master, Stuart Mordaunt. She had evidently been turning some things over in her mind.

For months there had been talk on the plantation, but nobody knew the inside of what was going on quite so well as she, for was she not Miss Eliza's mammy? Had she not cared for her every day of her life, from her birth until now, and was she not still her own child, her "Lammy"?

Indeed, at first she had entirely opposed the marriage of her young mistress to anybody, and had discouraged the attentions of young Stone Daniels when she thought he was "spa'kin' roun'"; but when Miss Eliza laid her head on her breast and blushingly told her all about it she surrendered. And the young mistress seemed as happy over mammy's consent as she had been over her father's blessing. Mammy knew all the traditions of the section, and the histories of all the families thereabouts, and for her to set the seal of approval upon young Daniels was the final glory.

The preparations for the great wedding had gone on merrily. There was only a little time now before the auspicious day. Aunt Tempe, chief authority and owner-in-general had been as busily engaged as any one. As the time had come nearer and nearer, though, her trouble had visibly increased, and it was the culmination of it which brought her hobbling out to chat with her master on that April evening. It must have been Maid Doshy that told her about the beautiful ceremony of giving away the bride, and described to her what a figure "Ol' Mas'" would make on the occasion, but it rankled in her mind, and she had thoughts of her own on the subject.

"Look hyeah, Mas' Stua't," she said, as she settled down on the veranda step at his feet; "I done come out hyeah to 'spute wid you."

"Well, Aunt Tempe," said Mordaunt placidly, "it won't be the first time; you've been doing that for many years. The fact is, half the time I don't know who's running this plantation, you or I. You boss the whole household round, and 'the quarters' mind you better than they do the preacher. Plague take my buttons if I don't think they're afraid you'll conjure them!"

"Conju'! Who conju'! Me conju'? Wha's de mattah wid you, Mas' Stua't? You know I ain't long haided. Ef I had 'a' been, you know I'd 'a' wo'ked my roots long 'fo' now on ol' Lishy, we'en he tuk up wid dat No'ton ooman." This had happened twenty-five years before, but Stuart Mordaunt knew that it was still a sore subject with the old woman—this desertion by her husband—so he did not pursue the unpleasant matter any further.

"Well, what are you going to ''spute' with me about, Tempe? Ain't I running the plantation right? Or ain't your mistress behaving herself as she ought to?"

"I do wish you'd let me talk; you des' keep a-jokin' an' a runnin' on so dat a body cain't git in a wo'd aigeways."

"Well, go on."

"Now you know dat Miss 'Liza gwine ma'y?"

"Yes, she has told me about it, though I suppose she asked your consent first."

"Nemmine dat, nemmine dat, you hyeah me. Miss 'Liza gwine ma'y."

"Yes, unless young Daniels runs off, or sees a girl he likes better."

"Sees a gal he lak' bettah! Run off! Wha's de mattah wid you?"

The master laughed cheerily, and the old woman went on.

"Now, we all's gwineter gin huh a big weddin', des' lak my baby oughter have."

"Of course, what else do you expect? You don't suppose I'm going to have her 'jump over the broom' with him, do you?"

"Now, you listen to me: we's gwineter have all de doin's dat go 'long wid a weddin', ain't we?"

Stuart Mordaunt struck his fist on the arm of his chair and said:

"We're going to have all that the greatness of the occasion demands when a Mordaunt marries."

"Da's right, da's right. She gwineter have de o'ange wreaf an' de ring?"

"That's part of it."

"An' she gwineter be gin' erway in right style?" asked Aunt Tempe anxiously.

"To be sure."

Aunt Tempe turned her sharp black eyes on her master and shot forth her next question with sudden force and abruptness.

"Now, whut I wanter know, who gwineter gin huh erway?"

Stuart Mordaunt straightened himself up in his chair with a motion of sudden surprise and exclaimed:

"Why, Tempe, what the—what do you mean?"

"I mean des' whut I say, da's whut I mean. I wanter know who gwineter gin my Miss 'Liza erway?"

"Who should give her away?"

The old woman folded her hands calmly across her neckerchief and made answer: "Da's des' de questun."

"Why, I'm going to give my daughter away, of course."

"You gwineter gin yo' darter erway, huh, is you?" Aunt Tempe questioned slowly.

The tone was so full of contempt that her master turned a surprised look upon her face. She got up, put her hands behind her in an attitude of defiance, and stood there looking at him, as he sat viciously biting the end of his cigar.

"You 'lows to gin huh erway, does you?"

"Why, Tempe, what the—who should give her away?"

"You 'lows to gin huh erway, I say?"

"Most assuredly I do," he answered angrily.

The old woman moved up a step higher on the porch and asked in an intense voice:

"Whut business you got givin' my chile erway? Huccome you got de right to gin Miss 'Liza to anybody?"

"Why—why—Tempe!"

"Who is you?" exclaimed Tempe. "Who raise up dat chile? Who nuss huh th'oo de colic w'en she cried all night, an' she was so peakid you didn't know w'en you gwine lay huh erway? Huh? Who do dat? Who raise you up, an' tek keer o' you, w'en yo' ol' mammy die, an' you wa'n't able even to keep erway f'om de bee-trees? Huh? Who do dat? You gin huh erway! You gin huh erway! Da's my chile, Mas' Stua't Mo'de'nt, an' ef anybody gin huh erway at de weddin', d' ain't nobody gwine do it but ol' Tempe huhself. You hyeah me?"

"But, Tempe, Tempe!" said the master, "that wouldn't be proper. You can't give your young mistress away."

"P'opah er whut not, I de only one whut got de right, an' I see 'bout dat!"

Mordaunt forgot that he was talking to a servant, and sprang to his feet.

"See about it! See about it!" he cried, "I'll let you know that I can give my own daughter away when she marries. You must think you own this whole plantation, and all the white folks and niggers on it."

Aunt Tempe came up on the porch and curtsied to her master.

"Nemmine, Mas' Stua't," she said; "nemmine." Her eyes were full of tears, and her voice was trembling. "Hit all right, hit all right. I 'longs to you, but Miss 'Liza, she my chile." Her voice rose again in a defiant ring, and lost its pathos as she exclaimed, "I show you who got de right to gin my chile erway!" And shaking her turbaned head, she went back into the house mumbling to herself.

"Well!" said Stuart Mordaunt, "I'll be blessed!" He might have used a stronger term, but just then the black-coated figure of the rector came round the corner of the veranda.

"How are you, how are you, sir!" said the Rev. Mr. Davis jocosely. "Are you the man who owns this plantation?"

Mordaunt hurled his cigar down the path, and replied grimly:

"I don't know; I used to think so."

Meanwhile Aunt Tempe had gone into the house to tell her troubles to her young mistress. She and her Miss Eliza were mutually the bearers of each other's burdens on all occasions. She told her story, and laid her case before the bride-to-be.

"Now you know, baby," she said, "ef anybody got de right to gin you erway, 'tain't nobody but me."

"Yes, yes, mammy," said the young woman consolingly; "they sha'n't slight you, that they sha'n't."

"No, indeed; I don't 'tend to be slighted."

"I'll tell you what I'll do, mammy," said Miss Eliza; "even if you can't give me away, you'll be where Doshy and Dinah and none of the rest can be."

"Whah dat, chile?"

"Why, before the ceremony I'll hide you under the portieres right back of where we're going to stand in the drawing-room."

"An' I cain't gin you erway, baby?" said the old woman sadly.

"We'll see about that, mammy; you know nobody ever knows what's going to happen."

The girl was comforting the old woman's distresses as mammy in the years gone by had quieted her childish fears. It was a putting off until to-morrow of the evils that seemed present to-day.

Aunt Tempe went away seemingly satisfied, but she thought deeply, and later she visited old Brother Parker, who used to know a servant in a preacher's family, and they talked long and earnestly together one whole evening.

Doshy saw them as they separated, and cried in derision:

"Look hyeah, Aunt Tempe, whut you an' ol' Brothah Pahkah codgin' erbout so long? 'Spec' fus' thing we knows we be gittin' slippahs an' wreafs fu you, an' you'll be follerin' Miss 'Liza's 'zample!"

"Huh-uh, chile," Aunt Tempe answered, "I ain't thinkin' nothin' 'bout may'in', case I's ol', but la, chile, I ol' in de haid, too!"

The preparations for the wedding were completed, and the time arrived. All the elite of the surrounding country were present. Mammy was allowed to put the last touches, insignificant though they were, to the bride's costume. She wept copiously over her child, but with not so much absorption as not to be alert when Miss Eliza took her down and slipped her behind the heavy portieres.

The organ pealed its march; the ceremony began and proceeded. The responses of the groom were strong, and those of the bride timid, but decisive and clear. Above all rose the resonant voice of the rector. Stuart Mordaunt had gathered himself together and straightened his shoulders and stepped forward at the words, "Who giveth this woman," when suddenly the portieres behind the bridal party were thrown asunder, and the ample form of Aunt Tempe appeared. The whole assemblage was thunderstruck. The minister paused, Mordaunt stood transfixed; a hush fell upon all of them, which was broken by the old woman's stentorian voice crying:

"I does! Dat's who! I gins my baby erway!"

For an instant no one spoke; some of the older ladies wiped tears from their eyes, and Stuart Mordaunt bowed and resumed his place beside his daughter. The clergyman took up the ceremony where he had left off, and the marriage was finished without any further interruption.

When it was all over, neither the father, the mother, the proud groom, nor the blushing bride had one word of reproach for mammy, for no one doubted that her giving away and her blessing were as effectual and fervent as those of the nearest relative could have been.

And Aunt Tempe chuckled as she went her way. "I showed 'em. I showed 'em."

Aunt Tempe's Revenge

LARAMIE BELLE—why she was Laramie Belle no one could ever make out— Laramie Belle had astonished the whole plantation. She came of stock that was prone to perpetrating surprises, and she did credit to her blood and breeding. When she was only two weeks old the wiseacres had said that no good could ever come to so outrageously a named child. Aunt Mandy had quite expressed the opinion of everyone, when she said: "Why, ef de chile had been named a puoh Bible name er a puoh devil name, she mought a' mounted to somep'n', but dat aih contraption, Laramie Belle, ain't one ner 'tothah. She done doomed a'ready." And here was Laramie Belle after eighteen years of a rather quiet life, getting ready to fulfill all the adverse prophecies.

There were, perhaps, two elements in the matter that made the Mordaunt plantation look upon it with less leniency even than usual. Of course, it was the unwritten law of the little community that alliances should not be contracted with people off the estate. But even they knew that love must go where it will, and a certain latitude might have been allowed the culprit had she not been guilty of another heresy that made her crime blacker. Incredible as it may seem, at the very time that Tom Norton began bestowing his impudent attentions upon her, Julius, the coachman, had also deigned to look at her with favor. For her to give the preference to the former was an offence not to be overlooked nor condoned. By so doing, she not only lost a golden matrimonial opportunity, but belittled the value of her own people.

There was another feeling that entered into the trouble, too, a vague, almost shadowy dislike to the man upon whom Laramie Belle had placed her affections. Although only a tradition to the younger servants, the memory was still vivid in the minds of the older heads of Aunt Tempe's desertion by her husband, when he took up with "the Norton woman." They remembered how Tempe, then a spirited, lively woman, had mourned and refused to be comforted, and they could not forget the bravery with which she had consented that Stuart Mordaunt should transfer her husband to Master Norton, in order that he might be with his new wife. She had mourned for weeks, yes, for months, and no one else had ever come into her heart. Was it not enough that this suffering had come to a Mordaunt through this Norton wench, without this man, this son of her and her stolen mate, taking away one of the plantation's buds of promise?

They talked much to Laramie Belle, but she was not a girl of many words, and only held her head down and made imaginary lines with her foot as she listened. She would not talk to them about it, but neither would she give up Tom and encourage Julius.

There were those who believed that she was encouraged in her stubbornness by her mother, that mother who had closed her ears to all advice, remonstrance, and prophecy when warned as to the naming of her baby. They were right, too, for Lucy did uphold her daughter's quiet independence. Indeed, there was a streak of strangeness in both of them that, in spite of the younger woman's popularity, placed them, as it were, in a position apart.

"You right, honey," said her mother to her, "ef you loves Tom No'ton you tek up wid him; don' keer whut de res' says. Yo' got to live wid him, yo' got to do his cookin' an' washin' an' i'nin', an' all you got to do is to git Mas' Stua't to say yes to you."

No one argued with Lucy, whatever they might say to her daughter. About the older woman there was a spirit fierce and free that would not be gainsaid. There was something of the wild nerve of African forests about her that had not yet been driven out by the hard hand of slavery, nor yet smoothed down by the velvet glove of irresponsibility. The essence of this, albeit subdued, refined, diluted, perhaps, was in her daughter, and that was why she kept her way in spite of all opposition.

As for Tom Norton, opposition only made him more determined, and nothing did him more good than to laugh in the face of Julius as he was leaving the Mordaunt place after a pleasant visit with Laramie.

As promiscuous visiting between the plantations was forbidden, Tom had had the good sense to secure both his master's and Stuart Mordaunt's consent, the latter's reluctantly given to these excursions. On the principle, however, that he who is given much may with safety take more, he often overstepped the bound and went to see his sweetheart when the permission was wanting. Julius found this out and determined to administer a severe lesson to his rival on the first occasion that he found him within his domain without his master's permission. So thinking, he laid his plans carefully, the first of them being to gain a friend and informant on the Norton place. This he succeeded in doing, and then, after confiding in a couple of trusted friends, he lay in wait for his unfortunate rival. He had a stout hickory stick in his hand, and he and his friends were stationed at short intervals of space along the road which Tom must cross to visit Laramie Belle.

It was a moonlit night. The watchers by the roadside heard the sound of his footsteps as their victim approached. But, with ghoulish satisfaction, they let him pass on. It was not now that they wanted him, but when he came back. Then they would have the fun of whipping him to his very gate, and he would not dare to tell. They possessed their souls in patience, and waited, chuckling ever and anon at the prospect as the first hour passed. They yawned more and chuckled less through the second hour. During the third, the yawns held exclusive sway. He was staying particularly late that night. It was in the gray dawn that, unsatisfied, sleepy, and angry, they took their way home. Their heads seemed scarcely to have touched the pillows when the horns and bells sounded the rising hour. Oh, misery! They had missed Tom, too.

Julius could not understand it. It was very simple, though. Man proposes, but woman exposes, and he had not learned to beware of a friend who had a wife. So, his secret had leaked out, Laramie Belle had had a chance to warn Tom, and, going by another road, he had been in bed and snoring when his watchers were wearily waiting for him by the roadside.

Even for the coachman's friends, the story was too good to keep, and before long big house and quarters were laughing to their hearts' content.

The unwelcome suitor was doubly unfortunate, however, for his action precipitated the result which he was so anxious to prevent. Seeing himself in danger of being the constant victim of intrigue and molestation, Tom Norton determined to press his suit and bring matters to a close. With this end in view he sought his master and laid the case before him, begging for his intercession. Norton, the master, promised to visit Stuart Mordaunt and talk the matter over with him.

He did so. He laid the case before Mordaunt plainly and clearly. A negro on his plantation was in love with one of his host's maids. What was to be done about it?

"Well, it's this way, Norton," said Mordaunt frankly. "You know I never have countenanced this mating of servants off the plantation. It's only happened once, and you know how that was."

"I know, but, Mr. Mordaunt, Tom likes that wench, and if he don't get her it'll make a bad darky out of him, that's all; and he'll be a trouble to your plantation as well as to mine."

"Oh, I can answer as to mine."

"Perhaps, but there's no telling what influence he might have over your people, and that's worth looking into."

"You're on the wrong road to accomplish your end with me, Norton."

"But you don't understand; I'm not talking for myself, but for the happiness of a boy that I like."

"You know how I handled a similar case."

"Yes; but I'm a poorer man than you, and I—well, I can't afford to be generous."

Mordaunt laughed coldly. "Well," he said, "I don't like the stock of that boy Tom. You know how his father treated Tempe, and—oh, well, Norton, see me again, I'm not in the mood to discuss this matter now," and he rose to dismiss his visitor.

"I'll sell Tom cheap," said Norton.

"In spite of your deep feeling for him?"

"My deep feeling for him prompts me to help him to happiness."

"Very considerate of you, Norton, but I'm not buying or selling darkies, Good-day."

Norton ground his teeth as he walked away. "That proud fool despises me," he murmured angrily, "but either he shall buy Tom or that nigger shall make him more than his money's worth of trouble."

Stuart Mordaunt went away from the interview with his neighbor with a sneer on his lips. He despised Aldberry Norton, not because he was a poorer man, but because he was a man with no principle. Once an overseer, now a small owner, he brought the manners of the lower position to the higher one.

"I'd buy Tom," he said to himself, "just to satisfy Laramie Belle, if it wasn't against my principle."

When the plantation, through some mysterious intelligence, heard how Tom's suit fared, it was exultant. After all, the flower of their girls was not to go away to mate with an inferior. They ceased to laugh at Julius behind his back. But there is no accounting for the ways of women, and at this time Laramie Belle ceased speaking to him—so, setting one off against the other, the poor coachman had little to pride himself upon.

The girl now had fewer words than ever. Her smiles, too, were fewer, and she was often in tears. Seeing her thus, the fierceness in her mother's face and manner increased until it grew to be a settled fact that one who cared for his life was not to bother Laramie Belle nor Lucy.

During all the trouble, Aunt Tempe had listened and looked on, unmoved. Everyone had expected her to take a very decided part against the welcome suitor, the son of her old rival and her defaulting husband; but she had not done so. She had stood aloof until this crisis came. Even now, she was strangely subdued. Only she cast inquiring glances at Laramie Belle's long, tear-saddened face whenever she passed her. Day by day she saw how the girl faded, and then came the wrath of the plantation upon her. When they saw that she would not yield, they cast her off. They would not associate with her, nor speak to her. She was none of theirs. Let her find her friends over at Norton's, they said. They laughed at her and tossed their heads in her face, and she went her way silent but weeping. Lucy's eyes grew fierce. Something strange, foreign, even wild within her seemed to rear itself and call for release. But she held herself as if saying, "A little while yet."

The day came, however, when Aunt Tempe could stand Laramie Belle's sad face no longer. It may have been the influence of Parker's words as he told of the command to do good to "dem dat spitefully use you," or it may have been the strong promptings of her own good heart that drove Tempe to seek her master out.

"Well, Tempe," said Mordaunt, as he saw that she had settled herself for a talk with him, "what now?"

"It's des' anothah one o' my 'sputes," said Tempe, with an embarrassment entirely new to her.

"Well, what's coming now?"

"Mas' Stua't, I's an' ol' fool, dat's what I is."

"Ah, Tempe, have you found that out? Then you begin to be wise. It's wonderful how as you and I get old we both arrive at the same conclusions."

"I aint jokin', Mas' Stua't, I's mighty anxious. I been thinkin' 'bout Tawm an' La'amie Belle."

"Now, Tempe!"

"Hol' on, Mas'. Yo' know de reason I got some right to think 'bout dem two. Mas' Stua't, my ol' man didn' do me right to leave me an' tek up wid anothah 'ooman."

"He was a hound."

"Look-a-hyeah, whut you talkin' 'bout? You heish. I was a gwine 'long to say dat my man didn' treat me right, but sence it's done, it's done, an' de only way to do is to mek de bes' of it."

"You've been doing that for a good many years."

"Yes, but it wasn't wid my willin' hea't. Brothah Pahkah say 'dough dat we mus' do good to dem what spitefully use us."

"What are you driving at, Tempe?"

"Mas' Stua't, sence Tawm No'ton, he my ol' man's boy, don't you reckon I's some kin' of a step-mammy to him?"

Stuart Mordaunt could not repress a chuckle as he answered, "Well, I can't just figure out any such kinship."

"I don' keer whut yo' figgers out. Hit's got to be so 'cause I feels it."

"It must be so, then."

"Well, de plantation done cas' La'amie Belle out 'cause she love Tawm, an' she cryin' huh eyes out. Tawm, he feel moughty bad 'bout it."

"Well?"

"Mas' Stua't, let 'em ma'y."

"Tempe, you know I object to the servants marrying off the plantation."

"I know, but—"

"And you know that I can't buy Tom."

"Won't you, des' dis time?"

"No, I won't; I'm not a nigger trader, and I won't have any one making me one. You let me alone, Tempe, and don't concern yourself in this business."

"Dey des two po' chillen, Mas' Stua't."

"I don't care if they are. I won't have anything to do with it, I tell you. I won't have my people marrying with Norton's, and if he can't make a fair exchange for the man I gave him, why, Tom and Laramie Belle will have to give each other up, that's all."

Aunt Tempe said no more, but went tearfully away, but out of the corner of her eye she saw her master pacing up and down long after she had left him, and she had the satisfaction of knowing he was uneasy.

"Confound Tempe," Mordaunt was saying. "Why can't she let me alone? Just as I quiet my conscience, here she comes and knocks everything into a cocked hat. I won't buy Tom. I won't, that's all there is about it. Her stepson, indeed!" He tried to laugh, but it ended lamely. "Confound Tempe," he repeated.

He was troubled for two or three days, and then with a very sheepish expression he went to Tempe's cabin.

"Tempe," he said, "you've served me long and faithfully, and I've been thinking about making you a present for some time."

"La, Mas' Stua't, wha's de mattah wid you?"

"You hush up. Here's some money, you can do with it as you please," and he thrust a roll of bills into her hand.

"W'y, Mas' Stua't Mo'da'nt, is you clean loony? What is I gwine to do wid all dis money?"

"Throw it in the fire, confound you, if you haven't got sense enough to know what use to put it to!" Stuart Mordaunt shouted, as he turned away. Then the light dawned on Aunt Tempe, and she sank to her knees with a prayer of thanks.

It took but a short time for her to have a less scrupulous man buy Tom for her, and then with a solemnity as great as his own, she presented him to her master, who received him, as he said, in the spirit in which he was given.

Lucy and Laramie Belle were present at the ceremony. The fierce light had died out of Lucy's eyes, and Laramie's face was aglow. When it was all over, Julius shook hands with Tom as an acknowledgment of defeat, and that gave the cue to the rest of the plantation, who forgot at once all its animosities against the new fellow-servant. But there were some things which the author of all this good could not forget, and on the night of the wedding, when the others rejoiced, Aunt Tempe wept and murmured: "He might 'a' been mine, he might 'a' been mine."

The Walls of Jericho

PARKER WAS SITTING alone under the shade of a locust tree at the edge of a field. His head was bent and he was deep in thought. Every now and then there floated to him the sound of vociferous singing, and occasionally above the music rose the cry of some shouting brother or sister. But he remained in his attitude of meditation as if the singing and the cries meant nothing to him.

They did, however, mean much, and, despite his outward impassiveness, his heart was in a tumult of wounded pride and resentment. He had always been so faithful to his flock, constant in attendance and careful of their welfare. Now it was very hard, at the first call of the stranger to have them leave their old pastor and crowd to the new exhorter.

It was nearly a week before that a free negro had got permission to hold meetings in the wood adjoining the Mordaunt estate. He had invited the negroes of the surrounding plantations to come and bring their baskets with them that they might serve the body while they saved the soul. By ones and twos Parker had seen his congregation drop away from him until now, in the cabin meeting house where he held forth, only a few retainers, such as Mandy and Dinah and some of the older ones on the plantation, were present to hear him. It grieved his heart, for he had been with his flock in sickness and in distress, in sorrow and in trouble, but now, at the first approach of the rival they could and did desert him. He felt it the more keenly because he knew just how powerful this man Johnson was. He was loud-voiced and theatrical, and the fact that he invited all to bring their baskets gave his scheme added influence; for his congregations flocked to the meetings as to a holy picnic. It was seldom that they were thus able to satisfy both the spiritual and material longings at the same time.

Parker had gone once to the meeting and had hung unobserved on the edge of the crowd; then he saw by what power the preacher held the people. Every night, at the very height of the service, he would command the baskets to be opened and the people, following the example of the children of Israel, to march, munching their food, round and round the inclosure, as their Biblical archetypes had marched around the walls of Jericho. Parker looked on and smiled grimly. He knew, and the sensational revivalist knew, that there were no walls there to tumble down, and that the spiritual significance of the performance was entirely lost upon the people. Whatever may be said of the Mordaunt plantation exhorter, he was at least no hypocrite, and he saw clearly that his rival gave to the emotional negroes a breathing chance and opportunity to eat and a way to indulge their dancing proclivities by marching trippingly to a spirited tune.

He went away in disgust and anger, but thoughts deeper than either burned within him. He was thinking some such thoughts now as he sat there on the edge of the field listening to the noise of the basket meeting. It was unfortunate for his peace of mind that while he sat there absorbed in resentful musings two of the young men of his master's household should come along. They did not know how Parker felt about the matter, or they never would have allowed themselves to tease him on the score of his people's defection.

"Well, Parker," said Ralph, "seems mighty strange to me that you are not down there in the woods at the meeting."

The old man was silent.

"I am rather surprised at Parker myself," said Tom Mordaunt; "knowing how he enjoys a good sermon I expected him to be over there. They do say that man Johnson is a mighty preacher."

Still Parker was silent.

"Most of your congregation are over there," Ralph resumed. Then the old exhorter, stung into reply, raised his head and said quietly:

"Dat ain't nuffin' strange, Mas' Ralph. I been preachin' de gospel on yo' father's plantation, night aftah night, nigh on to twenty-five years, an' spite o' dat, mos' o' my congregation is in hell."

"That doesn't speak very well for your preaching," said Ralph, and the two young fellows laughed heartily.

"Come, Parker, come, don't be jealous; come on over to the meeting with us, and let us see what it is that Johnson has that you haven't. You know any man can get a congregation about him, but it takes some particular power to hold them after they are caught."

Parker rose slowly from the ground and reluctantly joined his two young masters as they made their way toward the woods. The service was in full swing. At a long black log, far to the front, there knelt a line of mourners wailing and praying, while the preacher stood above them waving his hands and calling on them to believe and be saved. Every now and then someone voluntarily broke into a song, either a stirring, marching spiritual or some soft crooning melody that took strange hold upon the hearts of even the most skeptical listeners. As they approached and joined the crowd someone had just swung into the undulating lilt of

> "Someone buried in de graveyard,
>   Someone buried in de sea,
>   All come togethah in de mo'nin',
>   Go soun' de Jubilee."

Just the word "Jubilee" was enough to start the whole throng into agitated life, and they moaned and shouted and wailed until the forest became a pandemonium.

Johnson, the preacher, saw Parker approach with the two young men and a sudden spirit of conquest took possession of him. He felt that he owed it to himself to crystallize his triumph over the elder exhorter. So, with a glance that begged for approbation, he called aloud:

"Open de baskets! Rise up, fu' de Jericho walls o' sin is a-stan'in'. You 'member dey ma'ched roun' seven times, an' at de sevent' time de walls a-begun to shake an' shiver; de foundations a-begun to trimble; de chillen a-hyeahed de rum'lin' lak a thundah f'om on high, an' putty soon down come de walls a-fallin' an' a-crum'lin'! Oh, brothahs an' sistahs, let us a-ma'ch erroun' de walls o' Jericho to-night seven times, an' a-eatin' o' de food dat de Lawd has pervided us wid. Dey ain't no walls o' brick an' stone a-stan'in' hyeah to-night, but by de eye o' Christian faif I see a great big wall o' sin a-stan'in' strong an' thick hyeah in ouah midst. Is we gwine to let it stan'?"

"Oh, no, no!" moaned the people.

"Is we gwine to ma'ch erroun' dat wall de same ez Joshuay an' his ban' did in de days of ol', ontwell we hyeah de cracklin' an' de rum'lin', de breakin' an' de taihin', de onsettlin' of de foundations an' de fallin' of de stones an' mo'tah?" Then raising his voice he broke into the song:

> "Den we'll ma'ch, ma'ch down, ma'ch, ma'ch down,
>   Oh, chillen, ma'ch down,
>   In de day o' Jubilee."

The congregation joined him in the ringing chorus, and springing to their feet began marching around and around the inclosure, chewing vigorously in the breathing spaces of the hymn.

The two young men, who were too used to such sights to be provoked to laughter, nudged each other and bent their looks upon Parker, who stood with bowed head, refusing to join in the performance, and sighed audibly.

After the march Tom and Ralph started for home, and Parker went with them.

"He's very effective, don't you think so, Tom?" said Ralph.

"Immensely so," was the reply. "I don't know that I have ever seen such a moving spectacle."

"The people seem greatly taken up with him."

"Personal magnetism, that's what it is. Don't you think so, Parker?"

"Hum," said Parker.

"It's a wonderful idea of his, that marching around the walls of sin."

"So original, too. It's a wonder you never thought of a thing like that, Parker. I believe it would have held your people to you in the face of everything. They do love to eat and march."

"Well," said Parker, "you all may think what you please, but I ain't nevah made no business of mekin' a play show outen de Bible. Dem folks don' know what dey're doin'. Why, ef dem niggahs hyeahed anything commence to fall they'd taih dat place up gittin' erway f'om daih. It's a wondah de Lawd don' sen' a jedgmen' on 'em fu' tu'nin' His wo'd into mockery."

The two young men bit their lips and a knowing glance flashed between them. The same idea had leaped into both of their minds at once. They said no word to Parker, however, save at parting, and then they only begged that he would go again the next night of the meeting.

"You must, Parker," said Ralph. "You must represent the spiritual interest of the plantation. If you don't, that man Johnson will think we are heathen or that our exhorter is afraid of him."

At the name of fear the old preacher bridled and said with angry dignity:

"Nemmine, nemmine; he shan't nevah think dat. I'll be daih."

Parker went alone to his cabin, sore at heart; the young men, a little regretful that they had stung him a bit too far, went up to the big house, their heads close together, and in the darkness and stillness there came to them the hymns of the people.

On the next night Parker went early to the meeting-place and, braced by the spirit of his defiance, took a conspicuous front seat. His face gave no sign, though his heart throbbed angrily as he saw the best and most trusted of his flock come in with intent faces and seat themselves anxiously to await the advent of an alien. Why had those rascally boys compelled him for his own dignity's sake to come there? Why had they forced him to be a living witness of his own degradation and of his own people's ingratitude?

But Parker was a diplomat, and when the hymns began he joined his voice with the voices of the rest.

Something, though, tugged at Parker's breast, a vague hoped-for something; he knew not what—the promise of relief from the tension of his jealousy, the harbinger of revenge. It was in the air. Everything was tense as if awaiting the moment of catastrophe. He found himself joyous, and when Johnson arose on the wings of his eloquence it was Parker's loud "Amen" which set fire to all the throng. Then, when the meeting was going well, when the spiritual fire had been thoroughly kindled and had gone from crackling to roaring; when the hymns were loudest and the hand-clapping strongest, the revivalist called upon them to rise and march around the walls of Jericho. Parker rose with the rest, and, though he had no basket, he levied on the store of a solicitous sister and marched with them, singing, singing, but waiting, waiting for he knew not what.

It was the fifth time around and yet nothing had happened. Then the sixth, and a rumbling sound was heard near at hand. A tree crashed down on one side. White eyes were rolled in the direction of the noise and the burden of the hymn was left to the few faithful. Half way around and the bellow of a horn broke upon the startled people's ears, and the hymn sank lower and lower. The preacher's face was ashen, but he attempted to inspire the people, until on the seventh turn such a rumbling and such a clattering, such a tumbling of rocks, such a falling of trees as was never heard before gave horror to the night. The people paused for one moment and then the remains of the bread and meat were cast to the winds, baskets were thrown away, and the congregation, thoroughly maddened with fear, made one rush for the road and the quarters. Ahead of them all, his long coat-tails flying and his legs making not steps but leaps, was the Rev. Mr. Johnson. He had no word of courage or hope to offer the frightened flock behind him. Only Parker, with some perception of the situation, stood his ground. He had leaped upon a log and was crying aloud:

"Stan' still, stan' still, I say, an' see de salvation," but he got only frightened, backward glances as the place was cleared.

When they were all gone, he got down off the log and went to where several of the trees had fallen. He saw that they had been cut nearly through during the day on the side away from the clearing, and ropes were still along the upper parts of their trunks. Then he chuckled softly to himself. As he stood there in the dim light of the fat-pine torches that were burning themselves out, two stealthy figures made their way out of the surrounding gloom into the open space. Tom and Ralph were holding their sides, and Parker, with a hand on the shoulder of each of the boys, laughed unrighteously.

"Well, he hyeahed de rum'lin' an' crum'lin'," he said, and Ralph gasped.

"You're the only one who stood your ground, Parker," said Tom.

"How erbout de walls o' Jericho now?" was all Parker could say as he doubled up.

When the people came back to their senses they began to realize that the Rev. Mr. Johnson had not the qualities of a leader. Then they recalled how Parker had stood still in spite of the noise and called them to wait and see the salvation, and so, with a rush of emotional feeling, they went back to their old allegiance. Parker's meeting-house again was filled, and for lack of worshipers Mr. Johnson held no more meetings and marched no more around the walls of Jericho.

How Brother Parker Fell from Grace

IT ALL HAPPENED so long ago that it has almost been forgotten upon the plantation, and few save the older heads know anything about it save from hearsay. It was in Parker's younger days, but the tale was told on him for a long time, until he was so old that every little disparagement cut him like a knife. Then the young scapegraces who had the story only from their mothers' lips spared his dotage. Even to young eyes, the respect which hedges about the form of eighty obscures many of the imperfections that are apparent at twenty-eight and Parker was nearing eighty.

The truth of it is that Parker, armed with the authority which his master thought the due of the plantation exhorter, was wont to use his power with rather too free a rein. He was so earnest for the spiritual welfare of his fellow-servants that his watchful ministrations became a nuisance and a bore.

Even Aunt Doshy, who was famous for her devotion to all that pertained to the church, had been heard to state that "Brothah Pahkah was a moughty powah-ful 'zortah, but he sholy was monst'ous biggity." This from a member of his flock old enough to be his mother, quite summed up the plantation's estimate of this black disciple.

There was many a time when it would have gone hard with Brother Parker among the young bucks on the Mordaunt plantation but that there was scarcely one of them but could remember a time when Parker had come to his cabin to console some sick one, help a seeker, comfort the dying or close the eyes of one already dead, and it clothed him about with a sacredness, which, however much inclined, they dared not invade.

"Ain't it enough," Mandy's Jim used to say, "fu' Brothah Pahkah to 'tend to his business down at meetin' widout spookin' 'roun' all de cabins an' outhouses? Seems to me dey's enough dev'ment gwine on right undah his nose widout him gwine 'roun' tryin' to smell out what's hid."

Every secret sinner on the place agreed with this dictum, and it came to the preacher's ears. He smiled broadly.

"Uh, huh," he remarked, "hit's de stuck pig dat squeals. I reckon Jim's up to some'p'n right now, an' I lay I'll fin' out what dat some'p'n is." Parker was a subtle philosopher and Jim had by his remark unwittingly disclosed his interest in the preacher's doings. It then behooved his zealous disciple to find out the source of this unusual interest and opposition.

On the Sunday following his sermon was strong, fiery and convincing. His congregation gave themselves up to the joy of the occasion and lost all consciousness of time or place in their emotional ecstasy. But, although he continued to move them with his eloquence, not for one moment did Parker lose possession of himself. His eyes roamed over the people before him and took in the absence of several who had most loudly and heartily agreed with Jim's dictum. Jim himself was not there.

"Uh, huh," said the minister to himself even in the midst of his exhortations. "Uh, huh, erway on some dev'ment, I be boun'." He could hardly wait to hurry through his sermon. Then he seized his hat and almost ran away from the little table that did duty as a pulpit desk. He brushed aside with scant ceremony those who would have asked him to their cabins to share some special delicacy, and made his way swiftly to the door. There he paused and cast a wondering glance about the plantation.

"I des wondah whaih dem scoun'els is mos' lakly to be." Then his eye fell upon an old half-ruined smoke-house that stood between the kitchen and the negro quarters, and he murmured to himself. "Lak ez not, lak ez not." But he did not start directly for the object of his suspicions. Oh, no, he was too deep a diplomat for that. He knew that if there were wrongdoers in that innocent-looking ruin they would be watching in his direction about the time when they expected meeting to be out; so he walked off swiftly, but carelessly, in an opposite direction, and, instead of going straight past the kitchen, began to circle around from the direction of the quarters, whence no danger would be apprehended.

As he drew nearer and nearer the place, he thought he heard the rise and fall of eager voices. He approached more cautiously. Now he was perfectly sure that he could hear smothered conversation, and he smiled grimly as he pictured to himself the surprise of his quarry when he should come up with them. He was almost upon the smoke-house now. Those within were so absorbed that the preacher was able to creep up and peer through a crack at the scene within.

There, seated upon the earthen floor, were the unregenerate of the plantation. In the very midst of them was Mandy's Jim, and he was dealing from a pack of greasy cards.

It is a wonder that they did not hear the preacher's gasp of horror as he stood there gazing upon the iniquitous performance. But they did not. The delight of High-Low-Jack was too absorbing for that, and they suspected nothing of Parker's presence until he slipped around to the door, pushed it open and confronted them like an accusing angel.

Jim leaped to his feet with a strong word upon his lips.

"I reckon you done fu'got, Brothah Jim, what day dis is," said the preacher.

"I ain't fu'got nuffin," was the dogged reply; "I don't see what you doin' roun' hyeah nohow."

"I's a lookin' aftah some strayin' lambs," said Parker, "an' I done foun' 'em. You ought to be ashamed o' yo'se'ves, evah one o' you, playin' cyards on de Lawd's day."

There was the light of reckless deviltry in Jim's eyes.

"Dey ain't no h'am in a little game o' cyards."

"Co'se not, co'se not," replied the preacher scornfully. "Dem's des de sins that's ca'ied many a man to hell wid his eyes wide open, de little no ha'm kin'."

"I don't reckon you evah played cyards," said Jim sneeringly.

"Yes, I has played, an' I thought I was enjoyin' myse'f ontwell I foun' out dat it was all wickedness an' idleness."

"Oh, I don't reckon you was evah ve'y much of a player. I know lots o' men who has got u'ligion des case dey couldn't win at cyards."

The company greeted this sally with a laugh and then looked aghast at Jim's audacity.

"U'ligion's a moughty savin' to de pocket," Jim went on. "We kin believe what we wants to, and I say you nevah was no playah, an' dat's de reason you tuk up de Gospel."

"Hit ain't so. I 'low dey was a time when I could 'a' outplayed any one o' you sinnahs hyeah, but—"

"Prove it!" The challenge shot forth like a pistol's report.

Parker hesitated "What you mean?" he said.

"Beat me, beat all of us, an' we'll believe you didn't quit playin' case you allus lost. You a preachah now, an' I daih you."

Parker's face turned ashen and his hands gripped together. He was young then, and the hot blood sped tumultuously through his veins.

"Prove it," said Jim; "you cain't. We'd play you outen yo' coat an' back into de pulpit ag'in."

"You would, would you?" The light of battle was in Parker's eyes, the desire for conquest throbbing in his heart. "Look a'hyeah, Jim, Sunday er no Sunday, preachah er no preachah, I play you th'ee games fu' de Gospel's sake." And the preacher sat down in the circle, his face tense with anger at his tormentor's insinuations. He did not see the others around him. He saw only Jim, the man who had spoken against his cloth. He did not see the look of awe and surprise upon the faces of the others, nor did he note that one of the assembly slipped out of the shed just as the game began.

Jim found the preacher no mean antagonist, but it mattered little to him whether he won or not. His triumph was complete when he succeeded in getting this man, who kept the conscience of the plantation, to sin as others sinned.

"I see you ain't fu'got yo' cunnin'," he remarked as the preacher dealt in turn.

"'Tain't no time to talk now," said Parker fiercely.

The excitement of the onlookers grew more and more intense. They were six and six, and it was the preacher's deal. His eyes were bright, and he was breathing quickly. Parker was a born fighter and nothing gave him more joy than the heat of the battle itself. He riffled the cards. Jim cut. He dealt and turned Jack. Jim laughed.

"You know the trick," he said.

"Dat's one game," said Parker, and bent over the cards as they came to him. He did not hear a light step outside nor did he see a shadow that fell across the open doorway. He was just about to lead when a cold voice, full of contempt, broke upon his ear and made him keep the card he would have played poised in his hand.

"And so these are your after-meeting diversions, are they, Parker?" said his master's voice.

Stuart Mordaunt was standing in the door, his face cold and stern, while his informant grinned maliciously.

Parker brushed his hand across his brow as if dazed.

"Well, Mas' Stua't, he do play monst'ous well fu' a preachah," said his tempter.

The preacher at these words looked steadily at Jim, and then the realization of his position burst upon him. The tiger in him came uppermost and, with flaming eyes, he took a quick step toward Jim.

"Stop," said Mordaunt, coming between them; "don't add anything more to what you have already done."

"Mas' Stua't, I—I—" Parker broke down, and, turning away from the exultant faces, rushed headlong out of the place. His master followed more leisurely, angry and hurt at the hypocrisy of a trusted servant.

Of course the game was over for that day, but Jim and his companions hung around the smoke-house for some time, rejoicing in the downfall of their enemy. Afterward, they went to their cabins for dinner. Then Jim made a mistake. With much laughter and boasting he told Mandy all about it, and then suddenly awakened to the fact that she was listening to him with a face on which only horror was written. Jim turned to his meal in silence and disgust. A woman has no sense of humor.

"Whaih you gwine?" he asked, as Mandy began putting on her bonnet and shawl with ominous precision.

"I's gwine up to de big house, dat's whaih I's gwine."

"What you gwine daih fu'?"

"I gwine to tell Mas' Stua't all erbout hit."

"Don't you daih."

"Heish yo' mouf. Don't you talk to me, you nasty, low-life scamp. I's gwine tell Mas' Stua't, an' I hope an' pray he'll tek all de hide offen yo' back."

Jim sat in bewildered misery as Mandy flirted out of the cabin; he felt vaguely some of the hopelessness of defeat which comes to a man whenever he attempts to lay sacrilegious hands on a woman's religion or what stands to her for religion.

Parker was sitting alone in his cabin with bowed head when the door opened and his master came across the floor and laid his hand gently on the negro's shoulder.

"I didn't know how it was, Parker," he said softly.

"Oh, I's back-slid, I's fell from grace," moaned Parker.

"Nonsense," said his master, "you've fallen from nothing. There are times when we've got to meet the devil on his own ground and fight him with his own weapons."

Parker raised his head gladly. "Say dem wo'ds ag'in, Mas' Stua't," he said.

His master repeated the words, but added: "But it isn't safe to go into the devil's camp too often, Parker."

"I ain't gwine into his camp no mo'. Aftah dis I's gwine to stan' outside an' hollah in." His face was beaming and his voice trembled with joy.

"I didn't think I'd preach to-night," he said timidly.

"Of course you will," said Mordaunt, "and your mistress and I are coming to hear you, so do your best."

His master went out and Parker went down on his knees.

He did preach that night and the plantation remembered the sermon.

The Trousers

IT WAS A NASTY, rainy Sunday morning. The dripping skies lowered forbiddingly and the ground about the quarters was slippery with mud and punctuated with frequent dirty puddles where the rain had collected in the low spots. Through this Brother Parker, like the good pastor that he was, was carefully picking his way toward the log meeting house on the border of the big woods, for neither storm nor rain could keep him away from his duty however careless his flock might prove. He was well on his way when he was arrested by the sound of a voice calling him from one of the cabins, and Ike, one of the hands, came running after him. His wife, Caroline, was sick, and as she could not get to church, she desired the pastor's immediate spiritual ministrations at her own house.

The preacher turned back eagerly. His duty was always sweet to him and nothing gave him so keen a sense of pleasure as to feel that he was hurried to attend to all that needed him—that one duty crowded upon the heels of another. Moreover, he was a strong man of prayer in the sick room and some word that he should say might fall as a seed upon the uncultivated ground of Ike's heart, or if not, that he might heap coals of fire upon his head, for he was still a sinner.

With these thoughts and speculations in his mind, he started back to the cabin. But alas, for his haste, a sneaking, insidious piece of land lay in wait for him. Upon this he stepped. In another instant, his feet were pointing straight before him and he sat down suddenly in one of the biggest of the mud puddles. The tails of his long coat spread out about him and covered him like a blanket.

"Oomph!" he exclaimed as if the impact had driven the word from his lips, and for a moment he sat looking pitifully up into Ike's face as if to see if there were any laughter there. But there was no mirth in the younger man's countenance.

"Did you hu't yo'se'f, Brother Pahkah?" he asked, offering his hand.

"Well, seems like hit's shuck me up a leetle. But I reckon hit'll des' settle my bones mo' natchally fu' de grave."

"Hit's too bad I had to call you. Hit nevah would a' happened if it hadn't a been fu' dat."

"Heish, man. Hit's all right. De shephud muss answeh de call o' de lambs, don' keer whut de weathah an' whut de tribbilations, dat's what he fu'."

The old man spoke heroically, but he felt ruefully his soaking and damaged trousers even while the words were on his lips.

"Well, let's pu'su' ouah way."

He took up his hurried walk again and led Ike to his own door, the cloth of his garments sticking to him and the tails of his coat flapping damply about his legs.

It has been maintained, with some degree of authority to enforce the statement, that the Americanized African is distinctly averse to cold water. If this is true, Parker was giving a glowing illustration of the warmth of his religion or the strength of his endurance, for not once did he murmur or make mention of his wet clothes even when the sick woman, all unconscious of his misfortune, started in upon a long history of her bodily ailments and spiritual experiences. He gave her sound pastoral advice, condoled with her and prayed with her. But when his ministrations were over, something like a sigh of relief broke from the old man's breast.

He turned at once to Ike: "Brothah Ike," he said. "I's feared to go on to meetin' in dese pants. I's ol' an' dey ain't no tellin' but I'd tek col'. Has you got a spaih paih 'bout?"

Ike was suddenly recalled to himself, and his wife, upon hearing the matter explained, was for getting up and helping to brush and fix up the none too neat pair of trousers that her husband found for the preacher. Dissuaded from doing this, she was loud in denunciations of her innocent self for keeping brother Parker so long in his wet garments. But the old man, thankful to get out of them at last, bade her not to worry.

"I reckon it's de old hosses aftah all dat kin stan' de ha'des' whacks," he said, and with these cheery words hastened off to meeting.

As was to be expected, he was late in arriving, and his congregation were singing hymn after hymn as he came up in order to pass the time and keep themselves in the spirit. It warmed his heart as he heard the rolling notes and he was all ready to dash into his sermon as soon as he was seated before the table that did duty as a reading desk. He flung himself into the hymn with all the power that was in him, and even before his opening prayer was done, the congregation showed that it was unable to contain its holy joy.

"Ol' Brothah Pahkah sholy is full of de spirit dis mo'nin," Aunt Fanny whispered to Aunt Tempe, and Aunt Tempe whispered back, "I reckon he done been in his secut closet an' had a pensacoshul showah befo' he come."

"He sholy been a dwellin' on Mount Sinai. Seem lak he mus a'hyeahed de thundah."

"Heish, honey, he's a thunde'in hisself."

And so like the whisper of waves on a shore, the ripple of comment ran around the meeting house, for there were none present but saw that in some way the spirit had mysteriously descended upon their pastor.

Just as the prayer ended and the congregation had swung into another spiritual hymn, Ike entered with a scared look upon his face and took a seat far back near the door. He glanced sheepishly about the church, and then furtively at Brother Parker. Once he made as if to rise, but thinking better of it, ducked his head and kept his seat.

Now, if one thing more than another was needed to fire the exhorter, it was the voluntary presence of this sinner untouched by the gospel. His eyes glowed and his old frame quivered with emotion. He would deliver a message that morning that would be pointed straight at the heart of Ike.

To the observer not absorbed by one idea, however, there was something particularly strange in the actions of this last comer. Some things that he did did not seem to argue that he had come to the house of worship seeking a means of grace. After his almost stealthy entrance and his first watchful glances about the room, he had subsided into his seat with an attitude that betokened a despair not wholly spiritual. His eyes followed every motion the preacher made as he rose and looked over the congregation and he grew visibly more uneasy. Once or twice it seemed that the door behind him opened a bit and there is no doubt that several times he turned and looked that way, on one occasion giving his head a quick shake when the door was hastily, but softly closed.

When Parker began his sermon Ike crept guiltily to his feet to slip out, but the old preacher paused with his eyes upon him, saying, "I hope none o' de cong'ega-tion will leave de sanctua'y befo' de sehvice is ended. We is in now, an' gettin' up will distu'b de res'. Hit ain't gwine hu't none of us to gin one day to de Lawd, spechully ef dem what is neah an' deah unto us is layin' erpon de bed of affliction," and the man had sunk back miserably into his seat with the looks of all his fellows fixed on him. From then, he watched the preacher as if fascinated.

Parker was in his glory. He had before him a sinner writhing on the Gospel gridiron and how he did apply the fire.

Ike moved about and squirmed, but the old man held him with his eye while he heaped coals of fire upon the head of the sinner man. He swept the whole congregation with his gaze, but it came back and rested on Ike as he broke into the song,

"Oh, sinnah, you needn't try to run erway,
You sho' to be caught on de jedgment day"

He sung the camp meeting "spiritual" with its powerful personal allusions all through, and then resumed his sermon. "Oh, I tell you de Gospel is a p'inted swo'd to de sinnah. Hit mek him squi'm, hit mek him shivvah and hit mek him shek. He sing loud in de day, but he hide his face at night. Oh, sinnah, what you gwine to do on de gret day? What do de song say?

'W'en de rocks an' de mountains shell all flee erway,
W'y a you shell have a new hidin' place dat day.'

Oh, sinnah man, is you a huntin' fu' de new hidin' place? Is you a fixin' fu' de time w'en de rocks shell be melted an' de mountains shell run lak rivers?"

Parker had settled well down to his work. As his own people would have expressed it, "He'd done tried de watah an' waded out." They were shouting and crying aloud as he talked. A low minor of moans ran around the room, punctuated by the sharp slapping of hands and stamping of feet. On all sides there were cries of "Truth, truth!" "Amen!" "Amen!" and "Keep in de stream, Pahkah; keep in de stream!"

This encouragement was meat to the pastor's soul and he rose on the wings of his eloquence. The sweat was pouring down his black face. He put his hand back to his pocket to pull out his handkerchief to wipe his face. It came out with a flourish, and with it a pack of cards. They flew into the air, wavered and then fluttered down like a flock of doves. Aces, jacks, queens and tens settled all about the floor grinning wickedly face upward. Parker stopped still in the midst of a sentence and gazed speechless at the guilty things before him. The people gasped. It all flashed over them in a minute. They had heard a story of their pastor's fondness for the devil's picture books in his younger days and now it had come back upon him and he had fallen once more. Here was incontestable proof.

Parker, in a dazed way, put his hand again into his back pocket and brought forth the king of spades. His flock groaned.

"Come down outen dat pulpit," cried one of the bolder ones. "Come down!" Then Parker found his voice.

"Fo' de lawd, folks," he said, gazing sorrowfully at the king. "Dese ain't my pants ner my cyards." Then his eye fell upon Ike, who was taking advantage of the confusion to make toward the door and he thundered at him. "Come back hyeah, you rapscallion, an' claim yo' dev'ment! Come back hyeah."

Ike came shamefacedly back. He came forward and commenced to pick up the cards while Parker was making his explanations to the relieved flock. The sinner got all of the cards, except one and that one the preacher still held.

"Brothah Pahkah, Brother Pahkah," he whispered, "You's a hol'in' de king." The old man dropped it as if it had burnt him and grabbing it, the scapegrace fled.

Outside the door all things were explained. Several fellows with angry faces were waiting for Ike.

"Couldn't he'p it, boys," he said. "He done begun sehvice w'en I got in. I couldn't stop him, an' den w'en he dropped all the res' he held on to de king."

"Well, all I got to say," said the fiercest of the lot, "don' you nevah put dat deck in yo' pocket no mo' an' len' yo' pants. Come on, de game's been waitin' a houah, put' nigh."

The Last Fiddling of Mordaunt's Jim

WHEN THE SPIRIT has striven with a man year after year without success, when he has been convicted and then gone back, when he has been converted and then backslidden, it's about time to say of him that there is the devil's property, with his deed signed and sealed. All of these things had happened to Jim. He became serious and bowed his head in the meeting house, a sure sign of contrition and religious intention, but the very next night he had been caught "wingin'" behind the smokehouse with the rest of the unregenerate. Once he had actually cried out "Amen!" but it was afterwards found out that one of his fellows had trodden upon his foot, and that the "Amen" came in lieu of a less virtuous expletive.

Had it been that Jim's iniquities affected himself only he might have been endured, at least with greater patience, but this was not so. He was the prime mover in every bit of deviltry that set the plantation by the ears, and the most effectual destroyer of every religious influence that its master attempted to throw around it. His one fiddle had caused more backsliding, more flagrant defections from the faith than had any other invention of the devil that the plantation knew.

All of Parker's pleas and sermons had been unavailing—even his supreme exhortation, when he threatened the wicked with eternal fiddling, when their souls should be pining for rest and silence and never find it. Jim was there, but he appeared unmoved. He laughed when Parker broke out, "Fiddle on, you sinnahs, fiddle on! But de time'll come w'en you'll want to hyeah praih, an' you'll hyeah a fiddle; w'en you'll want to sing a hymn, an' you'll hyeah a fiddle; w'en you'll be list'nin' fu' de soun' of de angels' voices erbove de noise of earf, an' you'll hyeah a fiddle. Fiddle on, sinnahs, but w'en you hyeah de soun' of Jerdon a-dashin' on de rocks, w'en you hyeah de watah leapin' an' a-lashin', way up erbove dem all you'll hyeah de devil fiddlin' fu' you an' you'll follah him on an' into dat uttah da'kness whaih dey is wailin' an' gnash o' teef. Fiddle on, sinnah, fiddle on! dance on, sinnah, dance on! laugh on, sinnah, laugh on! but I tell you de time will come w'en dat laughin' will be tu'ned to weepin', an' de soun' of de fiddle shell be as de call of de las' trump in yo' yeahs." And Jim laughed. He went home that night and fiddled until nearly morning.

"'Pears to me," he said to his wife, "a good fiddle 'ud be a moughty fine t'ing to hyeah ez a body was passin' ovah Jerdon, ez ol' Pahkah calls it."

"Nemmine, Jim," said Mandy, solemn and shocked; "nemmine, you an' yo' dev'ment. Brothah Pahkah right, an' de time gwine come w'en dat fiddle gwine ter be to yo' soul ez a mill stone dat been cas' in de middle of de sea, dat'll bring fo'th tares, some fifty an' some a hund'ed fol'. Nemmine, all I got to say to you, you bettah listen to de Wo'd ez it is preached."

"Mandy," said Jim irreverently, "d'you 'membah dat ol' chune, 'Hoe co'n, an' dig pertaters?' Don't it go 'long somep'n' lak dis?"

"Lawsy, yes, honey, dat's hit," and before the poor deluded creature knew what she was doing she was nodding her head in time to the seductive melody, while Jim fiddled and chuckled within himself until the joke was too much for him, and he broke down and ended with a discord which brought Mandy to her sorrowing senses.

Her discretion came to her, though not before Parker's white inquisitive head had been stuck in at the door.

"Lawd, Sis' Mandy," he cried in dismay, "you ain't collogin' wid de spe'it of de devil, too, is you? Lawd a' mussy, 'pon my soul, an' you one of de faifful of de flock! My soul!"

"I ain't been collogin' wid de devil, Brothah Pahkah," said Mandy contritely, "but dat rapscallion, he fool me an' got my haid to gwine 'fo' I knowed whut I was 'bout."

"Uh, uh, uh," murmured the preacher.

Jim was convulsed. "Hit sho' is a mighty funny 'ligion you preaches, Brothah Pahkah, w'en one fiddle chune kin des' mortally lay out all o' yo' himes."

Parker turned on Jim with the old battle fire in his eyes. "Go on!" he cried. "Go on, but I lay you'll fiddle yo'se'f in hell yit!" And with out more ado he stamped away. He was very old, and his temper was shorter than it used to be.

The events of the next week followed each other in quick succession and there are many tales, none fully authenticated, about what really occurred. Some say that, hurt to the quick, Parker tramped around late that night after his visit to Jim's cabin. Others say that he was old and feeble and that his decline was inevitable. Whatever the truth about the cause of it, the old man was taken with a heavy cold which developed into fever. Here, too, chroniclers disagree, for some say that at no time was he out of his head, and that his wild ravings about fiddles and fiddlings were the terrible curses that a righteous man may put, and often does put, on a sinner.

For days the old man's life hung in the balance, and Jim grew contrite under the report of his sufferings and Mandy's accusations. Indeed, he fiddled no more, and the offending "box," as he called it, lay neglected on a shelf.

"Yes, you tryin' to git good now, aftah you mos' nigh killed dat ol' man, havin' him trompin' erroun' in de night aih lookin' aftah yo' dev'ment." Women are so cruel when they feel themselves in the right.

"He wan't trompin' erroun' aftah me. I ain't nevah sont fu' him," was always Jim's sullen reply.

"'Tain't no use beatin' erbout de bush; you knows you been causin' dat ol' man a heap er trouble, an' many's de time he mought 'a' been in baid takin' a good res' ef it hadn't been fu' yo' ca'in' on."

Jim grinned a sickly grin and lapsed into silence. What was the use of arguing with a woman anyway, and how utterly useless it was when the argument happened to be about her preacher! It is really a remarkable thing how, when it comes to woman, the philosophy of man in the highest and lowest grades of life arrives at the same conclusion. So Jim kept his mouth shut for several days until the one on which the news came that Parker had rallied and was "on the mend"; then he opened it to guffaw. This brought Mandy down upon him once more.

"I sholy don't know whut to mek o' you, Jim. Instid o' spreadin' dat mouf o' yo'n, you ought to be down on yo' knees a-thankin' de Lawd dat Brothah Pahkah ain't passed ovah an' lef' yo' 'niquities on yo' soul."

"La, chile, heish up; I's gwine celebrate Brothah Pahkah's 'cov'ry."

Jim busied himself with dusting and tuning his neglected instrument, and immediately after supper its strains resounded again through the quarters. It rose loud and long, a gladsome sound. What wonder, then, that many of the young people, happy in their old pastor's recovery, should gather before Jim's cabin and foot it gayly there?

But in the midst of the merriment a messenger hastened into the cabin with the intelligence that Brother Parker wanted Jim at his cabin. Something in the messenger's face, or in the tone of his voice, made Jim lay his fiddle aside and hurry to Parker's bedside.

"Howdy, Bud' Jim?" said Parker weakly.

"Howdy, Brothah Pahkah?" said Jim nervously; "how you come on?"

"Well, I's clothed an' in my right min' at las', bless Gawd. Been havin' a little frolic down to yo' cabin to-night?"

Jim twirled his piece of hat tremulously.

"Yes, suh, we was a kin' o' celebratin' yo' gittin' well."

"Dat uz a moughty po' way o' celebratin' fu' me, Jim, but I ain't gwine scol' you now. Dey say dat w'ile I wuz outen my haid I said ha'd tings erbout you an' yo' fiddlin', Jim. An' now dat de Lawd has giv' me my senses back ergin, I want to ax yo' pa'don."

"Brothah Pahkah," Jim interrupted brokenly, "I ain't meant no ha'm to'ds you. Hit des' mus' 'a' been natchul dev'ment in me."

"I ain't a-blamin' you, Jim, I ain't a-blamin' you; I only wanted to baig yo' pa'don fu' whutevah I said w'en my min' wan't mine."

"You don' need to baig my pa'don."

"Run erlong now, Jim, an' ac' de bes' you kin; so-long."

"So-long, Brothah Pahkah," and the contrite sinner went slowly out and back to the cabin, sorrow, fear, and remorse tugging at his heart.

He went back to his cabin and to bed at once, but he could not sleep for the vague feeling of waiting that held his eyes open and made him start at every sound. An hour passed with him under this nervous tension and then a tap came at the door. He sprang up to open it, and Mandy, as if moved by the same impulse, rose and began to dress hurriedly. Yes, his worst fears were realized. Parker was worse, and they sent for Mandy to nurse him in what they believed to be his last hours.

Jim dressed, too, and for a while stood in the door watching the lights and shadows moving over in the direction of the preacher's cabin. Then an ague seemed to seize him, and with a shiver he came back into the room and closed and bolted the door.

He had sat there, it seemed, a long while, when suddenly out of the stillness of the night a faint sound struck on his ears. It was as if someone far away were fiddling, fiddling a wild, weird tune. Jim sat bolt upright, and the sweat broke out upon his face in great cold drops. He waited. The fiddling came nearer. Jim's lips began moving in silent, but agitated, prayer. Nearer and nearer came the sound, and the face of the scapegrace alone in the cabin turned ashen with fear, then seizing his own fiddle, he smashed it into bits upon the chair, crying the while: "Lawd, Lawd, spaih me, an' I'll nevah fiddle ergin!" He was on his knees now, but the demon of the fiddle came so relentlessly on that he sprang up and hurled himself against the door in a very ecstasy of terror while he babbled prayer on prayer for protection, for just one more trial. Then it seemed that his prayer had been answered. The music began to recede. It grew fainter and fainter and passed on into silence.

Not, however, until the last note had passed away did Jim leave the door and sink helpless on his knees beside the broken fiddle. It seemed ages before he opened the door to Mandy's knock.

"Brothah Pahkah done daid," she said sadly.

"I know it," Jim replied; "I knowed it w'en he died, 'case de devil come fu' me, an' tried to fiddle my soul erway to hell, an' he 'u'd done it, too, ef I hadn't a-wrassled in praih."

"Jim, has you been visited?"

"I has," was the solemn reply, "an' I'll nevah fiddle no mo' ez long ez I live. Daih's de fiddle."

Mandy looked at the broken instrument, and the instinct of thrift drove out her superstition. "Jim," she cried out angrily, "whut you wan' 'o go brek up dat good fiddle fu'? Why'n't you sell it?"

"No, ma'am, no ma'am, I know whut's in dat fiddle. I's been showed, an' I ain't gwine temp' no man wid de devil's inst'ument."

From that moment Jim was a pious man, and at the great funeral which they gave Brother Parker a few days later there was no more serious and devout mourner than he. The whole plantation marveled and the only man who held the key to the situation could not tell the story. He was only a belated serenader who had fiddled to keep up his spirits on a lonely road.

But Parker's work was not without its fruition, for his death accomplished what his life had failed to do, and no more moral story was known or told on the plantation than that of the last fiddling of Mordaunt's Jim.

A Supper by Proxy

THERE WAS AN air of suppressed excitement about the whole plantation. The big old house stared gravely out as if it could tell great things if it would, and the cabins in the quarters looked prophetic. The very dogs were on the alert, and there was expectancy even in the eyes of the piccaninnies who rolled in the dust. Something was going to happen. There was no denying that. The wind whispered it to the trees and the trees nodded.

Then there was a clatter of horses' hoofs, the crack of a whip. The bays with the family carriage swept round the drive and halted at the front porch. Julius was on the box, resplendent in his holiday livery. This was the signal for a general awakening. The old house leered an irritating "I told you so." The quarters looked complacent. The dogs ran and barked, the piccaninnies laughed and shouted, the servants gathered on the lawn and, in the midst of it all, the master and mistress came down the steps and got into the carriage. Another crack of the whip, a shout from the servants, more antics from the piccaninnies, the scurrying of the dogs—and the vehicle rumbled out of sight behind a clump of maples. Immediately the big house resumed its natural appearance and the quarters settled back into whitewashed respectability.

Mr. and Mrs. Mordaunt were off for a week visit. The boys were away at school, and here was the plantation left in charge of the negroes themselves, except for the presence of an overseer who did not live on the place. The conditions seemed pregnant of many things, but a calm fell on the place as if everyone had decided to be particularly upon his good behavior. The piccaninnies were subdued. The butlers in the big house bowed with wonderful deference to the maids as they passed them in the halls, and the maids called the butlers "mister" when they spoke to them. Only now and again from the fields could a song be heard. All this was ominous.

By the time that night came many things were changed. The hilarity of the little darkies had grown, and although the house servants still remained gravely quiet, on the return of the field hands the quarters became frankly joyous. From one cabin to another could be heard the sound of "Juba, Juba!" and the loud patting of hands and the shuffling of feet. Now and again some voice could be heard rising above the rest, improvising a verse of the song, as:

> "Mas' done gone to Philamundelphy, Juba, Juba.
> Lef' us bacon, lef' us co'n braid, Juba, Juba.
> Oh, Juba dis an' Juba dat, an' Juba skinned de yaller cat
> To mek his wife a Sunday hat, Oh, Juba!"

Not long did the sounds continue to issue from isolated points. The people began drifting together, and when a goodly number had gathered at a large cabin, the inevitable thing happened. Someone brought out a banjo and a dance followed.

Meanwhile, from the vantage ground of the big house, the more favored servants looked disdainfully on, and at the same time consulted together. That they should do something to entertain themselves was only right and proper. No one of ordinary intelligence could think for a moment of letting this opportunity slip without taking advantage of it. But a dance such as the quarters had! Bah! They could never think of it. That rude, informal affair! And these black aristocrats turned up their noses. No, theirs must be a grave and dignified affair, such as their master himself would have given, and they would send out invitations to some on the neighboring plantations.

It was Julius, the coachman, who, after winning around the head butler, Anderson, insisted that they ought to give a grand supper. Julius would have gone on without the butler's consent had it not been that Anderson carried the keys. So the matter was canvassed and settled.

The next business was the invitations, but no one could write. Still, this was a slight matter; for neatly folded envelopes were carried about to the different favored ones, containing—nothing, while at the same time the invitations were proffered by word of mouth.

"Hi, dah!" cried Jim to Julius on the evening that the cards had been distributed; "I ain't seed my imbitation yit."

"You needn't keep yo' eyes bucked looking fu' none, neithah," replied Julius.

"Uh, puttin' on airs, is you?"

"I don't caih to convuss wid you jest now," said Julius pompously.

Jim guffawed. "Well, of all de sights I evah seed, a dahky coachman offen de box tryin' to look lak he on it! Go 'long, Julius, er you'll sholy kill me, man."

The coachman strode on with angry dignity.

It had been announced that the supper was to be a "ladies' an' gent'men's pahty," and so but few from the quarters were asked. The quarters were naturally angry and a bit envious, for they were but human and not yet intelligent enough to recognize the vast social gulf that yawned between the blacks at the "big house" and the blacks who were quartered in the cabins.

The night of the grand affair arrived, and the Mordaunt mansion was as resplendent as it had ever been for one of the master's festivities. The drawing-rooms were gayly festooned, and the long dining-room was a blaze of light from the wax candles that shone on the glory of the Mordaunt plate. Nothing but the best had satisfied Julius and Anderson. By nine o'clock the outside guests began to arrive. They were the dark aristocrats of the region. It was a well-dressed assembly, too. Plump brown arms lay against the dainty folds of gleaming muslin, and white stocked, brass-buttoned black counterparts of their masters strode up the walks. There were Dudley Stone's Gideon and Martha, Robert Curtis' Ike with Dely, and there were Quinn, and Doshy, and, over them all, Aunt Tempe to keep them straight. Of these was the company that sat down to Stuart Mordaunt's board.

After some rivalry, Anderson held the head of the table, while Julius was appeased by being placed on the right beside his favorite lady. Aunt Tempe was opposite the host where she could reprove any unseemly levity or tendency to skylarking on the part of the young people. No state dinner ever began with more dignity. The conversation was nothing less than stately, and everybody bowed to everybody else every time they thought about it. This condition of affairs obtained through the soup. Somebody ventured a joke and there was even a light laugh during the fish. By the advent of the entree the tongues of the assembly had loosened up, and their laughter had melted and flowed as freely as Stuart Mordaunt's wine.

"Well, I mus say, Mistah An'erson, dis is sholy a mos' salub'ious occasion."

"Thank you, Mistah Cu'tis, thank you; it ah allus my endeavoh to mek my gues'es feel deyse'ves at home. Let me give you some mo' of dis wine. It's f'om de bes' dat's in my cellah."

"Seems lak I remembah de vintage," said Ike, sipping slowly and with the air of a connoisseur.

"Oh, yes, you drinked some o' dis on de 'casion of my darter's ma'ige to Mas'—to Mistah Daniels."

"I ricollec', yes, I ricollec'."

"Des lis'en at dem dahkies," said the voice of a listening field hand.

Gideon, as was his wont, was saying deeply serious things to Martha, and Quinn whispered something in Doshy's ear that made her giggle hysterically and cry: "Now, Mr. Quinn, ain't you scan'lous? You des seem lak you possessed dis evenin'."

In due time, however, the ladies withdrew, and the gentlemen were left over their cigars and cognac. It was then that one of the boys detailed to wait on the table came in and announced to the host that a tramp was without begging for something to eat. At the same instant the straggler's face appeared at the door, a poor, unkempt-looking white fellow with a very dirty face. Anderson cast a look over his shoulder at him and commanded pompously:

"Tek him to de kitchen an' give him all he wants."

The fellow went away very humbly.

In a few minutes Aunt Tempe opened the dining-room door and came in.

"An'erson," she cried in a whisper.

"Madam," said the butler rising in dignity, "excuse me—but—"

"Hyeah, don't you come no foo'ishness wid me; I ain't no madam. I's tiahed playing fine lady. I done been out to de kitchen, an' I don' lak dat tramp's face an' fo'm."

"Well, madam," said Anderson urbanely, "we haven't asked you to ma'y him."

At this there was a burst of laughter from the table.

"Nemmine, nemmine, I tell you, I don' lak dat tramp's face an' fo'm, an' you'd bettah keep yo' eye skinned, er you'll be laughin' on de othah side o' yo' mouf."

The butler gently pushed the old lady out, but as the door closed behind her she was still saying, "I don' lak dat tramp's face an' fo'm."

Unused to playing fine lady so long, Aunt Tempe deserted her charges and went back to the kitchen, but the "straggler man" had gone. It is a good thing she did not go around the veranda, where the windows of the dining-room opened, or she would have been considerably disturbed to see the tramp peeping through the blinds—evidently at the Mordaunt plate that sparkled conspicuously on the table.

Anderson with his hand in his coat, quite after the manner of Stuart Mordaunt, made a brief speech in which he thanked his guests for the honor they had done him in coming to his humble home. "I know," he said, "I have done my po' bes'; but at some latah day I hopes to entertain you in a mannah dat de position an' character of de gent'men hyeah assembled desuves. Let us now jine de ladies."

His hand was on the door and all the gentlemen were on their feet when suddenly the window was thrown up and in stepped the straggler.

"W'y, w'y, how daih you, suh, invade my p'emises?" asked Anderson, casting a withering glance at the intruder, who stood gazing around him.

"Leave de room dis minute!" cried Julius, anxious to be in the fray. But the tramp's eyes were fastened on Anderson. Finally he raised one finger and pointed at him.

"You old scoundrel," he said in a well-known voice, as he snatched off his beard and wig and threw aside his disguising duster and stood before them.

"Mas' Stu'at!"

"You old scoundrel, you! I've caught you, have I?"

Anderson was speechless and transfixed, but the others were not, and they had cleared that room before the master's linen duster was well off. In a moment the shuffling of feet ceased and the lights went out in the parlor. The two stood there alone, facing each other.

"Mas' Stu'at."

"Silence," said Mordaunt, raising his hand, and taking a step toward the trembling culprit.

"Don' hit me now, Mas' Stu'at, don' hit me ontwell I's kin' o' shuk off yo' pussonality. Ef you do, it'll be des' de same ez thumpin yo'se'f."

Mordaunt turned quickly and stood for a moment looking through the window, but his shoulders shook.

"Well," he said, turning; "do you think you've at last relieved yourself of my personality?"

"I don't know, I don't know. De gyahment sho' do fit monst'ous tight."

"Humph. You take my food, you take my wine, you take my cigars, and now even my personality isn't safe.

"Look here, what on earth do you mean by entertaining half the darkies in the county in my dining-room?"

Anderson scratched his head and thought. Then he said: "Well, look hyeah, Mas' Stu'at, dis hyeah wasn't rightly my suppah noways."

"Not your supper! Whose was it!"

"Yo'n."

"Mine?"

"Yes, suh."

"Why, what's the matter with you, Anderson? Next thing you'll be telling me that I planned it all, and invited all those servants."

"Lemme 'splain it, Mas', lemme 'splain it. Now I didn't give dat suppah as An'erson. I give it ez Mas' Stu'at Mordaunt; an' Quinn an' Ike an' Gidjon, dey didn't come fu' deyse'ves, dey come fu' Mas' Cu'tis, an' Mas' Dudley Stone. Don' you un'erstan', Mas' Stu'at? We wasn' we-all, we was you-all."

"That's very plain; and in other words, I gave a supper by proxy, and all my friends responded in the same manner?"

"Well, ef dat means what I said, dat's it."

"Your reasoning is extremely profound, Anderson. It does you great credit, but if I followed your plan I should give you the thrashing you deserve by proxy. That would just suit you. So instead of that I am going to feed you, for the next day or so, by that ingenious method. You go down and tell Jim that I want him up here early to-morrow morning to eat your breakfast."

"Oh, Mas' Stu'at! Whup me, whup me, but don't tell dose dahkies in de quah-tahs, an' don't sta've me!" For Anderson loved the good things of life.

"Go."

Anderson went, and Mordaunt gave himself up to mirth.

The quarters got their laugh out of Anderson's discomfiture. Jim lived high for a day, but rumors from the kitchen say that the butler did not really suffer on account of his supper by proxy.

The Trouble about Sophiny

ALWAYS ON THE plantation there had been rivalry between Julius, the coachman, and Anderson, the butler, for social leadership. Mostly it had been good-natured, with now and then a somewhat sharper contest when occasion demanded it. Mostly, too, Anderson had come off victorious on account of certain emoluments, honestly or dishonestly come by, that followed his position. Now, however, they were at loggerheads and there seemed no possible way to settle the matter in the usual amicable manner. Anderson swore dire things against Julius, and the latter would be satisfied with nothing less than his enemy's destruction. There was no use in the peacemakers on the plantation trying to bring them together. They were sworn enemies and would have none of it. In fact, there was no way to adjudicate the affair, for it concerned no less a matter than who should have the right to take Miss Sophiny to the great ball that was to be given in her honor.

Perhaps you do not know that Miss Sophiny was maid to Mistress Fairfax, who was now on a visit to the Mordaunt plantation, and in the whole State the prettiest girl, black, brown, or yellow that had ever tossed her head, imitated her mistress and set her admirers wild. She was that entrancing color between brown and yellow which is light brown if you are pleasant and gingerbread if you want to hurt a body's feelings. Also, Sophiny had lustrous, big black eyes that had learned from her mistress the trick of being tender or languishing at their owner's will.

Mistress Fairfax and her maid had not been on the grounds a day before they had disrupted the whole plantation.

From the very first, Julius had paid the brown damsel devoted court. In fact, as the coachman, he had driven up from the station with her mistress and had the first chance to show her his gallantry. It is true that Anderson came into the lists immediately after, and found a dainty for her even before he had served her mistress, but it could not be denied that he was after Julius, and it was upon his priority of attention that the coachman based his claim to present precedence.

For days the contest between the two men was pretty balanced. Julius walked down the quarters' road with her, but Anderson stood talking with her on the back veranda for nearly an hour. She went to the stables with the coachman to look over the horses, in which he took a special pride; but she dropped into the butler's pantry to try his latest confection. She laughed at a joke by Julius, but said "You're right" to a wise remark that Anderson made. Altogether, their honors seemed dangerously even.

Then the big house gave the grand ball for Mistress Fairfax, and the servants' quarters could hardly wait to follow their example in giving something for the maid. It was here that the trouble arose. Their ball was to be a great affair. It was to be given in the largest of the cabins, and field and house were to unite to do honor to the fair one. But the question was: Who was to have the honor of escorting her to the ball?

Now it might be supposed that under ordinary circumstances such a matter would be left to the personal preference of the lady most concerned; but that is just where the observer makes his first mistake. His premise is wrong. This was no ordinary matter. Had the lady shown any decided preference for either one or the other of her suitors; had either even the shade of a hair an advantage over the other, it would all have been different. It would have resolved itself merely into a trial of personal influence and the vanquished would have laughed with his victor. But it was not so. Miss Sophiny had treated them both painfully alike. The one who took the lady would gain a distinct advantage over his fellow, and this must not be left to chance. They must settle outside their charmer's knowledge once and for all as to which should ask and, as a consequence, be her escort.

Now it was at this time that the mirth-loving master, Stuart Mordaunt, took note of the affair. He saw that there was bad feeling between his butler and his coachman, and he was not long in finding out the cause thereof. There were many with the story waiting on their lips and anxious to tell him. The little tale filled Mordaunt with mischievous joy. He hurried to the house with the news that there was trouble on the plantation

"Look a-here, Miss Caroline," he said to his visitor, "I had no idea your coming was going to cause such a commotion on my place. Why, I really believe that I'm threatened with an uprising, and all about that maid of yours. It's really doubtful whether we shall be able to drive anywhere, and I am beginning to tremble for the serving of my meals, for all the trouble seems to center in my coachman and my butler."

"Now, tell me, Mr. Stuart, what has that girl been doing now? Honestly, she's the plague of my life."

"Oh, no more than her mistress did last winter down at the capitol. It's really remarkable what a lot of human nature horses and niggers have."

"Aren't you ashamed of yourself, Mr. Mordaunt? Pray, what did I do last winter at the capitol?"

"The whole case is as bad as it was between Captain Carter and Willis Breckinridge, and I'm expecting the affair of honor between Julius and Anderson at any time. If you hear the sudden report of pistols you may all just know what it is and thank your maid Sophiny for bringing it about."

Miss Caroline laughed heartily at her host's bantering, but he went on in a tone of mock seriousness, "You may laugh, now, my lady, but I'll warrant you'll sing another tune if you have to go walking about this place or perchance have to set to work some of you and get your own dinners; and that's what it will come to if this matter goes on much longer."

The rivalry between the two servants had now run its course for some time, and as neither man seemed disposed to yield, it threatened to ruin the whole entertainment, which had been postponed from time to time to allow of an adjustment of the matter. Finally, when that night of pleasure was too visibly menaced, Jim, the unregenerate, came forward with a solution of the problem. "Why," he argued, "should Julius and Anderson be allowed to spoil the good time of the whole plantation by their personal disagreements and bickerings? What was it to the rest of them, who took Miss Sophiny, so she came and they had their dance? If the two must differ, why not differ like men and fight it out? Then, the one that whipped had the right to take the young lady." Jim was primitive. He was very close to nature. He did not argue it out in just these words, but his fellows took his meaning, and they said, "That's so."

Now, neither Julius nor Anderson much favored the idea of fighting. Each wanted to save himself and look his best on the momentous night. But the fact that unless the matter were soon settled there would be no such night, and because the force of opinion all around pressed them, they accepted Jim's solution of the problem and decided to fight out their differences.

Meanwhile there was an unholy twinkle in the eye of Miss Sophiny. She was not unmindful of all that was going on, but she kept her counsel.

Neither Julius nor his fellow servant was in particularly good fighting trim. One had been stiffened by long hours, both in winter and summer upon the carriage. The other had been softened by being much in the house and by over feeding. But as their disadvantages were equal these could not justly be taken into account and so are passed over.

As the plantation was manifesting a growing impatience for its festivities and the visitor's stay was drawing to a close, they set the time for the encounter on the night after the matter was proposed. It was soon, but not too soon for some solicitous one to inform the master of what was going on.

The place chosen was one remote from the big house and behind an old dismantled smoke-house in which the card games were usually played of a Sunday. At the appointed time, the few who were in the secret gathered and formed a ring about the rivals, who faced each other stripped to the waist. There was not a great show of confidence or eagerness in their bearing, and there would have been less could they have known that their master with Miss Caroline and several members of the family were hiding just around the corner of the smoke-house, convulsed with laughter.

The two men were a funny sight as they stood there in the ring fearfully facing each other. Julius was tall and raw-boned, while Anderson was short and fat from much feeding. When the preliminaries were all arranged the fight began without further ceremony. Julius led with a heavy awkward blow that caught his opponent just above where the belt should have been, and Anderson grunted with a sound like a half-filled barrel. This was enough. The blow was immediately returned by the butler's bending his head and butting his rival quickly and resoundingly. Before he could recover his upright position, however, the tall coachman had caught him under his arm and was trying to work havoc on his woolly pate. For a few minutes they danced around in this position, for all the world like two roosters when one shields his head under the other's wing.

"Brek aloose," cried Jim, excitedly, "brek aloose, dat ain't no fist fightin'."

The men separated and began to pummel each other at a distance and in good earnest. Anderson's nose was bleeding, and Julius' eye was closed to earthly scenes. They were both panting like engines.

At this juncture, thinking it had gone far enough, Mordaunt, with much ado to keep his face straight, emerged from behind the smoke-house. At first the combatants did not see him, so busily were they engaged, but the sound of scurrying feet as their spectators fled the scene, called them to themselves and they turned to meet the eyes of their master fixed upon them with a sternness that it was all he could do to maintain.

"Well, you are a pretty pair. Here, what is the meaning of this?"

The two men hung their heads. A giggle, pretty well-defined, came from behind the smoke-house, and they became aware that their master was not alone. They were covered with confusion.

"Get into your coats." They hustled into their garments. "Now tell me what is the meaning of this?"

"We was des' a fightin' a little," said Julius, sheepishly.

"Just for fun, I suppose?"

No answer.

"I say, just for fun?"

"Well, I seen huh fust," Julius broke out like a big boy.

"Don' keer ef yo' did, I did mo' talkin' to huh, an' I got de right to tek huh to th' pa'ty, dat's what I have."

"Well, you're a pretty pair," repeated the master. "Has it ever occurred to you that Sophiny herself might have something to say as to who went with her?"

"Well, dat's des' what I say, but Julius he want to ax huh fus' an' so does I."

"Anderson, I'm ashamed of you. Why ain't you got sense enough to go together and ask her, and so settle the matter peacefully? If it wasn't for the rest of the hands you should not have any dance at all. Now take yourselves to the house and don't let me hear any more of this business."

Mordaunt turned quickly on his heel as the combatants slipped away. His gravity had stood all that it could. As soon as he had joined the others he broke into a peal of laughter in which Miss Caroline and the rest joined him.

"Oh, you women," he exclaimed, "didn't I warn you that we should have an affair of honor on our hands? It's worse, positively worse than Carter and Breckinridge."

"Yes, it is worse," assented Miss Caroline, mischievously, "for in this encounter some blood was drawn," and they took their way merrily to the house.

Julius and Anderson were both glad of the relief that their master had brought to them and of the expedient he had urged for getting around their difficulty. They talked amicably of the plan as they pursued their way.

"I'll go fix my eye an' yo' ten' to yo' nose, an' den we'll go an' see Miss Sophiny togethah des' lak Mas' says."

"All right, I'll be ready in a minute."

When they had somewhat repaired the damage to their countenances the coachman and the butler together set out to find the object of their hearts' desire. Together, each one fearing to let the other talk too much, they laid their case before her.

Sophiny sat on the step of the back porch and swung one slender foot temptingly down and outward. She listened to them with a smile on her face. When they were through she laughed lightly and said, "Why, la, gentlemen, I done p'omised Mistah Sam long 'go. He axed me soon's he hyeahed 'bout it!" Then she laughed again.

Sam was a big field hand and not at all in the coachman's and the butler's social set. They turned away from the siren in silence and when they were some distance off they solemnly shook hands.

Mr. Groby's Slippery Gift

TWO MEN COULD hardly have been more unlike than Jim and Joe Mordaunt, and when it is considered that they were brothers brought up under the same conditions and trained by the same hand, this dissimilarity seems nothing less than remarkable. Jim was the older, and a better, steadier-going hand Stuart Mordaunt did not own upon the place, while a lazier, more unreliable scamp than Joe could not have been found within a radius of fifty miles.

The former was the leader in all good works, while the latter was at the head of every bit of deviltry that harassed the plantation. Everyone recognized the difference between these two, and they themselves did not ignore it.

"Jim, he's de 'ligious pa't o' de fambly," Joe used to say, "an' I's most o' de res' o' it." He looked upon his brother with a sort of patronizing condescension, as if his own wickedness in some manner dignified him; but nevertheless, the two were bound together by a rough but strong affection. The wicked one had once almost whipped a fellow-servant to death for saying that his brother couldn't out-pray the preacher. They were both field hands, and while Jim went his way and did his work rejoicing, Joe was the bane of the overseer's life. He would seize every possible chance of shirking, and it was his standing boast that he worked less and ate more than any other man on the place.

It was especially irritating to his master, because he was a fine-appearing fellow, with arms like steel bars, and the strength of a giant. It was this strength and a certain reckless spirit about him that kept the overseer from laying the lash to his back. It was better to let Joe shirk than to make him desperate, thought Mr. Groby. In his employer's dilemma, however, he suggested starvation as a very salutary measure, but was met with such an angry response that he immediately apologized. Stuart Mordaunt, while rejecting his employee's methods, yet looked to him to work an amendment in Joe's career. "For," said he, "that rascal will corrupt the whole plantation. Joe literally carries out the idea that he doesn't have to work, and is there a servant on the place who will work if he thinks he doesn't have to?"

"Yes, one—Joe's brother Jim," said the overseer, grinning. "He's what a nigger ought to be—as steady and as tireless as an ox."

"It's a wonder that brother of his hasn't corrupted him."

"Jim ain't got sense enough to be corrupted as long as he gets his feed."

"Maybe he's got too much sense," returned the master coldly. "But do you think that Joe really has notions?"

"Notions of freedom? No. He's like a balky horse. He'll stand in his tracks until you beat the life out of him, but he isn't the kind to run away. It would take too much exertion."

"I wish to Heaven he would run off!" said Mordaunt impatiently. "It would save me a deal of trouble. I don't want to deal harshly with him, but neither do I want the whole plantation stirred up."

"Why don't you sell him?"

Stuart Mordaunt's eyes flashed up at the overseer as he replied: "I haven't got down to selling my niggers down the river yet."

"Needn't sell him down the river. Sell him—"

"I'm no nigger-trader," the gentleman broke in.

"Listen to me," said Mr. Groby, insinuatingly. "My wife wants a good servant up at our house, and I'd be willing to take Joe off your hands. I think I could manage him." He looked for the moment as if he might manage the slave to the poor fellow's sorrow.

"But would you keep him right about here so that I could look after him if he got into trouble?"

"Certainly," said Mr. Groby, jingling the coins in his pocket.

"Then I'll give him to you," said Mordaunt coldly.

"I don't ask that; I—"

"I do not sell, I believe I told you. I'll give him to you."

The overseer laughed quietly when his employer was gone. "Oh, yes," he said to himself, "I think I can manage Joe when he's mine."

"I don't believe I ought to have done that," mused the master as he went his way.

Joe did not know what had happened until the papers transferring him were made out and Groby came and read them to him.

"You see, Joe," he said, "you're mine. I've wanted you for a long time. I've always thought that if you belonged to me I could make a good hand out of you. You see, Joe, I've got no sentiments. Of course you don't know what sentiments are, but you'll understand later. I feel as if I can increase your worth to the world," and Mr. Groby rubbed his hands and smiled.

The black man said nothing, but at night, humble and pleading, he went to see his old master. When Stuart Mordaunt saw him coming he did not feel altogether easy in his mind, but he tried to comfort himself by affecting to believe that Joe would be pleased.

"Well, Joe," he said, "I suppose you'll be glad to get away from the field?"

"Glad to git erway—oh, mastah!" He suddenly knelt and threw his arms about his master's knees, "Oh, Mas' Stua't," he cried, "don' gi' me to dat Mistah Groby; don' do it! I want to wo'k fu' you all de days o' my life. Don' gi' me to dat man!"

"Why, Joe, you never have been anxious before to work for me."

"Mas' Stua't, I knows I ain' been doin' right. I ain' been wo'kin', but I will wo'k. I'll dig my fingahs to de bone; but don' gi' me to dat man."

"But, Joe, you don't understand. You'll have a good home, easier work, and more time to yourself—almost the same as if you were up to the big house."

This was every field-hand's ambition, and Stuart Mordaunt thought that his argument would silence the refractory servant, but Joe was not to be silenced so. He raised his head and his black face was twitching with emotion. "I'd ravver be yo' fiel'-han' dan dat man Groby's mastah."

Mordaunt was touched, but his determination was not altered. "But he'll be good to you, don't you know that?"

"Good to me, good to me! Mas' Stua't, you don' know dat man!"

The master turned away. He had a certain discipline to keep on his place, and he knew it. "Perhaps I don't know him," he said, "but what I don't see with my own eyes I can't spy out with the eyes of my servants. Joe, you may go. I have given my word, and I could not go back even if I would. Be a good boy and you'll get along all right. Come to see me often."

The black man seized his master's hand and pressed it. Great fellow as he was, when he left he was sobbing like a child. He was to stay in the quarters that night and the next morning leave the fields and enter the service of Mrs. Groby.

It was a sad time for him. As he sat by the hearth, his face bowed in his hands, Jim reached over and slapped him on the head. It was as near to an expression of affection and sympathy as he could come. But his brother looked up with the tears shining in his eyes, and Jim, taking his pipe from his mouth, passed it over in silence, and they sat brooding until Mely took piece of "middlin'" off the coals for brother Joe.

When she had gone to bed the two men talked long, but it was not until she was snoring contentedly and the dogs were howling in the yard and the moon had gone down behind the trees that Mr. Groby's acquisition slipped out of the cabin and away to the woods, bearing with him his brother's blessing and breakfast.

It was near eleven o'clock the next morning when the overseer came to the big house, fuming and waving his papers in his hands. He was looking for his slave. But the big house did not know where he was any more than did the quarters, and he went away disappointed and furious.

Joe had rebelled. He had called the dark night to his aid and it had swallowed him up.

Against Mordaunt's remonstrances, the new-made master insisted upon putting the hounds on the negro's track; but they came back baffled. Joe knew Mr. Groby's methods and had prepared for them.

"It was a slippery gift you gave me, Mr. Mordaunt," said the overseer on the third day after Joe's escape.

"Even a slippery gift shouldn't get out of rough hands, Groby," answered Mordaunt, "and from what I hear your hands are rough enough."

"And they'd be rougher now if I had that black whelp here."

"I'm glad Joe's gone," mused Stuart Mordaunt as he looked at the overseer's retreating figure. "He was lazy and devilish, but Groby—"

It was just after that that Parker, the plantation exhorter, reported the backsliding of Jim. His first fall from grace consisted in his going to a dance. This was bad enough, but what was worse, although the festivities closed at midnight, Jim —and his wife Mely told it, too—did not reach his cabin until nearly daylight. Of course she was uneasy about it. That was quite natural. There were so many dashing girls on the plantations, within a radius of ten or twelve miles, that no woman's husband was safe. So she went to the minister about it, as women will about their troubles, and the minister went to his master.

"Let him alone," said Stuart Mordaunt. "His brother's absence has upset him, but Jim'll come round all right."

"But, mastah," said old Parker, pushing back his bone-bowed spectacles, "dat uz mighty late fu' Jim to be gittin' in—nigh daylight—ez stiddy a man ez he is. Don't you reckon dey's a 'ooman in it?"

"Look here, Parker," said his master; "aren't you ashamed of yourself? Have you ever known Jim to go with any other woman than Mely? If you preachers weren't such rascals yourselves and married less frequently you wouldn't be so ready to suspect other men."

"Ahem!" coughed Parker. "Well, Mas' Stua't, ef you gwineter question inter de p'ogatives o' de ministry, I'd bettah be gwine, case yo on dang'ous groun'," and he went his way.

But even an indulgent master's patience must wear out when a usually good servant lapses into unusually bad habits. Jim was often absent from the plantation now, and things began to disappear: chickens, ducks, geese, and even Jim's own family bacon, and now and then a shoat of the master's found its way off the place.

The thefts could be traced to but one source. Mely didn't mind the shoats, nor the ducks, nor the geese, nor the chickens—they were her master's, and he could afford to lose them—but that her husband should steal hers and the children's food —it was unspeakable. She caught him red-handed once, stealing away with a side of bacon, and she upbraided him loud and long.

"Oh, you low-down scoun'el," she screamed, "stealin' de braid outen yo' chillun's moufs fu' some othah 'ooman!"

Jim, a man of few words, stood silent and abashed, and his very silence drove her to desperation. She went to her master, and the next day the culprit was called up.

"Jim," said Mordaunt, "I want to be as easy with you as I can. You've always been a good servant, and I believe that it's your brother's doings that have got you off the handle. But I've borne with you week after week, and I can't stand it any longer. So mark my words: if I hear another complaint I'll have you skinned; do you hear me?"

"Yes, suh."

That night Jim stole a ham from the kitchen before Aunt Doshy's very eyes. When they told the master in the morning he was furious. He ordered that the thief be brought before him, and two whippers with stout corded lashes in their hands stood over the black man's back.

"What's the matter with you, anyhow?" roared Mordaunt. "Are you bound to defy me?"

Jim did not answer.

"Will you answer me?" cried the master.

Still Jim was silent.

"Who is this woman you're stealing for?"

"Ain't stealin' fu' no ooman."

"Don't lie to me. Will you tell?"

Silence.

"Do you hear me? Lay it on him! I'll see whether he'll talk!"

The lashes rose in the air and whizzed down. They rose again, but stopped poised as a gaunt figure coming from nowhere, it seemed, stalked up and pushed the whippers aside.

"Give it to me," said Joe, taking off his coat. "I told him jes' how it would be, an' I was comin' in to gi' myse'f up anyhow. He done it all to keep me f'om sta'vin'; but I's done hidin' now. I'll be dat Groby's slave ravver dan let him tek my blows." He ceased speaking and slipped out of his ragged shirt. "'Tain't no use, Jim," he added, "you's done all you could."

"Dah, now, Joe," said his brother in disgust, "you's done come hyeah an' sp'iled evaht'ing; you nevah did know yo' place."

"Whup away," said Joe.

But the master's hand went up.

"Joe!" he cried. "Jim, you—you've been taking that food to him! Why didn't you tell me?"

He kicked each one of the whippers solemnly, then he kicked Joe. "Get out of this," he said. "You'll be nobody's but mine. I'll buy you from Groby, you low-down, no-account scoundrel." Then he turned and looked down on Jim. "Oh, you fool nigger—God bless you."

When Mr. Groby heard of Joe's return he hastened up to the big house. He was elated.

"Ha," he said, "my man has returned."

Stuart Mordaunt looked unpleasant, then he said: "Your man, Mr. Groby, your man, as you call him, has returned. He is here. But, sir, your man has been redeemed by his brother's vicarious suffering, and I intend—I intend to buy Joe back. Please name your price."

And Mr. Groby saw the look in the gentleman's eye and made his price low.

Ash-Cake Hannah and Her Ben

CHRISTMAS EVE HAD come, and the cold, keen air with just a hint of dampness in it gave promise of the blessing of a white Christmas. A few flakes began sifting slowly down, and at sight of them a dozen pairs of white eyes flashed, and a dozen negro hearts beat more quickly. It was not long before the sound of grinding axes was heard and the dogs barked a chorus to the grindstones' song, for they, wise fellows that they were, knew what the bright glint of the steel meant. They knew, too, why Jake and Ike and Joe whistled so merrily, and looked over at the distant woods with half-shut eyes and smiled.

Already the overseers were relaxing their vigilance, the quarters were falling into indolence, and the master was guarding the key of a well-filled closet.

Negro Tom was tuning up his fiddle in the barn, and Blophus, with his banjo, was getting the chords from him, while Alec was away out in the woods with his face turned up to the gray sky, letting the kinks out of his tenor voice. All this because the night was coming on. Christmas Eve night was the beginning of a week of joy. The wind freshened and the snow fell faster. The walks were covered. Old gnarled logs that had lain about, black and forbidding, became things of beauty. The world was a white glory. Slowly, so slowly for a winter's night, the lights faded out and the lamps and candles and torches like lowly stars laughed from the windows of big house and cabin. In fireplaces great and small the hickory crackled, and the savory smell of cooking arose, tempting, persistent. The lights at the big house winked at the cabin, and the cabin windows winked back again. Laughter trickled down the night and good cheer was everywhere. Everywhere, save in one room, where Hannah—Ash-Cake Hannah, they called her—sat alone by her smouldering hearth, brushing the cinders from her fresh cake, mumbling to herself.

For her there was no Christmas cheer. There were only her dim, lonely cabin and the ash-covered hearth. While the others rejoiced she moaned, for she had taken as a husband a slave on a distant plantation, whose master was a hard man, and on many a Christmas he had refused permission to Ben to go and see his wife. So each year, as soon as Christmas Eve came, Hannah began to mope and fast, eating nothing but ash-cake until she knew whether or not Ben was coming. If he came, she turned to and laughed and made merry with the rest. If he did not, her sorrow and meagre fare lasted the week out, and she went back to her work with a heavy heart and no store of brightness for the coming year. To-day she sat, as usual, mumbling and moaning, for the night was drawing down, and no sign of Ben.

Outside the negroes from the quarters, dressed in their best, were gathering into line, two by two, to march to the big house, where every Christmas they received their presents. There was much pushing and giggling, with ever and anon an admonitory word from one of the older heads, as they caught some fellow's arm making free with a girl's waist. Finally, when darkness had completely come, they started briskly away to the tune of a marching song. As they neared and passed Hannah's cabin they lowered their voices out of respect to the sorrow they knew she was undergoing. But once beyond it they broke out with fresh gusto, stamping or tripping along through the damp snow like so many happy children. Then, as they neared the steps of the great house, the doors were thrown wide and a flood of yellow light flowed out upon the throng of eager faces. With their halting the marching song was stopped, and instantly a mellow voice swung into a Christmas hymn, one of their own rude spirituals:

Oh, moughty day at Bethlehem,
Who dat layin' in de manger?

De town, hit full, dey ain't no room;
Who dat layin' in de manger?

The old master had come forward to the front of the piazza and around him clustered his family and guests, listening with admiration to the full, rich chorus. When it was done the negroes filed through the hall, one by one, each with a "Me'y Chris'mus" and each receiving some token from the master and mistress. Laughing, joking, bantering, they went out to their holidays, some to their cabins to dance or eat, others to the woods with the dogs and the newly sharpened axes to look for game. One of the women stopped at Hannah's cabin with the gift for which she so seldom came. At her knock the lone watcher sprang up and flung the door wide, but sank down again with a groan at sight of the visitor. She did not even open the things which the messenger laid upon the bed, but bent again over her cheerless hearth.

The sound of merriment and song were dying away within the neighboring huts when her door was thrown suddenly open again and a huge negro stood before Ash-Cake Hannah. The slightly nibbled cake was hurled into a dark corner, and the woman sprang up with a heart-cry: "Ben!" She threw her arms about his neck and burst into happy tears, while Ben held her, grinned sheepishly, and kept glancing furtively toward the door.

"'Sh, 'sh," he said.

"What I want o' 'sh fu', w'en you's hyeah, Ben? I got a min' to hollah," she answered, laughing and crying.

"'Sh, 'sh," he repeated; "I's run off."

She stopped, and stood staring at him with wide, scared eyes.

"You's run off?" she echoed.

"Yes, Mas' Mason wouldn't let me come, so I tuk my chanst an' come anyhow."

"Oh, Ben, he'll mos' nigh kill you."

"I knows it, but I don' keer. It 'uz Chris'mus an' I was boun' to see you."

The woman fell to crying again, but he patted her shoulder, saying: "'Tain't no use to cry, Hannah. Hit's des' wastin' time. I got to pay fu' dis runnin' off anyhow, so I'd des' ez well have ez good a time ez I kin while hit las'. Fix me some suppah, an' den we'll go roun' a little an' see de folks."

As they went out the deadened sound of merriment came to them from the cabins.

"I don' know ez I ought to show myse'f des' now," said Ben stealthily, as they neared one of the places where the fun was at its height. "Ef I should tek a notion to go back, I mought git in widout Mas' Mason knowin' I been gone, 'dough he moughty sha'p-eyed."

"Le's des stan' outside hyeah, den, an, hol' han's an' listen; dat'll be enough fu' me, seen' you's hyeah."

They stationed themselves outside a cabin window whose shutter was thrown wide open to admit the air. Here they could see and listen to all that went on within. To them it was like starving within sight of food. Their hearts yearned to be enjoying themselves with their kind. But they only clutched each other's hands the tighter, and stood there in the square of yellow light thrown out by the candles and fat pine torches, drinking in all they could of the forbidden pleasures.

Now they were dancing to the tum-tum of a banjo and the scraping of a fiddle, and Ben's toes tingled to be shuffling. After the dance there would be a supper. Already a well-defined odor was arising from a sort of rude lean-to behind the cabin. The smell was rich and warm and sweet.

"What is dat, Hannah?" asked Ben. "Hit smell monst'ous familiah."

"Hit's sweet 'taters, dat's what it is."

Ben turned on her an agonized look. "Hit's sweet 'taters, an' p—" His lips were pouted to say the word, but it was too much for him. He interrupted himself in an attempt to pronounce that juicy, seductive, unctuous word, "possum," and started for the door, exclaiming: "Come on, Hannah; I'd des' ez well die fu' an ol' sheep ez fu' a lamb"; and in a moment he was being welcomed by the surprised dancers.

Ben and Hannah were soon in the very midst of the gayety.

"No ash-cake fu' Hannah dis Chris'mus!" shouted someone as he passed the happy woman in the dance.

Hannah's voice rang loud and clear through the room as she courtesied to her husband and answered: "No, indeed, honey; Hannah gwine live off'en de fat o' de lan' dis hyeah Chris'mus."

In a little while Fullerton, the master, came to the cabin with some of his friends who wanted to enjoy looking on at the negroes' pleasure. This was the signal for the wildest pranks, the most fantastic dancing and a general period of showing off. The happy-go-lucky people were like so many children released from their tasks. The more loudly their visitors applauded the gayer they became. They clapped their hands, they slapped their knees. They leaped and capered. And among them, no one was lighter-hearted than Ben. He had forgotten what lay in store for him, and his antics kept the room in a roar.

Fullerton had seen him and had expressed the belief that Ben had run away, for Mason Tyler would hardly have let him come without sending with him a pass; but he took it easily, glad to see Hannah enjoying herself, and no longer forced to moan and fast.

For a brief space the dancers had rested. Then the music struck up again. They had made their "'bejunce" and were swinging corners, when suddenly the clatter of horses' hoofs broke in on the rhythm of the music, which stopped with a discord. The people stood startled and expectant, each in the attitude in which he had stopped. Ben was grinning sheepishly and scraping his foot on the floor. All at once he remembered.

With a cry, Hannah ran across the room and threw herself at her master's feet. "Oh, Mas' Jack," she begged, "don' let Mas' Mason Tyler whup Ben! He runned off to be wid me."

"'Sh," said Fullerton quickly; "I'll do what I can."

In another moment the door was flung open and Mason Tyler, a big, gruff-looking fellow with a face red with anger, stood in the doorway. Over his shoulder peeped two negroes. He had a stout whip in his hand.

"Is my—oh, there you are, you black hound. Come here; I'm going to larrup you within an inch of your life."

"Good-evening, Mr. Tyler," broke in Fullerton's smooth voice.

"Oh, good-evening, Mr. Fullerton. You must excuse me; I was so taken up with that black hound that I forgot my manners."

Fullerton proceeded to introduce his friends. Tyler met them gruffly.

"Ben, here," he proceeded, "has taken it into his head that he is his own master."

"Oh, well, these things will happen about Christmas time, and you must over-look them."

"Nobody need tell me how to run my place."

"Certainly not, but I've a sort of interest in Ben on Hannah's account. How-ever, we won't talk of it. Come to the house, and let me offer you some refresh-ment."

"I haven't time."

"My friends will think very badly of you if you don't join us in one holiday glass at least."

Tyler's eyes glistened. He loved his glass. He turned irresolutely.

"Oh, leave Ben here for the little time you'll be with us. I'll vouch for him."

Mellowed already by pleasant anticipations, Mason Tyler allowed himself to be persuaded, and setting the two negroes who accompanied him to watch Ben, he went away to the big house.

It was perhaps two hours later when a negro groom was sent to bed Tyler's horse for the night, while one of his own servants was dispatched to tell his family that he could not be home that night.

Ben, perfectly confident that he was to "die for an old sheep," was making the best of his time, even while expecting every moment to be called to go home for punishment. But when the news of his master's determination to stay reached him, his fears faded, and he prepared to enjoy himself until fatigue stopped him. As for Hannah, she was joyous even though, woman-like, she could not shut her eyes to the doubtful future.

It was near twelve o'clock on the crisp, bright, Christmas morning that fol-lowed when Mason Tyler called for his horse to ride home. He was mellow and jovial and the red in his face was less apoplectic. He called for his horse, but he did not call for Ben, for during the night and morning Fullerton had gained several promises from him; one that he would not whip the runaway, the other, that Ben might spend the week. One will promise anything to one's host, especially when that host's cellar is the most famous in six counties.

It was with joyous hearts that Ash-Cake—now Happy—Hannah and Ben watched the departure of Tyler. When he was gone, Ben whooped and cut the pigeon-wing while Hannah, now that the danger was past, uttered a reproving: "You is de beatenes'! I mos' wish he'd 'a tuk you erlong now"; and turned to open her Christmas presents.

Dizzy-Headed Dick

THOSE WERE TROUBLOUS times on the plantation, both for master and for man. The master only should have been concerned; but nothing ever went on at the "big house" that "the quarters" did not feel and know. And they had good reason to know this. The master had been specially irritable that morning, and Dinah told Aunt Fannie that he had driven Jim, the valet, from the room, and had shaved himself—an unprecedented happening, for Bradley Fairfax had never before been known to refuse the delicate attentions of his favorite serving-man.

There was another reason, too, why the quarters should know all about the trouble, for was not Dinah herself the weathervane whose gyrations in the quarters had only to be watched to know which way the wind blew at the big house, and when Big Ben from the Norton plantation came over to visit her Emily, as he had been doing for a year past, had she not driven him from the place?

"I ain't a raisin' darters," she said indignantly, "to th'ow away on de likes o' dem No'ton niggahs; w'en Em'ly m'ay, I spec' huh to look fu' biggah game in tallah trees."

"But, Dinah," said Aunt Fannie, "yo' been lettin' Ben gallant Em'ly right erlong fu' mos' nigh a yeah; huccome yo' done change so quick?"

Dinah turned upon her interlocutor the look of disgust which is only possible with a matchmaking matron as she replied: "La, A'nt Fannie, chile, you don' know? I let huh go 'long o' him case I hadn't 'skivered yit dat de niggah had any 'tentions. Soon ez I did, I made him faihly fly."

Aunt Fannie laughed significantly, because she knew her people so well, and said with apparent irrelevance: "I ain't seed Mas' Tawm No'ton up to de big house fu' a day er so."

It was irrelevant, but confidential.

"Heish, honey; Mas' Bradley done driv' him away too long 'go to talk 'bout. He 'lows how ef Mis' Marg'et cain't find no bettah match fu' huhse'f dan Tawm No'ton she kin des' be a ol' maid, lak huh A'nt Marg'et."

"Whut's de mattah wid Mas' Tawm? He good quality an' mighty well off?"

"Whut's de mattah? W'y, he wil' ez a young deeh; whut wid hoss-racin' an' gwine down de ribber to Noo O'leans, he des' taihin' up awful Jack!"

"But hol' on; I don' see de rights o' dat. Ol' Phœbe say dat Mas' hisse'f was one o' de hoss-racin'est, travelin'-erroun'est young mans in de country w'en he was a-comin' erlong."

"Sh-sh; maybe he done been dat, but den Mas' he settled down."

"Den w'y don' he give Mas' Tawm a chanst? A hoss got to be a colt fus', ain't he?"

"Look hyeah, A'nt Fannie, whut's de mattah'd you? I don't keer ef a hoss uz got to be a colt fus'; nobody ain't gwine to buy no colt w'en he want a ca'ige hoss."

"No, indeedy, an' yo' cain't tell me! No ca'ige hoss ain't gwine to 'mount to nuffin' 'less'n he been a purty lively colt."

"Go 'long, A'nt Fannie!"

"Clah out, Dinah!"

Aunt Fannie was wiser than she seemed. She was the cook for the big house, and from the vantage ground of her kitchen, which sat just a little way off the back veranda, she saw many things. Besides, her son Dick was a house boy, and he told her others.

She and Dick had special reasons for loving and cherishing the young Miss Margaret, for, when angry at some misdemeanor of the black boy's, Bradley Fairfax had threatened to sell him down the river, it had been the young woman's prayers rather than Aunt Fannie's wailings that had turned him from his determination. So they worshiped her, and Dick would have died for her.

On the day that the storm rose to its height Dick slipped down to his mother's kitchen with the news.

"Whut's de mattah'd you, Dick?" asked his mother.

"Sh, mammy, but dey's goin's on up dah."

"Wha kin' o' gwine on, huh?"

"I hyeahd Mas' Bradley talkin' to young Mis' dis mo'nin', an' I tell you fu' a little w'ile it was mannahs."

"Whut'd he say to my little lammy?"

"Dey was talkin' 'bout Mas' Tawm No'ton, an' she tol' him dat Mas' Tawm wasn't so wil' ez he used to be, an' he uz a-settlin' down. Mas' he up an' said dat Tawm No'ton didn't come o' a settlin-down fambly, an' dey wouldn't be no weddin' in his house 'tween huh an' a No'ton. Den she ax him ef he an' Mas' Tawm's pa wa'n't great frien's w'en dey was young, an he say, c'ose; but dey had come to de pa'tin' o' de ways long befo' ol' man Tawm No'ton died.

"Mis' Marg'et, she 'plied up, 'Well, fathah, I hope you won't fo'ce yo' darter to steal away lak a thief in de night to ma'y de man she loves.'"

"'I ain't 'fraid,' ol' Mas' says; 'no Fairfax lady have evah done dat.' 'Den watch th'oo de day,' she answeh back, an' den I didn't hyeah no mo'. It 'pears lak to me Mas' Bradley ain't so sot ag'in Mas' Tawm No'ton, case he come out purty soon an' kicked Jim, an' w'en he right mad he don't ac' dat a-way. Seem lak he des' kin' o' whimsy an' stubbo'n; but it's goin' to mek somep'n happen."

"How yo' know whut it gwine to do?"

"'Case I saw Mis' Marg'et ride down to de big gate, an' w'en she thought nobody was lookin' tek a lettah out o' de post, an' w'en she rode back huh lips was a-set in de Fairfax way, so I'm gwine to keep my eye peeled th'oo de day."

"Oomph, is dat all you know?"

"Yes'm."

"Well, you clah out, you black rascal; you been eavesdrappin' ag'in, dat's whut you been doin'. You ought to be ashamed o' yo'se'f. Don' you come hyeah a'tellin' me no mo' o' yo' eavesdrappin' trash; clah out!"

"Yes'm, I'm a-goin', but you keep yo' eahs open, mammy, an' yo' eyes, too; an' mammy, 'membah hit's ouah Mis' Marg'et!"

"Clah out, I tell you!" and Dick went his way. "Ouah Mis' Marg'et; sic himpidence!" mused the old woman as she began to beat the dough for the biscuits; "ouah Mis' Marg'et—my po' little lamb!"

If Tom Norton had only known it, he had two strong allies in any designs he might have.

Aunt Fannie affected to ignore Dick's injunctions. Nevertheless, in the ensuing days she followed his advice and kept her eyes open. They were so wide open and so busy with diverse things that on two mornings she sent in burned biscuits to the big house, and was like to lose her reputation.

However, all waiting must sometime end, and Aunt Fannie's watchfulness was rewarded when she saw one morning a carriage and pair dash up the front drive, circle the house, and halt at the back veranda.

"I couldn't mek out whut was de mattah," she afterward told Dinah, "w'en I seed dat ca'ige flyin' roun' de house widout stoppin'; den all of a suddint I seed my lammy come a'runnin' out wid a mantilly ovah huh haid, an' I look at de ca'ige ag'in, an' lo an' behol'; dah stood young Mas' Tawm No'ton, hol'in' out his ahms to huh. She runned right past de kitchen, an' whut you think dat blessed chile do? She stop an' fling huh ahms roun' my ol' naik an' kiss me, an' hit's de livin trufe, I'd 'a' died fu' huh right dah. She wa'n't no mo' den ha'f way to de ca'ige w'en ol' Mas' come des' a-ragin' an' a-sto'min' to de do', an' Lawd, chile, 'fo' I knowed it I was a-hollerin', 'Run, baby, run!' She did run, too, an' Mas' Tawm he run to meet huh and tuk huh by de han'.

"Den I seed my Dick runnin', too, an' I hyeahed Mas' Bradley hollah: 'Cut de traces, Dick, cut de traces!' I stepped back an' reached fu' my meat cleavah. Ef dat boy'd 'a' teched dem traces I's mighty 'feahed I'd 'a' th'owed it at him an' cut ouah 'lationship in two, but I see Mis' Marg'et tu'n an' look back ovah huh shoulder der at him des' as she step in de ca'ige. She gin him a kin' o' 'pealin look, but hit a 'fidin' look, too, an' all of a suddint dat rascal's han's went up in de aih an' he fell flat on de grass. Ol' Mas' kept a'screamin' to him to cut de traces, but c'ose, 'fo' he could git up de hosses was a-sailin' down de road, an' Mis' Marg'et was a'wavin' huh han' kin' o' sad lak outen de ca'ige windah; but la' Mas' Tawm gin one look at Dick a-layin dah in de grass an' faihly split his sides wid laffin'. De las' I seed o' dem ez dey made de tu'n he was still a'hol'in' hisse'f."

"Well, Mas' Bradley he come a sto'min' down an' kick Dick. 'Git up,' he say, 'git up, you black scoun'el, 'an' Dick raise his haid kin' o' weak lak, an' say 'Huh?' Well, I lak to died; I didn't know de boy had so much dev'ment in him.

"Ol Mas' he grab him an' yank him up, an' he say: 'W'yn't you cut dem traces?' An' Dick he look up an' 'ply, des' ez innercent: 'W'y, Mas' Bradley, I was tuk wid sich a dizz'ness in my haid all o' de sudden hit seemed lak I was tu'nin' roun' and roun'.'

"'I give you dizz'ness in yo' haid,' ol' Mas' hollah; 'tek him up on de po'ch an' tie him to one o' dem pillahs!' So Bob an' Jim tuk him up an' tied him to one o' de pillahs, an' ol' Mas' went inter de house."

Here Dinah broke in: "I was in dah w'en he comed. Me an' ol' Mis' had des' got back f'om town, an' Mas' Bradley he say, 'Well, a fellah dat'll drive right up in a man's ya'd an' tek his darter f'om under his nose mus' have some'p'n in him,' an' ol' Mis' she laff an' cry altogethah. I spec' she uz in de secret. I ain' so down on Big Ben ez I was."

"La, Dinah, you is de beatenes'—But wait; lemme tell you—"

"Don' I know de res'?"

"You don't know 'bout de coffee?"

"No; whut 'bout de coffee?"

"Aftah w'ile Mas' Bradley sent a whole string o' little darkies down to my kitchen an' mek me give each of 'em a cup o' coffee; den he ma'ched 'em all in line up to Dick an' mek him drink all de coffee.

"'Whut you want me drink all dis coffee fu'?' Dick say, an' Mas' Bradley he look mighty se'ious an' 'ply: 'I's tryin' to cuoah dat dizzy haid o' yo'n.' Well, suh, I wish't yo'd 'a' hyeahed dem little rascallions. Dey des' rolled on de grass an' hollahed, 'Dizzy-haided Dick! Dizzy-haided Dick!' an' Mas' he tu'ned an' went in de house. I reckon dat name'll stick to de boy 'twell he die; but I don't keer, he didn't go back on his young Mis', dizzy haid er no dizzy haid, an' Mas' Bradley he gwine fu'give de young folks anyhow. Ef he ain't, huccome he didn't taih Dick all to pieces?"

The Conjuring Contest

THE WHOLE PLANTATION was shocked when it became generally known that Bob, who had been going with Viney for more than a year, and for half that time had publicly escorted her to and from meeting, had suddenly changed, and bestowed his affections upon another. It was the more surprising, for Viney was a particularly good-looking girl, while the new flame, Cassie, was an ill-favored woman lately brought over from another of the Mordaunt plantations.

It was one balmy Sunday evening that they strolled up from the quarters' yard together, arm in arm, and set wagging the tongues of all their fellow-servants.

Bob's mother, who was sitting out in front of her door, gave a sigh as her son passed with his ungainly sweetheart. She was still watching them with an unhappy look in her eyes when Mam' Henry, the plantation oracle, approached and took a seat on the step beside her.

"Howdy, Mam' Henry," said Maria.

"Howdy, Maria, how you come on?"

"Oh, right peart in my body, but I'm kin' o' 'sturbed in my min'."

"Huh, I reckon you is 'sturbed in yo' min'!" said the old woman keenly. "Maria, you sholy is one blin' 'ooman."

"Blin'? I don't know whut you mean, Mam' Henry; how's I blin'?"

"You's blin', I tell you. Now, whut you s'pose de mattah wid yo' Bob?"

"De mattah wid him? Dat des' whut trouble my min'. Mam' Henry, hit's to think dat dat boy o' mine 'u'd be so thickle-minded!"

"Uh!"

"Hyeah he was a-gwine 'long o' Viney, whut sholy is a lakly gal, an' a peart one, too; den all o' a sudden he done change his min', an' tek up wid dat ol' ha'd-time lookin' gal. I don' know whut he t'inkin' 'bout."

"You don' know whut he t'inkin' 'bout? Co'se you don' know whut he t'inkin' 'bout, an' I don' know whar yo' eyes is, dat you can't see somep'n' dat's des' ez plain ez de nose on yo' face."

"Well, I 'low I mus' be blin', Mam' Henry, 'ca'se I don' understan' it."

"Whut you reckon a lakly boy lak Bob see on dat gallus niggah?"

"I don' know, Mam' Henry, but dey do say she bake mighty fine biscuits, an' you know Bob's min' moughty close to his stomach."

"Biscuits, biscuits," snorted the old woman; "'tain't no biscuits got dat man crazy. Hit's roots, I tell you, hit's roots!"

"Mam' Henry, fo' de Lawd, you don' mean—"

The old woman leaned solemnly over to her companion and whispered dramatically: "He's conju'ed, dat's whut he is!"

Maria sprang up from the doorway and stood gazing at Mam' Henry like a startled animal, then she said in a hurried voice: "Whut! dat huzzy conju' my chile? I—I—I'll kill huh; dat's whut I will."

"Yes, you kill huh, co'se you will. I reckon dat'll tek de spell offen Bob, won't hit? Dat'll kep him f'om hatin' you, an' des pinin' erway an' dyin' fu' huh, won't hit, uh?"

Maria sank down again in utter helplessness, crying: "Conju'ed, conju'ed; oh, whut shell I do?"

"Fus' t'ing," said Mam' Henry, "you des set up an' ac' sensible. Aftah dat I'll talk to you."

"Go on, Mam' Henry; I's a-listenin' to you. Conju'ed, conju'ed, my boy! Oh, de—"

"Heish up, an' listen to me. Befo' Bob put on his shoes termorrer mornin' you slip a piece o' silvah in de right one, flat in de middle, whah he won' feel it. You want to fin' out how he's conju'ed, an' des' how bad it is. Ef she ain't done nuffin' but planted somep'n' roun' de do' fu' him, why I reckon des' sowin' salt'll brek de spell; but ef she's cotch him in his eatin's you'll have to see a reg'lar conju' doctah fo' you kin wo'k dat out. I ain't long-haided myse'l; but I got a frien' dat is."

"But, Mam' Henry, how I gwine tell how bad de conju' is?"

"Huh, gal, you don' know nuffin'! Ef de silvah tu'ns right black, w'y, he's cotched bad, an' ef it only tu'ns kin' o' green he's only middlin' tricked."

"How long I got to wait 'fo' I knows?"

"Let him wah de silvah th'ee er fo' days, an' den let me see it."

Maria did as she was told, placing a dime in the bottom of her son's shoe, and at the expiration of the allotted time, with eyes fear and wonder wide, she took the coin to her instructor. Whether from working in the field all day the soil had ground into Bob's shoe and discolored the coin, or whether it had attracted some subtle poison from the wearer's body, is not here to be decided. From some cause the silver piece was as dark as copper.

Mam' Henry shook her head over it. "He sho' is cotched bad," she said. "I reckon she done cotched him in his eatin's; dat de wuss kin'. You tek dat silvah piece an' th'ow it in de runnin' watah."

Maria hesitated; this was part of a store she was saving for a particular purpose.

"W'y does I has to do dat, Mam' Henry?" she asked. "Ain' dey no othah way?"

"Go 'long, gal; whut's de mattah wid you? You do ez I tell you. Don' you know dat anyt'ing you buy wid dat money'd be bad luck to you? Dat ah dime's chuck full o' goophah, clah to de rim."

So, trembling with fear, Maria hastened to the branch and threw the condemned coin into it, and she positively asserted to Mam' Henry on her return that the water had turned right black and thick where the coin sunk.

"Now, de nex' t'ing fu' you to do is to go down an' see my frien', de conju' doctah. He live down at de fo'ks o' de road, des' back o' de ol' terbaccer house. Hit's a skeery place, but you go dah ter-night, an' tell him I sont you, an' he lif' de spell. But don' you go down dah offerin' to pay him nuffin', 'ca'se dat 'stroy his cha'ms. Aftah de wo'k done, den you gin him whut you want, an' ef it ain't enough he put de spell back on ergin. But mustn' nevah ax a conju' doctah whut he chawge, er pay him 'fo' de cha'm wo'k, no mo'n you mus' say thanky fu' flowah seed."

About nine that night, Maria, frightened and trembling, presented herself at the "conju' doctah's" door. The hut itself was a gruesome looking place, dark and dilapidated. The yard surrounding it was overrun with a dense growth of rank weeds which gave forth a sickening smell as Maria's feet pressed them. The front window was shuttered, and the sagging roof sloped down to it, like the hat of a drunken man over a bruised eye.

The mew of a cat, the shuffling of feet and a rattle of glass followed the black woman's knock, and Maria pictured the terrible being within hastening to put away some of his terrible decoctions before admitting her. She was so afraid that she had decided to turn and flee, leaving Bob to his fate, when the door opened and the doctor stood before her.

He was a little, wizened old man, his wrinkled face the color of parchment. The sides of his head were covered with a bush of gray hair, while the top was bald and blotched with brown and yellow spots. A black cat was at his side, looking with evil eyes at the visitor.

"Is you de conju' doctah?" asked Maria.

He stepped back that she might enter, and closed the door behind her. "I's Doctah Bass," he replied.

"I come to see you—I come to see you 'bout my son. Mam' Henry, she sont me."

"'Well, le' m' hyeah all erbout it." His manner was reassuring, if his looks were not, and somewhat encouraged, Maria began to pour forth the story of her woes into the conjure doctor's attentive ear. When she was done he sat for a while in silence, then he said:

"I reckon she's got some o' his ha'r—dat meks a moughty strong spell in a 'ooman's han's. You go back an' bring me some o' de' 'ooman's ha'r, an' I fix it, I fix it."

"But how's I gwine git any o' huh ha'r?"

"Dat ain' fu' me to say; I des' tell you whut to do."

Maria backed out of the bottle-filled, root-hung room, and flew home through the night, with a thousand terrors pressing hard upon her heels.

All next day she wondered how she could get some of her enemy's hair. Not until evening did the solution of the problem come to her, and she smiled at its simplicity. When Cassie, her son's unwelcome sweetheart, came along, she stepped out from her cabin door and addressed her in terms that could mean but one thing —fight. Cassie attacked Maria tooth and nail, but Maria was a wiry little woman, and when Bob separated the two a little later his mother was bruised but triumphant, for in her hand she held a generous bunch of Cassie's hair.

"You foun' out a way to git de ha'r," said the conjure doctor to her that night, "an' you ain't spaihed no time a-gittin' it."

He was busy compounding a mixture which looked to Maria very much like salt and ashes. To this he added a brown thing which looked like the dried liver of some bird. Then he put in a portion of Cassie's hair. The whole of this he wrapped up in a snake's skin and put in a bag.

"Dat'll fetch him," he said, handing the bag to Maria. "You tek dis an' put it undah his baid whah he won' fin' it, an' sprinkle de res' o' dis ha'r on de blanket he lay on, an' let hit stay dah seven days. Aftah dat he come roun' all right. Den you kin come to see me," he added significantly.

Clasping her treasure, Maria hastened home and placed the conjure bag under her son's bed, and sprinkled the short, stiff hair as she had been directed. He came in late that night, hurried out of his clothes and leaped into bed. Usually he went at once to sleep, but not so now. He rolled and tossed, and it was far past midnight before his regular breathing signified to the listening mother that he was asleep. Then with a murmured, "De conju' is a-wokin' him," she turned over and addressed herself to rest.

The next morning Bob was tired and care-worn, and when asked what was the matter, responded that his dreams had been troubled. He was so tired when the day's work was over that he decided not to go and see Cassie that night. He was just about going to bed when a tap came at the cabin door, and Viney came in.

"Evenin', A'nt Maria," she said; "evenin', Bob."

"Evenin'," they both said.

"I des' run in, A'nt Maria, to bring you some o' my biscuits. Mam' Henry done gi' me a new 'ceipt fu' mekin' dem." She uncovered the crisp, brown rolls, and the odor of them reached Bob's nose. His eyes bulged, and he paused with his hand on his boot.

"La," said Maria, "dese sho' is nice, Viney. He'p yo'se'f, Bob."

Bob suddenly changed his mind about going to bed, and he and Viney sat and chatted while the biscuits disappeared. Maria discreetly retired, and she said to herself as she sat outside on the step: "Dey ain't no way fu' dat boy to 'sist dat goophah an' dem biscuits, too."

Bob's dreams were troubled again that night, and the next, and as the evenings came he still found himself too tired to go a-courting. All this was not lost on the watchful mother, and she duly reported matters to Mam' Henry, who transferred her information to Cassie in the following manner:

"Hit sholy don' seem right, Sis' Cassie, w'en Bob gwine 'long o' you, fu' him to be settin' up evah night 'long o' dat gal Viney."

And Cassie, who was a high-spirited girl, replied:

"Uh, let de niggah go 'long; I don' keer nuffin' 'bout him."

Next time she met Bob she passed without speaking to him, and, strange to say, he laughed, and didn't seem to care, for Mam' Henry's biscuit receipt had made Viney dearer to him than she had ever been. Up until the eighth night his dreams continued to be troubled, but on that night he slept easily, and dreamed of Viney, for Maria had removed the conjure bag and had thrown it into running water. What is more, she had shaken the hair out of the blanket.

The first evening that Bob felt sufficiently rested to go out skylarking it was with Viney he walked, and the quarters nodded and wondered. They walked up to the master's house, where the momentous question was asked and favorably answered. Then they came back radiant, and Viney set out some biscuits and preserves in her cabin to clinch it, and invited Maria and Mam' Henry to share them with Bob and her.

That night sundry things from the big house, as well as lesser things from Maria's cabin found their way to the "conju' doctah's." The things from the big house were honestly procured, but it took the telling of the whole story by Maria to get them.

When she had gone, her master, Dudley Stone, laughed to himself, and said with true Saxon incredulity: "That old rascal, Bass, is a sharp one. I think lying on Cassie's hair would trouble anybody's dreams, conjure or no conjure, and if Viney learned to make biscuits like Mammy Henry she needed no stronger charm."

Dandy Jim's Conjure Scare

DANDY JIM WAS very much disturbed when he came in that morning to shave his master. He was Dandy Jim, because being just his master's size, he came in for the spruce garments which Henry Desmond cast off. The dark-skinned valet took great pride in his personal appearance, and was little less elegant than the white man himself. He was such a dapper black boy, and always so light and agile on his feet that his master looked up in genuine surprise when he came in this morning looking care-worn and dejected, and walking with a decided limp.

To the question, "Why, what on earth is the matter with you, Jim?" he answered only with a doleful shake of his head.

"Why, you look like you'd been getting religion."

"No, I ain't quite as bad as dat, Mas' Henry. Religion 'fects de soul, but hits my body dats 'fected."

"You've been getting your feet wet, I reckon, and it's cold."

"I wish 'twas; I wish 'twas," said Jim sadly.

"You wish it was? Well, what is the matter with you?"

"Mas' Henry, kin you let me have a silver dime? I's been hurted."

"Jim!"

"I tell you I's been tricked."

"And you believe in that sort of thing after all I've tried to teach you?"

"Mas' Henry, I tell you, I's been tricked. Dey ain't no 'sputin' de signs, teachin' er no teachin'!"

"Well, I wish you'd tell me the signs so that I'd know them. It's just possible that I may have been tricked some time and didn't know it."

"Don' joke, Mas' Henry, don' joke. Dis is a se'ious mattah, an' 'f you'd 'a' evah been tricked an' hit doneright, you'd 'a' knowed, case dey 'ain't no 'sputin' de symptoms. Dey's mighty well known. W'en a body's tricked, dey's tricked, an' dat's de gospel truf."

"Do you claim to know them?"

"Don' I tell you I's a sufferin' f'om dem now?"

"Well, what are they?"

"Well, fu' one t'ing, I's got a mighty mis'ry in my back, an' I got de limb trim-bles, an' I's des creepy all ovah in spots, dat's a sho' sign, whenevah you feels spot-ted. I tells you, Mas' Henry, somebody's done laid fu' me an' cotch me. I wish you'd please, suh, gimme a piece o' silvah to lay on de place."

"What will that do?"

"W'y, I wants to be right sho', fo' I goes to a conju' doctah, an' ef I is tricked, de silvah, hit'll show it, 'dout a doubt. Hit'll tu'n right black."

"Jim," said the white man, as he handed over the silver coin, "I've never known you to talk this way before, and I believe you've got some other reason for believing you're conjured besides the ones you've given me. You rascal, you've been up to something."

The valet grinned sheepishly, hung his head and shuffled his feet in a way that instantly confessed judgment.

"Come, own up now," pressed his master, "what devilment have you been up to?"

"I don' see how it's any dev'ment fu' a body to go to see de gal he like."

"Uh-huh, you've been after somebody else's girl, have you? And he's fixed you, eh?"

"I didn't know 'Lize was goin' 'long o' anybody else 'twell I went in thaih de othah night to see huh, an' even den, she nevah let on nuffin'. We talked erlong, an' laughed, an' was havin' a mighty fine time. You see 'Lize, she got a powahful drawin' way erbout huh. I kep' on settin' up nighah an' nighah to huh, an' she kep' laughin', but she nevah hitched huh cheer away, so co'se I thought hit was all right, an' dey wa'nt nobody else a-keepin' comp'ny wid huh. W'en, lo, an' behol', des' as I was erbout to put my ahm erroun' huh wais', who should walk in de do' but one dem gret big, red-eyed fiel'-han's. Co'se I drawed erway, fu' dat man sho' did look dan-g'ous. Well, co'se, a gent'man got to show his mannahs, so I ups an' says, 'Good-evenin', suh,' an' meks my 'bejunce. Oomph, dat man nevah answered no mo'n I'd been a knot on a log, an' him anothah. Den 'Lize she up an say, 'Good evenin', Sam,' an' bless yo' soul, ef he didn't treat huh de same way. He des' went ovah in de cornder an' sot down an' thaih he sot, a-lookin' at us wid dem big red eyes o' his'n a-fai'ly blazin'! Well, I seed dat 'Lize was a-gittin' oneasy, an' co'se, hit ain't nevah perlite to be a inconwenience to a lady, so I gits up an' takes my hat, an' takes my departer."

"The fact, in other words, is, you ran from the man."

"No, suh, a pusson couldn't 'zactly say I run. I did come erway kind o' fas', but you see, I was thinkin' 'bout 'Lize's feelin's an' hit seemed lak ef I'd git out o' de way, it'd relieve de strain."

"Yes, your action does great credit to your goodness of heart and your respect for your personal safety, Jim."

Jim flashed a quick glance up into his master's face. He did not like to be laughed at, but his eyes met nothing but the most serious of expressions, so he went on: "Dat uz two nights ago, an' evah sence den, I been feelin' mighty funny. I des' mo'n 'low dat Sam done laid fu'me, an' cotch me in de back an' laig. You know, Mas' Henry, dem ah red-eyed people, dey mighty dang'ous, an' it don' do nobody no good to go 'long a-foolin' wid 'em. Ef I'd 'a' knowed dat Sam was a 'long o' 'Lize, I sholy would 'a' fed 'em bofe wid a long spoon. I do' want nobody plantin' t'ings fu' me."

"Jim, you're hopeless. Here I've tried my best to get that conjuring notion out of your head. You've been brought up right here in the house with me for three or four years, and now the first thing that happens, you fall right back to those old beliefs that would be unworthy of your African grandfather."

"Mas' Henry, I ain' goin' to 'spute none o' yo' teachin's, an' I ain' goin' to argy wid you, 'case you my mastah, an' it wouldn' be perlite, but I des' got one t'ing to say, dat piece o' silvah you gi' me, 'll tell de tale."

The valet now having finished his work and his complaints, went his way, leaving his master a bit disgusted, and a good deal amused. "These great overgrown children," he mused, "still frightened by fairy tales."

It was late in the afternoon before the master saw his servant again. Then he opened his eyes in astonishment at him.

Henry Desmond was sitting on the porch, when the black man hove in sight. He would have slipped round to the back of the house and entered that way had not his master called to him. Dandy Jim, a dandy no longer, approached and stood before his speechless owner. He was a figure for gods and men to behold. He was covered with dirt from head to foot. His clothes looked as though he might have changed raiment with an impoverished scarecrow. One sleeve was gone out of his coat, and the leg of his trousers was ripped from the knee down. A half a dozen scratches and bruises disfigured his face, and when he walked, it was with a limp more decidedly genuine than the one of the morning. But the feature that utterly surprised Henry Desmond, that took away his speech for a moment or two, was the beautiful smile that sat on Jim's countenance.

The master finally found his voice, "Jim, what on earth is the matter? You look like a storm had struck you."

"Oh, Mas' Henry, I ain' conjuahed, I ain' conjuahed!"

"You ain't conjured? Well, you look a good deal more like you'd been conjured than you did this morning. I should take it for granted that a whole convention of witches and hoodoos had sat on your case."

"No suh, no suh, I ain' conjuahed a-tall."

"Well, what's the matter with you, then?"

"W'y, suh, I's seed dat red-eyed fiel'-han' Sam, an' he pu't nigh walloped de life out o' me, yes, suh, he did."

"Well, you take it blessed cheerful."

"Dat's becase I knows I ain' conjuahed."

"Didn't the silver turn black? You know it might not have had time yet!"

"Mas' Henry, I ain' bothahed nuffin' 'bout de silvah, I ain' 'pendin' on dat. De reason I knows I ain' conjuahed, Sam, he done whupped me. I was a goin' down to de fiel' 'long 'bout dinnah time, an' who should I meet but Sam. 'Hol' on, Jim,' he say, a settin' down de bucket he was ca'in' to de fiel'. 'Hol' on,' he say, an' I stop 'twell he come up. 'Jim,' he say, 'you was down in the quahtahs a-settin' up to Miss 'Lize night befo' last', wasn't you?' 'Well, I was present,' say I, 'on dat occasion, w'en I had de pleasure o' meetin' you.' 'Nemmine dat, nemmine dat,' he say,' 'I do' want none o' yo' fine wo'ds what you lu'n up to de big house, an' uses crookid down in de quahtahs'; but bless yo' soul, Mas' Henry, dat wa'nt true—'I do' want none o' yo' fine wo'ds'; den he tuk off his hat, an' rolled up his sleeves—he sholy has got awful ahms. 'I's goin' to whup you,' says he, an', well, suh, he did. He whupped me mos' scan'lous. He des' walloped me all ovah de groun'. Oomph, I nevah shell fu'git it! W'y, dat man lak to wo' me out. Seemed lak, w'en he fust sta'ted, he was des' goin' to give me a little dressin' down, but he seemed to waken to de wo'k ez he pu'sued his co'se. W'en he got thoo, he say, 'Now ef evah I ketches you foolin' 'roun' Miss 'Lize agin, I'll brek you all ter pieces.' Den I come away rejoicin' 'case I knowed I wa'nt tricked."

"Well, you're the first man I ever saw rejoice over such a thrashing as you've had. What do you mean? How do you know you're not conjured?"

"W'y, Mas' Henry, what's de use o' conjuahin' a man w'en you can whup him lak dat? Hain't dat enough satisfaction? Dey ain't no need to go 'roun' wo'kin wid roots w'en you got sich fistes ez Sam got."

"But you had so much confidence in the silver this morning. What does the silver say?"

"La, Mas' Henry, aftah Sam whupped me dat 'way I was so satisfied in my min' dat I des' tuk off de silvah an bought lin'ment wid it. You kin cuoah bruises wid lin'ment, an' you allus knows des how to reach de case, but conjuah, dat's dif-f'unt." And Jim limped away to apply his lotion to his sore, but unconjured body.

The Memory of Martha

YOU MAY TALK about banjo-playing if you will, but unless you heard old Ben in his palmy days you have no idea what genius can do with five strings stretched over the sheepskin.

You have been told, perhaps, that the banjo is not an expressive instrument. Well, in the hands of the ordinary player it is not. But you should have heard old Ben, as bending low over the neck, with closed eyes, he made the shell respond like a living soul to his every mood. It sang, it laughed, it sighed; and, just as the tears began welling up into the listener's eyes, it would break out into a merry reel that would set one's feet a-twinkling before one knew it

Ben and his music were the delight of the whole plantation, white and black, master and man, and in the evening when he sat before his cabin door, picking out tune after tune, hymn, ballad or breakdown, he was always sure of an audience. Sometimes it was a group of white children from the big house, with a row of pickaninnies pressing close to them. Sometimes it was old Mas' and Mis' themselves who strolled up to the old man, drawn by his strains. Often there was company, and then Ben would be asked to leave his door and play on the veranda of the big house. Later on he would come back to Martha laden with his rewards, and swelled with the praise of his powers.

And Martha would say to him, "You, Ben, don' you git conceity now; you des' keep yo' haid level. I des' mo'n 'low you been up dah playin' some o' dem ongodly chunes, lak Hoe Co'n an' Dig 'Taters."

Ben would laugh and say, "Well, den, I tek de wickedness offen de banjo. Swing in, ol' 'ooman!" And he would drop into the accompaniment of one of the hymns that were the joy of Martha's religious soul, and she would sing with him until, with a flourish and a thump, he brought the music to an end.

Next to his banjo, Ben loved Martha, and next to Ben, Martha loved the banjo. In a time and a region where frequent changes of partners were common, these two servants were noted for their single-hearted devotion to each other. He had never had any other wife, and she had called no other man husband. Their children had grown up and gone to other plantations, or to cabins of their own. So, alone, drawn closer by the habit of comradeship, they had grown old together—Ben, Martha and the banjo.

One day Martha was taken sick, and Ben came home to find her moaning with pain, but dragging about trying to get his supper. With loud pretended upbraidings he bundled her into bed, got his own supper, and then ran to his master with the news.

"Marfy she down sick, Mas' Tawm," he said, "an' I's mighty oneasy in my min' 'bout huh. Seem lak she don' look right to me outen huh eyes."

"I'll send the doctor right down, Ben," said his master. "I don't reckon it's anything very serious. I wish you would come up to the house to-night with your banjo. Mr. Lewis is going to be here with his daughter, and I want them to hear you play."

It was thoughtlessness on the master's part; that was all. He did not believe that Martha could be very ill; but he would have reconsidered his demand if he could have seen on Ben's face the look of pain which the darkness hid.

"You'll send de doctah right away, Mas'?"

"Oh, yes; I'll send him down. Don't forget to come up."

"I won't fu'git," said Ben as he turned away. But he did not pick up his banjo to go to the big house until the plantation doctor had come and given Martha something to ease her. Then he said: "I's got to go up to de big house, Marfy; I be back putty soon."

"Don' you hu'y thoo on my 'count. You go 'long, an' gin Mas' Tawm good measure, you hyeah?"

"Quit yo' bossin'," said Ben, a little more cheerfully; "I got you whah you cain't move, an' ef you give me any o' yo' back talk I 'low I frail you monst'ous."

Martha chuckled a "go 'long," and Ben went lingeringly out of the door, the banjo in its ragged cover under his arm.

The plantation's boasted musician played badly that night. Colonel Tom Curtis wondered what was the matter with him, and Mr. Lewis told his daughter as he drove away that it seemed as if the Colonel's famous banjoist had been overrated. But who could play reels and jigs with the proper swing when before his eyes was the picture of a smoky cabin room, and on the bed in it a sick wife, the wife of forty years?

The black man hurried back to his cabin where Martha was dozing. She awoke at his step.

"Didn't I tell you not to hu'y back hyeah?" she asked.

"I ain't nevah hu'ied. I reckon I gin 'em all de music dey wanted," Ben answered a little sheepishly. He knew that he had not exactly covered himself with glory. "How's you feelin'?" he added.

"'Bout de same. I got kin' of a mis'ry in my side."

"I reckon you couldn't jine in de hymn to tek de wickedness outen dis ol' banjo?" He looked anxiously at her.

"I don' know 'bout j'inin' in, but you go 'long an' play anyhow. Ef I feel lak journeyin' wid you I fin' you somewhar on de road."

The banjo began to sing, and when the hymn was half through Martha's voice, not so strong and full as usual, but trembling with a new pathos, joined in and went on to the end. Then Ben put up the banjo and went to his rest.

The next day Martha was no better, and the same the next. Her mistress came down to see her, and delegated one of the other servants to be with her through the day and to get Ben's meals. The old man himself was her close attendant in the evenings, and he waited on her with the tenderness of a woman. He varied his duties as nurse by playing to her, sometimes some lively, cheerful bit, but more often the hymns she loved but was now too weak to follow.

It gave him an aching pleasure at his heart to see how she hung on his music. It seemed to have become her very life. He would play for no one else now, and the little space before his door held his audience of white and black children no more. They still came, but the cabin door was inhospitably shut, and they went away whispering among themselves, "Aunt Martha's sick."

Little Liz, who was a very wise pickaninny, once added, "Yes, Aunt Marfy's sick, an' my mammy says she ain' never gwine to git up no mo'." Another child had echoed "Never!" in the hushed, awe-struck tones which children use in the presence of the great mystery.

Liz's mother was right. Ben's Martha was never to get up again. One night during a pause in his playing she whispered, "Play 'Ha'k! F'om de Tomb.'" He turned into the hymn, and her voice, quavering and weak, joined in. Ben started, for she had not tried to sing for so long. He wondered if it wasn't a token. In the midst of the hymn she stopped, but he played on to the end of the verse. Then he got up and looked at her.

Her eyes were closed, and there was a smile on her face—a smile that Ben knew was not of earth. He called her, but she did not answer. He put his hand upon her head, but she lay very still, and then he knelt and buried his head in the bedclothes, giving himself up to all the tragic violence of an old man's grief.

"Marfy! Marfy! Marfy!" he called. "What you want to leave me fu'? Marfy, wait; I ain't gwine be long."

His cries aroused the quarters, and the neighbors came flocking in. Ben was hustled out of the way, the news carried to the big house, and preparations made for the burying

Ben took his banjo. He looked at it fondly, patted it, and, placing it in its covering, put it on the highest shelf in the cabin.

"Brothah Ben allus was a mos' p'opah an' 'sponsible so't o' man," said Liz's mother as she saw him do it. "Now, dat's what I call showin' 'spec' to Sis Marfy, puttin' his banjo up in de ve'y place whah it'll get all dus'. Brothah Ben sho is diff'ent f'om any husban' I evah had." She had just provided Liz with a third stepfather.

On many evenings after Martha had been laid away, the children, seeing Ben come and sit outside his cabin door, would gather around, waiting, and hoping that the banjo would be brought out, but they were always doomed to disappointment. On the high shelf the old banjo still reposed, gathering dust.

Finally one of the youngsters, bolder than the rest, spoke: "Ain't you gwine play no mo', Uncle Ben?" and received a sad shake of the head in reply, and a laconic "Nope."

This remark Liz dutifully reported to her mother. "No, o' co'se not," said that wise woman with emphasis; "o' co'se Brothah Ben ain' gwine play no mo'; not right now, leas'ways; an' don' you go dah pesterin' him, nuther, Liz. You be perlite an' 'spectable to him, an' make yo' 'bejunce when you pass."

The child's wise mother had just dispensed with her latest stepfather.

The children were not the only ones who attempted to draw old Ben back to his music. Even his master had a word of protest. "I tell you, Ben, we miss your banjo," he said. "I wish you would come up and play for us sometime."

"I'd lak to, Mastah, I'd lak to; but evah time I think erbout playin' I kin des see huh up dah an' hyeah de kin' o' music she's a-listenin' to, an' I ain't got no haht fu' dat ol' banjo no mo'."

The old man looked up at his master so pitifully that he desisted.

"Oh, never mind," he said, "if you feel that way about it."

As soon as it became known that the master wanted to hear the old banjo again, every negro on the plantation was urging the old man to play in order to say that his persuasion had given the master pleasure. None, though, went to the old man's cabin with such confidence of success as did Mary, the mother of Liz.

"O' co'se, he wa'n't gwine play den," she said as she adjusted a ribbon; "he was a mo'nin'; but now—hit's diffe'nt," and she smiled back at herself in the piece of broken mirror.

She sighed very tactfully as she settled herself on old Ben's doorstep.

"I nevah come 'long hyeah," she said "widout thinkin' 'bout Sis Marfy. Me an' huh was gret frien's, an' a moughty good frien' she was."

Ben shook his head affirmatively. Mary smoothed her ribbons and continued:

"I ust to often come an' set in my do' w'en you'd be a-playin' to huh. I was des' sayin' to myse'f de othah day how I would lak to hyeah dat ol' banjo ag'in." She paused. "'Pears lak Sis Marfy 'd be right nigh."

Ben said nothing. She leaned over until her warm brown cheek touched his knee. "Won't you play fu' me, Brothah Ben?" she asked pleadingly. "Des' to bring back de membry o' Sis Marfy?"

The old man turned two angry eyes upon her. "I don' need to play," he said, "an' I ain' gwineter. Sis Marfy's membry's hyeah," and tapping his breast he walked into his cabin, leaving Mary to take her leave as best she could.

It was several months after this that a number of young people came from the North to visit the young master, Robert Curtis. It was on the second evening of their stay that young Eldridge said, "Look here, Colonel Curtis, my father visited your plantation years ago, and he told me of a wonderful banjoist you had, and said if I ever came here to be sure to hear him if he was alive. Is he?"

"You mean old Ben? Yes, he's still living, but the death of his wife rather sent him daft, and he hasn't played for several years."

"Pshaw, I'm sorry. We laughed at father's enthusiasm over him, because we thought he overrated his powers."

"I reckon not. He was truly wonderful."

"Don't you think you can stir him up?"

"Oh, do, Col. Curtis," chorused a number of voices.

"Well, I don't know," said the Colonel, "but come with me and I'll try."

The young people took their way to the cabin, where old Ben occupied his accustomed place before the door.

"Uncle Ben," said the master, "here are some friends of mine from the North who are anxious to hear you play, and I knew you'd break your rule for me."

"Chile, honey—" began the old man.

But Robert, his young master, interrupted him. "I'm not going to let you say no," and he hurried past Uncle Ben into the cabin. He came out, brushing the banjo and saying, "Whew, the dust!"

The old man sat dazed as the instrument was thrust into his hand. He looked pitifully into the faces about him, but they were all expectancy. Then his fingers wandered to the neck, and he tuned the old banjo. Then he began to play. He seemed inspired. His listeners stood transfixed.

From piece to piece he glided, pouring out the music in a silver stream. His old fingers seemed to have forgotten their stiffness as they flew over the familiar strings. For nearly an hour he played and then abruptly stopped. The applause was generous and real, but the old man only smiled sadly, and with a far-away look in his eyes.

As they turned away, somewhat awed by his manner, they heard him begin to play softly an old hymn. It was "Hark! From the Tomb."

He stopped when but half through, and Robert returned to ask him to finish, but his head had fallen forward close against the banjo's neck, and there was a smile on his face, as if he had suddenly had a sweet memory of Martha.

Who Stand for the Gods

THERE WAS A warm flush of anger on Robert Curtis' face as he ran down the steps of the old Stuart mansion. Everyone said of this young man that he possessed in a marked degree the high temper for which the family was noted. And one looking at him that night would have said that this temper had been roused to the utmost.

This was not the first time Robert Curtis had ridden away from the Stuarts' in anger. Emily Stuart was a high-strung girl, independent, and impatient of control, and their disagreements had been many. But they had never gone so far as this one, and they had somehow always blown over. This time the young lover had carried away in his pocket the ring with which they had plighted their troth, and had gone away vowing never to darken those doors again, and Emily had been exasperatingly polite and cool, though her eyes were flashing as she assured him how little she ever wanted to look upon his face again.

It may have been the strain of keeping this self-possession that made her break down so completely as soon as her lover was out of sight. That she did break down is beyond dispute, for when Dely came in with a very much disordered waistband she found her mistress in tears.

With the quick sympathy and easy familiarity of a favorite servant she ran to her mistress exclaiming, "La, Miss Em'ly, whut's de mattah?"

Her Miss Emily waved her away silently, and drying her eyes stood up dramatically.

"Dely," she said, "Mr. Curtis will not come here any more after to-day. Certain things have made it impossible. I know that you and Ike are interested in each other, and I do not want the changed relations between Mr. Curtis and me to make any difference to you and Ike."

"La, Miss Em'ly," said Dely, surreptitiously straightening her waistband, "I don' keer nuffin' 'bout Ike; he ain't nuffin' 'tall to me."

"Don't fib, Dely," said Emily impressively.

"'Claih to goodness, Miss Em'ly, I ain't fibbin'; but even if Ike was anyt'ing to me you know I wa'n't nevah 'spectin' to go ovah to the Cu'tis plantatin 'ceptin' wid you, w'en you an' Mas' Bob—"

"That will do, Dely." Emily caught up her handkerchief and hurried from the room.

"Po' Miss Em'ly," soliloquized Dely; "she des natchully breakin' huh hea't now, but she ain't gwine let on. Ike, indeed! I ain't bothahed 'bout Ike," and then she added, smiling softly, "That scamp's des de same ez a b'ah; he mighty nigh ruined my ap'on at de wais'."

Robert Curtis was crossing the footbridge which separated the Curtis and Stuart farther fields before Ike rode up abreast of him. The bay mare was covered with dust and foam, and a heavy scowl lay darkly on the young man's face.

Finding his horse blown by her hard gallop, the white man drew rein, and they rode along more slowly, but in silence. Not a word was spoken until they alighted, and the master tossed the reins to his servant.

"Well," he said bitterly, "when you go to the Stuarts' again, Ike, you'll have to go alone."

"Then I won't go," said Ike promptly.

"Oh, yes, you will; you're fool enough to be hanging around a woman's skirts, too; you'll go."

"Whaih you don' go, I don' go."

"Well, I don't go to the Stuarts' any more, that's one thing certain." Robert was very young.

"Then I don' go," returned Ike doggedly; "don' you reckon I got some fambly feelin's?"

The young man's quick anger was melting in its own heat, and he laughed in spite of himself as he replied: "Neither family feelings nor anything else count for much when there's a woman in the case."

"Now, I des wonder," said Ike, as he led the horses away and turned them over to a stable boy, "I des wonder how long this hyeah thing's goin' on? De las' time they fell out fu' evah hit was fou' whole days befo' he give in. I reckon this time it might run to be a week."

He might have gone on deluding himself thus if he had not suddenly awakened to the fact that more than the week he had set as the limit of the estrangement had passed and he had not yet been commanded to saddle a horse and ride over to the Stuarts' with the note that invariably brought reconciliation and happiness.

He felt disturbed in his mind, and his trouble visibly increased when, on the next day, which was Sunday, Quin, who was his rival in everything, dressed himself with more than ordinary care and took his way toward the Stuarts'.

"Whut's de mattah wid you, Ike?" asked one of the house boys next day; "you goin' to let Quin cut you out? He was ovah to Stua'ts' yistiddy, an' he say he had a ta'in' down time wid Miss Dely."

"Oh, I don' reckon anybody's goin' to cut me out."

"Bettah not be so sho," said the boy; "bettah look out."

This was too much for Ike. He had been wavering; now his determination gave way, yet he tried to delude himself.

"Hit's a shame," he said. "I des know Mas' Bob is bre'kin' his hea't to git back to Miss Em'ly, an' hit do seem lak somep'n 'oughter be done to gin him a chancet."

It needed only the visit from his master that afternoon to decide him. He was out on the back veranda cleaning shoes, when his master came and stood in front of him, flicking his boots with his riding-whip.

"Ah, Ike, you haven't been over to Mr. Stuart's lately."

"No, suh; co'se not; I ain't been ovah."

"Well, I don't believe I'd do that, Ike. Don't let my affair keep you away; you go on and see her. You don't know; she might be sick or something, and want to see you. Here's fifty cents; take her something nice." And with the very erroneous idea that he had fooled both Ike and himself, Robert Curtis went down the steps whistling.

"What'd I tell you?" said Ike, addressing the shoe which sat upon his hand, and he began to hurry.

Dely was sitting on the doorstep of her mother's cabin as Ike came up. She pretended not to see him, but she was dressed as if she expected his coming.

"Howdy, Dely; how you this evenin'?" said Ike.

"La, Mistah Ike," said Dely, affecting to be startled, "I come mighty nigh not seein' you. Won't you walk in?"

"No, I des tek a seat on de do'step hyeah 'longside you."

She tossed her head, but made room for him on the step.

"I ain't seen you fu' sev'al days."

"You wasn' blin' ner lame."

"No, but you know," answered Ike rather doggedly.

"I don know nuffin'," Dely returned.

"I wasn' 'spected to come alone."

"Was you skeered?"

"Did you want me to come alone?"

Dely did not deign to answer.

"I wonder how long this is goin' on?" pursued Ike; "I'm gittin' mighty tiahed of it."

"They ain't no tellin'. Miss Em'ly she mighty high-strung."

"Well, hit's a shame, fu' them two loves one another, an' they ought to be brought togethah."

"Co'se they ought; but how anybody goin' to do it?"

"You an' me could try ef you was willin'."

"I'd do anything fu' my Miss Em'ly."

"An' I'd do anything fu' Mas' Bob. Come an' le's walk down by de big gate an' talk about it."

Dely rose, and together they walked down by the big gate, where they stood in long and earnest conversation. Maybe it was all about their master's and mistress' love affair. But a soft breeze was blowing, and the moon was shining in the way which tempts young people to consider their own hearts, however much they may be interested in the hearts of others.

It was some such interest which ostensibly prompted Robert Curtis to sit up for Ike that night. Ike came into the yard whistling. His master was sitting on the porch.

"Ike, you are happy; you must have had a good time."

Instantly Ike's whistle was cut short, and the late moonlight shone upon a very lugubrious countenance as he answered:

"Sometimes people whistles to drown dey sorrers."

"Why, what sorrows have you got? Wasn't Dely in a pleasant mood?"

"Dely's mighty 'sturbed 'bout huh Miss Em'ly."

"About her Miss Emily!" exclaimed the young master in sudden excitement; "what's the matter with Miss Emily?"

"Oh, Dely says she des seems to be a-pinin' 'bout somep'n'. She don' eat an' she don' sleep."

"Poor litt—" began Curtis, then he checked himself. "Hum," he said. "Well, good-night, Ike."

When Ike had gone in, his master went to his room and paced the floor for a long while. Then he went out again and walked up and down the lawn. "Maybe I'm not treating her just right," he murmured; "poor little thing, but—" and he clenched his fist and kept up his walking.

"Ike was here to-night?" said Miss Emily to Dely as the maid was brushing her hair that night.

"Yes'm, he was hyeah."

"Yes, I saw him come up the walk early, and I didn't call you because I knew you'd want to talk to him," she sighed.

"Yes'm, he wanted to talk mighty bad. He feelin' mighty 'sturbed 'bout his Mas' Bob."

The long, brown braid was quickly snatched out of her hand as her young mistress whirled swiftly round.

"What's the matter with his master?"

"Oh, Ike say he des seem to pine. He don' seem to eat, an' he don' sleep."

Miss Emily had a sudden fit of dreaming from which she awoke to say, "That will do, Dely; I won't need you any more to-night." Then she put out her light and leaned out of her window, looking with misty eyes at the stars. And something she saw up there in the bright heavens made her smile and sigh again.

It was on the morrow that Dely told her mistress about some wonderful wild flowers that were growing in the west woods in a certain nook, and Dely was so much in earnest about it that her mistress finally consented to follow her thither.

Strange to say, that same morning Ike accosted his young master with, "Look hyeah, Mas' Bob, de birds is sholy thick ovah yondah in that stretch o' beechwoods. I've polished up the guns fu' you, ef you want to tek a shot."

"Well, I don't mind, Ike. We'll go for a while."

It was in this way—quite by accident, of course, one looking for strange flowers, and the other for birds—that Emily and Robert, with their faithful attendants, set out for the same stretch of woods.

Miss Emily was quite despairing of ever finding the wonderful flowers, and Ike was just protesting that he himself had "seen them birds," when all of a sudden Dely exclaimed: "Well, la! Ef thaih ain't Mas' Cu'tis."

Miss Emily turned pale and red by turns as Robert, blushing like a girl, approached her, hat in hand.

"Miss Emily."

"Mr. Curtis."

Then they both turned to look for their attendants. Ike and Dely were walking up a side path together. They both broke into a laugh that would not be checked.

"It would be a shame to disturb them," Robert went on when he could control himself. "Emily, I've been a—"

"Oh, Robert!"

"Let us take the good that the gods provide."

"And they," said Emily, looking after the blacks, "stand for the gods."

A Lady Slipper

ON THAT PARTICULAR night in June it pleased Miss Emily Stuart to be gracious to Nelson Spencer. Robert Curtis was away, attending court at the county seat, and really, when one is young and beautiful and a woman, it is absolutely necessary that there should be some person upon whom to try one's charms. So the lady was gracious to her ardent, but oft-rejected lover. She was sitting on the step of the high veranda and he a little below her. Her tiny foot, shod in the daintiest of slippers, swung dangerously near him. She knew that he was looking admiringly at the glimpse of pointed toe which now and then he got from beneath her skirt, and it pleased her. She was rather proud of that pretty, aristocratic foot of hers, not so much because it was pretty and aristocratic as because it was hereditary in the family and belonged by right of birth to all the Stuarts.

It was a warm, soft night, a night just suited for love and dreams. The sky like a blue-black cup inverted, seemed pouring a shower of gems upon the earth, and the breeze was laden with the sweet smell of honeysuckle and the heavier odor of magnolia blossoms.

They were not talking much because it wasn't worthwhile. After an extended period of silence he looked up at her and sighed, perhaps because he wanted to, maybe because he couldn't help it.

"What are you sighing for?" she asked.

"Oh, just at the beauty of things."

"Why, that should make you smile."

"Not always. If there is sometimes a grief too deep for tears, there is at others a joy too great for smiles."

"You ought to have been a poet, Nelson, you are so sentimen—"

"Spare me that."

"No I shall not. You are sentimental to the last degree."

"Oh, well, I may be; if it is sentimentality to be willing to grovel in the dirt for a lady's slipper, then I am sentimental." Emily Stuart laughed.

"You know you would look very ridiculous groveling in the dirt. Would you really do it for my slipper?"

"Yes"

"I'll put you to the test, then; you shall have my slipper when I see you grovel."

He hesitated. "What," she laughed, "am I too literal?"

"No," he said; "I mean what I say," and he leaped from the porch to the road beyond and fell upon his knees in the dust of the carriageway.

The spectacle amused Emily, and disgusted her no little. A woman pretends that she wants a man to abase himself before her, but she never forgives him if he does. While he knelt there in the road she thought how differently Robert would have acted under the circumstances. Instead of groveling, he would probably have said, "I'll be hanged if I do," and she rather liked the thought of his saying that. She knew that so far as brains went, Robert could not compare with Nelson; she knew, too, that the wisest man has the greatest capacity for making a fool of himself.

After an interval, Nelson arose from his position and came back to the veranda.

"I claim my reward," he said.

"Do you think you can rightly call that groveling?"

"Yes, without a doubt."

"Then you shall not go unrewarded," and, turning, she went into the house to return with a slipper, a dainty little beribboned thing, which she handed to him. She was quite used to his extravagant protestations, and only thought to put a light significance upon his words. She was unprepared, then, to see him put the slipper into his pocket as if he really meant to keep it.

The evening passed away, and though they talked much, no reference was made to the slipper until he rose to go. Then Emily said, "Has your desire for my slipper been sufficiently satisfied?"

"Oh, no," he replied, "I shall keep this as the outward sign and the reward of my abasement."

"You are really not going to keep it?"

"Oh, but I am. You gave it to me."

"I did not mean it in that way."

"The sight of me groveling there in the road I gave you to remember for all time, and the gift that I ask in return is a permanent one."

"And it is of no use for me to argue with you?"

"None."

"Nor plead?"

"No."

"Very well," said Emily with a vain effort at calmness, "I wish you joy of your treasure. Good-night," and she went into the house. But she watched him from behind the curtain until he was quite gone; then she came flying out again and made her way hastily toward the quarters whither she knew her maid Dely had gone to spend the evening. When she had brought her to the big house, she exclaimed breathlessly:

"Oh, Dely, Dely, I am in such trouble!"

"Do tell we what is de mattah now?"

"Oh, Nelson Spencer has been here and—"

"Miss Em'ly," Dely broke in, "you been ca'in on wid dat man agin?"

"Why, Dely, how can you say such things? Carrying on, indeed! I was only trying to put him in his place by making him ridiculous, but I gave him my slipper, and he—he kept it."

"He got yo' slippah? Miss Em'ly, don' tell me dat."

"Oh, what shall I do, Dely, what shall I do? Suppose Robert should go there and see it on his bureau or somewhere—you know they are such friends—what would he say? He'd be bound to recognize it, you know. They're the ones with the silver buckles and satin bows that he liked so well. One could never explain to Robert; he's so impetuous. Dely, don't stand there that way. You must help me."

"What shell I do, Miss Em'ly? I reckon you'd bettah go an' have yo' pa frail dat slippah outen him."

"What? Papa? Why, I wouldn't have him to know anything about it for the world."

"Why, it ain't yo' fault, Miss Em'ly; you in de rights of de thing."

"Oh, yes, yes, I know, but a thing like that is so hard to explain. Dely, you must get that slipper."

"How I'm goin' to?"

"I don't know; you'll have to find some way. You'll find some way to get it before Robert comes. You will, won't you, Dely?"

"When do Mas' Robert come?"

"He'll surely be home in a couple of days."

"An he's mighty cu'ious, ain't he?"

"If he should happen to come across that slipper in Nelson Spencer's room, all would be over between us. Oh, Dely, you must find some way."

"Mas' Nelson Spencah is right sma't boas'ful, ain't he?"

"Oh, Dely."

"You don't reckon he'd show it to Mas' Robert, do you?"

"Dely, you're saying everything to frighten me; don't talk that way."

"Miss Em'ly, de truth is de light; but nevah min', I'll try an' git dat slippah fu' you."

"Oh, Dely, and you shall have that blue sprigged muslin dress of mine you liked so much."

Dely's eyes gleamed but she answered, "Nevah you min' about de dress, Miss Em'ly. What we wants is de slippah," and the maid departed to think.

For a long while she thought of everything she knew, and canvassed every resource within her power. Of course, she might make love to Harry, Spencer's valet, and have him get the prize for her, but then she knew that Ike would be sure to find that out and get angry with her. She might appeal to Carrie, one of the Spencer household, but she knew that Carrie hated her and would do anything rather than gratify her slightest wish, for Carrie herself had an eye on Ike. Then might she not steal it herself? But how to effect an entrance to the room of her mistress' enemy?

"Lawd bless me," she exclaimed suddenly, her eyes brightening, "I done fu'git young Mas' Roger. I spec he'll be snoopin' roun' some place to-morrer."

Now Dely knew that Nelson Spencer had a brother, a reckless, disobedient boy, who had just arrived at the unspeakable age. Something in this knowledge or rather in the sudden recollection, sent her flying to the kitchen, where for something over two hours she braved Aunt Hester's maledictions while she baked heap upon heap of crisp sweet cakes.

When, hot and tired, she had finished and placed them in a cloth-covered jar, she chuckled to herself with the remark, "Now, ef dat don't fetch dat slippah, I reckon Miss Em'ly bettah look out fu' anothah gallant; but I know dat boy."

On the following morning, the maid, carrying a bulging bag, wandered out in the direction of the Spencer place, hoping to meet young Roger somewhere in the open air, on his pony or nosing about the woods on foot. She had said that she knew that boy, and she did. Roger was a boy with a precocious appetite. He might be backward in everything else, but his ability to consume food was large beyond his years. He lived to eat. He went into the house to browse, and came out of it to forage. He was insatiable. When kitchen and orchard had done their part in vain, he had recourse to roots of the field and strange, unaccountable plants which would have proved his death but for the intervention of that Providence which is popularly supposed to take care of three certain irresponsible classes of humanity.

Dely was not mistaken in thinking he would be "snooping about" somewhere, for it was not long before she saw him walking along the road munching an apple and looking for more food. She hastened to catch up with him, and, like a sensible girl, approached him from the windward side.

"Howdy, Roger?" said Dely invitingly.

"Hullo, Dely."

"Whaih you goin'?"

"I don' know; where are you goin'?" eyeing the bag. Dely must have put ginger into those sweet cakes and Roger's scent was keen.

"Oh, I'm jest walkin' erroun'."

"What you got in your bag?"

"Now jest listen at dat chile," exclaimed Dely with a well-feigned surprise and admiration. "Now who'd a thought you'd tek notice o' dis hyeah ol' bag. Nev' you min' what I got in dis bag."

"Seems like I smell somethin' good."

"Don' bothah me, Roger; I ain't got no time to fool wid you. Seems to me lak you always want to be eatin' some'p'n."

"Then it is eatin', Dely?"

"Who said so? Dat's what I want to know; who said so?"

"Why, you did, you did, that's who," Roger cried gleefully.

"Did I? Well, la sakes! Who'd 'a' evah thought o' me givin' myself away dat away? I mus' be gittin' right rattle-brained. I don' b'lieve I said it."

"Oh, yes, you did. Let's see, Dely. Do let's see."

"Oh, I dassent," said the dissembler. "Hit's some'p'n fine."

Roger fairly danced with excitement. "Do, do," he pleaded; "just one little peep."

"I'm feared you'll want to eat some."

"Oh, no, I won't. Please let me look?"

Dely carefully opened the mouth of the bag and slowly inclined it toward the eager boy. Even before the brown beauty of the cakes broke on the boy's sight the fragrant odor of them had reached his nostrils. Then he saw them. Just one flash of russet and gold and the maid closed the bag with a jerk, but not before she was aware that she had a willing slave at her feet.

"Oh, Dely!" the boy gasped.

"Well, I mus' be gittin' 'long now."

"Dely, just one. Oh, Dely!"

"Now what'd I tell you? Didn't I say you'd be wantin' one? I cain't stop to bothah wid you. Dese is luck cakes."

"Luck cakes?" Roger's curiosity for the moment almost overcame his hunger. "What's luck cakes?"

Miss Emily's diplomat took one of them from the bag.

"You see dis hyeah cake," she said, holding it dangerously near Roger's nose, while his hands twitched, "you see dis hyeah cake. Well, ef you go out of a mornin' wid a bag of dese an' ef anybody can bring you a unmatched slippah befo' dey's all et up, you has luck fu' de rest o' yo' life, an' de pusson what brings de slippah gits de rest o' de cakes."

"Gets them all, Dely?" asked Roger faintly.

"All dat's lef'."

"Ain't you eatin' yourself, Dely?"

"No, I ain't 'lowed to eat 'em. It'll spile de chawm."

Just then Dely let the golden cake drop in his hand. When the last crumb had disappeared he asked, "Dely, what's an unmatched slipper?"

"Why, it's one dat ain't got no mate, of cou'se. Jest a one-footed slippah."

"Oh, I can get you one."

"You! De ve'y ideeh!"

"Yes, I can, too; mamma has lots of odd ones."

"No, no," said Dely hastily, "you musn't git yo' mammy's. No 'ndeedy. Dat 'u'd spile de chawm."

"Charms are funny things, ain't they?" said the boy.

"Mighty funny, mighty funny. You nevah know whaih dey goin' to break out. But 'bout dis chawm," and she handed him another cake, "you musn't git de slippah of no lady what belongs to you, ner of no man, ner you musn't let nobody know dat you teken' it, fu' dat 'u'd break de chawm, too. De bes' way is to go in yo' brothah Nelson's room an' look erroun' right sha'p, an' mebbe you might fin' a little weenchy slippah wid ribbons er some'p'n on it, an' dat'll be de luck slippah."

"Oh," exclaimed Roger, "I know there couldn't be such a slipper in brother Nelson's room."

Dely paused dramatically and closed her bag. "Well, I got to be goin'," she said. "I mus' fin' somebody else to bring me de luck slippah."

"I'll go, Dely, I'll go," cried Roger, starting; "but Dely, promise you won't let anybody else eat those cakes. It might spoil the charm."

"Well, I'll give you anothah one, jes' fu' strengf," and she laughed a laugh of triumph as the boy sped away.

"I 'low ef dey's any slippah thaih he'll fin' it, 'long ez he smell dese hyeah cakes in his min'."

Dely had not long to wait for her courier. Pretty soon he came bounding toward her waving something in his hand. He was radiant.

"I found it, Dely, I found it, just as you said. It was on the bureau. Now I may have the cakes, mayn't I?"

"It's de luck slippah, thank goodness," said Dely solemnly as she eagerly clutched the missing piece of foot-wear.

"Now I may have the cakes, mayn't I?" Roger was dancing again.

"Yes, ef you'll promise you'll never, never tell," said Dely, "so's 't'll not break de chawm."

"Hope m' die, Dely."

Then she poured the cakes on the ground beside him, and, leaving him to his joy, went home laughing to her mistress.

"How *did* you get it, Dely?" asked her mistress, clasping her accusing shoe.

"Oh, I wo'ked my chawms," Dely replied.

Miss Emily was walking along the road that evening with thoughtful eyes cast on the ground. She knew that Nelson Spencer was behind her.

"What are you looking for?" he asked as he overtook her.

"A flower," she said.

"A flower! What particular one?"

"A lady-slipper."

"Aren't you a little far south for it?" His house was to the north.

"I think I have found it," she said, facing him and planting both feet firmly within sight.

Spencer looked down, and, bowing low, passed on, but she could see the flush that started in his brow, spreading from cheek to neck, and she laughed cheerily.

Nelson Spencer went home to say unrepeatable things to his valet, the butler, the housekeeper and Carrie the maid, in fact, to everybody except Roger, who was, at the time, suffering the pangs of precocious indigestion.

A Blessed Deceit

As MARTHA SAID, "it warn't long o' any sma'tness dat de rapscallion evah showed, but des 'long o' his bein' borned 'bout de same time ez young mastah dat Lucius got tuk into de big house." But Martha's word is hardly to be taken, for she had a mighty likely little pickaninny of her own who was overlooked when the Daniels were looking about for a companion for the little toddler, their one child. Martha might have been envious. However, it is true that Lucius was born about the same time that his young Master Robert was, and it is just possible that that might have had something to do with his appointment, although he was as smart and likely a little darkey as ever cracked his heels on a Virginia plantation. Years after, people wondered why that black boy with the scarred face and hands so often rode in the Daniels' carriage, did so little work, and was better dressed than most white men. But the story was not told them; it touched too tender a spot in the hearts of all who knew. But memory deals gently with old wounds, and the balm of time softens the keenest sorrow.

Lucius first came to the notice of Mr. Daniels when as a two-year-old pickaninny he was rolling and tumbling in the sand about the quarters. Even then, he could sing so well, and was such a cheerful and good-natured, bright little scamp that his master stood and watched him in delight. Then he asked Susan how old he was, and she answered, "La, Mas' Stone, Lucius he 'bout two years old now, don't you ricollec'? He born 'bout de same time dat little Mas' Robert came to you-alls." The master's eyes sparkled, and he tapped the black baby on the head.

His caress was immediately responded to by a caper of enjoyment on the young-ster's part. Stone Daniels laughed aloud, and said, "Wash him, Susan, and I'll send something down from the house by Lou, then dress him, and send him on up." He turned away, and Susan, her heart bounding with joy, seized the baby in her arms and covered his round black body with kisses. This was a very easy matter for her to do, for he only wore one pitiful shift, and that was in a sadly dilapidated con-dition. She hurried to fulfill her master's orders. There was no telling what great glory might come of such a command. It was a most wonderful blue dress with a pink sash that Lou brought down from the house, and when young Lucius was ar-rayed therein, he was a sight to make any fond mother's heart proud. Of course, Lucius was rather a deep brunette to wear such dainty colors, but plantation tastes are not very scrupulous, and then the baby Robert, whose garments these had been, was fair, with the brown hair of the Daniels, and was dressed accordingly.

Half an hour after the child had gone to the big house, Susan received word that he had been appointed to the high position of companion in chief, and amuser in general to his young master, and the cup of her earthly joy was full. One hour later, the pickaninny and his master were rolling together on the grass, throwing stones with the vigorous gusto of two years, and the sad marksmanship of the same age, and the blue dress and pink sash were of the earth, earthy.

"I tell you, Eliza," said Stone, "I think I've struck just about the right thing in that little rascal. He'll take the best care of Robert, and I think that playing like that out in the sunshine will make our little one stronger and healthier. Why, he loves him already. Look at that out there." Mrs. Daniels did look. The young scion of the Daniels house was sitting down in the sand and gravel of the drive, and his companion and care taker was piling leaves, gravel, dirt, sticks, and whatever he could find about the lawn on his shoulders and head. The mother shuddered.

"But don't you think, Stone, that that's a little rough for Robert, and his clothes —oh my, I do believe he is jamming that stick down his throat!"

"Bosh," said Stone, "that's the way to make a man out of him."

When the two children were brought in from their play, young Robert showed that he had been taken care of. He was scratched, he was bruised, but he was flushed and happy, and Stone Daniels was in triumph.

One, two, three years the companionship between the two went on, and the love between them grew. The little black was never allowed to forget that he was his Master Robert's servant, but there is a democracy about childhood that over-steps all conventions, and lays low all barriers of caste. Down in the quarters, with many secret giggles, the two were dubbed, "The Daniels twins."

It was on the occasion of Robert's sixth birthday that the pair might have been seen "codgin'" under the lilac bush, their heads very close together, the same in-tent look on both the black and the white face. Something momentous was under discussion. The fact of it was, young Master Robert was to be given his first party that evening, and though a great many children of the surrounding gentry had been invited, provision had not been made for the entertainment of Lucius in the parlor. Now this did not meet with Robert's views of what was either right or proper, so he had determined to take matters in his own hands, and together with his black confederate was planning an amendment of the affair.

"You see, Lucius," he was saying, "you are mine, because papa said so, and you was born the same time I was, so don't you see that when I have a birthday party, it is your birthday party too, and you ought to be there?"

"Co'se," said Lucius, with a wise shake of the head, and a very old look, "Co'se, dat des de way it look to me, Mas' Robert."

"Well, now, as it's your party, it 'pears like to me that you ought to be there, and not be foolin' 'round with the servants that the other company bring."

"'Pears lak to me dat I oughter be 'roun' dah somewhah," answered the black boy.

Robert thought for awhile, then he clapped his little knee and cried, "I've got it, Lucius, I've got it!" His face beamed with joy, the two heads went closer together, and with many giggles and capers of amusement, their secret was disclosed, and the young master trotted off to the house, while Lucius rolled over and over with delight.

A little while afterwards Robert had a very sage and professional conversation with his father in the latter's library. It was only on state occasions that he went to Doshy and asked her to obtain an interview for him in that august place, and Stone Daniels knew that something great was to be said when the request came to him. It was immediately granted, for he denied his only heir nothing, and the young man came in with the air and mien of an ambassador bearing messages to a potentate.

What was said in that conversation, and what was answered by the father, it boots not here to tell. It is sufficient to say that Robert Daniels came away from the interview with shining eyes and a look of triumph on his face, and the news he told to his fellow conspirator sent him off into wild peals of pleasure. Quite as eagerly as his son had gone out to Lucius, Stone Daniels went to talk with his wife.

"I tell you, Eliza," he said, "there's no use talking, that boy of ours is a Daniels through and through. He is an aristocrat to his finger tips. What do you suppose he has been in to ask me?"

"I have no idea, Stone," said his wife, "what new and original thing this wonderful boy of ours has been saying now."

"You needn't laugh now, Eliza, because it is something new and original he has been saying."

"I never doubted it for an instant."

"He came to me with that wise look of his; you know it?"

"Don't I?" said the mother tenderly.

"And he said, 'Papa, don't you think as I am giving a party, an' my servant was born 'bout the same time as I was, don't you think he ought to kinder—kinder—be 'roun' where people could see him, as, what do you call it in the picture, papa?' 'What do you mean?' I said 'Oh, you know, to set me off.' 'Oh, a background, you mean?' 'Yes, a background; now I think it would be nice if Lucius could be right there, so whenever I want to show my picture books or anything, I could just say,

"Lucius, won't you bring me this, or won't you bring me that?" like you do with Scott.' 'Oh, but my son,' I said, 'a gentleman never wants to show off his possessions.' 'No, papa,' he replied, with the most quizzical expression I ever saw on a child's face, 'no, I don't want to show off. I just want to kinder indicate, don't you know, cause it's a birthday party, and that'll kinder make it stronger.'"

"Of course you consented?" said Mrs. Daniels.

"With such wise reasoning, how could a man do otherwise?" He replied, "Don't you see the child has glimmers of that fine feeling of social contrast, my dear?"

"I see," said Mrs. Daniels, "that my son Robert wants to have Lucius in the room at the party, and was shrewd enough to gain his father's consent."

"By the Lord!" said her husband, "but I believe you're right. Well, it's done now, and I can't go back on my word."

"The Daniels twins" were still out on the lawn dancing to the piping of the winds and throwing tufts of grass into the air and over their heads, when they were called in to be admonished and dressed. Peacock never strutted as did Lucius when, arrayed in a blue suit with shining brass buttons, he was stationed in the parlor near his master's chair. Those were the days when even children's parties were very formal and elegant affairs. There was no hurrying and scurrying then, and rough and tumble goings-on. That is, at first, there was not; when childhood gets warmed up though, it is pretty much the same in any period of the world's history. However, the young guests coming were received with great dignity and formality by their six-year-old host. The party was begun in very stately fashion. It was not until supper was announced that the stiffness and awe of the children at a social function began to wear off. Then they gathered about the table, cheerful and buoyant, charmed and dazzled by its beauty. There was a pretty canopy over the chair of the small host, and the dining-room and tables were decorated with beautiful candles in the silver candlesticks that had been heirlooms of the Daniels for centuries. Robert had lost some of his dignity and laughed and chatted with the rest as the supper went on. The little girls were very demure, the boys were inclined to be a little boisterous. The most stately figure in the room was Lucius where he was stationed stiff and erect behind his master's chair. From the doorway, the elders looked on with enjoyment at the scene. The supper was nearly over, and the fun was fast and furious. The boys were unable longer to contain the animal spirits which were bubbling over, and there began surreptitious scufflings and nudges under the table. Someone near Robert suddenly sprang up, the cloth caught in his coat, two candles were tipped over straight into the little host's lap. The melted wax ran over him, and in a twinkle the fine frills and laces about him were a mass of flames. Instantly all was confusion, the children were shrieking and rushing pell-mell from the table. They crowded the room in frightened and confused huddles, and it was this that barred Stone Daniels as he fought his way fiercely to his son's side. But one was before him. At the first sign of danger to his young master, Lucius had sprung forward and thrown himself upon him, beating, fighting, tearing, smothering, trying to kill the fire. He grabbed the delicate linen, he tore at the collar and jacket; he was burning himself, his clothes were on fire, but he heeded it not. He only saw that his master was burning, burning before him, and his boy's heart went out in a cry, "Oh, Mas' Bob, oh, Mas' Bob!"

Somehow, the father reached his child at last, and threw his coat about him. The flames were smothered, and the unconscious child carried to his room. The children were hurried into their wraps and to their homes, and a messenger galloped away for the doctor.

And what of Lucius? When the heir of the Daniels was in danger of his life no one had time to think of the slave, and it was not until he was heard moaning on the floor where he had crept in to be by his master's bedside, that it was found out that he also was badly burned, and a cot was fixed for him in the same room.

When the doctor came in he shook his head over both, and looked very grave indeed. First Robert and then his servant was bound and bandaged, and the same nurse attended both. When the white child returned to consciousness his mother was weeping over him, and his father with face pale and drawn stood at the foot of the bed. "Oh, my poor child, my poor child!" moaned the woman; "my only one!"

With a gasp of pain Robert turned his face toward his mother and said, "Don't you cry, mamma; if I die, I'll leave you Lucius."

It was funny afterwards to think of it, but then it only brought a fresh burst of tears from the mother's heart, and made a strange twitching about the father's mouth.

But he didn't die. Lucius' caretaking had produced in him a robust constitution, and both children fought death and gained the fight. When they were first able to sit up—and Robert was less inclined to be parted from Lucius than ever—the young master called his father into the room. Lucius' chair was wheeled near him when the little fellow began:

"Papa, I want to 'fess somethin' to you. The night of the party I didn't want Lucius in for indicatin', I wanted him to see the fun, didn't I Lucius?"

Lucius nodded painfully, and said, "Uh-huh."

"I didn't mean to 'ceive you, papa, but you know it was both of our birthdays —and—er—" Stone Daniels closed his boy's mouth with a kiss, and turned and patted the black boy's head with a tender look on his face, "For once, thank God, it was a blessed deceit."

That is why in years later, Lucius did so little work and dressed like his master's son.

The Brief Cure of Aunt Fanny

SOME PEOPLE GROW old gracefully, charmingly. Others with a bitter reluctance so evident that it detracts from whatever dignity might attach to their advanced period of life. Of this latter class was Aunt Fanny. She had cooked in the Mordaunt kitchen for more years than those hands who even claimed middle-age cared to remember. But any reference to the length of time she had passed there was keenly resented by the old woman. She had been good-looking in her younger days, sprightly, and a wonderful worker, and she held to the belief in her capabilities long after the powers of her youth and middle-age were gone. She was still young when her comrades, Parker, Tempe, Doshy and Mam Henry had duly renounced their sins, got religion and confessed themselves old. She had danced beyond the time when all her comrades had grown to the stage of settled and unfrivolous Christianity. Indeed, she had kept up her gayety until she could find no men old enough to be her partners, and the young men began to ignore her; then she went into the Church. But with the cooking, it was different. Even to herself, after years had come and brought their infirmities, she would not admit her feebleness, and she felt that she had never undergone a greater trial or endured a more flagrant insult than when Maria was put into the kitchen to help her with her work. Help her with her work, indeed! Who could help her? In truth, what need had she of assistance? Was she not altogether the most famous cook in the whole county? Was she not able by herself to cope with all the duties that could possibly devolve upon her? Resentment renewed her energy, and she did her work with an angry sprightliness that belied her years. She browbeat Maria and made her duties a sinecure by doing everything just as she had done before her rival's appearance.

It was pretty hard for the younger woman, who also was active and ambitious, and there were frequent clashes between the two, but Aunt Fanny from being an autocrat had gained a consciousness of power, and was almost always victorious in these bouts, "Uh huh!" she said to Tempe, discussing the matter. "They ain't gwine to put no upstart black 'ooman oveh me, aftah all de yeahs I's been in dat kitchen. I knows evah brick an' slat in it. It uz built fu' me, an' I ain't gwine let nobody tek it f'om me. No, suh, not ontwell de preacheah done tho'wed de ashes on dis haid."

"We's all gittin' ol', dough," said Tempe thoughtfully, "an' de young ones got to tek ouah place."

"Gittin' ol'! gittin' ol'!" Aunt Fanny would exclaim indignantly; "I ain't gittin' ol'. I des' ez spry ez I was w'en I was a gal." And by her work she made an attempt to bear out her statement.

It would not do, though; for Time has no illusions. Neither is he discreet, and he was telling on Aunt Fanny.

The big house, too, had felt for a long time that she was failing, but the old master had hesitated to speak to her, but now he felt that she was going from bad to worse, and that something must be done. It was hard speaking to her, but when morning after morning the breakfast was unpardonably late, the beaten biscuits were burned and the cakes tough, it appeared that the crisis had come. Just at this time, too, Maria made it plain that she was not being given her proper share of responsibility, and Stuart Mordaunt, the old master, went down to remonstrate with Aunt Fanny.

"Now, Fanny," he said, "you know we have never complained of your cooking, and you have been serving right here in this kitchen for forty years, haven't you?"

"Yes, I has, Mas' Stua't," said Aunt Fanny, "an' I wish I could go right on fu' fo'ty yeahs mo'."

"I wish so, too, but age is telling on you just as it is on me"; he put his hand to his white head. "It is no use your working so hard any more."

"I want to work hard," said Aunt Fanny tremulously; "hit's my life."

"But you are not able to do it," said Mordaunt forcibly; "you are too old, Fanny."

She turned on him a look eager, keen and argumentative.

"I's moughty sho' you older'n me, Mas' Stua't," she said.

"I know it," he said hastily. "Didn't I just say that age was telling on us both?"

"You ain't quit runnin' de plantation yit," was the calm reply.

The master was staggered for a moment, but he hurriedly rallied: "No, I haven't, but I am a good deal less active than I was twenty, ten, even five years ago. I don't work much, I only direct others—and that's just what I want you to do. Be around, direct others, and teach Maria what you know."

"It ain't in huh," sententiously.

"Put it in her; someone had to teach you."

"No, suh, I was a born cook. Nemmine, I see you want to git rid o me; nemmine, M'ria kin have de kitchen." The old woman's voice was trembling and tears stood in her eyes, big and glistening. Mordaunt, always gentle-hearted, gave in. "Well, confound it, Fanny," he broke in, "do as you please; I've nothing more to say. I suppose we'll have to go on eating your burned biscuits and tough batter-cakes as long as you please. That's all I have to say."

But with Maria there was no such easy yielding; for she knew that she had the power of the big house behind her, and in the next bout with Aunt Fanny she held her own and triumphed for the first time. The older woman's anger knew no bounds. She went sullenly to her cabin that night, and she did not rise the next morning when the horn blew. She told those who inquired that she was sick, and "I 'low," she invariably added, "dat I either got the rheumatiz or dat black wench has conju'ed me so's to git my kitchen, 'case she knowed dat was de only way to git it."

Now Aunt Fanny well knew that to accuse one of her fellow-servants of calling in the aid of the black art was to bring about the damnation of that other servant if the story gained credence, but even she doubted that the plantation could believe anything so horrible of one so generally popular, who, besides, had her own particular following. Among the latter Mam Henry was not wont to be numbered, but she was a woman who loved to see fair play, and after having visited Aunt Fanny in her cabin, she said in secret to Aunt Tempe:

"Fanny she don't look lak no conju'ed ooman to me, an' I's gwine fin' out whether dey's anything de matter wid huh a-tall 'case I don' b'lieve dey is. I b'lieve she's des' in one o' huh tantrums, 'case M'ria stood huh down 'bout de kitchen."

Aunt Tempe had answered: "Dey ain't no 'sputin' dat Fanny is gittin' ol' an' doty."

The sick woman or malingerer, whichever she was, did not see the subtle motive which prompted Mam Henry's offer to nurse and doctor her. She looked upon it as an evidence of pure friendship and a tribute to her own worth on the plantation. She saw in Mam Henry, a woman older even than herself, a trusted ally in revolt against the advances of youth, and she anticipated a sympathetic listener into whose ears she might pour her confidences. As to her powers as a curer and a nurse, while Mam Henry was not actually "long-headed," she was known to be both "gifted" and "wise," and was close in the confidence of Dr. Bass, the conjure man, himself.

Although Maria went her way about the kitchen, and made the most of her new-found freedom, she heard with grief and consternation, not unmingled with a wholesome fear, the accusations which her old enemy was making against her. She trembled for what the plantation would say and do, and for what her master would think. Some of her misgivings she communicated to Aunt Tempe, who reassured her with the remark, "Nevah you min', chile, you des go 'long an' do yo' wo'k, dey's things wo'kin' fu' you in de da'k."

Meanwhile Mam Henry had duly installed herself in her patient's cabin and entered upon her ministrations. The afflicted arm and leg were covered with greased jimson weed and swathed in bandages.

"'Tain't no use doin' dis, Mam Henry," Aunt Fanny protested, "'tain't a bit o' use. I's hyeah to tell you dat dis mis'ry I's sufferin' wid ain't no rheumatiz, hit's des plain conju', an' dey ain't nuffin' gwine to do no good but to meet trick wid trick."

"You lay low, chile," answered Mam Henry impressively. "I got my own idees. I's gwine to use all de rheumatiz cuohs, an' den ef you ain't no bettah, de sign will be sho' ez de wo'd dat you's been tricked. Den we gwine to use othah things."

Aunt Fanny closed her eyes and resigned herself. She could afford to wait, for she had a pretty definite idea herself what the outcome would be.

In the long hours that the old women were together it was quite natural that they should fall into confidences, and it was equally natural that Aunt Fanny should be especially interested in the doings of the kitchen and the big house. Her mistress had brought her some flannels, and good things to eat, and, while she had sympathized with her, she felt that nothing could have been more opportune than this illness that settled the question of the cooking once and forever. In one of their talks, Aunt Fanny asked her nurse what "Ol' Miss 'Liza say 'bout me bein' sick."

"She say she moughty so'y fu' you, but dat 'tain't no mo' den she 'spected anyhow, case de kitchen kin' o' open an' you gittin' too ol' to be 'roun', 'sposin' yo'se'f to all kin' o' draughts."

"Humph!" sniffed Aunt Fanny from the bed, and she flirted the rheumatic arm around in a way that should have caused her unspeakable pain. She never flinched, however.

"She don't b'lieve you conju'ed," Mam Henry went on. "She say dat's all foo'ishness; she say you des' got de rheumatiz, dat w'en you git up you gotter stay closah to yo cabin, an' not be flyin' 'roun' whaih you tek mo' col'."

This time the rheumatic leg performed some gyrations unheard of from such a diseased member.

"Mam Henry," said Aunt Fanny solemnly, "ain't it cu'ious how little w'ite folks know 'bout natur?"

"It sho is. Ol' Mas' he say he gwine 'tiah mos' of de ol' servants, an' let 'em res' fu' de balance o' dey days, case dey been faifful, an' he think dey 'serve it. I think so, too. We been wo'kin' all ouah days, an' I know ol' Time done laid his han' heavy on my back. Ain't I right?"

"Humph!" from the bed. "Some people ages quicker'n othahs."

"Dat's de Gospel. Now wid you an' me an' Tempe an' Pahkah an' Doshy, dey ain't been nuffin quick 'bout hit, case I tell you, Fanny, chile, we's been hyeah lo dese many days."

"How M'ria git erlong?" Aunt Fanny asked uneasily.

"Oh, M'ria she des' tickled to deaf. She flyin' 'roun' same ez a chicken wid his haid wrung off. She so proud o' huhse'f dat she des cain't res', she cain't do enough. She scourin' an' she cleanin' an' she cookin' all de time, an' w'en she ain't cookin' she plannin what she gwine to cook. I hyeah ol' mas' say dat she sholy was moughty peart, an' I 'low huh battah-cakes was somep'n scrumptious. Mas' Stua't et a mess; he 'low dat ef M'ria keep on mekin' such cakes as she mek in de mornin', de m'lasses bar'l ain't gwine hol' out no time."

Aunt Fanny looked nervously toward her brogans in the corner. The camel's back was being pretty heavily laden, and a faint smile flickered over Mam Henry's shrewd face.

"You des' ought to see de aihs M'ria teks on huhse'f. She allus struttin' erroun' wid a w'ite ap'on on soon's huh wo'k's done, an' she calls huhse'f de big house cook."

This was the last straw. The camel's back went with a figurative crash. The covers were thrown back, and Aunt Fanny sprang up and seated herself on the side of the bed.

"Han' me my shoes," she said.

"W'y, Fanny, fo' de Lawd!" cried Mam Henry in well-feigned surprise. "What you gwine do?"

"I's gwine git up f'om hyeah, dat's what I's gwine do. Han' me my shoes."

"But yo' rheumatiz, yo' rheumatiz?"

"I ain't got no rheumatiz. You done cuohed me," she said, slipping into her dress as she spoke.

"But you ain't gin me de chanst to try all de cuohs yit; s'posen you tu'ns out to be conju'ed aftah all."

"Ain't ol' miss done say hit all foolishness?"

"But you done say de w'ite folks don't know nuffin 'bout natur."

"I ain't got no time to bantah wo'ds wid you, Mam Henry, I got to go to my wo'k. I ain't gwine let my kitchen be all messed up an' my w'ite folks' appetites plum spiled by dat know-nuffin wench." And Aunt Fanny walking with an ease that bore out her statement that she was cured swept out of the house with scant courtesy to her nurse, who remained behind, shaking with laughter.

"I said so, I said so," she said to herself. "I knowed dey wa'nt nuffin' de mattah wid Fanny but de tantrums."

Maria was a good deal surprised and not at all pleased when, a little later, her old rival appeared upon the scene and began to take charge of things in the old way.

"W'y, Aunt Fanny," she said, "I t'ought you was sick?"

"You don't s'pose I's gwine to stay sick all de time, do you?" was the short response. "I wants you to know I's cuohed."

Then Maria bridled. Her unlimited authority in the last few days had put added spirit into her.

"Look a-hyeah, Aunt Fanny," she said, "I sees thoo you now. You des been sick 'case you couldn't have yo' own way, an' you wanted to mek b'lieve I conju'ed you so de folks would drive me out, didn't you? But sick er no sick, conju' er no conju', cuohed er no cuohed, dis is my kitchen, an' I ain't gwine gin it up to no 'ooman."

Later on the services of the master had to be called in again, and he also began to understand.

"Well, it's this way, Fanny," he said; "you might be cured now, but if you stay around here you are likely to be taken down again. You are apt to become subject to these attacks, so you had better go back to your cabin and stay around there. Maria is going to take charge of the kitchen now, and when we need you, you can come up and cook something special for your old Miss and me."

The old woman would have protested, but there was a firm ring in her master's voice which was not to be mistaken, and she went tearfully back to her cabin, where, though so suddenly "cuohed," she was immediately taken ill again, more seriously, if possible, than before.

The Stanton Coachman

THE MORNING SUN touched the little old-fashioned Virginia church with glory, while in the shadow of its vine-covered porch an old negro alternately mumbled to himself and dozed.

It was not yet time for the service to begin, and as I stood watching the bees go in and out of the honeysuckle vines there came up the road and halted at the door a strange equipage. Side by side upon the one seat of an ox-cart sat a negro, possibly fifty years of age, and an old white lady. No one could have mistaken her for one of the country women coming in from any of the adjoining farms, for she was unmistakably a lady, from the white hair which crowned her high-bred face to the patched and shabby shoe that peeped from under her dress as she alighted. The black man had leaped down and, holding in one hand the ropes that did duty as reins, helped her tenderly to the ground.

The grace and deference of his manner were perfect, and she accepted his service with a certain genial dignity that bespoke custom. She went her feeble way into the church, and I was surprised to see the dozing old negro wake into sudden life, spring up and doff his cap as she passed. Meanwhile, at the heads of the lazy oxen stood the shabby servitor, erect and fine-looking, even in the tattered garments that covered his form.

The scene would have been ludicrous if there had not been about it an air of dignified earnestness that disarmed ridicule. You could almost have imagined that black tatterdemalion there a coachman in splendid livery, standing by the side of his restless chargers, and that ox-cart with its one seat and wheels awry might have been the most dashing of victorias. What had I stumbled upon—one of those romances of the old South that still shed their light among the shadows of slavery?

The old negro in the porch had settled himself again for a nap, but I disregarded his inclination and, the service forgotten, approached him: "Howdy, Uncle."

"Howdy, son, howdy; how you come on?"

"Oh, I'm tol'able peart," I answered, falling easily into his manner of speech. "I was just wondering who the old lady was that went in church just now."

He looked up questioningly for a minute, and then being satisfied of my respect, replied, "Dat uz de Stanton lady—Ol Mis' Stanton."

"And the black man there?"

"Dat's Ha'ison; dat's de Stanton coachman. I reckon you ain't f'om hyeah?"

"No, but I should like to know about them."

"Oomph, hit's a wonder you ain't nevah hyeahed tell o' de Stantons, I don' know whah yo' been at, man. Why, evahbody knowed de Stantons roun' 'bout hyeah. Dey wuz de riches' folks anywhah roun'."

"Well to do, were they?"

"Well to do! Man, whut you talkin' 'bout? I tell you, dem people wuz rich, dey wuz scand'lous rich. Dey owned neahly all de dahkies in de county, an' dey wasn't no hi'in' out people, neithah. I didn't 'long to dem, but I allus wished I did, 'case—"

"But about Harrison?"

"Ez I were goin' to say, my ol' mastah hi'ed out, an' I wuz on de go mos' all de time, 'case I sholy wuz spry an' handy dem days. Ha'ison, he wuz de coachman, an' a proudah, finah-dressed dahky you nevah seed in all yore bo'n days. Oomph-um, but he wuz sta'chy! Dey had his lib'ry made at de same place whah dey made de ol' Cunnel's an' de young mastah's clothes, an' dey wuz sights. Such gol' buttons, an' long coats, an' shiny hats, an' boots—" The old man paused and shook his head, as if the final glory had been reached. "Dey ain't no mo' times lak dat," he went on. "Hit used to be des lak a pu'cession when Ha'ison come ridin' down de road on top o' de Stanton ca'ige. He sot up thar des ez straight, de hosses a prancin', an' de wheels a glistenin', an' he nevah move his naik to de right er de lef, no mo'n ef he wuz froze. Sometimes you could git a glimpse o' de mistus' face inside, an' she wuz allus beautiful an' smilin', lak a real lady ought to be, an' sometimes dey'd have de ca'ige open, an' de Cunnel would come a ridin' down 'longside o' hit on one o' his fine hosses, an' Ha'ison ud sit straightah dan evah, an' you couldn' a tol' wheddah he knowed de footman wuz a sittin' side o' him er not.

"Dey wuz mighty good to all de people, de Stantons wuz, an' dey faihly id'l-ized dem. Why, ef Miss Dolly had a stahted to put huh foot on de groun' any time she'd a had a string o' niggers ez long ez f'om hyeah to yandah a layin' daihse'ves in de paf fu' huh to walk on, fu' dey sholy did love huh. An' de Cunnel, he wuz de beatenes' man. He could nevah walk out on de plantation 'dout a whole string o' piccaninnies a followin' aftah him. Dey knowed whut dey wuz doin', fu' aftah while de Cunnel tu'n roun' an' th'ow 'em a whole lot o' coppers an' fips, an' bless yore hea't, sich anothah scram'lin' an' rollin' an' a tumblin' in de dus' you nevah seed. Well, de Cunnel, he'd stan' thar an' des natchelly crack his sides a-laffin' ontwell dey wuz thoo fightin', den he call up dem dat hadn't got nuffin' an' give 'em daih sheer, so's to see 'em all go off happy, a-hollerin' 'Thanky, Mas' Stant', thanky, mastah!' I reckon any fips dey gits now dey has to scratch fu' wuss'n dey did den. Dem wuz wunnerful times!

"Den come 'long de time o' de wah, an' den o' co'se I oughtn' say hit, but de Cunnel, he make a great big mistake; he freed all de niggahs. Hit wuz des dis away: de Stantons, dey freed all daih servants right in de middle o' de wah, an' o' cose nobody couldn' stan' ag'inst daih wo'd, so freedom des spread. Mistah Lincoln mought 'a' been all right, but he didn' have nothin' to do wid hit. Hit wuz Mas' Stanton, dat who it wuz. Ef hit wasn', huccome Mas' Stanton keep all de sarvants he want, eben ef he do pay 'em wages? Huccome he keep Ha'ison, 'ceptin' he writ home to his lady? He wuz at de wah, an' thar wasn' no mo folks on de place, 'ceptin' a sarvant, w'en hit all come up. Ha'ison he layin' flat on his back sick in his cabin, an' not able to do nuffin a-tall. Seemed lak dey'd a freed a no-count dahky lak dat;

but, no, suh, ol' Mis' sont Marfy to nuss him, an' sont him all kin' o' contraptions to git him well, an' ol' Doctah Ma'maduke Wilson he come to see him.

"Den w'en Ha'ison got up ol' Mis' went down to see him, an' tuk him his wages, an' 'sisted on payin' him fu' de th'ee months he'd been a-layin thar, 'case she said he wuz free an' he'd need all de money he could git. Den Ha'ison, he des broke down, an' cried lak a baby, an' said he nevah 'spected dat ol' Mis' 'ud evah put any sich disgrace erpon him, an' th'owed de money down in de dus' an' fell down on his knees right thar in all his unifo'm.

"Mis' Stanton, she cry, too, an' say she didn' mean no ha'm to him. Den she tell him to git up, an' he 'fuse to git up, 'ceptin she promise dat he allus gwine to drive huh des lak he been doin'. Den she say she spec' dey gwine to be po', an' he 'ply to huh dat he don' keer; so she promise, an' tek de money, an' he git up happy. Dat look lak de end o' hit all, but la, chile! dat wuz des de beginnin', an' de end o' hit ain't come yet.

"De middle paht come w'en de wah ended, an' de ol' Cunnel come back home all broke up f'om de battles, an' de young mans, dey nevah come back a-tall. Daih pappy, he wuz mighty proud o' dem, dough. He'd allus say dat he lef' his two boys wid daih feet to de foe. I reckon dat's de way dey bu'y dem. He wuz a invally hisse'f —dat's what dey call de sojers dat's gone down in de Valley an' de Shadder o' Def, an' he sholy wuz in de Valley a long w'ile. But Ha'ison he des keep on drivin' dem, dough de plantation wuz all to' up, an' dey'd got mighty po', an' daih fine ca'iges wuz sold, an' dey didn' have but one hoss, him a-lookin' lak a ol' crow-bait. Marfy patched an' patched huh man's lib'ry 'twell hit wuz one livin' sight to behol'.

"W'en dat ol' crow-bait o' a hoss died, him an' Marfy wouldn' let daih ol' Mis' go out a-tall, but Marfy, she'd wheel de Cunnel roun' in his cheer, w'ile huh man wuz a-hi'in' out so's to buy anothah hoss an' a spring wagin. Soon's dey got dat de ol' Missis 'menced comin' back to ch'uch ag'in, 'case she mighty 'ligious ooman, an' allus wuz. An Ha'ison he sat on dat wagin seat de same ez ef he wuz on de ol' ca'ige.

"'Ha'ison,' somebody say to him one time, 'w'yn't you go on away f'om hyeah an' mek somep'n' out yorese'f? You got 'telegence.' Ha'ison, he go 'long an' shet his mouf, an' don' say nuffin'. So dey say ag'in, 'Ha'ison, w'y don' you go 'long up Norf an' git to be a Cong'essman, er somep'n' 'nothah?' Den he say, 'I don' want to be no Cong'essman, ner nuffin else. I been a-drivin' ol' Mis' fu' lo, dese many yeahs, an' I don' want nuffin bettah den des to keep on drivin' huh.' W'y dat man, seemed lak he got proudah dan evah, 'case hit wuzn' de money he wuz lookin' aftah; hit wuz de fambly. Anybody kin git money, but Gawd got to gin yo' quality.

"I don' lak to talk 'bout de res' o' it. But, de spring wagin an' de hoss had to go w'en de Cunnel laid down in de Valley, an' hit wuz nigh onter a yeah fo' ol' Mis' Stanton come out to chu'ch ag'in. But Ha'ison done eahned dat team o' oxen an' de cyart, an' dey been comin' in dat evah sence. She des ez sweet an' ladyfied ez she evah wuz, an' dat niggah des ez proud. I tell you, man, you kin kiver hit up wid rags a foot deep, but dey ain' no way to keep real quality f'om showin'!"

The old man paused and got up, for the forgotten service was over and the people were filing out of church. When the old lady came out there were lifted hats and courtly bows all along her pathway, which she acknowledged with gentle gracefulness. Her coachman suddenly became alive again as he helped her into the rude cart and climbed in beside her. She gave her hand to a slim, fine-faced man as he stopped to bid her good-bye, then the oxen turned and moved off up the road whence they had come.

The Easter Wedding

THE BRIEF, SHARP winter had passed and Easter was approaching. As Easter Monday was a great day for marrying, Aunt Sukey's patience was entirely worn out with her master's hesitancy, for which she could see no reason. She had long ago given her consent, and young Liza had said "yes" to Ben too many days past to talk about, and the old woman could not see why the white man, the one least concerned, should either object or hesitate. She had lorded it in the family for so long that it now seemed very hard suddenly to be denied anything.

"I tell you, Mas' Lancaster," she said, "dem two chillum been gallantin' wid each othah too long to pa't dem now. How'd you 'a' felt w'en you spa'kin' Mis' Dolly ef somebody'd 'a' helt you apa't an' kep you fwom ma'yin', huh? Cose I knows you gwine say Ben and 'Lize des niggahs, but la' Mas' you'd be s'prised w'en hit come to lovin', dem two des de same ez white folks in dere feelin's."

It was perhaps this point in the old woman's argument that overcame Robert Lancaster's objections. He surrendered and gave his consent to the marriage of Sukey's Lize and his boy Ben on the Monday following Easter. Great were the rejoicings that attended the announcement of the affair, and because Sukey herself was a great person on the plantation and Ben his master's valet, the wedding was to be no small one.

As the days passed the preparations were hastened. The mistress herself went into town and purchased such a dress as only Sukey's daughter could have thought of wearing, even though both Easter and her wedding day came at the same time. The young mistress, she who had married early but was widowed and sad now, had brought out a once used orange wreath and a veil as filmy as a fairy spider's web, and both the white mother and daughter took as deep an interest in the affair as did the two black women. While Sukey and Liza spun and wove they laughed, chatted and sewed, and they could not understand why Robert Lancaster kept so close to his library and looked on at all the preparations with no gladness in his eyes and no mirth on his tongue. He was closeted often with strange men from town, but they thought very little of that. He was a popular man, and it was not to be wondered at that he should be visited by people who did not know him.

It may have been that Robert Lancaster was an arch dissembler or only that he was less transparent than his brother, the good and child-like rector, who cared for the souls of the whole country, and for the bodies of one-half its population and took no thought for the morrow. It was on his face that they first saw the cloud that hung over them all. Robert himself was slow to confess it, and when his wife went to him and taxed him with holding something from her, some trouble on his mind that he was bearing alone, he confessed all, and she took up the burden of it with him. For some time past things had gone badly with him. He had been careless of his crops and over-indulgent with his servants. A man drawn apart from the mere commercial pursuits of life to the quieter world of literature and art, he had paid little attention to the affairs of his plantation, and suddenly he awoke to find his overseer rich and himself poor. Little or nothing was left of all that had been his, except his wife, his daughter and his memories. But what grieved him most was that his slaves, beings whom he had treated almost as his own children, whom he had indulged and spoiled until they were not fit to work for any other master, would have to be put upon the block. He knew what that meant, and felt all the horror of it. He had fostered fidelity among them and he knew that now it would fall back upon them, bringing only suffering and pain, for wives and husbands who had been together for years must be separated and whole families broken up.

"It was for this reason, Dolly," he said, "that I objected to the marriage of Ben and Eliza. They are two, good, whole-souled darkies, and they love each other, I suppose, as well as we ever could have loved, and it seems hard to let them go into the farce of marrying with the chance of being separated again in three or four weeks."

"Won't you be able to keep them anyway, Robert?" asked his wife.

"No, I am sorry I cannot. I shall keep a few of the older servants who would be absolutely useless to a new master, but the greed of my creditors will swallow everything that is of any commercial value."

His wife put her arms about his neck and laid her cheek against his.

"Never mind, Robert," she said, "never mind. We have our Dolly still, and each other. Then there is James, so we shall get on very well, after all."

"But what of Ben and Eliza?"

"Well, let them dream their dream while they may. If the dream be short, it will at least be sweet."

"It is not right," her husband said, "it is not right. It is giving them a false hope which is bound to be dashed when the sale comes."

"Sufficient unto the day is the evil thereof," said his brother James, crossing the threshold. He joined his word to his sister-in-law's, and together they persuaded the broken man to let the marriage go on, to let the two servants sup whatever of joy there might be for them. "Perhaps," added the always sanguine rector, "some man will be good enough to buy the two together. Anyway, we can try."

By an effort his voice was cheerful and his manner buoyant, but on his face there was a deeper shadow than that which clouded the brows of his brother, for now when his all was gone from which so many had received bounty, what would the poor of the county do?

The sad conversation was hardly finished when Aunt Sukey came in. It was something more that she had to say about "de weddin' fixin's." She was delighted and garrulous.

"Tell you what, Mas' Lancaster," she said, "hit do seem to me lak ol' times agin, all dis fixin' an' ca'in on. 'Pears to me lak de day o' my man Jeems done come back agin. Yo' spe't, yo' mannah an' yo' dispersition an' evahthing des de spittin' image of yo' pa. 'Tain't no wunner day named you Robbut aftah him. I 'membah how he say to me w'en Jeems come a-courtin', 'Sukey,' he say, 'Sukey, you gwine ma'y Jeems right, you gwine ma'y him wid a preachah, an' you gwine to live wid him 'twell you die. Dain't gwine to be no jumpin' ovah de broom an' pa'tin' in a year on my plantation. You gwine to all de famblies. La, bless yo' soul! wen Jeems an' me ma'ied, we had de real preachah dah, an' we stood up an' helt han's an' 'peated ovah, "twell deaf do us pa't,' des lak white folks. It sho did mek me monst'ous happy an' glad w'en I foun' out you gwine to do de same wid 'Lize an' Ben. 'Lize she a good gal, an' Ben be stiddy, an' Mas' Jeems," she said, turning to the rector, "I know you ain't gwine 'fuse to ma'y 'em out on de po'ch des lak me an' Jeems was ma'ied. Hit'll do my ol' eyes good. I kin o' believe my soul be fit fu' glory den."

The clergyman cleared his throat to speak, but the old woman broke in. "You ain't gwine 'fuse, Mas' Jeems? 'Lize an' Ben dey loves one 'nothah in de real ma'in' way an' dey hea'ts des sot on you jinin' 'em."

The brothers gazed for a moment into each other's eyes, and then James said huskily: "All right, Aunt Sukey, I'll do it."

She went away happy, but over the inmates of the big house a gray pall of sorrow fell.

Easter radiant with flowers and birds and the glorious Southern sunshine came but 'Lize had another use for her holiday dress, and Ben was ashamed to go, so neither of them went to the church service; a gladder, holier service waited for them. There followed a happy Monday, then the night of the wedding came and the long procession of servants marched from Aunt Sukey's cabin in the quarters up to the big house. The porch was garlanded and festooned. Under the farther end, near where the bridal pair would stand, sat the master's family; the dark-robed widow, whose mind went back sadly to her own brief married life, the master, the mistress, and the rector. His face was pale and set, but as the strange, weird wedding song of the Negroes came to his ears and they marched up the steps, stiff, awkward, but proud, in the best clothes they could muster, he tried to call back to his features the far smile which had always been so ready to welcome them. Eliza and Ben led the way. She radiant in her new finery smiling and bridling, Ben shame-faced, head hung and shuffling, and behind them Aunt Sukey in all the glory of a new turban and happy as she had been with her Jeems years and years ago.

They halted before the preacher and he pressed his brother's hand and stood up. The servants gathered around them, eager and expectant. The wedding hymn died away into the night, a low minor sob, as much of sorrow in it as of joy, as if it foreshadowed all that this marriage was and was not. Just as the last faint echo died away into the woods that skirted the lawn and the waiting silence was most intense, the hoot of an owl smote upon their ears and Eliza turned ashen with fear. She gripped Ben's arm; it was the worst of omens. James Lancaster knew the superstitions of the people and as he heard the cry of the evil bird, his book shook in his hand. Was it prophetic? His voice trembled with more than one emotion as he began: "Dearly beloved—"

The ceremony ran on, a deep-toned solo with an accompaniment of the anxious breathing of the onlookers. Then the preacher hesitated. He turned for an instant and looked at his brother, and in the glance was all the agony of a wounded heart. His next words were uttered in a scarcely audible tone, "till death do us part." And after him they all unknowing, repeated, "'twell deaf do us pa't."

It was over. The couples reformed and followed the bridal pair down the steps, Aunt Sukey hardly containing her joy, but Ben and Eliza somehow subdued. As their feet touched the ground of the lawn, the owl hooted again, and ever and anon, his voice was heard as the procession wound its stately way to the place of the next festivities.

In silence, the family from the big house followed. The two men walked together. As they reached the door of the decorated barn, James paused and took his brother's hand.

"Till death do them part," he cried, "My God! will it be death or the block!" Then with hard, forced smiles, they turned into the room to open the dance and the fiddles struck up a merry tune.

The Finding of Martha

WHETHER ONE BELIEVES in predestination or not, the intenseness with which Gideon Stone went toward his destiny would have been a veritable and material proof of foreordination. Even before the old mistress had followed her husband to the silent land and the marriage of Miss Ellen had entirely broken up the home, he had begun to exhort among the people who were forming a free community about the old slave plantation. The embargo against negro education having been removed, he learned to read by hook and by crook, and night after night in his lonely room he sat poring over the few books that he could lay his hands upon.

Aside from the semi-pastoral duties which he had laid upon himself, his life was a lonely one. For Gideon was no less true to his love than he had been to his honor. Since Martha had left him, five years before, no other woman had been enshrined in his heart, and the longing was ever in him to go forth and search for her. But his duties and his poverty still held him bound, and so the years glided away. Gideon's powers, however, were not rusting from disuse. He was gaining experience and increasing his knowledge.

It was now that the wave of enthusiasm for the education of the blacks swept most vigorously over the South, and, catching him, carried him into the harbor of one of the new Southern schools. The chief business of these institutions then was the turning out of teachers and preachers. During the months of his vacations Gideon followed the former calling as a means of preparation for the latter. So he was imparting to others the Rule of Three very soon after he had learned it himself. He brought to both these new labors of his the same earnestness and seriousness that had characterized his life on the plantation. And in due course the little school sent him forth proudly as one of her brightest and best.

The course being finished, Gideon's first impulse was to go farther southward, where his duty toward his fellows was plain. But his plan warred with the longing that had been in his heart ever since he had seen the blue lines swing over the hills and away, and he knew that with them Martha was making her way northward. He had never heard of her since; but he did not blame her. She could not write herself, few of her associates could, and in the turmoil of the times it would not be easy to get a letter written, or, being written, get it to him. Not for one moment did he lose faith in her. He believed that somewhere she was waiting for him,—impatiently, perhaps, but still with trust. He would go to her. From that moment his search should begin. Washington was the Mecca for his people then. Perhaps among those who had flocked from the South to the nation's capital he might find the object of his search. It was worth the trying, so thither he turned his steps.

At that time, when the first desire for a minister with at least a little more knowledge than they themselves possessed was coming to the Negroes, it was not a difficult matter for Gideon to find a church. He was called to a small chapel very shortly after he arrived in Washington, and after pastoring that for a few months found himself over the larger congregation of Shiloh Church, which was the mother of his former charge.

He had an enthusiasm for his work that gave him influence over the people and made him popular both as a preacher and a pastor, while the voice that in the days gone by had sung "Gideon's Band" was mighty in its aid to the volunteer choir. His fame grew week by week, and he drew around him a larger and better crowd of his own people. But in it all, his occupations and his successes, he did not forget why he had come to the city. His eye was ever out for a glimpse of a familiar face. With no thought of self-aggrandizement, he yet did all in his power to spread his name abroad, for, thought he, "If Martha hears of me, she will come to me." He did not trust to this method alone, however, but went forth at all times upon his search.

"Hit do 'pear to me moughty funny," said one of his congregation to another one day, "dat a preachah o' Brotah Stone's ability do hang erroun' de deepo so."

"Hang erroun' de deepo! What you talkin' 'bout, Sis Mandy?"

"Dat des whut I say. Dat man kin sholy allus be foun' at one deepo er anothah, Sis Lizy."

"I don't know how dat come, case he sholy do mek his pasto'ial wisits."

"I ain't 'sputin' de wisits, ner I ain't a-blamin' de man, case I got all kin' o' faif in Brotah Gidjon Stone, but I do say, an' dey's othahs dat kin tell you de same, dat w'en he ain't a-wisitin' de sick er a-preachin', he stan' erroun' watchin' de steam-cyahs, an' dey say his eyes des glisten w'enevah a train comes in."

"Huh, uh, honey, dey's somep'n' behime dat."

"'Tain't fu' me to say. Cose I knows all edjicated people has dey cuhiousnesses, but dis is moughty cuhious."

It was indeed true, as Sister Mandy Belknap had said, that Gideon was often to be found at one or the other of the railway stations, where he watched feverishly the incoming and outgoing trains. Maybe Martha would be on one of them. She might be coming in or going out any day, and so he was miserable whenever he missed a day at his post. The station officials looked in wonder at the slim Negro in clerical dress who came day by day to watch with intense face the monotonous bustle of arrival and departure. Whoever he is, they thought, he has been expecting someone for a long time.

The trains went and the trains came, and yet Martha did not appear, and the eager look in Gideon's face grew stronger. The intent gaze with which he regarded the world without grew keener and more expectant. It was as if all the yearning that his soul had experienced in all the years had come out into his face and begged pity of the world. And yet there was none of this plea for pity in Gideon's attitude. On the contrary, he went his own way, and a brave, manly way it was, that asked less of the world than it gave. The very disappointment which he restrained made him more helpful to the generally disappointed and despised people to whom he ministered. When his heart ached within him, he took no time for repining, but measuring their pain by his own, set out to find some remedy for their suffering. Their griefs were mirrored in his own sorrow, and every wail of theirs was but the echo of his own heart cry. He drew people to him by the force of his sympathetic understanding of their woes, and even those who came for his help and counsel went away asking how so young a man could feel and know so much.

Meanwhile in Gideon's congregation a feeling of unrest seemed taking possession of the sisters. In the privacy of their families they spoke of the matter which troubled them to indifferent husbands, who guffawed and went their several ways as if a momentous question were not taxing their wives' minds. But the women would not be put off. When they found that the men, with the indifference of the sex, refused to be interested, they talked among themselves, and they concluded without a dissenting voice that there was something peculiar, something strange and uncanny, about the celibacy of the Reverend Gideon Stone. He was abnormal. He was the shining exception in a much-marrying calling.

A number of them were gathered at Sister Mandy Belknap's home one Friday evening, when the conversation turned to the preacher's unaccountable course.

"Hit seem mo' unnatchul lak, case preachahs is mos'ly de marryinest kin' o' men," said Sister Lizy Doke.

"To be sho'; dat what mek his diffuntness look so cuhious."

"Well, now, look-a-hyeah, sistahs," spoke up a widow lady who was now enjoying a brief interval of single-blessedness after a stormy parting with her fourth spouse; "don't you reckon dat man got a wife som'ers? You know men will do dat thing. I 'membah my third husban'. W'en I ma'ied him he had a wife in Tennessee, and anothah one in Fuginny. I know men."

"Brothah Gidjon ain't nevah been ma'ied," said Sister Mandy shortly.

"Huccome you so sho'?"

"He ain't got de look; dat's huccome me so sho'?"

"Huh, uh, honey, dey ain't no tellin' whut kin' o' look a man kin put on. I know men, I tell you."

"Brothah Gidjon ain't ma'ied," reiterated the hostess; "fust an' fo'mos', dey ain't no foolin' de pusson on de ma'ied look, an' he ain't got it. Den he ain't puttin' on no looks, case Brothah Gidjon is diffunt f'om othah men mo' ways den one. I knows dat ef I is only got my fust husban' an' is still livin' wid him."

The widow lady instantly subsided.

"You don' reckon Brothah Gidjon's been tekin' up any dese hyeah Cath'lic notions, does you?" ventured another speaker. "You know dem Cath'lic pries'es don' nevah ma'y."

"How's he gwine to have any Cath'lic notions, w'en he bred an' born an' raised in de Baptis' faif?"

"Dey ain't no tellin'. Dey ain't no tellin'. W'en colo'ed folks git to gwine to colleges, you nevah know what dey gwine lu'n. My mammy's sistah was sol' inter Ma'ylan', an', bless yo' soul, she's a Cath'lic to dis day."

"Well, I don' know nuffin' 'bout dat, but hit ain't no Cath'lic notions, I tell you. Brothah Gidjon Stone's too solid fu' dat. Dey's some'p'n else behime it."

The interest and curiosity of the women, now that they were fired, did not stop at these private discussions among themselves. They went even farther and broached the matter to the minister.

They suggested jocosely, but with a deep vein of earnestness underlying the statement, that they were looking for a wife for him. But they could elicit from him no response save "There's time enough; oh, there's time enough."

Gideon said this with an appearance of cheerfulness, but in his heart he did not believe it. He did not think that there was time. His body, his mind, his soul all yearned hotly for the companionship of the woman he loved. There are some men born to be husbands, just as there are some men born to be poets, painters, or musicians—men who, living alone, cannot know life. Gideon was one of these. Every instinct of his being drove him towards domestic life with unflagging insistency. But it was Martha whom he wanted. Martha whom he loved and with whom he had plighted his troth. What to him were the glances of other women? What the seduction in their eyes, and the unveiled invitation in their smiles? There was one woman in the world to him, and she loomed so large to his sight that he could see no other. How he waited; how he longed; how he prayed! And the days passed, the trains came and went, and still no word, no sight of Martha.

Strangers came to his church, and visitors from other cities came to him, and still nothing of her for whom he waited to make his life complete. Then one day in the silence of his own sorrow he fell upon his knees, crying, "My God, my God, why hast thou forsaken me?" And from then hope fled from him. She was dead. She must be, or she would have come to him. He had waited long, oh, so long, and now it was all over. For the rest of his days he must walk the way of his life alone or—could he, could he turn his eyes upon another woman? No, no, his heart cried out to him, and he felt in that moment as a man standing beside his wife's bier would feel should the thought of another obtrude itself.

He went to the trains no more. He searched no more; hope was dead; but the one object that had blinded him, that had given him single sight, being removed, he began to look around him and to see—at first it seemed almost a revelation— other women. Now he saw too their glances and their smiles. He heard the tender notes in their voices as they spoke to him, for all other sounds were no longer drowned by Martha's calling to him from the Unknown. When first he found himself giving fuller range to his narrow vision, he was startled, then apologetic, then defiant. The man in him triumphed. Martha was dead. He was alone. Must he always be? Was life, after all, to be but this bitter husk to him when he had but to reach forth his hand to find the kernel of it?

He had never even been troubled with such speculations before, but now he awoke to the fact that he was not yet old and that the long stretch of life before him looked dreary enough if he must tread it by himself.

In this crisis the tempter, who is always an opportunist, came to Gideon. Sister Mandy Belknap had always manifested a great deal of interest in the preacher's welfare, a surprising amount for a woman who had no daughter. However, she had a niece. Now she came to the pastor with a grave face.

"Brothah Stone," she said, "I got some talk fu' you."

"Yes, Sister Belknap?" said Gideon, settling himself complacently, with the expectation of hearing some tale of domestic woe or some history of spiritual doubt, for among his congregation he was often the arbiter in such affairs.

"Now, I's ol' enough fu' yo' mothah," Sister Mandy went on, and at the words the minister became suddenly alert, for from her introduction her visit seemed to be admonitory, rather than appealing. Evidently he was not to give advice, but to be advised. He was not to be the advocate, but the defendant; not the judge, but the culprit.

"I's seed mo' of life den you has, Brothah Gidjon, ef I do say hit myse'f."

"Not a doubt of it, my sister."

"An' I knows mo' 'bout men an' women den you does. Co'se you know mo' 'bout Scripter den I does, dough I ricollect dat de Lawd said dat it ain't good fu' man to be alone."

Gideon started. It was as if the old woman had by some occult power divined the trend of his thoughts and come to take part in the direction of them.

"The Bible surely says that, Sister Belknap," he said when the first surprise was over.

"It do, an' I want to know ef you ain't a-flyin' in de face o' Providence by doin' what hit say ain't good fu' a man?"

Gideon was a little bit puzzled, but in answer he began, "There are circumstances—"

"Dat's des' hit," said Sister Mandy impressively; "sarcumstances, sarcumstances, an' evah man dat wants to disobey de wo'd t'inks he's got de sarcumstances. Uh! I tell you de ol' boy is a moughty clevah han' at mekin' excuses fu' us."

"I don't reckon, sister, that we've got the same point of view," said Gideon nervously.

"'Tain't my p'int of view, 'tain't mine; hit's de Lawd A'mighty's. You young, Brothah Gidjon, you young, an' you don' see lak I does, but lemme tell you, hit ain't right fu' no man whut ain't ma'ied to be a-pasto'n no sich a flock. I don' want to meddle into yo' business, but all I got to say is, you bettah look erroun' you an' choose a wife fu' to be yo' he'pmeet. 'Scuse me fu' speakin' to you, Brothah. Go 'roun' an' see my niece. She kin p'int out some moughty nice women."

"It was mighty good of you to speak, and I am glad that you came to me. I will think over what you have said."

"'It is not good for man to be alone,'" mused Gideon when his visitor was gone. Was not this just the word of help and encouragement that he had wanted —indeed, the one that he had been waiting for? He had been faithful, he told himself. He had looked and he had waited. Martha had not come, and was it not true that "it is not good for man to be alone?" He went to bed that night with the sentence ringing in his head.

Mandy Belknap had done her work well, for on the following Sunday the preacher smiled on her niece, Caroline Martin, and on the Sunday after that he walked home to dinner with her.

What the gossips said about it at the time, how they gazed and chattered, and with what a feeling of self-satisfaction Sister Mandy went her way, are details that do not belong to this story. However, one cannot pass over Gideon's attitude in this new matter. It is true that he found himself liking Caroline better and better the more frequently he saw her. The girl's pretty ways pleased him. She was a member of his choir, and he thought often how like Martha's her voice was. Indeed, he was wont to compare her with this early love of his, and it did not occur to him that he cared for her not so much for what she was herself, but for the few points in which she resembled his lost sweetheart. He was not wooing (if wooing his attentions could be called) Caroline Martin as Caroline Martin, but only as a proxy for his own unforgotten Martha, for even now, in the face of hopelessness, his love and faith were stronger than he.

Caroline Martin was the most envied girl in Shiloh Church, for, indeed, hers was no slight distinction, to be singled out by the minister for his special attention after so long a period of indifference. But envy and gossip passed her by as the idle wind, for the very honor which had been accorded her placed her above the reach of petty jealousies. Her triumph, however, was to be brief.

It was on a rainy Sunday night in October, a late Washington October, which has in it all the possibilities of nastiness given to weather. Shiloh Chapel was well filled despite the storm without. Gideon was holding forth in his accustomed way, vigorously, eloquently, and convincingly. His congregation was warming up to a keen appreciation of his sermon, when suddenly the door opened, and a drabbled, forlorn-looking woman entered and sank into a back seat. One glance at her, and the words died on Gideon's lips. He paused for a moment and swayed upon his feet while his heart beat a wild tattoo.

It was Martha, his Martha, but, oh, how sadly changed! His heart fell a-bleeding for her as he saw the once proud woman sitting there crouched in her seat among the well-dressed people like the humblest of creatures. He wanted to stop right there in the midst of his sermon and go rushing to her, to take her in his arms and tell her that if the world had dealt hard with her, he at least was true.

It was a long pause he made, and the congregation was looking at him in surprise. Then he recovered himself, and went on with his exhortation, hastily, feverishly. He could scarcely wait to be done.

The last words of the benediction fell from his lips and he hastened down the aisle, elbowing his way through the detaining crowd, his face set toward one point. Someone spoke to him as he passed, but he did not hear; a hand was stretched out to him, but he did not see it. There was but one thought in his mind.

He reached the seat in the corner of which Martha had crouched. She was gone. He stood for a moment dazed, and then dashed out into the rain and darkness. Nothing was to be seen of her, and hatless he ran on down the street, hoping to strike the direction in which she had started and so overtake her. But she had evidently gone directly across the street or turned another way. Sad and dejected and wondering somewhat, he retraced his steps to the church.

It was Martha; there could be no doubt of that. But why such an act from her? It seemed as if she had purposely avoided him. What had he done to her that she should treat him thus? She must have some reason. It was not like Martha. Yes, there was some good reason, he knew. Faith came back to him then. He had seen her. She was living and he would see her again. His heart lightened and bounded. Martha was found.

Sister Belknap was waiting for him when he got back to the church door, and beside her the comely Caroline.

"Wy, Brothah Gidjon," said the elder woman, "what's de mattah wid you to-night? You des shot outen de do' lak a streak o' lightnin', an' baih-headed, ez I live! I lay you'll tek yo' death o' col' dis hyeah night."

"I saw an old friend of mine from the South in church and I wanted to catch her before she got away, but she was gone."

There was something in the minister's voice, a tone or an inflection, that disturbed Sister Belknap's complacency, and with a sharp, "Come on, Ca'line," she bade him good-night and went her way. He saw them go off together without a pang. As he got his hat and started home, his only thought was of Martha and how she would come again, and he was happy.

The next Sunday he watched every new-comer to the church with eager attention, and so at night; but Martha was not among them. Sunday after Sunday told the same story, and again Gideon's heart failed him. Maybe Martha did not want to see him. Maybe she was married, and his heart grew cold at that.

For over a month, however, his vigilance did not relax, and finally his faith was rewarded. In the midst of his sermon he saw Martha glide in and slip into a seat. He ended quickly, and leaving the benediction to be pronounced by a "local preacher," he hurried down the aisle and was at her side just as she reached the door ahead of everyone.

"Martha, Martha, thank the Lord!" he cried, taking her hand.

"Oh Gid—I mean Brothah—er—Reverent—I must go 'long." The woman was painfully embarrassed.

"I am going with you," he said firmly, still holding her hand as he led her protesting from the church.

"Oh, you mustn't go with me," she cried, shrinking from him.

"Why, Martha, what have I done to you? I've been waiting for you so long."

She had begun to sob now, and Gideon, without pausing to think whether she were married or not, put his arm tenderly about her. "Tell me what it is, Martha? What has kept you from me so long?"

"I ain't no fittin' pusson fu' you now, Gidjon."

"What is it? You're not—are you married?"

"No."

"Have you kept the light?"

"Yes, thank de Lawd, even wid all my low-downess, I's kept de light in my soul."

"Then that's all, Martha?"

"No, it ain't—it ain't. I wouldn't stay wid you w'en you axed me, an' I came up hyeah an' got po'er an' po'er, an' dey's been times w'en I ain't had nothin' ha'dly to go on; but I wouldn't sen' you no wo'd, case I was proud an' I was ashamed case I run off to fin' so much an' only foun' dis. Den I hyeahed dat you was edjicated an' comin' hyeah to preach. Dat made you furder away f'om me, an' I knowed you wasn' fu' me no mo'. It lak to killed me, but I stuck it out. Many an' many's de time I seen you an' could 'a' called you, but I thought you'd be ashamed o' me."

"Martha!"

"I wouldn' 'a' come to yo' chu'ch, but I wanted to hyeah yo' voice ag'in des once. Den I wouldn' 'a' come back no mo case I thought you reckernized me. But I had to—I had to. I was hongry to hyeah you speak. But go back now, Gidjon, I'm near home, an' I can't tek you to dat po' place."

But Gideon marched right on. A light was in his face and a springiness in his step that had been absent for many a day. She halted before a poor little house, two rooms at the most, the front one topped with a stove-pipe which did duty as a chimney.

"Hyeah's whaih I live," she said shamefacedly; "you would come."

They went in. The little room, ill furnished, was clean and neat, and the thread-bare carpet was scrupulously swept.

Gideon had been too happy to speak, but now he broke silence. "This is just about the size of the cabin we'd have had if the war hadn't come on. Can you get ready by to-morrow?"

"No, no, I ain't fu' you, Gidjon. I ain't got nothin', I don't know nothin' but ha'd work. What would I look lak among yo' fine folks?"

"You'd look like my Martha, and that's what you're going to do."

Her eyes began to shine. "Gidjon, you don't mean it! I thought when colo'ed folks got edjicated dey fu'got dey mammys an' dey pappys an' dey ol' frien's what can't talk straight."

"Martha," said Gideon, "did you ever hear 'Nearer, my God, to Thee' played on a banjo?"

"No."

"Well, you know the instrument isn't much, but it's the same sweet old tune. That's the way it is when old friends tell me their love and friendship brokenly. Can't you see?"

THEY TALKED LONG that night, and Gideon brought Martha to his way of thinking, though she held out for less haste. She exacted a week.

On the following Sunday the Reverend Gideon Stone preached as his congregation had never heard him preach before, and after the service, being asked to remain, they were treated to a surprise that did their hearts good. A brother pastor, mysteriously present, told their story and performed the ceremony between Gideon and Martha.

So many of them were just out of slavery. So many of them knew what separation and fruitless hope of re-meeting were, that it was an event to strike home to their hearts. Some, wept, some rejoiced, and all gathered around the pastor and his wife to grasp their hands.

And then Martha was back on the old plantation again and her love and Gideon's was young, and she never knew why she did it, but suddenly her voice, the voice that Gideon had loved, broke into one of the old plantation hymns. He joined her. Members from the old South threw back their heads, and, seeing the yellow fields, the white cabins, the great house, in the light of other days, fell into the chorus that shook the church, and people passing paused to listen, saying,—

"There's a great time at Shiloh to-day."

And there was.

The Defection of Maria Ann Gibbs

THERE HAD BEEN a wonderful season of grace at Bethel Chapel since the advent of the new minister, and the number of converts who had entered the fold put the record of other years and other pastors to shame. Seats that had been empty were filled; collections that had been meagre were now ample. The church had been improved; a coat of paint had been put on the outside, and the interior had been adorned by a strip of carpet down the two aisles and pink calcimining on the walls. The Rev. Eleazar Jackson had proved a most successful shepherd. The fact was shown by the rotundity of his form, which bespoke good meals, and the newness of his clothes, which argued generous contributions.

He was not only a very eloquent man, but had social attainments of a high order. He was immensely popular with the sisters, and was on such good terms with the brothers that they forgot to be jealous of him. When he happened around about an hour before dinner-time, and some solicitous sister killed for him the fattening fowl which her husband had been watching with eager eyes, Mr. Jackson averted any storm which might have followed by such a genial presence and such a raciness of narration at the table that the head of the house forgot his anger and pressed the preacher to have some more of the chicken.

Notwithstanding this equality of regard on the part of both brothers and sisters, it was yet noticeable that the larger number of the converts were drawn from the tenderer sex—but human nature is human nature, women are very much women, and the preacher was a bachelor.

Among these gentle converts none was more zealous, more ardent or more constant than Maria Ann Gibbs. She and her bosom friend, Lucindy Woodyard, had "come th'oo" on the same night, and it was a wonderful event. They shouted all over Bethel Chapel. When one went up one aisle the other came down the other. When one cried "Hallelujah" the other shouted "Glory!" When one skipped the other jumped, and finally they met in front of the altar, and binding each other in a joyous embrace, they swayed back and forth to the rhythm of the hymn that was rising even above their own rejoicings, and which asserted that,

> "Jedgement Day is a-rollin' roun',
> Er how I long to be there!"

It was a wonderfully affecting sight, and it was not long before the whole church was in a tumult of rejoicings. These two damsels were very popular among their people, and every young man who had looked with longing eyes at Lucindy, or sighed for the brown hand of Maria Ann, joined in the shouting, if he was one of the "saved," or, if he was not, hastened up to fall prostrate at the mourners' bench. Thus were the Rev. Eleazar Jackson's meetings a great success, and his name became great in the land.

From the moment of their conversion Lucindy and Maria Ann went hand in hand into the good work for the benefit of the church, and they were spoken of as especially active young members. There was not a sociable to be given, nor a donation party to be planned, nor a special rally to be effected, but that these two consulted each other and carried the affair to a successful issue. The Rev. Eleazar often called attention to them in his exhortations from the pulpit, spoke of the beautiful harmony between them, and pointed it out as an example to the rest of his flock. He had a happy turn for phrase-making, which he exercised when he called the two "twin sisters in the great new birth o' grace."

For a year the church grew and waxed strong, and the minister's power continued, and peace reigned. Then as the rain clouds creep slowly over the mountaintop and bring the storm thundering down into the valley, so ominous signs began to appear upon the horizon of Bethel's religious and social life. At first these warning clouds were scarcely perceptible; in fact, there were those unbelievers who said that there would be no storm; but the mutterings grew louder.

The first sign of danger was apparent in the growing coolness between Lucindy and Maria Ann. They were not openly or aggressively enemies, but from being on that high spiritual plane, where the outward signs of fellowship were not needed, and on which they called each other by their first names, they had come down to a level which required, to indicate their relations one to the other, the interchange of "Sister Gibbs" and "Sister Woodyard." There had been a time when they had treated each other with loving and familiar discourtesy, but now they were scrupulously polite. If one broke in upon the other's remarks in church council, it was with an "Excuse me, Sis' Gibbs," or "I beg yo' pa'don, Sis' Woodyard," and each seemed feverishly anxious to sacrifice herself to make way for the other.

Then they came to work no more together. The separation was effected without the least show of anger. They simply drifted apart, and Lucindy found herself at the head of one faction and Maria Ann in the lead of another. Here for a time a good-natured rivalry was kept up, much to the increase of Bethel's finances and its minister's satisfaction. But an uncertain and less genial note began to creep into these contests as the Rev. Eleazar Jackson continued to smile upon both the ardent sisters.

The pastor at Bethel had made such a glowing record as a financier that the Bishop had expressed his satisfaction by a special letter, and requested that at the June rally he make an extra effort to raise funds for the missionary cause. Elated at this mark of distinction, and with visions of a possible Presiding Eldership in his mind, Mr. Jackson sought out his two most attractive parishioners and laid his case before them. It was in the chapel, immediately after the morning service, that he got them together.

"You see, sisters," he said, "Bethel have made a record which she have to sustain. She have de reputation o' bein' one o' the most lib'l chu'ches in de Confer'nce. Now we don't want to disa'point the Bishop when he picks us out to help him in such a good cause. O' co'se I knowed who I could depend on, an' so I come right to you sisters to see if you couldn't plan out some'p'n that would make a real big splurge at de June rally."

He paused and waited for the sisters to reply. They were both silent. This made him uneasy, and he said, "What you think, Sister Gibbs?"

"Oh," said Maria Ann, "I'm waitin' to hyeah f'om Sis' Woodyard."

"Oh, no," said Sister Woodyard politely, "don' wait on me, Sis' Gibbs. 'Spress yo'se'f, 'spress yo'se'f."

But Maria Ann still demurred. "I couldn't think o' puttin' my po' opinions up 'fo' Sis' Woodyard," she said. "I'd a good deal ruther wait to hyeah f'om my elders." She laid especial stress on the last word.

Lucindy smiled a smile so gentle that it was ominous.

"I ain't holdin' back 'ecause I cain't think o' nothin'," she said, "but jes' 'ecause I ain't been used to puttin' myse'f forrard, an' I don't like to begin it so late." And she smiled again.

The minister began to feel uneasy. Figuratively speaking, both of the sisters seemed to be sparring for wind, and he thought it better to call the council to a close and see each one separately.

"Well," he said hurriedly, "I know you sisters will come to some conclusion, an' jes' 'po't to me on next Wednesday night, an' I will pass a kind o' 'view over yo' plans, an' offer a su'jestion, mebbe. We want to do some'p'n that will bring out de people an' mek 'em give gen'ously of their means for de benefit o' de heathen."

The two sisters bowed very politely to each other, shook the minister's hand, and went their different ways.

It must have been Satan himself who effected the result of having both women hit upon the same plan of action. Maria Ann was pleased at her idea, and hastened to church on Wednesday evening to report it to the pastor, only to find that Lucindy Woodyard had been before her with the same plan.

"I mus' congratulate you, sisters," said the Rev. Eleazar, "bofe upon yo' diligence an' yo' fo'thought. It must 'a' been P'ovidence that directed bofe yo' min's in de same channel."

Both the sisters were aghast. They had both suggested dividing the church into soliciting parties and giving a prize to the one collecting the highest amount of money. Perhaps the Devil was not so much concerned in making their minds revert to this as it appeared, as it is a very common device for raising money among negro churches. However, both the women were disappointed.

"I'd jes' leave draw out an' let Sis' Gibbs go on an' manage dis affair," said Lucindy.

"I'd ruther be excused," said Maria Ann, "an' leave it in Sis' Woodyard's han's."

But the minister was wily enough to pour oil on the troubled waters, and at the same time to suggest a solution of the problem that would enlist the sympathies and ambition of both the women.

"Now I su'jest," he said, "that bofe you sisters remains in dis contest, an' then, instid o' throwin' the competition open, you sisters by yo'se'ves each be de head o' a pa'ty that shall bring de money to you, an' the one of you that gets the most f'om her pa'ty shall have de prize."

Lucindy's eyes glittered, and Maria Ann's flashed, as they agreed to the contest with joyful hearts. Here should be a trial of both strength and prowess, and it would be shown who was worthy to walk the ways of life side by side with the Rev. Eleazar Jackson.

Joyfully they went to their tasks. Their enthusiasm inspired their followers with partisan energy. Side bantered side, and party taunted party, but the leaders kept up a magnificent calm. It was not they alone who knew that there was more at stake than the prize that was offered, that they had more in view than the good of the heathen souls. There were other eyes that saw and minds that understood besides those of Lucindy, Maria Ann and the preacher.

Pokey Williams, who was very warm in the Gibbs faction, called from the fence to her neighbor, Hannah Lewis, who was equally ardent on the other side: "How yo' collection come on, Sis' Lewis?"

"Oh, middlin', middlin'; de w'ite folks I wok fu' done p'omise me some'p'n, my grocery man he gwine give me some'p'n, an' I got fo' dollahs in little bits a'ready."

"Oomph," said Pokey, "you jes' boun' an' 'termine to ma'y Lucindy Woodyard to de preachah!"

"G'way f'om hyeah, Pokey, you is de beatenes'! How you gittin' on?"

"Heish, gal, my w'ite folks done gi' me ten dollahs a'ready, an' I'm jes' tacklin' evahbody I know."

"Ten dollahs! W'y, dey ain' no way fu' de preachah to git erway f'om Maria Ann Gibbs ef you keep on!"

The two waved their hands at each other and broke into a rollicking laugh.

The rally in June was the greatest the annals of Bethel Chapel had ever recorded. The prize decided upon was a gold watch, and on the evening that the report and decision were to be made, a hall had to be procured, for the chapel would not hold the crowd. A brief concert was given first to get the people in a good humor, and to whet their anxiety, and though the performers were well received, little attention was paid to them, for everyone was on the *qui vive* for the greater drama of the evening. The minister was in his glory.

When the concert was over, he welcomed Lucindy and Maria Ann to the stage, where they sat, one on either side of him. The reports began. First one from Lucindy's side, then one from Maria Ann's, and so alternately through. It was very close! The people were leaning forward, eager and anxious for the issue. The reports came thick and fast, and the excitement grew as the sums increased. The climax was to be the reports of the two leaders themselves, and here Lucindy had shown her shrewdness. Maria Ann's side had begun to report first, and so their leader was compelled to state her amount first. There was a certain little reserve fund in the pocket of her opponent with which young Mrs. Worthington was somewhat acquainted, and it was to be used in case Maria Ann should excel her. Maria Ann made her report, reading from her book:

"'Codin' to de returns made by my pa'ty, which you hev all hyeahed, they hev collected one hun'erd an' eight dollahs; addin' to that what I hev collected by my-se'f, fifty-two dollahs, I returns to de chu'ch one hun'erd an' sixty dollahs."

Down in her lap Lucindy did some quick, surreptitious writing. Then she stood up.

"'Co'din' to de returns which my pa'ty hev made, an' which you hev all hyeahed, they hev collected one hun'erd an' two dollahs, an' I, by my own individual effort"—she laid wonderful emphasis upon the last two words, "bring in sixty dollahs, mekin' the total one hun'erd and sixty-two dollahs, which I submit to de chu'ch."

There was a burst of applause from Lucindy's partisans, but Maria Ann was on her feet:

"I forgot," she said, "de last donation I received. Mrs. Jedge Haines was kin' enough to give me a check fu' ten dollahs, which I didn't add in at fust, an' it brings my collection up to one hun'erd an' seventy dollahs."

The volume of applause increased at Maria Ann's statement, but it wavered into silence as Lucindy arose. She smiled down upon Maria Ann.

"I'm mighty thankful to de sister," she said, "fu' mindin' me o' some'p'n I mos' nigh fu'got. Mis' Cal'ine Worthington desired to put her name down on my book fu' twenty dollahs, which brings my collection to one hun'erd an eighty dollahs."

Mrs. Worthington looked across at Mrs. Haines and smiled. That lady raised her chin. An ashen hue came into Maria Ann Gibbs' face.

With great acclamation the watch was awarded to Lucindy Woodyard, and in congratulating her the Rev. Eleazar Jackson held her hand perhaps a little longer than usual. Mrs. Worthington was standing near at the time.

"If I had known it meant this," she said to herself, "I wouldn't have given her that twenty dollars." The lady saw that she was likely to lose a good servant. When the meeting was out the preacher walked home with Lucindy.

On the following Thursday night the Afro-American Sons and Daughters of Hagar gave a dance at their hall on Main Street. Maria Ann Gibbs, the shining light of Bethel Church, went, and she danced. Bethel heard and mourned.

On the next Sunday she went to church. She walked in with Mose Jackson, who was known to be a sinner, and she sat with him near the door, in the seat of the sinners.

The Rev. Eleazar Jackson went past Lucindy's house and they walked to church together. Lucindy had increased her stock of jewelry, not only by the watch, but by a bright gold ring which she wore on the third finger of her left hand. But if Maria Ann cared, she did not show it. She had found in the tents of the wicked what she could not get in the temple of the Lord.

A Judgment of Paris

IT IS A VERY difficult thing at any time and in any place to be the acknowledged arbiter of social affairs. But to hold this position in "Little Africa" demanded the maximum of independence, discretion and bravery. I say bravery, because the civilization of "Little Africa" had not arrived at that edifying point where it took disapproval gracefully and veiled its feelings. It was crude and primitive, and apt to resent adverse comment by an appeal to force, not of the persuasive but of the vindictive kind.

It had fallen to the lot of Mr. Samuel Hatfield to occupy this delicate position of social judge, and though certain advantages and privileges accrued to him his place was in no wise a sinecure. There were times when his opinions on matters of great moment had been openly scoffed at, and once it had even happened when a decision of his had been displeasing that fleetness of foot alone had saved him from the violence of partisans. Little did it matter to the denizens of "Little Africa" that others might be put upon committees to serve with Mr. Hatfield in judging the merits of waltzers or of the qualities of rival quartets. He was the one who invariably brought in the report and awarded the prize, and on him fell the burden of approval or disapproval.

For some months he had gone on gloriously unannoyed, with no one to judge, and nothing to pass upon. In the absence of these duties, Cupid had stepped in and with one shaft laid him prone at the feet of Miss Matilda Jenkins. Of course, Mr. Hatfield did cast occasional glances at the charms of Miss Amarilla Jones, but Cupid, grown wise with the wisdom of the world, has somehow learned to tip his arrows with gold, and the wound of these is always fatal.

Now, the charms of these two maidens were equal, their brown beauty about the same, but Matilda Jenkins' father was a magnate in "Little Africa," and so—.

On a night in autumn the devil appeared to certain members of the trustees' board of Mt. Moriah Church, and said unto them: "You need money wherewith to run this church," and they answered and said: "Yes, good devil, we do."

The devil spoke again and said: "Give a calico festival and a prize to the woman wearing the prettiest calico dress." And much elated, they replied: "Yea, verily."

Thereupon the devil, his work being done, vanished with a crafty smile, leaving them to their deliberations.

Brother Jenkins and Brother Jones were both members of the "Boa'd," and when the contest was decided upon they looked across at each other with defiance shining in their eyes, because there was a strong rivalry between the two families. But there animosity apparently ended. Brother Jenkins dropped his eyes, for he was a little old man, and Brother Jones was "husky," which is the word that in their community indicated rude strength. The fight, however, for fight it was going to be, was on.

Within the next few days the shopkeepers of the town sold bolt upon bolt of calico. The buying of this particular line of goods was so persistent that one shop-keeper, who was a strong-tongued, rude man, laid it at the door of certain advocates of industrial education and began to denounce any doctrines which repressed in the negro his love of clothes far above his pocket, and thereby lowered profits.

As soon as Mr. Hatfield learned what was going on he became alarmed, for he saw more clearly than most people and he knew that it was all the invention of the devil. His good angel prompted him to flee from the town at once, but he lingered to think about it, and while he lingered the committee came upon him. They wanted him to be chairman of the awarding committee. He stammered and made excuses.

"You see, gent'mens, hit's des disaway. I 'low I got to go out o' town fu' my boss des 'bout de time dat dis hyeah's comin' off, an' I wouldn' lak to p'omise an' den disap'pint you."

"Dat's all right, dat's all right," said brother Jones, the spokesman; "I knows yo' boss, an' he teks a mighty intrus' in Mt. Moriah. I'll see him an' see ef he can't let you go befo' er after de en'tainment."

The sweat broke out on Mr. Hatfield's brow in painful beads.

"Oh, nevah min', nevah min'," he exclaimed hastily; "dis hyeah's private business, an' I wouldn' lak him to know dat I done spoke 'bout it."

"But we got to have you, Mr. Hatfield. You sholy mus' speak to yo' boss. Ef you don't, I'll have to."

"I speak to him, den, I speak to him. I see what he say."

"Den I reckon we kin count on yo' suhvices?"

"I reckon you kin," said the victim.

As the committee went its way, Hatfield was sure that he heard a diabolical chuckle and smelt sulphur.

The days that had dragged flew by and the poor social arbiter looked upon the nearing festivity as upon the approach of doom. With the clear perception of a man who knows his world, Mr. Hatfield already saw that all women in the contest besides Matilda Jenkins and Amarilla Jones were but figureheads, accessories only to the real fight between the rival belles. So, as an earnest of his intention to be impartial, he ceased for the time his attentions to Matilda Jenkins. This lady, though, was also wise in her day and generation. She offered no protest at the apparent defection of her lover. Indeed, when her father squeaked his disapproval of Hatfield's action, she was quick to come to his defense.

"I reckon Mr. Hatfield knows what he's about," she said loyally. "You know how de people talks erroun' hyeah. Den, ef he go an' gi' me de prize, dey des boun' to say dat it ain't 'cause I winned it, but 'cause he keepin' comp'ny wid me, an' ain' gwine to shame his own lady."

"Uh, huh," said the old man; "dat hadn't crost my min' befo'."

In the meantime a similar council was taking place between Miss Amarilla Jones and her father.

"I been noticin'," said the paternal Jones one day, "dat Sam Hatfield don' seem to be a-gwine wid Matildy Jenkins so much."

Amarilla modestly ducked—yes, that's the word—she ducked her head, but she smiled as she replied: "Mistah Hatfiel' been cas'in' sheep's-eyes at me fu' a long while now."

"Well, what good do dat do, less'n he up an' say some'p'n?"

"Nevah you min', pap; I 'lows I un'erstan' young men bettah dan you do. Ef he don' mean nuffin, how come he done give up Matildy Jenkins des at dis junction?"

"Hit's all mighty quare to me."

"Don' you see he got to jedge de contes', an' he cain go ag'in his own lady, so he gin huh up? Now, ef he gi' me de prize, he feel puffectly free to ax me to ma'y him."

"Whew-ee!" whistled the elder, entirely overcome with admiration at his daughter's sagacity; "you sholy has got a quick head on dem shoulders o' yo'n!"

At the time appointed the members and friends of Mt. Moriah assembled for the calico social. The church was crowded with a curiously-gowned throng of all conditions and colors, who tittered and chatted with repressed excitement. There was every conceivable kind of dress there among the contestants, from belted Mother Hubbards to their aristocratic foster-sisters, Empire gowns. There was calico in every design, from polka-dot to Dolly Vardens—and there was—anxiety.

Promptly at ten o'clock the judges, three pompous individuals with white ribbons in their buttonholes, strode in and took their seats just beneath the pulpit. Then there was a short address by the pastor, who, being a wily man and unwilling to put his salary in jeopardy, assured his hearers that if he were one of the judges he would "jest throw up his job an' give a prize to every lady in the room." This brought forth a great laugh and somewhat relieved the nervous tension, but it did not make the real judges feel any better over their difficult task. Indeed, it quite prostrated their chairman, who, in spite of his pompous entrance, sat huddled up in his chair, the sweat breaking out of every pore and the look of final despair in his eyes.

When the pastor was through with his driveling the organist took her place at the wheezy little cabinet organ and struck up a decorous-sounding tune to which the contestants marched round and round the room before the eyes of the bewildered arbiters. They stepped jauntily off, marking the time perfectly to show off their airs and graces as well as their clothing. It was like nothing so much as a sort of religious cake-walk. And the three victims of their own popularity presided over the scene with a solemnity that was not all dignity nor yet pride of place. Five times the contestants marched around and then, at a signal, they halted and ranged themselves in a more or less straight line before the judges.

After careful inspection, somewhat like that of prize cattle at a fair, they were dismissed, and three very nervous and perturbed gentlemen retired to consult.

Now, these people were lovers of music, and at the very promise that they were to hear their favorite singer, Miss Otilla Bell, they usually became enthusiastic. But to-night Miss Bell came out without a greeting, and sang her best without attention. There were other things occupying the minds of the audience. The vocalist was barely done warbling disappointedly when a burst of applause brought a smile to her face. But a glance in the direction toward which everyone was looking showed her that the acclamation was not for her, but for the returning judges.

The men took their seats until the handclapping ceased, and then Mr. Hatfield, in sorrowful case, arose to read the committee's report.

"We, de committee—" He paused and looked at the breathless auditors, then went on: "We de committee; I wish to impress dat on you. Dis ain't de decision of one man, but of a committee, an' one of us ain't no mo' 'sponsible den de otah. We, de committee, aftah carefully ezaminin' de costooms of de ladies hyeah assembled ez contestants in dis annual calico social" (It was not annual, but then it sounded well), "do fin'" (Here he cleared his throat again, and repeated himself) —"do fin' dat de mos' strikin' costoom was wo' by Miss Matilda Jenkins, who is daihfo' entitled to de prize."

A little patter of applause came from the Jenkins partisans.

"Will Miss Jenkins please come forward?"

Matilda sidled to the front with well-simulated modesty.

"Miss Jenkins, we, de committee—I repeat, we, de committee, teks great pleasure in pussentin' you wid de prize fu' yo' handsome costoom. It is dis beautiful photygraph a'bum. May you have nuffin' but de faces of frien's in it fu' de reason dat you has no inimies."

He bowed. She bowed. There was again the patter of perfunctory applause, and for that night, at least, the incident was closed.

Fear has second sight, and, albeit he trembled in his shoes, Mr. Hatfield was in nowise astonished when old man Jones called on him next morning at the hotel where he was employed.

"W'y, w'y, how do, Mistah Jones? How do?"

"Howdy?" growled the old man, and went on without pause: "Me an' 'Rilla wants to see you to-night."

"W'y, w'y, Mistah Jones," began Hatfield. "I—I—" But the other cut him short, his brow gathering.

"Me an' 'Rilla wants to see you," he said.

The scared waiter paused. What should he do? He must decide quickly, for the man before him looked dangerous. There must be no trouble there, because it would mean the loss of his place, and the fact that he was a head waiter was dear to him. Better promise to go and have it out where the presence of Amarilla might mitigate his punishment. So he stammered forth: "'Oh, well, co'se, ef you an' Miss Amarilla wants me, w'y, I'll come."

"All right," and the irate Jones turned away.

With trembling knees he knocked at the Jones door that night. The old man himself opened to him and received him alone in the front room. This was threatening.

"I reckon you reelizes, Mistah Hatfiel'," said Jones when they had seated themselves and disposed of the weather, "you reelizes dat I had some'p'n putic'lah to say er I wouldn' 'a' had you come hyeah?"

"I knows you's a man o' bus'ness, Mistah Jones."

"I is, suh; so let's come to bus'ness. You t'ought las' night dat Tildy Jenkins was bettah dressed den my daughter?"

Hatfield glanced at the glowering face and stammered: "Well, of co'se, you know, Mistah Jones, I wasn' de whole committee."

"Don't you try to beat erbout de bush wid me—answeh my question!" cried the father angrily.

"I don't des see how I kin answeh. You hyeahed de decision."

"Yes, I hyeahed it, an' I want to know des what you t'ought."

"Dey was two othah men 'long wid me."

Jones walked over and stood towering before his trembling victim. "I's gwine to ax you des once mo', did you t'ink Matildy's dress any puttier den my 'Rilla's?"

"No, no—suh," chattered the chairman of the committee.

"Den," thundered Amarilla's father—"den you own up dat you showed favoh to one side?"

"No, no—I didn' sho' no favoh—but—but de majo'ity, hit rules."

"Majo'ity, majo'ity! W'y, w'en I's in de Odd Fellows' meetin's, ef I's one ag'in fifty, I brings in a mino'ity repo't."

"But I don't reckon dat 'ud 'a' been fittin'."

"Fittin', fittin'! Don't you daih to set thaih an' talk to me erbout fittin', you nasty little rapscallion, you. No, suh! You's shamed my house, you's insulted my gal, an'—"

"Oh, no, Mistah Jones, no. W'y, d'ain't nobody I thinks mo' of den I does of Miss Amarilla."

"Dey hain't, eh? Well, dey's only one way to prove it," said Mr. Jones, sententiously; and then he called: "'Rilla, come hyeah. I'll be right outside de do'," he said, "an' we'll know putty soon how to treat you."

He went out and the vivacious 'Rilla entered.

"Good-evenin'," she said.

"Good-evenin'," said Hatfield in agony. "Oh, Miss 'Rilla, Miss 'Rilla," he cried, "I hope you don't think I meant any kin' o' disrespect to you?" She hung her head.

"You know dey ain't nobody dat I think any mo' of den I do of you." In his fervor he took her hand.

"This is so sudden," she said, "but I thought I unnerstood you all along. Ef you really does think so much o' me, I reckon I has to tek you even ef you was sich a naughty boy las' night," and she looked at him lovingly.

He stood with staring eyes, dumbfounded. She had taken his apology for a proposal of marriage, and he—he dared not correct her. He looked toward the door meditating flight, but remembered what was just behind it.

"Dear Miss Amarilla," he said, "dis is mo' den I expected."

The ponderous Mr. Jones did not bother them again that evening. He must have heard all.

Matilda Jenkins first heard the news upon the street. She came home directly and before taking off her hat picked up the red plush album and hurled it fiercely out into the yard, where it barely missed her father's head.

"What's dat?" he cried.

"Dat?" she shrieked. "Dat is de price o' Mistah Hatfiel'."

Silent Sam'el

MISS ANGELINA BROWN was a young woman of many charms. Everyone in Little Africa conceded that. No one who had seen her dash gracefully up the aisle of Mount Moriah Church to the collection-table with tossing head and rustling skirts; no one who had seen her move dreamily through the mazy dance at the hod-carriers' picnics could fail to admit this much. She was a tall, fine-looking girl, with a carriage that indicated that she knew her own worth, as she did.

What added to the glamour that hung about the name of the brown damsel was that she was the only daughter of a very solid citizen—a man who was known to have both "propity" and money. There was no disputing the solidity of the paternal Brown, as there was no question of his utter simplicity and unaffectedness. He had imparted to Angelina a deal of his own good sense, and though she did not flaunt it, she did not, like many others born hitherside the war, disdain the fact that her father had learned on his master's plantation the trade that supported them.

Under these circumstances it is easy to believe that the young woman had many suitors. There were many proper and stylish young men in the community who were willing to take the entrancing girl for herself in spite of the incubus of her riches. Indeed, there were frequent offers of such noble sacrifices; but Angelina was a shrewd high priestess, and she found it better to keep her victims in her train than to immolate them on the altar of matrimony. So it happened that there were few evenings when a light was not visible in the parlor of old Isaac Brown's house, and one or another of the young men of Little Africa did not sit there with Angelina.

It was of a piece with the usual good sense that governed this house that slow-going, unpretentious Samuel Spencer—"Silent Sam'el," they called him—made one of these evening sitters. Samuel was a steady-going, good-humored fellow, and a workman under the elder Brown. This may have accounted for Angelina's graciousness to him. For even when he was in her company he had never a word to say for himself, but sat, looked at the lamp, twirled his hat, and smiled. This was certainly not very entertaining for the girl, but then, her father had a high opinion of Samuel's ability. So she would make conversation, and endure his smiles, until old Isaac would call gruffly to him from the kitchen, and he would rise silently and go. Then Angelina was free to entertain whom she pleased for the rest of the evening, for the two men did not part until near midnight.

Once with his employer, Samuel would venture a remark now and then over the something like oily looking tea which they stirred round and round in their glasses. But usually he listened while the old man expounded his new plans and ideas, and every once in a while would shake his head in appreciation, or pat his knee in pure enjoyment. This happened every Wednesday, for that was Samuel's particular evening. Isaac Brown looked forward to it with more pleasure than Angelina. For as he said, when Samuel's silence was referred to, "You needn't say nothin' to me 'bout Sam'el Spencer. I reckon he talks enough fu' me; and 'sides dat, I's allus noticed dat hit took a might' sma't man to know how to keep his mouth shet. Hit's a heap easier to talk."

But there were others who were not so favorably disposed toward old man Brown's "pet," as they called him. Jim White, who was head waiter at the big hotel, and consequently widely conversant with men and things, said: "Huh, ol' Sam go down to ol' man Brown's, an' set up there fur an hour an' a half 'side Miss Angelina, her talkin' an' laughin' an' him lookin' like a bump on a log." And this same joke, though often repeated, never failed to elicit a shout of laughter from the waiters assembled about their leader, and anxious to laugh at anything the autocrat of the dining-room might condescend to say. Others went so far as to twit Samuel himself, but he bore all of this good-naturedly, and without attempting to change his manner, until one memorable night.

It was on the occasion of a great rallying festival at Mount Moriah Church, and a large part of Little Africa was gathered within the church walls, partaking of ice cream, oyster stews and coffee. As Angelina was one of those who had volunteered to help serve the company she had denied herself the pleasure of a "gentleman escort" and had gone early with her father and mother.

Jim White and Samuel Spencer were not the only ones who followed her about that evening with amorous glances. Young men bought oyster stews if she could serve them when they had eaten far beyond their normal capacities. Old men with just teeth enough left to ache gave themselves neuralgia with undesired ice cream.

Jim White had about him a crowd that he treated lavishly every time he could get Angelina's eye; and Samuel himself had already accomplished six oyster stews and was looking helplessly at his seventh.

There is no telling what might have happened had not the refreshments given out and the festival been forced to close. The young men and young women came together in twos and took their way home. But while Angelina stood counting her takings there were no less than six anxious beaus who stood waiting her pleasure.

Of these Sam was the nearest, and those who looked on were about to conclude that even slow as he was he would reach her this time first and gain permission to take her home, when just as a slight sinking of her head showed that her counting was done, Jim White stepped up and, with a bow, asked for "the pleasure." She looked around for a moment and her eye fell on her silent admirer. She hesitated, and then, turning, bowed to White.

The smile died on Sam's face, and he stood watching them blankly. Not until her escort had found her wraps and had put her in them and she had said a light good-night to those who waited did Sam awake from his stupor.

There were some titters as he passed out, and a few remarks such as, "Uh huh, Sam, you too slow fu' Jim. You got to move an' talk faster," or "You sholy was cut out dat time."

But he went on his way, though in spite of the smile that came back to his lips there was a determined look in his eyes. On the church steps he paused and looked after the retreating forms of Angelina and his rival, then with a short but not angry "Huh!" he went his way home.

There was in his mind the consciousness of something wrong, and that something was wrong, his far from dull wits told him, neither with Jim nor Angelina, but himself. He had a perfect right to speak to her first if he could, and she had a right to accept his company. He was bleakly just to everyone concerned, and yet he knew by rights he should have taken Angelina home, and then the thought came to him that he could have said nothing to her even had he taken her home. Jim could talk; he couldn't. The knowledge of his own deficiencies overwhelmed him, and he went to bed that night in no happy frame of mind.

For a long while he did not sleep, but lay thinking about Angelina. It was nearly morning when he got suddenly out of bed and began dancing a breakdown in his bare feet, whispering to himself, "By gum, that's it!"

The landlady knocked on the wall to know what was the matter. He replied that he had been attacked with cramp in his feet, but was better now, and so subsided.

From now on a change took place in Samuel's manner of proceeding. The first thing that marked this change was his unexpected appearance in the Brown parlor on the next Monday. Angelina was entertaining another caller, but she received him pleasantly and, so far as an occasional reference to him would suffice, drew him into the conversation. However, he did not stay long, and so his hostess concluded that he had just been passing and had casually dropped in. What was her surprise when promptly at the same hour on the next night Samuel again came smiling in and settled himself to listen to the talk of that night's caller. Angelina was astounded. What did he mean? Had he begun to spy upon her and her company? Wednesday was his acknowledged night, and of course he had a right to come, but when he turned up on Thursday she openly tossed her head and treated him with marked coldness. The young man who had the pleasure of sitting out the hours on Thursday brought her a bunch of flowers. Samuel was evidently taking lessons, for on Friday night he appeared with a wondrous bouquet.

For one whole week, including Sunday, he was by the side of his divinity some part of every evening. The other young men were provoked. Angelina was annoyed, but less seriously than she might have been when she found that Samuel had the consideration never to stay long. The most joyful one of all concerned was old Isaac Brown himself.

"When Sam'el sets out a cou'tin' he does it jes' like he does evahthing else. Huh, de way he sot his cap fu' Angie is a caution."

But the truth of it was, Samuel Spencer was deeper than those who knew him could fathom. His week's visit to Angelina had not been without reason or result, and its object might have been discovered as he mumbled to himself on the last night of his constant attendance: "Well, I've heard 'em all talk, but I reckon that little Scott fellow that comes on Friday night's about the slickest of the lot. He'll have to do my talkin' fur me." He chuckled a little, and shook his head solemnly, "Ef somebody else got to speak fur me," he added, "I do' want nothin' but the best talent."

The next week it appeared that Samuel's sudden passion must have burned itself out as suddenly as it had appeared, for not even Wednesday night saw his face in the Brown parlor. Then was Angelina uneasy, for she thought she had offended him; and she didn't want to do that, for he was her father's friend, anyway, even if he was nothing to her, and her father's—oh, well, her father's friend deserved respect. So she instructed the elder Brown to inquire the reason for the young man's sudden defection, and she was greatly soothed, even though she did not care for him, when her parent brought back the message that "Sam was all right, an' 'ud be 'roun'."

It was not until Friday night that he came and, contrary to his usual custom, he went directly back into the kitchen, where he spent the hours with the old man. Angelina was piqued, and she tossed her head as he came in just as Mr. Scott was leaving. He sat down and smiled at her for a little while, and then he said abruptly:

"I mean all he said."

She gazed at him in astonishment.

"I mean all he said," he repeated, and soon after bade her good-night.

Friday night after Friday night he came at one hour or another, and after Scott had poured out his heart to Angelina Samuel merely whispered in her ear that he meant all that. Now this was very shrewd of Samuel, for Mr. Scott was a very eloquent and fluent talker, and Angelina thought that if Samuel meant all the other said he must mean a good deal.

One night, with burning words, Scott asked the momentous question. Samuel was in the kitchen with Isaac Brown at the time his rival was making his impassioned plea. Angelina bade her wooer to wait until she had time to think, and when he had gone she awaited the coming of Samuel.

He came in smiling, as usual.

"I mean all he said," he asserted.

"How do you know, you do? You do' know what he said," retorted Angelina.

"I mean all he said," repeated Sam.

"La, Mr. Spencer, you are the beatenes' man! If you mean all he said, why don't you say it yo'se'f?"

"I can't,"said Sam simply.

"Well, Mr. Scott surely has said enough to-night."

"I mean all he said."

"I'm mighty 'fraid you'll want to back out when you hear it."

"I mean all he said," and Sam laid an emphasis on the "all." He was slowly working his way toward Angelina. His wits began to tell him what Scott had said.

"You ain't never ast me what he said."

"What?"

"Oh, I can't tell you; don't you know?"

By this time he had reached her and put his arm around her trim waist.

"I mean all he said."

"Well, then, I says yes to you fur what you means, even if you won't say it," and Angelina ducked her head on his breast.

Sam's eyes shone, and it was a good deal later before he left that night. As he stood at the gate he suddenly broke his silence and said, "I thought Scott was nevah goin' to git to the question."

The Way of a Woman

ANY MAN WHO has ever wooed in earnest, or thought so, knows how hard it is to have his suit repulsed time and time again. However the capricious one may smile at times, one "no" upsets the memory of many days of smiles.

The structure of Gabe Harris' hopes had fallen so often that he had begun to build it over again listlessly and mechanically enough, until one momentous day, when it seemed fallen for good.

He had come by, as usual, upon his cart that evening after work, and paused, as was his wont, for a chat with his desired one, Anna Maria Moore. He had been hard at work all day hauling from the clay-pits, and so was not a thing of beauty as to clothes. But if Anna Maria loved him—and he believed she did—love was blind, which left him all right in his own eyes and hers.

Perhaps he was right even thus far, and all would have gone well had not the plump, brown beauty of the girl overcome him as he stood chatting with her.

The realization of her charms, of her desirableness, swept over him with a rush of emotion. Instinctively he held out his arms to her. They were in the front yard, too. "W'en—w'en you gwine ma'y me, honey? Tell me."

Anna Maria froze at once. She grew as rigid as the seams in her newly starched calico.

"W'y—w'y, what's de mattah, Anna Maria?" stammered the discomfited Gabe.

"'Scuse me, Mistah Ha'is," said the lady, with dignity, "but I's not in de habit ob bein' spoke to in dat mannah."

"W'y, what's I done, Anna Maria?"

"What's you done, sah? What's you done? W'y you's scandalized me 'fo' de eyes ob de whole neighbo'hood," and the calico swished itself as well as its stiffness would allow into the house.

Gabe scratched his head. "Well, I'll be dad burned!" he ejaculated.

Just then Uncle Ike, Anna Maria's father, came up. He was Gabe's friend and ally, and the young fellow's bewilderment was not lost upon him.

"What's de mattah, Brothah Gabe?" he questioned.

"W'y, Unc' Ike, I done axed Anna Maria to ma'y, an she say I's insulted an' scandalized de neighbo'hood. Huccome dat?"

"Tsch, tsch, tsch, Brothah Gabe; you sholy doesn't knew de pherlosophy ob oomankin'."

"I reckon I ain't up on dat, Unc' Ike; seems I ain' had de spe'ence dat hab fell to yo' lot."

The present was Uncle Ike's fourth matrimonial venture, and he was supposed to know many things. He went on: "Now, Brothah Gabe, in co'tin' a ooman, less'n she's a widdah ooman, dey's th'ee t'ings you got to do; you got to satisfy huh soul, you got to chawm huh yeah, an' you got to please huh eye. 'Tain't no use doin' one ner tothah less'n you does all—dat is, I say, pervided it ain't a widdah lady; dey bein' easiah to please an' mo' unnerstannin' laik. Well, you come hyeah, aftah yo' day's wo'k, an' you talk to Anna Maria. She know you been a'wo'kin', an'll mak' a good perviderr; dat satisfy huh soul."

"Yes, suh; she smile w'en I was a-talkin' to huh, an' dat what mak me fu'git myse'f."

"Uh-huh," said the old man, wagging his head sagely and stroking the straggling beard upon his chin, "uh-huh, dat mean dat you chawm huh yeah; but hol' on, hol' on dey's one mo' t'ing. How in de name ob common sense you spec' to please huh eye a-comin' hyeah in sich togs ez deze? Ki yi, now you see."

Again Gabe had recourse to his signal of perplexity, and woolly head and grimy nails came together in a half-hearted scratch.

"Unc' Ike, you sholy hab opened my eyes," he said, as he went slowly out to his cart.

On the morrow he arrayed himself in his best, and hitching his mare to a buggy not yet too rickety to awe some of his less prosperous neighbors, started toward the home of his inamorata. Old Suke, accustomed to nothing lighter than her cart on workdays, first set her ears doubtfully at the unaccustomed vacation, and then, seeming to realize that it was really a vacation, a gala-day, she tossed her head and stepped out bravely.

In the heart of Gabe Harris a similar exultation was present. What now would check him in his quest of the fair one? He had fulfilled all the requirements laid down by Uncle Ike, and Uncle Ike knew. He had already satisfied her soul; he had done his duty as to "chawmin' her yeah," now he went forth a potential conqueror for the last great feat—the pleasing of her eyes. Gone were the marks and the memory of the clay-pits, gone was the ashiness of dust from his hardened hands. His self-abashing cap was replaced by an aggressive "stiff hat," while his black coat and waistcoat, with drab trousers, completed an invincible make-up.

It was an autumn day, the year was sighing toward its close, but there was a golden touch in the haze that overhung the mean streets where he passed, and somewhere up in a balsam poplar a bird would persist in singing, and something in Gabe's heart kept answering, answering, as he alighted and hitched Suke before Anna Maria's gate.

A little later she came out arrayed in all her glory. She passed through the gate which the smiling Gabe held open for her, and stepped lightly into the buggy. Suke turned one inquisitive glance over her shoulder, and then, winking slowly to herself, consented to be unhitched and to jog leisurely toward the country roads. What Gabe said to Anna Maria and what Anna Maria said to Gabe on that drive is not recorded. But it is evident that the lover had been preparing his lady for something momentous, for upon returning late that afternoon he paused as he helped her alight, and whispered softly: "I got sompin' mo' to say to you."

As they entered the house, the smell of baking biscuits and of frying pork assailed their nostrils. Aunt Hannah Moore also had recognized this as a gala-day, and was putting herself out to lay such a feast for her daughter's suitor as he should remember for many a day to come. Gabe sat down in the spick-and-span front room.

"Ma's biscuits cert'n'y does smell scan'lous," Anna Maria commented, agreeably.

Gabe's mind was too full of his mission to heed the remark. The momentous second had arrived—the second that held the fruition of all his ambitions, all his dreams. He plumped down on his knees at her feet. "Oh, Anna Maria," he cried, "Anna Maria, ain't you gwine hab me now?"

Anna Maria turned on him a look full of startled surprise, which soon turned to anger and disdain. "Look hyeah, Gabe," she said, wrathfully, "what's de mattah wid you? Is you done tuk leab oh yo' senses? Ain't you got no 'spect fo' a lady's feelin's? Heah I's tiahed an' hongry, an' you come 'roun talkin' sich foolishness ez dat. No, I ain't gwine hab you. Git up f'om daih, an' ac' sensible. I's hongry, I is."

Gabe got up sheepishly, dusting his knees. Anna Maria turned to the window. He took his hat, and let himself out of the door.

"Heyo, Brothah Gabe, wha you gwine? You ain't gwine 'way fo' suppah, am you? We got som monstous fine middlin' daih fryin' speshly fo' you," was the greeting from Anna Maria's father.

"D'you want to buy Suke? I's gwine 'way f'om hyeah."

"What's de mattah'd you?" was the old man's quick question.

"I's done filled all de 'quirements you tol' me, an' axed Anna Maria 'gain, an' she won't hab me, an' I's gwine 'way."

"No, y'ain't. Set down."

Gabe seated himself beside his adviser.

"W'en you ax Anna Maria?"

"Jes' now."

"Oomph, oomph, oomph," said the old man, reflectively; and he went on: "Gabe, fo' a ha'd wo'kin, money-savin', long-haided man you sholy has got less sense dan anybody I know."

"What's I done now?" said Gabe, disconsolately. "Ain't I filled all de 'quirements? Ain't I satisfied huh soul? Aain't I chawmed huh yeah? Ain't I pleased huh eye? Now wha' mo'—oh, 'tain't no use!"

"Hol' on, hol' on, I say; you done all dese t'ings. You's satisfied huh soul, you's chawmed huh yeah, you's pleased huh eye, an' she's jes ready fo' you, but Lawd a' massy 'pon me, ain't you got mo' sense dan to pop de question to a lady w'en she hungry? Gabe, you got lots to l'arn."

"'Tain't no use, Unc' Ike; ef she eat suppah an' git satisfied, den she ain't gwine need me."

"You set down an' wait till aftah suppah, I say."

Just then the call for supper came, and Gabe went in with the black Solomon. During the blessing Anna Maria was cold and distant, but when the first biscuit was passed to her her face brightened. She half smiled as she broke it open and filled its hot interior with rich yellow butter. The smile was on full force when she had tasted the brown crisp "middlin'," and by the time she had the "jackets" off two steaming potatoes her face was beaming.

With wonder and joy Gabe watched the metamorphosis take place, and Uncle Ike had constantly to keep nudging or kicking him under the table to keep him from betraying himself.

When the supper was done, and it went on to a merry ending, Aunt Hannah refused Anna Maria's help with mock fierceness, and Uncle Ike went out on the porch to smoke. Only the front room was left for Anna Maria and Gabe, and thither they went.

Gabe lingered for awhile on the brink, and then plunged in "Anna Maria, I's failed, an' failed, an' I's waited an' waited. Is you—is you—will you have me now?"

"La, Gabe Ha'is, you is de beatenes'!" But her hand slipped into his.

"Is you gwine have me, Anna Maria ?" he repeated.

"I reckon I'll have to," she said.

Out on the porch Uncle Ike waited long in the silence; then he said: "Well, dat's a moughty good sign, but it sholy time fu' it. Oomph, oomph, oomph, 'oomen an' colts, an' which is de wus, I don' know."

The Heart of Happy Hollow

Foreword

HAPPY HOLLOW; are you wondering where it is? Wherever Negroes colonise in the cities or villages, north or south, wherever the hod carrier, the porter, and the waiter are the society men of the town; wherever the picnic and the excursion are the chief summer diversion, and the revival the winter time of repentance, wherever the cheese cloth veil obtains at a wedding, and the little white hearse goes by with black mourners in the one carriage behind, there—there—is Happy Hollow. Wherever laughter and tears rub elbows day by day, and the spirit of labour and laziness shake hands, there—there—is Happy Hollow, and of some of it may the following pages show the heart.

THE AUTHOR.

The Scapegoat

I

THE LAW IS usually supposed to be a stern mistress, not to be lightly wooed, and yielding only to the most ardent pursuit. But even law, like love, sits more easily on some natures than on others.

This was the case with Mr. Robinson Asbury. Mr. Asbury had started life as a bootblack in the growing town of Cadgers. From this he had risen one step and become porter and messenger in a barber-shop. This rise fired his ambition, and he was not content until he had learned to use the shears and the razor and had a chair of his own. From this, in a man of Robinson's temperament, it was only a step to a shop of his own, and he placed it where it would do the most good.

Fully one-half of the population of Cadgers was composed of Negroes, and with their usual tendency to colonise, a tendency encouraged, and in fact compelled, by circumstances, they had gathered into one part of the town. Here in alleys, and streets as dirty and hardly wider, they thronged like ants.

It was in this place that Mr. Asbury set up his shop, and he won the hearts of his prospective customers by putting up the significant sign, "Equal Rights Barber-Shop." This legend was quite unnecessary, because there was only one race about, to patronise the place. But it was a delicate sop to the people's vanity, and it served its purpose.

Asbury came to be known as a clever fellow, and his business grew. The shop really became a sort of club, and, on Saturday nights especially, was the gathering-place of the men of the whole Negro quarter. He kept the illustrated and race journals there, and those who cared neither to talk nor listen to someone else might see pictured the doings of high society in very short skirts or read in the Negro papers how Miss Boston had entertained Miss Blueford to tea on such and such an afternoon. Also, he kept the policy returns, which was wise, if not moral.

It was his wisdom rather more than his morality that made the party managers after a while cast their glances toward him as a man who might be useful to their interests. It would be well to have a man—a shrewd, powerful man—down in that part of the town who could carry his people's vote in his vest pocket, and who at any time its delivery might be needed, could hand it over without hesitation. Asbury seemed that man, and they settled upon him. They gave him money, and they gave him power and patronage. He took it all silently and he carried out his bargain faithfully. His hands and his lips alike closed tightly when there was anything within them. It was not long before he found himself the big Negro of the district and, of necessity, of the town. The time came when, at a critical moment, the managers saw that they had not reckoned without their host in choosing this barber of the black district as the leader of his people.

Now, so much success must have satisfied any other man. But in many ways Mr. Asbury was unique. For a long time he himself had done very little shaving—except of notes, to keep his hand in. His time had been otherwise employed. In the evening hours he had been wooing the coquettish Dame Law, and, wonderful to say, she had yielded easily to his advances.

It was against the advice of his friends that he asked for admission to the bar. They felt that he could do more good in the place where he was.

"You see, Robinson," said old Judge Davis, "it's just like this: If you're not admitted, it'll hurt you with the people; if you are admitted, you'll move uptown to an office and get out of touch with them."

Asbury smiled an inscrutable smile. Then he whispered something into the judge's ear that made the old man wrinkle from his neck up with appreciative smiles.

"Asbury," he said, "you are—you are—well, you ought to be white, that's all. When we find a black man like you we send him to State's prison. If you were white, you'd go to the Senate."

The Negro laughed confidently.

He was admitted to the bar soon after, whether by merit or by connivance is not to be told.

"Now he will move uptown," said the black community. "Well, that's the way with a coloured man when he gets a start."

But they did not know Robinson Asbury* yet. He was a man of surprises, and they were destined to disappointment. He did not move uptown. He built an office in a small open space next his shop, and there hung out his shingle.

"I will never desert the people who have done so much to elevate me," said Mr. Asbury. "I will live among them and I will die among them."

This was a strong card for the barber-lawyer. The people seized upon the statement as expressing a nobility of an altogether unique brand.

They held a mass meeting and indorsed him. They made resolutions that extolled him, and the Negro band came around and serenaded him, playing various things in varied time.

All this was very sweet to Mr. Asbury, and the party managers chuckled with satisfaction and said, "That Asbury, that Asbury!"

Now there is a fable extant of a man who tried to please everybody, and his failure is a matter of record. Robinson Asbury was not more successful. But be it said that his ill success was due to no fault or shortcoming of his.

For a long time his growing power had been looked upon with disfavour by the coloured law firm of Bingo & Latchett. Both Mr. Bingo and Mr. Latchett themselves aspired to be Negro leaders in Cadgers, and they were delivering Emancipation Day orations and riding at the head of processions when Mr. Asbury was blacking boots. Is it any wonder, then, that they viewed with alarm his sudden rise? They kept their counsel, however, and treated with him, for it was best. They allowed him his scope without open revolt until the day upon which he hung out his shingle. This was the last straw. They could stand no more. Asbury had stolen their other chances from them, and now he was poaching upon the last of their preserves. So Mr. Bingo and Mr. Latchett put their heads together to plan the downfall of their common enemy.

The plot was deep and embraced the formation of an opposing faction made up of the best Negroes of the town. It would have looked too much like what it was for the gentlemen to show themselves in the matter, and so they took into their confidence Mr. Isaac Morton, the principal of the coloured school, and it was under his ostensible leadership that the new faction finally came into being.

Mr. Morton was really an innocent young man, and he had ideals which should never have exposed to the air. When the wily confederates came to him with

*Original reads "Asbury Robinson." We have corrected the name for consistency in the story.

their plan he believed that his worth had been recognised, and at last he was to be what Nature destined him for—a leader.

The better class of Negroes—by that is meant those who were particularly envious of Asbury's success—flocked to the new man's standard. But whether the race be white or black, political virtue is always in a minority, so Asbury could afford to smile at the force arrayed against him.

The new faction met together and resolved. They resolved, among other things, that Mr. Asbury was an enemy to his race and a menace to civilisation. They decided that he should be abolished; but, as they couldn't get out an injunction against him, and as he had the whole undignified but still voting black belt behind him, he went serenely on his way.

"They're after you hot and heavy, Asbury," said one of his friends to him.

"Oh, yes," was the reply, "they're after me, but after a while I'll get so far away that they'll be running in front."

"It's all the best people, they say."

"Yes. Well, it's good to be one of the best people, but your vote only counts one just the same."

The time came, however, when Mr. Asbury's theory was put to the test. The Cadgerites celebrated the first of January as Emancipation Day. On this day there was a large procession, with speechmaking in the afternoon and fireworks at night. It was the custom to concede the leadership of the coloured people of the town to the man who managed to lead the procession. For two years past this honour had fallen, of course, to Robinson Asbury, and there had been no disposition on the part of anybody to try conclusions with him.

Mr. Morton's faction changed all this. When Asbury went to work to solicit contributions for the celebration, he suddenly became aware that he had a fight upon his hands. All the better-class Negroes were staying out of it. The next thing he knew was that plans were on foot for a rival demonstration.

"Oh," he said to himself, "that's it, is it? Well, if they want a fight they can have it."

He had a talk with the party managers, and he had another with Judge Davis.

"All I want is a little lift, judge," he said, "and I'll make 'em think the sky has turned loose and is vomiting niggers."

The judge believed that he could do it. So did the party managers. Asbury got his lift. Emancipation Day came.

There were two parades. At least, there was one parade and the shadow of another. Asbury's, however, was not the shadow. There was a great deal of substance about it—substance made up of many people, many banners, and numerous bands. He did not have the best people. Indeed, among his cohorts there were a good many of the pronounced rag-tag and bobtail. But he had noise and numbers. In such cases, nothing more is needed. The success of Asbury's side of the affair did everything to confirm his friends in their good opinion of him.

When he found himself defeated, Mr. Silas Bingo saw that it would be policy to placate his rival's just anger against him. He called upon him at his office the day after the celebration.

"Well, Asbury," he said, "you beat us, didn't you?"

"It wasn't a question of beating," said the other calmly. "It was only an inquiry as to who were the people—the few or the many."

"Well, it was well done, and you've shown that you are a manager. I confess that I haven't always thought that you were doing the wisest thing in living down here and catering to this class of people when you might, with your ability, to be much more to the better class."

"What do they base their claims of being better on?"

"Oh, there ain't any use discussing that. We can't get along without you, we see that. So I, for one, have decided to work with you for harmony."

"Harmony. Yes, that's what we want."

"If I can do anything to help you at any time, why you have only to command me."

"I am glad to find such a friend in you. Be sure, if I ever need you, Bingo, I'll call on you."

"And I'll be ready to serve you."

Asbury smiled when his visitor was gone. He smiled, and knitted his brow. "I wonder what Bingo's got up his sleeve," he said. "He'll bear watching."

It may have been pride at his triumph, it may have been gratitude at his helpers, but Asbury went into the ensuing campaign with reckless enthusiasm. He did the most daring things for the party's sake. Bingo, true to his promise, was ever at his side ready to serve him. Finally, association and immunity made danger less fearsome; the rival no longer appeared a menace.

With the generosity born of obstacles overcome, Asbury determined to forgive Bingo and give him a chance. He let him in on a deal, and from that time they worked amicably together until the election came and passed.

It was a close election and many things had had to be done, but there were men there ready and waiting to do them. They were successful, and then the first cry of the defeated party was, as usual, "Fraud! Fraud!" The cry was taken up by the jealous, the disgruntled, and the virtuous.

Someone remembered how two years ago the registration books had been stolen. It was known upon good authority that money had been freely used. Men held up their hands in horror at the suggestion that the Negro vote had been juggled with, as if that were a new thing. From their pulpits ministers denounced the machine and bade their hearers rise and throw off the yoke of a corrupt municipal government. One of those sudden fevers of reform had taken possession of the town and threatened to destroy the successful party.

They began to look around them. They must purify themselves. They must give the people some tangible evidence of their own yearnings after purity. They looked around them for a sacrifice to lay upon the altar of municipal reform. Their eyes fell upon Mr. Bingo. No, he was not big enough. His blood was too scant to wash away the political stains. Then they looked into each other's eyes and turned their gaze away to let it fall upon Mr. Asbury. They really hated to do it. But there must be a scapegoat. The god from the Machine commanded them to slay him.

Robinson Asbury was charged with many crimes—with all that he had committed and some that he had not. When Mr. Bingo saw what was afoot he threw himself heart and soul into the work of his old rival's enemies. He was of incalculable use to them.

Judge Davis refused to have anything to do with the matter. But in spite of his disapproval it went on. Asbury was indicted and tried. The evidence was all against him, and no one gave more damaging testimony than his friend, Mr. Bingo. The judge's charge was favourable to the defendant, but the current of popular opinion could not be entirely stemmed. The jury brought in a verdict of guilty.

"Before I am sentenced, judge, I have a statement to make to the court. It will take less than ten minutes."

"Go on, Robinson," said the judge kindly.

Asbury started, in a monotonous tone, a recital that brought the prosecuting attorney to his feet in a minute. The judge waved him down, and sat transfixed by a sort of fascinated horror as the convicted man went on. The before-mentioned attorney drew a knife and started for the prisoner's dock. With difficulty he was restrained. A dozen faces in the court-room were red and pale by turns.

"He ought to be killed," whispered Mr. Bingo audibly.

Robinson Asbury looked at him and smiled, and then he told a few things of him. He gave the ins and outs of some of the misdemeanours of which he stood accused. He showed who were the men behind the throne. And still, pale and transfixed, Judge Davis waited for his own sentence.

Never were ten minutes so well taken up. It was a tale of rottenness and corruption in high places told simply and with the stamp of truth upon it.

He did not mention the judge's name. But he had torn the mask from the face of every other man who had been concerned in his downfall. They had shorn him of his strength, but they had forgotten that he was yet able to bring the roof and pillars tumbling about their heads.

The judge's voice shook as he pronounced sentence upon his old ally—a year in State's prison.

Some people said it was too light, but the judge knew what it was to wait for the sentence of doom, and he was grateful and sympathetic.

When the sheriff led Asbury away the judge hastened to have a short talk with him.

"I'm sorry, Robinson," he said, "and I want to tell you that you were no more guilty than the rest of us. But why did you spare me?"

"Because I knew you were my friend," answered the convict.

"I tried to be, but you were the first man that I've ever known since I've been in politics who ever gave me any decent return for friendship."

"I reckon you're about right, judge."

In politics, party reform usually lies in making a scapegoat of someone who is only as criminal as the rest, but a little weaker. Asbury's friends and enemies had succeeded in making him bear the burden of all the party's crimes, but their reform was hardly a success, and their protestations of a change of heart were received with doubt. Already there were those who began to pity the victim and to say that he had been hardly dealt with.

Mr. Bingo was not of these; but he found, strange to say, that his opposition to the idea went but a little way, and that even with Asbury out of his path he was a smaller man than he was before. Fate was strong against him. His poor, prosperous humanity could not enter the lists against a martyr. Robinson Asbury was now a martyr.

II

A year is not a long time. It was short enough to prevent people from forgetting Robinson, and yet long enough for their pity to grow strong as they remembered. Indeed, he was not gone a year. Good behaviour cut two months off the time of his sentence, and by the time people had come around to the notion that he was really the greatest and smartest man in Cadgers he was at home again.

He came back with no flourish of trumpets, but quietly, humbly. He went back again into the heart of the black district. His business had deteriorated during his absence, but he put new blood and new life into it. He did not go to work in the shop himself, but, taking down the shingle that had swung idly before his office door during his imprisonment, he opened the little room as a news- and cigar-stand.

Here anxious, pitying custom came to him and he prospered again. He was very quiet. Uptown hardly knew that he was again in Cadgers, and it knew nothing whatever of his doings.

"I wonder why Asbury is so quiet," they said to one another. "It isn't like him to be quiet." And they felt vaguely uneasy about him.

So many people had begun to say, "Well, he was a mighty good fellow after all."

Mr. Bingo expressed the opinion that Asbury was quiet because he was crushed, but others expressed doubt as to this. There are calms and calms, some after and some before the storm. Which was this?

They waited a while, and, as no storm came, concluded that this must be the after-quiet. Bingo, reassured, volunteered to go and seek confirmation of this conclusion.

He went, and Asbury received him with an indifferent, not to say, impolite, demeanour.

"Well, we're glad to see you back, Asbury," said Bingo patronisingly. He had variously demonstrated his inability to lead during his rival's absence and was proud of it. "What are you going to do?"

"I'm going to work."

"That's right. I reckon you'll stay out of politics."

"What could I do even if I went in?"

"Nothing now, of course; but I didn't know—"

He did not see the gleam in Asbury's half shut eyes. He only marked his humility, and he went back swelling with the news.

"Completely crushed—all the run taken out of him," was his report.

The black district believed this, too, and a sullen, smouldering anger took possession of them. Here was a good man ruined. Some of the people whom he had helped in his former days—some of the rude, coarse people of the low quarter who were still sufficiently unenlightened to be grateful—talked among themselves and offered to get up a demonstration for him. But he denied them. No, he wanted nothing of the kind. It would only bring him into unfavourable notice. All he wanted was that they would always be his friends and would stick by him.

They would to the death.

There were again two factions in Cadgers. The schoolmaster could not forget how once on a time he had been made a tool of by Mr. Bingo. So he revolted against his rule and set himself up as the leader of an opposing clique. The fight had been long and strong, but had ended with odds slightly in Bingo's favour.

But Mr. Morton did not despair. As the first of January and Emancipation Day approached, he arrayed his hosts, and the fight for supremacy became fiercer than ever. The schoolteacher* brought the school-children in for chorus singing, secured an able orator, and the best essayist in town. With all this, he was formidable.

Mr. Bingo knew that he had the fight of his life on his hands, and he entered with fear as well as zest. He, too, found an orator, but he was not sure that he was as good as Morton's. There was no doubt but that his essayist was not. He secured a band, but still he felt unsatisfied. He had hardly done enough, and for the schoolmaster to beat him now meant his political destruction.

It was in this state of mind that he was surprised to receive a visit from Mr. Asbury.

"I reckon you're surprised to see me here," said Asbury, smiling.

"I am pleased, I know." Bingo was astute.

"Well, I just dropped in on business."

"To be sure, to be sure, Asbury. What can I do for you?"

"It's more what I can do for you that I came to talk about," was the reply.

"I don't believe I understand you."

"Well, it's plain enough. They say that the schoolteacher is giving you a pretty hard fight."

"Oh, not so hard."

*The original text reads "The schoolteacher is giving you a pretty hard brought the school-children in for chorus singing, secured an able orator, and the best essayist in town." We have cut "is giving you a pretty hard" as it appears that this was part of a sentence nine paragraphs below that was inadvertently transposed into this position.

"No man can be too sure of winning, though. Mr. Morton once did me a mean turn when he started the faction against me."

Bingo's heart gave a great leap, and then stopped for the fraction of a second.

"You were in it, of course," pursued Asbury, "but I can look over your part in it in order to get even with the man who started it."

It was true, then, thought Bingo gladly. He did not know. He wanted revenge for his wrongs and upon the wrong man. How well the schemer had covered his tracks! Asbury should have his revenge and Morton would be the sufferer.

"Of course, Asbury, you know what I did I did innocently."

"Oh, yes, in politics we are all lambs and the wolves are only to be found in the other party. We'll pass that, though. What I want to say is that I can help you to make your celebration an overwhelming success. I still have some influence down in my district."

"Certainly, and very justly, too. Why, I should be delighted with your aid. I could give you a prominent place in the procession."

"I don't want it; I don't want to appear in this at all. All I want is revenge. You can have all the credit, but let me down my enemy."

Bingo was perfectly willing, and, with their heads close together, they had a long and close consultation. When Asbury was gone, Mr. Bingo lay back in his chair and laughed. "I'm a slick duck," he said.

From that hour Mr. Bingo's cause began to take on the appearance of something very like a boom. More bands were hired. The interior of the State was called upon and a more eloquent orator secured. The crowd hastened to array itself on the growing side.

With surprised eyes, the schoolmaster beheld the wonder of it, but he kept to his own purpose with dogged insistence, even when he saw that he could not turn aside the overwhelming defeat that threatened him. But in spite of his obstinacy, his hours were dark and bitter. Asbury worked like a mole, all underground, but he was indefatigable. Two days before the celebration time everything was perfected for the biggest demonstration that Cadgers had ever known. All the next day and night he was busy among his allies.

On the morning of the great day, Mr. Bingo, wonderfully caparisoned, rode down to the hall where the parade was to form. He was early. No one had yet come. In an hour a score of men all told had collected. Another hour passed, and no more had come. Then there smote upon his ear the sound of music. They were coming at last. Bringing his sword to his shoulder, he rode forward to the middle of the street. Ah, there they were. But—but—could he believe his eyes? They were going in another direction, and at their head rode—Morton! He gnashed his teeth in fury. He had been led into a trap and betrayed. The procession passing had been his—all his. He heard them cheering, and then, oh! climax of infidelity, he saw his own orator go past in a carriage, bowing and smiling to the crowd.

There was no doubting who had done this thing. The hand of Asbury was apparent in it. He must have known the truth all along, thought Bingo. His allies left him one by one for the other hall, and he rode home in a humiliation deeper than he had ever known before.

Asbury did not appear at the celebration. He was at his little news-stand all day.

In a day or two the defeated aspirant had further cause to curse his false friend. He found that not only had the people defected from him, but that the thing had been so adroitly managed that he appeared to be in fault, and three-fourths of those who knew him were angry at some supposed grievance. His cup of bitterness was full when his partner, a quietly ambitious man, suggested that they dissolve their relations.

His ruin was complete.

The lawyer was not alone in seeing Asbury's hand in his downfall. The party managers saw it too, and they met together to discuss the dangerous factor which, while it appeared to slumber, was so terribly awake. They decided that he must be appeased, and they visited him.

He was still busy at his news-stand. They talked to him adroitly, while he sorted papers and kept an impassive face. When they were all done, he looked up for a moment and replied, "You know, gentlemen, as an ex-convict I am not in politics."

Some of them had the grace to flush.

"But you can use your influence," they said.

"I am not in politics," was his only reply.

And the spring elections were coming on. Well, they worked hard, and he showed no sign. He treated with neither one party nor the other. "Perhaps," thought the managers, "he is out of politics," and they grew more confident.

It was nearing eleven o'clock on the morning of election when a cloud no bigger than a man's hand appeared upon the horizon. It came from the direction of the black district. It grew, and the managers of the party in power looked at it, fascinated by an ominous dread. Finally it began to rain Negro voters, and as one man they voted against their former candidates. Their organisation was perfect. They simply came, voted, and left, but they overwhelmed everything. Not one of the party that had damned Robinson Asbury was left in power save old Judge Davis. His majority was overwhelming.

The generalship that had engineered the thing was perfect. There were loud threats against the newsdealer. But no one bothered him except a reporter. The reporter called to see just how it was done. He found Asbury very busy sorting papers. To the newspaper man's questions he had only this reply, "I am not in politics, sir."

But Cadgers had learned its lesson.

One Christmas at Shiloh

MARTHA MARIA MIXON was a "widder lady." So she described herself whenever anyone asked her as to her status in life. To her more intimate friends she confided that she was not a "weed widder," but one of the "grass" variety. The story of how her husband, Madison, had never been "No 'count, even befo' de wah," and of his rapid degeneration thereafter, was vividly told.

"De fact of de mattah is," Mrs. Mixon was wont to say, "my man, Madison, was nevah no han' to wo'k. He was de settin'-downest man you evah seed. Hit wouldn't 'a' been so bad, but Madison was a lakly man, an' his tongue wah smoothah dan ile; so hit t'wan't no shakes fu' him to fool ol' Mas' 'bout his wo'k an' git erlong des erbout ez he pleased. Mas' Madison Mixon, hisse'f, was a mighty 'dulgent so't o' man, an' he liked a laugh bettah dan anyone in de worl'. Well, my man could mek him laugh, an' dat was enough fu' him. I used to lectuah dat man much 'bout his onshifless ways, but he des went erlong, twell bimeby hyeah come de wah an' evahthing was broke up. Den w'en hit come time dat Madison had to scramble fu' hisself, dey wa'nt no scramble in him. He des' wouldn't wo'k an' I had to do evahthing. He allus had what he called some gret scheme, but deh nevah seemed to come to nuffin, an' once when he got de folks to put some money in somep'n' dat broke up, dey come put' nigh tahin' an' featherin' him. Finally, I des got morchully tiahed o' dat man's ca'in' on, an' I say to him one day, 'Madison,' I say, 'I'm tiahed of all dis foo'ishness, an' I'm gwine up Norf whaih I kin live an' be somebody. Ef evah you mek a man out o' yo'se'f, an' want me, de Bible say "Seek an' you shell receive."' Cause even den I was a mighty han' to c'ote de Scripters. Well, I lef' him, an' Norf I come, 'dough it jes' nigh broke my hea't, fu' I sho did love dat black man. De las' thing I hyeahed o' him, he had des learned to read an' write an' wah runnin' fu' de Legislater 'twell de Klu Klux got aftah him; den I think he 'signed de nomernation."

This was Martha's story, and the reason that there was no Mr. Mixon with her when she came North, drifted from place to place and finally became one of New York's large black contingent from the South. To her the lessons of slavery had not been idle ones. Industrious, careful, and hard-working, she soon became prosperous, and when, hunting a spiritual home she settled upon Shiloh Chapel, she was welcomed there as a distinct addition to the large and active membership.

Shiloh was not one of the fashionable churches of the city, but it was primarily a church home for any Southern negro, for in it were representatives of every one of the old slaveholding States. Its pastor was one of those who had not yet got beyond the belief that any temporal preparation for the preaching of the Gospel was unnecessary. It was still his firm trust, and often his boast, that if one opened his mouth the Lord would fill it, and it grew to be a settled idea that the Lord filled his acceptably, for his converts were many and his congregation increased.

The Rev. Silas Todbury's education may have been deficient in other matters, but one thing he knew, and knew thoroughly—the disposition of his people. He knew just what weaknesses, longings, and desires their recent bondage had left with them, and with admirable shrewdness contrived to meet them. He knew that in preaching they wanted noise, emotion, and fire; that in the preacher they wanted free-heartedness and cordiality. He knew that when Christmas came they wanted a great rally, somewhat approaching, at least, the rousing times both spiritual and temporal that they had had back on the old plantation, when Christmas meant a week of pleasurable excitement. Knowing the last so well, it was with commendable foresight that he began early his preparations for a big time on a certain Christmas not long ago.

"I tell you people," he said to his congregation, "we's goin' to have a reg'lar 'Benjamin's mess'!"

The coloured folk, being not quite sure of the quotation, laughed heartily, exclaiming in admiration of their pastor, "Dat Todbu'y is sholy one mess hisse'f."

"Now any of de sistahs dat's willin' to he'p mek dis comin' Chris'mus a real sho 'nough one, 'll 'blige me by meetin' me in de basement of de chu'ch aftah services. De brothahs kin go 'long home 'twell dey called fu'."

There was another outburst of merriment at this sally, and it was a good-natured score or more of sisters who a little later met the pastor as agreed. Among them was Martha Maria Mixon, for she was very close to her pastor, and for many a day had joyed his clerical heart with special dinners.

"Ah," said the preacher, rubbing his hands, "Sistah Marthy, I see you's on han' ez usual to he'p me out, an' you, too, Sis Jinny, an' Sis Dicey," he added, quick to note the signs of any incipient jealousy, and equally ready to check it. "We's all hyeah, de faithful few, an' we's all ready fu' wo'k."

The sisters beamed and nodded.

"Well, we goin' to have some'p'n evah night, beginnin' wid Chris'mus night, straight on endurin' of de week, an' I want to separate you all into companies fu' to take chawge of each night. Now, I's a-goin' to have a powahful preachah f'om de Souf wid us, an' I want you all to show him what we kin do. On Chris'mus day we goin' to have a sermont at de chu'ch an' a festabal in de evenin' wid a Chris'mus tree. Sis' Marthy, I want you to boa'd de minister."

"La, Brothah Todbu'y, I don't scarcely feel lak I's 'portant 'nough fu' dat," said Mrs. Mixon modestly, "but I'll do de bes' I kin. I hatter be lak de widder's mice in de scuse o' meal."

"We ain't got no doubt 'bout what you able to do, Sis Marthy," and the pastor passed to the appointment of his other committees. After evening services the brothers were similarly called in consultation and appointed to their respective duties.

To the black people to whom these responsibilities were thus turned over, joy came, and with it the vision of other days—the vision of the dear old days, the hard old days back there in the South, when they had looked forward to their Christmas from year to year. Then it had been a time of sadness as well as of joy, for they knew that though the week was full of pleasure, after it was over must come separation and sadness. For this was the time when those who were to be hired out, loaned, or given away, were to change their homes. So even while they danced they sighed, and while they shouted they moaned. Now there was no such repressing fact to daunt them. Christmas would come. They would enjoy themselves, and after it was over would go back to the same homes to live through the round of months in the midst of familiar faces and among their own old loved ones. The thought gave sweetness to their labour, and the responsibilities devolving upon them imbued the sacred holiday with a meaning and charm that it had never had before for them. They bubbled over with importance and with the glory of it. A sister and a brother could not meet without a friendly banter.

"Hi, Sis' Dicey," Brother Williams would call out across the fence to his neighbour, "I don' believe you doin' anything to'ds dat Chris'mus celebration. Evah time I sees you, you's in de washtub tryin' to mek braid an' meat fo' dat no 'count man o' yo'n."

Sister Dicey's laugh rang out loud and musical before she replied, "Nevah you min', Brothah Williams. I don' see yo' back bowed so much by de yoke."

"Oh, honey, I's labo'in' even ef you do'n know it, but you'll see it on de day."

"I 'low you labo'in' de mos' to git dat wife o' yo'n a new dress," and her tormentor's guffaw seemed to admit some such benevolent intention.

In the corners of every house where the younger and more worldly-minded people congregated there was much whispering and giggling, for they had their own plans for Christmas outside of the church affair.

"You goin' to give me de pleasure of yo' comp'ny to de dance aftah de festabal?" some ardent and early swain would murmur to his lady love, and the whisper would fly back in well-feigned affright, "Heish, man, you want to have Brothah Todbu'y chu'chin' me?" But if the swain persisted, there was little chance of his being ultimately refused. So the world, the flesh, and the devil kept pace with the things of the spirit in the great preparation.

Meanwhile Martha Maria Mixon went her own way, working hard, fixing and observing. She had determined to excel herself this time, and not only should her part at the church be above reproach, but the entertainment which she would give that strange preacher would be a thing long to be remembered. And so, almost startled at all that Shiloh was preparing for his reception, hoary Christmas approached.

All New York was a dazzling bazar through which the people thronged ceaselessly, tumultuously. Everyone was a child again; holly wreaths with the red berries gleaming amid the green were everywhere, and the white streets were gay with laughter and bustle and life.

On the night before the great day Martha sat before her fire and hummed softly to herself. There was a smile upon her face, for she had worked and worked well, and now all was ready and to her entire satisfaction. Something which shall be nameless simmered in a tin cup on the back of the stove before her, and every now and then she broke her reverie to sip of it. It smelled sweet and pungent and suspicious, but, then—this was Christmas Eve. She was half drowsing when a brisk knock startled her into wakefulness. Thinking it was one of the neighbours in for a call she bade the visitor enter, without moving. There was a stamping of feet, and the door opened and a black man covered with snow stood before her. He said nothing. Martha rubbed her eyes and stared at him, and then she looked at the cup accusingly, and from it back to the man. Then she rubbed her eyes again.

"Wha—wha—" she stammered, rising slowly.

"Don' you know me, Marthy, don' you know me; an' don' you want to see yo' husban'?"

"Madison Mixon, is dat you in de flesh?"

"It's me, Marthy; you tol' me ef evah I made a man o' myse'f, to seek you. It's been a long road, but I's tried faithful."

All the memories of other days came rushing over Martha in an overwhelming flood. In one moment everything was forgotten save that here stood her long delinquent husband. She threw out her arms and took a step toward him but he anticipated her further advance and rushing to her clasped her ample form in a close embrace.

"You will tek me back!" he cried, "you will fu'give me!"

"Yes, yes, of co'se, I will, Madison, ef you has made a man of yo'se'f."

"I hopes to prove dat to you."

It was a very pleasant evening that they spent together, and like old times to Martha. Never once did it occur to her that this sudden finding of a husband might be awkward on the morrow when the visitor came to dinner. Nor did she once suspect that Madison might be up to one of his old tricks. She accepted him for just what he said he was and intended to be.

Her first doubt came the next morning when she began to hurry her preparations for church. Madison had been fumbling in his carpet bag and was already respectably dressed. His wife looked at him approvingly, but the glance turned to one of consternation when he stammered forth that he had to go out, as he had some business to attend to.

"What, on de ve'y fust day you hyeah, ain't you goin' to chu'ch wid me?"

"De bus'ness is mighty pressin', but I hopes to see you at chu'ch by de time de services begin. Waih does you set?" His hand was on the door.

Martha sank into a chair and the tears came to her eyes, but she choked them back. She would not let him see how much she was hurt. She told him in a faltering voice where she sat, and he passed out. Then her tears came and flooded away the last hope. She had been so proud to think that she would walk to church with her husband that morning for the first time in so long a while, and now it was all over. For a little while she thought that she would not go, and then the memory of all the preparations she had made and of the new minister came to her, and she went on with her dressing.

The church was crowded that morning when Martha arrived. She looked around in vain for some sight of Madison, but she could see nothing of him, and so she sank into her seat with a sigh. She could just see the new minister drooping in his seat behind the reading desk. He was evidently deep in meditation, for he did not get up during the hymn.

Then Martha heard the Rev. Silas Todbury speaking. His words did not affect her until she found that the whole of his closing sentence was flashing through her brain like a flame. "We will now be exho'ted by de Reverent Madison Mixon."

She couldn't believe her ears, but stared wildly at the pulpit where the new preacher stood. It was Madison. Her first impulse was to rise in her seat and stop him. It was another of his tricks, and he should not profane the church. But his look and voice silenced her and she sank back in amazement.

He preached a powerful sermon, and at its close told something of his life and who he was, and Martha found herself all at once the centre of attention; and her face glowed and her heart burned within her as the people about her nodded and smiled at her through their tears, and hurled "Amen" upon "Amen."

Madison hurried to her side after the services. "I des wanted to s'prise you a little, Marthy," he said.

She was too happy to answer and, pressing his arm very tightly, she walked out among her congratulating friends, and between her husband and the Rev. Silas Todbury went proudly home to her Christmas dinner.

The Mission of Mr. Scatters

IT TOOK SOMETHING just short of a revolution to wake up the sleepy little town of Miltonville. Through the slow, hot days it drowsed along like a lazy dog, only half rousing now and then to snap at some flying rumour, and relapsing at once into its pristine somnolence.

It was not a dreamless sleep, however, that held the town in chains. It had its dreams—dreams of greatness, of wealth, of consequence and of growth. Granted that there was no effort to realise these visions, they were yet there, and, combined with the memory of a past that was not without credit, went far to give tone to its dormant spirit.

It was a real spirit, too; the gallant Bourbon spirit of the old South; of Kentucky when she is most the daughter of Virginia, as was evidenced in the awed respect which all Miltonvillians, white and black alike, showed to Major Richardson in his house on the hill. He was part of the traditions of the place. It was shown in the conservatism of the old white families, and a certain stalwart if reflected self-respect in the older coloured inhabitants.

In all the days since the school had been founded and Mr. Dunkin's marriage to the teacher had raised a brief ripple of excitement, these coloured people had slumbered. They were still slumbering that hot August day, unmindful of the sensation that lay at their very doors, heedless of the portents that said as plain as preaching, "Miltonville, the time is at hand, awake!"

So it was that that afternoon there were only a few loungers, and these not very alert, about the station when the little train wheezed and puffed its way into it. It had been so long since anyone save those whom they knew had alighted at Miltonville that the loungers had lost faith, and with it curiosity, and now they scarcely changed their positions as the little engine stopped with a snort of disgust. But in an instant indifference had fled as the mist before the sun, and every eye on the platform was staring and white. It is the unexpected that always happens, and yet humanity never gets accustomed to it. The loafers, white and black, had assumed a sitting posture, and then they had stood up. For from the cars there had alighted the wonder of a stranger—a Negro stranger, gorgeous of person and attire. He was dressed in a suit of black cloth. A long coat was buttoned close around his tall and robust form. He was dead black, from his shiny top hat to his not less shiny boots, and about him there was the indefinable air of distinction. He stood looking about the platform for a moment, and then stepped briskly and decisively toward the group that was staring at him with wide eyes. There was no hesitation in that step. He walked as a man walks who is not in the habit of being stopped, who has not known what it is to be told, "Thus far shalt thou go and no further."

"Can you tell me where I can find the residence of Mr. Isaac Jackson?" he asked sonorously as he reached the stupefied loungers. His voice was deep and clear.

Someone woke from his astonishment and offered to lead him thither, and together the two started for their destination, the stranger keeping up a running fire of comment on the way. Had his companion been a close observer and known anything about the matter, he would have found the newcomer's English painfully, unforgivably correct. A language should be like an easy shoe on a flexible foot, but to one unused to it, it proves rather a splint on a broken limb. The stranger stalked about in conversational splints until they arrived at Isaac Jackson's door. Then giving his guide a dime, he dismissed him with a courtly bow, and knocked.

It was a good thing that Martha Ann Jackson had the innate politeness of her race well to the fore when she opened the door upon the radiant creature, or she would have given voice to the words that were in her heart: "Good Lawd, what is dis?"

"Is this the residence of Mr. Isaac Jackson?" in the stranger's suavest voice.

"Yes, suh, he live hyeah."

"May I see him? I desire to see him upon some business." He handed her his card, which she carefully turned upside down, glanced at without understanding, and put in her apron pocket as she replied:

"He ain't in jes' now, but ef you'll step in an' wait, I'll sen' one o' de chillen aftah him."

"I thank you, madam, I thank you. I will come in and rest from the fatigue of my journey. I have travelled a long way, and rest in such a pleasant and commodious abode as your own appears to be will prove very grateful to me."

She had been half afraid to invite this resplendent figure into her humble house, but she felt distinctly flattered at his allusion to the home which she had helped Isaac to buy, and by the alacrity with which the stranger accepted her invitation.

She ushered him into the front room, mentally thanking her stars that she had forced the reluctant Isaac to buy a bright new carpet a couple of months before.

A child was despatched to find and bring home the father, while Martha Ann, hastily slipping out of her work-dress and into a starched calico, came in to keep her visitor company.

His name proved to be Scatters, and he was a most entertaining and ingratiating man. It was evident that he had some important business with Isaac Jackson, but that it was mysterious was shown by the guarded way in which he occasionally hinted at it as he tapped the valise he carried and nodded knowingly.

Time had never been when Martha Ann Jackson was so flustered. She was charmed and frightened and flattered. She could only leave Mr. Scatters long enough to give orders to her daughter, Lucy, to prepare such a supper as that household had never seen before; then she returned to sit again at his feet and listen to his words of wisdom.

The supper progressed apace, and the savour of it was already in the stranger's nostrils. Upon this he grew eloquent and was about to divulge his secret to the hungry-eyed woman when the trampling of Isaac's boots upon the walk told him that he had only a little while longer to contain himself, and at the same time to wait for the fragrant supper.

Now, it is seldom that a man is so well impressed with a smooth-tongued stranger as is his wife. Usually his hard-headedness puts him on the defensive against the blandishments of the man who has won his better half's favour, and, however honest the semi-fortunate individual may be, he despises him for his attainments. But it was not so in this case. Isaac had hardly entered the house and received his visitor's warm handclasp before he had become captive to his charm. Business, business—no, his guest had been travelling and he must be both tired and hungry. Isaac would hear of no business until they had eaten. Then, over a pipe, if the gentleman smoked, they might talk at their ease.

Mr. Scatters demurred, but in fact nothing could have pleased him better, and the open smile with which he dropped into his place at the table was very genuine and heartfelt. Genuine, too, were his praises of Lucy's cooking; of her flaky biscuits and mealy potatoes. He was pleased all through and he did not hesitate to say so.

It was a beaming group that finally rose heavily laden from the supper table.

Over a social pipe a little later, Isaac Jackson heard the story that made his eyes bulge with interest and his heart throb with eagerness.

Mr. Scatters began, tapping his host's breast and looking at him fixedly, "You had a brother some years ago named John." It was more like an accusation than a question.

"Yes, suh, I had a brothah John."

"Uh, huh, and that brother migrated to the West Indies."

"Yes, suh, he went out to some o' dem outlandish places."

"Hold on, sir, hold on, I am a West Indian myself."

"I do' mean no erfence, 'ceptin' dat John allus was of a rovin' dispersition."

"Very well, you know no more about your brother after his departure for the West Indies?"

"No, suh."

"Well, it is my mission to tell you the rest of the story. Your brother John landed at Cuba, and after working about some years and living frugally, he went into the coffee business, in which he became rich."

"Rich?"

"Rich, sir."

"Why, bless my soul, who'd 'a evah thought that of John? Why, suh, I'm sho'ly proud to hyeah it. Why don't he come home an' visit a body?"

"Ah, why?" said Mr. Scatters dramatically. "Now comes the most painful part of my mission. 'In the midst of life we are in death.'" Mr. Scatters sighed, Isaac sighed and wiped his eyes. "Two years ago your brother departed this life."

"Was he saved?" Isaac asked in a choked voice. Scatters gave him one startled glance, and then answered hastily, "I am happy to say that he was."

"Poor John! He gone an' me lef'."

"Even in the midst of our sorrows, however, there is always a ray of light. Your brother remembered you in his will."

"Remembered me?"

"Remembered you, and as one of the executors of his estate,"—Mr. Scatters rose and went softly over to his valise, from which he took a large square package. He came back with it, holding it as if it were something sacred,—"as one of the executors of his estate, which is now settled, I was commissioned to bring you this." He tapped the package. "This package, sealed as you see with the seal of Cuba, contains five thousand dollars in notes and bonds."

Isaac gasped and reached for the bundle, but it was withdrawn. "I am, however, not to deliver it to you yet. There are certain formalities which my country demands to be gone through with, after which I deliver my message and return to the fairest of lands, to the Gem of the Antilles. Let me congratulate you, Mr. Jackson, upon your good fortune."

Isaac yielded up his hand mechanically. He was dazed by the vision of this sudden wealth.

"Fi' thousan' dollahs," he repeated.

"Yes, sir, five thousand dollars. It is a goodly sum, and in the meantime, until court convenes, I wish you to recommend some safe place in which to put this money, as I do not feel secure with it about my person, nor would it be secure if it were known to be in your house."

"I reckon Albert Matthews' grocery would be the safes' place fu' it. He's got one o' dem i'on saftes."

"The very place. Let us go there at once, and after that I will not encroach upon your hospitality longer, but attempt to find a hotel."

"Hotel nothin'," said Isaac emphatically. "Ef my house ain't too common, you'll stay right thaih ontwell co't sets."

"This is very kind of you, Mr. Jackson, but really I couldn't think of being such a charge upon you and your good wife."

"'Tain't no charge on us; we'll be glad to have you. Folks hyeah in Miltonville has little enough comp'ny, de Lawd knows."

Isaac spoke the truth, and it was as much the knowledge that he would be the envy of all the town as his gratitude to Scatters that prompted him to prevail upon his visitor to stay.

Scatters was finally persuaded, and the men only paused long enough in the house to tell the curiosity-eaten Martha Ann the news, and then started for Albert Matthews' store. Scatters carried the precious package, and Isaac was armed with an old shotgun lest anyone should suspect their treasure and attack them. Five thousand dollars was not to be carelessly handled!

As soon as the men were gone, Martha Ann started out upon her rounds, and her proud tongue did for the women portion of Miltonville what the visit to Matthews' store did for the men. Did Mrs. So-and-So remember brother John? Indeed she did. And when the story was told, it was a "Well, well, well! he used to be an ol' beau o' mine." Martha Ann found no less than twenty women of her acquaintance for whom her brother John seemed to have entertained tender feelings.

The corner grocery store kept by Albert Matthews was the general gathering-place for the coloured male population of the town. It was a small, one-roomed building, almost filled with barrels, boxes, and casks.

Pride as well as necessity had prompted Isaac to go to the grocery just at this time, when it would be quite the fullest of men. He had not calculated wrongly when he reckoned upon the sensation that would be made by his entrance with the distinguished-looking stranger. The excitement was all the most hungry could have wished for. The men stared at Jackson and his companion with wide-open eyes. They left off chewing tobacco and telling tales. A half-dozen of them forgot to avail themselves of the joy of spitting, and Albert Matthews, the proprietor, a weazened little brown-skinned man, forgot to lay his hand upon the scale in weighing out a pound of sugar.

With a humility that was false on the very face of it, Isaac introduced his guest to the grocer and the three went off together mysteriously into a corner. The matter was duly explained and the object of the visit told. Matthews burned with envy of his neighbour's good fortune.

"I do' reckon, Mistah Scatters, dat we bettah let de othah folks in de sto' know anything 'bout dis hyeah bus'ness of ouahs. I got to be 'sponsible fu dat money, an' I doesn't want to tek no chances."

"You are perfectly right, sir, perfectly right. You are responsible, not only for the money itself, but for the integrity of this seal which means the dignity of government."

Matthews looked sufficiently impressed, and together they all went their way among the barrels and boxes to the corner where the little safe stood. With many turnings and twistings the door was opened, the package inclosed and the safe shut again. Then they all rose solemnly and went behind the counter to sample something that Matthews had. This was necessary as a climax, for they had performed, not a mere deed, but a ceremonial.

"Of course, you'll say nothing about this matter at all, Mr. Matthews," said Scatters, thereby insuring publicity to his affair.

There were a few introductions as the men passed out, but hardly had their backs turned when a perfect storm of comment and inquiry broke about the grocer's head. So it came to pass, that with many mysterious nods and headshakings, Matthews first hinted at and then told the story.

For the first few minutes the men could scarcely believe what they had heard. It was so utterly unprecedented. Then it dawned upon them that it might be so, and discussion and argument ran rife for the next hour.

The story flew like wildfire, there being three things in this world which interest all sorts and conditions of men alike: great wealth, great beauty, and great love. Whenever Mr. Scatters appeared he was greeted with deference and admiration. Any man who had come clear from Cuba on such an errand to their fellow-townsman deserved all honour and respect. His charming manners confirmed, too, all that preconceived notions had said of him. He became a social favourite. It began with Mr. and Mrs. Dunkin's calling upon him. Then followed Alonzo Taft, and when the former two gave a reception for the visitor, his position was assured. Miltonville had not yet arisen to the dignity of having a literary society. He now founded one and opened it himself with an address so beautiful, so eloquent and moving that Mr. Dunkin bobbed his head dizzy in acquiescence, and Aunt Hannah Payne thought she was in church and shouted for joy.

The little town had awakened from its long post-bellum slumber and accepted with eagerness the upward impulse given it. It stood aside and looked on with something like adoration when Mr. Scatters and Mrs. Dunkin met and talked of ineffable things—things far above the ken of the average mortal.

When Mr. Scatters found that his mission was known, he gave up further attempts at concealing it and talked freely about the matter. He expatiated at length upon the responsibility that devolved upon him and his desire to discharge it, and he spoke glowingly of the great government whose power was represented by the seal which held the package of bonds. Not for one day would he stay away from his beloved Cuba, if it were not that that seal had to be broken in the presence of the proper authorities. So, however reluctant he might be to stay, it was not for him to shirk his task: he must wait for the sitting of court.

Meanwhile the Jacksons lived in an atmosphere of glory. The womenfolk purchased new dresses, and Isaac got a new wagon on the strength of their good fortune. It was nothing to what they dreamed of doing when they had the money positively in hand. Mr. Scatters still remained their guest, and they were proud of it.

What pleased them most was that their distinguished visitor seemed not to look down upon, but rather to be pleased with, their homely fare. Isaac had further cause for pleasure when his guest came to him later with a great show of frank confidence to request the loan of fifty dollars.

"I should not think of asking even this small favour of you but that I have only Cuban money with me and I knew you would feel distressed if you knew that I went to the trouble of sending this money away for exchange on account of so small a sum."

This was undoubtedly a mark of special confidence. It suddenly made Isaac feel as if the grand creature had accepted and labelled him as a brother and an equal. He hastened to Matthews' safe, where he kept his own earnings; for the grocer was banker as well.

With reverent hands they put aside the package of bonds and together counted out the required half a hundred dollars. In a little while Mr. Scatter's long, graceful fingers had closed over it.

Mr. Jackson's cup of joy was now full. It had but one bitter drop to mar its sweetness. That was the friendship that had sprung up between the Cuban and Mr. Dunkin. They frequently exchanged visits, and sat long together engaged in conversation from which Isaac was excluded. This galled him. He felt that he had a sort of proprietary interest in his guest. And any infringement of this property right he looked upon with distinct disfavour. So that it was with no pleasant countenance that he greeted Mr. Dunkin when he called on a certain night.

"Mr. Scatters is gone out," he said, as the old man entered and deposited his hat on the floor.

"Dat's all right, Isaac," said Mr. Dunkin slowly, "I didn't come to see de gen't'man. I come to see you."

The cloud somewhat lifted from Isaac's brow. Mr. Dunkin was a man of importance and it made a deal of difference whom he was visiting.

He seemed a little bit embarrassed, however, as to how to open conversation. He hummed and hawed and was visibly uneasy. He tried to descant upon the weather, but the subject failed him. Finally, with an effort, he hitched his chair nearer to his host's and said in a low voice, "Ike, I reckon you has de confidence of Mistah Scatters?"

"I has," was the proud reply, "I has."

"Hum! uh! huh! Well—well—has you evah loant him any money?"

Isaac was aghast. Such impertinence!

"Mistah Dunkin," he began, "I considah—"

"Hol' on, Ike!" broke in Dunkin, laying a soothing hand on the other's knee, "don' git on yo' high hoss. Dis hyeah's a impo'tant mattah."

"I ain't got nothin' to say."

"He ain't never tol' you 'bout havin' nothin' but Cubian money on him?"

Isaac started.

"I see he have. He tol' me de same thing."

The two men sat staring suspiciously into each other's faces.

"He got a hun'ed an' fifty dollahs f'om me," said Dunkin.

"I let him have fifty," added Jackson weakly.

"He got a hun'ed an' fifty dollahs f'om Matthews. Dat's how I come to git 'spicious. He tol' him de same sto'y."

Again that pregnant look flashed between them, and they both rose and went out of the house.

They hurried down to Matthews' grocery. The owner was waiting for them there. There was solemnity, but no hesitation, in the manner with which they now went to the safe. They took out the package hastily and with ruthless hands. This was no ceremonial now. The seal had no longer any fears for them. They tore it off. They tore the wrappers. Then paper. Neatly folded paper. More wrapping paper. Newspapers. Nothing more. Of bills or bonds—nothing. With the debris of the mysterious parcel scattered about their feet, they stood up and looked at each other.

"I nevah did believe in furriners nohow," said Mr. Dunkin sadly.

"But he knowed all about my brothah John."

"An' he sho'ly did make mighty fine speeches. Maybe we's missed de money." This from the grocer.

Together they went over the papers again, with the same result.

"Do you know where he went to-night, Ike?"

"No."

"Den I reckon we's seed de las' o' him."

"But he lef' his valise."

"Yes, an' he lef' dis," said Dunkin sternly, pointing to the paper on the floor. "He sho'ly is mighty keerless of his valybles."

"Let's go git de constable," said the practical Matthews.

They did, though they felt that it would be unavailing.

The constable came and waited at Jackson's house. They had been there about half an hour, talking the matter over, when what was their surprise to hear Mr. Scatters' step coming jauntily up the walk. A sudden panic of terror and shame seized them. It was as if they had wronged him. Suppose, after all, everything should come right and he should be able to explain? They sat and trembled until he entered. Then the constable told him his mission.

Mr. Scatters was surprised. He was hurt. Indeed, he was distinctly grieved that his friends had had so little confidence in him. Had he been to them anything but a gentleman, a friend, and an honest man? Had he not come a long distance from his home to do one of them a favour? They hung their heads. Martha Ann, who was listening at the door, was sobbing audibly. What had he done thus to be humiliated? He saw the effect of his words and pursued it. Had he not left in the care of one of their own number security for his integrity in the shape of the bonds?

The effect of his words was magical. Every head went up and three pairs of flashing eyes were bent upon him. He saw and knew that they knew. He had not thought that they would dare to violate the seal around which he had woven such a halo. He saw that all was over, and, throwing up his hands with a despairing gesture, he bowed graciously and left the room with the constable.

All Miltonville had the story next day, and waited no less eagerly than before for the "settin' of co't."

To the anger and chagrin of Miltonvillians, Fox Run had the honour and distinction of being the county seat, and thither they must go to the sessions; but never did they so forget their animosities as on the day set for the trial of Scatters. They overlooked the pride of the Fox Runners, their cupidity and their vaunting arrogance. They ignored the indignity of showing interest in anything that took place in that village, and went in force, eager, anxious, and curious. Ahorse, afoot, by ox-cart, by mule-wagon, white, black, high, low, old, and young of both sexes invaded Fox Run and swelled the crowd of onlookers until, with pity for the very anxiety of the people, the humane judge decided to discard the now inadequate court-room and hold the sessions on the village green. Here an impromptu bar was set up, and over against it were ranged the benches, chairs, and camp-stools of the spectators.

Every man of prominence in the county was present. Major Richardson, though now retired, occupied a distinguished position within the bar. Old Captain Howard shook hands familiarly with the judge and nodded to the assembly as though he himself had invited them all to be present. Former Judge Durbin sat with his successor on the bench.

Court opened and the first case was called. It gained but passing attention. There was bigger game to be stalked. A hog-stealing case fared a little better on account of the intimateness of the crime involved. But nothing was received with such awed silence as the case of the State against Joseph Scatters. The charge was obtaining money under false pretences, and the plea "Not Guilty."

The witnesses were called and their testimony taken. Mr. Scatters was called to testify in his own defence, but refused to do so. The prosecution stated its case and proceeded to sum up the depositions of the witnesses. As there was no attorney for the defence, the State's attorney delivered a short speech, in which the guilt of the defendant was plainly set forth. It was as clear as day. Things looked very dark for Mr. Scatters of Cuba.

As the lawyer sat down, and ere the case could be given to the jury, he rose and asked permission of the Court to say a few words.

This was granted him.

He stood up among them, a magnificent, strong, black figure. His eyes swept the assembly, judge, jury, and spectators with a look half amusement, half defiance.

"I have pleaded not guilty," he began in a low, distinct voice that could be heard in every part of the inclosure, "and I am not guilty of the spirit which is charged against me, however near the letter may touch me. I did use certain knowledge that I possessed, and the seal which I happened to have from an old government position, to defraud—that is the word, if you will—to defraud these men out of the price of their vanity and their cupidity. But it was not a long-premeditated thing. I was within a few miles of your town before the idea occurred to me. I was in straits. I stepped from the brink of great poverty into the midst of what you are pleased to deem a greater crime."

The Court held its breath. No such audacity had ever been witnessed in the life of Fox Run.

Scatters went on, warming to his subject as he progressed. He was eloquent and he was pleasing. A smile flickered over the face of Major Richardson and was reflected in the features of many others as the speaker burst forth:

"Gentlemen, I maintain that instead of imprisoning you should thank me for what I have done. Have I not taught your community a lesson? Have I not put a check upon their credulity and made them wary of unheralded strangers?"

He had. There was no disputing that. The judge himself was smiling, and the jurymen were nodding at each other.

Scatters had not yet played his trump card. He saw that the time was ripe. Straightening his form and raising his great voice, he cried: "Gentlemen, I am guilty according to the letter of the law, but from that I appeal to the men who make and have made the law. From the hard detail of this new day, I appeal to the chivalry of the old South which has been told in story and sung in song. From men of vindictiveness I appeal to men of mercy. From plebeians to aristocrats. By the memory of the sacred names of the Richardsons"—the Major sat bolt upright and dropped his snuff-box—"the Durbins"—the ex-judge couldn't for his life get his pince-nez on—"the Howards"—the captain openly rubbed his hands—"to the memory that those names call up I appeal, and to the living and honourable bearers of them present. And to you, gentlemen of the jury, the lives of whose fathers went to purchase this dark and bloody ground, I appeal from the accusation of these men, who are not my victims, not my dupes, but their own."

There was a hush when he was done. The judge read the charge to the jury, and it was favourable—very. And—well, Scatters had taught the darkies a lesson; he had spoken of their families and their traditions, he knew their names, and—oh, well, he was a good fellow after all—what was the use?

The jury did not leave their seats, and the verdict was acquittal.

Scatters thanked the Court and started away; but he met three ominous-looking pairs of eyes, and a crowd composed of angry Negroes was flocking toward the edge of the green.

He came back.

"I think I had better wait until the excitement subsides," he said to Major Richardson.

"No need of that, suh, no need of that. Here, Jim," he called to his coachman, "take Mr. Scatters wherever he wants to go, and remember, I shall hold you responsible for his safety."

"Yes, suh," said Jim.

"A thousand thanks, Major," said the man with the mission.

"Not at all, suh. By the way, that was a very fine effort of yours this afternoon. I was greatly moved by it. If you'll give me your address I'll send you a history of our family, suh, from the time they left Vuhginia and before."

Mr. Scatters gave him the address, and smiled at the three enemies, who still waited on the edge of the green.

"To the station," he said to the driver.

A Matter of Doctrine

THERE WAS GREAT excitement in Miltonville over the advent of a most eloquent and convincing minister from the North. The beauty about the Rev. Thaddeus Warwick was that he was purely and simply a man of the doctrine. He had no emotions, his sermons were never matters of feeling; but he insisted so strongly upon the constant presentation of the tenets of his creed that his presence in a town was always marked by the enthusiasm and joy of religious disputation.

The Rev. Jasper Hayward, coloured, was a man quite of another stripe. With him it was not so much what a man held as what he felt. The difference in their characteristics, however, did not prevent him from attending Dr. Warwick's series of sermons, where, from the vantage point of the gallery, he drank in, without assimilating, that divine's words of wisdom.

Especially was he edified on the night that his white brother held forth upon the doctrine of predestination. It was not that he understood it at all, but that it sounded well and the words had a rich ring as he champed over them again and again.

Mr. Hayward was a man for the time and knew that his congregation desired something new, and if he could supply it he was willing to take lessons even from a white co-worker who had neither "de spi'it ner de fiah." Because, as he was prone to admit to himself, "dey was sump'in' in de unnerstannin'."

He had no idea what plagiarism is, and without a single thought of wrong, he intended to reproduce for his people the religious wisdom which he acquired at the white church. He was an innocent beggar going to the doors of the well-provided for cold spiritual victuals to warm over for his own family. And it would not be plagiarism either, for this very warming-over process would save it from that and make his own whatever he brought. He would season with the pepper of his homely wit, sprinkle it with the salt of his home-made philosophy, then, hot with the fire of his crude eloquence, serve to his people a dish his very own. But to the true purveyor of original dishes it is never pleasant to know that someone else holds the secret of the groundwork of his invention.

It was then something of a shock to the Reverend Mr. Hayward to be accosted by Isaac Middleton, one of his members, just as he was leaving the gallery on the night of this most edifying of sermons.

Isaac laid a hand upon his shoulder and smiled at him benevolently.

"How do, Brothah Hayward," he said, "you been sittin' unner de drippin's of de gospel, too?"

"Yes, I has been listenin' to de wo'ds of my fellow-laborah in de vineya'd of de Lawd," replied the preacher with some dignity, for he saw vanishing the vision of his own glory in a revivified sermon on predestination.

Isaac linked his arm familiarly in his pastor's as they went out upon the street.

"Well, what you t'ink erbout pre-o'dination an' fo'-destination any how?"

"It sutny has been pussented to us in a powahful light dis eve'nin'."

"Well, suh, hit opened up my eyes. I do' know when I's hyeahed a sehmon dat done my soul mo' good."

"It was a upliftin' episode."

"Seem lak 'co'din' to de way de brothah 'lucidated de matter to-night dat evaht'ing done sot out an' cut an' dried fu' us. Well dat's gwine to he'p me lots."

"De gospel is allus a he'p."

"But not allus in dis way. You see I ain't a eddicated man lak you, Brothah Hayward."

"We can't all have de same 'vantages," the preacher condescended. "But what I feels, I feels, an' what I unnerstan's, I unnerstan's. The Scripture tell us to get unnerstannin'."

"Well, dat's what I's been a-doin' to-night. I's been a-doubtin' an' a-doubtin', a-foolin' erroun' an' wonderin', but now I unnerstan'."

"'Splain yo'se'f, Brothah Middleton," said the preacher.

"Well, suh, I will to you. You knows Miss Sally Briggs? Huh, what say?"

The Reverend Hayward had given a half discernible start and an exclamation had fallen from his lips.

"What say?" repeated his companion.

"I knows de sistah ve'y well, she bein' a membah of my flock."

"Well, I been gwine in comp'ny wit dat ooman fu' de longes'. You ain't nevah tasted none o' huh cookin', has you?"

"I has 'sperienced de sistah's puffo'mances in dat line."

"She is the cookin'est ooman I evah seed in all my life, but howsomedever, I been gwine all dis time an' I ain' nevah said de wo'd. I nevah could git clean erway f'om huh widout somep'n' drawin' me back, an' I didn't know what hit was."

The preacher was restless.

"Hit was des dis away, Brothah Hayward, I was allus lingerin' on de brink, feahful to la'nch away, but now I's a-gwine to la'nch, case dat all dis time tain't been nuffin but fo'-destination dat been a-holdin' me on."

"Ahem," said the minister; "we mus' not be in too big a hu'y to put ouah human weaknesses upon some divine cause."

"I ain't a-doin' dat, dough I ain't a-sputin' dat de lady is a mos' oncommon fine lookin' pusson."

"I has only seed huh wid de eye of de spi'it," was the virtuous answer, "an' to dat eye all t'ings dat are good are beautiful."

"Yes, suh, an' lookin' wid de cookin' eye, hit seem lak' I des fo'destinated fu' to ma'y dat ooman."

"You say you ain't axe huh yit?"

"Not yit, but I's gwine to ez soon ez evah I gets de chanst now."

"Uh, huh," said the preacher, and he began to hasten his steps homeward.

"Seems lak you in a pow'ful hu'y to-night," said his companion, with some difficulty accommodating his own step to the preacher's masterly strides. He was a short man and his pastor was tall and gaunt.

"I has somp'n' on my min', Brothah Middleton, dat I wants to thrash out to-night in de sollertude of my own chambah," was the solemn reply.

"Well, I ain' gwine keep erlong wid you an' pestah you wid my chattah, Brothah Hayward," and at the next corner Isaac Middleton turned off and went his way, with a cheery "so long, may de Lawd set wid you in yo' meddertations."

"So long," said his pastor hastily. Then he did what would be strange in any man, but seemed stranger in so virtuous a minister. He checked his hasty pace, and, after furtively watching Middleton out of sight, turned and retraced his steps in a direction exactly opposite to the one in which he had been going, and toward the cottage of the very Sister Griggs concerning whose charms the minister's parishioner had held forth.

It was late, but the pastor knew that the woman whom he sought was industrious and often worked late, and with ever increasing eagerness he hurried on. He was fully rewarded for his perseverance when the light from the window of his intended hostess gleamed upon him, and when she stood in the full glow of it as the door opened in answer to his knock.

"La, Brothah Hayward, ef it ain't you; howdy; come in."

"Howdy, howdy, Sistah Griggs, how you come on?"

"Oh, I's des tol'able," industriously dusting a chair. "How's yo'se'f?"

"I's right smaht, thankee ma'am."

"W'y, Brothah Hayward, ain't you los' down in dis paht of de town?"

"No, indeed, Sistah Griggs, de shep'erd ain't nevah los' no whaih dey's any of de flock." Then looking around the room at the piles of ironed clothes, he added: "You sutny is a indust'ious ooman."

"I was des 'bout finishin' up some i'onin' I had fu' de white folks," smiled Sister Griggs, taking down her ironing-board and resting it in the corner. "Allus when I gits thoo my wo'k at nights I's putty well tiahed out an' has to eat a snack; set by, Brothah Hayward, while I fixes us a bite."

"La, sisteh, hit don't skacely seem right fu' me to be a-comin' in hyeah lettin' you fix fu' me at dis time o' night, an' you mighty nigh tuckahed out, too."

"Tsch, Brothah Hayward, taint no ha'dah lookin' out fu' two dan it is lookin' out fu' one."

Hayward flashed a quick upward glance at his hostess' face and then repeated slowly, "Yes'm, dat sutny is de trufe. I ain't nevah t'ought o' that befo'. Hit ain't no ha'dah lookin' out fu' two dan hit is fu' one," and though he was usually an incessant talker, he lapsed into a brown study.

Be it known that the Rev. Mr. Hayward was a man of a very level head, and that his bachelorhood was a matter of economy. He had long considered matrimony in the light of a most desirable estate, but one which he feared to embrace until the rewards for his labours began looking up a little better. But now the matter was being presented to him in an entirely different light. "Hit ain't no ha'dah lookin' out fu' two dan fu' one." Might that not be the truth after all. One had to have food. It would take very little more to do for two. One had to have a home to live in. The same house would shelter two. One had to wear clothes. Well, now, there came the rub. But he thought of donation parties, and smiled. Instead of being an extravagance, might not this union of two beings be an economy? Somebody to cook the food, somebody to keep the house, and somebody to mend the clothes.

His reverie was broken in upon by Sally Griggs' voice. "Hit do seem lak you mighty deep in t'ought dis evenin', Brothah Hayward. I done spoke to you twicet."

"Scuse me, Sistah Griggs, my min' has been mighty deeply 'sorbed in a little mattah o' doctrine. What you say to me?"

"I say set up to the table an' have a bite to eat; tain't much, but 'sich ez I have' —you know what de 'postle said."

The preacher's eyes glistened as they took in the well-filled board. There was fervour in the blessing which he asked that made amends for its brevity. Then he fell to.

Isaac Middleton was right. This woman was a genius among cooks. Isaac Middleton was also wrong. He, a layman, had no right to raise his eyes to her. She was the prize of the elect, not the quarry of any chance pursuer. As he ate and talked, his admiration for Sally grew as did his indignation at Middleton's presumption.

Meanwhile the fair one plied him with delicacies, and paid deferential attention whenever he opened his mouth to give vent to an opinion. An admirable wife she would make, indeed.

At last supper was over and his chair pushed back from the table. With a long sigh of content, he stretched his long legs, tilted back and said: "Well, you done settled de case ez fur ez I is concerned."

"What dat, Brothah Hayward?" she asked.

"Well, I do' know's I's quite prepahed to tell you yit."

"Hyeah now, don' you remembah ol' Mis' Eve? Taint nevah right to git a lady's cur'osity riz."

"Oh, nemmine, nemmine, I ain't gwine keep yo' cur'osity up long. You see, Sistah Griggs, you done 'lucidated one p'int to me dis night dat meks it plumb needful fu' me to speak."

She was looking at him with wide open eyes of expectation.

"You made de 'emark to-night, dat it ain't no ha'dah lookin' out aftah two dan one."

"Oh, Brothah Hayward!"

"Sistah Sally, I reckernizes dat, an' I want to know ef you won't let me look out aftah we two? Will you ma'y me?"

She picked nervously at her apron, and her eyes sought the floor modestly as she answered, "Why, Brothah Hayward, I ain't fittin' fu' no sich eddicated man ez you. S'posin' you'd git to be pu'sidin' elder, er bishop, er somp'n' er othah, whaih'd I be?"

He waved his hand magnanimously. "Sistah Griggs, Sally, whatevah high place I may be fo'destined to I shall tek my wife up wid me."

This was enough, and with her hearty yes, the Rev. Mr. Hayward had Sister Sally close in his clerical arms. They were not through their mutual felicitations, which were indeed so enthusiastic as to drown the sound of a knocking at the door and the ominous scraping of feet, when the door opened to admit Isaac Middleton, just as the preacher was imprinting a very decided kiss upon his fiancée's cheek.

"Wha'—wha'" exclaimed Middleton.

The preacher turned. "Dat you, Isaac?" he said complacently. "You must 'scuse ouah 'pearance, we des got ingaged."

The fair Sally blushed unseen.

"What!" cried Isaac. "Ingaged, aftah what I tol' you to-night." His face was a thundercloud.

"Yes, suh."

"An' is dat de way you stan' up fu' fo'destination?"

This time it was the preacher's turn to darken angrily as he replied, "Look a-hyeah, Ike Middleton, all I got to say to you is dat whenevah a lady cook to please me lak dis lady do, an' whenevah I love one lak I love huh, an' she seems to love me back, I's a-gwine to pop de question to huh, fo'destination er no fo'destination, so dah!"

The moment was pregnant with tragic possibilities. The lady still stood with bowed head, but her hand had stolen into her minister's. Isaac paused, and the situation overwhelmed him. Crushed with anger and defeat he turned toward the door.

On the threshold he paused again to say, "Well, all I got to say to you, Hayward, don' you nevah talk to me no mor' nuffin' 'bout doctrine!"

Old Abe's Conversion

THE NEGRO POPULATION of the little Southern town of Danvers was in a state of excitement such as it seldom reached except at revivals, baptisms, or on Emancipation Day. The cause of the commotion was the anticipated return of the Rev. Abram Dixon's only son, Robert, who, having taken up his father's life-work and graduated at one of the schools, had been called to a city church.

When Robert's ambition to take a college course first became the subject of the village gossip, some said that it was an attempt to force Providence. If Robert were called to preach, they said, he would be endowed with the power from on high, and no intervention of the schools was necessary. Abram Dixon himself had at first rather leaned to this side of the case. He had expressed his firm belief in the theory that if you opened your mouth, the Lord would fill it. As for him, he had no thought of what he should say to his people when he rose to speak. He trusted to the inspiration of the moment, and dashed blindly into speech, coherent or otherwise.

Himself a plantation exhorter of the ancient type, he had known no school except the fields where he had ploughed and sowed, the woods and the overhanging sky. He had sat under no teacher except the birds and the trees and the winds of heaven. If he did not fail utterly, if his labour was not without fruit, it was because he lived close to nature, and so, near to nature's God. With him religion was a matter of emotion, and he relied for his results more upon a command of feeling than upon an appeal to reason. So it was not strange that he should look upon his son's determination to learn to be a preacher as unjustified by the real demands of the ministry.

But as the boy had a will of his own and his father a boundless pride in him, the day came when, despite wagging heads, Robert Dixon went away to be enrolled among the students of a growing college. Since then six years had passed. Robert had spent his school vacations in teaching; and now, for the first time, he was coming home, a full-fledged minister of the gospel.

It was rather a shock to the old man's sensibilities that his son's congregation should give him a vacation, and that the young minister should accept; but he consented to regard it as of the new order of things, and was glad that he was to have his boy with him again, although he murmured to himself, as he read his son's letter through his bone-bowed spectacles: "Vacation, vacation, an' I wonder ef he reckons de devil's goin' to take one at de same time?"

It was a joyous meeting between father and son. The old man held his boy off and looked at him with proud eyes.

"Why, Robbie," he said, "you—you's a man!"

"That's what I'm trying to be, father." The young man's voice was deep, and comported well with his fine chest and broad shoulders.

"You's a bigger man den yo' father ever was!" said his mother admiringly.

"Oh, well, father never had the advantage of playing football."

The father turned on him aghast. "Playin' football!" he exclaimed. "You don't mean to tell me dat dey 'lowed men learnin' to be preachers to play sich games?"

"Oh, yes, they believe in a sound mind in a sound body, and one seems to be as necessary as the other in fighting evil."

Abram Dixon shook his head solemnly. The world was turning upside down for him.

"Football!" he muttered, as they* sat down to supper.

Robert was sorry that he had spoken of the game, because he saw that it grieved his father. He had come intending to avoid rather than to combat his parent's prejudices. There was no condescension in his thought of them and their ways. They were different; that was all. He had learned new ways. They had retained the old. Even to himself he did not say, "But my way is the better one."

His father was very full of eager curiosity as to his son's conduct of his church, and the son was equally glad to talk of his work, for his whole soul was in it.

"We do a good deal in the way of charity work among the churchless and almost homeless city children; and, father, it would do your heart good if you could only see the little ones gathered together learning the first principles of decent living."

"Mebbe so," replied the father doubtfully, "but what you doin' in de way of teachin' dem to die decent?"

The son hesitated for a moment, and then he answered gently, "We think that one is the companion of the other, and that the best way to prepare them for the future is to keep them clean and good in the present."

"Do you give 'em good strong doctern, er do you give 'em milk and water?"

"I try to tell them the truth as I see it and believe it. I try to hold up before them the right and the good and the clean and beautiful."

"Humph!" exclaimed the old man, and a look of suspicion flashed across his dusky face. "I want you to preach fer me Sunday."

It was as if he had said, "I have no faith in your style of preaching the gospel. I am going to put you to the test."

Robert faltered. He knew his preaching would not please his father or his people, and he shrank from the ordeal. It seemed like setting them all at defiance and attempting to enforce his ideas over their own. Then a perception of his cowardice struck him, and he threw off the feeling that was possessing him. He looked up to find his father watching him keenly, and he remembered that he had not yet answered.

"I had not thought of preaching here," he said, "but I will relieve you if you wish it."

"De folks will want to hyeah you an' see what you kin do," pursued his father tactlessly. "You know dey was a lot of 'em dat said I oughtn't ha' let you go away to school. I hope you'll silence 'em."

---

*Text originally read "the."

Robert thought of the opposition his father's friends had shown to his ambitions, and his face grew hot at the memory. He felt his entire inability to please them now.

"I don't know, father, that I can silence those who opposed my going away or even please those who didn't, but I shall try to please One."

It was now Thursday evening, and he had until Saturday night to prepare his sermon. He knew Danvers, and remembered what a chill fell on its congregations, white or black, when a preacher appeared before them with a manuscript or notes. So, out of concession to their prejudices, he decided not to write his sermon, but to go through it carefully and get it well in hand. His work was often interfered with by the frequent summons to see old friends who stayed long, not talking much, but looking at him with some awe and a good deal of contempt. His trial was a little sorer than he had expected, but he bore it all with the good-natured philosophy which his school life and work in a city had taught him.

The Sunday dawned, a beautiful, Southern summer morning; the lazy hum of the bees and the scent of wild honeysuckle were in the air; the Sabbath was full of the quiet and peace of God; and yet the congregation which filled the little chapel at Danvers came with restless and turbulent hearts, and their faces said plainly: "Rob Dixon, we have not come here to listen to God's word. We have come here to put you on trial. Do you hear? On trial."

And the thought, "On trial," was ringing in the young minister's mind as he rose to speak to them. His sermon was a very quiet, practical one; a sermon that sought to bring religion before them as a matter of every-day life. It was altogether different from the torrent of speech that usually flowed from that pulpit. The people grew restless under this spiritual reserve. They wanted something to sanction, something to shout for, and here was this man talking to them as simply and quietly as if he were not in church.

As Uncle Isham Jones said, "De man never fetched an amen"; and the people resented his ineffectiveness. Even Robert's father sat with his head bowed in his hands, broken and ashamed of his son; and when, without a flourish, the preacher sat down, after talking twenty-two minutes by the clock, a shiver of surprise ran over the whole church. His father had never pounded the desk for less than an hour.

Disappointment, even disgust, was written on every face. The singing was spiritless, and as the people filed out of church and gathered in knots about the door, the old-time head-shaking was resumed, and the comments were many and unfavourable.

"Dat's what his schoolin' done fo' him," said one.

"It wasn't nothin' mo'n a lecter," was another's criticism.

"Put him 'side o' his father," said one of the Rev. Abram Dixon's loyal members, "and bless my soul, de ol' man would preach all roun' him, and he ain't been to no college, neither!"

Robert and his father walked home in silence together. When they were in the house, the old man turned to his son and said:

"Is dat de way dey teach you to preach at college?"

"I followed my instructions as nearly as possible, father."

"Well, Lawd he'p dey preachin', den! Why, befo' I'd ha' been in dat pulpit five minutes, I'd ha' had dem people moanin' an' hollerin' all over de church."

"And would they have lived any more cleanly the next day?"

The old man looked at his son sadly, and shook his head as at one of the unenlightened.

Robert did not preach in his father's church again before his visit came to a close; but before going he said, "I want you to promise me you'll come up and visit me, father. I want you to see the work I am trying to do. I don't say that my way is best or that my work is a higher work, but I do want you to see that I am in earnest."

"I ain't doubtin' you mean well, Robbie," said his father, "but I guess I'd be a good deal out o' place up thaih."

"No, you wouldn't, father. You come up and see me. Promise me."

And the old man promised.

It was not, however, until nearly a year later that the Rev. Abram Dixon went up to visit his son's church. Robert met him at the station, and took him to the little parsonage which the young clergyman's people had provided for him. It was a very simple place, and an aged woman served the young man as cook and caretaker; but Abram Dixon was astonished at what seemed to him both vainglory and extravagance.

"Ain't you livin' kin' o' high fo' yo' raisin', Robbie?" he asked.

The young man laughed. "If you'd see how some of the people live here, father, you'd hardly say so."

Abram looked at the chintz-covered sofa and shook his head at its luxury, but Robert, on coming back after a brief absence, found his father sound asleep upon the comfortable lounge.

On the next day they went out together to see something of the city. By the habit of years, Abram Dixon was an early riser, and his son was like him; so they were abroad somewhat before business was astir in the town. They walked through the commercial portion and down along the wharves and levees. On every side the same sight assailed their eyes: black boys of all ages and sizes, the waifs and strays of the city, lay stretched here and there on the wharves or curled on doorsills, stealing what sleep they could before the relentless day should drive them forth to beg a pittance for subsistence.

"Such as these we try to get into our flock and do something for," said Robert.

His father looked on sympathetically, and yet hardly with full understanding. There was poverty in his own little village, yes, even squalour, but he had never seen anything just like this. At home almost everyone found some open door, and rare was the wanderer who slept out-of-doors except from choice.

At nine o'clock they went to the police court, and the old minister saw many of his race appear as prisoners, receiving brief attention and long sentences. Finally a boy was arraigned for theft. He was a little, wobegone fellow hardly ten years of age. He was charged with stealing cakes from a bakery. The judge was about to deal with him as quickly as with the others, and Abram's heart bled for the child, when he saw a negro call the judge's attention. He turned to find that Robert had left his side. There was a whispered consultation, and then the old preacher heard with joy, "As this is his first offence and a trustworthy person comes forward to take charge of him, sentence upon the prisoner will be suspended."

Robert came back to his father holding the boy by the hand, and together they made their way from the crowded room.

"I'm so glad! I'm so glad!" said the old man brokenly.

"We often have to do this. We try to save them from the first contact with the prison and all that it means. There is no reformatory for black boys here, and they may not go to the institutions for the white; so for the slightest offence they are sent to jail, where they are placed with the most hardened criminals. When released they are branded forever, and their course is usually downward."

He spoke in a low voice, that what he said might not reach the ears of the little ragamuffin who trudged by his side.

Abram looked down on the child with a sympathetic heart.

"What made you steal dem cakes?" he asked kindly.

"I was hongry," was the simple reply.

The old man said no more until he had reached the parsonage, and then when he saw how the little fellow ate and how tenderly his son ministered to him, he murmured to himself, "Feed my lambs"; and then turning to his son, he said, "Robbie, dey's some'p'n in dis, dey's some'p'n in it, I tell you."

That night there was a boy's class in the lower room of Robert Dixon's little church. Boys of all sorts and conditions were there, and Abram listened as his son told them the old, sweet stories in the simplest possible manner and talked to them in his cheery, practical way. The old preacher looked into the eyes of the street gamins about him, and he began to wonder. Some of them were fierce, unruly-looking youngsters, inclined to meanness and rowdyism, but one and all, they seemed under the spell of their leader's voice. At last Robert said, "Boys, this is my father. He's a preacher, too. I want you to come up and shake hands with him." Then they crowded round the old man readily and heartily, and when they were outside the church, he heard them pause for a moment, and then three rousing cheers rang out with the vociferated explanation, "Fo' de minister's pap!"

Abram held his son's hand long that night, and looked with tear-dimmed eyes at the boy.

"I didn't understan'," he said. "I didn't understan'."

"You'll preach for me Sunday, father?"

"I wouldn't daih, honey. I wouldn't daih."

"Oh, yes, you will, pap."

He had not used the word for a long time, and at sound of it his father yielded.

It was a strange service that Sunday morning. The son introduced the father, and the father, looking at his son, who seemed so short a time ago unlearned in the ways of the world, gave as his text, "A little child shall lead them."

He spoke of his own conceit and vainglory, the pride of his age and experience, and then he told of the lesson he had learned. "Why, people," he said, "I feels like a new convert!"

It was a gentler gospel than he had ever preached before, and in the congregation there were many eyes as wet as his own.

"Robbie," he said, when the service was over, "I believe I had to come up here to be converted." And Robbie smiled.

The Race Question

SCENE—RACE TRACK. *Enter old coloured man, seating himself.*

"Oomph, oomph. De work of de devil sho' do p'ospah. How 'do, suh? Des tol'able, thankee, suh. How you come on? Oh, I was des a-sayin' how de wo'k of de ol' boy do p'ospah. Doesn't I frequent the racetrack? No, suh; no, suh. I's Baptis' myse'f, an' I 'low hit's all devil's doin's. Wouldn't 'a' be'n hyeah to-day, but I got a boy named Jim dat's long gone in sin an' he gwine ride one dem hosses. Oomph, dat boy! I sut'ny has talked to him and labohed wid him night an' day, but it was allers in vain, an' I's feahed dat de day of his reckonin' is at han'.

"Ain't I nevah been intrusted in racin'? Humph, you don't s'pose I been dead all my life, does you? What you laffin' at? Oh, scuse me, scuse me, you unnerstan' what I means. You don' give a ol' man time to splain hisse'f. What I means is dat dey has been days when I walked in de counsels of de ongawdly and set in de seats of sinnahs; and long erbout dem times I did tek most ovahly strong to racin'.

"How long dat been? Oh, dat's way long back, 'fo' I got religion, mo'n thuty years ago, dough I got to own I has fell from grace several times sense.

"Yes, suh, I ust to ride. Ki-yi! I nevah furgit de day dat my ol' Mas' Jack put me on 'June Boy,' his black geldin', an' say to me, 'Si,' says he, 'if you don' ride de tail offen Cunnel Scott's mare, "No Quit," I's gwine to larrup you twell you cain't set in de saddle no mo'.' Hyah, hyah. My ol' Mas' was a mighty han' fu' a joke. I knowed he wan't gwine to do nuffin' to me.

"Did I win? Why, whut you spec' I's doin' hyeah ef I hadn' winned? W'y, ef I'd 'a' let dat Scott maih beat my 'June Boy' I'd 'a' drowned myse'f in Bull Skin Crick.

"Yes, suh, I winned; w'y, at de finish I come down dat track lak hit was de Jedgment Day an' I was de las' one up! Ef I didn't race dat maih's tail clean off, I 'low I made hit do a lot o' switchin'. An' aftah dat my wife Mandy she ma'ed me. Hyah, hyah, I ain't bin much on hol'in' de reins sence.

"Sh! dey comin' in to wa'm up. Dat Jim, dat Jim, dat my boy; you nasty putrid little rascal. Des a hundred an' eight, suh, des a hundred an' eight. Yas, suh, dat's my Jim; I don' know whaih he gits his dev'ment at.

"What's de mattah wid dat boy? Whyn't he hunch hisse'f up on dat saddle right? Jim, Jim, whyn't you limber up, boy; hunch yo'se'f up on dat hoss lak you belonged to him and knowed you was dah. What I done showed you? De black raskil, goin' out dah tryin' to disgrace his own daddy. Hyeah he come back. Dat's bettah, you scoun'ril.

"Dat's a right smaht-lookin' hoss he's a-ridin', but I ain't a-trustin' dat bay wid de white feet—dat is, not altogethah. She's a favourwright too; but dey's sumpin' else in dis worl' sides playin' favourwrights. Jim bettah had win dis race. His hoss ain't a five to one shot, but I spec's to go way fum hyeah wid money ernuff to mek a donation on de pa'sonage.

"Does I bet? Well, I don' des call hit bettin'; but I resks a little w'en I t'inks I kin he'p de cause. 'Tain't gamblin', o' co'se; I wouldn't gamble fu nothin', dough my ol' Mastah did ust to say dat a honest gamblah was ez good ez a hones' preachah an' mos' nigh ez skace.

"Look out dah, man, dey's off, dat nasty bay maih wid de white feet leadin' right fu'm de pos'. I knowed it! I knowed it! I had my eye on huh all de time. Oh, Jim, Jim, why didn't you git in bettah, way back dah fouf? Dah go de gong! I knowed dat wasn't no staht. Troop back dah, you raskils, hyah, hyah.

"I wush dat boy wouldn't do so much jummying erroun' wid dat hoss. Fust t'ing he know he ain't gwine to know whaih he's at.

"Dah, dah dey go ag'in. Hit's a sho' t'ing dis time. Bettah, Jim, bettah. Dey didn't leave you dis time. Hug dat bay mare, hug her close, boy. Don't press dat hoss yit. He holdin' back a lot o' t'ings.

"He's gainin'! doggone my cats, he's gainin'! an' dat hoss o' his'n gwine des ez stiddy ez a rockin'-chair. Jim allus was a good boy.

"Confound these spec's, I cain't see 'em skacely; huh, you say dey's neck an' neck; now I see 'em! now I see 'em! and Jimmy's a-ridin' like— Huh, huh, I laik to said sumpin'.

"De bay maih's done huh bes', she's done huh bes'! Dey's turned into the stretch an' still see-sawin'. Let him out, Jimmy, let him out! Dat boy done th'owed de reins away. Come on, Jimmy, come on! He's leadin' by a nose. Come on, I tell you, you black rapscallion, come on! Give 'em hell, Jimmy! give 'em hell! Under de wire an' a len'th ahead. Doggone my cats! wake me up w'en dat othah hoss comes in.

"No, suh, I ain't gwine stay no longah, I don't app'ove o' racin', I's gwine 'roun' an' see dis hyeah bookmakah an' den I's gwine dreckly home, suh, dreckly home. I's Baptis' myse'f, an' I don't app'ove o' no sich doin's!"

A Defender of the Faith

THERE WAS A very animated discussion going on, on the lower floor of the house Number Ten "D" Street. House Number Ten was the middle one of a row of more frames, which formed what was put down on the real estate agent's list as a coloured neighbourhood. The inhabitants of the little cottages were people so poor that they were constantly staggering on the verge of the abyss, which they had been taught to dread and scorn, and why, clearly. Life with them was no dream, but a hard, terrible reality, which meant increasing struggle, and little wonder then that the children of such parents should see the day before Christmas come without hope of any holiday cheer.

Christmas; what did it mean to them? The pitiful little dark ragmuffins, save that the happy, well-dressed people who passed the shanties seemed further away from their life, save that mother toiled later in the evening at her work, if there was work, and that father drank more gin and prayed louder in consequence; save that, perhaps—and there was always a donation—that there might be a little increase in the amount of cold victuals that big sister brought home, and there might be turkey-dressing in it.

But there was a warm discussion in Number Ten, and that is the principal thing. The next in importance is that Miss Arabella Coe, reporter, who had been down that way looking mainly for a Christmas story, heard the sound of voices raised in debate, and paused to listen. It was not a very polite thing for Miss Coe to do, but then Miss Coe was a reporter and reporters are not scrupulous about being polite when there is anything to hear. Besides, the pitch to which the lusty young voices within were raised argued that the owners did not care if the outside world shared in the conversation. So Arabella listened, and after a while she passed through the gate and peeped into the room between the broken slats of a shutter.

It was a mean little place, quite what might be expected from its exterior. A cook stove sat in the middle of the floor with a smoky fire in it, and about it were clustered four or five black children ranging from a toddler of two to a boy of ten. They all showed differing degrees of dirt and raggedness, but all were far and beyond the point of respectability.

One of the group, the older boy, sat upon the bed and was holding forth to his brothers and sisters not without many murmurs of doubt and disbelief.

"No," he was saying, "I tell you dey hain't no such thing as a Santy Claus. Dat's somep'n dat yo' folks jes' git up to make you be good long 'bout Christmas time. I know."

"But, Tom, you know what mammy said," said a dreamy-eyed little chap, who sat on a broken stool with his chin on his hands.

"Aw, mammy," said the orator, "she's jes' a-stuffin' you. She don' believe in no Santy Claus hersel', less'n why'nt he bring huh de dress she prayed fu' last

Christmas." He was very wise, this old man of ten years, and he had sold papers on the avenue where many things are learned, both good and bad.

"But what you got to say about pappy?" pursued the believer. "He say dey's a Santy Claus, and dat he comes down de chimbly; and—"

"Whut's de mattah wid you; look at dat stove pipe; how you s'pose anybody go'n' to git in hyeah th'oo de chimbly?"

They all looked up at the narrow, rusty stove pipe and the sigh of hopelessness brought the tears to Arabella's eyes. The children seemed utterly nonplussed, and Tom was swelling at his triumph. "How's any Santy Claus go'n' to come down th'oo that, I want to know," he repeated.

But the faith of childhood is stronger than reason. Tom's little sister piped up, "I don't know how, but he comes th'roo' that away anyhow. He brung Mamie Davith a doll and it had thoot on it out o' de chimbly."

It was now Tom's turn to be stumped, but he wouldn't let it be known. He only said, "Aw," contemptuously and coughed for more crushing arguments.

"I knows dey's a Santy Claus," said dreamy-eyed Sam.

"Ef dey is why'n't he never come here?" retorted Tom.

"I jes' been thinkin' maybe ouah house is so little he miss it in de night; dey says he's a ol' man an' I 'low his sight ain' good."

Tom was stricken into silence for a moment by this entirely new view of the matter, and then finding no answer to it, he said "Aw" again and looked superior, but warningly so.

"Maybe Thanty's white an' don' go to see col'red people," said the little girl.

"But I do know coloured people's houses he's been at," contended Sam. "Aw, dem col'red folks dat's got the money, dem's de only ones dat Santy Claus fin's, you bet."

Arabella at the window shuddered at the tone of the sceptic; it reminded her so much of the world she knew, and it was hard to believe that her friends who prided themselves on their unbelief could have anything in common with a little coloured newsboy down on "D" Street.

"Tell you what," said Sam again, "let's try an' see if dey is a Santy. We'll put a light in the winder, so if he's ol' he can see us anyhow, an' we'll pray right hard fu' him to come."

"Aw," said Tom.

"Ith been good all thish month," chirped the little girl.

The other children joined with enthusiasm in Sam's plan, though Tom sat upon the bed and looked scornfully on.

Arabella escaped from the window just as Sam brought the smoky lamp and set it on the sill, but she still stood outside the palings of the fence and looked in. She saw four little forms get down on their knees and she crept up near again to hear.

Following Sam's lead they began, "Oh, Santy," but Tom's voice broke in, "Don't you know the Lord don't 'low you to pray to nobody but Him?"

Sam paused, puzzled for a minute, then he led on: "Please 'scuse, good Lord, we started wrong, but won't you please, sir, send Santy Clause around. Amen." And they got up from their knees satisfied.

"Aw," said Tom as Arabella was turning wet-eyed away.

It was a good thing the reporter left as soon as she did, for in a few minutes a big woman pushed in at the gate and entered the house.

"Mammy, mammy," shrieked the children.

"Lawsy, me," said Martha, laughing, "who evah did see sich children? Bless dey hearts, an' dey done sot dey lamp in de winder, too, so's dey po' ol' mammy kin see to git in."

As she spoke she was taking the lamp away to set it on the table where she had placed her basket, but the cry of the children stopped her. "Oh, no, mammy, don't take it, don't take it, dat's to light Santy Claus in."

She paused a minute bewildered and then the light broke over her face. She smiled and then a rush of tears quenched the smile. She gathered the children into her arms and said, "I's feared, honey, ol' man Santy ain' gwine fin' you to-night."

"Wah'd I tell you?" sneered Tom.

"You hush yo' mouf," said his mother, and she left the lamp where it was.

As Arabella Coe wended her way home that night her brain was busy with many thoughts. "I've got my story at last," she told herself, "and I'll go on up and write it." But she did not go up to write it. She came to the parting of the ways. One led home, the other to the newspaper office where she worked. She laughed nervously, and took the former way. Once in her room she went through her small store of savings. There was very little there, then she looked down ruefully at her worn boots. She did need a new pair. Then, holding her money in her hand, she sat down to think.

"It's really a shame," she said to herself, "those children will have no Christmas at all, and they'll never believe in Santa Claus again. They will lose their faith forever and from this it will go to other things." She sat there dreaming for a long while and the vision of a very different childhood came before her eyes.

"Dear old place," she murmured softly, "I believed in Santa Claus until I was thirteen, and that oldest boy is scarcely ten." Suddenly she sprung to her feet. "Hooray," she cried, "I'll be defender of the faith," and she went out into the lighted streets again.

The shopkeepers looked queerly at Arabella that night as she bought as if she were the mother of a large and growing family, and she appeared too young for that. Finally, there was a dress for mother.

She carried them down on "D" Street and placed them stealthily at the door of Number Ten. She put a note among the things, which read: "I am getting old and didn't see your house last year, also I am getting fat and couldn't get down that little stove pipe of yours this year. You must excuse me. Santa Claus." Then looking wilfully at her shoes, but nevertheless with a glow on her face, she went up to the office to write her story.

There were joyous times at Number Ten the next day. Mother was really surprised, and the children saw it.

"Wha'd I tell you," said dreamy Sam.

Tom said nothing then, but when he went down to the avenue to sell the morning papers, all resplendent in a new muffler, he strode up to a boy and remarked belligerently, "Say, if you says de ain't no Santy Claus again, I'll punch yo' head."

Cahoots

IN THE CENTRE of the quaint old Virginia grave-yard stood two monuments side by side—two plain granite shafts exactly alike. On one was inscribed the name Robert Vaughan Fairfax and the year 1864. On the other was the simple and perplexing inscription, "Cahoots." Nothing more.

The place had been the orchard of one of the ante-bellum mansions before the dead that were brought back from the terrible field of Malvern Hill and laid there had given it a start as a cemetery. Many familiar names were chiselled on the granite head-stones, and anyone conversant with Virginia genealogy would have known them to belong to some of the best families of the Old Dominion. But "Cahoots,"—who or what was he?

My interest, not to say curiosity, was aroused. There must be a whole story in those two shafts with their simple inscriptions, a life-drama or perhaps a tragedy. And who was more likely to know it than the postmaster of the quaint little old town. Just after the war, as if tired with its exertions to repel the invader, the old place had fallen asleep and was still drowsing.

I left the cemetery—if such it could be called—and wended my way up the main street to the ancient building which did duty as post-office. The man in charge, a grizzled old fellow with an empty sleeve, sat behind a small screen. He looked up as I entered and put out his hand toward the mailboxes, waiting for me to mention my name. But instead I said: "I am not expecting any mail. I only wanted to ask a few questions."

"Well, sir, what can I do for you?" he asked with some interest.

"I've just been up there walking through the cemetery," I returned, "and I am anxious to know the story, if there be one, of two monuments which I saw there."

"You mean Fairfax and Cahoots."

"Yes."

"You're a stranger about here, of course."

"Yes," I said again, "and so there is a story?"

"There is a story and I'll tell it to you. Come in and sit down." He opened a wire door into his little cage, and I seated myself on a stool and gave my attention to him.

"It's just such a story," he began, "as you can hear in any of the Southern States—wherever there were good masters and faithful slaves. This particular tale is a part of our county history, and there ain't one of the old residents but could tell it to you word for word and fact for fact. In the days before our misunderstanding with the North, the Fairfaxes were the leading people in this section. By leading, I mean not only the wealthiest, not only the biggest land-owners, but that their name counted for more in social circles and political councils than any other hereabout. It is natural to expect that such a family should wish to preserve its own name down a direct line. So it was a source of great grief to old Fairfax that his first three children were girls, pretty, healthy, plump enough little things, but girls for all that, and consequently a disappointment to their father's pride of family. When the fourth child came and it proved to be a boy, the Fairfax plantation couldn't hold the Fairfax joy and it flowed out and mellowed the whole county.

"They do say that Fairfax Fairfax was in one of his further tobacco fields when the good news was brought to him, and that after giving orders that all the darkies should knock off work and take a holiday, in his haste and excitement he jumped down from his horse and ran all the way to the house. I give the story only for what it is worth. But if it is true, it is the first case of a man of that name and family forgetting himself in an emergency.

"Well, of course, the advent of a young male Fairfax would under any circumstances have proven a great event, although it was afterwards duplicated, but there would have been no story to tell, there would have been no 'Cahoots,' if by some fortuitous circumstance one of the slave women had not happened to bring into the world that day and almost at the same time that her mistress was introducing young Vaughan Fairfax to the light, a little black pickaninny of her own. Well, if you're a Southern man, and I take it that you are, you know that nothing ever happens in the quarters that the big house doesn't know. So the news was soon at the white father's ears and nothing would do him but that the black baby must be brought to the house and be introduced to the white one. The little black fellow came in all rolled in his bundle of shawls and was laid for a few minutes beside his little lord and master. Side by side they lay blinking at the light equally strange to both, and then the master took the black child's hand and put it in that of the white's. With the convulsive gesture common to babyhood the little hands clutched in a feeble grasp.

"'Dah now,' old Doshy said—she was the nurse that had brought the pickaninny up—'dey done tol' each othah howdy.'

"'Told each other howdy nothing,' said old Fairfax solemnly, 'they have made a silent compact of eternal friendship, and I propose to ratify it right here.'

"He was a religious man, and so there with all the darkies clustered around in superstitious awe, and with the white face of his wife looking at him from among the pillows, he knelt and offered a prayer, and asked a blessing upon the two children just come into the world. And through it all those diminutive specimens of humanity lay there blinking with their hands still clasped.

"Well, they named the white child Robert Vaughan, and they began calling the little darky Ben, until an incident in later life gave him the name that clung to him till the last, and which the Fairfaxes have had chiseled on his tomb-stone.

"The incident occurred when the two boys were about five years old. They were as thick as thieves, and two greater scamps and greater cronies never tramped together over a Virginia plantation. In the matter of deviltry they were remarkably precocious, and it was really wonderful what an amount of mischief those two could do. As was natural, the white boy planned the deeds, and the black one was his willing coadjutor in carrying them out.

"Meanwhile, the proud father was smilingly indulgent to their pranks, but even with him the climax was reached when one of his fine young hounds was nearly driven into fits by the clatter of a tin can tied to its tail. Then the two culprits were summoned to appear before the paternal court of inquiry.

"They came hand in hand, and with no great show of fear or embarrassment. They had gotten off so many times before that they were perfectly confident of their power in this case to cajole the judge. But to their surprise he was all sternness and severity.

"'Now look here,' he said, after expatiating on the cruel treatment which the dog had received. 'I want to know which one of you tied the can to Spot's tail?'

"Robert Vaughan looked at Ben, and Ben looked back at him. Silence there, and nothing more.

"'Do you hear my question?' old Fairfax asked with rising voice.

"Robert Vaughan looked straight ahead of him, and Ben dug his big toe into the sand at the foot of the veranda, but neither answered.

"'Robert Vaughan Fairfax,' said his father, 'who played that trick on Spot? Answer me, do you hear?'

"The Fairfax heir seemed suddenly to have grown deaf and dumb, and the father turned to the black boy. His voice took on the tone of command which he had hardly used to his son. 'Who played that trick on Spot? Answer me, Ben.'

"The little darky dug harder and harder into the sand, and flashed a furtive glance from under his brows at his fellow-conspirator. Then he drawled out, 'I done it.'

"'You didn't,' came back the instant retort from his young master, 'I did it myself.'

"'I done it,' repeated Ben, and 'You didn't,' reiterated his young master.

"The father sat and looked on at the dispute, and his mouth twitched suspiciously, but he spoke up sternly. 'Well, if I can't get the truth out of you this way, I'll try some other plan. Mandy,' he hailed a servant, 'put these boys on a diet of bread and water until they are ready to answer my questions truthfully.'

"The culprits were led away to their punishment. Of course it would have just been meat to Mandy to have stolen something to the youngsters, but her master kept such a close eye upon her that she couldn't, and when brought back at the end of three hours, their fare had left the prisoners rather hungry. But they had evidently disputed the matter between themselves, and from the cloud on their faces when they reappeared before their stern judge, it was still unsettled.

"To the repetition of the question, Vaughan answered again, 'I did it,' and then his father tried Ben again.

"After several efforts, and an imploring glance at his boy master, the little black stammered out:

"'Well, I reckon—I reckon, Mas', me an' Mas' Vaughan, we done it in cahoots.'

"Old Fairfax Fairfax had a keen sense of humour, and as he looked down on the strangely old young darky and took in his answer, the circumstance became too much for his gravity, and his relaxing laugh sent the culprits rolling and tumbling in the sand in an ectasy of relief from the strained situation.

"'Cahoots—I reckon it was "Cahoots,"' the judge said. 'You ought to be named that, you little black rascal!' Well, the story got around, and so it was, and from that day forth the black boy was 'Cahoots.' Cahoots, whether on the plantation, at home, in the halls of the Northern College, where he accompanied his young master, or in the tragic moments of the great war-drama played out on the field of Malvern.

"As they were in childhood, so, inseparable through youth and young manhood, Robert Fairfax and Cahoots grew up. They were together in everything, and when the call came that summoned the young Virginian from his college to fight for the banner of his State, Cahoots was the one who changed from the ease of a gentleman's valet to the hardship of a soldier's body-servant.

"The last words Fairfax Fairfax said as his son cantered away in his gray suit were addressed to Cahoots: 'Take good care of your Mas' Vaughan, Cahoots, and don't come back without him.'

"'I won't, Mastah,' Cahoots flung back and galloped after his life-long companion.

"Well, the war brought hard times both for master and man, and there were no flowery beds of ease even for the officers who wore the gray. Robert Fairfax took the fortunes of the conflict like a man and a Virginia gentleman, and with him Cahoots.

"It was at Malvern Hill that the young Confederate led his troops into battle, and all day long the booming of the cannon and the crash of musketry rising above the cries of the wounded and dying came to the ears of the slave waiting in his tent for his master's return. Then in the afternoon a scattered fragment came straggling back into the camp. Cahoots went out to meet them. The firing still went on.

"'Whah's Mas' Bob?' his voice pierced through the cannon's thunder.

"'He fell at the front, early in the battle.'

"'Whah's his body den, ef he fell?'

"'We didn't have time to look for dead bodies in that murderous fire. It was all we could do to get our living bodies away.'

"'But I promised not to go back without him.' It was a wail of anguish from the slave.

"'Well, you'll have to.'

"'I won't. Whah did he fall?'

"Someone sketched briefly the approximate locality of Robert Fairfax's resting place, and on the final word Cahoots tore away.

"The merciless shot of the Federals was still raking the field. But amid it all an old prairie schooner, gotten from God knows where, started out from the dismantled camp across the field. 'Some fool going to his death,' said one of the gray soldiers.

"A ragged, tattered remnant of the wagon came back. The horses were bleeding and staggering in their steps. The very harness was cut by the balls that had grazed it. But with a light in his eyes and the look of a hero, Cahoots leaped from the tattered vehicle and began dragging out the body of his master.

"He had found him far to the front in an abandoned position and brought him back over the field of the dead.

"'How did you do it?' They asked him.

"'I jes' had to do it,' he said. 'I promised not to go home widout him, and I didn't keer ef I did git killed. I wanted to die ef I couldn't find Mas' Bob's body.'

"He carried the body home, and mourned at the burial, and a year later came back to the regiment with the son who had come after Robert, and was now just of fighting age. He went all through this campaign, and when the war was over, the two struck away into the mountains. They came back after a while, neither one having taken the oath of allegiance, and if there were any rebels Cahoots was as great a one to the day of his death as his master. That tomb-stone, you see it looks old, was placed there at the old master's request when his dead son came home from Malvern Hill, for he said when Cahoots went to the other side they must not be separated; that accounts for its look of age, but it was not until last year that we laid Cahoots—Cahoots still though an old man—beside his master. And many a man that had owned his people, and many another that had fought to continue that ownership, dropped a tear on his grave."

The Promoter

EVEN AS EARLY as September, in the year of 1870, the newly emancipated had awakened to the perception of the commercial advantages of freedom, and had begun to lay snares to catch the fleet and elusive dollar. Those controversialists who say that the Negro's only idea of freedom was to live without work are either wrong, malicious, or they did not know Little Africa when the boom was on; every little African, fresh from the fields and cabins, dreamed only of untold wealth and of mansions in which he would have been thoroughly uncomfortable. These were the devil's sunny days, and early and late his mowers were in the field. These were the days of benefit societies that only benefited the shrewdest man; of mutual insurance associations, of wild building companies, and of gilt-edged land schemes wherein the unwary became bogged. This also was the day of Mr. Jason Buford, who, having been free before the war, knew a thing or two, and now had set himself up as a promoter. Truly he had profited by the example of the white men for whom he had so long acted as messenger and factotum.

As he frequently remarked when for purposes of business he wished to air his Biblical knowledge, "I jest takes the Scripter fur my motter an' foller that ol' passage where it says, 'Make hay while the sun shines, fur the night cometh when no man kin work.'"

It is related that one of Mr. Buford's customers was an old plantation exhorter. At the first suggestion of a Biblical quotation the old gentleman closed his eyes and got ready with his best amen. But as the import of the words dawned on him he opened his eyes in surprise, and the amen died a-borning. "But do hit say dat?" he asked earnestly.

"It certainly does read that way," said the promoter glibly.

"Uh, huh," replied the old man, settling himself back in his chair. "I been preachin' dat t'ing wrong fu' mo' dan fo'ty yeahs. Dat's whut comes o' not bein' able to read de wo'd fu' yo'se'f."

Buford had no sense of the pathetic or he could never have done what he did —sell to the old gentleman, on the strength of the knowledge he had imparted to him, a house and lot upon terms so easy that he might drowse along for a little time and then wake to find himself both homeless and penniless. This was the promoter's method, and for so long a time had it proved successful that he had now grown mildly affluent and had set up a buggy in which to drive about and see his numerous purchasers and tenants.

Buford was a suave little yellow fellow, with a manner that suggested the training of some old Southern butler father, or at least, an experience as a likely houseboy. He was polite, plausible, and more than all, resourceful. All of this he had been for years, but in all these years he had never so risen to the height of his own uniqueness as when he conceived and carried into execution the idea of the "Buford Colonizing Company."

Humanity has always been looking for an Eldorado, and, however mixed the metaphor may be, has been searching for a Moses to lead it thereto. Behold, then, Jason Buford in the rôle of Moses. And equipped he was to carry off his part with the very best advantage, for though he might not bring water from the rock, he could come as near as any other man to getting blood from a turnip.

The beauty of the man's scheme was that no offering was too small to be accepted. Indeed, all was fish that came to his net.

Think of paying fifty cents down and knowing that some time in the dim future you would be the owner of property in the very heart of a great city where people would rush to buy. It was glowing enough to attract a people more worldly wise than were these late slaves. They simply fell into the scheme with all their souls; and off their half dollars, dollars, and larger sums, Mr. Buford waxed opulent. The land meanwhile did not materialize.

It was just at this time that Sister Jane Callender came upon the scene and made glad the heart of the new-fledged Moses. He had heard of Sister Jane before, and he had greeted her coming with a sparkling of eyes and a rubbing of hands that betokened a joy with a good financial basis.

The truth about the newcomer was that she had just about received her pension, or that due to her deceased husband, and she would therefore be rich, rich to the point where avarice would lie in wait for her.

Sis' Jane settled in Mr. Buford's bailiwick, joined the church he attended, and seemed only waiting with her dollars for the very call which he was destined to make. She was hardly settled in a little three-room cottage before he hastened to her side, kindly intent, or its counterfeit, beaming from his features. He found a weak-looking old lady propped in a great chair, while another stout and healthy-looking woman ministered to her wants or stewed about the house in order to be doing something.

"Ah, which—which is Sis' Jane Callender," he asked, rubbing his hands for all the would like a clothing dealer over a good customer.

"Dat's Sis' Jane in de cheer," said the animated one, pointing to her charge. "She feelin' mighty po'ly dis evenin'. What might be yo' name?" She was promptly told.

"Sis' Jane, hyeah one de good brothahs come to see you to offah his suvices if you need anything."

"Thanky, brothah, charity," said the weak voice, "sit yo'se'f down. You set down, Aunt Dicey. Tain't no use a runnin' roun' waitin' on me. I ain't long fu' dis worl' nohow, mistah."

"Buford is my name an' I came in to see if I could be of any assistance to you, a-fixin' up yo' mattahs er seein' to anything for you."

"Hit's mighty kind o' you to come, dough I don' 'low I'll need much fixin' fu' now."

"Oh, we hope you'll soon be better, Sistah Callender."

"Nevah no mo', suh, 'til I reach the Kingdom."

"Sis' Jane Callender, she have been mighty sick," broke in Aunt Dicey Fairfax, "but I reckon she gwine pull thoo', the Lawd willin'."

"Amen," said Mr. Buford.

"Huh, uh, children, I done hyeahd de washin' of de waters of Jerdon."

"No, no, Sistah Callendah, we hope to see you well and happy in de injoyment of de pension dat I understan' de gov'ment is goin' to give you."

"La, chile, I reckon de white folks gwine to git dat money. I ain't nevah gwine to live to 'ceive it. Des' aftah I been wo'kin' so long fu' it, too."

The small eyes of Mr. Buford glittered with anxiety and avarice. What, was this rich plum about to slip from his grasp, just as he was about to pluck it? It should not be. He leaned over the old lady with intense eagerness in his gaze.

"You must live to receive it," he said, "we need that money for the race. It must not go back to the white folks. Ain't you got nobody to leave it to?"

"Not a chick ner a chile, 'ceptin' Sis' Dicey Fairfax here."

Mr. Buford breathed again. "Then leave it to her, by all means," he said.

"I don' want to have nothin' to do with de money of de daid," said Sis' Dicey Fairfax.

"Now, don't talk dat away, Sis' Dicey," said the sick woman. "Brother Buford is right, case you sut'ny has been good to me sence I been layin' hyeah on de bed of affliction, an' dey ain't nobody more fitterner to have dat money den you is. Ef de Lawd des lets me live long enough, I's gwine to mek my will in yo' favoh."

"De Lawd's will be done," replied the other with resignation, and Mr. Buford echoed with an "Amen!"

He stayed very long that evening, planning and talking with the two old women, who received his words as the Gospel. Two weeks later the *Ethiopian Banner,* which was the organ of Little Africa, announced that Sis' Jane Callender had received a back pension which amounted to more than five hundred dollars. Thereafter Mr. Buford was seen frequently in the little cottage, until one day, after a lapse of three or four weeks, a policeman entered Sis' Jane Callender's cottage and led her away amidst great excitement to prison. She was charged with pension fraud, and against her protestations, was locked up to await the action of the Grand Jury.

The promoter was very active in his client's behalf, but in spite of all his efforts she was indicted and came up for trial.

It was a great day for the denizens of Little Africa, and they crowded the court room to look upon this stranger who had come among them to grow so rich, and then suddenly to fall so low.

The prosecuting attorney was a young Southerner, and when he saw the prisoner at the bar he started violently, but checked himself. When the prisoner saw him, however, she made no effort at self control.

"Lawd o' mussy," she cried, spreading out her black arms, "if it ain't Miss Lou's little Bobby."

The judge checked the hilarity of the audience; the prosecutor maintained his dignity by main force, and the bailiff succeeded in keeping the old lady in her place, although she admonished him: "Pshaw, chile, you needn't fool wid me, I nussed dat boy's mammy when she borned him."

It was too much for the young attorney, and he would have been less a man if it had not been. He came over and shook her hand warmly, and this time no one laughed.

It was really not worth while prolonging the case, and the prosecution was nervous. The way that old black woman took the court and its officers into her bosom was enough to disconcert any ordinary tribunal. She patronised the judge openly before the hearing began and insisted upon holding a gentle motherly conversation with the foreman of the jury.

She was called to the stand as the very first witness.

"What is your name?" asked the attorney.

"Now, Bobby, what is you axin' me dat fu'? You know what my name is, and you one of de Fairfax fambly, too. I 'low ef yo' mammy was hyeah, she'd mek you 'membah; she'd put you in yo' place."

The judge rapped for order.

"That is just a manner of proceeding," he said; "you must answer the question, so the rest of the court may know."

"Oh, yes, suh, 'scuse me, my name hit's Dicey Fairfax."

The attorney for the defence threw up his hands and turned purple. He had a dozen witnesses there to prove that they had known the woman as Jane Callender.

"But did you not give your name as Jane Callender?"

"I object," thundered the defence.

"Do, hush, man," Sis' Dicey exclaimed, and then turning to the prosecutor, "La, honey, you know Jane Callender ain't my real name, you knows dat yo'se'f. It's des my bus'ness name. W'y, Sis' Jane Callender done daid an' gone to glory too long 'go fu' to talk erbout."

"Then you admit to the court that your name is not Jane Callender?"

"Wha's de use o' my 'mittin', don' you know it yo'se'f, suh? Has I got to come hyeah at dis late day an' p'ove my name an' redentify befo' my ol' Miss's own chile? Mas' Bob, I nevah did t'ink you'd ac' dat away. Freedom sutny has done tuk erway yo' mannahs."

"Yes, yes, yes, that's all right, but we want to establish the fact that your name is Dicey Fairfax."

"Cose it is."

"Your Honor, I object—I—"

"Your Honor," said Fairfax coldly, "will you grant me the liberty of conducting the examination in a way somewhat out of the ordinary lines? I believe that my brother for the defence will have nothing to complain of. I believe that I understand the situation and shall be able to get the truth more easily by employing methods that are not altogether technical."

The court seemed to understand a thing or two himself, and overruled the defence's objection.

"Now, Mrs. Fairfax—"

Aunt Dicey snorted. "Hoomph? What? Mis' Fairfax? What ou say, Bobby Fairfax? What you call me dat fu'? My name Aunt Dicey to you an' I want you to un'erstan' dat right hyeah. Ef you keep on foolin' wid me, I 'spec' my patience gwine waih claih out."

"Excuse me. Well, Aunt Dicey, why did you take the name of Jane Callender if your name is really Dicey Fairfax?"

"W'y, I done tol' you, Bobby, dat Sis' Jane Callender was des' my bus'ness name."

"Well, how were you to use this business name?"

"Well, it was des dis away. Sis' Jane Callender, she gwine git huh pension, but la, chile, she tuk down sick unto deaf, an' Brothah Buford, he say dat she ought to mek a will in favoh of somebody, so's de money would stay 'mongst ouah folks, an' so, bimeby, she 'greed she mek a will."

"And who is Brother Buford, Aunt Dicey?"

"Brothah Buford? Oh, he's de gemman whut come an' offered to 'ten' to Sis' Jane Callender's bus'ness fu' huh. He's a moughty clevah man."

"And he told her she ought to make a will?"

"Yas, suh. So she 'greed she gwine mek a will, an' she say to me, 'Sis Dicey, you sut'ny has been good to me sence I been layin' hyeah on dis bed of 'fliction, an' I gwine will all my proputy to you.' Well, I don't want to tek de money, an' she des mos' nigh fo'ce it on me, so I say yes, an' Brothah Buford he des sot an' talk to us, an' he say dat he come to-morrow to bring a lawyer to draw up de will. But bless Gawd, honey, Sis' Callender died dat night, an' de will wasn't made, so when Brothah Buford come bright an' early next mornin', I was layin' Sis' Callender out. Brothah Buford was mighty much moved, he was. I nevah did see a strange pusson tek anything so hard in all my life, an' den he talk to me, an' he say, 'Now, Sis' Dicey, is you notified any de neighbours yit?' an' I said no I hain't notified no one of de neighbours, case I ain't 'quainted wid none o' dem yit, an' he say, 'How erbout de doctah? Is he 'quainted wid de diseased?' an' I tol' him no, he des come in, da's all. 'Well,' he say, 'cose you un'erstan' now dat you is Sis' Jane Callender, caise you inhe'it huh name, an' when de doctah come to mek out de 'stiffycate, you mus' tell him dat Sis' Dicey Fairfax is de name of de diseased, an' it'll be all right, an' aftah dis you got to go by de name o' Jane Callender, caise it's a bus'ness name you done inhe'it.' Well, dat's whut I done, an' dat's huccome I been Jane Callender in de bus'ness 'sactions, an' Dicey Fairfax at home. Now, you un'erstan', don't you? It wuz my inhe'ited name."

"But don't you know that what you have done is a penitentiary offence?"

"Who you stan'in' up talkin' to dat erway, you nasty impident little scoun'el? Don't you talk to me dat erway. I reckon ef yo' mammy was hyeah she sut'ny would tend to yo' case. You alluse was sassier an' pearter den yo' brother Nelse, an' he had to go an' git killed in de wah, an' you—you—w'y, jedge, I'se spanked dat boy mo' times den I kin tell you fu' hus impidence. I don't see how you evah gits erlong wid him."

The court repressed a ripple that ran around. But there was no smile on the smooth-shaven, clear-cut face of the young Southerner. Turning to the attorney for the defence, he said: "Will you take the witness?" But that gentleman, waving one helpless hand, shook his head.

"That will do, then," said young Fairfax. "Your Honor," he went on, addressing the court, "I have no desire to prosecute this case further. You all see the trend of it just as I see, and it would be folly to continue the examination of any of the rest of these witnesses. We have got that story from Aunt Dicey herself as straight as an arrow from a bow. While technically she is guilty; while according to the facts she is a criminal according to the motive and the intent of her actions, she is as innocent as the whitest soul among us." He could not repress the youthful Southerner's love for this little bit of rhetoric.

"And I believe that nothing is to be gained by going further into the matter, save for the purpose of finding out the whereabouts of this Brother Buford, and attending to his case as the facts warrant. But before we do this, I want to see the stamp of crime wiped away from the name of my Aunt Dicey there, and I beg leave of the court to enter a *nolle prosse*. There is only one other thing I must ask of Aunt Dicey, and that is that she return the money that was illegally gotten, and give us information concerning the whereabouts of Buford."

Aunt Dicey looked up in excitement, "W'y, chile, ef dat money was got illegal, I don' want it, but I do know whut I gwine to do, cause I done 'vested it all wid Brothah Buford in his colorednization comp'ny." The court drew its breath. It had been expecting some such *dénouement*.

"And where is the office of this company situated?"

"Well, I des can't tell dat," said the old lady. "W'y, la, man, Brothah Buford was in co't to-day. Whaih is he? Brothah Buford, whaih you?" But no answer came from the surrounding spectators. Brother Buford had faded away. The old lady, however, after due conventions, was permitted to go home.

It was with joy in her heart that Aunt Dicey Fairfax went back to her little cottage after her dismissal, but her face clouded when soon after Robert Fairfax came in.

"Hyeah you come as usual," she said with well-feigned anger. "Tryin' to sof' soap me aftah you been carryin' on. You ain't changed one mite fu' all yo' bein' a man. What you talk to me dat away in co't fu'?"

Fairfax's face was very grave. "It was necessary, Aunt Dicey," he said. "You know I'm a lawyer now, and there are certain things that lawyers have to do whether they like it or not. You don't understand. That man Buford is a scoundrel, and he came very near leading you into a very dangerous and criminal act. I am glad I was near to save you."

"Oh, honey, chile, I didn't know dat. Set down an' tell me all erbout it."

This the attorney did, and the old lady's indignation blazed forth. "Well, I hope to de Lawd you'll fin' dat rascal an' larrup him ontwell he cain't stan' straight."

"No, we're going to do better than that and a great deal better. If we find him we are going to send him where he won't inveigle any more innocent people into rascality, and you're going to help us."

"W'y, sut'ny, chile, I'll do all I kin to he'p you git dat rascal, but I don't know whaih he lives, case he's allus come hyeah to see me."

"He'll come back some day. In the meantime we will be laying for him."

Aunt Dicey was putting some very flaky biscuits into the oven, and perhaps the memory of other days made the young lawyer prolong his visit and his explanation. When, however, he left, it was with well-laid plans to catch Jason Buford napping.

It did not take long. Stealthily that same evening a tapping came at Aunt Dicey's door. She opened it, and a small, crouching figure crept in. It was Mr. Buford. He turned down the collar of his coat which he had had closely up about his face and said:

"Well, well, Sis' Callender, you sut'ny have spoiled us all."

"La, Brothah Buford, come in hyeah an' set down. Whaih you been?"

"I been hidin' fu' feah of that testimony you give in the court room. What did you do that fu'?"

"La, me, I didn't know, you didn't 'splain to me in de fust."

"Well, you see, you spoiled it, an' I've got to git out of town as soon as I kin. Sis' Callender, dese hyeah white people is mighty slippery, and they might catch me. But I want to beg you to go on away from hyeah so's you won't be hyeah to testify if dey does. Hyeah's a hundred dollars of yo' money right down, and you leave hyeah to-morrer mornin' an' go erway as far as you kin git."

"La, man, I puffectly willin' to he'p you, you know dat."

"Cose, cose," he answered hurriedly, "we col'red people has got to stan' together."

"But what about de res' of dat money dat I been 'vestin' wid you?"

"I'm goin' to pay intrus' on that," answered the promoter glibly.

"All right, all right." Aunt Dicey had made several trips to the little back room just off her sitting room as she talked with the promoter. Three times in the window had she waved a lighted lamp. Three times without success. But at the last "all right," she went into the room again. This time the waving lamp was answered by the sudden flash of a lantern outside.

"All right," she said, as she returned to the room, "set down an' lemme fix you some suppah."

"I ain't hardly got the time. I got to git away from hyeah." But the smell of the new baked biscuits was in his nostrils and he could not resist the temptation to sit down. He was eating hastily, but with appreciation, when the door opened and two minions of the law entered.

Buford sprang up and turned to flee, but at the back door, her large form a towering and impassive barrier, stood Aunt Dicey.

"Oh, don't hu'y, Brothah Buford," she said calmly, "set down an' he'p yo'se'f. Dese hyeah's my friends."

It was the next day that Robert Fairfax saw him in his cell. The man's face was ashen with coward's terror. He was like a caught rat though, bitingly on the defensive.

"You see we've got you, Buford," said Fairfax coldly to him. "It is as well to confess."

"I ain't got nothin' to say," said Buford cautiously.

"You will have something to say later on unless you say it now. I don't want to intimidate you, but Aunt Dicey's word will be taken in any court in the United States against yours, and I see a few years hard labour for you between good stout walls."

The little promoter showed his teeth in an impotent snarl. "What do you want me to do?" he asked, weakening.

"First, I want you to give back every cent of the money that you got out of Dicey Fairfax. Second, I want you to give up to every one of those Negroes that you have cheated every cent of the property you have accumulated by fraudulent means. Third, I want you to leave this place, and never come back so long as God leaves breath in your dirty body. If you do this, I will save you—you are not worth the saving—from the pen or worse. If you don't, I will make this place so hot for you that hell will seem like an icebox beside it."

The little yellow man was cowering in his cell before the attorney's indignation. His lips were drawn back over his teeth in something that was neither a snarl nor a smile. His eyes were bulging and fear-stricken, and his hands clasped and unclasped themselves nervously.

"I—I—" he faltered, "do you want to send me out without a cent?"

"Without a cent, without a cent," said Fairfax tensely.

"I won't do it," the rat in him again showed fight. "I won't do it. I'll stay hyeah an' fight you. You can't prove anything on me."

"All right, all right," and the attorney turned toward the door.

"Wait, wait," called the man, "I will do it, my God! I will do it. Jest let me out o' hyeah, don't keep me caged up. I'll go away from hyeah."

Fairfax turned back to him coldly, "You will keep your word?"

"Yes."

"I will return at once and take the confession."

And so the thing was done. Jason Buford, stripped of his ill-gotten gains, left the neighbourhood of Little Africa forever. And Aunt Dicey, no longer a wealthy woman and a capitalist, is baking golden brown biscuits for a certain young attorney and his wife, who has the bad habit of rousing her anger by references to her business name and her investments with a promoter.

The Wisdom of Silence

JEREMIAH ANDERSON WAS free. He had been free for ten years, and he was proud of it. He had been proud of it from the beginning, and that was the reason that he was one of the first to cast off the bonds of his old relations, and move from the plantation and take up land for himself. He was anxious to cut himself off from all that bound him to his former life. So strong was this feeling in him that he would not consent to stay on and work for his one-time owner even for a full wage.

To the proposition of the planter and the gibes of some of his more dependent fellows he answered, "No, suh, I's free, an' I sholy is able to tek keer o' myse'f. I done been fattenin' frogs fu' othah people's snakes too long now."

"But, Jerry," said Samuel Brabant, "I don't mean you any harm. The thing's done. You don't belong to me any more, but naturally, I take an interest in you, and want to do what I can to give you a start. It's more than the Northern government has done for you, although such wise men ought to know that you have had no training in caring for yourselves."

There was a slight sneer in the Southerner's voice. Jerry perceived it and thought it directed against him. Instantly his pride rose and his neck stiffened.

"Nemmine me," he answered, "nemmine me. I's free, an' w'en a man's free, he's free."

"All right, go your own way. You may have to come back to me some time. If you have to come, come. I don't blame you now. It must be a great thing to you, this dream—this nightmare." Jerry looked at him. "Oh, it isn't a nightmare now, but some day, maybe, it will be, then come to me."

The master turned away from the newly made freeman, and Jerry went forth into the world which was henceforth to be his. He took with him his few belongings; these largely represented by his wife and four lusty-eating children. Besides, he owned a little money, which he had got working for others when his master's task was done. Thus, burdened and equipped, he set out to tempt Fortune.

He might do one of two things—farm land upon shares for one of his short-handed neighbours, or buy a farm, mortgage it, and pay for it as he could. As was natural for Jerry, and not uncommendable, he chose at once the latter course, bargained for his twenty acres—for land was cheap then, bought his mule, built his cabin, and set up his household goods.

Now, slavery may give a man the habit of work, but it cannot imbue him with the natural thrift that long years of self-dependence brings. There were times when Jerry's freedom tugged too strongly at his easy inclination, drawing him away to idle when he should have toiled. What was the use of freedom, asked an inward voice, if one might not rest when one would? If he might not stop midway the furrow to listen and laugh at a droll story or tell one? If he might not go a-fishing when all the forces of nature invited and the jay-bird called from the tree and gave forth saucy banter like the fiery, blue shrew that she was?

There were times when his compunction held Jerry to his task, but more often he turned an end furrow and laid his misgivings snugly under it and was away to the woods or the creek. There was joy and a loaf for the present. What more could he ask?

The first year Fortune laughed at him, and her laugh is very different from her smile. She sent the swift rains to wash up the new planted seed, and the hungry birds to devour them. She sent the fierce sun to scorch the young crops, and the clinging weeds to hug the fresh greenness of his hope to death. She sent—cruellest jest of all—another baby to be fed, and so weakened Cindy Ann that for many days she could not work beside her husband in the fields.

Poverty began to teach the unlessoned delver in the soil the thrift which he needed; but he ended his first twelve months with barely enough to eat, and nothing paid on his land or his mule. Broken and discouraged, the words of his old master came to him. But he was proud with an obstinate pride and he shut his lips together so that he might not groan. He would not go to his master. Anything rather than that.

In that place sat certain beasts of prey, dealers, and lenders of money, who had their lairs somewhere within the boundaries of that wide and mysterious domain called The Law. They had their risks to run, but so must all beasts that eat flesh or drink blood. To them went Jerry, and they were kind to him. They gave him of their store. They gave him food and seed, but they were to own all that they gave him from what he raised, and they were to take their toll first from the new crops.

Now, the black had been warned against these same beasts, for others had fallen a prey to them even in so short a time as their emancipation measured, and they saw themselves the re-manacled slaves of a hopeless and ever-growing debt, but Jerry would not be warned. He chewed the warnings like husks between his teeth, and got no substance from them.

Then, Fortune, who deals in surprises, played him another trick. She smiled upon him. His second year was better than his first, and the brokers swore over his paid up note. Cindy Ann was strong again and the oldest boy was big enough to help with the work.

Samuel Brabant was displeased, not because he felt any malice toward his former servant, but for the reason that any man with the natural amount of human vanity must feel himself agrieved just as his cherished prophecy is about to come true. Isaiah himself could not have been above it. How much less, then, the uninspired Mr. Brabant, who had his "I told you so," all ready. He had been ready to help Jerry after giving him admonitions, but here it was not needed. An unused "I told you so," however kindly, is an acid that turns the milk of human kindness sour.

Jerry went on gaining in prosperity. The third year treated him better than the second, and the fourth better than the third. During the fifth he enlarged his farm and his house and took pride in the fact that his oldest boy, Matthew, was away at school. By the tenth year of his freedom he was arrogantly out of debt. Then his pride was too much for him. During all these years of his struggle the words of his master had been as gall in his mouth. Now he spat them out with a boast. He talked much in the market-place, and where many people gathered, he was much there, giving himself as a bright and shining example.

"Huh," he would chuckle to any listeners he could find, "Ol' Mas' Brabant, he say, 'Stay hyeah, stay hyeah, you do' know how to tek keer o' yo'se'f yit.' But I des' look at my two han's an' I say to myse'f, whut I been doin' wid dese all dese yeahs—tekin' keer o' myse'f an' him, too. I wo'k in de fiel', he set in de big house an' smoke. I wo'k in de fiel', his son go away to college an' come back a graduate. Das hit. Well, w'en freedom come, I des' bent an' boun' I ain' gwine do it no mo' an' I didn't. Now look at me. I sets down w'en I wants to. I does my own wo'kin' an' my own smokin'. I don't owe a cent, an' dis yeah my boy gwine graduate f'om de school. Dat's me, an' I ain' called on ol' Mas' yit."

Now, an example is always an odious thing, because, first of all, it is always insolent even when it is bad, and there were those who listened to Jerry who had not been so successful as he, some even who had stayed on the plantation and as yet did not even own the mule they ploughed with. The hearts of those were filled with rage and their mouths with envy. Some of the sting of the latter got into their re-telling of Jerry's talk and made it worse than it was.

Old Samuel Brabant laughed and said, "Well, Jerry's not dead yet, and although I don't wish him any harm, my prophecy might come true yet."

There were others who, hearing, did not laugh, or if they did, it was with a mere strained thinning of the lips that had no element of mirth in it. Temper and tolerance were short ten years after sixty-three.

The foolish farmer's boastings bore fruit, and one night when he and his family had gone to church he returned to find his house and barn in ashes, his mules burned and his crop ruined. It had been very quietly done and quickly. The glare against the sky had attracted few from the nearby town, and them too late to be of service.

Jerry camped that night across the road from what remained of his former dwelling. Cindy Ann and the children, worn out and worried, went to sleep in spite of themselves, but he sat there all night long, his chin between his knees, gazing at what had been his pride.

Well, the beasts lay in wait for him again, and when he came to them they showed their fangs in greeting. And the velvet was over their claws. He had escaped them before. He had impugned their skill in the hunt, and they were ravenous for him. Now he was fatter, too. He went away from them with hard terms, and a sickness at his heart. But he had not said "Yes" to the terms. He was going home to consider the almost hopeless conditions under which they would let him build again.

They were staying with a neighbour in town pending his negotiations and thither he went to ponder on his circumstances. Then it was that Cindy Ann came into the equation. She demanded to know what was to be done and how it was to be gone about.

"But Cindy Ann, honey, you do' know nuffin' 'bout bus'ness."

"T'ain't whut I knows, but whut I got a right to know," was her response.

"I do' see huccome you got any right to be a-pryin' into dese hyeah things."

"I's got de same right I had to w'ok an' struggle erlong an' he'p you get whut we's done los'."

Jerry winced and ended by telling her all.

"Dat ain't nuffin' but owdacious robbery," said Cindy Ann. "Dem people sees dat you got a little some'p'n, an' dey ain't gwine stop ontwell dey's bu'nt an' stoled evah blessed cent f'om you. Je'miah, don't you have nuffin' mo' to do wid 'em."

"I got to, Cindy Ann."

"Whut fu' you got to?"

"How I gwine buil' a cabin an' a ba'n an' buy a mule less'n I deal wid 'em?"

"Dah's Mas' Sam Brabant. He'd he'p you out."

Jerry rose up, his eyes flashing fire. "Cindy Ann," he said, "you a fool, you ain't got no mo' pride den a guinea hen, an' you got a heap less sense. W'y, befo' I go to ol' Mas' Sam Brabant fu' a cent, I'd sta've out in de road."

"Huh!" said Cindy Ann, shutting her mouth on her impatience.

One gets tired of thinking and saying how much more sense a woman has than a man when she comes in where his sense stops and his pride begins.

With the recklessness of despair Jerry slept late that next morning, but he might have awakened early without spoiling his wife's plans. She was up betimes, had gone on her mission and returned before her spouse awoke.

It was about ten o'clock when Brabant came to see him. Jerry grew sullen at once as his master approached, but his pride stiffened. This white man should see that misfortune could not weaken him.

"Well, Jerry," said his former master, "you would not come to me, eh, so I must come to you. You let a little remark of mine keep you from your best friend, and put you in the way of losing the labour of years."

Jerry made no answer.

"You've proved yourself able to work well, but Jerry," pausing, "you haven't yet shown that you're able to take care of yourself, you don't know how to keep your mouth shut."

The ex-slave tried to prove this a lie by negative pantomime.

"I'm going to lend you the money to start again."

"I won't—"

"Yes, you will, if you don't, I'll lend it to Cindy Ann, and let her build in her own name. She's got more sense than you, and she knows how to keep still when things go well."

"Mas' Sam," cried Jerry, rising quickly, "don' len' dat money to Cindy Ann. W'y ef a ooman's got anything she nevah lets you hyeah de las' of it."

"Will you take it, then?"

"Yes, suh; yes, suh, an' thank 'e, Mas' Sam." There were sobs some place back in his throat. "An' nex' time ef I evah gets a sta't agin, I'll keep my mouf shet. Fac' is, I'll come to you, Mas' Sam, an' borry fu' de sake o' hidin'."

The Triumph of Ol' Mis' Pease

Between the two women, the feud began in this way: When Ann Pease divorced her handsome but profligate spouse, William, Nancy Rogers had, with reprehensible haste, taken him for better or for worse. Of course, it proved for worse, but Ann Pease had never forgiven her.

"'Pears lak to me," she said, "dat she was des a-waitin' fu' to step inter my shoes, no mattah how I got outen 'em, whethah I died or divo'ced."

It was in the hey-day of Nancy Rogers' youth, and she was still hot-tempered, so she retorted that "Ann Pease sut'ny did unmind huh' o' de dawg in de mangah." The friends of the two women took sides, and a war began which waged hotly between them—a war which for the first few weeks threatened the unity of Mt. Pisgah Church.

But the church in all times has been something of a selfish institution and has known how to take care of itself. Now, Mt. Pisgah, of necessity, must recognise divorce, and of equal necessity, re-marriage. So when the Rev. Isaiah Johnson had been appealed to, he had spread his fat hands, closed his eyes and said solemnly, "Whom God hath j'ined, let no man put asundah;" peace, or at best, apparent peace, settled upon the troubled waters.

The solidity of Mt. Pisgah was assured, the two factions again spoke to each other, both gave collections on the same Sunday; but between the two principals there was no abatement of their relentless animosity.

Ann Pease as it happened was a "puffessor," while the new Mrs. Pease was out of the fold; a gay, frivolous person who had never sought or found grace. She laughed when a black wag said of the two that "they might bofe be 'peas,' but dey wasn't out o' de same pod." But on its being repeated to Sister Pease, she resented it with Christian indignation, sniffed and remarked that "Ef Wi'yum choosed to pick out one o' de onregenerate an' hang huh ez a millstone erroun' his neck, it wasn't none o' huh bus'ness what happened to him w'en dey pulled up de tares f'om de wheat."

There were some ultra-malicious ones who said that Sister Pease, seeing her former husband in the possession of another, had begun to regret her step, for the unregenerate William was good-looking after all, and the "times" that he and his equally sinful wife had together were the wonder and disgust, the envy and horror of the whole community, who watched them with varying moods of eagerness.

Sister Ann Pease went her way apparently undisturbed. Religion has an arrogance of its own, and when at the end of the year the good widow remained unmarried she could toss her head, go her way, and look down from a far height upon the "po' sinnahs"; indeed, she had rather the better of her frailer sister in the sympathies of the people.

As one sister feelingly remarked, "Dat ooman des baihin' dat man in huh prayahs, an' I 'low she'll mou'n him into glory yit."

One year of married life disillusions, and defiant gaiety cannot live upon itself when admiration fails. There is no reward in being daring when courage becomes commonplace. The year darkened to winter, and bloomed to spring again. The willows feathered along the river banks, and the horse-chestnuts budded and burst into beautiful life. Then came summer, rejoicing, with arms full of flowers, and autumn with lap full of apples and grain, then winter again, and all through the days Nancy danced and was gay, but there was a wistfulness in her eyes, and the tug of the baby no longer drew her heart. She had come to be "Wi'yum's Nancy," while the other, *that* other was still "Sister Pease," who sat above her in the high places of the people's hearts.

And then, oh, blessedness of the winter, the revival came; and both she and William, strangely stricken together with the realisation of their sins, fell at the mercy seat.

"There is more joy over one sinner that repenteth,"—but when Will and Nancy both "came through" on the same night—well, Mt. Pisgah's walls know the story.

There was triumph in Nancy's face as she proclaimed her conversion, and the first person she made for was Sister Pease. She shook her hands and embraced her, crying ever aloud between the vociferations of the congregation, "Oh, sistah, he'p me praise Him, he'p me praise Him," and the elder woman in the cause caught the infection of the moment and joined in the general shout.

Afterwards she was not pleased with herself. But then if she hadn't shouted, wouldn't it have been worse?

The Rev. Isaiah was nothing if not dramatic in his tendencies, and on the day when he was to receive William and Nancy Pease into full membership with the church, it struck him that nothing could make upon his congregation a profounder impression for good than to have the two new Peases joined by the elder one, or as the wag would have put it, all in one pod. And it was so ordered, and the thing was done.

It is true that the preacher had to labour some with Sister Ann Pease, but when he showed her how it was her Christian duty, and if she failed of it her rival must advance before her in public opinion, she acquiesced. It was an easier matter with "Sister Wi'yum Pease." She agreed readily, for she was filled with condescending humility, which on every occasion she took the opportunity of displaying toward her rival.

The Rev. Isaiah Johnson only made one mistake in his diplomatic manoeuvring. That was when he whispered to Sister Ann Pease, "Didn't I tell you? Des see how easy Sister Wi'yum give in." He was near to losing his cause and the wind was completely taken out of his sails when the widow replied with a snort, "Give in, my Lawd! Dat ooman's got a right to give in; ain't she got 'uligion an' de man, too?"

However, the storm blew over, and by the time service was begun they were all seated together on a front bench, Sister Nancy, William, and Sister Ann.

Now was the psychological moment, and after a soul-stirring hymn the preacher rose and announced his text—"Behold how good and how pleasant it is for brethren to dwell together in unity."

Someone in the back part of the church suggested trinity as a substitute and started a titter, but the preacher had already got his dramatic momentum, and was sweeping along in a tumultuous tide of oratory. Right at his three victims did he aim his fiery eloquence, and ever and again he came back to his theme, "Behold how good and how pleasant it is for brethren to dwell together in unity," even though Ann Pease had turned her back on William, whose head was low bowed, and Nancy was ostentatiously weeping into a yellow silk handkerchief.

The sermon spurred on to a tempestuous close, and then came the climax when the doors of the church were opened. William and Nancy immediately went up to end their probation, and after a few whispered remarks the minister shook hands with each of them, then raising his voice he said: "Now, brothahs and sistahs, befo' you all gives dese lambs de right han' o' fellowship to welcome dem to de fol', I want Sister Ann Pease to come up an' be de first to bid 'em God speed on the gospel way." Ann Pease visibly swelled, but she marched up, and without looking at either, shook hands with each of her enemies.

"Hallelujah, praise de Lord," shouted the preacher, clapping his hands, "Behold how good and how pleasant it is; and now let the congregation in gineral come aroun' and welcome Brothah and Sistah Pease."

His rich bass voice broke into "Bless Be the Tie that Binds," and as the volume of the hymn, swelled by the full chorus of the congregation, rolled away to the rafters of the little church, the people rose and marched solemnly round, shaking hands with the new members and with each other.

Brother and Sister Pease were the last to leave church that day, but they found Ann waiting for them at door. She walked straight up to them and spoke: "Nancy Rogers," she said, "I know you; I kin see claih thoo you, and you ain't a foolin' me one bit. All I got to say is dat I has done my Christian duty, an' I ain't gwine do no mo', so don' you speak to me fo'm dis day out."

For the brief space of a second there was something like a gleam in Nancy's eyes, but she replied in all meekness, "I's a full-blown Christian now, an' I feel it my bounden duty to speak to you, Sis' Pease, an' I's gwine t' speak."

Ignoring this defiance the other woman turned to her former husband. She looked at him with unveiled contempt, then she said slowly, "An' ez fu' Wi'yum, Gawd he'p you."

Here all intercourse between these warring spirits might have ended but for Nancy Pease's persistent civility. She would speak to her rival on every occasion, and even call upon her if she could gain admittance to the house. And now the last drop of bitterness fell into the widow's cup, for the community, to distinguish between them, began calling her "Ol' Sis' Pease." This was the climax of her sorrows, and she who had been so devout came no more to the church; she who had been so cheerful and companionable grew morose and sour and shut her doors against her friends. She was as one dead to her old world. The one bit of vivid life about her was her lasting hatred of the woman who bore her name. In vain the preacher sought to break down the barrier of her animosity. She had built it of adamant, and his was a losing fight. So for several years the feud went on, and those who had known Ann in her cheerier days forgot that knowledge and spoke of her with open aversion as "dat awful ol' Mis' Pease." The while Nancy, in spite of "Wi'yum's" industrial vagaries, had flourished and waxed opulent. She continued to flaunt her Christian humility in the eyes of her own circle, and to withhold her pity from the poor, lonely old woman whom hate had made bitter and to whom the world, after all, had not been over-kind. But prosperity is usually cruel, and one needs the prick of the thorn one's self to know how it stings his brother.

She was startled one day, however, out of her usual placidity. Sister Martin, one of her neighbours, dropped in and settling herself with a sigh announced the important news, "Well, bless Gawd, ol' Sis' Pease is gone at last."

Nancy dropped the plate she had been polishing, and unheeded, it smashed into bits on the floor.

"Wha'—what!" she exclaimed.

"Yes'm," Sister Martin assured her, "de ol' lady done passed away."

"I didn't know she was sick; w'en she die?"

"She done shet huh eyes on dis worl' o' sorror des a few minutes ago. She ain't bin sick mo'n two days."

Nancy had come to herself now, and casting her eyes up in an excess of Christian zeal, she said: "Well, she wouldn't let me do nuffin' fu' huh in life, but I sut'ny shell try to do my duty by huh in death," and drying her hands and throwing a shawl over her head, she hastened over to her dead enemy's house.

The news had spread quickly and the neighbourhood had just begun to gather in the little room which held the rigid form. Nancy entered and made her way through the group about the bed, waving the others aside imperiously.

"It is my Christian duty," she said solemnly, "to lay Sis' Pease out, an' I's gwine do it." She bent over the bed. Now there are a dozen truthful women who will vouch for the truth of what happened. When Nancy leaned over the bed, as if in obedience to the power of an electric shock, the corpse's eyes flew open, Ann Pease rose up in bed and pointing a trembling finger at her frightened namesake exclaimed: "Go 'way f'om me, Nancy Rogers, don't you daih to tech me. You ain't got de come-uppance of me yit. Don't you daih to lay me out."

Most of this remark, it seems, fell on empty air, for the room was cleared in a twinkling. Women holding high numerous skirts over their heavy shoes fled in a panic, and close in their wake panted Nancy Pease.

There have been conflicting stories about the matter, but there are those who maintain that after having delivered her ultimatum, old Mis' Pease immediately resumed the natural condition of a dead person. In fact there was no one there to see, and the old lady did not really die until night, and when they found her, there was a smile of triumph on her face.

Nancy did not help to lay her out.

The Lynching of Jube Benson

GORDON FAIRFAX'S LIBRARY held but three men, but the air was dense with clouds of smoke. The talk had drifted from one topic to another much as the smoke wreaths had puffed, floated, and thinned away. Then Handon Gay, who was an ambitious young reporter, spoke of a lynching story in a recent magazine, and the matter of punishment without trial put new life into the conversation.

"I should like to see a real lynching," said Gay rather callously.

"Well, I should hardly express it that way," said Fairfax, "but if a real, live lynching were to come my way, I should not avoid it."

"I should," spoke the other from the depths of his chair, where he had been puffing in moody silence. Judged by his hair, which was freely sprinkled with gray, the speaker might have been a man of forty-five or fifty, but his face, though lined and serious, was youthful, the face of a man hardly past thirty.

"What, you, Dr. Melville? Why, I thought that you physicians wouldn't weaken at anything."

"I have seen one such affair," said the doctor gravely, "in fact, I took a prominent part in it."

"Tell us about it," said the reporter, feeling for his pencil and note-book, which he was, nevertheless, careful to hide from the speaker.

The men drew their chairs eagerly up to the doctor's, but for a minute he did not seem to see them, but sat gazing abstractedly into the fire, then he took a long draw upon his cigar and began:

"I can see it all very vividly now. It was in the summer time and about seven years ago. I was practising at the time down in the little town of Bradford. It was a small and primitive place, just the location for an impecunious medical man, recently out of college.

"In lieu of a regular office, I attended to business in the first of two rooms which I rented from Hiram Daly, one of the more prosperous of the townsmen. Here I boarded and here also came my patients—white and black—whites from every section, and blacks from 'nigger town,' as the west portion of the place was called.

"The people about me were most of them coarse and rough, but they were simple and generous, and as time passed on I had about abandoned my intention of seeking distinction in wider fields and determined to settle into the place of a modest country doctor. This was rather a strange conclusion for a young man to arrive at, and I will not deny that the presence in the house of my host's beautiful young daughter, Annie, had something to do with my decision. She was a beautiful young girl of seventeen or eighteen, and very far superior to her surroundings. She had a native grace and a pleasing way about her that made everybody that came under her spell her abject slave. White and black who knew her loved her, and none,

I thought, more deeply and respectfully than Jube Benson, the black man of all work about the place.

"He was a fellow whom everybody trusted; an apparently steady-going, grinning sort, as we used to call him. Well, he was completely under Miss Annie's thumb, and would fetch and carry for her like a faithful dog. As soon as he saw that I began to care for Annie, and anybody could see that, he transferred some of his allegiance to me and became my faithful servitor also. Never did a man have a more devoted adherent in his wooing than did I, and many a one of Annie's tasks which he volunteered to do gave her an extra hour with me. You can imagine that I liked the boy and you need not wonder any more that as both wooing and my practice waxed apace, I was content to give up my great ambitions and stay just where I was.

"It wasn't a very pleasant thing, then, to have an epidemic of typhoid break out in the town that kept me going so that I hardly had time for the courting that a fellow wants to carry on with his sweetheart while he is still young enough to call her his girl. I fumed, but duty was duty, and I kept to my work night and day. It was now that Jube proved how invaluable he was as a coadjutor. He not only took messages to Annie, but brought sometimes little ones from her to me, and he would tell me little secret things that he had overheard her say that made me throb with joy and swear at him for repeating his mistress' conversation. But best of all, Jube was a perfect Cerberus, and no one on earth could have been more effective in keeping away or deluding the other young fellows who visited the Dalys. He would tell me of it afterwards, chuckling softly to himself. 'An', Doctah, I say to Mistah Hemp Stevens, "'Scuse us, Mistah Stevens, but Miss Annie, she des gone out," an' den he go outer de gate lookin' moughty lonesome. When Sam Elkins come, I say, "Sh, Mistah Elkins, Miss Annie, she done tuk down," an' he say, "What, Jube, you don' reckon hit de—" Den he stop an' look skeert, an' I say, "I feared hit is, Mistah Elkins," an' sheks my haid ez solemn. He goes outer de gate lookin' lak his bes' frien' done daid, an' all de time Miss Annie behine de cu'tain ovah de po'ch des' a laffin' fit to kill.'

"Jube was a most admirable liar, but what could I do? He knew that I was a young fool of a hypocrite, and when I would rebuke him for these deceptions, he would give way and roll on the floor in an excess of delighted laughter until from very contagion I had to join him—and, well, there was no need of my preaching when there had been no beginning to his repentance and when there must ensue a continuance of his wrong-doing.

"This thing went on for over three months, and then, pouf! I was down like a shot. My patients were nearly all up, but the reaction from overwork made me an easy victim of the lurking germs. Then Jube loomed up as a nurse. He put everyone else aside, and with the doctor, a friend of mine from a neighbouring town, took entire charge of me. Even Annie herself was put aside, and I was cared for as tenderly as a baby. Tom, that was my physician and friend, told me all about it afterward with tears in his eyes. Only he was a big, blunt man and his expressions did not convey all that he meant. He told me how my nigger had nursed me as if I were a sick kitten and he my mother. Of how fiercely he guarded his right to be the sole one to 'do' for me, as he called it, and how, when the crisis came, he hovered, weeping, but hopeful, at my bedside, until it was safely passed, when they drove him, weak and exhausted, from the room. As for me, I knew little about it at the time, and cared less. I was too busy in my fight with death. To my chimerical vision there was only a black but gentle demon that came and went, alternating with a white fairy, who would insist on coming in on her head, growing larger and larger and then dissolving. But the pathos and devotion in the story lost nothing in my blunt friend's telling.

"It was during the period of a long convalescence, however, that I came to know my humble ally as he really was, devoted to the point of abjectness. There were times when for very shame at his goodness to me, I would beg him to go away, to do something else. He would go, but before I had time to realise that I was not being ministered to, he would be back at my side, grinning and pottering just the same. He manufactured duties for the joy of performing them. He pretended to see desires in me that I never had, because he liked to pander to them, and when I became entirely exasperated, and ripped out a good round oath, he chuckled with the remark, 'Dah, now, you sholy is gittin' well. Nevah did hyeah a man anywhaih nigh Jo'dan's sho' cuss lak dat.'

"Why, I grew to love him, love him, oh, yes, I loved him as well—oh, what am I saying? All human love and gratitude are damned poor things; excuse me, gentlemen, this isn't a pleasant story. The truth is usually a nasty thing to stand.

"It was not six months after that that my friendship to Jube, which he had been at such great pains to win, was put to too severe a test.

"It was in the summer time again, and as business was slack, I had ridden over to see my friend, Dr. Tom. I had spent a good part of the day there, and it was past four o'clock when I rode leisurely into Bradford. I was in a particularly joyous mood and no premonition of the impending catastrophe oppressed me. No sense of sorrow, present or to come, forced itself upon me, even when I saw men hurrying through the almost deserted streets. When I got within sight of my home and saw a crowd surrounding it, I was only interested sufficiently to spur my horse into a jog trot, which brought me up to the throng, when something in the sullen, settled horror in the men's faces gave me a sudden, sick thrill. They whispered a word to me, and without a thought, save for Annie, the girl who had been so surely growing into my heart, I leaped from the saddle and tore my way through the people to the house.

"It was Annie, poor girl, bruised and bleeding, her face and dress torn from struggling. They were gathered round her with white faces, and, oh, with what terrible patience they were trying to gain from her fluttering lips the name of her murderer. They made way for me and I knelt at her side. She was beyond my skill, and my will merged with theirs. One thought was in our minds.

"'Who?' I asked.

"Her eyes half opened, 'That black—' She fell back into my arms dead.

"We turned and looked at each other. The mother had broken down and was weeping, but the face of the father was like iron.

"'It is enough,' he said; 'Jube has disappeared.' He went to the door and said to the expectant crowd, 'She is dead.'

"I heard the angry roar without swelling up like the noise of a flood, and then I heard the sudden movement of many feet as the men separated into searching parties, and laying the dead girl back upon her couch, I took my rifle and went out to join them.

"As if by intuition the knowledge had passed among the men that Jube Benson had disappeared, and he, by common consent, was to be the object of our search. Fully a dozen of the citizens had seen him hastening toward the woods and noted his skulking air, but as he had grinned in his old good-natured way they had, at the time, thought nothing of it. Now, however, the diabolical reason of his slyness was apparent. He had been shrewd enough to disarm suspicion, and by now was far away. Even Mrs. Daly, who was visiting with a neighbour, had seen him stepping out by a back way, and had said with a laugh, 'I reckon that black rascal's a-running off somewhere.' Oh, if she had only known.

"'To the woods! To the woods!' that was the cry, and away we went, each with the determination not to shoot, but to bring the culprit alive into town, and then to deal with him as his crime deserved.

"I cannot describe the feelings I experienced as I went out that night to beat the woods for this human tiger. My heart smouldered within me like a coal, and I went forward under the impulse of a will that was half my own, half some more malignant power's. My throat throbbed drily, but water nor whiskey would not have quenched my thirst. The thought has come to me since that now I could interpret the panther's desire for blood and sympathise with it, but then I thought nothing. I simply went forward, and watched, watched with burning eyes for a familiar form that I had looked for as often before with such different emotions.

"Luck or ill-luck, which you will, was with our party, and just as dawn was graying the sky, we came upon our quarry crouched in the corner of a fence. It was only half light, and we might have passed, but my eyes had caught sight of him, and I raised the cry. We levelled our guns and he rose and came toward us.

"'I t'ought you wa'n't gwine see me,' he said sullenly, 'I didn't mean no harm.'

"'Harm!'

"Some of the men took the word up with oaths, others were ominously silent.

"We gathered around him like hungry beasts, and I began to see terror dawning in his eyes. He turned to me, 'I's moughty glad you's hyeah, doc,' he said, 'you ain't gwine let 'em whup me.'

"'Whip you, you hound,' I said, 'I'm going to see you hanged,' and in the excess of my passion I struck him full on the mouth. He made a motion as if to resent the blow against even such great odds, but controlled himself.

"'W'y, doctah,' he exclaimed in the saddest voice I have ever heard, 'w'y, doctah! I ain't stole nuffin' o' yo'n, an' I was comin' back. I only run off to see my gal, Lucy, ovah to de Centah.'

"'You lie!' I said, and my hands were busy helping the others bind him upon a horse. Why did I do it? I don't know. A false education, I reckon, one false from the beginning. I saw his black face glooming there in the half light, and I could only think of him as a monster. It's tradition. At first I was told that the black man would catch me, and when I got over that, they taught me that the devil was black, and when I had recovered from the sickness of that belief, here were Jube and his fellows with faces of menacing blackness. There was only one conclusion: This black man stood for all the powers of evil, the result of whose machinations had been gathering in my mind from childhood up. But this has nothing to do with what happened.

"After firing a few shots to announce our capture, we rode back into town with Jube. The ingathering parties from all directions met us as we made our way up to the house. All was very quiet and orderly. There was no doubt that it was as the papers would have said, a gathering of the best citizens. It was a gathering of stern, determined men, bent on a terrible vengeance.

"We took Jube into the house, into the room where the corpse lay. At sight of it, he gave a scream like an animal's and his face went the colour of storm-blown water. This was enough to condemn him. We divined, rather than heard, his cry of 'Miss Ann, Miss Ann, oh, my God, doc, you don't t'ink I done it?'

"Hungry hands were ready. We hurried him out into the yard. A rope was ready. A tree was at hand. Well, that part was the least of it, save that Hiram Daly stepped aside to let me be the first to pull upon the rope. It was lax at first. Then it tightened, and I felt the quivering soft weight resist my muscles. Other hands joined, and Jube swung off his feet.

"No one was masked. We knew each other. Not even the culprit's face was covered, and the last I remember of him as he went into the air was a look of sad reproach that will remain with me until I meet him face to face again.

"We were tying the end of the rope to a tree, where the dead man might hang as a warning to his fellows, when a terrible cry chilled us to the marrow.

"'Cut 'im down, cut 'im down, he ain't guilty. We got de one. Cut him down, fu' Gawd's sake. Here's de man, we foun' him hidin' in de barn!'

"Jube's brother, Ben, and another Negro, came rushing toward us, half dragging, half carrying a miserable-looking wretch between them. Someone cut the rope and Jube dropped lifeless to the ground.

"'Oh, my Gawd, he's daid, he's daid!' wailed the brother, but with blazing eyes he brought his captive into the centre of the group, and we saw in the full light the scratched face of Tom Skinner—the worst white ruffian in the town—but the face we saw was not as we were accustomed to see it, merely smeared with dirt. It was blackened to imitate a Negro's.

"God forgive me; I could not wait to try to resuscitate Jube. I knew he was already past help, so I rushed into the house and to the dead girl's side. In the excitement they had not yet washed or laid her out. Carefully, carefully, I searched underneath her broken finger nails. There was skin there. I took it out, the little curled pieces, and went with it to my office.

"There, determinedly, I examined it under a powerful glass, and read my own doom. It was the skin of a white man, and in it were embedded strands of short, brown hair or beard.

"How I went out to tell the waiting crowd I do not know, for something kept crying in my ears, 'Blood guilty! Blood guilty!'

"The men went away stricken into silence and awe. The new prisoner attempted neither denial nor plea. When they were gone I would have helped Ben carry his brother in, but he waved me away fiercely, 'You he'ped murder my brothah, you dat was *his* frien', go 'way, go 'way! I'll tek him home myse'f.' I could only respect his wish, and he and his comrade took up the dead man and between them bore him up the street on which the sun was now shining full.

"I saw the few men who had not skulked indoors uncover as they passed, and I—I—stood there between the two murdered ones, while all the while something in my ears kept crying, 'Blood guilty! Blood guilty!'"

The doctor's head dropped into his hands and he sat for some time in silence, which was broken by neither of the men, then he rose, saying, "Gentlemen, that was my last lynching."

Schwalliger's Philanthropy

THERE IS NO adequate reason why Schwalliger's name should appear upon the pages of history. He was decidedly not in good society. He was not even respectable as respectability goes. But certain men liked him and certain women loved him. He is dead. That is all that will be said of the most of us after a while. He was but a weak member of the community, but those who loved him did not condemn him, and they shut their eyes to his shortcomings because they were a part of him. Without his follies he would not have been himself.

Schwalliger was only a race-horse "tout." Ah, don't hold up your hands, good friends, for circumstances of birth make most of us what we are, whether poets or pickpockets, and if this thick-set, bow-legged black man became a "tout" it was because he had to. Old horsemen will tell you that Schwalliger—no one knew where he got the name—was rolling and tumbling about the track at Bennings when he was still so short in stature that he got the name of the "tadpole." Naturally, he came to know much of horses, grew up with them, in fact, and having no wealthy father or mother to indulge him in his taste or help him use his knowledge, he did the next best thing and used his special education for himself in the humble capacity of voluntary adviser to aspiring gamesters. He prospered and blossomed out into good clothes of a highly ornate pattern. Naturally, like a man in any other business, he had his ups and downs, and there were times when the good clothes disappeared and he was temporarily forced to return to the occupation of rubbing down horses; but these periods of depression were of short duration, and at the next turn of fortune's wheel he would again be on top.

"No, thuh," he was wont to say, with his inimitable lisp—"no, thuh, you can't keep a good man down. 'Tain't no use a-talkin', you jeth can't. It don't do me no harm to go back to rubbin' now an' then. It jeth nachully keepth me on good termth with de hothes."

And, indeed, it did seem that his prophecies were surer and his knowledge more direct after one of these periods of enforced humility.

There were various things whispered about Schwalliger; that he was no more honest than he should be, that he was not as sound as he might be; but though it might be claimed, and was, that he would prophesy, on occasion, the success of three different horses to three different men, no one ever accused him of being less than fair with the women who came out from the city to enjoy the races and increase their excitement by staking small sums. To these Schwalliger was the soul of courtesy and honour, and if they lost upon his advice, he was not happy until he had made it up to them again.

One, however, who sets himself to work to give a racehorse tout a character may expect to have his labour for his pains. The profession of his subject is against him. He may as well put aside his energy and say, "Well, perhaps he was a bad lot, but—." The present story is not destined to put you more in love with the hero of it, but—

The heat and enthusiasm at Saratoga and the other race-courses was done, and autumn and the glory of Bennings had come. The ingratiating Schwalliger came back with the horses to his old stamping ground and to happiness. The other tracks had not treated him kindly, and but for the kindness of his equine friends, whom he slept with and tended, he might have come back to Washington on the wooden steps. But he was back, and that was happiness for him. Broke?

"Well," said Schwalliger, in answer to trainer's question, "I ain't exactly broke, Misthah Johnthon, but I wath pretty badly bent. I goth awa jutht ath thoon ath I commenth to feel mythelf crackin', but I'm hyeah to git even."

He was only a rubber again, but he began to get even early in the week, and by Saturday he was again as like to a rainbow as any of his class. He did not, however, throw away his rubber's clothes. He was used to the caprices of fortune, and he did not know how soon again he should need them. That he was not dressed in them, and yet saved them, made him capable of performing his one philanthropy.

Had he not been gorgeously dressed he would not have inspired the confidence of the old Negro who came up to him on Tuesday morning, disconsolate and weeping.

"Mistah," he said deferentially through his tears, "is you a spo't?"

Mr. Schwalliger's chest protruded, and his very red lips opened in a smile as he answered: "Well, I do' know'th I'm tho much of a thpo't, but I think I knowth a thing or two."

"You look lak a spo'tin' gent'man, an' ef you is I thought mebbe you'd he'p me out."

"Wha'th the mattah? Up againtht it? You look a little ol' to be doin' the gay an' frithky." But Schwalliger's eyes were kind.

"Well, I'll tell you des' how it is, suh. I come f'om down in Ma'lan', 'case I wanted to see de hosses run. My ol' mastah was moughty fon' of sich spo't, an' I kin' o' likes it myse'f, dough I don't nevah bet, suh. I's a chu'ch membah. But yistiddy aftahnoon dee was two gent'men what I seen playin' wid a leetle ball an' some cups ovah it, an' I went up to look on, an' lo an' behol', suh, it was one o' dese money-mekin' t'ings. W'y, I seen de man des' stan' dere an' mek money by the fis'ful. Well, I 'low I got sorter wo'ked up. De men dee axed me to bet, but I 'low how I was a chu'ch membah an' didn' tek pa't in no sich carryin's on, an' den dee said 'twan't nuffin mo' den des' a chu'ch raffle, an' it was mo' fun den anyt'ing else. I des' say dat I could fin' de little ball, an' dee said I couldn't, an' if I fin' it dee gin me twenty dollahs, an' if I didn' I des' gin 'em ten dollahs. I shuk my haid. I wa'n't gwine be tempted, an' I try to pull myse'f erway. Ef I'd 'a' gone den 'twould 'a' been all right, but I stayed an' I stayed, an' I looked, an' I looked, an' it did seem lak it was so easy. At las', mistah, I tried it, an' I didn' fin' dat ball, an' dee got my ten dollahs, an' dat was all I had."

"Uh, huh," said Schwalliger grimly, "thell game, an' dey did you." The old man shuffled uneasily, but continued:

"Yes, suh, dee done me, an' de worst of it is, I's 'fraid to go home, even ef I could get dere, 'case dee boun' to axe me how I los' dat money, an' dee ain't no way fu' me to hide it, an' ef dee fin' out I been gamblin' I'll git chu'ched fu' it, an' I been a puffessor so long—" The old man's voice broke, and Schwalliger smiled the crooked smile of a man whose heart is touched.

"Whereth thith push wo'kin'?" he said briefly.

"Right ovah thaih," said the old Negro, indicating a part of the grounds not far distant.

"All right, you go on ovah thaih an' wait fu' me; an' if you thee me, remembah, you don't thee me. I don't know you, you don't know me, but I'll try to thee you out all right."

The old man went on his way, a new light in his eyes at the hope Schwalliger had inspired. Schwalliger himself made his way back to the stables; his dirty, horsy, rubber's outfit was there. He smiled intelligently as he looked at it. He was smiling in a different manner when, all dressed in it, he came up nearer to the grand stand. It was a very inane smile. He looked the very image of simplicity and ignorance, like a man who was anxious and ready to be duped. He strolled carelessly up to where the little game with the little ball was going on, and stood there looking foolishly on. The three young men—ostensibly there was only one—were doing a rushing business. They were playing very successfully on that trait of human nature which feels itself glorified and exalted when it has got something for nothing. The rustics, black and white, and some who had not the excuse of rusticity, were falling readily into the trap and losing their hard-earned money. Every now and then a man—one of their confederates, of course, would make a striking winning, and this served as a bait for the rest of the spectators. Schwalliger looked on with growing interest, always smiling an ignorant, simple smile. Finally, as if he could stand it no longer, he ran his hand in his pocket and pulled out a roll of money— money in its most beautiful and tempting form, the long, green notes. Then, as if a sudden spirit of prudence had taken possession of him, he put it back into his pocket, shook his head, and began working his way out of the crowd. But the operator of the shell game had caught sight of the bills, and it was like the scent of blood to the tiger. His eye was on the simple Negro at once, and he called cheerfully:

"Come up, uncle, and try your luck. See how I manipulate this ball. Easy enough to find if you're only lucky." He was so flippantly shrewd that his newness to the business was insolently apparent to Schwalliger, who knew a thing or two himself. Schwalliger smiled again and shook his head.

"Oh, no, thuh," he said, "I don't play dat."

"Why, come and try your luck anyhow; no harm in it."

Schwalliger took out his money and looked at it again and shook his head. He began again his backward movement from the crowd.

"No," he said, "I wouldn' play erroun' hyeah befo' all thethe people, becauthe you wouldn't pay me even ef I won."

"Why, of course we would," said the flippant operator; "everybody looks alike to us here."

Schwalliger kept moving away, ever and anon sending wistful, inane glances back at his tempter.

The bait worked admirably. The man closed up his little folding table, and, winking to his confederates, followed the retreating Negro. They stayed about with the crowd, while he followed on and on until Schwalliger had led him into a short alley between the stables. There he paused and allowed his pursuer to catch up with him.

"Thay, mithtah," he said, "what you keep on follerin' me fu'? I do' want to play wid you; I ain't got but fo'ty dollahs, an' ef I lothe I'll have to walk home."

"Why, my dear fellow, there ain't no way for you to lose. Come, now, let me show you." And he set the table down and began to manipulate the ball dexterously. "Needn't put no money down. Just see if you can locate the ball a few times for fun."

Schwalliger consented, and, greatly to his delight, located the little ball four times out of five. He was grinning now and the eye of the tempter was gleaming. Schwalliger took out his money.

"How much you got?" he said.

"Just eighty-five dollars, and I will lay it all against your forty."

"What you got it in?" asked Schwalliger.

"Four fives, four tens, and five five-dollar gold-pieces." And the man displayed it ostentatiously. The tout's eyes flashed as he saw his opponent put his money back into his waistcoat pocket.

"Well, I bet you," he said, and planked his money down.

The operator took the shells and swept the pea first under one then under the other, and laid the three side by side. Schwalliger laid his hand upon one. He lifted it up and there was nothing there.

"Ha, ha, you've had bad luck," said the operator—"you lose, you lose. Well, I'm sorry for you, old fellow, but we all take chances in this little game, you know." He was folding up his table when all of a sudden a cry arose to heaven from Schwalliger's lips, and he grappled with the very shrewd young man, while shriek on shriek of "Murder! Robber! Police!" came from his lips. The police at Bennings were not slow to answer a call like this, and they came running up, and Schwalliger, who, among other things, was something of an actor, told his story trembling, incoherently, while the operator looked on aghast. Schwalliger demanded protection. He had been robbed. He had bet his eighty-five dollars against the operator's forty, and when he had accidentally picked out the right shell the operator had grabbed his money and attempted to escape. He wanted his money. He had eighty-five dollars, he said. "He had fo' fiveth, fo' tenth, and five five-dollar gold-pieceth, an' he wanted them."

The policeman was thorough. He made his search at once. It was even as Schwalliger had said. The money was on the gambler even as the Negro had said. Well, there was nothing but justice to be done. The officers returned the eighty-five dollars to Schwalliger, and out of an unusual access of clemency bade the operator begone or they would run him in.

When he had gone, Schwalliger turned and winked slowly at the minions of the law, and went quietly into a corner with them, and there was the sound of the shuffling of silken paper. Later on he found the old man and returned him his ten, and went back to don his Jacob's coat.

Who shall say that Schwalliger was not a true philanthropist?

The Interference of Patsy Ann

PATSY ANN MERIWEATHER would have told you that her father, or more properly her "pappy," was a "widover," and she would have added in her sad little voice, with her mournful eyes upon you, that her mother had "bin daid fu' nigh onto fou' yeahs." Then you could have wept for Patsy, for her years were only thirteen now, and since the passing away of her mother she had been the little mother for her four younger brothers and sisters, as well as her father's housekeeper.

But Patsy Ann never complained; she was quite willing to be all that she had been until such time as Isaac and Dora, Cassie and little John should be old enough to care for themselves, and also to lighten some of her domestic burdens. She had never reckoned upon any other manner of release. In fact her youthful mind was not able to contemplate the possibility of any other manner of change. But the good women of Patsy's neighbourhood were not the ones to let her remain in this deplorable state of ignorance. She was to be enlightened as to other changes that might take place in her condition, and of the unspeakable horrors that would transpire with them.

It was upon the occasion that little John had taken it into his infant head to have the German measles just at the time that Isaac was slowly recovering from the chicken-pox. Patsy Ann's powers had been taxed to the utmost, and Mrs. Caroline Gibson had been called in from next door to superintend the brewing of the saffron tea, and for the general care of the fretful sufferer.

To Patsy Ann, then, in ominous tone, spoke this oracle. "Patsy Ann, how yo' pappy doin' sence Matildy died?" "Matildy" was the deceased wife.

"Oh, he gittin' 'long all right. He was mighty broke up at de fus', but he 'low now dat de house go on de same's ef mammy was a-livin'."

"Oom huh," disdainfully; "Oom huh. Yo' mammy bin daid fou' yeahs, ain't she?"

"Yes'm; mighty nigh."

"Oom huh; fou' yeahs is a mighty long time fu' a colo'd man to wait; but we'n he do wait dat long, hit's all de wuss we'n hit do come."

"Pap bin wo'kin right stiddy at de brickya'd," said Patsy, in loyal defence against some vaguely implied accusation, "an' he done put some money in de bank."

"Bad sign, bad sign," and Mrs. Gibson gave her head a fearsome shake.

But just then the shrill voice of little John calling for attention drew her away and left Patsy Ann to herself and her meditations.

What could this mean?

When that lady had finished ministering to the sick child and returned, Patsy Ann asked her, "Mis' Gibson, what you mean by sayin' 'bad sign, bad sign?'"

Again the oracle shook her head sagely. Then she answered, "Chil', you do' know de dev'ment dey is in dis worl'."

"But," retorted the child, "my pappy ain' up to no dev'ment, 'case he got 'uligion an' bin baptized."

"Oom-m," groaned Sistah Gibson, "dat don' mek a bit o' diffunce. Who is any mo' ma'yin' men den de preachahs demse'ves? W'y Brothah 'Lias Scott done tempted matermony six times a'ready, an' 's lookin' roun' fu' de sebent, an' he's a good man, too."

"Ma'yin'," said Patsy breathlessly.

"Yes, honey, ma'yin', an' I's afeared yo' pappy's got notions in his haid, an' w'en a widower git gals in his haid dey ain' no use a-pesterin' wid 'em, 'case dey boun' to have dey way."

"Ma'yin'," said Patsy to herself reflectively. "Ma'yin'." She knew what it meant, but she had never dreamed of the possibility of such a thing in connection with her father. "Ma'yin'," and yet the idea of it did not seem so very unalluring.

She spoke her thoughts aloud.

"But ef pap 'u'd ma'y, Mis' Gibson, den I'd git a chanct to go to school. He allus sayin' he mighty sorry 'bout me not goin'."

"Dah now, dah now," cried the woman, casting a pitying glance at the child, "dat's de las' t'ing. He des a feelin' roun' now. You po', ign'ant, mothahless chil'. You ain' nevah had no step-mothah, an' you don' know what hit means."

"But she'd tek keer o' the chillen," persisted Patsy.

"Sich tekin' keer of 'em ez hit 'u'd be. She'd keer fu' 'em to dey graves. Nobody cain't tell me nuffin 'bout step-mothahs, case I knows 'em. Dey ain' no ooman goin' to tek keer o' nobody else's chile lak she'd tek keer o' huh own," and Patsy felt a choking come into her throat and a tight sensation about her heart while she listened as Mrs. Gibson regaled her with all the choice horrors that are laid at the door of step-mothers.

From that hour on, one settled conviction took shape and possessed Patsy Ann's mind; never, if she could help it, would she run the risk of having a step-mother. Come what may, let her be compelled to do what she might, let the hope of school fade from her sight forever and a day—but no step-mother should ever cast her baneful shadow over Patsy Ann's home.

Experience of life had made her wise for her years, and so for the time she said nothing to her father; but she began to watch him with wary eyes, his goings out and his comings in, and to attach new importance to trifles that had passed unnoticed before by her childish mind.

For instance, if he greased or blacked his boots before going out of an evening her suspicions were immediately aroused and she saw dim visions of her father returning, on his arm the terrible ogress whom she had come to know by the name of step-mother.

Mrs. Gibson's poison had worked well and rapidly. She had thoroughly inoculated the child's mind with the step-mother virus, but she had not at the same time made the parent widow-proof, a hard thing to do at best. So it came to pass that with a mysterious horror growing within her, Patsy Ann saw her father black his boots more and more often and fare forth o' nights and Sunday afternoons.

Finally her little heart could contain its sorrow no longer, and one night when he was later than usual she could not sleep. So she slipped out of bed, turned up the light, and waited for him, determined to have it out, then and there.

He came at last and was all surprise to meet the solemn, round eyes of his little daughter staring at him from across the table.

"W'y, lady gal," he exclaimed, "what you doin' up at 'his time?"

"I sat up fu' you. I got somep'n' to ax you, pappy." Her voice quivered and he snuggled her up in his arms.

"What's troublin' my little lady gal now? Is de chillen bin bad?"

She laid her head close against his big breast, and the tears would come as she answered, "No, suh; de chillen bin ez good az good could be, but oh, pappy, pappy, is you got gal in yo' haid an' a-goin' to bring me a step-mothah?"

He held her away from him almost harshly and gazed at her as he queried, "W'y, you po' baby, you! Who's bin puttin' dis hyeah foolishness in yo' haid?" Then his laugh rang out as he patted her head and drew her close to him again. "Ef yo' pappy do bring a step-mothah into dis house, Gawd knows he'll bring de right kin'."

"Dey ain't no right kin'," answered Patsy.

"You don' know, baby; you don' know. Go to baid an' don' worry."

He sat up a long time watching the candle sputter, then he pulled off his boots and tip-toed to Patsy's bedside. He leaned over her. "Po' little baby," he said; "what do she know about a step-mothah?" And Patsy saw him and heard him, for she was awake then, and far into the night.

In the eyes of the child her father stood convicted. He had "gal in his haid," and was going to bring her a step-mother; but it would never be; her resolution was taken.

She arose early the next morning and after getting her father off to work as usual, she took the children into hand. First she scrubbed them assiduously, burnishing their brown faces until they shone again. Then she tussled with their refractory locks, and after that she dressed them out in all the bravery of their best clothes.

Meanwhile her tears were falling like rain, though her lips were shut tight. The children off her mind, she turned her attention to her own toilet, which she made with scrupulous care. Then taking a small tin-type of her mother from the bureau drawer, she put it in her bosom, and leading her little brood she went out of the house, locking the door behind her and placing the key, as was her wont, under the door-step.

Outside she stood for a moment or two, undecided, and then with one long, backward glance at her home she turned and went up the street. At the first corner she paused again, spat in her hand and struck the watery globule with her finger. In the direction the most of the spittle flew, she turned. Patsy Ann was fleeing from home and a step-mother, and Fate had decided her direction for her, even as Mrs. Gibson's counsels had directed her course.

The child had no idea where she was going. She knew no one to whom she might turn in her distress. Not even with Mrs. Gibson would she be safe from the horror which impended. She had but one impulse in her mind and that was to get beyond the reach of the terrible woman, or was it a monster? who was surely coming after her. On and on she walked through the town with her little band trudging bravely along beside her. People turned to look at the funny group and smiled good-naturedly as they passed, and one man, a little more amused than the rest, shouted after them, "Where you goin', sis, with that orphan's home?"

But Patsy Ann's dignity was impregnable. She walked on with her head in the air, the desire for safety tugging at her heart.

The hours passed and the gentle coolness of morning turned into the fierce heat of noon, and still with frequent rests they trudged on, Patsy ever and anon using her divining hand, unconscious that she was doubling and redoubling on her tracks. When the whistles blew for twelve she got her little brood into the shade of a poplar tree and set them down to the lunch which, thoughtful little mother that she was, she had brought with her. After that they all stretched themselves out on the grass that bordered the sidewalk, for all the children were tired out, and baby John was both sleepy and cross. Even Patsy Ann drowsed and finally dropped into the deep slumber of childhood. They looked too peaceful and serene for passers-by to bother them, and so they slept and slept.

It was past three o'clock when the little guardian awakened with a start, and shook her charges into activity. John wept a little at first, but after a while took up his journey bravely with the rest.

She had just turned into a side street, discouraged and bewildered, when the round face of a coloured woman standing in the doorway of a whitewashed cottage caught her eye and attention. Once more she paused and consulted her watery oracle, then turned to encounter the gaze of the round-faced woman. The oracle had spoken and she turned into the yard.

"Whaih you goin', honey? You sut'ny look lak you plumb tukahed out. Come in an' tell me all 'bout yo'se'f, you po' little t'ing. Dese yo' little brothas an' sistahs?"

"Yes'm," said Patsy Ann.

"W'y, chil', whaih you goin'?"

"I don' know," was the truthful answer.

"You don' know? Whaih you live?"

"Oh, I live down on Douglass Street," said Patsy Ann, "an' I's runnin' away f'om home an' my step-mothah."

The woman looked keenly at her.

"What yo' name?" she said.

"My name's Patsy Ann Meriweather."

"An' is yo' got a step-mothah?"

"No," said Patsy Ann, "I ain' got none now, but I's sut'ny 'spectin' one."

"What you know 'bout step-mothahs, honey?"

"Mis' Gibson tol' me. Dey sho'ly is awful, missus, awful."

"Mis' Gibson ain' tol' you right, honey. You come in hyeah and set down. You ain' nothin' mo' dan a baby yo'se'f, an' you ain' got no right to be trapsein' roun' dis away."

Have you ever eaten muffins? Have you eaten bacon with onions? Have you drunk tea? Have you seen your little brother John taken up on a full bosom and rocked to sleep in the most motherly way, with the sweetness and tenderness that only a mother can give? Well, that was Patsy Ann's case to-night.

And then she laid them along like ten-pins crosswise of her bed and sat for a long time thinking.

To Maria Adams about six o'clock that night came a troubled and disheartened man. It was no less a person than Patsy Ann's father.

"Maria! Maria! What shall I do? Somebody don' stole all my chillen."

Maria, strange to say, was a woman of few words.

"Don' you bothah 'bout de chillen," she said, and she took him by the hand and led him to where the five lay sleeping calmly across the bed.

"Dey was runnin' f'om home an' dey step-mothah," said she.

"Dey run hyeah f'om a step-mothah an' foun' a mothah." It was a tribute and a proposal all in one.

When Patsy Ann awakened, the matter was explained to her, and with penitent tears she confessed her sins.

"But," she said to Maria Adams, "ef you's de kin' of fo'ks dat dey mek step-mothahs out o' I ain' gwine to bothah my haid no mo'."

The Home-Coming of 'Rastus Smith

THERE WAS A great commotion in that part of town which was known as "Little Africa," and the cause of it was not far to seek. Contrary to the usual thing, this cause was not an excursion down the river, nor a revival, baptising, nor an Emancipation Day celebration. None of these was it that had aroused the denizens of "Little Africa," and kept them talking across the street from window to window, from door to door, through alley gates, over backyard fences, where they stood loud-mouthed and arms akimboed among laden clothes lines. No, the cause of it all was that Erastus Smith, Aunt Mandy Smith's boy, who had gone away from home several years before, and who, rumour said, had become a great man, was coming back, and "Little Africa," from Douglass Street to Cat Alley, was prepared to be dazzled. So few of those who had been born within the mile radius which was "Little Africa" went out into the great world and came into contact with the larger humanity that when one did he became a man set apart. And when, besides, he went into a great city and worked for a lawyer whose name was known the country over, the place of his birth had all the more reason to feel proud of her son.

So there was much talk across the dirty little streets, and Aunt Mandy's small house found itself all of a sudden a very popular resort. The old women held Erastus up as an example to their sons. The old men told what they might have done had they had his chance. The young men cursed him, and the young girls giggled and waited.

It was about an hour before the time of the arrival of Erastus, and the neighbours had thinned out one by one with a delicacy rather surprising in them, in order that the old lady might be alone with her boy for the first few minutes. Only one remained to help put the finishing touches to the two little rooms which Mrs. Smith called home, and to the preparations for the great dinner. The old woman wiped her eyes as she said to her companion, "Hit do seem a speshul blessin', Lizy, dat I been spaihed to see dat chile once mo' in de flesh. He sholy was mighty nigh to my hea't, an' w'en he went erway, I thought it 'ud kill me. But I kin see now dat hit uz all fu' de bes'. Think o' 'Rastus comin' home, er big man! Who'd evah 'specked dat?"

"Law, Mis' Smif, you sholy is got reason to be mighty thankful. Des' look how many young men dere is in dis town what ain't nevah been no 'count to dey pa'ents, ner anybody else."

"Well, it's onexpected, Lizy, an' hit's 'spected. 'Rastus allus wuz a wonnerful chil', an' de way he tuk to work an' study kin' o' promised something f'om de commencement, an' I 'lowed mebbe he tu'n out a preachah."

"Tush! yo' kin thank yo' stahs he didn't tu'n out no preachah. Preachahs ain't no bettah den anybody else dese days. Dey des go roun' tellin' dey lies an' eatin' de whiders an' orphins out o' house an' home."

"Well, mebbe hit's bes' he didn' tu'n out dat way. But f'om de way he used to stan' on de chaih an' 'zort w'en he was a little boy, I thought hit was des what he 'ud tu'n out. O' co'se, being' in a law office is des as pervidin', but somehow hit do seem mo' worl'y."

"Didn't I tell you de preachahs is ez worldly ez anybody else?"

"Yes, yes, dat's right, but den 'Rastus, he had de eddication, fo' he had gone thoo de Third Readah."

Just then the gate creaked, and a little brown-faced girl, with large, mild eyes, pushed open the door and came shyly in.

"Hyeah's some flowahs, Mis' Smif," she said. "I thought mebbe you might like to decorate 'Rastus's room," and she wiped the confusion from her face with her apron.

"La, chil', thankee. Dese is mighty pu'tty posies." These were the laurels which Sally Martin had brought to lay at the feet of her home-coming hero. No one in Cat Alley but that queer, quiet little girl would have thought of decorating any-body's room with flowers, but she had peculiar notions.

In the old days, when they were children, and before Erastus had gone away to become great, they had gone up and down together along the byways of their locality, and had loved as children love. Later, when Erastus began keeping company, it was upon Sally that he bestowed his affections. No one, not even her mother, knew how she had waited for him all these years that he had been gone, few in reality, but so long and so many to her.

And now he was coming home. She scorched something in the ironing that day because tears of joy were blinding her eyes. Her thoughts were busy with the meeting that was to be. She had a brand new dress for the occasion—a lawn, with dark blue dots, and a blue sash—and there was a new hat, wonderful with the flowers of summer, and for both of them she had spent her hard-earned savings, because she wished to be radiant in the eyes of the man who loved her.

Of course, Erastus had not written her; but he must have been busy, and writ-ing was hard work. She knew that herself, and realised it all the more as she penned the loving little scrawls which at first she used to send him. Now they would not have to do any writing any more; they could say what they wanted to each other. He was coming home at last, and she had waited long.

They paint angels with shining faces and halos, but for real radiance one should have looked into the dark eyes of Sally as she sped home after her contribution to her lover's reception.

When the last one of the neighbours had gone Aunt Mandy sat down to rest herself and to await the great event. She had not sat there long before the gate creaked. She arose and hastened to the window. A young man was coming down the path. Was that 'Rastus? Could that be her 'Rastus, that gorgeous creature with the shiny shoes and the nobby suit and the carelessly-swung cane? But he was knocking at her door, and she opened it and took him into her arms.

"Why, howdy, honey, howdy; hit do beat all to see you agin, a great big, grown-up man. You're lookin' des' lak one o' de big folks up in town."

Erastus submitted to her endearments with a somewhat condescending grace, as who should say, "Well, poor old fool, let her go on this time, she doesn't know any better." He smiled superiorly when the old woman wept glad tears, as mothers have a way of doing over returned sons, however great fools these sons may be. She set him down to the dinner which she had prepared for him, and with loving pa-tience drew from his pompous and reluctant lips some of the story of his doings and some little word about the places he had seen.

"Oh, yes," he said, crossing his legs, "as soon as Mr. Carrington saw that I was pretty bright, he took me right up and gave me a good job, and I have been working for him right straight along for seven years now. Of course, it don't do to let white folks know all you're thinking; but I have kept my ears and my eyes right open, and I guess I know just about as much about law as he does himself. When I save up a little more I'm going to put on the finishing touches and hang out my shingle."

"Don't you nevah think no mo' 'bout bein' a preachah, 'Rastus?" his mother asked.

"Haw, haw! Preachah? Well, I guess not; no preaching in mine; there's nothing in it. In law you always have a chance to get into politics and be the president of your ward club or something like that, and from that on it's an easy matter to go on up. You can trust me to know the wires." And so the tenor of his boastful talk ran on, his mother a little bit awed and not altogether satisfied with the new 'Rastus that had returned to her.

He did not stay in long that evening, although his mother told him some of the neighbours were going to drop in. He said he wanted to go about and see something of the town. He paused just long enough to glance at the flowers in his room, and to his mother's remark, "Sally Ma'tin brung dem in," he returned answer, "Who on earth is Sally Martin?"

"Why, 'Rastus," exclaimed his mother, "does yo' 'tend lak yo' don't 'member little Sally Ma'tin yo' used to go wid almos' f'om de time you was babies? W'y, I'm s'prised at you."

"She has slipped my mind," said the young man.

For a long while the neighbours who had come and Aunt Mandy sat up to wait for Erastus, but he did not come in until the last one was gone. In fact, he did not get in until four o'clock in the morning, looking a little weak, but at least in the best of spirits, and he vouchsafed to his waiting mother the remark that "the little old town wasn't so bad, after all."

Aunt Mandy preferred the request that she had had in mind for some time, that he would go to church the next day, and he consented, because his trunk had come.

It was a glorious Sunday morning, and the old lady was very proud in her stiff gingham dress as she saw her son come into the room arrayed in his long coat, shiny hat, and shinier shoes. Well, if it was true that he was changed, he was still her 'Rastus, and a great comfort to her. There was no vanity about the old woman, but she paused before the glass a longer time than usual, settling her bonnet strings, for she must look right, she told herself, to walk to church with that elegant son of hers. When he was all ready, with cane in hand, and she was pausing with the key in the door, he said, "Just walk on, mother, I'll catch you in a minute or two." She went on and left him.

He did not catch her that morning on her way to church, and it was a sore disappointment, but it was somewhat compensated for when she saw him stalking into the chapel in all his glory, and every head in the house turned to behold him.

There was one other woman in "Little Africa" that morning who stopped for a longer time than usual before her looking-glass and who had never found her bonnet strings quite so refractory before. In spite of the vexation of flowers that wouldn't settle and ribbons that wouldn't tie, a very glad face looked back at Sally Martin from her little mirror. She was going to see 'Rastus, 'Rastus of the old days in which they used to walk hand in hand. He had told her when he went away that some day he would come back and marry her. Her heart fluttered hotly under her dotted lawn, and it took another application of the chamois to take the perspiration from her face. People had laughed at her, but that morning she would be vindicated. He would walk home with her before the whole church. Already she saw him bowing before her, hat in hand, and heard the set phrase, "May I have the pleasure of your company home?" and she saw herself sailing away upon his arm.

She was very happy as she sat in church that morning, as happy as Mrs. Smith herself, and as proud when she saw the object of her affections swinging up the aisle to the collection table, and from the ring she knew that it could not be less than a half dollar that he put in.

There was a special note of praise in her voice as she joined in singing the doxology that morning, and her heart kept quivering and fluttering like a frightened bird as the people gathered in groups, chattering and shaking hands, and he drew nearer to her. Now they were almost together; in a moment their eyes would meet. Her breath came quickly; he had looked at her, surely he must have seen her. His mother was just behind him, and he did not speak. Maybe she had changed, maybe he had forgotten her. An unaccustomed boldness took possession of her, and she determined that she would not be overlooked. She pressed forward. She saw his mother take his arm and heard her whisper, "Dere's Sally Ma'tin" this time, and she knew that he looked at her. He bowed as if to a stranger, and was past her the next minute. When she saw him again he was swinging out of the door between two admiring lines of church-goers who separated on the pavement. There was a brazen yellow girl on his arm.

She felt weak and sick as she hid behind the crowd as well as she could, and for that morning she thanked God that she was small.

Aunt Mandy trudged home alone, and when the street was cleared and the sexton was about to lock up, the girl slipped out of the church and down to her own little house. In the friendly shelter of her room she took off her gay attire and laid it away and then sat down at the window and looked dully out. For her, the light of day had gone out.

The Boy and the Bayonet

IT WAS JUNE, and nearing the closing time of school. The air was full of the sound of bustle and preparation for the final exercises, field day, and drills. Drills especially, for nothing so gladdens the heart of the Washington mother, be she black or white, as seeing her boy in the blue cadet's uniform, marching proudly to the huzzas of an admiring crowd. Then she forgets the many nights when he has come in tired out and dusty from his practice drill, and feels only the pride and elation of the result.

Although Tom did all he could outside of study hours, there were many days of hard work for Hannah Davis, when her son went into the High School. But she took it upon herself gladly, since it gave Bud the chance to learn, that she wanted him to have. When, however, he entered the Cadet Corps it seemed to her as if the first steps toward the fulfilment of all her hopes had been made. It was a hard pull to her, getting the uniform, but Bud himself helped manfully, and when his mother saw him rigged out in all his regimentals, she felt that she had not toiled in vain. And in fact it was worth all the trouble and expense just to see the joy and pride of "little sister," who adored Bud.

As the time for the competitive drill drew near there was an air of suppressed excitement about the little house on "D" Street, where the three lived. All day long "little sister," who was never very well and did not go to school, sat and looked out of the window on the uninteresting prospect of a dusty thoroughfare lined on either side with dull red brick houses, all of the same ugly pattern, interspersed with older, uglier, and viler frame shanties. In the evening Hannah hurried home to get supper against the time when Bud should return, hungry and tired from his drilling, and the chore work which followed hard upon it heels.

Things were all cheerful, however, for as they applied themselves to the supper, the boy, with glowing face, would tell just how his company "A" was getting on, and what they were going to do to companies "B" and "C." It was not boasting so much as the expression of a confidence, founded upon the hard work he was doing, and Hannah and the "little sister" shared that with him.

The child often, listening to her brother, would clap her hands or cry, "Oh, Bud, you're just splendid an' I know you'll beat 'em."

"If hard work'll beat 'em, we've got 'em beat," Bud would reply, and Hannah, to add an admonitory check to her own confidence, would break in with, "Now, don't you be too sho', son; dey ain't been no man so good dat dey wasn't somebody bettah." But all the while her face and manner were disputing what her words expressed.

The great day came, and it was a wonderful crowd of people that packed the great baseball grounds to overflowing. It seemed that all of Washington's coloured population was out, when there were really only about one-tenth of them there. It was an enthusiastic, banner-waving, shouting, hallooing crowd. Its component parts were strictly and frankly partisan, and so separated themselves into sections differentiated by the colours of the flags they carried and the ribbons they wore. Side yelled defiance at side, and party bantered party. Here the blue and white of Company "A" flaunted audaciously on the breeze beside the very seats over which the crimson and gray of "B" were flying, and these in their turn nodded defiance over the imaginary barrier between themselves and "C's" black and yellow.

The band was thundering out "Sousa's High School Cadet's March," the school officials, the judges, and reporters, and some with less purpose were bustling about, discussing and conferring. Altogether doing nothing much with beautiful unanimity. All was noise, hurry, gaiety, and turbulence. In the midst of it all, with blue and white rosettes pinned on their breasts, sat two spectators, tense and silent, while the breakers of movement and sound struck and broke around them. It meant too much to Hannah and "little sister" for them to laugh and shout. Bud was with Company "A," and so the whole programme was more like a religious ceremonial to them. The blare of the brass to them might have been the trumpet call to battle in old Judea, and the far-thrown tones of the megaphone the voice of a prophet proclaiming from the hill-top.

Hannah's face glowed with expectation, and "little sister" sat very still and held her mother's hand save when amid a burst of cheers Company "A" swept into the parade ground at a quick step, then she sprang up, crying shrilly, "There's Bud, there's Bud, I see him," and then settled back into her seat overcome with embarrassment. The mother's eyes danced as soon as the sister's had singled out their dear one from the midst of the blue-coated boys, and it was an effort for her to keep from following her little daughter's example even to echoing her words.

Company "A" came swinging down the field toward the judges in a manner that called for more enthusiastic huzzas that carried even the Freshman of other commands "off their feet." They were, indeed, a set of fine-looking young fellows, brisk, straight, and soldierly in bearing. Their captain was proud of them, and his very step showed it. He was like a skilled operator pressing the key of some great mechanism, and at his command they moved like clockwork. Seen from the side it was as if they were all bound together by inflexible iron bars, and as the end man moved all must move with him. The crowd was full of exclamations of praise and admiration, but a tense quiet enveloped them as Company "A" came from columns of four into line for volley firing. This was a real test; it meant not only grace and precision of movement, singleness of attention and steadiness, but quickness tempered by self-control. At the command the volley rang forth like a single shot. This was again the signal for wild cheering and the blue and white streamers kissed the sunlight with swift impulsive kisses. Hannah and Little Sister drew closer together and pressed hands.

The "A" adherents, however, were considerably cooled when the next volley came out, badly scattering, with one shot entirely apart and before the rest. Bud's mother did not entirely understand the sudden quieting of the adherents; they felt vaguely that all was not as it should be, and the chill of fear laid hold upon their hearts. What if Bud's company, (it was always Bud's company to them), what if his company should lose. But, of course, that couldn't be. Bud himself had said that they would win. Suppose, though, they didn't; and with these thoughts they were miserable until the cheering again told them that the company had redeemed itself.

Someone behind Hannah said, "They are doing splendidly, they'll win, they'll win yet in spite of the second volley."

Company "A," in columns of fours, had executed the right oblique in double time, and halted amid cheers; then formed left halt into line without halting. The next movement was one looked forward to with much anxiety on account of its difficulty. The order was marching by fours to fix or unfix bayonets. They were going at a quick step, but the boys' hands were steady—hope was bright in their hearts. They were doing it rapidly and freely, when suddenly from the ranks there was the bright gleam of steel lower down than it should have been. A gasp broke from the breasts of Company "A's" friends. The blue and white drooped disconsolately, while a few heartless ones who wore other colours attempted to hiss. Someone had dropped his bayonet. But with muscles unquivering, without a turned head, the company moved on as if nothing had happened, while one of the judges, an army officer, stepped into the wake of the boys and picked up the fallen steel.

No two eyes had seen half so quickly as Hannah and Little Sister's who the blunderer was. In the whole drill there had been but one figure for them, and that was Bud, Bud, and it was he who had dropped his bayonet. Anxious, nervous with the desire to please them, perhaps with a shade too much of thought of them looking on with their hearts in their eyes, he had fumbled, and lost all that he was striving for. His head went round and round and all seemed black before him.

He executed the movements in a dazed way. The applause, generous and sympathetic, as his company left the parade ground, came to him from afar off, and like a wounded animal he crept away from his comrades, not because their reproaches stung him, for he did not hear them, but because he wanted to think what his mother and "Little Sister" would say, but his misery was as nothing to that of the two who sat up there amid the ranks of the blue and white holding each other's hands with a despairing grip. To Bud all of the rest of the contest was a horrid nightmare; he hardly knew when the three companies were marched back to receive the judges' decision. The applause that greeted Company "B" when the blue ribbons were pinned on the members' coats meant nothing to his ears. He had disgraced himself and his company. What would his mother and his "Little Sister" say?

To Hannah and "Little Sister," as to Bud, all of the remainder of the drill was a misery. The one interest they had had in it failed, and not even the dropping of his gun by one of Company "E" when on the march, halting in line, could raise their spirits. The little girl tried to be brave, but when it was all over she was glad to hurry out before the crowd got started and to hasten away home. Once there and her tears flowed freely; she hid her face in her mother's dress, and sobbed as if her heart would break.

"Don't cry, Baby! don't cry, Lammie, dis ain't da las' time da wah goin' to be a drill. Bud'll have a chance anotha time and den he'll show 'em somethin'; bless you, I spec' he'll be a captain." But this consolation of philosophy was nothing to "Little Sister." It was so terrible to her, this failure of Bud's. She couldn't blame him, she couldn't blame anyone else, and she had not yet learned to lay all such unfathomed catastrophes at the door of fate. What to her was the thought of another day; what did it matter to her whether he was a captain or a private? She didn't even know the meaning of the words, but "Little Sister," from the time she knew Bud was a private, that that was much better than being captain or any of those other things with a long name, so that settled it.

Her mother finally set about getting the supper, while "Little Sister" drooped disconsolately in her own little splint-bottomed chair. She sat there weeping silently until she heard the sound of Bud's step, then she sprang up and ran away to hide. She didn't dare to face him with tears in her eyes. Bud came in without a word and sat down in the dark front room.

"Dat you, Bud?" asked his mother.

"Yassum."

"Bettah come now, supper's puty 'nigh ready."

"I don' want no supper."

"You bettah come on, Bud, I reckon you mighty tired."

He did not reply, but just then a pair of thin arms were put around his neck and a soft cheek was placed close to his own.

"Come on, Buddie," whispered "Little Sister," "Mammy an' me know you didn't mean to do it, an' we don' keer."

Bud threw his arms around his little sister and held her tightly.

"It's only you an' ma I care about," he said, "though I am sorry I spoiled the company's drill; they say "B" would have won anyway on account of our bad firing, but I did want you and ma to be proud."

"We is proud," she whispered, "we's mos' prouder dan if you'd won," and pretty soon she led him by the hand out to supper.

Hannah did all she could to cheer the boy and to encourage him to hope for next year, but he had little to say in reply, and went to bed early.

In the morning, though it neared school time, Bud lingered around and seemed in no disposition to get ready to go.

"Bettah git ready fer school," said Hannah cheerily to him.

"I don't believe I want to go any more," Bud replied.

"Not go any more? Why ain't you shamed to talk that way! O' cose you a goin' to school."

"I'm ashamed to show my face to the boys."

"What you say about de boys? De boys ain't a-goin' to give you no edgication when you need it."

"Oh, I don't want to go, ma; you don't know how I feel."

"I'm kinder sorry I let you go into dat company," said Hannah musingly; "'cause it was de teachin' I wanted you to git, not de prancin' and steppin'; but I did t'ink it would make mo' of a man of you, an' it ain't. Yo' pappy was a po' man, ha'd wo'kin', an' he wasn't high-toned neither, but from the time I first see him to the day of his death I nevah seen him back down because he was afeared of anything," and Hannah turned to her work.

"Little Sister" went up to Bud and slipped her hand in his. "You ain't a-goin' to back down, is you, Buddie?" she said.

"No," said Bud stoutly, as he braced his shoulders, "I'm a-goin'."

But no persuasion could make him wear his uniform.

The boys were a little cold to him, and some were brutal. But most of them recognised the fact that what had happened to Tom Davis* might have happened to any one of them. Besides, since the percentage had been shown, it was found that "B" had outpointed them in many ways, and so their loss was not due to the one grave error. Bud's heart sank when he dropped into his seat in the Assembly Hall to find seated on the platform one of the blue-coated officers who had acted as judge the day before. After the opening exercises were over he was called upon to address the school. He spoke readily and pleasantly, laying especial stress upon the value of discipline; toward the end of his address he said: "I suppose Company 'A' is heaping accusations upon the head of the young man who dropped his bayonet yesterday." Tom could have died. "It was most regrettable," the officer continued, "but to me the most significant thing at the drill was the conduct of that cadet afterward. I saw the whole proceeding; I saw that he did not pause for an instant, that he did not even turn his head, and it appeared to me as one of the finest bits of self-control I had ever seen in any youth; had he forgotten himself for a moment and stopped, however quickly, to secure the weapon, the next line would have been interfered with and your whole movement thrown into confusion." There were a half hundred eyes glancing furtively at Bud, and the light began to dawn in his face. "This boy has shown what discipline means, and I for one want to shake hands with him, if he is here."

When he had concluded the Principal called Bud forward, and the boys, even his detractors, cheered as the officer took his hand.

"Why are you not in uniform, sir?" he asked.

"I was ashamed to wear it after yesterday," was the reply.

"Don't be ashamed to wear your uniform," the officer said to him, and Bud could have fallen on his knees and thanked him.

There were no more jeers from his comrades now, and when he related it all at home that evening there were two more happy hearts in that South Washington cottage.

"I told you we was more prouder dan if you'd won," said "Little Sister."

"An' what did I tell you 'bout backin' out?" asked his mother.

Bud was too happy and too busy to answer; he was brushing his uniform.

*The text originally read "Tom Harris." We have changed his last name to match his mother's.

II

Uncollected Stories

Dialect Stories

(*New York Journal and Advertiser,*
September 26–October 17, 1897)

Buss Jinkins Up Nawth

A HUMAN NATURE SKETCH OF
REAL DARKEY LIFE IN NEW YORK

[IT HAD] BEEN three [years] since Mat [had br]oken away [from] the narrow [town] of Parksville, [a]nd made her [way] Northward. [She] had always [been a]mbitious to [see] the "Nawth" [wher]e she heard [that] her people [were] so much bet[ter off h]ere and were [able] to come and [go as] they liked.

["O-o]mph," she [frequ]ently said to [her] friend, "I tell [you] gal, I's gwine [to g]it away f'om [this] little ol' slow [town] jez ez soon [ez I] kin get a [star]t. Dey ain't [nuffi]n hyeah fu' [sho']ly. De white [folks] is like pisen [and d]e colo'ed folks [ain'] no bettah. [You] cain't go no-[whar] an' you cain't [do n]uffin. I's a-[goin'] away fr'm [here,] I tell you; [I'm] gwine to go [whar] colo'ed peo[ple k]in be free an' [comfort]able, same ez [white] folks. Dis [town] is too slow fu' [me;] I wasn't [born] fu' it."

So when the opportunity did come to go to New York with a white lady who wanted a servant, she had gladly seized it and come. At last her dreams were realized, and she was a dweller in the enchanted Northland. The heart of the black girl was happy. Her mistress was kind, and as time passed Mat found friends among her own people. To be sure, they did not live as magnificently as had been pictured to her, and she found that there were no mansions in the part of Twenty-eighth street, which she visited. But she was pleased, nevertheless. It was all so new and strange to her.

All four of the *New York Journal and Advertiser* stories are taken from microfilm that was poorly photographed; each story has at least one column that was partially cut off in the process. Unfortunately, we have thus far been unable to locate any surviving copies of the *New York Journal and Advertiser;* microfilm seems to be the only remaining source for these stories. Bracketed insertions mark the places where we have attempted to restore the original text.

She made friends with a girl named Lizzie, who introduced her to other colored people. Her circle of acquaintances widened and she began to know young men who wore creased trousers and derby hats, in direct contrast to the jeans and slouches worn by her old admirers. It was very nice, too, to be called "Miss Jinkins" by them, instead of "Mat," as the boys did down home.

The Southern girl looked on and joined her friends with half-frightened admiration as they walked into ice cream parlors and ordered what they wanted "just like white folks."

The first year her letters were full of church socials, ice cream parties and the marvelous sermons she heard from the lips of the great preachers. These epistles were written painfully, for Mat was too proud to have anyone write for her, but she had the graphic touch in her descriptions, and those who read at Parksville commented among themselves that "Mat was sholy flyin' high."

"Ain' nevah even techin' de groun'," said Cepas Johnson, her old admirer; "I reckon she done clean fu'got ol' Ceph fu' good an' all."

"Don't you min' dat, Ceph," Mat's mother had retorted. "Mat ain't a-gwine to fu'git nobody—hit ain't like huh. All I's 'fred of, she's runnin' wif dem white folks, an' dey'll teach dev'ment. She ought to stay 'mong huh own colah. I don' believe in dis mixin' up; tain't nachul, nohow."

Meantime a change began to take place in Mat's letters.

"O-omph," said Cephas, "she do say a mighty lot about dat Mistah Thompson; I reckon he mus' be de bes' man wif huh."

Then began to creep into the letters allusions to "ladies' night at the club," and the balls she had been to.

"It ain't Mistah Thompson I's afred of," replied her mother, "I's mighty 'feared de gal done gone an' backslid. Whut bus'ness she got goin' to balls?"

The change in the girl's letters increased and they grew fewer and fewer. Finally, she ceased to write altogether. Cephas and her mother wrote to her to come home, but she did not come and she did not answer them.

"I reckon she done gon on wif dat Mistah Thompson," said Cephas, but her mother was silent, for mothers feel things without knowing.

For two years Mat had gone on well. As a servant she was irreproachable. She was quick and tidy, and above all, honest. Her mistress trusted her implicitly. But now, of a sudden, there was a change. Every now and then small peculations occurred which could be traced but to one source. At first Mrs. Morton doubted, but the evidence was too strong. She became convinced that Mat—her trusted Mat—was stealing. She talked to the girl, who promised to do better, and she was retained. But, after an interval, the thefts recommenced, and it was money, always money. Little insignificant amounts, which could do the girl no good, were taken. It was a great blow to Mrs. Morton—she had trusted Mat so. It was as if a terrible disease had suddenly manifested itself in a perfectly healthy child.

Once again she tried her, but with a like result. Then she reluctantly discharged her.

From that moment Mat became a wanderer. She would frequent the employ-ment offices day by day, until she had found a place. But she was seldom in any one house more than two weeks at a time. She was bright and apt, but she would steal —and it was money, always money. It seemed that the silver and copper fascinated her, and she could not keep her hands from it. During all this time she never took large amounts, and it was only the annoyance that her habit caused that kept her moving from place to place.

"Martha, why can't you do better?" asked one mistress, who had given her more than one trial. "I wish you would do better, Martha, my girl."

"Don't call me Marfy," the girl had replied, sullenly; "I's tiahed of all dese Nawthe'n aihs; I's Mat—jes' plain Mat."

"Well, won't you try and do better then, Mat."

"Yass'm, I will—I will do bettah; jes' gi' me a chanst."

But this chance ended like all the rest, and she was soon hunting a new place. It was all the more surprising to her mistresses that Mat did not seem to spend a great deal of money upon herself. Could it be that she played policy or had a lover who gambled? Love and craps will account for so much.

But at last Mat found a less yielding mistress, and one day she was in court charged with the theft of a small amount of money. The evidence was all against her—indeed, she did not once deny taking the money. Her past record was brought up, and the judge had already determined to make an example of the girl. But he was listening to the plea of one of the earnest women who work in the commoner districts for the fallen of their sex.

She was saying: "I will do what I can for her, Your Honor, if you will leave her to me. I will place her in one of the mission houses"—when Mat broke in: "I ain't a-gwine to no mission house. Sen' me to jail ef you want to, but I ain't a-gwine to go none o' them places. All I wants"—She broke down and began to sob.

"If you don't go to a home, as this lady suggests, I will fine you and commit you," said the judge, sternly.

"I don't keer—all I wants is to go back to Pa'ksville, an' see mammy and Cephas"—

Suddenly a stir went through the court-room. A negro stood up, and pointing at the weeping girl, said: "Fine dat gal, jedge, fine huh; I pay huh fine."

"Who are you?" thundered His Honor.

"I's Cephas, jedge, an' I's from Pa'ksville."

The girl had started up with a sudden joy.

"Ceph, dat ain't you."

"'Tis," said Cephas, grinning.

The Court was smiling.

"Cephas, kin you take me back to Pa'ksville?"

"Cose I kin; dat's whut I cum fu', an' you jes' save yo'se'f by ment'nin' me; ef you'd a' said Thompson, I'd 'a' been gone. Fine huh, jedge."

"Prisoner discharged."

"Hol' on, jedge," said Mat, going down into her stocking for something. "I's a-gwine to do right. I got dis book wif evah cent I took f'om evahbody sot down in it. I got all dat money yet. It's hid. I was a-savin' it to go back home. I was a-longin' fu' 'em all down thaih, an' wage comes slow. I 'spected to pay it all back when I was home; but I had to go—I jes' had to. Jedge, thaih's the book wif evahbody's name an' the 'mount I owes 'em. I'll git de money ef you let me go."

The judge took the book. His face was very red. "You can pay this money into court," he said. "Call the next case."

Mat and Cephas went out of the court-room together.

"Dey sells ice-cream down in Pa'ksville now, an' hit's gittin' mighty like de Nawth."

"I don't keer," said Mat, "I wants ol' Pa'ksville an' mammy an' you."

Yellowjack's Game of Craps

A CHARACTER SKETCH OF
REAL DARKY LIFE IN NEW YORK

IT IS HARD to tell just where Mr. Durton found John Jackson. But he picked him up somewhere in his rambles about the Tenderloin. Mr. Durton was earnest and enthusiastic and religious; besides, he was a friend of the colored race. So when he saw the condition of the people in the overcrowded districts where they colonized his heart was sore and he saw nothing better to be done for them than start a mission right among them.

This he did, and Sunday after Sunday found him in the narrow room, his dark-skinned retainers about him, leading in the songs and prayers and exhortations.

Then he came across John Jackson, and his heart was full of joy, for it seemed that this young man had been especially sent by Providence to help in the good work.

John was a yellow boy, and he was bright of mind. According to his own account he was from "Fuginia."

"Oh, yes, sah; yes, sah," he told Mr. Durton, "I was quite a membah of Mount Pigsah Chu'ch down in Fuginia, an' I ust to be de superintendent of de Sunday-school. I'm sholy glad to get up hyeah an' fall into de same wuk. It rests on us young men's shouldahs to do all we kin for de elevation of ouah race."

To say that Mr. Durton was delighted is putting it very mildly indeed. A white man's idea of a colored man's intelligence is very apt to rise in proportion to the latter's proximity to the Caucasian type, and, as I have said, John was yellow. Also, he proved himself worthy of his friend's admiration. He was invaluable at the mission. He knew the most spirited songs and could lead them with a gusto that roused the congregation to wild enthusiasm. When his rich, mellow Southern voice swung into the line of "Children, you shall be free," and the full chorus joined him, as one old lady expressed it, "it was mannahs fu' sho!"

Then, he could rattle out a very good accompaniment to the songs on the piano as long as the singers kept within his somewhat limited repertoire. He was resolute, and when the mission gave its little entertainment, as it sometimes did, John, besides being master of ceremonies, could sing a funny song or deliver a stump speech, as occasion demanded. So the mission grew and flourished, and the name of John Jackson became famous in the district.

One Sunday after an especially spirited service, Mr. Durton paused for a talk with his protege.

"Well, John," said he, "you've been of inestimable value to me in this work."

"Pshaw, Mistah Durton, don't say nothin' about that. Why, I've jist been in my element working hyeah."

"Yes, and your influence has been all for good. I believe that your people will accept your leadership sooner than mine; they know that you can have no ulterior motive, and have perfect confidence in you."

The yellow Mr. Jackson was all humility.

"Now, I have decided to spread this work, so I am going on further up town and start another, and leave you here in charge of this one. If you will agree."

"If I'll agree! why you couldn't do nothin' that 'ud please me better. I have had this same plan in my mind for some time. 'Cose de good work ought to be spread."

"I should like to have you devote all your time to the work, but I know a man must live, so you'll continue to devote a part of each Sunday collection to your own support, and I'll make up the rest."

"Oh, now, Mistah Durton, 'cose while de wuk is a-strugglin'"—

"Yes, John, that's all right; I appreciate your feeling, and commend you for it; but, then, you must remember that you are struggling yourself, and that the servant is worthy of his hire."

Mr. Jackson reluctantly allowed himself to be persuaded into taking this added compensation for his services, and so the conference ended.

Under Mr. Jackson's care the mission continued in the most promising state, and it was wonderful what a knack he had for getting good collections.

▨ ▧

THERE WAS A very warm game on that night at "Jig" Moore's, and the colored sports were out there, each expecting to "make a killin'."

It was ten o'clock, and the game was already in pretty lively progress when the door was opened quietly by the guard and a young man entered. He was a yellow young man.

A cry arose as his presence in the room became known.

"Lawd, hyeah come ol' yallah Jack, ready to bus' de game agin," yelled one fellow.

"An' look at de 'mp'dence of de niggah comin' right down hyeah, wif 'Jig' Mo's money on his back."

"Lawd, I'm hoodooed a'ready," yelled another; "gi' me my hat. Yellah Jack ain't go'n' to ca'y my money away in his clothes dis Sunday night."

"'Scuse me, gentlemen; I'm a little late to-night," said the newcomer, "but I knowed you was go'n' to try to do me fu' what I did to you las' Sunday, so I wanted to be heavy wif de green. Dat kep' me singin' a little longer over de collection."

"O-o-mph, niggah runnin' a gospel j'int up tharh, an' makin' a millin' evah week."

"Well, I had to do somep'n after my baby th'owed me down. How's de game?"

"Too wa'm fu' a chile like you," said a fellow shaking the dice.

"Well, I do' know; what's yo' p'int?"

"What's it to you; I'm already faded."

"That do' make no diffe'nce; what's yo' p'int?"

"Six."

"Dollar you can't come," said the yellow boy, casting the jingling coin on the floor; "we'll see how game you are."

"O-o-m-oumph! ol' Yellah Jack done started in bad."

"I got you," said the challenged one, tossing another coin on the floor, and he rattled the dice.

"Come, good dice, an' don' lie," he exclaimed, as the bones clicked together in his hand. Then they fell out on the floor. A shout went up. He had sevened.

"I thought you wasn't no devil," said Yellow Jack, as he took the dice and blew on them. "I feel lucky to-night, niggah. I don't believe I kin lose; huh! got me faded a'ready; you mus' be anxious to win somep'n, huh?" He rolled the dice. He won on seven. Again he rolled them and eleven came up. Again and again he won without losing his throw.

"Stand back, niggahs," he cried, "I tol' you I had my luck right with me. I tol' you I couldn't lose."

"He's a wa'm boy!"

"Jes' look at him!"

"He'll be wahin' silk stocks evah day when he gits thro'."

The exclamations were suddenly cut short by Yellow Jack's first opponent leaning quickly forward and picking up one of the dice.

"Put dem bones down!" cried the yellow boy, menacingly, and he reached inside his coat.

"Horses!" yelled his opponent, handing the crooked dice to another. There was a sudden outburst of anger. But the yellow boy was up to it all. He saw that everything was against him. He took his hand out of his pocket and something gleamed in it. Then he dashed toward the door. One man barred his way—"Jig" Moore. A quick movement of a yellow wrist, a man's cry of pain, the door was flung, and the yellow boy dashed out into the darkness.

Some one yelled "P'leece!" and the lights went out, while the gamblers scurried for the exits.

THE OFFICERS LOOKED for John Jackson next day among the rabbit burrows of the Tenderloin, but they did not find him.

Of course, it [was] all in [the papers, as] the papers get everything. Mr. Durton saw it. Of course, it couldn't be his John Jackson. He didn't believe the papers when they said the criminal ran a mission, but then he would go and see. He went to John's room, but John was out. All that week he went there, but with the same success.

Then he ventu[red] to go in. Th[ere] was little in [the] place. He wa[s still] unconvinced. [Maybe] be the boy was [still] in a hospital [and] had left some[thing.] Why had h[e not] thought of thi[s be]fore? He we[nt to a] drawer and [opened] it. Ah! h[e saw] some pa[per and] picked it up.

[Here the last paragraph is almost completely cut off; all that remains is: "It was . . . policy . . . Under i . . . of "ho . . . other . . . dra . . ."]

How George Johnson "Won Out"

A CHARACTER SKETCH OF
REAL DARKY LIFE IN NEW YORK

OTHER MEN HAD courted Melinda Jones, courted her assiduously, but, without success. They had been men of parts, too; men who had money, men who had bucked the tiger successfully or ridden a horse to a winning finish—but all their wooing had been in vain. Melinda Jones was a hard-hearted, obdurate, cruel flirt.

Against her obstinancy a yellow [jo]ckey had no more [po]wer than a black [coun]t. All were her [vic]tims.

[M]elinda Jones [wa]s the brown-[skin]ned Cleopatra [of] the Tenderloin. [No A]ntony had yet [appea]red.

[The]n Mistah [Georg]e Johnson [arrived on] the scene. [George] Johnson [was born] in Ken[tucky . . .] [Here the rest of the paragraph has been cut off except for a few fragments of words.] . . . admirers who followed her with their eyes.

"I's gwine to make dat black gal mine," hummed Mr. Johnson, and the crowd greeted his presumption with a guffaw.

"Why don't you go in an' win huh, Gawge, you say you're sich a good man, an' they aint been nobody wahm enough fur huh yet?"

"I win huh. I win huh if I sets my head to it."

"Oomph, niggah, what you 'spose Melinda Jones wants wif you less'n she put a red suit on you an' led you around by a string?"

"Keep on yo' stringin', ol' man, but I tell you, Mistah Gawge Johnson win dat gal if he jest put his mind down to it, an' you'll all be goin' aroun' hyeah in mou'nin'. I take my banjo an' play in front o' huh house an' she'll jump out o' the winder to me."

"Oh, I do' know, you needn't think that you're the sun, just because yo' face is shinin'."

Mistah George Johnson took out a red silk pocket handkerchief, and slowly wiped the perspiration from his shiny black face. "Dat's all right," he said. "Dat's all right, jolly to yo' heart's content now, fur you'll be cryin' after while."

"It'll be at yo' fun'al then."

That night there was a long conference between Mr. Johnson and his friend, Billy Black. Billy was a popular boy. Everybody liked him, even Melinda Jones, supposedly because he didn't try to court. Well, the two talked long together, and later on the dulcet strains of a banjo were heard under the charmer's window, and Mr. Johnson was singing a tender strain.

Melinda promptly blew out her light. This did not seem like encouragement, but the serenader went away chuckling to himself: "That's a good start, sho'."

Billy Black's form was on the belle's sofa next evening, and he was saying: "Law, Miss Lindy, you don't mean to tell me that you blowed out yo' light while he was singin'?"

"Of cose I did. I didn't want that niggah singin' under my window. I don't know nothin' 'bout him."

"Don't know nothin' 'bout him! Whew!" whistled Billy, "don't you tell nobody else that—they'd set yo' down as jest plum ign'ant, that's what they would."

"Why, who is he? He aint so many, I guess."

"Aint so many! Well I reckon he's a purty good few, yo' do' know who you'se a-foolin' with."

"I never seen him before."

"No, course you never, that's because he don't hang out around no sich parts o' the town as this very much. He lives up among God's people." The lady began to show an accession of interest in the subject, and her informer went on: "Why that's Mr. Composer Johnson, you'd ought to heard tell of him."

"No, I aint never heard his name. What did he ever compose, I'd like to know?"

"Why, barrels o' songs; makes 'em up right out of his own head, po'try an' all. You jest say to him: 'Gawge, sing us a 'riginal song,' he'll just set there an' think a minute, an' then he'll pick up that ol' banjo of his an' the way he'll sing to you'll be a caution—an' somep'n new, too. He can make any song you want him to. Why, that man's the greatest musical genius in New York, only they're holdin' him back on account of his colah."

"I aint never heard none of his songs."

"You aint? Well, you ought to be around to the club some night when they're givin' a smoker"—

"I oughtn't to be nowhere of the kind, Mistah Billy Black."

"Well, I mean there is where you'd get a chanst to hear 'em."

"I guess I can get 'em in sheet music, can't I?"

Billy was stumped for a moment, but he rose to the occasion: "Naw," he said, "you can't git 'em in sheet music. Don't suppose Gawge is goin' to put out his songs that-away so's anybody could go around singin' 'em."

"If he's goin' to make any money out of them, that's what he'll have to do."

"Well, I guess he will print one, an' I bet it'll make his fortune, too. Look at the money that fellow made that wrote 'After the Ball,' an' some o' Gawge's songs is hotter 'n that. He kin do them coon songs to a nevah quit, an' you know, they're all the rage now."

"You must bring your friend by sometime, Mistah Black. I'm ve'y much int'rested in music."

"Oh, I don't think he'll come now, Miss Lindy, ef you put out the light while he was singin'."

"Mebbe he would if he thought I took him fur somebody else—I do admiah yo' cuff buttons so, Mistah Black."

"Yes'm—mebbe he would come. I'll try him, anyhow."

Billy Black took his departure with a very serious face as if he were carefully weighing the chances for and against the success of the mission which Miss Melinda had given him. But the remark that fell from his lips as soon as he had left the charmer's presence belied the lugubrious expression of his face. "Pshaw," he said, "why ol' Gawge is jest boun' to win in a walk; what a lot o' human nature thaih is in a colo'ed woman."

About an hour afterward, perhaps by accident, Billy and Mr. Johnson happened to meet directly in front of the female's house and under her open window. Of course they could not know that she happened at that very moment to be sitting at her window in the darkness listening to the varied sounds of Thirtieth street. Among the varied sounds she heard this:

"How'd do, Mistah Johnson? I jest been talkin' 'bout you."

"How d' do, Billy? Who you been talkin' wif?"

"The lady in this house"—in a stage whisper.

"I do' know what that lady could have to say about me. She aint treated me right."

"That's all right now, Mistah Johnson. I knows all about that, an' it was a mistake. She took you for somebody else."

"Me fu' somebody else—me, Gawge Johnson? Oomph, that's wuss still. She mus' be very"—

"'Sh'—sh'; don't get riled now. I wish you go with me to call on her some day."

"Not on yo' life; nobody that insults me that way."

"But, I tell you, she didn't mean it for you, an' that's diff'rent."

"Yes, that is diff'rent—well, mebbe some day I'll go wif you."

They moved off down the street. Here was what the fair listener in the window above did not hear: "Well, now, look heah, Gawge, if you expect to win out in this game, you've got to push mattahs."

"If I make a killin' to-night, we'll do it to-morrow, an' I'll stake you fu' true, my boy."

It was evident on the morrow that George Johnson had made a killin'. He came down the street in an entirely new outfit—check suit, patent leathers, new hat and cane—he was gorgeous.

Billy Black was standing conveniently at Miss Melinda's window. "Law!" he exclaimed, "jest look at ol' Gawge Johnson, aint he wahm? I'll bet a dollah he's done sent a song away."

The damsel turned her eyes upon the approaching spectacle and gasped in admiration. She stepped back from the window, "Get him to come in," she gasped.

"Hyeah Gawge," Billy hailed from the window, "you must a-been sendin' away one of yo' songs at last."

"Yes, I sent one away."

"Well, you'se purty wahm."

"Yes, I'm too hot to hold, but this is only the advance anticipation—when that song comes out, they'll have to send a fire company with me when I come down the street to keep me from scorchin' the houses."

"Come on in, Gawge."

"Well, I do' know, I will drop in fu' a minute."

In a few minutes more the gorgeous Mr. Johnson was bowing before Miss Jones, and she was murmuring how happy she was "to fawm his acquaintance." Then Billy found it convenient to leave.

It need not be chronicled what words passed between the two, but there is one word in love's Summertime vocabulary which George Johnson knew and uttered. It was—ice cream.

When Melinda passed the barber shop on the arm of her admirer, the idle crowd in wonder forgot to laugh, and they did not recover until they noticed George's new hat sweeping toward the ground in profound salute, as he passed them.

George took Billy's advice and pushed matters, and in less than ten days' time there was a wedding at the home of Widow Jones, her daughter and Mr. Johnson being the high-contracting parties. The groom's song, for some reason, did not appear, but he makes a "killin'" now and then, and the widow keeps a restaurant, so they get on. Billy Black is always welcome in the Johnson household.

The Hoodooing of Mr. Bill Simms

A DARKY DIALECT STORY

"You don't believe in conju'in' does you? Oomp, huh, you go on foolin' an' I lay you fin' out."

"Oh, pshaw, that's all black despatch an' colo'ed people's sup'stition. That's de reason ouah folks don' git along no bettah, they so owdacious sup'stitious. They won't staht a job o' work on Friday, cause it's a bad day, an' while they're a-waitin', some othah man steps in an' gits de job."

"Yes, yes, that's just de way ol' Sam Davis talk, but you bet yo' life he sing a diff'ent tune aftah ol' Mis' Middleton git a-holt o' him."

"Ol' Mis' Middleton, humph! What kin she do?"

"What kin she do, niggah, what kin she do? You stan' tharh [and] ax me dat? I tell [you] what she kin' do, she kin mek you crawl, dat's what she kin do. Ol' Mis' Middleton long headed, an' it's me that knows it."

"Huh, uh, Bud Lewis, you sho'ly kill me; I reckon you'd tu'n back if a cat was to cross yo' paf."

"No, I wouldn't nuther, less'n it was a black cat, den I'd tu'n back, cose I would."

"They hain't but one kin' o' cat that could tu'n me back when I'd done stahted any wharh, an' that's a wil' cat."

"Ol' Bill Simms is a devil," said an admirer in the crowd that were seated about the tables in the little restaurant.

"I ain't no devil, but I ain't afeared o' none these hyeah foolish things that people talk about. I thinks it's just notions they git into they heads when they's childern, an' caint git 'em out no mo'."

"That's all it is," the same admirer assented.

Simms, emboldened by this encouragement, went on: "An' ez fu' talkin' about ol' Mis' Middleton an' all that. I wouldn't give a snap o' my fingahs fu' that ol' hag an' all her conju's. Why she jest"—

There was a sudden silence on the part of Simms, and he sat staring straight out of the door as if he had been frozen by the appearance of a sudden apparition. All eyes followed those of the man who had been speaking, and the sight that met their gaze startled his hearers as much as it had Bill Simms. For just outside the door stood ol' Mis' Middleton looking into the room, and straight at the man who had defied her power. There was not another word spoken, and in a moment or two the old woman shambled off, muttering to herself.

For awhile the silence continued, while Simms still stared straight before him. Then some one said: "She's done fixed him, he conju'ed."

"Cose, she was a puttin' de evil eye on him. I see huh eyes jes' a battin' an' a-snappin' like snakes' eyes."

"Yus, an' I hyeah huh a-mumblin' to huhse'f one o' them chahms, but ez soon ez I hyeah that I crossed my feet an' my fingahs."

"That niggah jes' ez well go kill hisse'f 'cause he nevah will have no mo' luck."

By this time Simms had partially recovered from his fright, although his face was still ashen. "Oh, git out," he said, "ol' Mis' Middleton wasn't a-doin' nothin' but jest talkin' to huhse'f. She didn't hyeah what I said about huh."

"Didn't hyeah! She do' need to hyeah, she jus' know what anybody a'saying about huh."

Simms laughed derisively, but the ring of sincerity had gone from his braggadocio. He was scared. "Well, if I am conju'd, nobody aint a-goin' to say that ol' Bill Simms didn't die game. I'll see all you fellows to-night, an' if my 'baby' stakes me I'll be with you jest ez hot ez evah; then look out fu' me, an' bring yo' rabbits' foots wif you, fu' I'm goin' to break ol' Mis' Middleton's charm or go broke," and the conju'ed man swaggered out.

"Ol' Bill tryn' ha'd to keep up his en' o' de line, but anybody kin see he's most skeered to death. I wouldn' play wif him, 'cause when a man's got a spell put on him he kin give et to somebody else, an' I do' want none o' ol' Mis' Middleton's evil eye on me."

Bud Lewis had been sitting there in deep thought throughout this colloquy. He spoke now: "I play wif him," he said, "I play wif him. Dat coon's got a wahm baby, an' ef she stakes him up, he'll come back hyeah jus' lousy wif de coin, an' I aint a-going to lose no chanst to pick him."

He went home to his "mamma" bubbling over with his enterprise.

"Look hyeah, Ca'line," he burst forth, "you mus' stake me, an' stake me quick. I got a cinch, a regular walkover. I'm goin' out o'hyeah to-night, an' when I come in evahthing's got lay away befo' Mistah Lewis, 'cause h'll be purty middlin'."

"Wha's de mattah 'd you, Bud?"

"Don' ax me what's de mattah wif me, woman, but stake me, I tell you, don' ax no questions, you spoil my luck."

"You a fool man. I ain' goin' to th'ow away my hahd-earned money don't knowin' whaih it's a-goin' to."

"It aint a-goin' no-whaih. It's comin' right back hyeah, an' bring some mo' along fu' company."

"How you know that so awful well?"

"I tell you. We was settin' in ol' Armstead's rest'rant awhile ago talkin' 'bout conju'rn', an' Bill Simms he up an' says he don' believe in nothin' o' that kin', an' then I tells him 'bout ol' Mis' Middleton an' huh doin's. Well, he jes' laffs, an', mun', it was the beatenes' thing I evah see. Jes' ez he was a-th'owin' the hooks into the ol' lady good an' strong, up she walks to de do' an' stan's tharh a-lookin' at him, fiah jes' a-flashin' outen huh eyes an' huh lips movin' jes' so—she was p'nouncin' a cuss on him. So you see he boun' to lose his luck; but he's p'tendin' to be game. He goin' home an' have that wahm baby o' his'n stake him, then he comin' back to play, an' I'm de man that'll play wif him. Cose now that he's conju'ed they aint no way fu' him to win. I'll take a few dollahs an' go up against that spo't an' what I'll do to him'll be a planty."

"La! Bud, you'se mos' nigh ez long-headed ez ol' Mis' Middleton," said Caroline, going down into her stocking.

"Il' gal, I'm thaih when it comes to schemin' fu' de coin."

"Thaih's ten plunkers; go in an' do him."

"Well, I guess this'll hold him fu' awhile."

"Go on. Bud, you'se a caution, an' I hope when these few lines reach you they'll fin' you well—when you comin' back?"

"Co'din' to how much money he has. Hya, hya. When I does come back, baby, you kin have that new silk dress you been a-wantin' an' that hat wif de feathers."

"Go 'way, man; you make my mouf watah. Go 'long. I'll be out on de avenoo an' back befo' you git hyeah."

A long, low room, full of the fumes of liquor and tobacco—a greasy calico curtain, setting apart the place where a grimy bar is situated. A dilapidated billiard table, and bending over its green cloth two eager men. About them a crowd of men as tense and eager as the two—there are men with white faces and black faces and brown and yellow—but all bear the same look of expectancy and excitement. Frantically the rolling of the dice goes on. A drunken man who has been asleep in the corner awakes, rises and staggers over to join the throng of onlookers. His heavy breathing, the click of the dice as they roll out and hit the wooden sides of the table, mingle with the voices of the men as they propose and accept their bids. The watchman at the door gives a warning whistle, but the game goes on, his warning unheeded. He gives the signal of "safe," but this is alike unnoticed. The battle is on between Bud Lewis and the conjured man. As Lewis had antici[pated,] Simms [was] "lo[usy" . . .] [Here two lines are cut off of the text.] . . . dollar Caroline's "stake" went, but he borrowed from those about him and played on. Surely the conjuration would wo[rk] in his favor at last.

Finally, with [an] oath he staked [his] last cent. He [was] promptly "fad[ed"] and saw it swep[t away] where the othe[rs had] gone. The crowd [gave] a gasp of relie[f, for] it had hel[d it's] breath throu[ghout the] whole contest.

"I was [conjured] was I?" [said Bill] Simms, trium[phantly.] [Here the last two short paragraphs are cut off; all that remains is: "Well, I . . . bettah . . . [con]ju'ed so . . . lookers . . . with d . . . "H . . . lan . . . "W . . . giv . . .]

Ohio Pastorals

(*Lippincott's,* August–December 1901)

The Mortification of the Flesh

FIRST IN A SERIES OF OHIO PASTORALS

NATHAN FOSTER AND his life-long friend and neighbor, Silas Bollender, sat together side by side upon the line fence that separated their respective domains. There were both whittling away industriously, and there had been a long silence between them. Nathan broke it, saying, "'Pears to me like I've had oncommon good luck this year."

Silas paused and carefully scrutinized the stick he was whittling into nothing at all, and then resumed operations on it before he returned: "Well, you have had good luck, there ain't no denyin' that. It 'pears as though you've been ee-specially blest."

"An' I know I ain't done nothin' to deserve it."

"No, of course not. Don't take no credit to yoreself, Nathan. We don't none of us deserve our blessin's, however we may feel about our crosses: we kin be purty shore o' that."

"Now look," Nathan went on; "my pertater vines was like little trees, an' nary a bug on 'em."

"An' you had as good a crop o' corn as I've ever seen raised in this part o' Montgomery County."

"Yes, an' I sold it, too, jest before that big drop in the price."

"After givin' away all the turnips you could, you had to feed 'em to the hogs."

"My fruit trees jest had to be propped up, an' I've got enough perserves in my cellar to last two er three winters, even takin' into consideration the drain o' church socials an' o' cherity."

"Yore chickens air fat an' sassy, not a sign o' pip among 'em."

"Look at them cows in the fur pasture. Did you ever seen anything to beat 'em fur sleekness?"

"Well, look at the pasture itself: it's most enough to make human bein's envy the critters. You didn't have a drop o' rain on you while you was gettin' yore hay in, did you?"

"Not a drop."

"An' I had a whole lot ruined jest as I was about to rick it."

So, alternately, they went on enumerating Nathan's blessings, until it seemed that there was nothing left for him to desire.

"Silas," he said solemnly, "sich luck as I'm a-havin' is achilly skeery; it don't seem right."

Silas had a droll humor of his own, and his eyes twinkled as he said: "No, it don't seem right fur a religious man like you, Nathan. Ef you was a hard an' graspin' sinner it 'u'd be jest what a body'd 'spect. You could understand it then: the Lord 'u'd jest be makin' you top-heavy so's yore fall 'u'd be the greater."

"I do' know but what that's it anyhow. Mebbe I'm a-gittin' puffed up over my goods without exactly knowin' it."

"Mebbe so, mebbe so. Them kind o' feelin's is mighty sneaky comin' on a body. O' course, I ain't seen no signs of it yit in you; but it 'pears to me you'll have to mortify yore flesh yit to keep from bein' purse-proud."

"Mortify the flesh," repeated Nathan seriously.

"O' course, you can't put peas in yore shoes er git any of yore friends to lash you, so you'll have to find some other way o' mortifyin' yore flesh. Well, fur my part, I don't need to look fur none, fur I never had too many blessin's in my life, less'n you'd want to put the children under that head."

Silas shut up his jack-knife with a snap and, laughing, slid down on his side of the fence. In serious silence Nathan Foster watched him go stumping up the path toward his house. "Silas seems to take everything so light in this world," he breathed half aloud. "I wonder how he can do it."

With Nathan, now, it was just the other way. Throughout his eight-and-forty years he had taken every fact of life with ponderous seriousness. Entirely devoid of humor, he was a firm believer in signs, omens, tokens, and judgments. Though the two men had grown up together and been friends from a boyhood spent upon their fathers' adjoining farms, their lives had been two very different stories. Silas, looking on everything cheerily, had married early and was the father of a houseful of children. His wife ruled him with a rod of iron, but he accepted her domination quite as a matter of course and went merrily on his way. He had never been a very successful man, but he had managed to hold the old homestead and feed and clothe his family. This seemed entirely to satisfy him.

On the other hand, to Nathan marriage had always seemed an undertaking fraught with so much danger that he had feared to embark upon it, and although in his younger days his heart had often burned within him when he contemplated some charming damsel, these heart-burnings had gone unknown to anyone but himself until someone else had led the girl to the altar. So he was set down as not a marrying man. He was essentially a cautious man, and through caution and industry his means had grown until from being well-to-do the people of Montgomery County spoke of him as a rich old bachelor. He was a religious man, and with the vision of Dives in his mind his wealth oppressed and frightened him. He gave to his church and gave freely. But he had the instinct for charity without the faculty for it. And he was often held back from good deeds by a modesty which told him that his gifts would be looked upon as "Alms to be seen of men."

As usual, he had taken his friend's bantering words in hard earnest and was turning them over in his mind. When the bell rang, calling him in to supper, he flung the stick which he had been whittling into the middle of the potato patch and stood watching abstractedly where it fell. Then, as if talking to it, he murmured, "Mortification of the flesh," and started moving slowly to the kitchen.

The next morning, when Nathan and Silas met to compare notes, the former began, "I been thinking over what you said last night, Silas, about me mortifying my flesh, and it seems to me like a good idee."

Silas looked at him quizzically from beneath bent brows, but Nathan went on, "I wrassled in prayer last night, and it was shown to me that it wa'n't no more'n right fur me to make some kind o' sacrifice fur the mercies that's been bestowed upon me."

"Well, I do' know, Nathan; burnt offerings air a little out now."

"I don't mean nothin' like that; I mean some sacrifice of myself; some—"

His sentence was broken in upon by a shrill voice that called from Silas Bollender's kitchen door: "Si, you'd better be gittin' about yore work instid o' standin' over there a-gassin' all the mornin'. I'm shore I don't have no time to stand around."

"All right, Mollie," he called back to his wife, and then, turning to Nathan, he said, "Speakin' of mortifyin' the flesh an' makin' a sacrifice of yoreself, why don't you git married?"

Nathan started.

"Then, you see," Silas continued, "you'd be shore to accomplish both. Fur pure mortification of the flesh, I don't know of nothin' more thorough-goin' er effectiver than a wife. Also she is a vexation of the sperrit. Look at me an' Mis' Bollender, fur instance. Do you think I need a hair shirt when I think I'm gittin' overfed? No. Mis' Bollender keeps me with a meek an' subdued sperrit. You raaly ought to marry, Nathan."

"Do you think so?"

"It looks like to me that that 'u'd be about as good a sacrifice as you could make, an' then it's sich a lastin' one."

"I don't believe that you realize what you air a-sayin', Silas. It's a mighty desprit step that you're advisin' me to take."

Again Mrs. Bollender's voice broke in, "Si, air you goin' to git anything done this mornin', er air you goin' to stand there an' hold up that fence fur the rest o' the day?"

"Nathan," said Silas, "kin you stand here an' listen to a voice an' a speech like that an' then ask me ef I realize the despritness of marriage?"

"It's desprit," said Nathan pensively, "but who'd you advise me to marry, Silas, ef I did,—that is, ef I did make up my mind to marry,—an' I don' jest see any other way."

"Oh, I ain't pickin' out wives fur anybody, but it seems to me that you might be doin' a good turn by marryin' the Widder Young. The Lord 'u'd have two special reasons fur blessin' you then; fur you'd be mortifyin' yore flesh an' at the same time a-helpin' the widder an' orphans."

Nathan turned his honest gray eyes upon his friend, but there was a guilty flush upon his sunburned cheek as he said, "That's so." For the world, he couldn't admit to Silas that he had been thinking hard of the Widow Young even before he had thought of mortifying his flesh with a wife. Now that he had an added excuse for keeping her in his mind, he was guiltily conscious of trying to cheat himself,—of passing off a pleasure for a penance. But his wavering determination was strengthened by the reflection that it was about Mrs. Young, not as a widow, but as a wife and a means of grace, that he was concerned, and the memory of what Silas had said about wives in general had put him right with his conscience again.

The widow was a lively, buxom woman who had seen forty busy summers pass. She had been one of the prettiest and most industrious girls of the village, and it had seemed that Nathan, when a young man, had serious intentions toward her. But his extreme caution had got the better of his inclination, and she had been retired to that limbo where he kept all his secret heart-burnings. She had married a ne'er-do-weel, and until the day of his death, leaving her with two children on her hands, she had had need of all her thrift.

Nathan thought of all these things and a lively satisfaction grew up in his mind. He thought of the good his money would do the struggling woman, of the brightness it would bring into her life. "Well, it's good," he murmured; "I'll be killin' two birds with one stone."

Once decided, it did not take him long to put his plans into execution. But he called Silas over to the fence that evening after he had dressed to pay a visit to the widow.

"Well, Silas," he began, "I've determined to take the step you advised."

"Humph, you made up yore mind quick, Nathan."

Nathan blushed, but said, "I do' know as it's any use a-waitin'; ef a thing's to be done, it ought to be done an' got through with."

"I'll have to ask you, now, ef you realize what a desprit step you're a-takin'?"

"I've thought it over prayerfully."

"I don't want nothin' that I said in lightness of mind to influence you. I do' know as I take sich things as serious as I ought."

"Well, I own up you did start the idee in my head, but I've thought it all over sence an' made up my mind fur myself, an' I ain't to be turned now. What I want partic'lar to know now is, whether it wouldn't be best to tell Lizzie—I mean the widder—that I want her as a means of mortification."

"Well, no, Nathan, I do' know as I would do that jest yit; I don't believe it 'u'd be best."

"But ef she don't know, wouldn't it be obtainin' her under false pertenses ef she said yes?"

"Not exactly the way I look at it, fur you've got more motives fur marryin' than one."

"What! Explain yoreself, Silas, explain yoreself."

"I mean you want to do her good as well as subdue yore own sperrit."

"Oh, yes, that's so."

"Now, no woman wants to know at first that she's a vexation to a man's sperrit. It sounds scriptural, but it don't sound nooptial. Now look at me an' Mis' Bollender, I never told her untell we'd been married more'n six months. Fact is, it never occurred to me before. But she didn't believe it then, an' she won't believe it tell this day. She admits that she's my salvation, but not in that way."

Silas chuckled and his friend chewed a straw and thought long. Finally he said: "Well, I'll agree not to tell her right away, but ef she consents, I must tell her a week er so after we're married. It'll ease my conscience. Ef I could tell her now, it 'ud be a heap easier in gittin' 'round to the question. I don't know jest how to do it without."

"Oh, you won't have no trouble in makin' her understand. Matrimony's a subjic' that women air mighty keen on. They can see that a man's poppin' the question ef he only half tries. You'll git through all right."

Somewhat strengthened, Nathan left his friend and sought the widow's house. He found her stitching merrily away under the light of a coal-oil lamp with a red shade. Even in his trepidation he found secret satisfaction in the red glow that filled the room and glorified the widow's brown hair.

"La, Nathan," said the widow when he was seated, "who'd 'a' expected to see you up here? You've got to be sich a home body that no one don't look to see you outside o' yore own field an' garden."

"I jest thought I'd drop in," said Nathan.

"Well, it's precious kind o' you, I'm shore. I was a-feelin' kind o' lonesome. The children go to bed with the chickens."

For an instant there was a picture in his mind of just such another evening as this, with the children all in bed and the widow sitting across from him or even beside him in another room than this. His heart throbbed, but the picture vanished before his realization of the stern necessity of saying something.

"I jest thought I'd drop in," he said. Then his face reddened as he remembered that he had said that before. But the widow was fully equal to the occasion.

"Well, it does remind me of old times to see you jest droppin' in informal-like, this way. My, how time does fly!"

"It is like old times, ain't it?"

Here they found a common subject, and the talk went on more easily, aided by story and reminiscence. When Nathan began to take account of the time, he found with alarm that two hours had passed without his getting any nearer to his object. From then he attempted to talk of one thing while thinking of another and failed signally. The conversation wavered, recovered itself, wavered again, and then it fell flat.

Nathan saw that his time had come. He sighed, cleared his throat, and began: "Widder, I been thinkin' a good deal lately, an' I been talkin' some with a friend o' mine." He felt guiltily conscious of what that friend had counseled him to keep back. "I've been greatly prospered in my day; in fact, 'my cup runneth over.'"

"You have been prospered, Nathan."

"Seems's ef—seems's ef I'd ought to sheer it with somebody, don't it?"

"Well, Nathan, I do' know nobody that's more generous in givin' to the pore than you air."

"I don't mean jest exactly that way: I mean—widder, you're the morti—I mean the salvation of my soul. Could you—would you—er—do you think you'd keer to sheer my blessin's with me—an' add another one to 'em?"

The Widow Young looked at him in astonishment; then, as she perceived his drift, the tears filled her eyes and she asked, "Do you mean it, Nathan?"

"I wouldn't 'a' spent so much labor on a joke, widder."

"No, it don't seem like you would, Nathan. Well, it's sudden, mighty sudden, but I can't say no."

"Fur these an' all other blessin's make us truly thankful, oh Lord, we ask for His name's sake—Amen!" said Nathan devoutly. And he sat another hour with the widow, making plans for the early marriage, on which he insisted.

The marriage took place very soon after the brief wooing was done. But the widow had been settled in Nathan's home over a month before he had even thought of telling her of the real motive of his marriage, and every day from the time it occurred to him it grew harder for him to do.

The charm and comfort of married life had wrapped him about as with a mantle, and he was at peace with the world. From this state his conscience pricked him awake, and on a night when he had been particularly troubled he sought his friend and counselor with a clouded brow. They sat together in their accustomed place on the fence.

"I'm bothered, Silas," said Nathan.

"What's the matter?"

"Why, there's several things. First off, I ain't never told the widder that she was a mortification, an' next, she ain't. I look around at that old house o' mine that ain't been a home sence mother used to scour the hearth an' it makes me feel like singing fur joy. An' I hear them children playin' around me—they're the beatenest children; that youngest one called me daddy yistiddy—well, I see them playin' around an' my eyes air opened, an' I see that the widder's jest another blessin' added to the rest. It looks to me like I had tried to cheat the Almighty."

With a furtive glance in the direction of his house, Silas took out his pipe and filled it, then between whiffs he said: "Well, now, Nathan, I do' know as you've got any cause to feel bothered. You've done yore duty. Ef you've tried to mortify yore flesh an' it refused to mortify, why, that's all you could do, an' I believe the Lord'll take the will fur the deed an' credit you accordin'ly."

"Mebbe so, Silas, mebbe so; but I've got to do more o' my duty, I've got to tell her."

He slipped down from the fence.

"Nathan," called his crony, but Nathan hurried away as if afraid to trust time with his will. "That's jest like him," said Silas, "to go an' spoil it all"; and he walked down his field-path grumbling to himself.

When the new husband reached the house his courage almost failed him, but he rushed in exclaiming, "Widder, I've got to tell you, you're a mortification of the flesh an' a vexation to the sperrit; long may you continuer fur the good of my soul."

Then, his duty being done and his conscience quieted, he kissed her and took one of the children on his knee.

The Independence of Silas Bollender

SECOND IN THE SERIES OF OHIO PASTORALS

THE ANNUAL FAIR was on in the town which was the seat of Montgomery County, and the expectations of those who farmed and of those who toiled otherwise were raised to the highest pitch. It was still early enough in the life of the State of Ohio for such an affair to be the prime attraction of the season. Even the metropolis of the State, which took great airs upon itself and was spoken of in all the provincial districts as "the city," did not deem it beneath her dignity to hold such a fête.

It was the great gathering place of the toilers of the section, who now found leisure for a little rest and sport. Sometimes it came too near on harvest time. And then what struggling there was! What knitting of sweaty brows and doing of double stints! For this fair, this thing of puppet shows, prize vegetables, and cattle, this carnival of cider-drinking, dancing, and horse-racing, was a matter not to be missed for the lack of a hand, or, at most, a few hours' overwork.

The first days of the fair were not so popular, as it was generally supposed that then all the attractions were not in, but yet coming; so, as the new Ohioan, informed with the spirit of his Yankee progenitors, wanted the fullest for his money, he came on the third or the fourth day. Usually it was the fourth, for the shrewd country people knew that some who must visit other places would leave Friday anyway, and they wanted all—all. Knowing this, the authorities of the Fair Association redoubled their efforts on those days, as did the cheap showmen and fakirs. Accordingly, on Wednesday and Thursday the races were more and better; the music finer; the wheel-of-fortune buzzed constantly and merrily; the cheap jacks shouted more engagingly, and wherever one turned, he might see for himself and the price of admission that wonder of the sea, a mermaid,—a mermaid in rainwater in a glass box. But they paid their money, gaped in wonder, and went their ways, convinced that now they knew more than ever of the world's mysteries.

It was with no care for the loud-mouthed fakirs nor the deep-sea wonders that the now happy benedict, Nathan Foster, made up his mind to go. Contrary to custom, which Nathan, however, cared little about, he decided to go on Monday, and for once, without considering the morality of his action, he went over to discuss the matter with Silas Bollender.

"Wouldn't go a Monday, 'f I's you, Nathan," said Silas; "they ain't never much goin' on then. You see, folks air jest gittin' in an' settin' things to rights."

"I do' know, Silas," replied Nathan, rubbing his chin reflectively. "I 'low I'll go a Monday, an' I got jest three reasons fur it. Fust an' foremos', 'f they advertise the fair to begin on a Monday, 'pears like, somehow er other, it ought to begin; then I got a lot o' work on hand, so I want to git the journey over an' done with; an' last, I hear tell down to Lem Baker's store that a whole passel o' people passed through Enon last Saturday with their stock and their patent machines all on the way to the fair. So I 'low I won't be disapp'inted,—leastways, not much."

"Well, there ain't no use talkin' to you. Ef you're sot to go, of course, you're sot."

"Better come along with me; 'pears like there's goin' to be a powerful sight o' interestin' things there."

"Do' know ef I'll get there, Nathan, but ef I do, it won't be 'fore about Thursday—that's the big day."

"I'd be glad of your company," said Nathan a bit forlornly, for he was by nature sociable, and hated the ordeal of travelling alone.

"The widder—Mis' Foster's—a-goin' with you, ain't she?"

"No, she 'lows she'd better stay home an' take keer o' the house."

"You don't say you're a-goin' alone?"

"I jest am."

"Nathan Foster, I 'low I had about ez much to do with you marryin' ez anybody."

"Well, Silas, they ain't no disputin' you had ez much to do with it ez anybody, essept Providence, an' I hain't never forgot to give you yore share o' the praise."

"I don't want no praise, Nathan, not a bit, but all I got to say to you is that you're a mighty lucky man." Just then he heard his wife's voice calling him, as usual, and he went away shaking his head and repeating, "Yes, you're a mighty lucky man."

So on the next day Nathan went to the fair, and through the long hours walked about enjoying the sights. He knew what he had gone to see, and nothing else tempted him, not even the glittering wheel and its promise of sudden fortune. He heard from the distance the thud of the horses' hoofs and the shouts of a scanty first day's crowd, but the races had no charm for him. He was perfectly happy as he walked about among the vegetables, cattle, and farming machines, now and then taking a "snack" from the generous lunch which his thrifty wife had put up for him. Night found him on his way home, weary but joyful, and bubbling over with the news of the great things he had seen. It was too late to see Silas that night, so he bided his time till the morrow, and meanwhile regaled Lizzie with tales of his experiences.

Silas was as anxious to hear of his neighbor's exploits in the city as Nathan was to tell them, so it was not to be wondered at that both men found work to do early the next morning near the fence which separated their land. They were both properly diligent for awhile, and then Silas leaned on the handle of the hoe, with which he had been making feints at the ground, and grinned across, "Well, you went to the fair, did you, Nathan?"

Nathan straightened up and answered gleefully, "Well, I jest did."

"An' what fur time did you have?"

"You ain't no idee, Silas Bollender; it was jest plum bully. Why, there was one hog there that it was wo'th goin' any kind o' distance to see. Actually, man, you never see such a animal in all yore life. He were that fat that it looked like the sun would jest render him, an' turn him out lard then and there."

"He must 'a' been a wonderful beast," assented the listener.

"Silas, it does seem almost onreligious to call that animal a beast, he was so well appearin'. It's a fact. Why, man, he took two premiums, a blue and a red."

"Pshaw!"

"Yes, indeed, an' he looked jest ez proud ez his owner. But let me tell you about the steers an' the cows an'—oh, yes, them great big punkins." And so Nathan rambled on to his friend's delight until Silas was wild to see the sights for himself, and vowed then and there that he would go too, and alone.

"You went alone," he told Nathan, "an' I'm jest goin' to make my Mollie follow Mis' Foster's example. An' say, Nathan," he added slily, "I reckon you didn't see none o' the shows ner the hoss-racin' ner nothin'?"

"Silas Bollender, I don't 'low I have to furgit my Christian duty jest because I go to a fair."

"Oh, no offense, Nathan, no offense; I was jest a-jokin'."

"An' I do say," Nathan went on indomitably, "that ef it's them things you're a-goin' to the fair fur, you'd better take yore wife along er stay at home, fur there's many a snare there fur the wicked an' onwary."

"Don't you mind me, Nathan, I kin take keer o' myself ef I go."

"'Let him that thinketh he stand take heed lest he fall,'" was the solemn reply.

"Ah, Nathan, I ain't allus a-goin' on like you, mortifyin' my flesh."

"Well, well, Silas, go yore way, but ricollect that many a man who won't learn to mortify his flesh, ends up by mortifying his flesh and blood."

But Silas was determined, and went away laughing to announce his intention to Mollie, his wife. But the laugh seemed to die away as he came before his wife's stern visage, where she was bustling about the kitchen.

"I see you an' Nathan Foster a-hobnobbin' ez ushul over the fence. I do wonder what you two men find to be talkin' about so much. You're worse than a pair o' ol' grannies, I do declare."

Silas raised his eyes to the level of his wife's waist-band. He dared not meet her gaze as he replied, "Nathan was a-tellin' me about the fair. He went yistiddy."

"Humph, ef he did, I 'low he had more time than his wife had fur sich foolishness."

"'Tain't foolishness," retorted Silas with some show of boldness, "it's instruction."

"Instruction, fiddlesticks! Silas Bollender, you'd better be out instructin' some o' the work there is to do about this place, instead o' standin' here a-talkin' idleness with me."

"Idleness er no idleness, I'm a-goin' to that fair Thursday!"

"You're a-goin' to that fair? You go to a fair! I kin say fur Nathan Foster that he kin take keer of hisself most anywhere. But you, why, you ain't got the gumption of a three-year-old baby. You go to a fair! Why, like ez not I'd have you back on my hands robbed, an' mebbe murdered. You'd run into everything you see. Now, all I got to say is, you go ef you want to; but I don't take no responsibility of it. I wash my hands of the whole thing."

Silas was wofully abashed, but he managed to say, "I do' want you to take no responsibility. I'm tired o' bein' tied to yore apern-strings, an' I'm goin' to be independent fur once."

Mollie Bollender, quite contrary to her custom, closed her lips in a stony silence. This revolt of her husband's against her ever-undisputed control was too much for words. Silas hurried away to the barn. He felt his triumph, and it was sweet to his soul, but he had his misgivings. As soon as he could do so properly, he saw Nathan, and told him slily, "The ol' lady got on her high hoss when I told her I was goin'."

But some of the joy of conquering was taken out of him as Nathan replied with shaking head, "I don't know what's goin' to come of it all. I don't know what's goin' to come of it."

"Pleg gone it, Nathan," exclaimed Silas, "you talk like I didn't have no sense, an' jest ez ef I was a-goin' out robbin' instead o' to the fair. You do' know what's goin' to come of it? Why, nothin' didn't come o' yore goin'. You put me jest in mind o' Mollie," and then Silas's naturally humorous disposition triumphed, and he laughed in spite of himself. "Blessed ef I don't b'lieve you an' her air some kin to one another."

But Nathan did not laugh, he only said, "You got a mighty fur-seein' wife, Silas; you ought to consider her a blessin'."

"I do, Nathan, I do, but I must say that sometimes the Lord does disguise His blessin's most wonderful."

"Silas, that's open disrespect to yore wife."

"Then Lord furgive me, fur I don't mean it," said the other seriously, "fur she's a good wife to me. But sometimes—sometimes there ain't no doubtin' that she's a little bit over-keer-takin'," and something suspiciously like a twinkle returned to his eye.

Nothing is worse for a man or boy who sets out either on a journey or in life under the prediction that he must turn out badly. Usually he is very likely to fulfil the prophecy out of pure discouragement. Sometimes he does not, but, nevertheless, his position is all the worse for him. Under such a cloud as this it was that on Thursday morning, dressed in his stiffest and most uncomfortable clothes, Silas set off for the fair.

There was a sheepish look upon his face, for he knew that he was a culprit already condemned, and felt no confidence in himself. A bad boy playing truant could not have gone forth more guiltily than he. Even the people whom he met on the road seemed to know that his was a forbidden holiday and to look at him askance.

But when he reached the city where the fair was going on something of the same truant boy in his nature took possession of him, and, giving himself up, he entered heart and soul into the pleasures of the festival. Many tales were told about him after Silas's return home. But the first thing he did, and this upon no less authority than Abram Judkins himself, was to take a ride upon the Flying Dutchman.

"Yes, sir," said Judkins afterwards, "the fust thing I see of Brother Silas, he was a-settin' on one o' them prancin' hosses, with a paper o' gingerbread in one hand, an' with the other a-hol'n' to his steed fur dear life. At fust I thinks to myself, the man's took leave of his senses, an' then I see him git off ez peart ez anybody, until he takes a step er two, an' then here he goes fust this way an' then that. 'Is Brother Silas under the influence?' says I to myself; but purty soon, I'm happy to say, I sees sich is not the case, fur he soon recovered hisself, an' I see it was the motion of that onrighteous machine. 'Anyhow,' says I, 'this man is shorely took peculiar.'"

It was all true. Silas had forgotten himself. It is possible that he did go for instruction, that he wanted to know more of short-horn cattle, draft horses, and the methods of fattening hogs. It is barely possible that he wanted to see the wonderful corn and the enormous pumpkins of which Nathan had told him, but the truant in him had got the better of the investigator, and he had fallen by the wayside.

It may be that all the years of hard work and repression, the restraint, first, of a plodding boyhood, and then of a narrow married life, had slipped off his shoulders as the miles had rolled away between him and his home, and he had found for the first time what freedom meant. Anyway, he enjoyed himself. He ate gingerbread, rode the merry-go-round, and someone even saw him coming out of one of the many minstrel shows with a seraphic smile on his face.

It was at the track-side, whither Silas had strayed, perhaps innocently, but now guiltily remained, that the catastrophe happened. There was a big crowd, a great excitement, when in the crush he felt someone tug at his chain. He put his hand hastily at his side. His watch was gone. He saw a man hastening away and rushed after him, crying "Stop thief!" Somebody tripped him up, and when he got to his feet the thief was gone.

There were tears of shame and grief in his eyes as he looked at the smiling crowd. Then he turned and blundered his way out from among them, bruised in mind and sore from his fall. He would go home, he told himself, and never leave it again. Mollie was right, after all. Bless her! How he'd like to be there in the kitchen with her right then. He'd take her a present back; yes, he would. He put his hand into his pocket for his wallet. It was gone. A sickness came over him, and he staggered as if he had been struck. That wallet had six dollars in it.

Fearfully and tremblingly he took off his hat, in the sweat-band of which his return-ticket had been placed. Thank Heaven! it was safe, and with a gladder heart than a piece of pasteboard had ever before inspired he went to his train.

They were mingled thoughts which passed through poor Silas's mind as he neared home, all his money gone, and his watch, an old timepiece that had come down from his father. He lingered around until it was quite late before he ventured to go into his house. Mollie was sitting up for him.

"Well, Silas?" she said.

"It was a great fair," he said sheepishly.

"Hum—you're late enough. I'm su'prised to see you get home alive. What time is it?"

There it was. The blow had come without any warning, and with no chance for him to work up to it.

With grim horror Mollie heard through the recital of his woes, and then she sat looking at him like an avenging Fate.

"There, what did I say? Yore watch, an' six dollars in money!"

"You're right, Mollie, you're allus right."

"I 'low you'll listen to me next time, an' not go junketin' around for all the world like a idiot."

"I'll allus listen to you after this," he said humbly.

"You'd better, instead o' runnin' around after hoss-racin' an' sich like, an' losin' yore children's substance. Oh, what a woman does have to bear in this world!"

"Don't, Mollie, don't feel bad about it. I—" He broke down and hid his eyes on his arm, like a child.

Something soft came into Mrs. Bollender's own eyes, but she tried to disguise it in her voice as she said, "Go to bed, Silas, I'm shore it's time."

"Yes, Mollie."

"An' don't you dare run over an' tell Nathan Foster about yore capers. It's enough fur me to know."

So it is that only the merry-go-round riding and show-going of Silas are known to his friends thereabouts until to-day. And all that Nathan Foster could say next day was, "Well, Silas, it's a mercy you're back all right; you never did take things serious enough."

Anyway, Mollie Bollender was loyal.

The White Counterpane

THIRD IN THE SERIES OF OHIO PASTORALS

IT WAS THE late afternoon. The sun was low in the west, and the coolness of approaching evening had succeeded the scorching heat of the summer's day. The haymakers in the great Judkins field were wiping their perspiring brows and preparing to go home. The huge wain went lumbering up the field-road and through the big gateway, the horses sniffing food and rest in the evening air.

A woman stood in the middle of the field apart from the rest, and, leaning upon her rake, looked dreamily away to the horizon. A man came by and touched her arm. She started, and then, falling into his step, walked on with him.

"Howdy, John," she said. "You like to skeered me."

"What was you thinkin' about?" he asked.

"Oh, nothin', I was jest a-studyin'; I was too tired even to think."

"It is tiresome work fur a woman. I wisht——"

"It ain't easy," she replied, unheeding his embarrassed halt, "but a body's got to do something."

"Yes, something," he said lamely. "But"—he gathered boldness—"there's other things fur women to do besides workin' out in the hay-field along with the men."

"None o' my folks ain't never gone into house service, an' I guess my mother 'u'd turn over in her grave ef I was to go into anybody else's kitchen."

There was a weary note in Maria Holden's voice. John Stearns detected it, and his voice trembled as he rejoined, "Every woman ought to have a kitchen of her own to be in."

"Of course she ought, but ef she hasn't, or can only be in her own after serving somebody else, what then?"

Her eyes fell on the man's face with the starved expression which comes to the countenance of woman when her hungry soul is feeding on itself. John Stearns answered it with a look as hopeless and a deprecating gesture.

"Ef I had my way," he said, "you should have a kitchen of yore own, and you should never serve anybody but yoreself. But——"

"I know, John, I know," she broke in. "I understand it all; but it don't do any good to talk about these things: it only makes us dissatisfied and rebellious." The woman laid her rake across her shoulder and quickened her pace, as if to outrun her thoughts. John hastened to catch up with her.

"I know it don't do no good to talk about it, an' I don't never say no more than I can help, but there is times when the words jest naturally spill out of my heart, and it's a sort of satisfaction to let them spill. I've been raised peculiar, M'ri'."

"I know that too, John, an' you can't help yore raisin'—mind, I ain't a-blamin' yore folks, now; but I can't lay the blame on you."

"Seems's ef somebody ought to be blamed, don't it?"

"Yes, it does."

"Here we been a-waitin' year in an' year out. You're thirty-five, M'ri'." It sounded like an accusation. "We been goin' along steady an' sober a-mindin' our own business an' hopin'—that is, hopin' fur the best," he added, coloring. "We've seen lots o' people younger than us grow up an' marry, but it don't seem to be intended fur us."

"No, it don't, John, it don't seem to be intended fur us, ever."

"I know what folks say," he went on bitterly. "I know that everybody thinks that ef I was any kind of a man I would go ahead an' take the intentions into my own hands and make 'em what I wanted 'em to be. But I can't! I can't! I tell you I've been raised peculiar, and what's growed into a man's bones from childhood up it's hard to git out o' him. It allus seems to me like ef I'd go ag'in' my mother's wishes, it 'u'd jest be like puttin' her aside when she was helpless. It used to be when I was a child that she could spank me and make me mind; but jest as soon as I git beyond the spankin' age I take the first chance I can git o' showin' off an' shamin' her. Don't you see, M'ri', how it 'u'd look?"

"I do see, an' I wouldn't want you to do any other way than what you're a-doin'. I've been raised peculiar too, John. Most of us in these parts has. And there's somethin' I feel that you don't seem to see at all. It does look to me like I was jest a-kinder standin' around waitin' fur yore mother to die. Now I don't want to be a-hankerin' fur no dead woman's place, so don't you think that we'd both better give up an' stop thinkin' about it?"

"Give up! oh, I couldn't do that! It's the only thing that's held me up fur the last ten years. No, M'ri', let's jest go on hopin' that mother'll come round at last. You don't know my mother: she's got a mighty good heart."

"I ain't sayin' ner thinkin' a thing ag'in' yore mother, John. I'm only talkin' ag'in' things. It ain't yore mother no more than anybody else. It's—it's—things—I can't explain it, but it's the way things turn out."

The hopeless note in her voice grated on his ear, but it did more than that: it sent a shaft of pain to his heart that stung him almost into action. He was filled with a sudden shame at himself, and a pitying love for the hardworked, restrained woman who had waited for him so long.

"M'ri'," he said, "couldn't we,—couldn't we—sort o' fix things?"

"How?"

"Couldn't we slip away an' git married on the quiet like?" He trembled at his own boldness as he spoke. She turned and looked at him half in anger. All the primitive pride in her being flamed up in her eyes.

"I ain't waited so long fur you, John Stearns, to slip away like a thief to marry you at last. No, ef ever we two air j'ined, it'll be open and above-board, in church and before the people that's seen and laughed at my waitin'. An' what's more,"— she drew herself up with a sudden motion,—"it's been you all the time that's held back; now it'll be fur me to say, an' I won't never marry you until you've got yore mother's consent full and free."

"Don't say that, M'ri'. You don't know what it means."

"Yes, I do; but I mean it."

His head drooped abjectly. "I didn't go to hurt yore feelin's," he faltered.

"You ain't hurt my feelin's, John," she said. "I've jest commenced to feel that I got feelin's. I been a-goin' along like an animal a-takin' hurts and only knowin' in a dull sort of a way that they was hurts. But I feel keener now, and mebbe on that account things'll pass me by. They say the Lord tempers the wind to the shorn lamb; mebbe He tempers His blows to a thin skin." She laughed without mirth.

"I'm sorry," he said, "I'm sorry."

"La!" exclaimed one of two women as John and Maria passed them, "ef I don't believe them two's been spattin'. Who ever heard tell o' sich a thing fur them."

"Well, it 'u'd be a good thing ef M'ri' did wake up and give him a right good tongue-lashin'. Mebbe he'd learn some sense—enough, anyhow, to let that mother o' his'n know that he'd come of age."

"Don't say a word, Tillie. I reely pity John more'n I blame him. I know jest how he feels. When they've been mother's boys all their lives, it's mighty hard to cut loose all of a sudden."

"Mebbe it is, but what I think is that it's all right fur them to be mother's boys as long as they are in short pants, but when they grow I want to see them grow into men. It ain't nothin' but conceit nohow that makes them mother's boys. They hear people a-praisin' them an' sayin' how good they air fur doin' jest what they'd ought to do, lookin' after their mothers, an' it spoils 'em. They're allus doin' somethin' fur folks to see, a-tryin' to live up to their reputation even ef it goes to the len'th o' keepin' a faithful woman waitin' year in an' year out an' breakin' her heart at last. Look at M'ri' Holden, how old she looks. Why, I remember when she was the purtiest girl in this town. It ain't hard work so much that makes a woman old, fur she kin work an' toil an' grub fur them she loves an' still come up smilin' an' rosy, but it's waitin' an' hopin' an' starvin' that ages 'em."

"I don't know but what I should kinder hate to see my boy marry an' furgit me. Mothers' hearts air purty tender on them points, you know."

"I'm a mother too, Esther Meriweather, an' I guess I'm about as lovin' a one as most, but I tell my Willie that when he gits notions in his head, I want him to go along an' do the right thing an' not keep no woman pinin' after him. It's because I am a mother that I kin feel fur some other mother's daughter."

"There's a good deal of truth in what you've said, Tillie, but—"

"But what?"

"I'd feel a good deal better in this case ef I hadn't seen ol' Mis' Stearns's blind move jest now. It ain't a-goin' to make her any yieldener to see John an' M'ri' together."

"Mebbe it ain't, but it'll make her useter to it. For my part, I hope she will see 'em—there, that's jest like M'ri' Holden to turn off at the corner instid o' passin' the gate with him. Ef that 'u'd 'a' been me, I'd 'a' walked 'spang' past the house."

But Maria Holden did not need to walk "spang past the house" to be seen by the ever-watchful eyes of Mrs. Stearns. The moving blind had hidden her form and shut out from scrutinizing eyes the look of hurt anxiety that came into her face when she saw the couple part at the corner.

Outside with Maria, John had felt injured and a bit heroic, but once in the presence of his mother, his feelings underwent a total change. A glance at her face —for in the long and close intimacy between mother and son they had learned to read each other well—told him that she had seen him with his companion. The sigh that forced itself between her tight-shut lips indicated with equal plainness that the sight had not been an agreeable one.

"Supper ready, mother?" he asked.

Another sigh came forth to follow its brother. "Oh, yes," she replied very gently, "supper's ready. As soon as you're ready to set down, I'll come an' help yore plate."

"Ain't you goin' to eat nothin' yoreself?"

"No, I don't believe I keer about anything myself. I ain't hungry. I jest want to see you satisfied."

The very tone in which Mrs. Stearns spoke was an accusation against her son. "Behold," it said, "what a mother am I. How gentle. How solicitous of my son's well-being. Did the world ever see such another one? Can anyone imagine a son's supplanting such a mother by a wife? Surely never."

John went through the house to the yard behind, where with much splashing he washed and cooled his flushed face. When he sat down to the table his mother paused only long enough beside her chair to say grace, and then bustled away to serve him. Each knew what was lying uppermost in the other's mind, but neither spoke. It was unpleasant, John thought, this being treated as a culprit without being given the chance of a defence. He wished that his mother would say something, so that he might answer and reason with her. But the longer the silence continued, the more abject he grew. If it went on much longer, he knew that when the inevitable argument should come he would not have a leg to stand on, and would meekly give up, as it had been his wont to do.

Finally, to save himself, he spoke: "It was a awful hot day in the field to-day."

"I 'lowed it must 'a' been."

"I noticed M'ri' Holden give down and have to rest several times."

"Um?"

"I was talkin' to her. It must be pretty hard on her, workin' out in the field sich weather as this. Me and her walked down the road together."

"I noticed."

This reticence disconcerted John, but he struggled bravely on, spurred to effort by the determination to have it over and done with once for all.

"I was a-tellin' her that field work wasn't fit fur no woman to do."

"I ca'cilate she agreed with you."

"Why, yes, o' course, leastways she couldn't very well help it. It was me a-makin' the statement and she couldn't contradict me out and out." Then, as if the point of his affirmation had been assailed and was the only thing that needed defence, he repeated, "And field work ain't no fittin' thing fur a woman to be a-doin'."

"I did it," said his mother firmly.

"Yes, but—but in them days—" He paused, confused and at a loss to go on.

"In them days," she took him up, "women was content to live by what their hands could earn, an' didn't have to try an' gobble up the first man that looked like he could take keer o' them."

The color mounted to the son's brow and made a little line of red where his hat-brim had warded off the tan.

"Ef you mean that fur M'ri' Holden," he said, "she ain't gobbled up ner been willin' to gobble up the first man that'll take care o' her. She'd had plenty of offers when I said my say to her, and I couldn't promise her as much as some o' the others, neither, but she chose to wait fur me even when I was oncertain. Well, she's had a waitin' time of it and she's showed herself a true woman ef ever one has. I wish to the Lord I was as much a man!"

"Be a man, John Stearns, be a man! Far be it from me to lay a straw in yore way. I ain't never told you what to do neither one way ner the other. I've allus tried my level best to make you comfortable an' happy, an' you sha'n't say now that I sp'iled yore pleasure in life."

"I think I owe somethin', mother, to the woman that's been a-spoilin' her life a-waitin' fur me all these years."

"O' course you do, o' course; an' you don't owe nothin' to yore mother that's toiled an' slaved all her life fur you: when a man gits marryin' in his head he furgits all that." Usually John capitulated here and the argument ended, but to-night, contrary to his common usage, he went on: "I ain't a-furgittin' you, mother. I wouldn't do that. No more would M'ri': she'd be more like a help and comfort to you."

"Don't say no more to me, John. I ain't told you not to marry M'ri' Holden, an' I ain't a-goin' to tell you so now."

"We been waitin' so long," he said plaintively. "Jes look," and he threw back the hair that lay over his brow, showing the streaks of gray that sprinkled it. The movement was eloquent with the pathos of his hard, unsatisfied life. "Sich things mean more to a woman than they do to a man," he continued.

"I ain't got nothin' more to say, only I do say that I think ef M'ri' wanted my house an' my things, she might 'a' waited till my head was cold before she went to reachin' fur 'em."

John rose from the table and, taking his hat, went out without a word. His slow, unemotional nature had been aroused, and a storm was raging within him. As his mother had said, she had never told him not to marry Maria Holden, but it was such scenes as this through which he had just passed that had checked and crushed him and dominated his patient will.

His father had died when he was yet very young, and, an only child, ever under the care and command of his mother, he had grown to manhood believing devoutly in her strength and wisdom. Now, it needed something more than an ordinary wrench to make him stand forth in opposition to her wishes. But to-night he felt equal to any manner or degree of revolt. In this mood he wandered down to the little river that wound its peaceful way through the village, and sat down upon the bank to think the matter out.

John had not been gone long, and his mother was still sitting in a brown study across from the uncleared table, when a visitor knocked and entered. She was a little old lady with a face as mild and innocent as a child's.

Mrs. Stearns visibly brightened as she said, "Why, howdy do, Mother Judkins; take a chair."

"Howdy, Jerushy, child," said the visitor, sinking into a rush-bottomed seat. "How air you an' John a'stan'in' the hot weather?"

"Oh, middlin'. John, he was complainin' some this evenin'."

"I see him goin' down the street jes' now, and says I to myself, there goes as stiddy a boy as ever was. He'll make some woman a good husband."

Mrs. Stearns pursed her lips, but Mother Judkins, whose mild, kindly eyes never saw anything, went blindly on: "It does seem to me so funny that every harum-scarum young scamp that you can't put no dependence on ups an' gits married, while the stiddy, solid men go along single."

"Humph!"

"It did jest seem like a special providence that Nathan Foster woke up at last and took Lizzie Young; but, mercy sakes, what a long time he was a-comin' to it!"

The old lady had seated herself for a chat, and she heeded no storm signals. Had her husband, Abe Judkins, been there, he would have stopped her, for he said, "Mother allus needed someone along to keep her from speakin' out in meetin'." So she wandered on, and when she rose to go she was all unconscious that her simple words had helped increase a brewing storm. Mrs. Stearns followed her to the door, and then hastily shut it and hurried back into the room. She was wrought to a high pitch by jealousy and anger. Her love and care for her son had grown into selfishness, but she did not know it. She only saw in herself all of the maternal virtues. Her son, despite the gray hair, was but a boy to her still, and a boy to be watched over, guarded, commanded, and repressed. She continued to hold herself responsible for anything he might do, and she looked with equal horror on any effort of his to be free either from her care or control. The revolt of the night had meant to her the shifting of the very foundation of things. In all their former contests upon this same subject he had never been so strenuous and outspoken in his opposition to her will. She saw in this new departure the strong hold which another love had taken upon him. And, oh, a mother's heart is a jealous one, whether it beats under the homespun of a peasant or the velvet of a grand dame. Mrs. Stearns flamed with sudden anger.

"M'ri' Holden's been a-pisenin' my son's mind ag'in me." The hot tears rushed to her eyes and hid from sight the old blue china that sparkled and gleamed on the presses about her, and the familiar look of the dear old furniture which had been the gathering of her struggling life. She rose up with a sudden resolution and forced back the bold drops. "Ef she does take him," she exclaimed, "not one bit of all I've labored fur shall she have. She kin work fur her own, an' mebbe when she's raised a child and toiled fur comforts to have around him, she'll learn, like I have, what it is to have another woman step in and take all the pleasure an' joy out o' life. No, she sha'n't have a thing o' mine. Pore John! pore child!" and the tears started afresh. "I know he'll suffer not havin' the things he's been used to all his life, an' ef it wasn't fur her, I'd—but I'll do it! I'll do it!"

There was determination in her step as she passed out of the kitchen and up the stairs to the garret. "Little did I think," she said as she delved into the drawers of a time-honored press,—"little did I think when I put my will away up here that I'd be lookin' fur it ag'in to cut off my own son. But ef we make our beds, we must lay in them."

The old press was filled with a motley assortment of yellow papers with seals and stamps of every variety of antiquity,—the house's documentary accumulations for three or four generations. There were old, long-forgotten wills, deeds, conveyances, and letters written by hands that had been dust for half a century, all tossed aimlessly together, a musty, pathetic, yellow heap. Among these the old woman's eyes glanced and her hands fumbled. A bundle of old letters met her gaze and she picked it up. She knew the handwriting even after all those years. Could she forget it, that hard, cramped scrawl, the best effort of a hand more used to the plough than the pen? She drew one from its faded and worn envelope and went to the window to read it by the failing light. As she perused it a glow came into her tanned and wrinkled cheeks, and moisture kept hiding the yellowed page from her. The memories of the past, of her own girlhood and its love, came over her with a rush of tender feeling.

The swain had laboriously spelled out:

"Dere Annie: Father's put the 'dition to the house an' bort the field jinin' ours. Mother's give me her white counterpin fur you, an' I've got fifty dollars saved up an' our waitin' is over. I'm happy, ain't you? Set the day, now, an' make it soon. Yores,

JIM.

"P.S. Uncle Syphax has give me a colt."

Her eyes were swimming. How well she remembered it all, and what joy that letter had brought her! What great items in her existence that counterpane and colt had been. The counterpane had long ago been worn out and its place supplied by a finer one, and Barney the colt had died in a green old age,—and Maria and John were waiting now as she and his father had done then. All the bitterness of the years rolled away from her. The callousness that a life of toil had laid heavily upon her heart was there no more, and she was a young widow again with her baby boy at her breast, mourning for the husband stricken down in the bloom of his youth. With a cry she pressed the letter to her bosom, and so she sat for a space with her mind roaming the green pastures of the past. After awhile, the will forgotten, she rose and went softly downstairs, the letter tightly clasped in her hand.

By the bank of the river John had sat and thought it all out. He was wrong. After all, she was his mother, and if set in her ways and peculiar, it was for him to bear in patient silence. This was his conclusion, but it left him with a sore and hopeless heart as he turned away from the little stream and bent his steps homeward.

There was no light in the kitchen when he got there, but his mother was sitting by the window. The last ember of his wrath died out as he looked at her through the gloom and thought that she was mourning over his words to her.

"We won't say nothin' more about M'ri', mother," he said.

"Never mind, John," she broke in upon him, "you hush; we jest air goin' to say some more about M'ri'." She got up and put her arm about his neck, an unwonted show of affection in this undemonstrative woman. "I were wrong," she went on with trembling voice. "I were wrong, John, but I've—I've repented."

"Don't you say that, mother," he cried in alarm, "there ain't nothin' to repent of. I ain't a-goin'—"

"You're a-goin' to bring me a darter into this house, that's what you're a-goin' to do, an', the good Lord helpin' me, I kin take two children into my heart. Don't say nothin' now; I—I've laid out my white counterpane."

His hand was trembling as he wiped the perspiration from his forehead.

"I didn't mean to hurt yore feelin's, mother," he pleaded.

"You ain't hurt my feelin's: you've opened my eyes; an'—an'—I found a old letter of yore father's, John. I been blind, but—there, there's my white counterpane fur M'ri'!"

The Minority Committee

FOURTH IN THE SERIES OF OHIO PASTORALS

THE COMMITTEE OF the minority that had been "settin'" at Abe Judkins's rose from its deliberations, and the talk became formal and desultory as they filed out of the stiff front room into the yard.

"I calcilate that we've fixed up a report that'll settle 'em some," said old Elisha Harvey as he halted and leaned against a convenient tree. "I reckon they did 'low to walk plumb over the wishes of the older heads, but I calcilate we'll stir 'em up some."

"I do' know, Brother Harvey," piped Mrs. Hemenway, or "Ol' Mis' Hemenway," as she was known throughout the length and breadth of the town,—"I do' know ef that's jest the right sperit to look at the matter in."

"Sperit er no sperit, Mis' Hemenway, I feel like rejoicin' an' cryin' aloud, 'How air the mighty fallen!'"

Abram spoke up slowly: "We ain't none of us shore that there's any cause fur rejoicin' yit. We ain't nothin' but a minority, an' they ain't no certainty that our report with all its repersentations is a-goin' to bring the majority over to our side."

Mrs. Judkins spoke at last: "Well," she said, "you know I ain't never been so sot ag'in' the young people's plans as the rest o' you older heads, fur I think mebbe we're a little old-fashioned, an' the young generation has a right to have what it wants; but you've all done yore best accordin' to yore lights."

"I'd be bound fur you, mother," said Abram affectionately, dropping his arm about the old lady's waist. "Ef all of us had as much cherity in our hearts an' lived up to our lights like you do, I reckon there wouldn't be much need o' minority reports er rejoicin' over our enemies."

And the committee said, "That's so," as it resumed its march towards the gate.

That there should be any necessity for the meeting of a minority committee was all the work of the young people and the advanced thinkers of Apostle's Chapel. For forty years the church had gone on its plodding, old-fashioned way, and there had been harmony within its walls. But now some agitating, restless spirits had decided that more harmony was wanted, and had brought forward the idea of placing an organ in the church. They argued that while Apostle's Chapel was the oldest organization of its kind in the town, that newer churches had outstripped it both in influence and size on account of its obsolete ways. They said too that if something were not done to hold them, the young people would leave the church and go where they could keep pace with modern ideas of worship.

To this the conservative part of the congregation, collectively known as "the older heads," had calmly replied that their present manner of worship had been good enough for their fathers and was good enough for them; also, if the young people wanted to go out after strange gods, let them go. The Apostle's should remain as it had been. The chorister would go on giving the tunes and raising the hymn, and the latter, on rare occasions, still might be "lined out."

The advanced thinkers' only reply to this was to call a church-meeting and appoint a committee from among themselves to report to the congregation upon the feasibility of purchasing an organ to assist in the services. This, then, was the cause of being of the body that met that Wednesday afternoon at Abram Judkins's. It was peculiarly fitting too that it should meet at this house, for, of all the conservatives, Abram was the most strenuous in his opposition to the new movement, and the most outspoken in his denunciation of it.

"No, sir," he said at the gate as the party was about to say good-by, "it may be like mother, here, says; I ain't sayin' it is so, an' I ain't sayin' it ain't. Mebbe we've had our day, an' it's time fur the younger generation to have their innin's, but all I've got to say to that is, let 'em wait tell we're dead. We ain't got many more years on top o' ground, an' after we're gone they kin worship the Lord in any new-fangled way they please. But while I live I don't expect to see no organ a-shamin' that old church. No, sirree. Ef yore soul's right, there's music enough there, an' you don't need no made insterment a-blowin' the grace o' song into you. Why, next thing you know, they'll be havin' fiddles in the sanctuary."

"Mercy me!" cried old Mrs. Hemenway as she clasped her half-mittened hands together, "don't let us ever think of sich a onreligious desecration, Brother Judkins."

"Well, that's what it's a-comin' to, 'pears like to me."

"We'll hope it ain't, anyhow, Abram," said his old wife gently.

"Yes, we'll hope, mother, we'll hope. Don't any of you committee people furgit to turn out to-night. We've got to impress 'em with our sperit an' stren'th ef we want to carry our point," was his last remark.

"We won't furgit!" floated back the answer.

The committee of the minority had put off the meeting and the drafting of its report until the afternoon of the very day on which the church-meeting was to be held. So that the words of their resolutions came hot from their hearts, and were expected to sway all who heard them. Perhaps too Abram Judkins planned so late a meeting—for it was his suggestion—in order not to alarm the enemy and make him too wary. If this was his idea, it was well conceived and deserved success. But he forgot, or did not know, that he was pitted against an enemy who did not need alarming, but was voluntarily alert. His spies were out reconnoitring, and their eyes were upon the committee itself when it marched staidly away from Abram's gate with his parting injunction ringing in its ears.

The afternoon wore slowly away. To many an anxious soul whose mental vision was set forward like an alarm-clock to the time of the meeting it seemed that it would never pass. Abram Judkins was one of these. For the life of him, try as he would, he could not possess his soul in patience. He was first in the house and then out. At one time he was rummaging in the attic; five minutes later he was in the barn talking church management to the old mare.

"I do declare, Abram," said Mother Judkins, "I never did see you in sich a fidget before. I will cert'n'y be glad when this meetin's over an' things decided one way er t'other, so you kin git off o' this strain. Ef you don't, I do believe you'll be took down sick."

At supper, in his abstraction, Abram asked the blessing twice, burned his mouth with the tea, and finally rose from the table, having eaten scarcely anything, although his favorite dish of fried apples steamed before him.

At the opening stroke of the first bell he put on his hat, and, hurrying his wife along, made his way to church. As was to be expected, they were the first ones there, and the old man had to sit and nurse his impatience for a good ten minutes before anyone else joined them. But then the church began to be filled fast, and by the time the last notes of the second bell had died away an eager and expectant crowd had gathered within its sacred walls.

A glance about the crowd told Abram what had been done. The church had been "packed" with young people favoring the new movement. But the old man sighed with satisfaction as his mind ran back over that part of the church discipline which required in such cases a vote by ballot, and he reflected that this crowd of outsiders could only have effect in a viva-voce vote.

A hymn was sung, and as soon as it was finished the superintendent of the Sunday-school, a young man and an indefatigable worker for the organ, was on his feet with the suggestion that before proceeding to business the pastor open the doors of the church. The plan that was to be followed immediately flashed across the minds of the committee of the minority, and Elisha Harvey at once rose to speak for them. It was his opinion, he said in substance, that this was a business meeting and hardly the time for taking in members. The superintendent replied that he was quite aware that it was a business meeting, but he hoped never to see the day when Apostle's Chapel should behold lambs standing at the gate of the fold and refuse to let them come in, on the chance of their never being persuaded again.

There were some "Amens" to this, and to the surprise of his immediate associates Abram Judkins joined his word to the "young brother's request that the doors of the church be opened." It was accordingly done, and a dozen or fifteen young people went forward and joined. There were radiant faces among the advanced thinkers. The pastor announced that the right hand of fellowship would be extended to the new accessions on the following Sunday, and they rose and resumed their seats.

They were then ready to proceed to business. And in a very business-like way did the secretary of the majority committee read his report setting forth the various reasons why it was not only expedient, but necessary, that they should have an instrument of music with the services.

In a not less stirring manner did Abram Judkins read his report and deduce his opposing conclusions. His thunder told too, but he had more in reserve. At the end of his reading he said, "And now, Mr. Chairman, as I understand we are to take a vote, which the discipline says is to be by written ballot, I suggest that the new accessions, having come into the church without letter or recommendation, and therefore being only probationers, or under our watch-care, I suggest that they be put to theirselves until the votin' is over, as the rule of our body provides."

"Quite right, quite right," said the pastor-chairman, who was a simple man and a good deal confused by all this manoeuvering.

The little superintendent turned white, but he kept still, for he knew that any attempt to fight or to distort the revered discipline would be rewarded by a defection of his followers. One of the new accessions giggled as they were retired to the back part of the church.

Since the matter of the reports resolved itself merely into the question of an organ or no organ, it was moved and carried that the ballots be prepared in this form. The slips of paper were passed around, and for a few minutes there was a tense and ominous scratching of pencils, and whispers across from one seat to the other of "How do you spell the last part of organ, with a 'o' or a 'i'?"

In her seat over on the women's side Mother Judkins laboriously penciled away. Intent upon her work, she looked neither to the right nor the left, for writing was no easy task to this gentle old soul. No fingers were defter than hers when the heel of a sock was turning and the knitting-needles flashed back and forth, but when a pencil was put in her fingers they suddenly grew rigid and reluctant.

At last the scratching pencils ceased, the basket was passed around, and the slips gathered. The tellers took their places and the count began. There was a hush over the house that told how deeply the people were interested in the contest. Even the girls forgot to whisper and titter, and strained to hear every word that fell from the lips of the men who sat to them as arbiters of fate. The rasp of the paper slips and the voices of the tellers alone made war upon the silence. "Organ, no organ; organ, no organ; organ, organ; no organ, no organ." Thus steadily on, so even, so well-balanced. Neither side seemed to hold the victory. For a momentary gain for the one or the other there was always an equal subsequent loss. At last only half a dozen slips remained in the basket. The people had begun to get up and crane their necks forward. The beads of perspiration stood out on Abram Judkins's face. Elisha's Harvey's mouth twitched nervously, and the little superintendent was quite white. When the last slip was reached, "Organ!" said the teller. He conferred with his colleague, who had kept tally, and then announced, "Those for the organ have it by one vote."

There was no applause, but a great sigh welled up from the people, as though through it all they had been holding their breath. Abram Judkins groaned and, rising, staggered out of the church. Mother Judkins hurried down the aisle and went out after him. There was a frightened look in her quaint, kindly old face, and she clutched nervously at her dress as she went out of the door. She overtook her husband as he reached their own home. "Go in, honey," she said, putting her arm around him. "I didn't have no idee you would take it so hard."

"Take it hard," he replied huskly; "why, they've ruined the church. They've let down the bars to the devil an' all his troop. They'll never git 'em up ag'in."

"Don't take on so, Abram; mebbe it was fur the best."

"Don't tell me it was fur the best. Don't I say it was the devil's own work? He prepared the material and sent it there to-night." He buried his head in his hands and groaned. Mother Judkins paled.

"Abram," she said, "I want to tell you something. I—I voted fur the organ."

He raised his head and looked at her in a dazed sort of way, as if he could not fully take in what she was saying.

"Don't look at me that way, husban'. I voted fur it 'cause I thought my one little vote wouldn't count much among so many, an' the young people did seem so sot on it that I kind o' wanted to give them my speritual support, never thinkin' what it 'ud come to." There was a suspicious quaver in her voice.

"You don't mean it?" he said, still looking at her.

"I do. I do, but I did it fur the best, I tell you"; and then the old woman broke down and began to sob.

"There! there! don't cry, mother," he said, drawing her down beside him on the settee, where he had dropped. "Don't cry; you did it fur the best, but—but— Ain't it awful? It seems like a special chastisement from the Lord. My own wife! I wouldn't 'a' keered so much ef it had been a outsider, but—well, I 'low I went there puffed up in my own conceit, an' I've been scourged,—but by my own wife, my own wife!" His head fell into his hands again, and, bowed together thus, with their gray hair touching, the two old people wept out the heaviness of their hearts. When they arose to go to bed, they went hand-in-hand and in silence.

There was yet some months' grace for Abram Judkins, during which he might attend divine service without the interference of the abhorred music. Since Apostle's Chapel had taken the step, it decided to go as far as possible, so a small pipe-organ was ordered, and while it was being builded and put in place Abram came eagerly and hungrily to church, as if he were storing up sufficient grace to carry him over some period when he should be remote from the base of supplies. This too was the fact, for on the Sabbath morning when the organ was opened he was absent from his seat. His wife came and sat silent and subdued throughout the service. The same thing happened Sunday after Sunday. A sadness seemed to fall upon the old man as soon as the church-bells began to ring, and when his wife was gone he would shut up the house lest some stray note of the music should float in to him, and there he would sit brooding until the service was over. It might have gone on this way indefinitely had not Mother Judkins's fears for her husband's salvation prompted her to speak to him.

"Abram," she said, "do you think that you kin go on this way without speritual food an' keep up yore speritual stren'th?"

"I do' know, mother, I do' know; but I ain't a-goin' to eat the Lord's bran mixed with the devil's mash,—not me."

"But you're a-starvin' yore soul."

"I'm a-crucifyin' it fur its own good."

"But it ain't necessary, husban', it ain't necessary; there's other feedin' places." It cost the old lady an effort to say this, for her heart was set upon her own church.

"I hadn't ever thought o' that," he said, lifting up his head and looking at her queerly. "It'll look funny fur me, but I'll do it. Ef I can't git unmixed food one place, mebbe I kin another."

So the next Sunday found Abram sitting under a new preacher in a church where the singing was without music because they were too poor to purchase an organ. He was a liberal contributor, and his new associates, seeing this, made such strenuous efforts to get him to join them that he dropped the new church in disgust. But this renewed taste of grace had whetted his appetite, and he felt that he could no longer do without his regular soul-food. His heart yearned for his own church and his own preacher, to whose well-worn sermons he had been so long accustomed. There was but one thing to do,—compromise,—and this he did. He tried it one Sunday, and it worked so admirably that he continued it. He would slip into the church after the conclusion of the opening hymns, remain during the service in a back seat, and then glide out again when he saw the organist begin to turn the leaves of his music. It was not altogether satisfactory to him, but then he got his food unmixed.

However, he was soon denied even this consolation, for as winter approached, Mother Judkins was taken with an illness that confined her to the house and kept her husband by her side much of the time. He did not murmur, but would sit contentedly by her bed, reading to her or simply holding her hand. They had never been blessed with children, and the old couple had grown to be all in all to each other. Each gave to the other a double love, the connubial and the parental. And never was the flower fairer or its fragrance sweeter than in those days when the old man sat by his wife's side and saw her slip away from him, not knowing, unable to believe, that she was going to leave him.

When the truth came home to him that she was dead he gave down utterly. All his faculties seemed to fail him. All he could do was to walk back and forth about the room looking at the still form, his throat parched and his eyes dry. Others made his arrangements for the funeral; he could do nothing; and when the day came, bowed, broken, and tearless, the solitary old man followed his wife's body into the chapel, where it went for the last time. He did not see the people about him. He did not know what they were doing. He was conscious only of the persistent, dull ache in his heart and the gray outlook of life before him. And then in a soft flood of harmony he could distinguish the tune that the voices were taking up:

"Asleep in Jesus, blessed sleep,
    From which none ever wake to weep."

It was Mother Judkins's favorite hymn. He listened as they sang, and he seemed to hear his old wife's voice quavering up among the rest. Higher and higher it seemed to go, until she seemed to be singing away in the skies. He bowed his head, and the long-reluctant tears burst forth. But his heart grew calmer and a sad peace came over him.

When they had laid the old woman away, some of the neighbors came home with Abram to help put things to rights and to break the new loneliness of the house. He sat for a long time by the fire thinking. Then he spoke. Elisha Harvey was nearest to him.

"Elishy," he said, "them organs air a great invention. They kin express more glory in a minute than a whole congregation kin in a week. I was all wrong about it, but mother's jest showed me. Why, I could hear her singin' to-day jest as plain, an' then all the differ'nt sounds in that insterment was jest a-helpin' her to say all that she was feelin' an' all her su'prise an' pleasure at the beauty o' Heaven. An' to think I fit a-puttin' it in, while she—God bless her!—that vote o' hern was the workin' of a special Providence. Well, Elishy, I've been showed, an' from this time on I want to hear that music every Sunday. It'll take me nearer to her. I want 'em to open it up wide an' to pull out all them little spools in front an' jest nachully let her pipe salvation to the skies. I know mother'll understand that I've changed and be glad."

And the next Sunday he went early and sat under the sound of the organ with rapt face, as though above and beyond it he heard a farther, sweeter music.

The Visiting of Mother Danbury

FIFTH IN THE SERIES OF OHIO PASTORALS

IN THE SMALL village everybody is interested in everybody's else doings,—not always with a malicious concern, as some would have us believe. For among primitive folk there may be kindly prying, and gossip is sometimes gentle.

There was no lack of this village meddling, if meddling it might be called, when Felix Danbury, he who was son of the Widow Danbury and chorister at Cory church, led Martha Dickson to the altar. He it was who had led the fight for an organ to be used in the house of worship, and some of the older heads were still sore upon the subject; but when it was generally known that at last the day was set when he was to leave the state of bachelorhood, all animosities were put aside in the general enthusiasm to assist in such an event.

There was some sorrow too in all this interest, for the marriage of Felix meant his loss to the community. Martha lived at Baldwin's Ford, and thither her betrothed had promised to go and take up his abode. Usually the woman follows the man, but in this instance old Mrs. Dickson, who was also a widow, had protested so loud and long against separation from her only child that the lover was compelled to assure her that she would gain a son rather than lose a daughter. It was very noble indeed, and there had been a beautiful scene in which old Mrs. Dickson had wept on Felix's shoulder and blessed him.

"You're a good boy," she had told him. "I know that the folks air a-goin' to say that you're desertin' yore mother, but 'tain't so; she'll come over here a-visitin', an' we'll go over there, an' it'll be jest like one family; an', besides, yore mother wouldn't be lonely like me, for she's got Melissy."

"Melissy" was Felix's married sister, and on his marriage it was with her that his mother went to live.

There were those who came to condole with Mother Danbury upon the loss of her son, but she was very brave, and they had their trouble for their pay.

"No, no," she would say, rocking complacently, "a man ought to have a wife, an' ef he can't git her to come to him, he's got to go to her. I don't blame Widder Dickson now a bit about Marthy. 'Tain't like me, that's blessed with two children to be the support of my declinin' years."

"But why couldn't she 'a' come over here?" her gossips protested.

"'Twouldn't 'a' been fair to ask her that; for she'd 'a' had to tore up root an' branch, while I ain't got nothin' to do scarcely but to slip out o' my house into Melissy's. An' then it ain't as ef Felix was gone fur good. You see Baldwin's Ford ain't fur away, an' I kin run over an' drop in on 'em almost anytime."

And so, placidly, the old lady went on with her knitting day by day, looking under and over her glasses as often as through them as she paused for little chats with the neighbors or to murmur gentle admonition to Melissy's children.

Outwardly she was calm, but her soul longed for a sight of this son, whose form had gladdened her eyes every evening as he returned from work, and the honeymoon was hardly over before she had "dropped over" to spend a day with her two dear children.

The day was a joyous one for her—for them all. Felix was radiant, his wife shyly happy, and the Widow Dickson brought out and spread for her visitor the best that her larder afforded.

All that bothered Mother Danbury was that the Widow insisted upon making company of her. She had assumed an air of possession over Felix that left a little sting in the mother's heart.

Mother Danbury did not want to be company, and she did want to be allowed a part in her son, and, above all, she did not want to sit in the front room and look at the staring wax flowers under their glass case and the shell houses on the mantel, even if she did have on her best alpaca. But when she first essayed forth with her dress tucked up around her waist and her sleeves rolled up, she was conducted —nay, almost carried—back to her prison with many and profuse protestations of horror at letting their guest do anything.

This was all very well for a time. She sat still and knitted, alone save for a minute's peep in from one or the other of her hostesses, until she heard the clatter and clucking of the fowls in the yard. Then she rebelled and, resolutely laying down her knitting, went forth to usefulness. She helped feed the chickens, and after that they all sewed together or knitted. She helped get supper. Felix came home again, as it seemed to her, almost as he used to do. Now, what could the gossips say? thought Mother Danbury.

They would not hear of her leaving that night, and the boy Jeff, who had driven her over in the spring-wagon, went early to his unemotional slumbers in the attic. Star, the jogging old mare, contentedly munched her hay in the barn, while the four sat out on the little porch in the soft spring night.

This was the first of a series of such visits made at short intervals, and sometimes of a Sunday returned by all the family from Baldwin's Ford. At such times Cory's church heard Felix's voice again, and it rejoiced too that he was not entirely lost to its service.

The village looked on at the pretty romance and smiled because there had been so many to prophesy that it could not be. The tongues of gossip had been wagging pretty freely. Some had said that Mother Danbury would never go to Baldwin's Ford; others that the Baldwin's Fordists would never return the visit. One side held that Felix would forget his mother in a month, and the others, with equal assurance, gave Martha a little more than that time to leave her native town, and both gave what to them were adequate reasons.

So the village looked on and smiled as month after month passed and these prophecies came to naught. The simple folk still had their ideals, and there is nothing in life so satisfactory as having one's ideals realized.

In the fulness of time there came good news from Baldwin's Ford, and there was much bustle and flutter about Melissy's house and running in of the neighbor women. When they emerged it was with nods and smiles and knowing winks, as if they were bubbling over with some glad, momentous intelligence. The spring-wagon was hastily rolled out, and old Star, stepping more lively than she had done for a dozen years, was hastily put between the shafts. Jeff deposited a mysterious bundle in the wagon's bed and then leaped to the seat. Then Mother Danbury came out, all smiling anxiety, and with fluttering ribbons and nods to the assembled people she was borne away towards Baldwin's Ford.

How the women gathered and chatted about it and wondered. It became a village event. Even the parson's wife walked down far enough to say that she hoped everything would come out all right, and if there were any "flannins" needed, there was her store to draw from. "Melissy's" house became a public hall, and her two little tow-headed youngsters were relegated to stern oblivion in face of the tremendous fact of a new-comer at Baldwin's Ford. Only their father, when he came home in the evening and found them disconsolate among the crowd of women waiting for the news, nestled them to his breast and soothed them, whispering, "Fawther don't care how many children are born, just so he's got baby buntings."

Hereupon the "baby buntings" took consoling fingers from dejected mouths and ran riot over the form of their one friend. They were shaken into startled silence, though, when Jeff arrived, grinning and shamefaced, to announce, "It's a girl, and Mis' Danbury says it weighs nine pounds."

Then Babel. The little ones fled. Their father fled. Jeff was before them, and the men on the street, after hearing the news, chuckled and walked away, pretending they had not been interested. But the women—bless them! They made no attempt to dissemble.

"The little dear, bless her heart!"

"Nine pounds! What a girl!"

"Wonder if her father was disappointed at her bein' a girl?"

"Disappointed! He'd better be glad that he's a father an' that poor wife o' his'n a-gittin' along. Disappointed!"

"Oh, Marthy'll git along, robust as she is an' with two such nurses as the Widder an' Mother Danbury to look after her."

"Hope the child won't cause no trouble in this family," said the voice of the inevitable croaker.

"Trouble in the family! The very idea of that innercent little thing a-causin' trouble, 'cept in the usual way."

"I don't know, but there ain't anything more likely to make disputes between people than the bringin' up of a child." The voice was persistent.

"Oh, do hush. Let's don't even think of such a thing. Why, I think it's lovely. A baby with two grandmothers to nurse it is just born with a silver spoon in its mouth."

Meanwhile there was rejoicing also in the village of Baldwin's Ford. Felix was joyfully tearful, and bustlingly glad the grandmothers, while Martha, all white from her travail, lay nursing her babe to her bosom. The house had already become a kingdom, and the mite of a girl was ruling it ruthlessly with her little pink hands. When she opened her mouth her ready minions flew to her side and stood there, trembling with anxiety to know what she wanted. More than likely it was only to yawn, and then they laughed at themselves and their fears and voted her a remarkable infant, as if no baby had ever twisted its head inconsequently and yawned before. Oh, the delight, the pain, the joy, the sorrow, the pride, and the fear over a first baby!

"Don't you think the little dear is wrapped up a little too heavy?" whispered Mother Danbury to the Widow.

"Too heavy," sniffed the Widow; "no, indeed. Why, when my Marthy was two days old I had her wrapped in twice that much stuff."

"But Marthy was born in the winter."

"That don't make no difference; a baby's a baby. I've had one."

"I've had three," was Mother Danbury's quiet retort.

"One of 'em's dead, though."

"She didn't die till she growed to be quite a girl, so it was the will o' Providence an' no fault o' mine."

"La, Mother Danbury, I didn't say it was."

This was a trifle conciliatory, but Felix's mother was hurt, and the Widow Dickson was put into an attitude of defence as to her rights over her daughter's child.

The next day, when the doctor came, the Widow Dickson forestalled Mother Danbury in questioning him, and took all the responsibility of caring for the child upon herself.

"I don't want to take the child from you, Martha Ann Dickson, I only want to help you. It's my son's child as well as your daughter's," said Mother Danbury.

"My daughter had all the pain o' bearin' this child."

"Well—well—" The other old lady stopped. She had nothing to say that quite fitted the occasion.

Day after day Mrs. Dickson bathed and cuddled the baby while her visitor was compelled to stand by and look on. Finally one morning when the baby was nearly three weeks old wagon-wheels were heard in the yard, and Mother Danbury came into the room with her bonnet-strings tied and her duster on.

"Well, I guess I'll be goin', Marthy," she said to her daughter-in-law.

"Why, Mother Danbury, you ain't a-goin', are you?"

"Oh, the baby's doin' first-rate, an' it seems I ain't needed here any more."

Marthy began to cry. "But I want you," she said.

Then Mrs. Dickson broke in with many tears. "It does seem strange to me, Marthy, that you should be a-cryin' after somebody else after the mother I've been to ye! That's all the thanks a mother gets."

"Never mind, never mind, you'll get along all right, both o' you, an' you know there's Melissy an' the children at home to look after."

"But what will Felix say?" moaned Marthy, for Felix's mother had chosen a safe time, when he was away, to take her departure.

"Felix is my son too," said the Widow sternly.

Then Mother Danbury turned on her for one brief moment.

"Fair exchange is no robbery, Martha Ann Dickson," she said, and went out at once to the wagon, where she tied down her veil, though the day was hot.

The baby smiled in its sleep. It is a pretty fallacy that says babies smile thus because angels are whispering to them. In most cases, as in this, the little ones, wise from other scenes, are smiling at the foibles of those greater infants whom we are pleased to call grown people.

The return of Mother Danbury was a source of great wonder to the community, and again tongues flew freely and inquiries were rife. The flying rumors could not but come to the ears of their subject, and some of the overbold even went so far as to question her. But they could elicit no more definite reply than, "Marthy an' the baby was a-gettin' along all right, an' I could do more good at home." Then she closed her lips.

The voice of the croaker was decidedly suspicious as she said, "I smell a rat."

It remained, however, for the Widow Dickson, who was not blessed with the gift of reticence, to let it be known just how matters stood.

"You see," she said to an intimate, after duly cautioning her to let it go no further, "you see, Mother Danbury is a good old woman, but she is set in her ways. Now, nobody could make me believe that she really meant to walk over me in my own house; but it is hard to see someone tryin' to come between you an' yore only child."

In a day the news was abroad. It came to the village the same night. There had been a breach, and the voice of the croaker said complacently, "I told you so."

After that Mother Danbury paid no more visits to Baldwin's Ford, nor did she speak of its people unless she were compelled.

On a morning, though, other news was brought, and the old lady's indifference fell from her like a cloak. With tearful eyes she made her way towards the forbidden place, and as she stepped into the wagon there were none who had the heart to be there and wave a good-by, for the word said the baby was dying.

She came like an angel of peace to the stricken household. The Widow was ready for a scene, but firmly and gently the stronger woman put her away. She kissed Martha and soothed her as the hysterical Widow could not do. Then she turned to her son.

"Felix," she said, "ain't there no hope?"

"No, none."

"'The Lord giveth an' the Lord taketh away'—" But she could go no further. An hour later the child breathed its last in her arms. It was she who bathed it and put it in its little gown and laid it silent in the cradle. The Widow had no remonstrance to offer, but she came later and said, "Oh, Mother Danbury, I'm afeared it's a jedgment. I was so hard an' jealous about the pore little creeter. I've done wrong, an' the Lord's took it. Fergive me, fergive me!"

She fell upon her knees. Mother Danbury lifted her, and her own tears fell now. "You see how little all our feelin's an' wills air compared to His," she said. "The child wasn't ours, it was His, an' He has showed us His sign."

The afternoon sun stole in and kissed the little, wax-like face as the old women stood with clasped hands looking down upon the dead grandchild.

His Bride of the Tomb

"You might consent to spend one day with me Violet, knowing that I have so little time to be with you," he said. "You may just as well lay aside your foolish prejudices and go with us, Philip, for I am determined upon going," replied Violet Harcourt; she was speaking to her betrothed husband Philip Trevelyn. The gay party with which she was spending a week or two in a quaint little out-of-the-way village, had in an overflow of thoughtless mischief determined upon picnicing in an old and long unused grave-yard; after dinner they were to amuse themselves by reading the rude epitaphs and visiting the gray old tombs, where "the rude fore-fathers of the hamlet sleep."

"I can't see," said Trevelyn, "what pleasure people can find in scampering over graves or picnicing among them, it shows very scant respect for the dead, to say the least." "Well every one doesn't choose to look at it in that way, Philip, you oughtn't to expect the whole world to think as you do, although you are Philip Trevelyn esquire, a rising young lawyer," she replied with almost a sneer. "There are some opinions in the world besides your own, although you don't seem to think so," she went on with rising anger.

"I am doing what I believe to be right, Violet, and you will acknowledge it some day," he said coolly. "Oh, of course you're always in the right, no one is ever right but you; well, at any rate I shall go to-morrow whether you choose to go or not."

"Violet, let me ask you, nay, beg you not to go; you will not enjoy it"; but with averted face she answered, "I shall go."

"Then," he replied flushing with anger, "Violet Harcourt, I command you as my betrothed wife not to go." She was hasty and willful, and, turning on him with a defiant look, she murmured, rather than spoke, "I shall disobey you, no man shall

This story was signed "Philip Louis Denterly." It has been attributed to Dunbar by, among others, Robert Bone in *Down Home* (310), Eugene W. Metcalf Jr. in *Paul Laurence Dunbar: A Bibliography* (76), and Herbert Woodward Martin and Ronald Primeau in *In His Own Voice* (224–27).

ever have the right to command me; I am my own mistress; if you want me for a slave, take back your ring"; and slipping the glittering band from her finger she held it out to him; for a moment he stood as though dazed, and then taking the ring, he placed it in his pocket and slowly turned away, just as Fred Tracy sauntered up saying, "It is our dance, Miss Harcourt." She placed her hand in his arm and entered the house, where the music of Strauss' "Merry Waltz" was filling the air with its beautiful rhythm.

It was an informal party which the young people were giving in the parlors of the one hotel which the village afforded, and the rooms were full of light and merriment. But Violet Harcourt's heart was heavy. Her companion's conversation became odious to her, and she began to think what abominable music that city orchestra was making.

She was a beautiful girl, dark-haired, with rich complexion slightly dark, that betrayed the Spanish blood in her veins, though even had that been less indicative, her great lustrous black eyes must have told upon her; her mother was a Spaniard and from her she had inherited all the fire and ardent passions of that race. For nearly a year she had been the betrothed wife of Philip Trevelyn, and she loved him with her whole soul. But he was proud and she was proud and they quarreled often, though never before had they come to such a point.

Violet was a divine dancer, but to-night she could not dance; the music seemed to drag; she was angry and sick at heart; no gayety could dispel the gloom that was gathering over her. "Are you ill?" asked her companion. "I am not!" she answered angrily. He should have been warned and not pursued the subject further but, Tracy unconscious that he was walking on forbidden ground remarked, "You do not seem to be in your accustomed spirits this evening." She deigned no reply, but the deadly look she gave him made the young man tremble.

When he left her, Philip Trevelyn walked rapidly trying to make his feet keep pace with his thoughts, cursing his fate and gnawing his cigar as though it had been the author of all his trouble. A man in this state is always likely to be more or less unjust. So there being no one else present, he cursed himself for ever coming to the village, he let his cigar go out and then cursed the cigar for going out. Before he got through his cursing he had reached the little grave-yard which had been the innocent cause of all his pain, so, to end it all, he cursed the ring in his pocket, and taking it out, threw it as far into the grave-yard as he could, and turned his steps homeward; a light rain began to fall as he went along. "Humph," he muttered, "it isn't enough for me to be scorned but even the heavens are conspiring against me. This rain will just make it cool and pleasant for those frivolous picnicers to-morrow, and I had hoped that they would be scorched by a blazing sun while they were scampering among the graves and laughing at my foolish notions."

And as he went on the rain fell more heavily and he distinctly heard the ominous sighing of the weeping willows in the grave-yard, sighing that sounded like the half suppressed groan of a spirit damned.

The morning dawned in great beauty, the air was cool and fresh, the trees full of birds singing thankfulness for the little shower. Philip Trevelyn did not rise early;

he had passed a sleepless night, so when, at nine o'clock, the picnic party started away he was not up to see them off.

A very similar night Violet Harcourt had spent, weeping and chiding herself. For awhile she was determined to go to Philip and confess herself in the wrong, but the demon Pride rose and quenched the desire; it was with very red and swollen eyes that she left her bed to dress for the picnic, half-doubting that the affair of last night was real, that it had not all been a troublous dream; but the sight of her bare finger, where had sparkled Philip Trevelyn's ring, was conclusive evidence that it was not all a dream. With heavy heart she donned her hat, as she heard Fred Tracy's voice at the door asking, "Are you ready?" "In a moment," she answered, and her voice sounded unnatural even to her own ears. She was bewitchingly beautiful in dead white and as she stepped out, Tracy glanced at her with a smile of pleasure, saying, "You are rivaling the morning in beauty"; and then he walked down the little corridor by her side singing cheerily,

"My love she's a beauty, but oh she's proud.
And many a quarrel have we."

"Where did you get that abominable song, Mr. Tracy?" said Violet. "It's perfectly harrowing."

"Well," he laughed in reply, "you're not very complimentary to my composition. I confess that the song is my own and I was foolish enough to think that it had quite a sweet melody."

"Tastes differ greatly," she said.

"*De gustibus non disputandum,*" he replied, "but if you do not like my song it shall never be heard again, although I had hoped great things for it." "Oh," said Violet, indifferently, "my opinion of it can have no influence over what others may think." By this time they had reached the street; she quietly entered the vehicle which waited to take them to the solemn seat of their gayety, and as one person cannot keep up a conversation, the short ride was a very silent one. The little cemetery was gloomy but beautiful even in its gloom, the weeping willows, nature's ever constant mourners hung over the sunken graves caressingly, and their drooping branches swept the green carpet of the ground. But notwithstanding the beauties of nature, the day was not what the picnicers expected it to be, and so, soon after dinner they by common consent decided to return, they were to walk home and were far upon the way when some one remarked the absence of Violet Harcourt. "Oh," said Tracy, "she's been in a bad humor all day, so I suppose she went home some time ago and left me to my fate." At this there was a general laugh as they walked home without her.

Just before they had started for home, Violet noticed a gray stone tomb with a heavy iron door which stood open; anxious to explore it and fearless, she entered and looked around for awhile at the dark caskets that seemed to frown at her boldness. But without a moment's warning the heavy door swung to and she heard the bolt outside as it fell into place. At first she was almost unable to realize her position, but as it dawned upon her that she was imprisoned with the dead, she raised her voice in a frantic cry for help. But the walls only seemed to hurl back the sound with redoubled force to her own ears, and then, when there seemed no help, she fell upon the floor in a dead faint. How long she lay there she did not know, but when she opened her eyes on the dense darkness again, she knew that her only escape lay in a continual cry for help, which might attract some passer's attention. As cry after cry went up, she suddenly heard a step and the latch was lifted, the door swung open, and she staggered out into Philip Trevelyn's arms. The past was forgotten, "Oh, Philip, my savior," she cried. He laughed for very joy and pressed her to his heart saying, "There was a providence in our quarrel last night; if I had not quarreled with you and forbidden your coming I would not have been here now to save you. I was looking for the ring you returned and which, in my anger, I threw into this grave-yard, will you help me find it, darling?" "Yes," she murmured, "but oh, Philip, can you forgive me?" He caught her to his arms again crying, "There is nothing to forgive, my bride of the tomb!"

His Failure in Arithmetic

WHILE THE PROFESSOR of West Branch academy was busy "working sums" for one of the Peterson boys a red "hided" man from Hallelujah Springs entered the school house, approached the professor, and said:

"Air you the man that runs this here erfair?"

The professor put down his slate and pencil, studied the features of the visitor, and then replied:

"That's what I came here for."

"Ah hah, my name's Jowerson."

"Glad to meet you, Mr. Jowerson."

"Well, you must not be glad agin, I'm done with you. My son has been going to school to you. Little feller's name's Tom."

"Oh, yes," said the professor, "I believe I remember him."

"Yes, reckon you do. Tuther day you whaled him with an oak split. I've come to maul you."

"My dear sir," said the professor, "I did whip your son with a white oak split, but he deserved it. During a recitation in arithmetic, I asked him this question: 'If

This story has been attributed to Dunbar by Robert Bone in *Down Home* (310).

you were to go with a jug to fill it, and there was a still-house a half mile away and a spring a quarter of a mile away, what would you bring back?' He studied a moment, and said 'water.' Then I took up a white oak split and whipped him."

"Wall," said the visitor, "I must be goin.' In the transaction that we was jes' talkin' about I agree with you all but one thing. A boy that didn't have no more sense than my chap has, deserves hickery instead of white oak."

His Little Lark

"GOOD NIGHT" SAID Mr. Sylvester, with an effort as he reached his own house. "Hope you won't find your wife sitting up f-for you. Mine u-used to, but I got her out of that notion pretty quick. She's sound asleep now, I'll warrant, and no make-believe either. I might fire off a Gatling gun alongside of her best ear and she'd never know it."

Mr. Sylvester parted from his neighbor and entered his own house, opening and shutting the door with some trouble and a great deal of noise. Then he extinguished the hall light, fell up stairs one step at a time and went into the front room, which was dimly lighted. And there he saw his wife sitting in a rocking chair by the dressing table. Her back was toward him and she did not look up or speak—both bad signs.

"Lizbeth," said Mr. Sylvester with much dignity, sitting down on the side of the bed unsteadily, "what are you doing there?"

No response.

"Lizbeth, haven't I told you never to set 'em up, I mean set—sit up f' me? It isn't proper. I'm old enough to come home w-when I please, Lizbeth. I c-command you not to do it again. Why don't you say something, Lizbeth?"

Mrs. Sylvester preserved a discreet silence. Mr. Sylvester resumed:

"Lizbeth, I command you to speak. It isn't treating me with proper respect to sit there s' mum. What have I done to be treated like this? Will you speak, Lizbeth?"

There was silence only more profound.

"Very well, Lizbeth, you'll be sorry f'r this in the morning. I shall now retire to my—bless my soul, Lizbeth, who is this?"

We are attributing this story to Dunbar because of the similarity between this story and "His Failure in Arithmetic."

Mr. Sylvester stood up very straight and stared at the bed, on the edge of which he was sitting. There lay his excellent wife sound asleep, her bangs done up in tissue paper and a smile of placid contentment on her lips.

"Who's that other woman?" stammered Mr. Sylvester in a sotto voce tone. Then he took up courage to approach and pluck her by the sleeve. Pshaw. She came to pieces in his hands. It was only Mrs. Sylvester's clothes which she had arranged handy in case of fire.

And Sylvester murmured: "Saved again, b'gosh!" as he tucked himself in his little bed, while his wife continued to sleep the sleep of the just.

From Impulse

IT WAS A divine summer's evening, in the middle of that most pleasant of all pleasant months, June. We were standing, Hallie and I, beneath a gnarled oak, through whose branches a soft wind blew, rustling the leaves over our heads, and the stars coming out blinked knowingly at us. Impetuous youngster that I was, could I help what occurred? When I saw the moonlight shining on Hallie's sweet little face, crowned with its cluster of golden curls, and the blue eyes looking love into mine, could I help kissing her and asking for a love which I knew was already my own?

We were only sixteen, and it was the same old story—I was poor and she was poor; and so I told her, but with a sly little glance, she said, "I shall be content to share your poverty as well as your love."

"But," said I, half crazed with delight, "It has always been my settled determination never to take a wife, until I was able to care for her properly."

"It would be so easy for us to live comfortably together," she said, "Even though we are poor."

But I was obdurate and when a few weeks after, a letter came to me from my uncle, I was sure that it held good news, and without opening it, I sought Hallie, so that we might read it together. As I broke the seal and ran my eyes along the lines, a cry of pain broke from Hallie's lips. Thus the letter ran.

This story was signed Frank Mayne Templeton. We are attributing this story to Dunbar because the similarity in theme of earnest love between this story and "His Bride of the Tomb" points to their being written by the same hand. Bracketed insertions mark the places where the original text has deteriorated and we have attempted to restore it.

DEAR BERT:—Your father and I have been scheming for your welfare for some time, but he tells me that you are getting spooney over some little country lass around there. Bert, my boy, [don't for the Lord's sake,] for if there is anything in this world that I, Silas Marchmont, do hate, it is calf love. Run up to the city for a time and take a place in my counting house instead of following the plow horses. I believe you have a common education. I can break you no doubt of your affection for the little country girl, at least, I shall try very earnestly to do that. You know I have no heirs and there's no telling what might happen, if you should please me. I, Silas Marchmont, am the one to be pleased. Your aunt was saying to-day what a fine lad you were, so you see there is not much doubt how you will be received by her. You can make something here, so throw up your little sweetheart, and come to your uncle.   SILAS MARCHMONT, Esq.

"The conceited, pompous, worldly, old rascal, throw you up indeed!" I burst forth excitedly.

"Shall you go, Bert?" asked Hallie.

"Go to be sure, I shall show him whom he has to deal with. Let him try to break me from you, if he dare. Does he think that when I won your heart, I was like a baby grasping a toy, to be deprived of my bauble at will? I will show him; I will show him!" I answered hotly.

"And you will go any how?" asked Hallie.

"I would not miss this opportunity for lowering my uncle's pride for worlds," I said. "I shall go, and what is more, I shall stay for a long time to show that egotistical old rascal, Silas Marchmont, how constant the heart of a boy may be in a case of 'calf love,' as he calls it."

"Your heart may wax less constant than you imagine, when we are parted."

"Shall yours?"

"No."

"And do you distrust me?" I asked angrily.

"No, no," she hastily answered, "but you do not know what influences they may bring to bear upon you."

"Do not fear for that, Hallie, they can bring nothing that will outweigh my love for you."

How big and manly I felt, as I said those words, standing there in the twilight, with the open letter fluttering in my hand, while the soft cooing of Hallie's pet pigeons floated to my ears as though by its gentleness trying to calm the fiery passions that burned within me.

"Hallie," I continued, "you are my first love." She smiled at the idea that one so young should have had many.

That smile sugared me and I exclaimed tragically, "You know that I come of a family, who will not break a promise; you must believe me when I say that nothing shall ever separate us. I promise to be faithful, I may go even farther, if you demand it, I swear!"

"You need not take an oath, Malbert, I can trust you; your promise is enough."

How many times in the after years, when I was struggling hand to hand with temptation, did those words come to me! "I can trust you; your promise is enough."

And how often did I blush and bend my head like a culprit, when the consciousness of how [unwor]thy I was of such trust, c[ame over] me.

It was all settled, and [with my] heart full of joy, notwithst[anding] my parting with those I lo[ved, I] left my happy home, the hom[e of] my boyhood, for the labors, [cares] and turmoil of the city. Still I was joyful, for was I not going to purchase happiness for Hallie?

My uncle received me into his family as a son, "and all went merry as a marriage bell" until near the last part of my first year with him, when one day he exclaimed, slapping me familiarly on the back, "Well Bert, my boy, you've forgotten your little country girl, [at] last, haven't you?"

"You would not think [so if] you should see the piles o[f her] perfumed letter with [which] my trunk is filled;" I[aughing] at the look of utter asto[nishment] which came over my uncl[e's face.]

"Thunder! boy, you m[ean to] say that she writes you?"

"Yes sir, I do, and I mean also to say that I write her in return."

His face clouded and his hands worked nervously as he said, "That will never do in the world; it must be stopped."

"It must not and shall not be stopped," I replied.

"I say it must be stopped."

"Humph, I don't see how it will be stopped."

"You young scamp, I forbid you to write to her."

Glancing coldly at him, I answered, "Sir, during business hours I am yours to command; you have a right to tell me then to whom I shall write. Outside of that time I reserve the privilege to do as I please, and to write to whoever I please, free from your dictation."

"You scapegrace, do you know that I am a rich man, and that your father hasn't a cent in the world to leave you?"

"I came here to work for you, sir, not to discuss my father's private affairs!" and turning on my heel I strode away from him as majestically as a boy of my age (I was seventeen then) could, leaving him boiling over with wrath, and murmuring something about, "me, Silas Marchmont, Esq.," and "to think," and "bundle him off on the next train."

However nothing serious resulted from our little war, and uncle soon gained his accustomed serenity, although he was deeply chagrined that any one should dare to disregard his command, in a house where he was used to abject obedience, where his will was law.

And now five years had passed, spent by me in my uncle's employ, with occasional visits to my country home to see my family and Hallie, when we received a visit from a distant relative of Mrs. Marchmont's. I was at the office when she came, but uncle chanced to casually remark that she wasn't pretty, but that I would do well to fall in love with her, as she had about two hundred thousand in her own right.

I did not answer him then, but my looks plainly said that I should do nothing of the kind.

I went home that evening, with the full determination of showing Miss Lelia Dalton all the coldness that courtesy would allow.

But my plan failed woefully.

I had gone expecting to meet a stiff, prim, young lady, with haughtiness showing itself in her every movement.

Instead, I was introdu[ced to] a creature whose little b[rown head] reached about to my [shoul]der, and who insisted [on callin]g me "Cousin Mal." fro[m the fir]st. As the weeks passed [I beg]an to think how comm[on looking] and stupid Hallie would be [beside] Lelia Dalton, who was both beautiful as a fairy, lively and accomplished.

We rode out in uncle's phaeton together, which was only large enough for two, and were, therefore not troubled with Aunt Marchmont.

We sang together and she would weep quietly as I read the sad stories of maidens who died of love unrequited.

While all the time [(I di]d not notice it then) uncle [looked o]n in [g]rim satisfaction, as t[his l]ittle maiden wove her net [around] my heart. At last I aw[oke and foun]d that I was madly and p[rofoundly] in love with Lelia Dalto[n with m]y heart and hand pledged to another.

What should I do? Should I cling to the one whom I had plighted my faith, in the days of indiscretion, or should I ask for release, and worship at the shrine of my new found love? It was a sad and difficult case. Love versus honor.

But I determined the best thing to do would be to come to an understanding with Hallie at once. Then like other guilty souls, I began to try to quiet the pleading of my conscience by making excuses for my actions. Might not she have repented also of her folly? Might not a real love have come to her also? Thus I reasoned, and having secured leave of absence for a short time, I boarded the train and went whirling away from the city, determined to ask release from my vows; repeating to myself ever and anon, as the cars bounded over the rails, "She has repented also." And then Hallie's words flashed across my memory. I seemed to hear them in the "click-click" of the rails, in the stirring breeze which floated past the window, in the engine's shrill whistle, and in its labored breathing, as it dragged the long train of cars up the hill. They seemed to be written, standing out in bold relief, across the face of everything on which I looked, "I can trust you; your promise is enough."

With these thoughts coursing through my brain I arrived at the country way station, and wended my way homewards. I felt gloomy, and the cordial greeting that met me only seemed a mockery to my misery. I was filled with a feverish excitement until I had torn myself from the family and started toward Hallie's house. As I neared the place, I saw her seated in the yard sewing; the branches of the trees waving over her, and the colored flowers blooming around her made a picture meet for an artist's brush.

My heart failed me, but as Hallie advanced toward me, I bowed and spoke coldly. Then as I saw the look of pain that crossed her face, clasped her in my arms, and—well, I didn't ask her to release me from my vows at all; and she, in her joy, forgot my momentary coldness.

I wrote to my uncle that evening after I had left Hallie, asking for a month's leave of absence, as, "My little country lass" and I were to be married at the end of that time. I had come back to be released from, but from the impulse of the moment, had confirmed the vows made when a boy affected with "calf-love."

The Tenderfoot

BACK IN THE '50s, we old miners didn't hev much respect fur them weak-kneed, white-handed chaps, thet you call "dudes" now. They was rank pisen to us an' one of 'em never struck our camp without hevin' so many tricks played on him thet arter awhile he was glad enough to git away.

We thought that a "dude," "tenderfoot" we called him, didn't hev no rights which a miner was bound to respect, an' we treated him accordin'ly. Even in them days we had the barroom bummer who didn't do nothin' all day long but hang aroun' the tavern doin' odd jobs fur his meals an' watchin' fur the stage to come jest as anxious as if he was waitin' fur friends.

Sich sort o' chap was Jerry Malcolm, he was the most shiftless sort o' cuss I ever seen. He wouldn't work under no circumstances, exceptin' jest enough to feed him.

Jerry would stand at thet tavern winder all afternoon, waitin' fur the stage to come in, with no reason in the world fur doin' so, thet is, as anybody could see. The boys used to rig him a good deal about it, but he never seemed to care much—took it all good natured as you please.

He wasn't a bad sort o' fellow, drunkard nor nothin' o' thet kind; but jest natchelly shiftless and don't-care-like.

One day, jest arter time fur the stage to come in, a half a dozen or so us fellows was su'prized clean out o' our wits to see Jerry Malcolm come a tearin' down the trail leadin' to the mine whar we was a workin', both hands throwed up and his feet goin' like wings.

"Wonder what's the matter with Jerry?" said Dan McCoy, shadin' his eyes with his hand and lookin' up the trail.

"Somethin' mighty pertickler's goin' on to make Jerry lift them feet o' hisn thet away."

"Mebbe Mulligan's gang has struck the camp again," said Tom Haydon, laying his hand on the butt of his revolver as he spoke. Every other man instinctively made the same movement as the thought flashed across their minds; for another visit from Tim Mulligan's dare-devils wasn't a very pleasant outlook.

So in silence we waited till Jerry come up out o' breath, puffin' and blowin' like a steam engine. "Boys," says he, "what d'you think?"

"We ain't thinkin' a tall," said Haydon, gruffly. "We're waitin' to hear, so spit it out as quick as you kin."

"Thar's a tenderfoot just landed from the stage," gasped Jerry, between puffs. "A tenderfoot!"

We was a good deal relieved, but we didn't let on t' each other, an' each fellow laughed an' he went back to his work an' began to hatch some divilment in his mind agin' that pore "tenderfoot."

Well, work jest flew along thet arternoon, fur we wanted to git done and go down to the tavern. When quittin' time come, you never seen men drop their tools an' make fur camp quicker in your life. We couldn't git to the tavern quick enough; but even when we did git there, we was disappointed, fur there wasn't a sign of a "tenderfoot" in sight. They said he had shelled out of his store clothes and gone out in the hills prospectin.' It was a hard strain on us but we had to sit down to supper without seein' him.

When the meal was about half over, Jerry Malcolm came a tiptoein' in like he was afraid he'd wake hisself, an' said kind o' low like; "He's a comin', fellers." Every eye turned toward the door. It opened sort o' quick like an' in stepped our man. Wall, we'd all been kind o' holden' our breath, an' all of a sudden we let it go with a gasp. Man alive! There was six foot of as good a man in that tenderfoot's clothes as ever I seen.

He was togged out in a rough workin' suit, but his hands give him away, fur they looked soft an' tender an' there wasn't nothin' like sunburn on 'em to spoil their whiteness. He didn't look like a very likely feller to fool with, an' I guess all the boys must a thought the same, fur none of them said anything to him.

Like as not, nothin' wouldn't ever hev bin said if it hadn't bin fur thet devil, Tom Haydon, who spoke up and says, "Wall, stranger, you've cast in your lot amongst us; you might as well git acquainted. Who are you and what's your business?"

"I'm an assayer, an' my name's Fred Bender," the young feller answered, very polite.

But Tom wasn't satisfied; he wanted to take the feller down, so he said, with a kind of sneer: "Oh, you're one of them college-taught miners, are you, a' squintin' around the rocks with a lead pencil an' microscope."

The young feller didn't make no answer, but I saw his eyes kind o' gleam in a way thet would 'a' warned most men. But Haydon went on: "What d'you expect to find here anyhow, gold or brass?" laughin' an' winkin' at the other fellers.

"If I'd ben lookin' fur brass," said the stranger, lookin' Haydon straight in the eyes, "I wouldn't have had to go far to find it after meetin' you."

Haydon was a good deal took back but he laughed with the rest of us an' nothin' more was said thet evenin'.

But anyone thet knowed him could 'a' told thet he wasn't satisfied; fur he was one o' these kind o' fellers thet hold a grudge agin' you if you git a little ahead of 'em even in fun.

Fur two months, things moved along smooth enough. The tenderfoot was still amongst us and he'd begun to grow into consid'able favor, fur we found thet he was a plain sort o' unassumin' man thet knowed his business an' tended to it. He was friendly, but not familiar, an' so we all kind o' took a likin' to him.

It was a rainin' like blazes one mornin' when we got up, an' the boys thought it was too wet to do much work; so we all got together in the big bare barroom of the tavern to amuse ourselves the best we could. One of the fellows had a banjo an' played an' sung whilst some of the others danced jigs an' breakdowns in their rough fashion. Fred Bender had joined us an' seemed to be enjoyin' the fun as much as anybody.

At last some one proposed havin' a wrasslin' match.

Now anyone thet ever knowed a camp o' miners knows thet's jes the thing fur 'em; so we hailed the idee with a shout an' cleared space fur a ring.

Haydon was the champion strong man of the camp, so he was put up agin all comers. Dan McCoy first faced him, an' in five minutes was on his back on the floor. Then Barney O'Shea, a jolly young Irishman, tackled the champion and went down the same way.

He hed throwed his fourth man, the whole crowd was hoarse with hollerin', an' he was tickled to death with his victory, when some one ups and says: "What's the matter with you tryin' him, Bender? You're about one size."

Bender kind o' hesitated an' I guess would hev refused, if Haydon hadn't o' sneered out: "Wall, I reckon I kin lay a tenderfoot in about half the reglar time."

At this the young feller got up and said he guessed he'd try his muscle anyhow. They was so nigh one size thet the fellers like to 'a' went crazy jest anticipatin' what a match it 'ud be.

Wall, sir, they grappled an' went to work in earnest, twistin' and strainin' like two big sarpents. The crowd kept gettin more an' more excited; those on the outside of the ring craned their necks an' pressed for'ard; those on the inside laid back an' hollered: "Give 'em room; give 'em a show."

But it wasn't no use they jest pressed up until they was packed together like a lot o' sardines.

In the ring the struggle was growin' fiercer an' fiercer; the fighters acted like they was in earnest, their faces was red, their [eyes] they was goin' to bust, an' the sawdust flying from under their feet in a perfec' cloud.

Then, I don't know how it happened, it was done so quick, but one of them went down. Fur a few minutes, in the confusion and dust, no one could tell who it was. But as the men began to git up the crowd saw his face an' a rousin' cheer went up. It was Haydon.

There was a very unpleasant look on his face as he turned an' left the room without a word.

Bender took his vict'ry in a very quiet way, an' the men hed soon furgot the matter turnin' their attention to cards an' dice. 'Bout three o'clock Haydon come in agin, an' begun a loadin' up purty heavy with sperrits. We all begun to expec' mischief, but he laid our fears to rest by goin' out agin without trouble.

"Them's strange actions fur Tom Haydon," says Dan McCoy; an' they was, too.

About sunset we heard a terrible clatter out o' doors an' every man rushed to the door to see what it was.

An' thar, down the road, came Tom Haydon on one o' them devilish little mustangs, brandishin' a gun, right an' left above his head. He'd made his plans well, an' it all flashed on our minds in a second. He knowed that the noise 'ud bring us all out, an' then he would pick out his man easy enough.

We knowed who the doomed man was an' so we didn't take the trouble to git out o' the way fur Tom Haydon was a sure shot an' wouldn't fail to hit the right one.

All of a sudden somethin' mes our gaze, right in the path o' the gallopin' critter; it was Tom Haydon's little gal Bess, only four years old. Right in the path air, an' that pony almost layin' flat in his mad gallop. Every man seemed froze with fear; we give one shout, Tom was blind and deaf to all but one thing. He hed his eyes fixed on Fred Bender, the tenderfoot, never movin' 'em as he bore down on his own child. I would a hid my eyes from the sight but somehow I couldn't. I was jest kind o' fascinated.

Then like a flash we saw a streak o' blue shirt right across the pony's path, a child flyin' away off to one side, a man down under the horse's feet, an' an instant later, "*ping*," went a bullet from Tom Haydon's revolver right into the door post whar Bender had been standin.'

All was confusion fur a minute or so an' then the men went out an' picked pore Bender up. He was hurt purty bad an' a gaspin' hard.

Wall, I never seen a man sober up as Haydon did in all my life. As soon as he could stop the pony, he jumped off an' come a runnin' back. He'd seen what had happened jest at the last moment. "My God!" said he, "he saved my child, my little Bess, an' me a tryin' to kill him." An' then, pushin' the men aside, he took Bender up in his arms as tender as a mother liftin' her sick baby.

He carried him into his own cabin, which was right across the street from the tavern, an' then leavin' his wife to make the pore feller easy, jumped on the pony an' went tearin' away after a doctor.

The first thing the tenderfoot gasped when he opened his eyes was: "Is the kid all right?"

Wall, sir, fur four months Tom Haydon an' his wife nussed that tenderfoot like their own brother an' he furgive Tom jest as if nothin' had happened an' didn't put on no airs 'bout his sacrifice.

The miners purty nigh worshiped him. He stopped his business o' jest assayin' and went to minin' fur all that's out, and to-day you can't git inside the border o' Californy without hearin' o' Fred Bender, president o' the Bender-Haydon Minin' Company. An' it's him that was the tenderfoot.

Little Billy

WHEN CONSUMPTION TOOK ol' Mis' Sanders off she left a pore, little, sickly baby boy, not more'n two year ol' fur her husband to raise. It was a turrible trial to a man workin' like Bill Sanders had to work, to hev a puny, cryin' baby on his hands. Ef it had a be'n one o' these great big strappin' childern thet kin knock about anywheres, it wouldn't a' be'n so bad; but it look purty hard to be hampered with one thet needed tender nussin' all the time.

To a' looked at Bill Sanders, you'd 'a' thought thet he couldn't be tender enough to nuss a sick elephant. He was a great big rough-lookin' feller with a voice like a foghorn an' hands as hard an' horny as a weather-beaten rock.

But somewhere, away down under all the rough shell, he had a heart brimful o' gentleness and kindness. He didn't take no great flarin' way o' showin' it, but you didn't hev to know him long to find it out.

There's some men thet hev to do big things to show how much heart they've got, but he didn't; a body jest naturally seemed to feel it. Fur two or three days arter his mother's death, the little boy didn't do nothin' but holler an' cry all the time, until you'd 'a' thought Bill's soul was almost worried out o' him.

When the fun'l was over an' pore Sally Sanders laid away forever, the women folks gathered to decide which of 'em should take the boy. Wall, you know how women are when there is any good act to be done, they all want to be the one to do it. An' so there was several willin' to take the child. They couldn't decide which of 'em was to hev him, an' so it was agreed thet the offer should be made to Sanders fur all of 'em an' left for him to choose between 'em.

Bill was touched by their kindness, but shook his head in answer to the offer. "No," says he, "Sally told me allus to keep little Bill with me 'cause he was sickly, an' I promised I would; I couldn't break a promise made to my dead wife fur no reason in the world."

"But you can't give the pore little feller the care he orter hev," said Tim Hodge's wife, who hed be'n sent to do the talkin.'

"I'll do the best I kin," answered Bill, "an' thet's all anybody could do."

It wasn't no use to try to shake his determination; what he said he meant an' stuck to. He made the child a little cart in which, wrapped up warm, he hauled him to the mines every day, an' then, stowing him in a safe place he would go on to work, runnin' back every little while to see thet he was gettin' 'long all right.

In spite of all the toys an' things thet Bill raked up, it couldn't help but be lonesome an' tiresome fur the child; but the litter feller seemed to know thet his father was doin' the best he could fur him an' he didn't make much trouble.

At first it was a kind o' funny sight to see the great big man goin' to his work every mornin' draggin' the cart with thet little peaked baby in it. People said that a man wouldn't stand anything like thet very long an' prophesied thet it wouldn't last.

But it did, an' big Bill haulin' the little Bill to work growed to be a common sight. An' how the women went on about him, holdin' him up as a model to their husbands an' pointin' him out as the only true man thet ever lived.

Wall, the air must 'a' done the child good, fur it commenced to grow stronger lookin.' It was wonderful how it filled out, an' Bill got as proud of him as a peacock of his tail. He hed allus be'n kind an' gentle to him, but he hedn't be'n so powerful affectionate.

With his sole care of the child, it hed kinder growed around his heart. His eyes would take on the softest look an' his voice would sink so low an' lovin' when he talked to little Billy thet every action showed how he was bound up in him.

When the boy was seven or eight years ol' a thing turned up thet showed thet Sanders' feelins hedn't changed a bit. A gang o' youngsters broke into the tool house, an' stole a lot o' the men's tools. They wasn't found for a long time, but arter awhile some boys was traced into a cave which was dug in the side of the hill. Two or three men followed an' raided the place, an' there was the tools, everyone of 'em, an' about a dozen young shavers layin' around.

Among 'em was little Billy, big as anybody.

Wall, they bagged every one of 'em an' marched 'em into camp, pretendin' they was a goin' to try 'em. They was as bad skeered a set o' boys as ever you seed 'cause they knowed what happened to thieves when they was ketched 'round there. They was most all a snivelin' an' pleadin' 'cept little Billy. He was game an' went along with his mouth shet as tight as wax.

They hed to come right up past a place where a lot o' the men was standin', laughin' at the sight. In the crowd was Bill Sanders; as his eyes fell on little Billy he jumped for'ard, sayin': "What's the meanin' o' this?"

"Oh, these are the fellers what stole them tools from the tool house an' we're a goin' to make 'em up an' try 'em," says Hank Simms.

"Didn't steal no tools, dad," little Billy bawled out.

His father went up to him and takin' his arm drawed him away from the crowd. Turnin' to Hank he says, in a low, dry voice: "I don't want no such darned foolishness with my boy. He didn't help steal them tools; he says so, an' I'd believe his word again' any of you; there ain't a drop o' lyin' or stealin' blood in his veins."

"Why, it's only fun, Bill," said Hank.

"Fun or what not, I don't like it," and Sanders took little Billy an' went home.

Mebbe Sanders was a little too particular, but every hen knows best how to cover her own chickens.

Boys in them days struck out soon fur themselves, an' when little Billy was about sixteen he left the camp an' went somewheres where he thought he could do better an' make more money. For a time Sanders heerd from him reg'lar an' he was allus a gettin' along well; but by 'n' by the letters commenced fallin' off. An' as he got further an' further away from the ol' man, they got slacker an' slacker ontil they quit entirely.

Not a word could be heerd from him; nobody even knowed where he was. But Sanders didn't worry or take on as you might 'a' expected he would. He was allus calm, for he said he knowed wherever little Billy was he was safe an' doin' well, 'cause he was honest an' willin' to work an' he hed hed good raisin.'

I tell you he hed lots o' faith in thet boy, a good deal more than anybody else hed, fur there was several times when he was in camp thet purty mean tricks was laid at his door, an' thet upon good proof, too; but he always managed to get out of it somehow or other, an' knowin' how his father doted on him, most everybody hated to press a thing against him. There's be'n more boys than one saved trouble thet way. But arter while, little Billy was furgot an' even Sanders himself hed stopped tellin' every listener the good points "o' thet boy Billy." Fact is we hed to furget everything in them rushin' times. The minin' camp hed growed into a town with reg'lar gov'nment an' a court an' jedge thet got in his work on offenders whenever his flourishin' an' expeditious rival Jedge Lynch giv him a chance.

An' there was plenty of work for both of 'em, 'cause every kind of thief under the sun was layin' 'round, waitin' fur a chance to nab the dust o' some onsuspectin' miner. An' now, hoss thieves, had be'n added to the list. Several valuable animals belongin' to different folks in the town hed walked off in a very mysterious manner.

Now, you know, thet is our sore point—hoss thieves!

We hate 'em worse 'n murderers, 'cause they're sneakin'er about their work. Wall, this yere thief was about the cutest one that ever laid fingers on hoss flesh; didn't leave no tracks, seemed to jest pick the animals up an' fly away with 'em.

We come to the conclusion thet it wasn't no gang, but jest one powerful slick man by hisself. No gang could 'a' moved so quiet an' mysterious an' be'n quick at the same time. We tried every way to ketch him, but he was too slick fur us. But at last we got desp'rate an' vowed we'd ketch thet feller ef it took every bit o' dust we hed an' our lives to boot. We studied an' studied to think how we could fix it, an' at last Bill Sanders hisself hit on a plan which we all agreed to.

So the next night seen in his own stable the finest hoss thet a heavy collection taken up amongst us could buy, an' a score o' determined men hid 'round in the dark. Now a really fine hoss draws a hoss thief like a magnet does steel, an' we knowed thet we hed the chap dead sure.

Wall, not a leaf stirred the first night an' we was considerable disappointed, so durin' the follerin' day the horse was driv' around the town to show him off to any watchers thet might be lurkin' about, an' we watched thet night in hopes, but it was like the first, no go. Fur ten solid days we watched without success an' then the men began to drop off, ontil the guard hed be'n entirely broken up.

We believed thet the hoss thief hed left us an' for good too. But I reckon thet chap was even slicker then we thought; fur one night arter we'd growed keerless, Sanders, who was a mite more keerful then the rest of us, heerd the hoss whinny. He was out to the stable in a minute. There was a man beside the hoss; at the sight of him, Sanders darted in but the feller vaulted into the saddle an' lettin' drive a shot thet took Bill in the shoulder, dashed out o' the back door.

Furgittin' the pain of his wound, Sanders was on a mustang an' arter him like a flash, alarmin' the town as he passed through, cryin', "Hoss thief, hoss thief, hoss thief!" Them thet looked out *seen* two hosses gallopin' past, but *heard* only one. The first hoss must 'a' hed his hoofs padded heavy.

It wasn't long before about twenty-five or thirty men hed jined the chase an' wen' gallopin' arter the sound o' the second hoss. But the thief hed a purty good start ahead, an' it was two good hours before even Sanders was sighted. In another hour the crowd overtook him. His face showed pale in the moonlight an' he looked like he could hardly keep his saddle an' his hoss was purty nigh wore out; but there was a sullen determination in the way he urged the pore beast on. Away off in the front a shadow could be seen movin' whenever the foremost rider passed between the moon an' a cluster o' rocks an' now an' then the sound of a hoof strikin' the stony ground could be heard. The hoss hed wore through or throwed off one of his pads.

The sight o' the prey made the men more eager 'n ever an' they spared neither lash nor spur. The hosses staggered an' stumbled under the strain, but thet wasn't the time fur pityin' brutes with a subject fur lynchin' a mile ahead.

So clatter an' dash over short spaces o' level land an' longer tracts o' hilly road, we went; up an' down over the bowlders that blocked our way an' gainin' not more 'n an inch in a hundred feet. When day broke, we was still a-goin'. Steady, steady. A foot at every hundred. Two feet. Three. But our hosses was gone up; they began to slow down. We would lose the gained ground, but we were in shootin' distance. Bill Sanders, who is still in the lead, raises his gun. It is our only chance, so a number follow suit. A report: twelve bullets fly on their mission. The man in advance throws up his arms an' falls back out of his saddle an' the hoss droops away riderless.

We ride up to where the body lay, face upward.

Bill Sanders glances at it an' then gives sech a cry as I never heerd before, an' God grant may never hear again.

"My God!" he screams. "My son; my little Billy!" and flingin' himself from his hoss he drops down beside the body.

How, in one glance, he ever recognized his son Billy in thet bronzed, scarred man, I can't see. I reckon mebbe there's sympathetic chords in the hearts o' parents an' children thet throb when they're brought together.

Like a brute thet laps the wounds of the injured young one, so Sanders fondled the body of his dead son, callin' him by name an' kissin' the bearded face. But the eyes were fast glazin' an' the lips were closed in the last silence.

We would a' taken the body up, but, springin' up, he stood over it like a tiger at bay. "Go 'way, go 'way, leave me alone with the son I hev murdered." An' we hed to obey.

We stood to one side as alone he strapped the sad load to the back o' the stolen hoss, then, mountin' his own an' leadin' the other, silent he led the way into town.

The End of the Chapter

"AND YOU ARE going to be married next week?"

"Yes. For the last half-year we have both known it would be, but it does seem startling, doesn't it?"

"I hope you will be very happy with Helen," she said. "I know you will."

"Helen is a dear girl. We men never half deserve the women we get."

"Wise youth," she said, smiling. "Have you learned that so soon? You give promise of growing into a fairly good husband just before you die."

"Don't be cynical, Margaret: there are times when it sets well on you, but it doesn't to-day, when—"

"I don't want to be cynical, Philip, but the idea possesses me. Widows weep so sorely for their husbands because—because it is only in *articulo mortis* that men show what possibilities of decency there are in them."

"And yet, have I not been pretty decent in this—in this—well—friendship of ours?"

"What a man it is to talk of himself!" she retorted, smilingly.

"But I want to talk of myself, and I want to talk of you, and our past, and of—"

"Our future," she said, significantly.

"Don't," he cried; and he put his hand up as if to ward off a blow.

"It should be very happy for us both," she said. "We are going to marry the ones our hearts have chosen."

"Margaret!" He possessed himself of her hand.

"Don't, Philip, don't; remember next week, and remember that we promised each other the chapter should close to-day." She disengaged her hand from his, and clasped it within the other behind her head. Her arms, so, were between her face and the man at her side.

He sat silent for a while, looking at her, taking in all the magnificent curves of her strong, lithe figure, the exquisite moulding of her arms and hands, the graceful sweep of her limbs in the soft gown she wore. Then he turned his eyes for a moment to the window. It was gray and gloomy outside, with a promise of rain in the air. He shivered, and turned again to her. She had not changed her position. He took hold of her hand again, and drew down her arm. She turned her eyes upon him. They were shining with unshed tears.

"Philip," she said, "have you not promised that the chapter should end to-day?"

He stood up, and looked down into her face, but he did not relinquish her hand.

"Then you do care?" he said.

"I am a conservative," she replied, trying to smile, "and of course I do not like change. Come, let us talk of something else."

"I want to talk of this."

"You are a very obstinate man."

"You are a very strong woman."

"I am as weak as the rest."

"Would that you were weak enough to—"

"Philip, be careful what you say."

"Oh, Margaret, you know what is in my heart."

"Perhaps; but put into words it becomes irrevocable."

"I don't care. I must say it."

"You must not say it. You must not say anything that would make you blush when you look into Helen's eyes. You must not say anything that with calm thought would make you think less of yourself. Don't let me be more loyal to Helen than her betrothed. Don't let me be more loyal to you than you are to yourself."

"Has it all meant nothing to you, then?"

"It has meant much. Our friendship has been very pleasant,—the pleasantest I have ever known. I wish it might have gone on this way,—but—"

"I was too weak to stand the test."

"Listen. When we began to be friends, a few months ago, each of us knew that the other was betrothed. But what of that? We had tastes in common, and found pleasure in each other's society. No harm could come of that. We freely talked to each other of our loved ones. That made us feel secure. Our friendship grew. Helen being away, and Ben frequently absent, we were much together. We furnished entertainment for each other. And the wise old world was shaking its head before we even realized that there was any danger in our association. Well, it has been a pleasant chapter, and we have enjoyed reading it. If there are a few sighs at the end, shall we blame the author?"

"Why need it end?" he asked.

"Now it is ended," she replied.

"Can we not turn back a page?"

"No; in this book we must read right on to finis." She rose. "Good-by," she said.

"Must it be good-by?"

She thought a moment. "Well, no; not necessarily. If you will remember that this chapter is ended, then it is only *auf wiedersehen*."

"But shall we not begin another?"

"Yes, when Helen is here to read it with us."

He bowed and went.

"Poor Philip," she said, as she watched him go down the steps; and with a rush of tears, she cried, "and poor me."

She wept silently, but long, as if her heart was overcharged; then, drying her eyes, she said, "And now I must write to Ben."

Lafe Halloway's Two Fights

THE WINTER HAD been one of extreme spiritual activity in the little town which claimed the Halloways as citizens. There were Martin Halloway, an honest and sturdy carpenter, his wife and their son, Lafe, or Lafayette, as he was written in the great family Bible. Martin and his gentle wife Annie had for a number of years been steady and devoted members of the little Methodist church, whose chapel reared its quiet front near the center of the town, and it had long been the hope of their hearts that their boy might come into the same communion with them. But, besides the ordinary admonitions of the Christian parent, they never strove with their son or asked of him the thing that was in their hearts.

"Let him be fully persuaded in his own mind," said Martin Halloway, when he and his wife talked the matter over as they often did.

"I would rather see him remain out of the Church than go in it out of a sense of obedience or even respect for the words of his parents." And the gentle wife had always agreed, only she would add: "But it will come all in God's own time."

Great, then, was the joy in that household when Lafe was enrolled among the number of converts. The mother's face was transfigured with an unusual radiance as she held her boy to her bosom and with quiet tears thanked God for the safety of her son. She fancied that she saw a new light in his eyes. The father was undemonstrative, but his pride showed in his very step, as father and son went their way together.

Lafe was a strapping young fellow of twenty. He had learned his father's trade and worked side by side with him day after day. As he went to and from the shop there was another woman's eye besides his mother's that watched him with new love. It was Alice Staniland, who was to preside over his home some day, and no one had been happier than this demure little lassie over Lafe's entrance upon the spiritual life.

The soft winter was succeeded by an early spring, and even as early as March the church-goers had begun to prepare for the event of the coming month, when the probation of the new converts would be over and they would be accepted into the full communion of the Church. It was looked forward to by both saint and sinner with equal eagerness; the former with the ardent desire to be endowed with all the churchly powers, the latter with a curiosity to see how many would "hold out"; and never was the church more happy over the conquest of a soul than these over the capture of one "backslider." When one had repudiated his vows of faith, he was always more defiant and aggressive than those who had never made any pretensions to grace.

This spring, through various weaknesses, several had already fallen by the wayside before the term of probation had ended, and their only desire seemed to be to make the lives of their former companions in grace miserable. One of these, a great, heavy-faced fellow named Tom Randall, took Lafe Halloway as his especial target, and on every occasion fired at him taunts and jeers. But the young man went his way unmoved in the pride of conscious rectitude.

Randall never offered his insults in the presence of any of the older or more staid members of the community, for he feared their rebuke, and, too, from them he had nothing to win. They were long and hard tried in the faith.

But before his own satellites he was boldness itself. The corner grocery store was a great gathering place for these fellows, and woe unto the luckless victim who had to pass the place alone. He must go through a perfect fire of raillery.

It is not an easy thing to be the target for the scorn of the petty scoffers of a small town. To say that they are ignorant only means that the weapons of ridicule they use are more blunt and they bruise rather than cut. A cut smarts, but a bruise aches and grows black.

Many a day Lafe went home with clenched teeth and white face. But he made no sign. His mother saw and understood, but she kept her counsel. The ultimate triumph which she believed her son capable of achieving was worth fighting for. If the father understood he also held his peace. The boy had all of the vigorous energy and animal strength which are the attributes of his age and condition in life, and he would have liked nothing better than to turn on his tormentors and give them the thrashing which they deserved. But this he knew to be the very concession which they demanded of him, and so he held his hand.

However, one day, as he was coming down the street toward the grocery, he spied Alice Staniland just ahead of him, and he quickened his steps to overtake her. The usual crowd was standing and lounging about in front. As Alice neared them, Tom Randall, grown desperate with constant resistance, stepped out and spoke to her. Lafe saw the girl shrink away and burst into tears as she hurried on. In a moment, with white face and compressed lips he was in front of Randall.

"What did you say to her?" he asked breathlessly, as the crowd of gazers gathered around.

"None o' yer bus'ness, Mr. Hymn-singer, you hear." There were no more words. Lafe's fist shot out and delivered a blow upon the scoffer's face that staggered him. Another followed hard upon it. Then Randall righted himself and began to reciprocate. He was no mean antagonist. They clinched. They fell and for a few moments that seemed like hours to the tense expectations of the watching crowd, the battle wavered. Then the mass upon the ground began to assume definiteness and it was seen that Lafe was on top. He did not strike his antagonist again, but pressing his face down into the dust, cried hoarsely, "Eat dirt, you beast, eat dirt, and learn to let women alone."

The crowd, ever with the strong and victorious, now jeered and taunted its fallen chief and even danced in the fullness of its delight. Suddenly there was a hush and Lafe felt a hand laid upon his shoulder and looked up to meet the grieving eyes of the old Methodist minister, whose gentle words had led him into the fold of the Church.

"Come with me, my son," said the old man, and his voice was very gentle, but oh, so sorrowful. The boy arose and turned away with his pastor. His antagonist made no attempt to follow him or renew the fight. He slunk into the grocery unobserved, for the crowd was wonderingly watching the old man and the young man as they went away together, and for once it was silent and not altogether comfortable.

"I guess he's backslid at last," said one.

"I ain't so sure about that," another replied. "He wasn't a-fightin' on his own account, an' besides he never cussed none." So, wavering between opinions as to the spiritual status of Lafe Halloway, the crowd broke up into little knots of three and four and so went its way.

The fire had not sufficiently left Lafe's blood for him fully to realize the equivocal position in which he had placed himself. For a time he walked on in silence, which was finally broken in upon by the preacher's voice. "I am sorry," he said, "so sorry, for I had hoped and expected much of you." These words brought the boy to himself, but he did not attempt to excuse his action. He simply told the straightforward, unbiased truth as it was. "Before I had time to think what to do, I had done it," he said, "but I don't know that it would have been different even with thought, you know I—we—our family, think a lot of Allie, and it was awful to have that—" His lips tightened again and the blood mounted to his forehead.

The old minister offered no admonition, no advice. He only repeated, "I am sorry, so sorry." But the pressure that he gave the boy's hand as he left him at the gate was warm and tender and fatherly. Perhaps his mind had gone back to his own youth and to the woman that had for a few years brightened his life, but was now sleeping at the foot of an old moss-grown stone in the little church-yard. Memories like this will not let a man be hard.

When he entered the house Lafe saw by the look on his mother's face that the news had preceded him down the street. She and his father sat at supper.

"I know you both know all, mother. Gossip runs fast in this town," he said.

"Yes, my son, I know all; but I hope that you didn't hurt him and that you are not hurt either—physically," she added, sorrowfully.

"Oh, we're both all right that way," he returned. He sat down to the table, but he couldn't eat for the lump in his throat. "I am sorry it happened," he went on, "but you know how it was, mother. It's kind o' hard for a fellow to stand by and see his girl insulted, and then Allie is such a quiet little body. Nobody but a brute would think of troubling her." He could say no more, but, man that he was, burst into sobs.

"My poor boy, my poor boy," cried the mother, "you have been sorely tried." Martin Halloway rose and went over to his son and laid his hands upon his shoulders. "Look, up boy," he said, "you did right, and I'd have done the same thing in your place if it had been me. With a man's arms and a man's feelin's you couldn't have done anything else. I don't believe that the Lord wants his lovers to be walked over rough-shod by the children of the devil. I do believe, tho, that 'Christian soldier' means Christian soldier in every sense of the word, and if the man that raises his hand to protect a woman sins against the right, I for one can't see it."

Lafe was braced by his father's words, and comforted by the fact that there was no reproof in his mother's face as she smiled and said: "Don't you think, Martin, it would be better to let Lafe fight his own fight, search his own heart and find out what is demanded of him?"

"You are always a safe adviser, Annie," said her husband. "Lafe, I've given you a few points in the war, but fight the rest out for yourself."

And Lafe determined to.

The fight was not long in beginning. All that night the young man's mind was in a turmoil of doubt. What had he done? Where did he stand? To what degree was he culpable? These thoughts harassed him and kept him tossing, sleepless, upon his bed, wrestling with his doubts as of old Jacob wrestled with the angel. The morning brought with it no decision and tired, silent and disturbed he went to work. His father had kept his promise and was letting him fight his battle alone.

The night for class-meeting came around, and Mr. and Mrs. Halloway, as was their wont, began early their preparations to go, but Lafe did not move from his chair. Seven o'clock came, and with his hand on the door Martin Halloway turned to his son and asked, "Not coming to class-meeting, eh?" "Not to-night, father," answered the boy, and his parents passed out.

Lafe had been the shining light of the class-room since his conversion. The older members were wont to greet him with a murmured "Bless the young soldier," or "Help him grow in grace," as he rose to recount his brief experience of the Christian life. He thought of all this, and of the pleasure he took in the meetings and then asked himself if in his first real battle he must fall out of the ranks. Once he rose, took up his hat and stood irresolute. Then he laid it down again, sinking into his chair and covering his face with his hands. When his parents came home, he had gone to bed. They could not tell him of the expectant look in the old minister's face as he caught sight of them, and of the look of disappointment which followed as he noticed the vacancy in their pew. Nor could they tell him of the tender prayer in which the old man pleaded earnestly, almost plaintively, for light and guidance to the young of the flock. But that night at their own bedside they remained longer upon their knees, and when they arose and looked into each other's faces, the eyes of both were moist.

It was a couple of days after this that, as he was going down the street, Lafe saw Tom Randall coming directly toward him. Here was the place where a decision must be made, and at once. Should he speak to him or not? Was it his duty to speak? Into his mind flashed the words: "If thy right hand offend thee, cut it off." How many there are who, having been wronged or having wronged some one and being without the grace either to forgive or ask forgiveness, have taken refuge in this sentence. Lafe did not feel entirely satisfied and still undecided, he raised his eyes, but Randall had also seen him coming and, shrinking from the encounter, turned out of his way. The young man breathed freer, although in his heart he knew that the ordeal had not been passed, but avoided, the question not settled, but postponed.

Meanwhile Communion Sunday was drawing painfully near. Indeed, it was the last week before the day. As the time went on Lafe's distress was visibly increased. It was about this period that he was walking with Alice one evening, when she suddenly said: "Lafe, I can't keep still any longer. I have been trying so hard not to speak, but my heart is too full of sorrow." She hesitated for a moment and then proceeded with trembling voice, "I know that I am the cause of all your troubles and it pains me to think of it. I feel as if I were guilty of a willful sin. If it had not been for me you would never have struck Tom Randall, but," laying her hand on his arm in a sudden burst of admiration, "it was noble of you." She stopped again and blushed. "I don't mean quite that," she said, "for you know, Lafe, it was very wrong, but then it was so brave and manly, and—and—it was—for me." The "for me" was hesitating, but very gentle and her hand stole into his restfully and trustfully.

A great glow came round Lafe's heart. His bosom swelled and he felt that for this he could thrash a score of bullies. "It wasn't anything great for me to do," he replied, "any fellow would have done it that didn't want to see him 'pick on' you."

Alice saw that her words had not had the effect which she had intended to produce. She must not let him feel that he had done right.

"I had so hoped, though, Lafe, that we would be admitted to full membership together, and now it is all through me that your trouble has come. I am so sorry. Next Sunday is the day, and we were all to be so happy—then this had to occur! Oh, you don't know how I have suffered since."

"You have suffered, Alice? Suffered about me?"

"Yes, Lafe, because it was all my fault."

"It wasn't your fault. It was just the fault of my own heart, and its lack of grace. I struck Tom Randall for you and here I've been hurting you worse than he ever could. I'm a brute and a great stubborn-hearted sinner."

"Lafe, Lafe," cried the girl, "you must not say that. You are not a sinner, you—"

"Yes I am," he said, "but you shan't suffer any more on my account. I see as I have never seen before. I have been too proud to do the right thing."

Alice said nothing, but there were tears of thankfulness in her eyes, for, as she parted with Lafe at her own gate she saw the light of a new determination in his face.

As soon as he had left Alice, the young man turned his steps toward the grocery where his altercation with Randall had taken place. The usual loungers were there, inside and out. The place was crowded and dingy. The smells of kerosene, tobacco, mackerel and red herring were struggling for supremacy. As Lafe stepped into the place the men looked with curiosity at his set face. Some of the outsiders followed him in. Tom Randall was seated carelessly on a barrel at one end of the place. A startled expression came into his face as he saw Lafe coming straight toward him and he half rose. All talk had suddenly hushed. There was quiet except for the sputtering of the yellow oil-lamp.

"I have come in to ask you to forgive me, Tom Randall," said Lafe, offering his hand, "for my action the other day. I was wrong, all wrong, both as a man and a Christian, and I am sorry for what I did. Will you shake hands with me and be friends?"

Tom Randall paused a moment. He was so taken aback that he could not speak at first. Then he slowly took the offered hand and said, "That's all right, Lafe, I guess I was the most wrong." Some one wanted to raise a cheer, but the deeper feelings of the rest repressed him. Lafe went on speaking: "I am going to make public confession of my wrong at general class Friday night. If it will satisfy you more, Tom, come."

"Oh, you needn't do that," began the other, but Lafe stopped him with a gesture. "I feel that I owe it to the church whose name I disgraced," he said, and shaking again the hand of his ertswhile enemy, he passed out amid the silence of the crowd, and went home feeling happier over his new victory.

It took but a short time for the news to get abroad that at the meeting on Friday night Lafe Halloway intended to make public confession of his sin, and it caused great stir. The incident of his altercation with Tom Randall was known far and near in the town, and speculation had been rife as to what stand the young convert would take. When it was known that it was all to be settled thus, and that he was to ask the church's forgiveness, the meeting of Friday sprung into a sudden prominence which tried issue as to popularity with Sunday's events. People could hardly wait the natural course of time, and if the hours could have been pushed up so that they would have tumbled over each other it would certainly have been done in that town.

Now that Lafe was once set in his purpose he asked advice of no one, but went on as if nothing had happened or were about to happen. He told his father and mother what he had done and what he intended to do, and received their quiet approval. Good, sensible, common folk, they made him neither a hero nor a martyr.

Well, Friday night came and with it a crowd to the little Methodist chapel. There were the devout, who always came for a renewal of their vows and the interchange of religious experiences. But the number of these was augmented by the addition of many mere curiosity seekers drawn thither by the hope of a sensation. The face of the gentle pastor was stern with rebuke as he looked over the assembly and divined the cause of the presence of many. Some must have inwardly at least winced when he prayed that all who were there might have come with right thoughts in their minds and right purposes in their hearts.

The meeting proceeded as usual. Sweet hymns were sung and interesting testimony given, but on the part of the crowd there was a tense waiting. The evening was drawing to its close and Lafe Halloway had not spoken yet and anxiety was giving way to disappointment. Maybe, after all, he wouldn't say anything. Perhaps he had backed down. There he sat, quietly between his father and mother, who had both spoken. Just as disappointment was being succeeded by disgust, he rose and the hush that followed was painful. But the boy's face, turned toward the minister, was quiet and his voice was calm. "My brothers and sisters," he said, "I have come to ask your prayers and your forgiveness in weakness. I have sinned. Pray for me, and forgive me, as I know our Heavenly Father has done." There were a few quiet "amens."

The old pastor rose and said, "What the Lord has given we cannot withhold; let us join in singing 'Praise God, from Whom All Blessings Flow.'"

The congregation rose and sang the doxology with a will. The benediction was pronounced, and the meeting was out. It had been all so brief, so quiet. The curiosity seekers went away feeling that they had been cheated of a sensation that rightfully belonged to them and they resented it.

To his credit let it be said that Tom Randall was not present.

The Halloways that night were a happy family. "Ah, Lafe," said his mother, with tears, "this second fight was the hardest, but oh, it was best!"

Martin Halloway was beyond speech.

It had been the especial desire of both Mrs. Halloway and Lafe that he be immersed, and on Sunday morning as he went down into the water with the glory of perfect joy and peace upon his face, with the low sung hymn ringing in his ears, there was no dove that alighted upon him. There was no voice that descended from Heaven, but in the heart of a moist-eyed mother was running these words, old as the Gospel of Jesus itself: "This is my beloved son in whom I am well pleased!"

The Emancipation of Evalina Jones

DOUGLASS STREET WAS alive with people, and astir from one dirty end to the other. Flags were flying from houses, and everything was gay with life and color. Every denizen of Little Africa was out in the street. That is, every one except Evalina Jones, and even she came as far as the corner, when with banners flying, and the sound of the colored band playing "'Rastus on Parade," the "Hod-Carriers' Union," bright in their gorgeous scarlet uniforms, came marching down. It was a great day for Little Africa, the 22d of September, and they were celebrating the emancipation of their race. The crowning affair of the day was to be this picnic of the "Hod-Carriers' Union," at the fair grounds where there was to be a balloon ascension, dancing, feasting and fireworks, with a speech by the Rev. Mr. Barnett, from Greene County, a very famous orator, who had been in the legislature, and now aspired to be a Bishop.

Evalina looked on with eyes that sparkled with the life of the scene, until the last of the pageant had passed, and then the light died out of her face and she hurried back to her home as she saw a man coming toward her up the street. She was bending over her wash-tub when he came into the house.

"Got any money, Evalina?" he asked, leering at her.

"I got fifty cents, Jim, but what do you want with that?" she replied.

"Nevah you mind what I want with it, give it to me."

"But Jim, that's all I got to go to the picnic with, an' I been hu'yin' thoo so I could git sta'ted."

"Picnic," he said "picnic, I'll picnic you. You ain't goin' a step f'om this house. What's the mattah with you, ain't you got that washin' to finish?"

"Yes, but I kin get throo in time, an' I want to go Jim, I want to go. You made me stay home last yeah, an' yeah befo', and I'm jes' the same ez a slave, I am."

"You gi' me that money," he said menacingly. Evalina's hand went down into the pocket of her calico dress, and reluctantly drew forth a pitiful half dollar.

"Umph," said her worse half. "This is a pretty looking sum fu' you to have, pu'tendin' to wo'k all the time," and he lurched out of the door.

Evalina stopped only long enough to wipe a few tears from her eyes, and then she went stolidly on with her washing. She had been married to Jim for five years, and for that length of time he had bullied her, and made her his slave. She had been a bright, bustling woman, but he had killed all the brightness in her and changed her bustling activity into mere stolid slavishness. Cheerfully she bore it at first, for a little child had come to bless her life. But when, after two pain-ridden years, the little one had passed away, she took up her burden sullenly, and without relief. People knew that Jim abused her, but she never complained to them; she was close-mouthed and patient. The very firmness with which she set her mouth when things went particularly hard, indicated that she might have beat her husband at his own game, had she tried. But somehow she never tried. There was a remarkable reserve force about the woman, but it needed something strong, something thrilling, to stir it into action.

Now and again, as she bent over the tub, her tears fell and mingled with the suds. They fell faster as the image of the little grave, which she had worked so hard to have digged outside the confines of Potter's Field, would arise in her mind. Then a tap came at her door.

"Come in," she said. A woman entered, bright in an array of cheap finery.

"Howdy, Evalina," she said.

"Howdy, yo'se'f, Ca'line," was the response.

"Oh, I middlin.' Ain't you goin' to the picnic?"

"No, I reckon I ain't. I got my work to do. I ain't got no time fu' picnics."

"Why, La, chile, this ain't no day fu' wo'k—Celebration Day! Why, evahbody's goin'; I even see ol' Aunt Maria Green hobblin' out wid huh cane, an' ol' Uncle Jimmy Hunter."

"I reckon they got time," said Evalina; "I ain't."

She looked the woman over with an unfriendly eye. She knew that this creature who made of life so light and easy a thing, stood between her and any joy that she might have found in her bare existence. She knew that Jim liked Caroline Wilson, and compared his wife unfavorably with her. She looked at the flashy ribbons and the brilliant hat, and then involuntarily glanced down at her own shabby gown, torn and faded and suds-splashed, and an anger, the heat of which she had never known before, came into her heart. Her throat grew dry and throbbed, but she said huskily,

"'Taint fu' me to go to picnics, it's fu' nice ladies what live easy, an' dress fine. I mus' wo'k an' dig an' scrub."

"Humph," said the other, "of co'se there's a diffunce in people."

"Well, that's one thing I kin thank Gawd fu'," said Evalina, with grim humor.

Caroline Wilson bridled. "I hope you ain't th'owin' out no slurs at me, Evalina Jones, cause I wants you to know I's a lady, myse'f."

"I ain't th'owin' out no slurs at nobody," said Evalina, slowly. "But all I kin say is thet ef that shoe fits you, put it on and waih it."

Her visitor was angry, and she showed it. She stood up, and the spirit of battle was strong in her. But she gave a glance first at her finery, and then at the strong arms which her hostess had placed akimbo as she looked at her, and she decided not to bring matters to an issue.

"Well, of co'se," temporized Caroline, "I'd like to see you go, but it ain't none o' my business. I allus got along wid my po' hu'ban' w'en he was livin.'"

"Oh, I ain't 'sputin' that, I ain't 'sputin' that. They ain't no woman that knows you goin' 'ny you got wunnerful pow'rs fu' handlin' men."

"Well, I does know how to keep what I has."

"Yes, an' you knows how to git what you hasn't." The light was growing greatly in Evalina's eyes, and Caroline saw it. She wasn't a coward, not she. But she looked at her finery again. It did look so flimsy and delicate to her eyes; then she said, "I mus' be goin', goo'-bye."

"Goo'-bye. Well, ef I didn't have a min' to frail that 'ooman, I ain't hyeah," and Evalina went back to her work with a shaking head and a new spirit.

Some instinct drew her to the door, and feeling that she might at least avail herself of a little breathing space, she walked as far as the corner of the now entirely deserted street. It was good that she had come, for the sight that she saw there aroused the life in her that had lain dead for the five years that she had been Jim's wife. She stood at the corner, and gazed down at the street that ran at right angles. Her arms unconsciously went akimbo, and she grinned a half-mouthed grin, showing the white gleam of her upper teeth like a dog when someone has robbed him of his precious bone.

"Oom—hoomph, Ca'line," she said, "oom—humph, Jim, I caught you." There was no shade of the anger she felt in her heart expressed in her tones. They were dry, hard and even, but she grinned that dog-like grin which boded no good to Jim and Caroline, who, all unconscious of it, walked on down the street towards the Fair Grounds.

She was done by eleven o'clock. Then she put on the best dress she had, and even that best was shabby, for Jim "needed" most of her money, and went up town to see Mrs. Wharton, for whom she worked. Mrs. Wharton was a little woman, with a very large spirit.

"Why, Evalina," she said, when she saw the black woman, "why on earth aren't you at the picnic?"

"That's jes' what I come hyeah to talk to you about," was the reply.

"Well, do let me hear! If you didn't have the money, why didn't you come to me? That's just what I say about you, you never open your mouth when you need anything. You know I'd have helped you out," rushed on the little lady.

"'Taint that, 'taint that," replied Evalina, "I'd a spoke to you this week. 'Taint the money, Mis' Wharton, it's Jim."

"Jim, Jim, what's that great hulking lazybones got to do with your going to the picnic?"

"He say I ain't to go."

"Ain't to go! Well, we'll show him whether you're to go or not."

At this sign of encouragement, Evalina brightened up. "Mis' Wharton," she burst out, "you don't know what I been bearin' f'om that man, an' I ain't nevah said nothin', but I cain't hol' in any longer. I ain't got a decent thing to wear, an' this very day, Jim tuk my las' cent o' money, an' walked off to the Fair Grounds wid another ooman."

"Come into the sewing-room, Evalina," said Mrs. Wharton with sudden energy. "You'll go to that picnic, and if that brute interferes with you, I'll put him where the rain won't touch him."

In the sewing-room, where Mrs. Wharton led the bewildered and delighted Evalina, there was wonderful letting out of seams, piecing of short skirts, and stretching over of scanty folds. But the washer-woman came out from there smiling and happy, well dressed and spirited. Say not that clothes have nothing to do with the feeling of the average human being. She felt that she could meet a dozen

Jims and out-face them all. The day of her awakening had come, and it had been like the awakening of a young giantess.

Jim was enjoying himself in a quadrille with Caroline when Evalina reached the dancing hall. He was just in the midst of a dashing farandole, much to the delight of the crowd, when he caught a glimpse of his wife arrayed in all her glory; he suddenly stopped. The people about thought he had paused for applause, and they gave it to him generously, but he failed to repeat his antics. He was surprised out of a desire for their approval. He gazed at his slave, and she, his slave no longer, gazed back at him calmly. For the rest of that quadrille he proved a most spiritless partner, and at its close Caroline, with a toss of her head, yielded herself to some more desirable companion. Then, with a surprise which he could not suppress, struggling for expression on his lowering brow, Jim went over to Evalina.

"What you doin' out hyeah?" he said roughly.

"Enjoyin' myse'f, like you is," replied Evalina.

"Didn't I tell you not to come?"

"What diffunce do yo' tellin' make?"

"I show you what diffunce my tellin' make," he said threateningly.

"You ain't goin' to show me not a pleg-goned thing," was the reply which startled him out of his senses, as Evalina started away on the arm of a partner, who had come to claim her for the next dance. Jim leaned up against a post to get his breath. He had expected Evalina to be scared, and she was not. There was some mistake, surely. This was not the Evalina whom he had known and married. Suddenly all of his traditions had been destroyed, and his mind reached out for something to grasp and hold to, and found only empty air. Meanwhile his wife, all her youthful lightness seeming to have come back to her, was whirling away in the mazes of the dance, stepping out as he had seen her step, when she had charmed him years ago. He stood and looked at her dully. He hadn't even energy enough to seek another partner and so show his resentment.

When the dance was over, Jim went up to Evalina and said, shamefacedly, "Well, sence you're out hyeah, folks are goin' to 'spec' us to dance togethah, I reckon?"

"Don't you min' folks," she said, "you jes' disapp'int 'em. Thaih's Ca'line ovah thaih waitin' fu' you," and she bowed graciously to a robust hod-carrier, who was on the other side asking "fu' de pleasure."

Jim could stand it no longer. He wandered out of the dance hall, and walked down by the horse stables alone, thinking of the change that had come to Evalina. He felt grieved, and a great wave of self-pity surged over him. His wife wasn't treating him right. He was a very much ill-used man.

Then it was time for the speaking, and he went back to the stand, to find his recreant wife the center of a number of women-folk, drawn about her by the unaccustomed fineness of her quiet gown. She was chatting, as he remembered she had chatted before he had discouraged all lightness of talk in her. When the speaker began there was no applause readier than her own. The Rev. Mr. Barnett was a very witty man. In fact, it was his wit, rather than his brains or his morals, that had sent him to the legislature; and when he scored a good point, Jim heard her laugh ring out, clear, high and musical. He could not help but wonder. It dazed him. Evalina had not laughed before since her little one had died, and when the speaking was over she was on the floor again, without a glance for him.

"That's the way with women," he told himself. "Hyeah I is, walkin' 'roun' hyeah all alone, an' she don't pay no mo' 'tention to me then if I was a dog." So he wandered over to the place where they were selling drinks, but they would not give him credit there, and feeling worse abused than ever, he went back to stand a silent witness of his wife's pleasure.

Evalina did not approve of remaining until after dark at the Fair Grounds, when the rougher element began to come in, so she left before Jim. She had finished her supper, and was sitting at the door when he came home. He passed her sullenly and went into the house, where he dropped into a chair. She was humming a light tune and paid no attention to him. Finally he said:

"You treated me nice to-day, didn't you? Dancin' 'roun', without payin' no 'tention to me, an' you my own lawful wife!"

This was too much for Evalina, it was too unjust. She got up and faced him, "Yo' own lawful wife," she said, "I don't reckon you thought o' that this mornin' when you tuk my las' cent, an' went out thaih wid Ca'line Wilson. Yo' lawful wife! You been treatin' me lak a wife, ain't you? This is the fust 'Mancipation Day I've had since I ma'ied you, but I want you to know I'se stood all I'se goin' to stan' f'om you, an' evah day's goin' to be 'Mancipation Day aftah this."

Jim was aghast. Rebellion cowed him. He wanted to be ugly, but he was crushed.

"I don't care nothin' 'bout Ca'line Wilson," he said.

"An' I don't care nothin' 'bout you," she retorted.

Jim's voice trembled. This was going too far. "That's all right, Evalina," he said, "that's all right. Mebbe I ain't no angel, but that ain't no way to talk to me; I's yo' husban.'" He was on the verge of maudlin tears. Somewhere he had found credit, and his conquered condition softened Evalina.

"You ain't been very keerful how you talk to me," she said in an easier tone, "But thaih's one thing suttain, aftah this you got to walk straight,—you hyeah me! Want some supper?"

"Yes," said Jim humbly.

The Lion Tamer

MRS. DE COURCEY-HARTWELL—hyphen Hartwell, if you please—was a patron of the arts. Of course, envious people said she was a lion hunter; but this statement may be taken with a grain of salt when it is considered that those who made it were just on the outer edge, in fact, on the very fringe of that society of which the De Courcey-Hartwells formed the brilliant and resplendent center.

It is quite true that the lady in question had a somewhat inordinate fancy for people who had done something. But much may be forgiven one who has good manners, a better cook and a surpassing cellar. When, added to all this, one's family has been wealthy for a half-century—twenty years puts an American out of the class of the *nouveau riche*—all the arrows of criticism are turned.

The young men who went to Mrs. De Courcey-Hartwell's lectures, literary evenings and strange, unaccountable musicals were a little prone to laugh over the affairs; for a brief moment to envy the lion his share of the girls' adoring attention, and then to wander off to the smoking room, whence they would emerge, after the program, to congratulate their hostess on the success of her entertainment.

This devoted patron of the arts was not only fair, but was wise for the thirty-eight years to which she owned, and she was not fooled. She used to say to Archie Courtney, who was a famous shirker: "Ah, never mind, Archie, if the mental pabulum I have provided was not to your taste; take heart, supper is now on." So it came to pass that they separated her foibles from herself, and laughed at them, but never at her.

Mrs. De Courcey-Hartwell's husband was in leather, as his father and his grandfather—he had a grandfather—had been before him. He looked on complacently at his wife's artistic endeavors, ever ready to pay the bills, which, whatever the catechism may say, is man's highest duty, especially if that man be a husband. Some malicious gossips said that they were still in love with each other after fifteen years of married life. But most of their acquaintances were charitable enough to give them the benefit of the doubt, even though the fact that the husband enjoyed himself at his own home looked dark. Perhaps, however, it was only a pose, just because they were rich enough to be odd.

"WELL, WHAT HAS our hostess on for tonight?" asked Forsythe Brandon of Archie Courtney as they went bowling up the street; "is it a reformed burglar, a captured Mahatma or an African Prince?"

"Oh, chuck it!" said Archie, scornfully. "Why, old man, you're talking in your sleep."

"It can't be, it can't be; oh, don't tell me that it is a party without a lion!"

"Certainly not. Didn't you read your card?"

"No, I just glanced at it and saw that it was the De Courcey-Hartwells', knew that there would be something good to eat, cried 'My tablets, my tablets!' and here I am."

"Glutton."

"Oh, most worthy exemplar!"

Archie laughed.

"Well, it's a real card this time. We're invited to meet that new writer who has been making such a stir. Worthington is his name."

"Whew!" whistled Brandon; "you don't say! Why, I thought he was playing the high and mighty, scorning society and all that!"

"I suppose he has been, but they say his appearance tonight is all Tom Van Kleek's doing. He and Tom are as thick as thieves."

"A strange pair."

"I don't know whether it's the author's liking for the Van or for the man."

"Possibly the Van."

"I don't know; Van Kleek's rather a white chap."

Brandon murmured something about Whitechapel, but Archie could not countenance the remark, and immediately froze into unconsciousness.

EXCEPT FOR Tom Van Kleek it seems hardly possible that Worthington and Mrs. De Courcey-Hartwell could have met, the man and the woman were so dissimilar in character.

Worthington had come down from Canada a few years before, when his books began to succeed in the United States. He made good acquaintances, but went out very little. There was something of the freedom and breeziness of his own woods about him—something charming but untamable—and he did not talk about his ART. He loved nothing quite so much as to get into a disreputable smoking-jacket, through the pocket of which the fire from his old brier had burned a volcanic-looking hole, and to loll in slippered ease alone with a book or with a few choice spirits.

He did not pose, or seem to pose, save that he wore a great shock of unruly black hair. When his friends twitted him about this he told them, with a laugh, that he was "knot pated," and did not dare to wear his hair short. They smiled, and in revenge he had his hair cut, after which a committee waited upon him to beg him not to do it again. The chairman of this committee plainly told him that he looked like a phrenologist's specially prepared subject, and they were all sorry for two weeks. From that time his hair went unmolested and unremarked.

He was a sociable fellow, outside of society, easy and gracious. The boys called him Dick, but he was Richard Barry Worthington under his stories, poems and articles and on the title pages of the books that had made him famous. Literary men put in all the name they can, presumably to add weight to whatever they offer the heartless editor.

It was Dick, rather than Richard Barry, who entered Mrs. De Courcey-Hartwell's drawing room with Tom Van Kleek on the night when a few friends had been invited to meet him. Forsythe Brandon was standing beside Helen Archer.

"Heavens!" he exclaimed, "the man is well dressed!"

"Why, why not?"

"And he hasn't stumbled over his feet once."

"Mr. Brandon, aren't you ashamed of yourself?"

"Not in the least. Just look at that bow; and he didn't forget to speak to his hostess."

"I think you are very silly, and I do think he is in very good form."

"That's just it; that's what I resent. Don't you know it's very bad form for a genius to be good form? He might, at least, have respected tradition enough to be shabby and have red hands—" And he sighed tragically.

Helen laughed, and moved away.

Much later in the evening Tom Van Kleek wandered disconsolately in from the smoking room, where the lion had taken refuge as in his lair; someone had mentioned a reading, and he had incontinently fled.

"What's the matter, Tom?" asked Millicent Martin. "You look like a hired mourner at a funeral."

"Don't joke, Millicent. I'm in an awful fix. You know I am partly responsible for Worthington's being here. But I'm afraid I've offended both him and our hostess. Everyone is expecting him to read something. Mrs. De Courcey-Hartwell sends me to feel him on the subject, and he absolutely refuses to do a thing."

"In other words," laughed Millicent, "the lion refuses to roar."

"Quite so."

"Where is he?"

"In the smoking room, yarning it with a lot of fellows."

"Oh, well, don't be disheartened. I'll help you out."

"Can you?"

"We'll try. Can you get him in? Say there is to be some reading. I'll do the rest. Mrs. De Courcey-Hartwell shall not be disappointed."

Millicent's eyes were twinkling as she made her way toward her hostess, and Tom Van Kleek went back into the smoking room with hope in his heart.

"Say, old man," he addressed Worthington, "come in with me. There's to be some doings, and they'll expect you. Oh, that's all right," he said, in answer to a questioning look; "they're not going to call on you to read."

"All right, I'll go, if I'm to be entertained," the author replied, bluntly, but with a smile in his eyes.

There was quite a little flutter when he re-entered the drawing room—the complacent sound of rustling silks.

The hostess was always very simple in her announcements. She said now only: "Miss Millicent Martin has kindly consented to recite for us."

There was faint patter of applause and a few disappointed looks. It was well that Worthington did not see the roguish look in Millicent's eyes as she began:

"I know that I am very daring, but in honor of the guest whom our hostess has so kindly invited us to meet"—here she bowed slightly to Worthington—"I will recite his exquisite poem, 'The Troubadour.'"

Worthington groaned in spirit, but his escape was cut off.

Millicent began. Her elocution was—well, bad; oh, but it was bad, and the author almost wept. When she was half through, he whispered, in an agonized voice: "Oh, Tom, Tom, don't let her do it again! I'll do anything; tell them I'll read. I'll do anything, but don't let that girl do it again!"

Van Kleek beamed. "Awfully good of you, old man!" he said, but Worthington only sighed.

When Millicent was done it fell to Van Kleek's lot to inform the assembled guests of the author's condescension. Then Worthington rose. He read well always, but tonight he was magnificent in his fury. He was defending himself against the insinuation of insipidity that the girl's interpretation had put upon his work, and all the fire and earnestness of his nature went into his rendition of the lines. The women from the halls and the men from the smoking room crowded the doorways, and there was a storm of applause as he sat down.

"I have always maintained that you should be called 'Militant,'" whispered Van Kleek as Millicent passed him.

As for Worthington, he was angry with himself, and altogether felt very much the fool. People had congratulated him until he was tired.

"I shall be spouting at afternoon teas next," he told his friend, savagely, when they were alone for a moment; but just then Millicent came up, and Tom moved guiltily away.

"I enjoyed it so much," she said, holding out her hand.

"Thank you."

She waited, smiling up into his face.

"And have you nothing to say of my work?"

"It—it—was charming," he stammered.

"Which, translated, means abominable."

He wondered why that girl should stand there laughing at him with her marvelous eyes. It annoyed him, and it pleased him. He answered:

"I am very, very sure you underrate yourself."

"Fie! Mr. Worthington, fie! I know it was abominable, because I tried to make it so."

He looked up quickly.

"I hope you will forgive me, for I have a confession to make. I am not heroic or self-sacrificing, and I want you to know that I can read better than I did, and that I felt what I read more deeply than I expressed. But—but—you are a lion, you know."

"Oh, am I?"

He was beginning to see, and the red mounted to his face.

"Yes," she said, "and you were very unsatisfactory; you would not roar, so I read badly, to compel you to read in self-defense. There!"

He struggled between anger and admiration at her audacity. The latter triumphed. He laughed a low, amused laugh. "If I am a lion, you are a lion tamer," he said. "May I come to see you some day?"

Her apprehensions fled, and she joined in his merriment.

"Will you promise not to be very fierce?"

"I promise to 'roar me as gently as a sucking dove.'"

"Then you may come," she said. "Good night, Sir Lion."

"Good night, my Lady Lion Tamer."

Nathan Makes His Proposal

NATHAN SAW THAT his time had come. He sighed, cleared his throat and began:

"Widder, I been thinkin' a good deal lately, an' I been talkin' some with a friend o' mine." He felt guiltily conscious of what that friend had counseled him to keep back. "I've been greatly prospered in my day; in fact, 'my cup runneth over.'"

"You have been prospered, Nathan."

"Seems ef—seems ef I'd ought to sheer it with somebody, don't it?"

"Well, Nathan, I do' know nobody that's more generous in givin' to the pore than you air."

"I don't mean jest exactly that way; I mean—widder, you're the morti—I mean the salvation of my soul. Could you—would you—er—do you think you'd keer to sheer my blessin's with me—an' add another one to 'em?"

The Widow Young looked at him in astonishment; then, as she perceived his drift, the tears filled her eyes and she asked, "Do you mean it, Nathan?"

"I wouldn't 'a' spent so much work on a joke, widder."

"No, it doesn't seem like you, Nathan. Well, it's sudden, mighty sudden, but I can't say no."

"For these and all other blessin's make us truly thankful. O Lord, we ask fur his name's sake—amen!" said Nathan devoutly. And he sat another hour with the widow, making plans for the early marriage, on which he insisted.

This story was an excerpt from "The Mortification of the Flesh," published in *Lippincott's Monthly Magazine* in August 1901. The heading of the story in this version notes that "Remarks of the Suitor Were 'Sudden Like' to the Widow," as well as that this was a new story by Paul Laurence Dunbar appearing in *Lippincott's*.

In a Circle

"OF COURSE, NOW, Ned, you must see for yourself how utterly impossible it is." She said it with decision and finality.

"I must confess that it had not occurred to me before, but, really, you have put it very clearly."

"I do hope you're not going to be sarcastic, Ned. It isn't nice, and then—oh, anybody can be sarcastic who is nasty enough."

"But I'm not sarcastic, though. Here is a problem, a hard one, let us confess, and I, stupid fellow that I am, cannot see through it. A bright little lady appears upon the scene and talks to me for ten minutes, and, presto, it is all perfectly lucid."

"Yes," she said doubtfully, and then more bravely, "I am so glad that you see and understand."

"It is all due to you."

"It would never do in the wide world."

"You are right, as you always are."

Her foot was tapping the floor impatiently.

"In such matters one must be practical."

"Practical, certainly."

"It must sound horribly worldly, but—"

"Oh, not in the least."

"In the first place, Ned, you are very poor—"

"As a church mouse."

"And I am so extravagant."

"Horribly so."

"Ned!"

"Oh, pardon me; I thought—"

"Oh, never mind," a little sharply. "You could never get me the things I wanted."

"No."

"And people would say you married me for my money."

"Yes, they would."

"One must always mind what people say, you know, even in affairs of this kind."

"Yes, even in affairs of this kind one must always manage to be to the windward of the gossips."

The tears were very near her eyes, but she struggled on.

"To be sure, I've always liked you, Ned."

Her breath caught.

"Yes, we've been such good friends, but we can still be."

"But will we?"

"Yes, indeed."

"Always?"

"Always."

"You'll marry some good girl who is better fitted than I to be a poor man's wife."

"I had never thought of that, but I suppose so."

"Laura Madison, for instance?"

"Good."

"And you'll be very, very happy?"

Slowly, "I—suppose—so."

"While I—"

"While you'll marry some jolly, rich—"

Hotly, "I shall never marry at all!"

"No?"

"O Ned, can't you see? It would be utterly impossible for me to marry you."

"Utterly impossible, I agree."

In a broken voice, and using her handkerchief, "You never loved me."

"I have always adored you."

Angrily, "Then I don't see how you can find it so utterly impossible to marry me."

"You have just shown me. I am poor."

"Oh, I hate a coward. Haven't you got two hands, and haven't I got just more than I want?" Tears.

"You are very extravagant."

"I could learn to be economical for the man I loved."

"But people would say I married you for your money."

"Oh, who cares what people say? I—I hate gossip, and everybody would know it isn't true, for you are miles and miles better than I am, and I ought to be glad—O Ned!"

"But even in affairs of this kind one must mind what people say."

"Oh, such a sentiment from a man! I—I—"

"And the girls who would make such wives for poor men."

"They would drag you down—they—they are impossible."

"Laura Madison?"

"Never speak her name to me again—the cat!"

"Well—"

"Ned, if you wish to say you don't want to marry me, say it. I am humiliated enough already."

"But I've just proposed to you, and it was impossible."

"Impossible! O Ned!"

Just here the curtain should fall, but two minutes afterward there should be a gurgle and a voice should say, "O Ned, if you're very, very poor, let's have a little cottage and—and—only ourselves." Then the voice should be smothered suddenly, as if some one were kissing the speaker's mouth.

Jethro's Garden

THE TWO OLD men were standing close to the line fence that separated their yards and their gardens. Their broken voices clattered on the morning air in harsh, dry laughter at the ancient jokes and well worn stories that they with much gusto were recounting one to the other.

Jethro Harding leaned on his hoe and his yellow old face, looking stiff like leather was creased into a hundred wrinkles of merriment. What was it to him that it was the middle of May, that rain was threatening and that the weeds were a good deal more forward than the lettuce and onions? It was better to lean on a hoe than over it. That was Jethro's philosophy of life, and it was the practice and exploitation of this creed that kept him in trouble with his persistent better half, Betsey.

Betsey believed in work for work's sake, and the gospel thereof she preached night and day. Now Jethro believed in work for no sake at all. He looked upon it as an evil necessity which was to be avoided whenever possible.

They were just at the height of their mirth. His neighbor, Ezra Horn, was saying, "An I tol' Hiram—" when a strong voice broke across their merriment with a loud and strident, "Jethrow, Jethrow, I wish you'd stop gassin' and git to that garden. A rain's a comin' up an' while the groun's too wet to work, the weeds'll walk off with everything. Ezry Horn, you'd better be attendin' to them beans o' yore'n, instead o' keepin' comp'ny with Jethrow."

Jethro bent quickly over the hoe and fell to work muttering to himself, while Ezra ducked behind his own fence with equal alacrity. The admonishing voice subsided, however, and its owner disappeared into the house. But the old man kept on with his work, until he heard his neighbor's stealthy voice saying, "I tell you, Jethrow, you must have a mighty sight of patience, or you jest never could stand bein' hectored that-a-way."

Jethro straightened up at this evidence of sympathy, "It's jest Christain grace, Ezry," he said, "I've got a powerful amount o' that, but sometimes it does seem as ef my cross was a leetle too heavy to bear."

"I know I couldn't bear it," Ezra replied, "but then I ca'c'late I've got more sperrit 'n you have."

"More sperrit, more sperrit! No, siree. Nary mite more. Why, I'm plumb runnin' over with sperrit, but I've got grace as well."

"So have I, but not enough for that," and Ezra shook his head doubtfully.

Further conversation was impossible for the present, as each of the old men was hoeing away from the fence and even the high-spirited Ezra was not willing to shout his strictures against Mrs. Harding in a voice loud enough to reach that dame's ears.

All the way to the other side of the garden Jethro was in deep thought. And it must have been of a vigorous and resentful kind if one could judge by the viciousness with which he cut at the offending weeds. At the turn, the mood seemed to grow upon him and he worked with such angry energy that he reached the dividing fence again long before his neighbor. There was a look of stern determination on his face as Ezra reached him and he flung his hoe far over into a corner with a gesture of unmistakable decision.

"Doggone it, Ezry," he exclaimed, "I jest ain't a-goin' to stand it, that's all. Ef I want to stand here and talk to you, I ain't a-goin' to let no woman in the world pester me out of it."

His friend stared at him in open-mouthed wonder. "Why, Jethrow," he said, "ain't you a-gittin' a leetle rash?"

"No, I ain't, Ezry," he said, "and they ain't no use fur you to stand there an' stare at me, go on with yore story right where you left off."

Evidently Jethro had been right about the amount of "sperrit" he possessed, and his neighbor went on lamely with his story, albeit he cast numberless fearful glances at the door across from him. But nothing happening, he warmed to the tale and, losing fear, kept Jethro in agonies of laughter.

It is of the nature of men that if one tells a story, another must cap it and this the rebel gardener proceeded to do.

Meanwhile, the forces that wait upon the tales of no man were vigorously at work piling the storm clouds black and high. A fresh wind came up in the west; the young leaves trembled, and the sunlight darkened, but still the interchange of banter went on. A few warning drops of rain pattered down, but teller and listener were just in the midst of an exceptionally good yarn and these cloud messages went unheeded. Not until a brisk downpour made shelter a necessity did they return to their senses.

"Lawsy, Jethrow, what'd d'ye think o' that?" exclaimed Ezra as he broke for the house shouting back over his shoulder, "I'll git it, too, now."

Jethro turned around upon his garden, green with arrogant weeds that seemed to nod defiance and a despairing look took possession of his face.

"Well," he said, "I done it," and with reluctant steps he made his way toward the house. Arriving at the kitchen window, he crept stealthily up and looked in, half expecting to encounter the accusing eyes of Betsey searching the plot for him. But he was mistaken. No Betsey appeared, and with a sigh half of surprise and half relief he went round from the window to the door and shuffled in. His spirit was considerably weakened by the wetting he had got and his courage considerably shaken by the fear of what his wife would say to him.

"Betsey," he called timidly, advancing toward the door of the "settin' room." "Betsey." But there was no answer. A sudden unnamed fear gripped the old man's knees, and his leathern face began to pale. Betsey not home? It raining, so, too, and the sturdy dame was no gadabout in the best of weathers.

He pushed open the door and went into the sitting room. It was vacant as the kitchen. Then with quaking heart and filling throat he passed into the parlor, then into the side bedroom. No Betsey.

The old man sank down on a chair and with his hands clenched on his bony knees sat staring out into the pouring rain. The remembrance of many threats that Betsey had made in his hours of shiftlessness now came to him with stunning force and he saw now in her absence their fruition.

"Oh, Betsey, Betsey," he muttered between broken, half-sobbing breaths, "ye allus said ye'd leave me; but I didn't believe it, I didn't think ye'd leave me after all these years together."

Against the pane the rain rapped maliciously and outside everything was drenched into bleak cheerlessness.

The old man's thought went on in their gloomy vein. "Me at this age, without Betsey—to think of it—an' all about an old garden, too." Then a sudden light came into his eyes and he got up stiffly. "Dodgast that garden, I'll hoe it now jest fur spite ef it kills me."

He hastened out of doors and seizing his hoe began to ply it vigorously, if unavailingly, in the water-thickened soil, punctuating his efforts with such remarks as "doggone yore time, you'll make Betsey leave me, will ye," and "ye'll leave me a widower, will ye," "I'll hoe ye, ef I bust," while the tears streamed down his weatherbeaten cheeks,

The May rain laughed tauntingly as it beat down upon his unprotected shoulders, while it followed behind him whipping flat the earth and weeds where he had turned them up; but he went on unheeding, making his sacrifice, paying his penalty.

To Ezra Horn, standing at his kitchen window, looking out meditatively at the storm, came the vision of his neighbor bending over his hoe in the driving rain.

"Well, I'll be—" His mouth closed with a snap, and seizing an umbrella, he made his way out of the house, down the walk and across the garden rows to the fence.

"Jethrow," he whispered fearfully.

But Jethro went on with his work.

"Jethrow," again whispered Ezra raising his voice a little. "Did she make you do it?"

Then Jethro straightened his form majestically. "No," he said, "she didn't make me do it, I'm doin' it of my own accord." He resumed his work upon the soil.

"Well, I'll be dodgasted!" By now Ezra had come to believe that his neighbor had taken leave of his senses. He came nearer the fence and said very gently, as soothingly as he would have spoken to a child.

"Don't you 'low ye'd better go into the house an' git her to make you some boneset tea? That's mighty good fur sudden 'tacks o' this kind."

"Don't talk to me 'bout tea an' sudden 'tacks an' her. There ain't no 'her' no more," and Jethro broke down.

"There ain't no her—why—why—" Ezra was quite helpless now and open-mouthed with wonder and surprise.

"No, ther' ain't no her. I've driv' from home the best woman the Lord ever give a man."

"Driv' from home—out in the rain! Why, man, what made you do it? Me an' my wife have our leetle differences, but—"

"Ezry Horn," interrupted the bereaved, and his voice was tragically accusing, "don't you talk to me. You helped me."

"I—I—helped you? Jethrow, ye'd better go in an' git that tea."

"I don't want no tea. Betsey's left me, an' it's all about this blamed garden, an' I'll hoe it now, rain er no rain, ef it kills me. Ef so be she should come back she'll find them rows clean er my body a-laying here." He pointed tragically to the earth, wiped his face on his sleeve and fell to work.

Now all this tragedy was too much for Ezra's simple mind, so with a muttered "M-m-m" he went back to the house. He would have liked to ask his wife's advice about it, but he knew his wife's capacity for domestic monologue, and he foresaw the deadly comparisons that she could make and the sickening moral that she could draw. So he maintained a discreet silence while flattening his nose against the pane. Then he jumped.

"Land sakes alive!" floated out from Jethro's kitchen door. Jethro threw down his hoe with a glad start and then a sudden shamefacedness overtook him.

"Jethrow Harding," again came Betsey's voice, "what in the name of common sense air you doin' out there in the rain?"

"I was weedin' the garden."

"Weedin' the garden? Have you gone clean out o' yore senses? Come in here this minute. Well, of all men!" as Jethro shuffled in.

She was already bustling about, putting the kettle on the stove while she kept up a running fire of talk.

"Git out o' them wet things as soon as you kin. Tsch, tsch, tsch! Sich a man, Sich a man. Here I can't even run 'crost the street to 'tend to Miss Bollender's poor sick child, but you must go an' do something foolish. Jethrow, whatever in the world made you do sich a foolish thing?"

"Why you was so set on havin' it done, Betsey," he announced weakly.

"I wasn't set on havin' you laid up with the rheumatiz. Better let the garden go," and there was a softer note in her voice. "I'm goin' to fill you up on hot tea an' bundle you into bed before you git to hackin' or limpin' around, but you shall have a nice warm stew, too."

It was while she was bathing his feet with mustard water that he bent over and laid his hand tenderly on her head and said: "Betsey, I ain't nothin' but a good-for-nothin' ol'—"

"Jethrow Harding," broke in his wife, "will you set still?" But she kept her head down, and it was a long time before she remembered that she was rubbing one toe.

When he was safely in bed, Betsey bent over him with motherlike solicitude murmuring. "Sich a man, sich a man," while Jethro lay there smiling with a sense of self-righteousness quite disproportionate to his deserts.

The Vindication of Jared Hargot

THE SUN SHONE very brightly again for Ellen Hargot these October days. She was as free to run about and chatter as the squirrels which fill the old oaks on the bluffs at the edge of the town. It had not been so for some time, and now she was happy in her freedom. Not that she had not been happy before in the labor of love that she was doing. But now the work was done and she had double reason for rejoicing.

One cannot help, even in the mechanical making of a book, absorbing some of the author's creative enthusiasm and delegating to one's self a partnership in the work. The amanuensis who copies the page for the press speaks with pride of "our book," while it is "our book" to the boy who carries it to the post office.

This had been Ellen Hargot's role. At first she had copied in her plain, fair hand; then she had helped him to read the returned proof (there had been no long delay in hunting a publisher; he published for himself). Finally on a day, inordinately proud, she had opened the first copy of *Morning-Stars and Morning-Glories,* and kissed her father ecstatically to find it dedicated to herself.

If there was one thing above another in which Ellen Hargot had faith, it was her father's poetical genius, and it was her praise and encouragement of him that had at last persuaded Jared Hargot to collect and publish the verses which for years he had been writing upon all sorts of occasions. The files of the *Eagle* for a score of years back, the memorial pictures and family Bibles of friends, were called into requisition, and *Morning-Stars and Morning-Glories* was the result.

Dorbury too had faith in Jared Hargot. Had he not in the hours of their joy or sorrow touched their hearts time and again by personal tributes, infinitely tender, to their loved ones? So thought Abram Judkins. For did he not know almost by heart the beautiful piece that Jared wrote when Mother Judkins passed away? And had not Jared borrowed it from him to put into the book? Ah, yes, he must have a dozen of those books, some for friends in the next county and some for the family of his son, who was living out West, in Illinois, and one, always one, for himself. And the mothers, the birth of whose babes he had celebrated—they must have the book, so that John or Clarissa, when they grew up, might see under what bright stars they were born.

So *Morning-Stars and Morning-Glories* sold. Not that Jared would have offered a single copy for sale. He would have given them away as freely as if he could afford it, had it not been for Ellen's restraining hand. She took the matter of distribution into her own hands, and hesitated at giving complimentary copies even to the newspapers. When the Cincinnati papers said no more of it than to give a bare announcement of its receipt she felt that she had been defrauded, and would really have liked to send for the book's return. But there really was a great compensation in considering that their book had been out but three weeks and two hundred copies had already been sold. Contemplating that, she could stand the silence of the reviewers, though she did expect something of their home paper, the *Eagle*.

Jared was content with what had come to him. He was not hoping to make much of a stir, and his one evidence of literary vanity evinced itself in a new tendency to wear his lead pencil behind his ear as if it must be ever ready to catch and prison a fleeting fancy. But such are the forgivable vagaries of poets.

If in all Dorbury there was anybody who was almost as interested in the book as the author himself and his daughter, that person was Nathan Foster, whom Jared had rallied in good-humored verse upon his marriage with the widow. Nathan was about with the book, a self-constituted agent, ramming it down the throats of his friends and buying them himself till the widow had to stop him.

He it was who was most indignant over the indifference of the press, and he was loud in his complaints because the *Eagle* had had nothing to say about their fellow citizen who had "writ a book out of his own head."

At last he confided in angry secrecy to his friend, Silas Bollender, "I tell you, Si, ef they don't print somethin' purty soon about Jared's book, I'm a-goin' to stop my paper."

But this catastrophe was fortunately averted, for on a certain Saturday, nearly a month after the publication of the book, the *Eagle* came out with glowing headlines: "A New Richmond in the Poetic Field—*Morning-Stars and Morning-Glories* —Work of a Fellow-Townsman." Nathan seized upon the paper with avidity, skimmed the opening paragraphs, and then hastened with it to Jared before anyone else could bear him the joyful news.

The wind was whispering secrets to the trees and the trees were nodding their understanding. White clouds were scudding across a field of blue, and the corn in the fields, with its mock swords, played the old war game—old as the oldest autumn.

It was a glorious afternoon. Jared was standing at his front gate, his pencil behind his ear and a meditative look in his deep-set eyes. His gaze was on the gleaming line of the river, which shimmered silver in the sun. Over him brooded ineffable content. It was the attitude of one who looks upon his finished work and says, "It is good." Softly through the golden silence came the wash of the stream against the shore, and the song of the flitting birds upon the bank broke partly through his dream and then melted into it.

A little later Nathan also broke through the dream, but not to melt into it. The dream was shattered immediately upon his excited appearance. He came brandishing the paper and mopping his brow.

"Jared, Jared," he said, "there's somethin' in the paper about you."

Jared's face brightened and he grew interested.

"It's all about the book, and he puts you 'way up,' Jared."

"I'll have the farther to fall down then, Nathan," said Jared, smiling as he took the paper.

"I 'low I been lookin' for that piece longer'n anybody else, an' ef anybody seen it before I did they must 'a' kept a good lookout."

The poet shook the paper out. "Well, let's see what he says about me an' my book, an' how high he 'puts me up.'"

Nathan, replete with satisfaction, leaned on the fence, smiling happily as his friend began to read.

At the first lines of the review Jared's face took on a delighted smile, and he read on, eager and happy as a child. Then, slowly, the smile faded, the paper shook in his hands, and a gray look came into his old face.

"Why, why," he stammered, "he's a-makin' fun o' me."

"Oh, no, Jared," said Nathan, adjusting his glasses and peering over his neighbor's shoulder again. "I didn't read it all, 'cause I'm kind of a slow hand at readin', but don't you see he says, 'We have the pleasure of presentin' to the readin' public a volume for which it has long waited. As our review comes late, the literary world must know of this book, so it seems almost superfl'ous to state that we refer to that effusion of poetic genius, *Morning-Stars and Morning-Glories,* written and published (let us add) by our distinguished fellow-townsman, Mr. Jared Hargot'?"

Nathan took off his glasses contentedly and wiped them. "I don't see what better praise you want than that, Jared. The trouble is you're too modest, and the feller is a little hifalutin' in his talk, but he means well."

"If it was praise, I wouldn't want nothin' better an' I wouldn't deserve that much; but it ain't praise; he's a-pokin' fun at me an' he thinks I am such a fool that I can't see it. I knowed what I wrote wasn't no great shakes fer poetry when it comes to comparing with the big things, but it emptied somethin' out o' me an' it gave me satisfaction, an' sometimes I believe when folks' dear ones had died a few of those lines o' mine gave 'em comfort, but now—" He gave a despairing gesture.

"But I tell you you're all wrong," insisted Nathan earnestly. "I'm a poor reader or I'd read it all myself. You go on an' read it all down from where I left off."

It was like asking a man to read his own death warrant, but with a bravery that his quivering voice and ashen face emphasized, Jared Hargot read on.

It was one of those flippantly sarcastic reviews written by very youthful reporters on small papers where the ridicule is half-veiled under an appearance of friendly praise. It was the sort of thing that is the pride of its writer, who chuckles over it in secret, and the joy of a thoughtless reader. But it was the kind of thing that makes a sensitive soul sick and stabs to death the heart of the man whose effort, whose dream, has called it forth.

A dream is a dream, however rude and impossible of fulfillment it may be. To write poetry had been the dream of Jared Hargot. He longed modestly for the simple, gentle expression of himself, and the feeling was entirely at one with the fine frenzy of a great poet, the fever to sing the songs of humanity, to chant its sorrows in time and tune to the beat of his own heart. And this dream a flippant youngster's ruthless hand had shattered.

"It has long been known," the article continued, "that the fires of poetic fancy and thought burned in the brain of our good citizen, Mr. Hargot, but never did we surmise with what a brilliant blaze until this matchless—this peerless—volume fell into our hands."

"Well, now," broke in Nathan, "I don't see nothin' wrong about that. 'Pears to me he's a-puttin' you up purty high."

"That's just it, Nathan, it's too high to be true. Can't you see he's a-laughin' behind his hand all the time?"

"No, I can't, an' I jest think it's nothin' but your consarned modesty, Jared, that makes you think so."

"No, no, Nathan, I know that every word he says here he means to be taken just the other way."

"Well, I don't believe it, but ef he does, he ought to be sued for libel—yes, sir, he ought to be sued for libel. You been a poet too long fur to have your reputation attackted. Go on and see what else he says."

"While we shall not take the liberty of eulogizing or commenting upon the literary form of any of the individual productions, we must confess that Mr. Hargot's style, while being perfectly free and easy, is singularly unique. It is all his own. No one can ever accuse him of plagiarism, for in all our experience of literature we have never come across a poet like him. He stands all alone in rugged unconventionality. In this day of straightlaced and mincing lines, it is good to say that in these poetic flights of our local bard his feet never hamper his wings. Shelley, Byron, Keats, and no other of the great singing throng which now comes to our mind was so entirely untrammeled. It was their misfortune.

"Mr. Hargot's verses are most simple and domestic ones. He treats mostly of birth, marriage, and death, the elemental facts of existence, and many of his friends whose names we recognize in the book as solid members of this community have profited by the power of his pen. He seldom touches upon the divine passion,—he seems to feel himself superior to its demoralizing influence,—but when he does, it is with a master's hand.

"We welcome this new addition to our literature and this new star in the galaxy of poets. All hail, Jared Hargot, author of *Morning-Stars and Morning-Glories!*"

"Good, good, that's talkin'," burst out Nathan excitedly.

Jared seized him by the shoulder and shook him. "Man, man," he said, "don't you know he means all o' that for a joke, an' there'll be a score of youngsters laughin' over it this evenin'?"

The man's voice shook with emotion,—the stress of grief,—but there was the thrill of anger in his tones.

"Well, Jared, I hope you're mistaken, but ef you ain't, it's a outrage, that's all I got to say. It's a outrage, an' you ought to have the law on him."

"The law can't stop their laughin', and it can't make that stuff I wrote poetry," said Jared bitterly.

"I don't keer whether the law can do it or not, yore friends'll believe it's poetry till the last gun kicks, an' I jing,—I'll say that much, though I am a perfesser,—I jing it, what's a body's friends good fur if they can't believe in you when other people's a-doubtin'? Anyhow, who's got any right to judge whether yore poetry is poetry or not, 'ceptin' yore friends? That's what I say."

Nathan had worked himself into a fine heat.

"Never mind, never mind, Nathan. When a man's too old for criticism to teach him, he ought to be too old for it to hurt him." And he turned slowly into the house, all the sunshine gone from his day, while Nathan went on down the street toward home, his head shaking in indignant protest.

It was in the silence of his own house—Ellen was out—that Jared had the greatest fight with himself. All the bitterness of disappointment rose in his soul in a floodtide and threatened to overwhelm all the sweetness and gentleness that had been his life's treasure. Somehow he had within him a sense of infinite injury. He felt like a child whose proffered gift of loved but sticky sweets some tactless person spurns. In pure free-heartedness he had offered the world his best, and it had been thrown back to him with jeers. He had asked of the great, cruel public nothing save that it take what he gave it—with a smile, perhaps, but not with a sneer. The hurt was the more poignant that his accusers—he could put it no other way—seemed to think that he expected more of them than he really did expect. Well, at least he could show them all how little he valued his own poor efforts.

He hurried to the kitchen and lighted a fire in the stove. The smoke curled up and the blaze went well. He stood silently contemplating the anxious flames, his eyes all sadness and his lips trembling.

In the corner of what by courtesy he called his library, closely packed, stood the remaining volumes of his edition of *Morning-Stars and Morning-Glories*. He took one and laid it upon the flame.

As the fire caught it and it curled and crisped something seemed to grasp his heart. He gasped, and his hand made an involuntary motion as though to rescue the precious volume from his own rashness. But he drew back again and with tense lips watched it burn. Then, as if spurred on by the accomplishment of this first sacrifice, with feverish haste he seized the books by armloads and stuffed them into the grinning stove.

As the last one shriveled and turned from the red glow of incandescence to the grayness of ash the door opened and Ellen entered. Her pale and haggard face showed that she already knew all. But she smiled bravely and held out her arms to her father.

"We don't care, do we? We have faith still, whatever they say." And then, suddenly, the smoke was in her eyes and nostrils.

"Why, father, what—what have you been doing?" she cried, her eyes growing wide with expectant horror.

"Wiping out an old man's folly," he said calmly but quietly. She turned swiftly and sped into the library. There, empty, mournful, tragic, the corner where the books had been stared blankly at her. With a despairing cry, she ran again to the kitchen and threw herself into her father's arms.

WHEN MR. NATHAN FOSTER, in the goodness of his heart, came to purchase a half-dozen more of *Morning-Stars and Morning-Glories* and found out the catastrophe that had taken place he was at first cast down to the very depths of despair.

But after a half-hour's indignant meditation he brightened, a smile overspread his face, and he left Jared's presence in a condition of plain exultation.

For the next few days Nathan was very busy among his old friends and cronies, while an air of mystery and suppressed excitement seemed to follow him into whatever region he went. Jared Hargot could not help notice it, for whenever he appeared, groups that had been gathered together in earnest converse would suddenly break up, and the very irrelevance of their subsequent talk was sufficient evidence that it had nothing to do with what they had been saying before. But he was so utterly miserable and distressed that he did not care. Suppose they were talking about him. What did it matter? He was a thing to be talked about, to be laughed at, to be pointed at. Ah, well!

But one thing he could not understand was the attitude of his daughter. She had always sympathized with him in every sorrow, even in every mood. At first when his trouble had come she had been all sorrow, all understanding of his hurt. Now, however, she was a different girl. She laughed, she sang, her footsteps skimmed the ground, and even while she tried to smooth the wrinkles of misery out of his brow she herself was radiant with joy.

Matters went on this way for weeks, and then, on the evening of a day that had been especially full of mystery, Ellen began to complain of her father's shabby appearance, and partly by persuasion, partly by tender bullying, she got him into his best suit and made him agree to accompany her to the Free Methodist Church, where something was "going on."

As he went along the street Jared wondered at the crowds which he saw flocking to the church.

"It's strange," he said, "I ain't heard anything of this."

"There's to be speaking or something," said Ellen with a little quiver in her voice.

Once in the church, Jared found all eyes upon him, and in those eyes a gleam of friendly roguishness. His blood beat fast as he was hustled forward to the platform and seated in a vacant chair between Nathan Foster and Abram Judkins. Besides these there were Silas Bollender, the pastor, and John Hardaway, who sat at a little table on which was a pitcher of water.

Jared wondered, but a number of closely wrapped parcels in one corner of the stage caught and held his attention. He coughed nervously and looked at Nathan, but Nathan, humorously solemn, was contemplating the beauty of a whitewashed ceiling. He turned to Abram, but Abram was busy chewing the end of his beard and seemed afraid that he would lose a bite.

Then the choir sang, and before he knew what was going on Abram Judkins had announced that they had met to pay honor to "their distinguished fellow citizen, their good friend and their well-beloved poet,"—he laid stress on the word,— "Jared Hargot," and he introduced the speaker of the evening, John Hardaway.

In deliberate terms Hardaway reviewed the work of Jared Hargot. He recalled and recited some of his poems, and the young lawyer's well-trained and sonorous voice gave them a new power. He told of the good those simple songs had done, of the joy or consolation they had carried to many hearts. Then, rising on the wings of his eloquence, he said: "He has chanted his dirges beside the bier of our well-beloved. He has sung his paeans at the cradle side of our newly born, and if he has not walked the high and rugged hills of song, he has piped him sweetly in the smiling vale. In the depths of his self-humiliation he would have taken from us the treasure which he gave, but others have reckoned better than he, and still shine his 'Morning-Stars'—still bloom his 'Morning-Glories.'"

At the word he stepped to one of the mysterious packages and tore aside the paper covering. A score of books bound in blue and gold fell clattering to the floor. The lawyer picked one up and handed it to the author, and the audience broke into applause.

Jared had sipped to the full the honey of appreciation, and now he could no longer contain himself. A sob of joy broke from him and he bowed his head over his book.

They sang the Doxology that night in the church as they had never sung it before, and as Nathan wrung Jared's hand at the close of the service he said expressively, "I jing, Jared, I jing! Talk about reviewers! I jing!"

The Way of Love

To BE PASSIVELY moral without an open confession of faith is, in the minds of some people, equivalent to being actively unreligious. Ever under the tongues of them rolls that sweet morsel, "He that is not for me must be against me." They spit it out at their victims and then draw it in again just for the pleasure of the taste of it.

John Hardaway was not a bad man. He did not steal, he did not lie,—that is, not more than an honest young lawyer should,—and his morals were above reproach. In spite of a certain haughty reserve of demeanor, which accorded ill with the simplicity of Dorbury, he was fairly well liked by the townspeople, and the fact that he was one of the unregenerate would hardly have penetrated their placid minds had it not been for the wonderful wave of religious enthusiasm that swept over the village that winter.

John Hardaway was not a professing Christian, although he attended church regularly on Sunday, joined in the singing (maybe that was because he held to one side of Ellen Hargot's hymn book), and paid his dues as a young man with ambitions ought to do. But when the Free Methodist Church inaugurated a protracted meeting his doom stared him in the face.

The Free Methodists were determined to convert the whole town—men, women, and children,—and to this end they had secured the services of the fiercest and most terrible of evangelists to aid the regular pastor. This gentleman fell upon Dorbury like an avenging angel, but instead of a flaming sword he possessed a huge fist, with which he pounded the Bible into pulp, and an equally huge voice, which tremendously called sinners to repentance. Such was the Rev. Abijah Center.

John Hardaway did not attend these meetings, and as nearly everyone else did, and many were falling before the great religious storm, he suddenly became the target for the shots of all the zealous proselytes who were working for God's glory, and perhaps their own. Indeed, it would have been a fine thing to say, "It was my persuasion that led him to seek salvation," or "It was my presentation of the case to him that opened his eyes." But, as it happened, none of the anxious old brothers and sisters of the church would have this satisfaction.

At first the attention which he excited annoyed him, and then he began to regard it with grim amusement. But when Silas Bollender, who was known to have gone to see play-acting at a certain county fair, exhorted him that he must be snatched as a "brand from eternal burning" he laughed outright.

"If any 'brand' needs 'snatching,' Mr. Bollender," he said laughingly, "I certainly am that one, but being snatched so young would keep me from so many pleasures."

"That's jest it," exclaimed Silas heatedly, "pleasure—"

"Such as a county fair," went on the young man imperturbably, "and"—but Silas, though now he sat starched and solemn in the "amen corner," was already fully routed. He said later to Nathan Foster,—

"Nathan, I'm afeared that Jawn's a-goin' to hell with his eyes wide open."

"Air you?" asked Nathan. "Well, I dunno; you know what our doctern is, 'Between the stirrup and the ground'—you know the rest."

But Silas only shook his head.

Nathan took his religion as he took life, seriously but calmly. Nevertheless, this did not prevent his going to call on John to see what he could do to bring this stubborn sinner to grace.

"John," he said to the smiling young man, "don't you want to be saved?"

"Why, why, Uncle Nathan! saved? Well, at least I want to be safe."

"Unhuh, well, that's jest it; git on the safe side, then, git on the safe side. I ain't no hand to preach, John Hardaway, but I hain't got no fear about your salvation. Ef you're a goin' to be floored, the Lord A'mighty'll floor you; don't you make no mistake about that; He'll find the way to do it."

When Nathan left there was a wry pucker about the young lawyer's lips, and it wasn't exactly mirth.

Then to himself, "Nonsense," he said, "am I giving way to the influence of this insanity-afflicted atmosphere?" He shook himself, put on his hat, and went out.

He believed he would go over to Ellen Hargot and tell her his joke on Si Bollender; she couldn't help but enjoy it, for she had humor and common sense.

He found Ellen with a smile upon her face and singing about her work, but there were traces of recent tears upon her lashes. Somehow she seemed to be, and yet not to be, the person by whom his little joke would be appreciated. Her eyes were glad, but with a peculiarly serious gladness. With some hesitation he told his story, and only got in return a serious sighing—

"Poor Mr. Bollender."

"Why, Ellen, surely you don't sympathize with that old hypocrite; why, he—"

"We cannot judge. He is doing all that he can do, and that is more than some of us with the light right before us can say."

"Ellen," broke in John Hardaway, "you don't mean to say that you too have come under the spell of this junketing mountebank's conjuring!"

"Don't say that, John. I have indeed been sitting for some nights under the outpouring of Elder Center's gospel—"

"It certainly is *his* gospel. The Lord wouldn't own it."

"And I have thought and prayed and professed religion at home to-day."

"You!"

"Yes. Oh John! don't look that way. I am so happy."

Hardaway sat dumb. He seemed as one on whom a sudden blow had fallen. Then he roused himself and began to think—to feel. Resentment surged up in his breast. Ellen, his Ellen, going through that emotional mockery! Oh, it was too much! He felt humiliated, defeated, defrauded of something that was rightfully his, —her sympathy,—and now she had put him entirely beyond the pale of it. Worst of all, away back in one corner of his consciousness he knew that in any cause to which she allied herself Ellen would be unflagging in her zeal and relentless in her disapproval of those who opposed her. He himself would be arrayed, whether he would or no, on one side or the other. If he were not wholly for her, he must certainly be against her.

With a half laugh and a poor attempt at lightness he approached her. "I'm sorry, Ellen, that you take your religion so hard. I'm afraid, dear, that you will never get over it. Remember too that it may be catching and I am exposed."

John Hardaway had made the mistake of his life. You may with more impunity flog a woman than make fun of her religion.

Ellen Hargot stiffened. She eluded John's outstretched hand.

"I could never marry a man who could scoff at religion," she said, slipping the little gold circlet from her finger and reaching it towards him.

"Why, Ellen, Ellen," he said, "I—I didn't mean to scoff at you. You will not give me up in this way, will you?"

For answer she pressed the ring into his hand and turned away with sad eyes.

He stood gazing for a moment at the little gold band, the sign and symbol of their love and betrothal; its return the reminder of his love rejected, thrown back upon him; then he cried passionately, "Well, if this is religion, then I say—"

"John," she cried in an awe-struck voice, and he paused, the rash words dying on his tongue.

"Take the ring, Ellen," he said softly, "it hasn't done you any harm and can't do you any."

But she only shook her head. "Not now, John," she said.

A sudden, sullen anger seized John Hardaway, and putting the ring into his pocket he hurried to the door. Then he paused, and his voice had something of a ring of challenge in it as he said: "Ellen, I think you had better read your gospel again. I believe that you will find somewhere that the great Exemplar says: 'I come not to save the righteous, but to bring sinners to repentance.' The later method seems to push the sinners to the wall so that the good may revel in their own virtue."

"John!"

But the door had closed behind him, leaving her with an aching thought in her mind.

NATHAN FOSTER was a genial meddler. The very generosity of his soul made everybody's business his business, and he pried into the most secret matters with so naive an innocence that he disarmed resentment. He always wanted to know. Be it said too that he was as free with the details of his own business as he expected everyone to be with theirs. He never had a secret in his life and didn't know why anybody else should.

So when he saw John Hardaway coming up from the Hargots' and looking as desolate as a prairie at dusk he made a mental note, "John's either under conviction or Ellen's given him the mitten, an' I'm a-goin' to find out which."

True to his resolution, he let but a short time pass before presenting himself at Ellen's door. The girl was full of deep and troubled thought, and she welcomed this simple old man both as a diversion and a possible helper in her dilemma.

Nathan Foster was no diplomat, neither had he the art of dissembling or of mincing matters. He had hardly seated himself and got settled with crossed knees when he ventured, "I see John a-comin' away from here awhile ago."

"Yes, he was here awhile this afternoon."

"Seemed like he didn't seem jest like himself, somehow."

"No?"

"John's under conviction," said Nathan to himself, "or she'd 'a' flared at that."

"He ain't been to any o' Brother Center's meetin's, has he?"

"Not that I know of. He doesn't seem much interested."

"She's give him the mitten," this time the old man commented secretly; then aloud, "Oh, there's time fur him yet."

"Yes, and it's a soul worth saving."

"Well, I'm stumped," mentally ejaculated Nathan.

But he was soon to know. Out of the fullness of her sorrow Ellen told the old man her joy and her grief, her pleasure and her trouble, and out of the sweetness of his old mellow life he replied: "I'm afeared you was a little hard on him, Ellen.

It's mighty hard work a-drivin sinners into the Christian fold, you got to lead 'em. I knowed an old sheep once that Si Bollender had, and when the rest o' the flock 'u'd go through the bars, he'd hang around and bungle about until someone took an' led him through. Folks air like sheep in more'n one perticilar. Now that little ring o' your'n you give him back might 'a' bin jest the little leadin' he needed to bring him in. Never push a mule; you're bound to git on the wrong side of him."

"Oh, Uncle Nathan," the girl cried, "I hadn't thought of it that way and I believe I was hard on him. I ought to have shown him that religion makes us tenderer."

"That's it exactly. There ain't no use bein' a Pharisee even if you are thankin' the Lord under yore breath that you ain't like Brother or Sister So-and-so."

The old man's simple words were as a sermon to the girl, and she looked often and sadly at her bare finger before it was time for church that night.

It was a period of unusual interest at the meeting-house, because the series of services were drawing to a speedy close, and many who had held aloof were hastening to make their peace before being finally shut out. And as the evangelist told them, none knew whether this chance to come into the fold would ever be offered again.

It was among this class that the local gossips put John Hardaway when he was seen that night seated in the church for the first time since the "protracted meeting" began.

"He's weakened at last," the whisper went round.

"From the looks on his face, he's under conviction."

"Well, if anybody could fetch him, Brother Center should."

Meanwhile the evangelist poured the fiery coals of his eloquence upon poor John's head. It had become a personal matter with him. Above all things he wanted the conversion of this young man as the one crowning triumph that should be the climax of his labors. He pleaded, he threatened, he cajoled, and through it all to the end John sat unmoved, impassive, and Brother Center dismissed services that night with a very unchristian-like disgust written on his countenance.

Ellen glanced wistfully at John, but he eluded her and slipped away by himself, and the Free Methodist Church saw him no more during the progress of the meeting.

It was a week after the close of the series that Ellen met John walking towards the river with head bent. It was his favorite route.

"May I walk with you?" she stopped to ask.

"Yes, yes," he said, "but I guess I am pretty poor company nowadays; even my dog won't follow me."

She said nothing until they reached the bank of the stream. Then she stopped. "John," she cried, with a catch in her voice, "I was hard and unjust to you and altogether unchristian, and—and—may I have my ring back?"

It was hard for the woman. But for the man, his hands trembled so that he could hardly take the little circlet from the pocket where it had reposed since the fateful day.

He managed to slip it on her finger, and then—well—the elms screened them from public view, and for some reason an impertinent bird overhead sang, "Sweet, sweet."

After awhile he said, "Well, if religion can bring this sort of happiness, it's worth looking into."

The Churching of Grandma Pleasant

It was Seraphiny Higgins who first heard her, and she really could not believe her ears, but when she heard her again, Seraphiny was sure that she could not be mistaken. Her kitchen window let right out on Mrs. Pleasant's back porch, and there was no doubt that there was someone sitting there and singing "Comin' Through the Rye."

Of course, Seraphiny is no woman to pry into other people's business, but as the Pleasants are such awfully religious people, she couldn't resist the temptation of lookin' out to see who it was. Of course, she was perfectly sure of seein' Mandy Jane or Katy Lou, but, lo and behold! who should it be but Gramma Pleasant herself a-settin' on the back porch, and not only a-singin', but a-pattin' her foot.

"My sakes," says Seraphiny, "is the world comin' to an end?"

Bless you, she hadn't no more'n got the words out of her mouth when the old woman stops, and Seraphiny, a-thinkin' that mebbe she had seen her a-lookin', felt condemned, though the old lady is as nearsighted as can be, but Seraphiny, being no inquisitive character, did not want to take any chances, so back she steps, a-lookin' for Gramma to git up and kite into the house; but nothin' of the kind, she jest stopped to take a breath to change her tune, and what do you suppose it was? She hadn't no more'n stopped "Comin' Through the Rye," than she commenced "Hoe Corn and Dig Potatoes."

That was too much for Seraphiny, and she broke out of the house and went for Mis' Gillam and Mis' Warner to come and hear. She fairly flew, because she was afraid the old lady would stop again before she got back, but, as luck would have it, when they got back to the house the old lady was still a-singin', and she had switched into one of the old plantation songs that they used to sing nigh on to fifty years ago, and it had a regular devil's jig into the tune of it.

"Well," Mis' Gillam says, "who would have thought it?"

Mis' Warner's breath was clean gone, but Seraphiny she "'lowed that it was the old lady's Maryland blood, and what else could you expect of folks that had once owned slaves. She wouldn't put it past her to see her settin' down smokin' a pipe an' a-fiddlin'."

The other women gasped at such bold speech, although they knew that Seraphiny had always been possessed of a sharp tongue. Meanwhile, the old lady had turned into a half-religious tune, "Singin' in the Skies," but a most unreligious patting of her foot went with it, and the horrified women behind the shades of Seraphiny's house believed that there must have been a time when Gramma Pleasant had even danced.

"It ought to be reported in session," says Seraphiny.

"But la, Seraphiny," replied Mis' Warner, "Gramma Pleasant is so old."

"She is nigh on to eighty," added Mis' Gillam.

"All the worse for her to be a-committin' such frivolity an' a-settin' a bad example before the younger members of the flock," says Seraphiny grimly.

"It 'ud break her heart if she was turned out of the church at this time of life," Mis' Warner returned.

"Sometimes it's good to break a heart in order to save a soul," was the stern response, and so these calm religious spies stood and listened to the old woman childishly voicing her joy, until Nathan Foster came up to the gate and stopped also to listen. Finally, he opened the gate and went in. There was a broad grin on his face. Seraphiny gasped.

"Jest look at Nathan Foster," she says, "a-grinnin' at them songs, and and he supposed to be such a strong man in Israel. Mebbe he's grinnin' jest to catch her."

But Nathan came up to the porch where the old lady sat and gave a hearty, unforced laugh.

"There, there now, Granny, I ketched you."

The old woman laughed and said, "Go way now, Nathan, you ain't a-goin' to tell on me?"

"What's the use o' tellin'?" he said. "There ain't no harm in that I jest tell you them old-time songs kind o' stirs up things in ye that ye ain't felt for a long while, and I vum I like 'em."

The three women behind the window-shades grasped one another's aprons and stared, horror-stricken. Then the vitriolic Seraphiny whispered tragically:

"Nathan Foster a-sayin' he likes them songs! The old hypocrite. If I don't do anything to Gramma Pleasant I'll have him up before session anyhow," and the others solemnly shook their heads in acquiescence and dumb amazement. The very foundation of their belief had been shaken. All the traditions of their narrow religious life had been uprooted, and they could not have been more disturbed, more disconcerted, more utterly unsettled in mind, had they seen the parson dancing.

It is only an evidence of how news may travel when one comes to know that the story of Gramma Pleasant's defection was soon rumored all over town. Seraphiny says it was not she who told it, Mis' Warner that it was not she who told it, and Mis'

Gillam swears with all the Methodist oaths that she never mentioned a word of it to anybody. Well, it wasn't Nathan Foster, because he was mixed up in the affair.

Everything might have gone right, but Mr. Simpson, the pastor of the church, got wind of it, and he was an awful strict man,—all Dorbury was strict,—and he just determined that he was going to make an example of those people. He said just what Seraphiny said, that it was all the worse because Gramma Pleasant was old enough, after reaching eighty years, to know better, and that he did want to save the young lambs of the flock from the demoralizing influence of the old ewes, so the Rev. Mr. Simpson rubbed his bony hands and decided that there must be a church meeting to set upon the case of Gramma Pleasant.

Meanwhile, perfectly happy, Gramma Pleasant chewed her gums and sang, "Union Forever, Hurrah, Boys, Hurrah!" although she had formerly been a very good rebel.

Well, Seraphiny now thought it was her duty to go and see Gramma Pleasant and to labor with her. Seraphiny always was conscientious, and she went the next day through the back gate, down the little alley, and into the Pleasants' yard. Gramma was out "grubbin'," as she would have termed it, when the righteous proselyte approached her. She was going to forestall the preacher.

"Howdy, honey?" said Gramma Pleasant.

"Howdy-do?" was returned to her.

"'Pears like we're a-goin' to have some rain. I'm tryin' to git these things into some sort o' condition to 'preciate it."

"La, Gramma," in a soft, pious voice said Seraphiny, "there's other more important things in this world that we got to work at."

"Yes, you're right, chil'," Gramma replied, "there's my quiltin' that I ain't done the right thing by for I don't know how long."

"'Tain't quiltin'," says Seraphiny.

"Yes, and the cannin'," Gramma replied.

"'Tain't cannin'," says Seraphiny kind o' sharp.

"Oh chil', you ain't thinkin' 'bout makin' a rag cyhapet—you got plenty o' time for that."

Then Seraphiny's religion exploded, and she said:

"Gramma, you ain't got your mind set on nothin' but worl'ly things. I wasn't thinkin' 'bout nothin' worl'ly, but somp'n that our Heavenly Master will be concerned with."

Before she answered, the old lady worked her gums, and as industriously worked her hoe about a tender young plant that was dying for want of attention:

"Well, I ain't botherin' nothin' 'bout that, 'ca'se I know the Lawd'll 'tend to that, and they ain't no use in tryin' to 'tend to His business, 'ca'se ye cyarn't."

She went on grubbing with her hoe. Defeated, insulted, disappointed, Seraphiny turned about and went home. She had meant it well, but the Word had come to Gramma Pleasant and she would not receive it. Gramma Pleasant went on grubbing with her hoe. She did not know that she had Mr. Simpson to reckon with.

The envelope which bore her name was addressed in a very strong, fine hand, and Gramma was immensely proud at receiving the letter. Her daughter Hannah read it, and Gramma was not so pleased. It was a call to a church meeting, where Sister Ann Maria Pleasant was the culprit, under the charge of "conduct unbecoming a Christian."

The old lady was hardly cognizant of what it really meant and worked her gums nervously as she tried to make it all out. Her daughter was in tears to think that at that age Gramma had been doing something that she really ought'nt to do, but Gramma kept on gumming and kept calmer than most of the rest of the folk.

The basement of the church where these spiritual executions were held was crowded with people who counted themselves on the Lord's side. The preacher, gaunt, grim, and gray, sat stern at the little desk which did duty as a prisoner's dock. Gramma Pleasant was very near his side and was smiling at the honor that had been done her in setting her near the preacher at this meeting.

The meeting hung fire; no one seemed willing to accuse until one old lady who was said to be weak-minded, and hardly accountable for what she said, started up a half song, half chant:

"Here, thou poor criminal, where's thine accusers?"

Then the Rev. Mr. Simpson arose. He put his hands together with the ends of his fingers very carefully joined and began,—

"My dear brethren and sisters, we have met here upon a very important occasion."

Gramma Pleasant went on gumming and smiling.

"We have assembled ourselves together for the purpose of making an example to the young members of the flock of one of the old mothers in Israel."

Gramma Pleasant grew anxious and alert.

"We can forgive," and here the minister raised his eyes piously, "the shortcomings of the young, but when it comes to frivolity—frivolity, I say," and he stretched his long arms far out of his coat-sleeves, "in our older members, we feel that the time has come to call a halt—I say, to call a halt. Mother Pleasant has been among us for many a long year, and we have looked up to and esteemed her, but it comes to us upon good authority that lately—yes, even within the present week—she has been heard by those in good standing in the church singing upon her own porch 'Comin' Through the Rye' and 'Hoe Corn and Dig Potatoes,' and we feel that it is our clerical duty to ask the church's opinion upon this matter."

There was a gasp of astonishment on the part of the church, with the exception of Seraphiny, Mis' Gillam, and Mis' Warner, and then one old soured sister arose and said:

"I move that Sister Pleasant, old as she is, be disciplined for the good of the younger members, for what she will do, they will do and wuss."

Someone equally sour seconded the motion, and then way back in the church a slender form arose and the preacher said,—

"I recognize Brother Nathan Foster."

Nathan cleared his throat. "I ain't no speaker," he said, "but I jest tell you I wish the Lord you had a-heerd Gramma Pleasant a-singin' them songs. You kin call it conduc' unbecomin' a Christian if ye want to, but it give me a mighty Christian feelin', and I ain't goin' to tell no lie at that, and I went home and tried to sing 'em to the widder, but the widder made me stop 'cause I never could carry a tune."

"What was she singin'?" somebody asked.

Then Seraphiny had to up and speak:

"The first I heerd her singin' was 'Comin' Through the Rye,'" and then Sandy Sanderson, the only Scotchman in the community, rose slowly and unfolded his gaunt length.

"If there is ony mon here that takes exception to thot song, 'Comin' Through the Rye,' he can juist come out of the dure wi' me," and he sat down.

No one accepted the cordial invitation of Sandy, and then Gramma Pleasant got up and plead for herself. She did not know, nor did she care, that Rye was a river and not a field of grain; it was all one to her; it was the music, it was the swing of it, it was the love of melody in her old age, and she said:

"Well, brethren and sisters, if ye want to turn me out, all right, but I don't know that a body could be any closter to Gawd than by bein' closter to what Gawd made, and I didn't know that there was any difference in singin' 'Comin' Through the Rye' an' 'When All Thy Mercies, Oh My Lord.' That's the reason I sang it. I thought I was gettin' clost to the Lord, but if you people feel that you're closter, why, jest shet the gate on me, an' I reckon that sometime the Lord Himself's goin' to open it."

Nobody knows whether it was old man Judkins or Nathan Foster that started "Praise God from Whom All Blessings Flow," but someone did, and Gramma Pleasant found herself standing up by the preacher's side getting the right hand of fellowship.

The Case of Cadwallader

"SPEAKING OF CHANGES in men," said the miner, although no one had been speaking of them, "now there's the case of Cadwallader, Henry Cadwallader, have you ever heard of him? Spelt his name C-a-d-w-a-l-l-a-d-e-r and called himself Calder. But he was an all right fellow, anyhow. He was an Englishman of good family, but a younger son. It seems as if his folks wanted him to take orders, but Cadwallader

Undated manuscript from *The Paul Laurence Dunbar Papers* signed "Paul Laurence Dunbar/ Congressional Library/Washington, D.C." Previously unpublished.

preferred to take chances. So he got his belongings together and came to America to try his luck. It seems strange to me that some of those families will persist in having younger sons when they see how hard they are to dispose of." The speaker rolled his cigar in his mouth and settled himself back into comfortable story-telling position.

"Well, when the Englishman struck the States, he came straight west. I met him first in one of the upper California camps when the first rush was over and we were just settling down to business. He had only been over a month then, and a rawer 'tenderfoot' you never saw in all your life. He was about twenty-three at that time, and not overly big and brawny looking as men wont in those parts. But he looked like a man who was well put together, and who would know how to handle his fists if occasion should demand. He was fair with light brown hair which he combed in a manner that would have attested his greenness even if that had not already been perfectly apparent in the brand newness of his mining clothes. But, in spite of all his inexperience, there was something about the fellow that made a man like him and want to put him on to all the wrinkles that he needed. He was a good shot, a fair rider, and when the glasses were clinking he could hold his own with the rest of the boys. He could tell a rattling good story, and was the best of company.

"In our locality, half camp, half town, there was one of two things that must happen to such a fellow. He would either be elected mayor or fall into bad company. Well, he wasn't elected mayor. He had come out prospecting. He had a little money, and so fell in with a gang of fellows who played poker every night of the week by way of diversion, being mainly occupied during the day with sleeping off the effects of the last night's diversion, spinning yarns and marking cards. Of course, the natural thing happened. He lost; then he got reckless. He drank more than was good for him and was going to the devil at a pretty rapid rate, without a hand to check him.

"I had taken something of a liking to the young fellow, so when he went broke, I got him to leave his lodgings at the 'Blue Lion,' and bunk up with me. That was long before I had 'struck it rich' in the '*Bon Marie.*' He came, and in the day time helped me about my work. He was as decent as I had expected and a good deal stronger than I had thought for. He had been to Oxford or some place where he had done considerable in athletics, and the training had left his muscles like steel. This much I picked out of him, for he wasn't much of a fellow to talk about himself.

"I had only one fault to find with him—but that wasn't my business, however —as soon as he got a few dollars in his hands, he was right back at his old tricks, down to the 'Blue Lion' bucking against the men who had skinned him. It wasn't any use to talk to him. He was determined as a setting hen.

"'I'm looking for revenge,' he used to say to me, 'and it will come some day, I know.'

"'That's the way many a man has gone to the devil,' I always answered.

"'Well, Jenks, old boy,' Cadwallader would retort, 'if a fellow must go to the devil, as well go with good grace and a steady face.'

"I never liked the way he laughed when he said those things. 'But,' I thought, '"what can't be cured must be endured,"' and I learned to keep my mouth shut.

"One of the steadiest opponents Cadwallader had was Mike Brady, big Mike we always called him. He stood six feet-two in his socks and was broad in proportion. He had been in the camp for about two years, having come out from New York on the pretext of prospecting, but as he had never 'prospected' any farther than the green tables of the 'Blue Lion,' it was generally supposed that he had come to Saunder's Gulch for reasons best known to himself,—which was our polite western way of designating a fugitive from justice. Brady had his wife with him and a more perfect contrast between a husband and wife I never seen before in all my life. While he was a big, bold blustering fellow, she was the littlest, quietest, scaredest looking woman I ever saw. In spite of her timid looks, though, she was pretty, with fair hair and a good complexion. By her manners, she was a lady and no one could understand why under the sun she had ever tied up to a big brute like Mike. She was as much loved for her gentleness as he was feared and hated for his brutality and fierceness.

"Well, from the first that Cadwallader struck the camp, Brady viewed him with disfavor. While he did not hesitate to play with him and win his money, he took every opportunity of guying and annoying the young fellow. But the boy was good natured, and besides he had a good deal of wit and would 'rap' back at Brady so sharply that more than half the time, he came out with the laugh on his side. At these times, the big fellow, instead of taking his own medicine like a man, would get ugly and lose his temper. But he never had recourse to violent measures. He had too much sense to kill the goose that laid the golden egg, and the Englishman was one of the regular sources of his revenue.

"Finally Cadwallader's luck turned. Either fortune got ashamed of her treatment of him, or he got on to some of the tricks by which his opponents won. Any way he began to bring his wages back home and something of a stake besides them. With this, his spirits rose. He used to chuckle and say to me, 'I told you, Jenks, old boy, that I was going to get my revenge. I am doing it now, and I'm going to keep right on until I have won back every cent I lost, you see if I don't; then I'll throw up the game forever.'

"I shook my head. 'Maybe you'll do it, Cadwallader, and maybe you won't. I've seen men before you try the same trick. You'll begin to lose again pretty soon, and then you'll be fighting to get that back. You will win sometimes again just long enough to give you hope, and draw you on; then you will lose again, and so on to the end of the story—God only knows what that end will be.'

"He laughed a boyish, cheerful laugh.

"'That's all right, old man, don't you have any fears about me—just you keep on sleeping at night, and dreaming quiet dreams. I'll pull through all right.' But in spite of his reassurance, I could not feel easy about him.

"The first intimation I had that trouble was brewing was one day when Sandy Townsend came up to my place and began to talk the matter over.

"'I tell you, Jenks,' said he, 'you'd better warn that young friend of yours to be careful and look a little out for himself; he ain't safe.'

"'What's up now?' I asked in some alarm, for I knew that Townsend was not the man to interfere in the affairs of others without very good reason.

"'There's nothing up yet,' replied Sandy a trifle tentatively, 'but there will be or I miss my guess. The Englishman's been winning here of late and big Mike Brady's getting nasty. It was all right as long as he won; then he could keep from sending your young friend to "Kingdom Come"; but now that he's losing, it's "a horse of another color."'

"I saw through it all immediately. Mike Brady would not hesitate to kill the bird that no longer laid for him.

"'Look here, Cadwallader,' I said to him that evening as he was preparing to seek his usual haunts, 'if I were you, I wouldn't go to the "Blue Lion" anymore.'

"'This will be my last night if I win, for I intend to keep my promise to you and quit playing the cursed game forever.'

"'You may not have a chance to quit,' I said significantly.

"'What do you mean?' he asked, and I narrated to him what I had heard. He smiled quietly but there was a steely glitter in his gray eyes.

"'A thousand thanks for your warning,' he said, 'but no where better than here in America should you know that there is competition in all businesses, even in the business of killing.'

"'And you will go in spite of what I have told you?'

"'I will go in spite of the devil,' he flashed back, 'do you think I am to be frightened by a big bully like Brady? Let him look out for himself also.' He swung out of the door with an independent air, and somehow I felt less fear for him than I had before. He seemed so strong and active and self-sufficient. But I determined, nevertheless, to follow him and be near in case of attempted treachery to see that the boy had fair play.

"So, when I had finished up my evening's work, I took my way down to the 'Blue Lion,' and sought the room where the clink of the chips and the flip of the cards told me that the game was going on. I shall never forget the scene.

"The room was long and low, and but for the tables and chairs, was rather bare of furniture. The floor was deep with sawdust and here and there were placed square boxes of the dust as spittoons, for half the men in the room were indulging in our national nastiness of tobacco chewing. The air was clouded with smoke, but beside the closeness caused by these vapours, the atmosphere had a tenseness of its own, which seemed like an exhalation from the heated spirits of the players. Every once in awhile, the curse of some loser would rise above the general hum, or some man would slip from his seat and, having tried vainly to borrow a new 'stake' from someone, would stalk out trying to look unconcerned. There were a number of tables about, but the one upon which my attention was centered sat against the wall to one side of the room. It was covered with a green cloth tacked on with brass-headed nails, as were all the others in the room. It was semicircular in form, and within the hollow center sat the dealer.

"About the semicircle, sat a number of intense, eager-faced men deep in the mysteries of poker. Among them sat Mike Brady and Cadwallader. Brady's lips were trembling, though he handled his cards with steady fingers, and his eyes were bloodshot. His face twitched as if he were under a terrible nervous strain.

"There was a slight flush upon the Englishman's face, but among the excited men, he looked irritatingly cool and collected. He was winning surely and steadily. One by one, the men rose and left the table as their last chips disappeared into the pile which Cadwallader had collected before him. Every time one of his opponents left, the young man smiled; but he did not raise his eyes from his cards. Brady's gaze was fastened upon him with the look of a hungry panther; but Cadwallader did not seem to see him. He was playing a terribly bold, reckless, but relentless game. He had, now, good resources to draw from and was able to 'freeze' his antagonists out one by one. When he held bad cards, he bluffed and bluffed successfully.

"Brady, though he was losing at every turn of the cards, was holding on doggedly. At last, the inevitable thing occurred, the two were left alone at the table, facing each other—Brady at one end of the semicircle, and the Englishman at the other.

"The defeated players had begun to gather expectantly about the table, watching the two. The flush had deepened in Cadwallader's face, and Brady's awful expression was augmented by a scowl like a thunder-cloud.

"Finally, when the stakes had been piling up in the middle of the table at a great rate, with a growl of triumph, as he threw the last of his chips into the pile, the big fellow exclaimed, 'Now, you English snoozer, you've been bluffing all the evening; let's see what you've got, I call you.'

"With the same quiet smile, Cadwallader laid down his hand. Brady looked at it and his eyes bulged.

"'A straight flush, Mr. Brady,' said the Englishman coolly and reaching over, he swept in the stakes. Brady's eyes followed the last of his chips as they were mixed with his opponent's and his face grew livid. The cards dropped from his hands, showing the four aces that he had banked all upon. He sat as if he were dazed, until the Englishman's voice saying, 'I'll just cash in now, Mr. Dealer' roused him.

"'No, by the devil, you won't,' he cried, springing up and taking a step forward from around his side of the table.

"'Oh, I won't,' retorted Cadwallader, 'well, we'll see,' and I saw that same steely glitter in his eyes that I had seen before.

"'There's hell in the boy,' thinks I to myself, 'and Brady had better look out.'

"'Yes, we will see,' roared the defeated gambler, 'I ain't going to be cheated by any half strained Britisher. Put those chips down.'

"The young one didn't weaken a bit. He drew his breath in through his teeth with such a sound as a locomotive makes when the steam is escaping. 'I'll see you in hell first,' he replied.

"Brady made a rush across the intervening distance and lunged at his opponent with his huge fist. But the young fellow stepped lightly aside. I did not see the blow, it was too quick. But I did hear a short sharp crack as the Englishman's hard knuckles struck the bully's face and I saw Brady go to the floor like a felled beef. He was up again in a moment, white with fury. His revolver was out. There were two reports so close together that a person could hardly say now was one, then was the* other. We did not know what had happened until the smoke had cleared away, and we saw Cadwallader standing unharmed with his smoking pistol in his hand. He was untouched, but as pale as death, and on the floor lay Brady shot through the heart.

"'Served him right,' said half a dozen voices.

"'What will his wife do?' asked one. But no one answered.

"The 'Blue Lion' being the common gathering place at Saunder's Gulch, a good many of the choice spirits of the camp were there. The shots had called the coroner, who was drinking in the bar-room, and he ordered the body to be carried out. The sheriff had been momentarily aroused from an intense game of seven-up which he had been playing in one corner of the room; but when the coroner came, he resumed his occupation. Cadwallader walked over to him, and offering his wrists, said, 'Well, I am ready to go with you, sir.' The official waved him aside with an impatient motion and shuffled the cards before he said, 'Just sit down a minute; we stand six and six and it's my deal.' Justice was a little bit peculiar out there in those days.

"To make a long story short, the sheriff did not take the trouble to arrest Cadwallader. He lost his game and began another, while the patient prisoner waited. After a while he looked up.

"'What, you still here?' he said. 'It'll be all right. You just run on up home with Jenks and stay until you're wanted.'

"So Cadwallader and I went home together. We walked along in silence. His head was bowed. When he got into the house, he threw himself upon the bed and burst into tears. I went out without saying anything to him, only I pressed his hand as I left the room to let him know that I was with him. Talk doesn't do any good in such a time as that was.

"After that night, we worked on about as usual. The young fellow, true to his promise, did not again enter the 'Blue Lion.' But in vain we waited for the sheriff, until his failure to turn up was explained to us one day by one of the boys who came up.

"'Oh,' said he in answer to my question about the delay, 'the sheriff's got nothing to do with it. The coroner sat on the remains that same night, and the jury brought in a verdict of killed in a fair fight by the pistol of one Cadwallader by Providence appointed.'

"Well, I confess that I laughed outright, and I hugged Cadwallader. I couldn't help it, you know, even though I had felt all along that the boys were too just to punish him for what was obviously not his fault. But he was grave and silent.

*In the original manuscript, the page numbers skip from 8 to 10 at this point, although there does not appear to be a break in the story itself.

"After our visitor had gone, he said, 'Jenks, I've got to do something to help Brady's widow, since I've killed her only support.'

"I didn't say no to him and that night I saw him tie up all his winnings in a bag and start out. Why, doggone it, a great big lump came up in my throat, and I guess I thought then that Cadwallader was about the biggest man I had ever known. But later on, he came back looking glum and dissatisfied. 'She wouldn't take it,' he said. 'She said she didn't need it, but I am going to try and prevail on her.'

"Well, he did, and I guess he must have liked prevailing, for he got to going pretty often and I was left alone as much as when he was gambling at the 'Blue Lion.' Finally he took to going with her to the little frame meeting house, and you could hear him singing bass to her treble any Sunday you might happen to be near the place. It was all mystery to me. Only I did know that the little girl looked better than I had ever seen her before. She seemed to have gotten her spirit back and a good color came with it.

"One night, Cadwallader came rushing in, and woke me up. I saw that he was excited and so stifled the very natural growl with which I felt like greeting his interruption of my slumbers.

"'It's all right, old man,' he cried.

"'What's all right?' I asked.

"'She's consented, Mary's consented.'

"'Look here, Cadwallader,' I said, 'will you talk sense, and tell me what you mean by all this nonsense about consenting?'

"'Why, Mary Brady has consented to marry me.' I sat up in bed and rubbed my eyes, though it was my ears that I mistrusted. 'The devil,' I ejaculated.

"'You see, I kept on trying to prevail on her to let me help and try in some way to make up for the loss of her husband.'

"'Well, you've done that,' I said, 'and with a vengeance.'

"'But she wouldn't hear to it. Finally, she told me her story and I sympathized with her more deeply than ever. Then I found out that it was more than sympathy, and—and—, well it's all over now.'

"He was disgustingly happy, and I own that I felt a little malicious; I could not spare him one little shot. 'Oh, when one is brave enough to make a widow, he surely ought to be able to marry her.'

"'You'll forgive me all that, old man, when you hear the story. That poor little girl is a martyr.'

"'Oh, yes, women usually are.'

"'Now don't be cynical; a sneer doesn't set well with the peculiarly benevolent curve of your mouth.' His happy good humor was so infectious that I had to laugh and listen to his story.

"'Mary was forced into marrying Brady. The scoundrel had gotten her brother into a scrape. The youngster was in a bank and, like some other fools that I have known—went the pace. He got into debt, and finally over the gaming table, he fell in with Brady, who was then a man of good address and sporting proclivities, and having made a friend of him, took him to his home. The big fellow was promptly discountenanced by Mary's family, but he had fallen in love with her at first sight and determined to win her. With this end in view, and with the promise of relieving his embarrassment, he got the young fool of a brother to do certain things that would not bear the light of day, such as forging a check or two. The checks he got into his possession and then boldly demanded the sister's hand in return for her brother's honor. Of course, he won easily; but he had to skip, so he brought her west to this hole, and her life has been hell ever since. I'm going to take her back east. Poor thing, I hope to make it a good deal easier for her.'

"They married at the little church, and the boys gave them a great send-off. They went east, and after some years, I lost sight of Cadwallader. But I suppose he's all right, for the last thing I heard of him he was superintendent of a Sunday-School.

"From gambler at the 'Blue Lion,' Saunder's Gulch to a Sunday-School superintendency is rather a big change in a man, ain't it?" But we've got many like it out in that western land of ours.

Jimmy Weedon's Contretemps

HAD YOU ASKED any one in his set, he would have told you with a polite uplifting of the brows, "Oh, yes, Jimmy Weedon is a little wild, but then—" You would not have asked, though. First off, because if you had belonged to his set you would have known all that his friends knew, and if you happened to be one of those ordinary mortals outside of that rare sphere, you would never have dared to approach one of the elect.

Jimmy was wild, though, and rather more so than Mama or Papa Weedon knew, or any of his world suspected. He was sowing his wild oats, and heredity was strong. So, like his father in his commercial enterprises, Jimmy chose a wide field of action. As far as people knew, he was not so bad as young men go, and they rather winked at the rumors of his little escapades, for he was such a favorite in his particular set, and then he was only to have his freedom for a little while longer, because under parental persuasion, aided by threats as to the non-payment

Undated manuscript from *The Paul Laurence Dunbar Papers* signed "Paul Laurence Dunbar." First published by Martin and Primeau in *In His Own Voice* (238–43). Dated circa 1895 by Martin and Primeau.

of certain debts, he had finally agreed to propose to Helen Greville, and had been accepted.

Now did young Weedon groan in spirit. Until the last, he had hoped against hope that Helen would refuse him. Not that Helen was not a nice girl. On the contrary, she was very nice. And even putting aside the snug fortune that was hers, she was much too good for Jimmy, and moreover, Jimmy knew it.

It is all very well, this marrying a woman who is one's superior, if, as the writers say, after the wedding she will stand still and let the man equal and then surpass her, but it is possible that he may continue to come out second in the race to the end of his days, and then—well, a man needs to do a deal of thinking before he consents to be the husband of somebody.

Two people were never more unlike than Jimmy and Helen. He was a good looking chap, fleshly and easy-going who excused his own faults and evaded responsibility with a calm that would have been startling to moralists. On the other hand, Helen was a serious girl, who looked everything, her faults, virtues, duties, everything except her prejudices, in fact, squarely in the face. She had not the saving grace of humor, and there were those who even accused her of being strait-laced. On the score of dignity she had disapproved of Jimmy's taking part in a cake walk, and was not sure it was nice for him to want to do so. She accepted him because he was thoroughly likable, and no one had moved her more than he, but she did not understand him. How could she? The vague rumors about him disturbed her. If he did do awful things, she thought that when they were married, her influence would change—she would not say, "reform" him. This was all very foolish, had Helen only known it, because there was no common ground where she could meet her fiancé to analyze his doings. She had never met a temptation and Jimmy had never resisted one. Just now, he was finding particular pleasure in certain excursions down into the shady districts of New York, where he could have a good time, be a prince of good fellows, and at the same time, be under none of the galling restrictions that hampered him in his own world.

Be it said, however, that Jimmy's predilection for low life had been of short duration, and was usually emphasized after the earlier part of the evening had been spent in pursuit of higher game. Then when his head was ringing, his cheeks flushed, and he felt in his heart the joy of possessing the whole world, he would hie himself to his favorite cabman and go down to inspect the lower half of his domain. There was one thing about Jimmy, though, a thing that will please men. He never deceived himself as to why he sought out these lowly companions and their abodes. Never for an instant did he soothe his conscience or excuse his tastes, by thinking that he was searching for types or studying conditions. The life of these people so far from his own amused him and he went among them without moralizing about it. He cared nothing about their types or conditions except as they appealed to his humor. He was as honest in his motives for slumming as was Helen, who went in for charity—spiced.

Charity hideth a multitude of curiosities. Also the pursuit hath in it much of that variety of life which is supposed to put ginger into existence. Virtue is its own reward, of course, and a certain joy comes from the very doing of a good deed, but when this same righteous accomplishment is accompanied by the sight of various zest-giving things that could not otherwise come within the range of one's experience, the pleasure is measurably increased. Not one of the companions of Helen who poked about with her among the tenements and dives of the poor and depraved would have confessed that he or she was actuated by any save the highest motives. They must see and diagnose the disease ere they could provide a remedy for it, and any suggestion of curiosity as a main spring of action or morbid pleasure in the unusual would have been met with indignant denial.

Mrs. Carrington was one of those who indulged in the complacent dissipation of charity. She was also original, and so her friends were glad to accept her invitation to a slum dinner with a mysterious entertainment afterward. It was to be a very simple affair as befitted the motive behind it. They were not to dress for the occasion and they were to have but two wines. What greater proof of sincerity could there be in this self denial?

When the simple dinner was over, Mrs. Carrington made a politely hesitating little speech: "I, ah—felt," she said, "that—ah—the special need of us, ah—who have the well being of the poor at heart to—ah—be—a closer—that is, a—ah, more intimate insight into their needs and their disabilities. What we want fully to realize is—ah—the—ah—real brotherhood of man, and so I have asked you to this simple little—ah—I can hardly call it a dinner," a deprecating little laugh, "in order to show our sympathy with the people who are on the underside. I did not tell you—ah—what we should do afterward because I wanted it to come—ah—in the nature of a surprise. Officer Mulligan of the oth precinct has—ah—consented to come and go with us through some of the dwellings and—ah—amusement places of the poorer classes in order that—ah—we may see for ourselves just the types and ah—ah—conditions that obtain there."

There was a buzzing murmur of applause that brought the roses of pleasure to the face of the hostess.

"Isn't it sweet of her?" said a little lady in Helen's ear, "and how clever, we don't have to dress."

"It is noble of her," said Helen, "and what an opportunity she gives us for seeing just where and how we can do good."

After the necessary flutterings attending upon any feminine movement, Detective Mulligan in plain clothes and a state of contempt, with the nervous young rector of St. Asaphs, led them out to their carriages, which by the way, were to await them at a convenient distance from their place of research, so as not to give the lowly brother any aggressive idea of luxury.

By some fortuitous circumstance, it happened to be Jimmy Weedon's off night, and he had decided to go slumming on his own account without a detective or a charitable motive. This was bad for Jimmy. One hour after the lowly peregrinations of the Carrington party had begun, he bade Teddy Van Guysen good bye over their thirteenth high ball, went airily down the steps of the club and gave a whispered direction to his confidential cabman. Now if Jimmy had only stopped with his twelfth high ball, this story might never have been told, but he didn't. He took one more, and thirteen is an unlucky number. He was the most inconsequently happy man that New York held that night. He hummed gaily as he rolled along, and tried, unsuccessfully, to be sure, to twirl his stick in the cab. He had the cabman stop at several glittering places along the way, where he added others to the thirteen, and one would have thought that it would have broken the "hoodoo," but it didn't. The "thirteen" had gotten in its work.

When he was within the radius which for the evening he intended to grace with his presence, Jimmy leaped from the cab and dropped into a little chop house that he knew. Here people of rather a different cast from himself hailed him joyously as a man and brother, for there were always good times for the less fortunate when gay young Weedon was doing the town. Moreover, Jimmy was one of the few of his class who could so utterly merge his personality in his surroundings as never to invite suspicion and resentment. He was never superior. When one accepted a treat from him it was really by way of doing him a favor.

"Say," said one of his confidential friends, "dey's a big time over to Reddy Blake's dance-hall to-night. Don't you want to go? He's givin' a free blow-out, an' dey'll be lots o' de goils an' boys down?"

"Don't care if I do, if they don't throw me out."

"T'row you out? Ah, gwan. De guys won't do nuttin' to yer because dey knows yer."

"All right."

A short time later, Mr. Weedon with his friend, who went under the simple name of Mike, rolled luxuriously up to the door of Reddy Blake's dance hall. Blake welcomed Jimmy as if he had been an alderman, while Mike, in the moments when he was not his companion's shadow, got around among those of his set who were inclined to be offish, and "copped off" his protégé as "dead game, an' a all roun' swell guy."

Jimmy entered at once into the spirit of things and as the night wore on apace, the fun grew fast and furious. He was somewhat of a speiler, and the way he swung those girls around was a matter of disgust or admiration according to whether his critic were jealous or generous.

"AND NOW," said Mrs. Carrington, "we have seen a great deal, and I know you must all be tired. We will go to just one more place, a dance hall." Up at Reddy Blake's Jimmy's good angel neglected him, but he danced on. One can judge the needs of the masses by the way they amuse themselves as well as by the way they live.

"This is practical work," said the little rector of St. Asaphs.

"How instructive," murmured Helen, and under the guidance of Mr. Mulligan, they made their way to Reddy Blake's.

The floor was very full when they entered, but their embarrassing presence caused some of the dancers to withdraw leaving the dancing place less crowded.

The aristocrats huddled together and looked on at the novel sight of the poor amusing themselves.

"They seem to be having a good time," whispered Mrs. Carrington, "but it is all—ah—so different from us."

"Quite different, quite," murmured Helen, "not only temperamentally, but—ah—every way."

"One couldn't conceive of a person in our class enjoying this however," said the rector.

"There is one good dancer if only he weren't so wild, there, that young man with the slender girl, coming this way."

Jimmy was waltzing wildly down the floor to the closing strains of the music. The playing stopped, and laughing and flushed he paused directly in front of the group. There was a gasp in concert, and looking up, he met Helen's horrified eyes. He gazed dumbfounded. Then he grinned, and there is no telling what other sort of fool he might have made of himself, had not Mrs. Carrington saved the day by hustling Helen away with a brisk, "Come, we've had enough of this, now to supper."

She cast only one backward glance at Jimmy, that destroyer of complacent theories and then swept out. The rector of St. Asaph's coughed and looked unhappy.

Helen went white at first and then red as she tugged at the ring under her glove. The women were subdued. The few men who lagged indifferently with the party, smiled behind their hands, and conversation languished. The supper was not a success.

As for Jimmy, with the philosophical reflection that one had as well die for an old sheep as for a lamb, he went on dancing.

It was the next morning when he received a cold note from Helen accompanied by his ring. His head was aching, and there were dark lines under his eyes. But he smiled as he read the curt note: "After what has happened, etc., etc." He put the towel to his head again. "It's an ill wind," he murmured cheerily.

And that night there was a supper at Reddy Blake's over which Jimmy presided and to which none but the elect of that quarter came.

Ole Conju'in Joe

IF THERE WAS any house in all the "black creek district" which more than another, the negroes young and old dreaded to pass, it was the little hut of old Joe Haskins, "Old Conju'in Joe," they called him; and not a one of them but would walk a half mile out of his way to avoid passing the proscribed shanty.

It was indeed a gruesome looking place and it was no wonder that it had fallen into disrepute. The house itself was slowly rotting away; the roof was battered and rough looking minus half its shingles, and the shutters, which were always kept tightly closed, were fastened to the framework of the house by strips of old leather in lieu of the hinges which had long since rusted away. The gate had dropped from its place and the fence sagged away from the perpendicular as if the rails and posts were sadly inebriated. The yard was choked up with many years' growth of rank weeds, save in one spot where a little kitchen garden struggled for life. The whole scene was anything but an inviting one, and it might well have been the abode of a devotee of the black art.

And yet, Joe Haskins had not always been thus, an avoided and dreaded outcast from his kind. Time was when the whole countryside rang with his praises, when the white aristocracy favored him and the black belles adored him. When never a dance was complete without Joe Haskins to lead the music, for the fame of his skill as a fiddler—that skill which was at the same time, the envy and delight of all who knew him, had gone forth among all the community. His earnings were such that after awhile he was enabled to purchase his freedom and begin work for himself. In spite of the prejudice exercised in those days against free negroes, his success suffered no falling off on account of his liberated condition, and he was soon able to build himself a little cabin on his own ground, for Joe, be it said, was both industrious and frugal. His cabin was adorned with that luxury unheard of among negro huts, of a shingled roof. You can imagine that all this prosperity had the effect of making Joe more popular among the belles of his race.

For a long time, he seemed to be impervious to Cupid's shafts; but after awhile, the attentions he began paying to Almarnia, one of old Jack Venable's slave girls, gave evidence sufficient that he had succumbed to the skill of the blind archer. The trend of his intentions became conclusive when he began negotiating with Almarnia's master for the purpose of buying her freedom. The bargain was made, and Joe began his task. Never did man labor so cheerily as did Joe, working all day, and fiddling all night to earn money enough to pay off the sum that kept his bride from him. And at last it was accomplished. Almarnia was paid for and her "free papers" signed; Joe's bliss was at its height, for the wedding was to be celebrated

Undated manuscript, University of Dayton Rare Book Collection. First published by Martin and Primeau in *In His Own Voice* (219–23).

in two weeks; the preparations had been made and even the preacher spoken to, when a great change occurred in the prospective bridegroom.

No one knew what caused it. The first intimation which anyone received indicating all was not right with Joe, came through his refusal to play for the great dance up to Colonel Dare's. Through all his life, there had been no better friend to Joe than his old master's favorite cousin, Harrison Dare, and for him to refuse to play for this man, especially at a function where the black fiddler knew all the "quality" of the county would be present, was a wonderful surprise. But the messenger who returned several times could get no answer from him other than the stubbornly repeated statement, "I'se too po'ly to play fo' Mas' Harry, too po'ly." And even this answer came through a door opened only about three inches.

From this time, Joe left off playing and was rarely seen. The negroes, prone to give everything they did not understand a supernatural bearing, said that he was having intercourse with Satan, "a learnin' to conju'" and they began to avoid him. The poor whites inclined to the same idea, while the better classes merely decided that he had become mentally deranged and left him to himself.

Then came the stormy days of the rebellion, when the peace and pleasure of southern homes were blighted and destroyed forever. The hurried answer of the call to arms; the parting from loved ones, sons, lovers, and brothers, and the return of the wounded and dead; the four years of fiery struggle, of blood and tears, and then peace and reconstruction.

But in the rushing times of war and the subsequent changes that took place in the conditions of both blacks and whites, Joe was forgotten. Unmolested, he had lived his life; year after year, the weeds had grown up about his shanty, and the house itself had fallen into decay all unnoticed.

It was long after the close of the war that an unusual incident called attention to the place and renewed some of the old interest in him who had once been its occupant. Someone passing within unaccustomed proximity to the house, heard sounds as of someone singing. It was so unusual coming from the long silent place that the matter was instantly reported, and all the tongues of the town began to wag. The old idea about Joe was renewed and someone said that he was singing songs of propitiation to the Devil. Several others now ventured near enough to hear or imagine they heard his weird incantations, and the old cry of "Joe, Joe conju'in' Joe" was taken up on again.

It was very evident that he was doing quite serious work, so many of them said, "fur dat showed f'um his goin's on, as plain as day," and when Uncle Frog Martin's barn burned down, everyone knew just where to lay the blame. The old women sighed and said "Lawd, Lawd, how long," and the old men said, "Look a hyeah, chillun, whut's dis world a comin' to, any how!" The Baptist preacher said in his Sunday sermon that "de Lawd was a lettin' loose his almighty wrat' upon de people a, an' de debbil was unchained a an' a going' about a lak a rabenin' lion a seekin' who he mought devour a." And everyone knew he referred to Joe.

So, when Jabes Harlem, the most public-spirited citizen in the whole place, went around trying to organize an indignation meeting to protest against the toleration of such a nuisance in their midst, public opinion was worked up to such a pitch that all the community readily agreed with him and the meeting was held. It was opened by the parson with an address emphatic in expression and powerful in influence.

"Bruddahs an' Sistahs," said he, "I ain't got nothin' again' no man, and I wouldn't by wud, ner deed harm nuther chick nor child, but I jes' rises to ax dis one question, what is we gwine to, whar is we gwine to? You 'member in bible days, conju's an' sich things was bu'ned, but sine de Lawd hab come, He hab taught a new lesson an' in dese days ob humility, we ain't got no oddah way but to vanish all such wo'kers ob iniquity f'um ouah midst. De man whut tries to hindah his feller man is a walkin' in de shades ob da'kness and de Lawd ain't agwine countenance no such doin's, so I moves you, Mistah Cha'man, if so be's I kin git a second, dat it be de consensus ob dis meetin' dat a sut'n pusson—no name, no blame—dat a sut'n pusson libin' in dat old to' down shanty at de end ob town, be notified to leab de place, an' dat a c'mittee be appointed to dat effec'."

After the parson's influential speech, there was nothing further to be said, save to second, put and carry the motion. On the notification committee, the chairman appointed first, the Reverend Ebenezer Clay and then the injured Frog Martin, with sage Uncle Silas Marplot as a sapient third.

Never did men walk with more dignity, and less courage, than did the members of the "committee" as they strode up the door of "Conju'in' Joe." They knocked. No answer. They knocked again. Still no answer. And again with the same result. Then the Reverend Ebenezer Clay swallowed something in his throat and said: "Conju'in' Joe, we is de c'mittee, open de do'!" The door opened a few inches, and a trembling voice said, "Is yo' cullud?"

"We is," said Parson Clay, "the Lawd had made us so agin' ouah will."

Back swung the door. "Den come in," said Joe, bravely.

The "c'mittee" stalked in, solemn, silent, and scared. The importance of their mission shone in their faces. The Parson was spokesman, and they waited for him to begin. But in vain. With his finger pointing straight before him, he was standing transfixed. They followed his gaze and their tongues froze in their mouths. For upon the unkempt bed lay a corpse, seemingly but just dead. As their eyes fell upon it and they stood rooted to the spot with terror, Joe gave a half triumphant, half simple laugh and spoke.

"He's done past yo' reckenin' now, po' runaway niggah, he come to me a huntin' fo' freedom, an' I couldn't tu'n him away, you kin had me whupped and bu'ned, but Sam, po' Sam has enjoyed him freedom and he's past bein' tuk back into slabery. He wanted freedom, dat's why I shet up my cabin, dat's why I quit fiddlin' ha, ha, ha, I've cheated his master out ob one good niggah; tell him, he can hab him now fo' he caint hyeah him cuss ner feel his whup. Po' Sam, po' Sam, jes' befo' he died I sung fo' him. 'I want to be a sojer in de army ob de Lawd,' praise de Lawd, he's gone to be a sojer now!"

The committee stood speechless for a minute. Then Parson Clay said "Joe, ain't yo' heard about de wah?"

"De wah?" said Joe.

"Joe, de white people's done had a wah, a wah, and wese all free."

A blank expression came over the face of the ex-slave and he rubbed his head wildly as if to waken himself. "Free, free" he murmured, and then the dawn of comprehension seemed to break through his benighted mind, and he clasped his arms, crying "Free, free."

"Yes, free," said the preacher.

"You ain't afoolin' me, is yo'," said Joe, "you know yo' caint bring him back now."

"It's true," said the parson.

Joe fell on his knees beside the bed and the room shook with his convulsive sobs.

"We hab be'n free dese ten yeahs," the preacher added.

"Ten yeahs, ten yeahs," moaned Joe, "oh, praise de Lawd, praise de Lawd, an' me a hidin' po' Sam all dis time, too, you ain't a foolin' me, is you? Free, free, niggahs free, why, Lawd A'mighty, youse be'n on ea'th, sho' 'nough, don't fool me, you won't fool me, will yo.' Free, free, no, yes, ha, ha, ha, praise de Lawd! Sam, Sam, wake up, don't be dead, why, chile, youse free, arter a waitin' all dese yeahs de Lawd hab come to yo' deliberance. Come out in de light, Sam, come out an' show yo'se'f, nobody cain't hu't yo' fo' youse free now, ha, ha. Tell me, is your mastahs all slabes? No, well praise de Lawd, anyhow, ha, ha, ha; free, Sam, free." He seized the corpse's hand, his head sunk down upon the dead man's breast, "We don't need to hide now, Sam, we'se free, free," he murmured.

The committee tenderly lifted him up and laid him beside his dead comrade. He did not speak. They felt his heart, it had ceased to beat; for "Ole Conju'in Joe" had passed to that land where all are free indeed.

A Prophesy of Fate

I WAS HALF drowsing over my cup of strong coffee that morning; supping it slowly, meditatively. There must have been that far-away look in my eyes, which writers always ascribe to the optics of people in deep thought.

Through the haze of the years which have intervened, it all comes back to me so plainly now. The gray dreariness of the time, the heavy oppressive stillness; the very objects in the room seeming to take on an aspect corresponding to my mood.

I was feeling mean that morning—yes that comes nearer expressing it than anything else—mean, decidedly mean.

There had been nothing yet in the course of the day to ruffle me. It was but nine o'clock. And yet I was possessed by that half sad, half angry, and utterly vague feeling, which I can only denominate, mean.

Now I am not a superstitious person by any means. I should not hesitate to allow a cat to cross my path, without the remedy of taking nine steps backward; I would willingly break a looking-glass, if some one else would pay the expense; ghosts and night have no terrors for me; and, call it foolhardy if you will, I am even prone to disregard the prophetic howling of a dog.

But I must confess, that at this time a sense of peculiar creepiness had attacked me, in reference to a dream of the preceding night.

I had gone to bed under auspices, which one would adjudge unfavorable to vivid dreams. I had eaten but a light supper and it was early when I retired. There had been no heavy mental labor to weary my mind, for leisure was then my *sine qua non*. But yet I had dreamed and the vivid events clung with startling distinctness in my mind.

I was a somewhat active member of a club, called "The Diners Out," which every now and then, gave entertainments of a more or less pretentious sort to their male acquaintances.

I dreamed that it was at one of these gatherings, I sat among the fellows drinking in deep draughts of pleasure, with more moderate sips of champagne; the toasts were bright, and the laughter boisterous. The time was never so merry. How the room shook with the bursts of mirth; and with what smiling approbation, the crowd of flushed, merry faces looked up into mine, as I responded to the time-worn toast of "Wine, Wit, and Women"; for I was one of the club's crack speakers, and it was their bounden duty to laugh and applaud me, whether I said anything worth it or not. As I was closing my remarks the lights seemed suddenly to darken and swim about me. While weaving itself among the merry final words of my

Undated manuscript from *The Paul Laurence Dunbar Papers*. Manuscript marked "rejected" at the top of the first page. "Paul Laurence Dunbar" typed at end, but is signed "Laurence G. Mial." First published in Martin and Primeau's *In His Own Voice* (250–55). Bracketed insertions mark the places where the original text has deteriorated and we have attempted to restore it.

toast, seeming to struggle for utterance, the ill-foreboding phrase, "the last time," obtruded itself.

I could not tell what it meant. But when I sat down, I was more fully possessed by the terrible fancy. A voice seemed to whisper in my ear, "This is the last time you will sit among them, the last time." I tried to disregard it and shake off the feeling, but it only grew more and more upon me as the feast progressed. I retained presence of mind enough to laugh and appear merry, but all within, my heart was burning with a strange sadness.

Often I wished to break out and tell the assembled company how I felt, but I feared that my speaking of the prophesy would dispel the half doubt which I felt in regard to it. And I looked forward to the time when people would say with shaking heads; "Poor fellow, he foresaw his own death and spoke of it there that last night." And I tried to avert the impending calamity by keeping silent regarding it. Never was mortal man so beridden by dread; even now I shudder as I think of it.

At last I could bear it no longer, and, excusing myself on a plea of sudden illness, left the company.

It is strange with what regular, natural sequence, events follow each other in that unconscious life which we call dreaming.

The walk home only continued the former feelings, and I moved with the consciousness that I was going home to die. I tried to doubt it. I could not. It was a stern fact. I turned my mind and looked the startling situation in the face, but my vague, indefinite dread was not quieted.

I reached home. The dark shadows hung about my door like mourning draperies, and just as I ascended the steps and entered,—a dog howled. Another time, I would not have noticed such a thing, but this was the very signal bell of my doom.

The fire in my room was low, the embers were just dying to ashes, anon a spark sprang up trying to revive the former brightness, but sank down again overwhelmed by the surrounding gloom.

I sat down before the grate and pondered. My thoughts went back over all my past life; I could hide nothing in my soul from my soul's eye. The relentless light of consci[ence's] sun was turned upon my every deed good or bad. Oh, the menace in the faces of the stern procession which passed before my eyes. I raised my hands to my head. It was burning with fever. I felt of my lips, they were parched.

The blood coursing through my veins was hot and cold by turns. My hands trembled. The sound known as the death bell began ringing in my ears.

The clock struck twelve. The dog howled again. I was ill unto death and I could not shut out the truth from myself. My breath came in gasps; my blood seemed to clot.

My God! was I dying thus alone! I could not speak or cry out, and though I strained as though I should burst my heart I could not move a finger. Thank heaven great agonies are not long-lived!

With one last gasp, I fell backward from my chair. A horror of icy gloom fell about me. In my last throes, I burst the terrible bonds of silence and cried aloud! "Is this death?" The sound of my own voice awoke me, trembling and perspiring.

[I had] dreamed.

And that morning the dark mantle of my vivid vision still hung about me, touching me with its cold, damp, clammy folds, making me shudder even while I reproached myself for my weakness. I will think no more about it. I began to muse; "What fools, we can—"

"Ding," goes the door-bell. I hear the door open—and then shut. Then Robert, my valet, brings me a note. It is from Tom Hilliard, president of the Diners Out. It runs:

Dear Vesey:

Be sure and be around to the club tonight; a few of the boys have conceived the idea of giving an informal banquet to young Danvers, of Chicago, who is in town.

Yours etc.
Tom Hilliard

The note made me uneasy; it seemed to be a kind of, "by-the-way-apropos-of-your-dream," affair. I sat dangling it in my hand asking myself, should I go.

Why not? Those dream fantasies might be reason enough to cause some superstitious fools to remain at home; but what effect should they have on a man of enlightened mind. I would go.

It was not without many misgivings that I went about my few duties during the day. And when night came, my excitement was in no manner abated. It seemed as I dressed for the banquet, that I was going to test a prophesy of fate, and I trembled for the result.

It was not a good night for the banquet, the sky was murky and a cold drizzling autumn rain was falling. A good strong cocktail taken on the road set me nearer right. I felt better and as I approached the club house and saw the friendly lights shining out into the streets, my spirits rose.

Once within, the bright happy surroundings made me forget my gloom, I laughed and joked with the rest. Not a shadow was there of my former distress to oppress me. Nor did I even think of it until some one proposed the toast "Wine, Wit, and Women" and I was asked to respond. The coincidence struck me, but I was in too happy a frame of mind to pay any particular attention to it then.

You know the effect of anything upon a man is always according to his mood. I spoke and spoke as I felt, the laughter became infectious, for there's nothing so contagious as joy,—unless, perchance, it is fear. But suddenly, even as in my dream, the lights began to darken around me and the sickening prophetic dread, felt before in my dream, to seize me. I struggled against it and talked on more wildly, recklessly. I was confident that it was but the effect of my dream and would soon wear away. But still, the laughter with which my words were greeted began to sound harshly in my ears; the chink of the glasses, and the twinkle of the lights seemed far away, while like an echo from the grave, those dismal dream words came darting through my mind,—"the last time."

But what need to repeat it all; detail after detail was the precise counterpart of what it had been in the dream. Even to leaving on the pretense of illness; the walk home; the shadows over my door; the dying fire. As I sat before the grate, the long low howl of a d[og came thr]ough the open window. As I rose to close it, shutting myse[lf away fr]om all outside sounds, I said to myself "It is fate, there is no [need to] fight it; my destiny is sealed and has been shown to me."

Tu[rni]ng out the gas, I sat down again wrapped in gloom and depression. So far I had followed, without deviation each event of my dream and now some power seemed to be forcing me to still follow in its ways by going into that retrospection of my life which had not been satisfactory even to my sleep ridden brain. Thus I sat thinking and thinking until, as a result of entire mental exhaustion, a heavy drowsiness came over me. I closed my eyes and I knew this was not death, for I could not feel the flutter of the dark wings.

How long I drowsed—it was not sleep—I do not know; but I was at last awakened by a difficulty in breathing. My head ached in a dull way and every breath came with a gasp. I knew that I was reenacting the last scene of the dream, that I was dying. And it was with a kind of grim satisfaction that I gasped out, "at last!"

Breathing became more difficult; the air about me seemed to grow denser and denser; all terror had left me and I calmly waited for the end, for it was fate.

A knock at the door partially aroused me, and I could hear a voice, far off it seemed,—saying, "Let me in Vesey, I want to spend the night with you, it's so late I'm locked out and I hate to disturb the old folks."

I felt perfectly helpless, but the thought that I would not have to die alone, seemed to pierce through the dull chaos of my mind and give me strength. With one final effort, I rose, tottered across the room and unlocked the door. It opened, a great rush of air came in, I turned to reach my chair again but fell prostrate.

And then the far off voice exclaimed "thunderation man, the room's full of gas!" A window was thrown up and I knew no more until I found myself next morning lying upon my bed, with a physician and my friend Jack [Munford bending] over me.

"He's coming around all right now," said the former as I opened my eyes.

"Well, it was a pretty close shave," replied the other.

"How could it have happened?" asked the Doctor.

"Why, it seems that he had turned the gas out, but not entirely off, and the room, being close, soon filled with it. It's a blamed good thing that I didn't want to disturb the old folks last night and so sought lodging with him."

"It was very fortunate," answered the doctor gravely.

WHEN I was well enough to explain, I told Jack that after I turned out the gas, I went to sleep and so did not notice its presence.

But I did not admit to him what was really the truth, that my nose was so busy hunting out my destiny from foolish dreams, and my mind so deep in morbid thought, that I couldn't tell the smell of gas from the hand of fate.

I [had] been so worried over the happenings of the night, coinciden[tally a part] of the dream, that my mind was hardly about me when I [faced tomor]row against a dog's howl, to harbor a more silent, but [equally real] enemy.

[So I m]ay still say that my dream was a prophesy of fate.

Sister Jackson's Superstitions

THERE WAS A deep metaphysical discussion one day last week in a little Washington restaurant kept by a lady of color. The participants were the proprietress, a real bit of Old Maryland, a believing brother from the same state, a skeptical sister from the west, and a wholly unbelieving brother from the Old Dominion.

The whole matter had risen in the skeptical sister's inadvertently or rather innocently calling on sister Jackson on Monday before twelve o'clock. Now anybody who is thoroughly informed knows that this is the worst luck in the world. But when informed of the horrible thing which she had done, sister Towers, the western skeptic, had the temerity to be doubtful and amused.

"Well, well," she ejaculated, "I've heerd tell o' lots o' things, but that do beat all."

This brought down upon her head a torrent of warnings and instances of the awful consequences of unbelief which had come under the notice of her hostess.

"I tell you, Sister Towers, I's seed people doubt befo' dis, an' I knows what's happens to 'em."

"Yass'r indeed," said the believing brother, "I's seed too, wid dese hyeah two eyes o' mine."

"Oh that's all ol' Fuginia," said the unbeliever. "Look hyeah, Mistah, whaih you f'om? Ain't you from Fuginia?"

"No, suh, I isn't."

"Well I thought you mus' be to believe all dem things. Whaih is you from?"

"Ma'yland, suh: dat's whaih I f'om."

Here the hostess broke in: "You needn't be talkin' 'bout Fuginia, brother Curtis, you f'om thaih yo'se'f, an' hit's bad luck fu' a ooman to come to yo' house on Monday mo'nin' befo' a man's been in, Fuginia er no Fuginia."

Undated manuscript from *The Paul Laurence Dunbar Papers* signed: "Paul Laurence Dunbar/ Congressional Library/Washington, D.C." First published by Jay Martin and Gossie H. Hudson in *The Paul Laurence Dunbar Reader* (103–6). Dated circa 1898 by Martin and Hudson.

"Well," said Sister Towers again, "I nevah did hyeah dat befo': but den a bidy got to learn new things ez long ez dey live. I'm go'n' to keep dat in my min.'"

"Don't you do nothin' of de kin', sistah," said Mr. Curtis. "I tell you, hit ain't nothin' but ol' Fuginia. Why, my ol' mothah used to believe all dem things."

"Yes, an' yo' ol' mammy had de truf, too, even ef she did have a onbelievin' son!" interjected sister Jackson.

"Why, befo' I come away f'om Fuginia, dey had my head full of all dem things, too. But evah sence I been in Washington, hit's kep' me so busy jumpin' erroun' to mek a livin' dat I ain't had time to 'membah all dem signs an' sup'stitions."

"You'd bettah 'membah 'em, fu' I tell you dey's true."

"Yass'm, dey is true, evah one of 'em," said the believing brother from Maryland.

A great chuckle welled up from the ample bosom of the western sister and called forth a disapproving frown and headshake from her hostess.

"You go on yo' way rejoicin', sistah Towers, but some day you fin' out."

"I cain't he'p it," said that sister contritely. "I do' mean no dis'spect, but I 'claih hit do tickle me. I reckon ef I'd been raised dat-away I'd 'a' believed all dis too, but we got to live an' learn. It may be true, but I ain't nevah heerd tell of all dis befo'," and she chuckled again, to the discomfiture and displeasure of her friend.

"Well," said the latter, "I knows what's true an' what ain't. 'Cose I don't b'lieve in evahthing lak some people. 'Cause some people dee say dat dee kin put things down fu' you to walk ovah dat'll pisen you; but dee ain't nothin' in it. Nobidy can't pisen you less'n dee git somep'n' inside o' you. I know nobidy cain't pisen me by layin' nothin' down less'n I pick it up an' eat hit."

This brought forth a duet of approval from the believing brother and the skeptical sister.

But Mr. Curtis said banteringly, "I kin pisen you."

"How?" sister Jackson challenged him.

"Why, by plantin' roots fu' you,—dat's how." And he burst into a peal of laughter that was so infectious that even his opponents joined him.

"Oomph-ph!" said the believing brother patting his foot and shaking his gray head, "Brother Curtis sholy is a case."

"Lawd, how long!" moaned the skeptical sister when her merriment had subsided.

"Nemmine," sister Jackson went on, "some folks don' know de truf when dee sees it, but I does. I used to tell my husband, when my lef' han' each, 'Mark, I's go'n' to git some money', an' hit's a sho sign. Ef dat lef' han' each I git money sho's you bo'n. I might not git it dat day ner dat week, but it'ud come aftar while. Now what else you call dat but a sign?"

"What han' you say?" said the believing brother.

"My lef' han'—when my lef' han' each."

"An you gits de money, don't you?

"Deed does I."

"Oomph-ph!" said he as if the final word had been spoken, "dat's a sign sho'."

"Oh, pshaw!" exclaimed Curtis, "ef de money's goin' to come, it's goin' to come."

"Cose it is, cose it is: but de sign come befo' an' let me know. Now I know jes' de same when my lef' foot each."

"How 'bout dat?"

"Jes' 's sho' 's my lef' foot each, I go'n' to foller some o' my kinfolks to de grave, —dat is ef it each so I have to tek off my shoe. I know one day my foot git to eachin', an' I say to a ooman what come in, 'la me, my foot do each so, I hatter git a piece of ol' i'on an' rub it on' an' she say which foot? an' I say de lef' foot; den she say, 'la, Mis' Jackson, you go'n' to foller some o' yo' kinfolks to de grave.' Well, I nevah did think no mo' 'bout hit: I jes' went 'long. Well 'm, in 'bout a week, Mistah Jackson, he come in an' say, 'Marfy, you bettah go down home, sis' Sallie see'n' hu' las',' an' suh, she died an' I nevah been to see huh. Well, my husband, he went to de fun'al wid me an' aftah dat my lef' foot hit each agin, an' I tek off my shoe an' git an' ol' rusty hatchet an' scratch dat foot. Aftah dat Mistah Jackson nevah did git out to ma'ket wid me no mo.' He tuk down, an' I know a month aftah my foot each, my husband was a co'pse, an' I ain't nevah been troubled wid my foot eachin' sence. Now what you call dat?"

"Oomph!" grunted sister Towers.

"I call hit ol' Fuginia," said Curtis.

"Which foot was hit?" said the Maryland brother.

"De lef' foot, I tell you, mun!"

"An' de man he die?"

"He die, I tell you."

"Hit was a sign," said the Maryland brother conclusively.

"An' what 'bout when yo' right foot each?" asked the doubter.

"You go'n walk on strange ground. I don't keer whain it is, ef it's jes' some place hyeah in Washington whaih you ain't nevah been befo' hit's strange groun.' But I ain' bothahed nothin' 'bout my right foot, 'cause hit ve'y easy fu' anybidy to walk on groun' dee ain' nevah been on befo'."

Then the conversation shifted to speculations upon the war.

Sources

Alphabetical List of Stories

Collections

Folks from Dixie. New York: Dodd, Mead and Co., 1898.
The Heart of Happy Hollow. New York: Dodd, Mead and Co., 1904.
In Old Plantation Days. New York: Dodd, Mead and Co., 1903.
The Strength of Gideon and Other Stories. New York: Dodd, Mead and Co., 1900.

Short Stories

"Anner 'Lizer's Stumblin' Block." *Folks from Dixie,* 3–26. Previously appeared in *Independent* 47 (May 23, 1895): 706–7.
"Ash-Cake Hannah and Her Ben." *In Old Plantation Days,* 108–19. Previously appeared in *Saturday Evening Post* 173 (December 8, 1900): 16–17.
"At Shaft 11." *Folks from Dixie,* 205–31.
"Aunt Mandy's Investment." *Folks from Dixie,* 159–67.
"Aunt Tempe's Revenge." *In Old Plantation Days,* 12–26. Previously appeared in *New York Evening Post,* October 13, 1900, 15, and *Boston Beacon,* November 3, 1900.
"Aunt Tempe's Triumph." *In Old Plantation Days,* 1–11.
"A Blessed Deceit." *In Old Plantation Days,* 190–202.
"The Boy and the Bayonet." *The Heart of Happy Hollow,* 293–309.
"The Brief Cure of Aunt Fanny." *In Old Plantation Days,* 203–16.
"Buss Jinkins Up Nawth: A Human Nature Sketch of Real Darkey Life in New York." *New York Journal and Advertiser,* September 26, 1897, 18.
"Cahoots." *The Heart of Happy Hollow,* 145–59.
"The Case of Cadwallader." Undated typed fourteen-page manuscript. Signed "Paul Laurence Dunbar/Congressional Library/Washington, D.C." In *The Paul Laurence Dunbar Papers,* roll 4, box 12, frames 220–32. Previously unpublished.
"The Case of 'Ca'line.'" *The Strength of Gideon,* 107–12.
"The Churching of Grandma Pleasant." *Lippincott's Monthly Magazine* 75 (March 1905): 337–42.
"The Colonel's Awakening." *Folks from Dixie,* 69–79.
"The Conjuring Contest." *In Old Plantation Days,* 130–41. Previously appeared in *Saturday Evening Post* 172 (July 8, 1899): 30.
"A Council of State." *The Strength of Gideon,* 317–38.
"Dandy Jim's Conjure Scare." *In Old Plantation Days,* 142–51.
"The Defection of Maria Ann Gibbs." *In Old Plantation Days,* 259–72. Previously appeared in *Saturday Evening Post* 172 (September 9, 1899): 172.
"A Defender of the Faith." *The Heart of Happy Hollow,* 133–42. Previously appeared in *San Francisco Chronicle,* December 22, 1901, 8.
"The Deliberation of Mr. Dunkin." *Folks from Dixie,* 235–63. Previously appeared in *Cosmopolitan* 24 (April 1898): 678–85.
"Dizzy-Headed Dick." *In Old Plantation Days,* 120–29.
"The Easter Wedding." *In Old Plantation Days,* 226–35.
"The Emancipation of Evalina Jones." *The People's Monthly* 1.2 (April 1900): 8–9.

"The End of the Chapter." *Lippincott's Monthly Magazine* 63 (April 1899): 532–34.

"The Faith Cure Man." *The Strength of Gideon*, 307–14. Previously appeared in *New York Journal and Advertiser*, December 11, 1898.

"A Family Feud." *Folks from Dixie*, 137–56. Previously appeared in *Outlook* 58 (April 23, 1898): 1016–20.

"The Finding of Martha." *In Old Plantation Days*, 236–58. Previously appeared in *Lippincott's Monthly Magazine* 69 (March 1902): 375–84.

"The Finding of Zach." *The Strength of Gideon*, 287–94.

"The Finish of Patsy Barnes." *The Strength of Gideon*, 115–27. Previously appeared in *Saturday Evening Post* 172 (August 12, 1899): 98–99.

"From Impulse." *Dayton Tattler*, December 20, 1890. Signed Frank Mayne Templeton. In *The Paul Laurence Dunbar Papers*, roll 3, box 9, frame 107.

"The Fruitful Sleeping of the Rev. Elisha Edwards." *The Strength of Gideon*, 75–86.

"His Bride of the Tomb." *Dayton Tattler*, December 13, 1890. Signed Philip Louis Denterly. In *The Paul Laurence Dunbar Papers*, roll 3, box 9, frame 103.

"His Failure in Arithmetic." *Dayton Tattler*, December 20, 1890. In *The Paul Laurence Dunbar Papers*, roll 3, box 9, frame 104.

"His Little Lark." *Dayton Tattler*, December 20, 1890. In *The Paul Laurence Dunbar Papers*, roll 3, box 9, frame 104.

"The Home-Coming of 'Rastus Smith." *The Heart of Happy Hollow*, 277–90.

"The Hoodooing of Mr. Bill Simms, A Darkey Dialect Story." *New York Journal and Advertiser*, October 16, 1897, 21.

"How Brother Parker Fell from Grace." *In Old Plantation Days*, 39–49. Previously appeared in *Saturday Evening Post* 173 (July 21, 1900): 11 and *San Francisco Chronicle*, August 4, 1900.

"How George Johnson 'Won Out': A Character Sketch of Real Darkey Life in New York." *New York Journal and Advertiser*, October 9, 1897, 22.

"In a Circle." *Metropolitan Magazine* 14 (October 1901): 460–62.

"The Independence of Silas Bollender." *Lippincott's Monthly Magazine* 68 (September 1901): 375–81. Second in "Ohio Pastorals" series.

"The Ingrate." *The Strength of Gideon*, 89–103. Previously appeared in *New England Magazine* 20 (August 1899): 676–81.

"The Interference of Patsy Ann." *The Heart of Happy Hollow*, 259–73.

"The Intervention of Peter." *Folks from Dixie*, 171–81.

"Jethro's Garden." *Era* 10 (July 1902): 78–80.

"Jimmy Weedon's Contretemps." Undated typed nine-page manuscript. Signed "Paul Laurence Dunbar." In *The Paul Laurence Dunbar Papers*, roll 4, box 12, frames 243–51. First published by Martin and Primeau in *In His Own Voice* (238–43).

"Jimsella." *Folks from Dixie*, 113–21. Partial version of story previously appeared in *Current Literature* 24 (July 1898): 15.

"Jim's Probation." *The Strength of Gideon*, 165–75.

"Johnsonham, Junior." *The Strength of Gideon*, 297–304. Previously appeared in *Saturday Evening Post* 172 (January 6, 1900): 597.

"A Judgment of Paris." *In Old Plantation Days*, 273–86. Previously appeared in *Saturday Evening Post* 174 (May 24, 1902): 3–4.

"A Lady Slipper." *In Old Plantation Days*, 175–89. Previously appeared in *Saturday Evening Post* 173 (September 15, 1900): 11, 19.

"Lafe Halloway's Two Fights." *Independent* 51 (September 7, 1899): 2417–22.

"The Last Fiddling of Mordaunt's Jim." *In Old Plantation Days*, 60–70. Previously appeared in *Saturday Evening Post* 175 (August 30, 1902): 11.

"The Lion Tamer." *Smart Set* 3 (January 1901): 147–50.

"Little Billy." Sold to A. N. Kellogg Newspaper Co. between 1891 and 1893. In *The Paul Laurence Dunbar Papers*, roll 4, box 15, frames 725–26.

"The Lynching of Jube Benson." *The Heart of Happy Hollow*, 223–40.

"Mammy Peggy's Pride." *The Strength of Gideon*, 27–49.

"A Matter of Doctrine." *The Heart of Happy Hollow*, 87–101.

"The Memory of Martha." *In Old Plantation Days*, 152–63.

"A Mess of Pottage." *The Strength of Gideon*, 241–53. Previously appeared in *Saturday Evening Post* 172 (December 16, 1899): 516–17.

"The Minority Committee." *Lippincott's Monthly Magazine* 68 (November 1901): 617–24. Fourth in "Ohio Pastorals" series.

"The Mission of Mr. Scatters." *The Heart of Happy Hollow*, 53–84.

"The Mortification of the Flesh." *Lippincott's Monthly Magazine* 68 (August 1901): 250–56. First in "Ohio Pastorals" series.

"Mr. Cornelius Johnson, Office-Seeker." *The Strength of Gideon*, 209–27. Previously appeared in *Cosmopolitan* 26 (February 1899): 420–24.

"Mr. Groby's Slippery Gift." *In Old Plantation Days*, 95–107.

"Mt. Pisgah's Christmas 'Possum." *Folks from Dixie*, 125–33.

"Nathan Makes His Proposal." *Pittsburgh Chronicle Telegraph*, August 10, 1901, 10. Partial version of "The Mortification of the Flesh," which appeared in *Lippincott's Monthly Magazine*.

"Nelse Hatton's Vengeance." *Folks from Dixie*, 185–202.

"Old Abe's Conversion." *The Heart of Happy Hollow*, 105–21.

"An Old-Time Christmas." *The Strength of Gideon*, 231–38.

"Ole Conju'in Joe." Undated manuscript, University of Dayton Rare Books Collection. First published by Martin and Primeau in *In His Own Voice* (219–23).

"One Christmas at Shiloh." *The Heart of Happy Hollow*, 35–49.

"One Man's Fortunes." *The Strength of Gideon*, 131–61.

"The Ordeal at Mt. Hope." *Folks from Dixie*, 29–65.

"The Promoter." *The Heart of Happy Hollow*, 163–88.

"A Prophesy of Fate." Undated typed four-page manuscript. Typed "Paul Laurence Dunbar" at end, but signed "Laurence G. Mial." In *The Paul Laurence Dunbar Papers*, roll 4, box 12, frames 258–61. First published by Martin and Primeau in *In His Own Voice* (250–55).

"The Race Question." *The Heart of Happy Hollow*, 125–30.

"The Scapegoat." *The Heart of Happy Hollow*, 3–31.

"Schwalliger's Philanthropy." *The Heart of Happy Hollow*, 243–56.

"Silas Jackson." *The Strength of Gideon*, 341–62. Previously appeared in *New York Evening Post*, Feb. 10, 1900, 8.

"Silent Sam'el." *In Old Plantation Days*, 287–98. Previously appeared in *Saturday Evening Post* 172 (June 16, 1900): 1181.

"Sister Jackson's Superstitions." Undated typed six-page manuscript. Signed "Paul Laurence Dunbar/Congressional Library/Washington, D.C." In *The Paul Laurence Dunbar Papers*, roll 4, box 12, frames 262–67. First published by Jay Martin and Gossie H. Hudson in *The Paul Laurence Dunbar Reader* (103–6).

"The Stanton Coachman." *In Old Plantation Days*, 217–25.

"The Strength of Gideon." *The Strength of Gideon*, 3–24. Previously appeared in *Lippincott's Monthly Magazine* 64 (October 1899): 617–25.

"A Supper by Proxy." *In Old Plantation Days*, 71–82. Previously appeared in *Saturday Evening Post* 173 (November 10, 1900): 27.

"The Tenderfoot." Sold to A. N. Kellogg Newspaper Co. in 1891 or 1892. In *The Paul Laurence Dunbar Papers*, roll 4, box 15, frames 731–32.

"The Tragedy at Three Forks." *The Strength of Gideon*, 269–83.

"The Trial Sermons on Bull-Skin." *Folks from Dixie*, 83–109.

"The Triumph of Ol' Mis' Pease." *The Heart of Happy Hollow*, 207–20.

"The Trouble about Sophiny." *In Old Plantation Days*, 83–94.

"The Trousers." *In Old Plantation Days*, 50–59. Previously appeared in *St. Louis Mirror*, March 2, 1902.

"The Trustfulness of Polly." *The Strength of Gideon*, 257–65.

"Uncle Simon's Sundays Out." *The Strength of Gideon*, 179–205.

"The Vindication of Jared Hargot." *Lippincott's Monthly Magazine* 73 (March 1904): 374–81.

"Viney's Free Papers." *The Strength of Gideon*, 53–71.

"The Visiting of Mother Danbury." *Lippincott's Monthly Magazine* 68 (December 1901): 746–51. Fifth in "Ohio Pastorals" series.

"The Walls of Jericho." *In Old Plantation Days*, 27–38. Previously appeared in *Saturday Evening Post* 173 (April 8, 1901): 14–15.

"The Way of a Woman." *In Old Plantation Days*, 299–307.

"The Way of Love." *Lippincott's Monthly Magazine* 75 (January 1905): 68–73.

"The White Counterpane." *Lippincott's Monthly Magazine* 68 (October 1901): 500–508. Third in "Ohio Pastorals" series.

"Who Stand for the Gods." *In Old Plantation Days*, 164–74.

"The Wisdom of Silence." *The Heart of Happy Hollow*, 191–204.

"Yellowjack's Game of Craps: A Character Sketch of Real Darkey Life in New York." *New York Journal and Advertiser*, October 2, 1897, 29.

Chronological List of Stories

Dated stories and collections are listed in order of first publication. Collected stories are listed under the titles of the respective collections; stories that appeared independently before they were published in a collection are listed by date of first publication as well. For further bibliographic details and archival source information, see the preceding alphabetical list of stories.

Undated

"The Case of Cadwallader." Typed fourteen-page manuscript. Signed "Paul Laurence Dunbar/Congressional Library/Washington, D.C." In *The Paul Laurence Dunbar Papers*, roll 4, box 12, frames 220–32. Previously unpublished.

"Jimmy Weedon's Contretemps." Typed nine-page manuscript. Signed "Paul Laurence Dunbar." In *The Paul Laurence Dunbar Papers*, roll 4, box 12, frames 243–51. First published by Martin and Primeau in *In His Own Voice* (238–43).

"Ole Conju'in Joe." Manuscript, University of Dayton Rare Books Collection. First published by Martin and Primeau in *In His Own Voice* (219–23).

"A Prophesy of Fate." Typed four-page manuscript. Typed "Paul Laurence Dunbar" at end, but signed "Laurence G. Mial." In *The Paul Laurence Dunbar Papers*, roll 4, box 12, frames 258–61. First published by Martin and Primeau in *In His Own Voice* (250–55).

"Sister Jackson's Superstitions." Typed six-page manuscript. Signed "Paul Laurence Dunbar/Congressional Library/Washington, D.C." In *The Paul Laurence Dunbar Papers*, roll 4, box 12, frames 262–67. First published by Jay Martin and Gossie H. Hudson in *The Paul Laurence Dunbar Reader* (103–6).

1890

"His Bride of the Tomb." *Dayton Tattler*, December 13.
"His Failure in Arithmetic." *Dayton Tattler*, December 20.
"His Little Lark." *Dayton Tattler*, December 20.
"From Impulse." *Dayton Tattler*, December 20.

1891–93

"The Tenderfoot." Sold to A. N. Kellogg Newspaper Co. in 1891 or 1892.
"Little Billy." Sold to A. N. Kellogg Newspaper Co. between 1891 and 1893.

1895

"Anner 'Lizer's Stumblin' Block." *Independent* 47 (May 23): 706–7.

1897

"Buss Jinkins Up Nawth: A Human Nature Sketch of Real Darkey Life in New York." *New York Journal and Advertiser*, September 26, 18.

"Yellowjack's Game of Craps: A Character Sketch of Real Darkey Life in New York." *New York Journal and Advertiser*, October 2, 29.

"How George Johnson 'Won Out': A Character Sketch of Real Darkey Life in New York." *New York Journal and Advertiser*, October 9, 22.

"The Hoodooing of Mr. Bill Simms, A Darkey Dialect Story." *New York Journal and Advertiser*, October 16, 21.

1898

Folks from Dixie. New York: Dodd, Mead and Co.

> Anner 'Lizer's Stumblin' Block
> The Ordeal at Mt. Hope
> The Colonel's Awakening
> The Trial Sermons on Bull-Skin
> Jimsella
> Mt. Pisgah's Christmas 'Possum
> A Family Feud
> Aunt Mandy's Investment
> The Intervention of Peter
> Nelse Hatton's Vengeance
> At Shaft 11
> The Deliberation of Mr. Dunkin

"The Deliberation of Mr. Dunkin." *Cosmopolitan* 24 (April): 678–85.

"A Family Feud." *Outlook* 58 (April 23): 1016–20.

"Jimsella." *Current Literature* 24 (July): 15. Partial version of story.

"The Faith Cure Man: A Pathetic Story of a Colored Mammy." *New York Journal and Advertiser*, December 11.

1899

"Mr. Cornelius Johnson, Office-Seeker." *Cosmopolitan* 26 (February): 420–24.

"The End of the Chapter." *Lippincott's Monthly Magazine* 63 (April): 532–34.

"The Conjuring Contest." *Saturday Evening Post* 172 (July 8): 30.

"The Ingrate." *New England Magazine* 20 (August): 676–81.

"The Finish of Patsy Barnes." *Saturday Evening Post* 172 (August 12): 98–99.

"Lafe Halloway's Two Fights." *Independent* 51 (September 7): 2417–22.

"The Defection of Maria Ann Gibbs." *Saturday Evening Post* 172 (September 9): 172.

"The Strength of Gideon." *Lippincott's Monthly Magazine* 64 (October): 617–25.

"A Mess of Pottage." *Saturday Evening Post* 172 (December 16): 516–17.

1900

The Strength of Gideon and Other Stories. New York: Dodd, Mead and Co.

> The Strength of Gideon
> Mammy Peggy's Pride
> Viney's Free Papers
> The Fruitful Sleeping of the Rev. Elisha Edwards
> The Ingrate
> The Case of "Ca'line"
> The Finish of Patsy Barnes
> One Man's Fortunes
> Jim's Probation
> Uncle Simon's Sundays Out
> Mr. Cornelius Johnson, Office-Seeker
> An Old-Time Christmas
> A Mess of Pottage
> The Trustfulness of Polly
> The Tragedy at Three Forks
> The Finding of Zach
> Johnsonham, Junior
> The Faith Cure Man
> A Council of State
> Silas Jackson

"Mt. Pisgah's Christmas 'Possum" reprinted in *Werner's Readings and Recitations,* no. 25, ed. Rachel Bauman. New York: Edgar S. Werner & Co., 127–32.

"Johnsonham, Junior." *Saturday Evening Post* 172 (January 6): 597.

"Silas Jackson." *New York Evening Post,* February 10, 8.

"The Emancipation of Evalina Jones." *The People's Monthly* 1.2 (April): 8–9.

"Silent Sam'el." *Saturday Evening Post* 172 (June 16): 1181.

"How Brother Parker Fell from Grace." *Saturday Evening Post* 173 (July 21): 11 and *San Francisco Chronicle,* August 4.

"A Lady Slipper." *Saturday Evening Post* 173 (September 15): 11, 19.

"Aunt Tempe's Revenge." *New York Evening Post,* October 13, 15, and *Boston Beacon,* November 3.

"A Supper by Proxy." *Saturday Evening Post* 173 (November 10): 27.

"Ash-Cake Hannah and Her Ben." *Saturday Evening Post* 173 (December 8): 16–17.

1901

"The Lion Tamer." *Smart Set* 3 (January): 147–50.

"The Walls of Jericho." *Saturday Evening Post* 173 (April 8): 14–15.

"The Mortification of the Flesh." *Lippincott's Monthly Magazine* 68 (August 1901): 250–56. First in "Ohio Pastorals" series. Reprinted in *Werner's Readings and Recitations,* no. 34, ed. Elise West. New York: Edgar S. Werner & Co., 129–35.

"Nathan Makes His Proposal." *Pittsburgh Chronicle Telegraph,* August 10, 10. Partial version of "The Mortification of the Flesh."

"The Independence of Silas Bollender." *Lippincott's Monthly Magazine* 68 (September): 375–81. Second in "Ohio Pastorals" series.

"In a Circle." *Metropolitan Magazine* 14 (October): 460–62.

"The White Counterpane." *Lippincott's Monthly Magazine* 68 (October): 500–508. Third in "Ohio Pastorals" series.

"The Minority Committee." *Lippincott's Monthly Magazine* 68 (November): 617–24. Fourth in "Ohio Pastorals" series.

"The Visiting of Mother Danbury." *Lippincott's Monthly Magazine* 68 (December): 746–51. Fifth in "Ohio Pastorals" series.

"A Defender of the Faith." *San Francisco Chronicle*, December 22, 8.

1902

"The Finding of Martha." *Lippincott's Monthly Magazine* 69 (March): 375–84.

"The Trousers." *St. Louis Mirror*, March 2.

"A Judgment of Paris." *Saturday Evening Post* 174 (May 24): 3–4.

"Jethro's Garden." *Era* 10 (July): 78–80.

"The Last Fiddling of Mordaunt's Jim." *Saturday Evening Post* 175 (August 30): 11.

1903

In Old Plantation Days. New York: Dodd, Mead and Co.

> Aunt Tempe's Triumph
> Aunt Tempe's Revenge
> The Walls of Jericho
> How Brother Parker Fell from Grace
> The Trousers
> The Last Fiddling of Mordaunt's Jim
> A Supper by Proxy
> The Trouble about Sophiny
> Mr. Groby's Slippery Gift
> Ash-Cake Hannah and Her Ben
> Dizzy-Headed Dick
> The Conjuring Contest
> Dandy Jim's Conjure Scare
> The Memory of Martha
> Who Stand for the Gods
> A Lady Slipper
> A Blessed Deceit
> The Brief Cure of Aunt Fanny
> The Stanton Coachman
> The Easter Wedding
> The Finding of Martha
> The Defection of Maria Ann Gibbs
> A Judgment of Paris
> Silent Sam'el
> The Way of a Woman

1904

The Heart of Happy Hollow. New York: Dodd, Mead and Co.

> The Scapegoat
> One Christmas at Shiloh
> The Mission of Mr. Scatters
> A Matter of Doctrine
> Old Abe's Conversion
> The Race Question
> A Defender of the Faith
> Cahoots
> The Promoter
> The Wisdom of Silence
> The Triumph of Ol' Mis' Pease
> The Lynching of Jube Benson
> Schwalliger's Philanthropy
> The Interference of Patsy Ann
> The Home-Coming of 'Rastus Smith
> The Boy and the Bayonet

"The Vindication of Jared Hargot." *Lippincott's Monthly Magazine* 73 (March): 374–81.

1905

"The Way of Love." *Lippincott's Monthly Magazine* 75 (January): 68–73.
"The Churching of Grandma Pleasant." *Lippincott's Monthly Magazine* 75 (March): 337–42.

Works Cited

Blight, David W. *Race and Reunion: The Civil War in American Memory*. Cambridge, MA: Belknap Press of Harvard University Press, 2001.

Bone, Robert. *Down Home: Origins of the Afro-American Short Story*. New York: Columbia University Press, 1975.

Brawley, Benjamin. *The Best Stories of Paul Laurence Dunbar*. New York: Dodd, Mead and Company, 1938.

———. *Paul Laurence Dunbar, Poet of His People*. Port Washington, NY: Kennikat Press, 1967.

Braxton, Joanne M. Introduction to *The Collected Poetry of Paul Laurence Dunbar*, ed. Joanne M. Braxton. Charlottesville: University Press of Virginia, 1993.

Brown, Sterling A. "Negro Character as Seen by White Authors." *Journal of Negro Education* 2 (April 1933): 179–203.

Colbron, Grace Isabel. "Across the Color Line." *Bookman* 8 (December 1898): 338–41.

Cunningham, Virginia. *Paul Laurence Dunbar and His Song*. New York: Dodd Mead, 1947.

Dunbar, Paul Laurence. *The Life and Works of Paul Laurence Dunbar*. Microfilm: 9 rolls. St. Paul, Minn.: 3M Company, 1969.

———. *The Paul Laurence Dunbar Papers*, ed. Sara S. Fuller. Microfilm: 9 rolls. Columbus: The Ohio Historical Society, 1972.

"*Folks from Dixie* [Review]." *Independent*, June 2, 1898, 726.

"*Folks from Dixie* [Review]." *New York Times*, June 18, 1898, 397.

"*Folks from Dixie* [Review]." *Outlook*, May 7, 1898, 86.

Gaines, Francis Pendleton. *The Southern Plantation: A Study in the Development and the Accuracy of a Tradition*. New York: Columbia University Press, 1925.

Gentry, Tony. *Paul Laurence Dunbar*. New York: Chelsea House, 1989.

Henry, Thomas Millard. "Old School of Negro 'Critics' Hard on Paul Laurence Dunbar." In *The Messenger Reader*, ed. Sondra Kathryn Wilson, 277–81. New York: Modern Library, 2000.

Howells, William Dean. "Life and Letters [review of *Majors and Minors*]." *Harper's Weekly*, June 27, 1896, 630.

Johnson, James Weldon. Preface to *The Book of American Negro Poetry*, ed. James Weldon Johnson. Rev. ed. New York: Harcourt Brace & World, 1959.

Jones, Gavin. *Strange Talk: The Politics of Dialect Literature in Gilded Age America*. Berkeley and Los Angeles: University of California Press, 1999.

Kallenbach, Jessamine S., ed. *Index to Black American Literary Anthologies*. Boston: G. K. Hall, 1979.

"*The Love of Landry* [Review]." *Bookman* 12 (January 1901): 512–13.

Martin, Herbert Woodward, and Ronald Primeau, eds. *In His Own Voice: The Dramatic and Other Uncollected Works of Paul Laurence Dunbar*. Athens: Ohio University Press, 2002.

Martin, Jay, ed. *A Singer in the Dawn: Reinterpretations of Paul Laurence Dunbar*. New York: Dodd, Mead & Co., 1975.

Martin, Jay, and Gossie H. Hudson, eds. *The Paul Laurence Dunbar Reader: A Selection of the Best of Paul Laurence Dunbar's Poetry and Prose, including Writings Never Before Available in Book Form*. New York: Dodd, Mead & Co., 1975; repr., Baltimore: Gateway Press, 1999.

Metcalf, Eugene W., Jr. "The Letters of Paul and Alice Dunbar: A Private History." PhD diss. University of California, Irvine, 1973.

———. *Paul Laurence Dunbar: A Bibliography*. Metuchen, NJ: Scarecrow Press, 1975.

Mixon, Wayne. *Southern Writers and the New South Movement, 1865–1913*. Chapel Hill: University of North Carolina Press, 1980.

Mott, Frank Luther. *A History of American Magazines, 1865–1885*. Vol. 3. Cambridge: Harvard University Press, 1938.

"Negro Stories [Review of *The Heart of Happy Hollow*]." *New York Times*, December 24, 1904, 916.

Nettels, Elsa. *Language, Race, and Social Class in Howells's America*. Lexington: University Press of Kentucky, 1988.

"Paul Dunbar's New Romance." *New York Times*, December 8, 1900, 902.

Preston, George. "*Folks from Dixie* [Review]." *Bookman* 7 (June 1898): 348–49.

Raboteau, Albert J. *Slave Religion: The "Invisible Institution" in the Antebellum South*. New York: Oxford University Press, 1978.

Revell, Peter. *Paul Laurence Dunbar*. Twayne's United States Authors Series. Boston: Twayne Publishers, 1979.

[Review of *Folks from Dixie*.] *Critic*, June 25, 1898, 413.

[Review of *Majors and Minors*.] *Bookman* 4 (September 1896): 18–19.

[Review of *The Strength of Gideon*.] *New York Times*, May 19, 1900, 324.

Simon, Myron. "Dunbar and Dialect Poetry." In *A Singer in the Dawn: Reinterpretations of Paul Laurence Dunbar*, ed. Jay Martin. New York: Dodd, Mead and Company, 1975.

Story, Ralph. "Paul Laurence Dunbar: Master Player in a Fixed Game." *CLA Journal* 27 (September 1983): 30–55.

Tracy, Susan Jean. *In the Master's Eye: Representations of Women, Blacks, and Poor Whites in Antebellum Southern Literature*. Amherst: University of Massachusetts Press, 1995.

Turner, Darwin. "Paul Laurence Dunbar: The Rejected Symbol." *Journal of Negro History* 52 (January 1967): 1–13.

———. *Black American Literature: Fiction*. Columbus, Ohio: C. E. Merrill., 1969.

———. *Black American Literature: Essays, Poetry, Fiction, Drama*. Columbus, Ohio: Merrill, 1970.

"Unpublished Letters of Paul Laurence Dunbar to a Friend." *Crisis* 20 (June 1920): 73–76.

Wagner, Jean. *Black Poets of the United States: From Paul Laurence Dunbar to Langston Hughes*. Urbana: University of Illinois Press, 1973.

Warfel, Harry Redcay, and George Harrison Orians, eds. *American Local-Color Stories*. New York, Cincinnati: American Book Company, 1941.

Washington, Booker T. *Up from Slavery: An Autobiography*. New York: Doubleday, Page & Co., 1901.

Wiggins, Linda Keck, ed. *The Life and Works of Paul Laurence Dunbar*. Naperville, IL: J. L. Nichols and Company, 1907; repr., New York: Kraus Reprint Co., 1971.

Wonham, Henry B. *Playing the Races: Ethnic Caricature and American Literary Realism*. New York: Oxford University Press, 2004.

Index of Titles

DATE DUE

Feb 07			